FROM
High
School
To
Work

150
GREAT TECH PREP CAREERS

Ferguson Publishing Company
Chicago, Illinois

Copyright © 1998 Ferguson Publishing Company
ISBN 0-89434-264-9

Library of Congress Cataloging-in-Publication Data
From high school to work : 150 great tech prep careers (Revised edition)
          p.   cm.
   ISBN 0-89434-264-9
   1. Vocation education--United States. 2. Technical education-
-United States. 3. School-to-work transition--United States.
4. Education, Cooperative--United States. 5. Occupations--United
States.
LC1045.F69 1998   97-25936
370.11'3'0973--dc21   CIP

Printed in the United States of America

Published and distributed by
Ferguson Publishing Company
200 West Madison Street, Suite 300
Chicago, Illinois 60606
800-306-9941
Web site: http://www.fergpubco.com

X-1

Table of Contents

Editor's Note:

Revision of the outlook sections in *From High School to Work* was largely based upon information presented in the U.S. Department of Labor Statistic's *1998-99 Occupational Outlook Handbook*. A short explanation of the terminology used follows.

If the statement reads:	Employment is projected to:
Grow much faster than the average	increase 36 percent or more
Grow faster than the average	increase 21 to 35 percent
Grow about as fast as the average	increase 10 to 20 percent
Grow more slowly than the average, or little or no change	increase 0 to 9 percent
Decline	decrease 1 percent or more

Introduction

The Problems

Today's graduates face fierce competition for jobs. Too many of them lack the basic skills and knowledge to be successful or even get a job. The world of work has become more competitive, globally focused, and technologically advanced.

The Conclusion

Our educational system is not adequately preparing our students for the challenges they will face as adult workers.

The Solution

A new philosophy of education has emerged. *School-to-Work* seeks to create an atmosphere of early career awareness by linking a student's educational development with the world of work. From kindergarten through high school, students will get the chance to explore and learn about careers. They will be taught the basic skills necessary to be successful in the workplace, and they will understand how their schoolwork relates to work done on the job (finally, an answer to the age-old question: Why are we learning this stuff anyway?).

The concept of linking school-learning with career preparation is not new. Most public high schools have a vocational education program, while some high schools are chartered as Vocational-Technical schools. In these programs, students have been learning "applied" education for years, that is, specific skills, such as auto repair and knowledge of machine tools, that can give them a head start in their area of interest. Moreover, as technology has increased the complexity of the tools and machinery we use daily, technicians are increasingly in demand to bridge the gap between the highly trained scientist and the unskilled worker. Once stereotyped as the place to put the "underachievers" who weren't going to college, vocational education has gained a new prominence and respect in the field of education. Now more fashionably known as *Tech Prep,* vocational education is upheld as one of the testaments of the School to Work paradigm. Meanwhile, it continues to do what it has always done best: train students for skilled jobs.

Today's Tech Prep prepares students with all types of educational goals, from those seeking advanced degrees to those interested in a two-year or technical education, to students who want to enter the workforce right after graduation. Whichever educational track they choose, Tech Prep students get practical training and experience that prepares them for the demands of the workplace and helps them make better decisions about what they really want to do. Employers, meanwhile, save time and money on employee training and get more qualified workers who can better compete in the global marketplace.

Newly revised to reflect the latest salary and job outlook information presented in the 1998-99 *Occupational Outlook Handbook, From High School to Work: 150 Great Tech Prep Careers* presents information on a wide variety of careers that fall under the broad category of Tech Prep. Similar in format and content to our well-respected *Encyclopedia of Careers and Vocational Guidance,* Ferguson's *High School to Work* includes information on the Nature of the Work, Requirements, Advancement, Methods of Entering, and Conditions of Work for 150 different careers. For students currently in a Tech Prep program, or for those considering one, this volume presents a range of choices not found anywhere else. As the old adage says, "If you don't know where you're going, any road will get you there." While we can't provide a map of all the possible roads for them, we hope this volume helps students make better decisions about where they're going in the first place.

The Editors

Aerobics Instructors and Fitness Trainers

Definition

Aerobics instructors and *fitness trainers* teach proper exercise techniques to people interested in physical fitness. Aerobics instructors choreograph and teach aerobics classes of varying types. Classes are geared toward people with general good health as well as to specialized populations, including the elderly or those with health problems, such as heart disease, that affect their ability to exercise. Men as well as women enjoy the lively exercise routines set to music.

Depending on where they are employed, fitness trainers help devise conditioning programs for individual clients, who may be weight trainers or athletes, both amateur and professional. Fitness trainers motivate their clients to follow their exercise programs and monitor their progress. When injuries occur, either during training or sporting events, fitness trainers determine the extent of injury and administer first aid for such things as blisters, bruises, and scrapes; following more serious injury, they may work with a physical therapist to help the athlete perform rehabilitative exercises.

Nature of the Work

There are three general levels of aerobics classes: low-impact, moderate, and high-intensity. A typical class starts with warm-up exercises—slow stretching movements to aid flexibility—followed by thirty-five minutes of nonstop activity to raise the heart rate and ending with a cool-down period of stretching and slower movements. Instructors teach class members to monitor their heart rates and to listen to their bodies for information on personal progress.

Aerobics instructors prepare activities prior to their classes. They choose exercises to work different muscles and music to

School Subjects
Health
Physical education

Personal Interests
Helping people: physical health/medicine
Teaching

Work Environment
Primarily indoors
Primarily one location

Minimum Education Level
High school diploma (aerobics instructors)
Bachelor's degree (fitness trainers)

Salary Range
$15,000 to
$25,000 to
$90,000

Certification or Licensing
Required for certain positions

Outlook
Faster than the average

DOT
153

GOE
10.02.02

NOC
5254

motivate students during each phase of the program—upbeat music for the all-out exercise portion and more soothing music for the cool-down phase. Instructors demonstrate each step of the routine until the class can follow along. They then incorporate the routines into a sequence that is set to music. This is usually an ongoing process, with new routines added as the class progresses. Some classes are the drop-in type, with new students starting at any time. The instructor either faces the class or a mirror in order to observe the students' progress and to ensure that they do the exercises correctly. Many aerobics instructors also lead toning and shaping classes. Although the emphasis is not on aerobic activity but on working particular areas of the body, the instructor begins the class with a brief aerobic period followed by stretching exercises that warm and loosen the muscles and thereby prevent pulled or strained muscles or other injuries.

In a health club, fitness trainers evaluate their client's fitness level with physical examinations and fitness tests. Using various pieces of testing equipment, they determine such things as percentage of body fat and optimal heart and pulse rate. Clients fill out a questionnaire about their medical background, general fitness level, and fitness goals. The fitness trainer uses this information to design a customized workout plan utilizing weights and other exercise options such as swimming and running to help clients meet these goals. Trainers also advise clients on weight control, diet, and general health.

To start clients' exercise programs, the trainer often demonstrates the proper use of weight lifting equipment to reduce the chance of injury, especially for beginners. The trainer observes clients as they use the equipment; this enables him or her to correct any problems before injury occurs.

Fitness trainers who work for professional, college, or high school athletic teams are known as *athletic trainers*. Athletic trainers generally perform the same types of activities as fitness trainers, but on a more specialized level. They work with athletes to strengthen certain muscles to improve their performance level.

Fitness and athletic trainers also tape weak or injured hands, feet, knees, or other parts of the body at risk for injury. This helps strengthen the body part and keeps it in the correct position to prevent further injury or strain. Many fitness trainers help athletes with therapy or rehabilitation, using special braces or other equipment to support or protect the injured part until it heals. Trainers ensure that the athlete does not overdo the exercise, risking further damage.

Requirements

Aerobics instructors need a high school diploma; many also have a college degree in dance exercise or a related field such as exercise physiology. For high school students, courses in physical education, biology, and anatomy are particularly helpful.

Because it is virtually impossible to be hired unless certified, potential aerobics instructors must first become certified by an organization such as the IDEA Foundation, which is recognized worldwide. Interested persons should request a copy of the dance exercise instructor manual, study it, and then take a three-and-a-half hour test. The information needed to pass the test covers such topics as how medications affect the body, the role of nutrition in performance, how to teach special populations, and how to handle injuries in class. Aerobics instructors also must be certified in CPR (cardiopulmonary resuscitation).

Other organizations that offer certification include the Aerobics and Fitness Association of America (AFAA) and the American College of Sports Medicine (ACSM).

Students interested in becoming fitness trainers need a bachelor's degree from an accredited athletic training program or a related program such as physical education or health. This, however, requires an additional 1,800 hours in an internship with a certified fitness or athletic trainer. To prepare, high school students should take general science, chemistry, biology, physiology, mathematics, and physics.

College-level courses include anatomy, biomechanics, chemistry, first aid, health, kinesiology, nutrition, physics, physiology, physiology of exercise, practicum in athletic training, psychology, and safety.

For those interested in working as a trainer for a college or professional team, a master's degree is generally required; many go on to receive doctoral degrees.

Some states require fitness trainers to be state licensed; other states are expected to follow suit. In addition, the National Athletic Trainers' Association and the American Athletic Trainers Association certify fitness trainers who have graduated from accredited college programs or have completed the necessary internship following a degree in a related field. Candidates for certification generally need Red Cross certification in CPR or as an emergency medical technician (EMT).

Whichever career path they follow, aerobics instructors and fitness trainers are expected to remain updated in their fields, becoming thoroughly familiar with the most recent knowledge and safety practices. They must take continuing education courses and participate in seminars to keep their certification current.

Aerobics instructors and fitness trainers are expected to be physically fit, but not necessarily specimens of human perfection. For example, members of an aerobics class geared to overweight people might feel more comfortable with a heavier instructor; a class geared towards the elderly may benefit from an older instructor.

Opportunities for Experience & Exploration

A visit to a health club, park district, or YMCA aerobics class is a good way to observe the work of fitness trainers and aerobics instructors. Part-time or summer jobs are sometimes available for high school students in these facilities, and it may be possible to volunteer in a senior citizen center where aerobics classes are offered.

If possible, enroll in an aerobics class or train with a fitness trainer to experience firsthand what their jobs entail and to see what makes a good instructor.

Aerobics instructor workshops are taught to help prospective instructors gain experience. These are usually offered in adult education courses at such places as the YMCA. Unpaid apprenticeships are also a good way for future instructors to obtain supervised experience before teaching classes on their own. The facility may allow prospective aerobics instructors to take their training class for free if there is a possibility that they will work there later on.

Opportunities for student fitness trainers are available in schools with fitness trainers on staff. This is an excellent way for students to observe and assist a professional fitness trainer on an ongoing basis and to decide if the job is for them.

Methods of Entering

Students should utilize their schools' placement office for information on available jobs. Often the facility that provided their training or internship will hire them or can provide information on available job openings in the area. Students can also find jobs through classified ads and by applying to health and fitness clubs, YMCAs, YWCAs, JCCs (Jewish Community Centers), local schools and colleges, park and recreation districts, church groups and organizations, and any other likely sponsor of aero-

bics classes or fitness facilities. Because exercise is understood to be a preventative measure for many health and medical problems and diseases, insurance companies often reward with lower insurance rates those companies and corporate centers that offer fitness facilities to their employees. Students should not overlook nearby companies for prospective positions or be afraid to suggest that a position be created to teach classes or supervise the use of equipment.

Advancement

Experienced aerobics instructors can become instructor trainers, providing tips and insight on how to present a class and what routines work well.

A bachelor's degree in either sports physiology or exercise physiology is especially beneficial for those who wish to advance to *health club director* or to teach corporate wellness programs.

Fitness trainers working at schools can advance from assistant positions to *head athletic director;* sometimes this requires changing to another school. Fitness trainers may go on to instruct new fitness trainers on the college level. Some work in sports medicine facilities, usually in rehabilitation work. In health clubs, fitness trainers can advance to become health club directors or work in administration. Often, fitness trainers who build up a reputation and a clientele go into business for themselves as personal trainers.

Employment Outlook

Because of the country's ever-expanding interest in physical well-being and fitness, the job outlook for aerobics instructors should remain strong through the year 2006.

Fitness trainers are also in strong demand, especially at the high school level. Currently, some states require high schools to have a fitness trainer on staff. The glamour jobs in professional sports are very competitive; less than five percent of all trainers work in the professional leagues.

Earnings

Aerobics instructors are usually paid by the class and generally start out at about $10 per class. Experienced aerobics instructors can earn up to $50 or $60 per class. Health club directors usually earn about $30,000 per year.

Fitness trainers earn between $15,000 and $35,000 per year, depending on geographic location and number of years of experience. High school athletic trainers who are also high school teachers earn a teacher's salary plus an extra payment to serve as trainer, from $2,500 to $4,000 per year. Those who serve as trainers for professional athletic teams earn between $40,000 to $90,000 per year or more. Although a sports season lasts only about six months, the athletes train year-round to remain in shape and require the trainers to guide them.

Conditions of Work

Most weight training and aerobics classes are done indoors. Athletic trainers must work outdoors during sporting events such as baseball and football and in cold skating rinks for hockey games. The position often calls for quite a bit of travel, especially when the team plays away games, or, in the case of professional athletes, when they head to training camp.

Both aerobics instructors and fitness trainers need a positive, outgoing personality in order to motivate people to exercise. The aerobics instructor helps class members, who may be at different fitness levels, become physically fit. This includes making the class enjoyable yet challenging so that its members will return class after class. The instructor also needs to be unaffected by complaints of class members, some of whom may find the routines too hard or too easy

or who may not like the music selections. Instructors need to realize that these complaints are not personal attacks.

Fitness trainers need to be able to work on a one-to-one basis with both amateur and professional athletes. They often must work with athletes who are in pain after an injury and must be able to coax them to use muscles they would probably rather not. They must possess patience, especially for beginners or those who are not athletically inclined, and offer encouragement to help them along. Most trainers find it rewarding to help others achieve their fitness goals.

Sources of Additional Information

American College of Sports Medicine
PO Box 1440
Indianapolis, IN 46206-1440
Tel: 317-637-9200

IDEA Foundation
The Association for Exercise Professionals
6190 Cornerstone Court East, Suite 204
San Diego, CA 92121-4729
Tel: 619-535-8979

National Athletic Trainers' Association
2952 Stemmons Freeway, Suite 200
Dallas, TX 75247
Tel: 214-637-6282
WWW: http://www.nata.org

Agricultural Equipment Technicians

Definition

Agricultural equipment technicians work with modern farm machinery. They assemble, adjust, operate, maintain, modify, test, and even help design it. This machinery includes automatic animal feeding systems; milking machine systems; and tilling, planting, harvesting, irrigating, drying, and handling equipment. They work on farms or for agricultural machinery manufacturers or dealerships. They often supervise skilled mechanics and other workers who keep machines and systems operating at maximum efficiency.

Nature of the Work

Agricultural equipment technicians work in a wide variety of jobs both on and off the farm. In general, most agricultural equipment technicians find employment in one of three areas: equipment manufacturing, equipment sales and services, and on-farm equipment management.

Equipment manufacturing technicians are involved primarily with the design and testing of agricultural equipment such as farm machinery; irrigation, power, and electrification systems; soil and water conservation equipment; and agricultural harvesting and processing equipment. There are two kinds of technicians working in this field: the *agricultural engineering technician* and the *agricultural equipment test technician*.

Agricultural engineering technicians work under the supervision of design engineers. They prepare original layouts and complete detailed drawings of agricultural equipment. They also review plans, diagrams, and blueprints to ensure that new products comply with company standards and design specification. In order to do this they must use their knowledge of biological, engineering, and design principles. They also must keep current on all of the new equipment and materials being developed for the industry to make sure the machines run at their highest capacity.

School Subjects
Agriculture
Shop (Trade/Vo-tech education)

Personal Interests
Building things
Fixing things

Work Environment
Indoors and outdoors
Primarily multiple locations

Minimum Education Level
Some postsecondary training

Salary Range
$13,312 to
$21,736 to
$40,560

Certification or Licensing
None

Outlook
Decline

DOT
624

GOE
05.05.09

NOC
7316

Agricultural equipment test technicians test and evaluate the performance of agricultural machinery and equipment. In particular, they make sure the equipment conforms with operating requirements, such as horsepower, resistance to vibration, and strength and hardness of parts. They test equipment under actual field conditions on company-operated research farms and under more controlled conditions. They work with test equipment and recording instruments such as bend-fatigue machines, dynamometers, strength testers, hardness meters, analytical balances, and electronic recorders.

Test technicians are also trained in methods of recording the data gathered during these tests. They compute values such as horsepower and tensile strength using algebraic formulas and report their findings using graphs, tables, and sketches.

After the design and testing phases are complete, other agricultural equipment technicians work with engineers to perform any necessary adjustments in the equipment design. By performing these functions under the general supervision of the design engineer, technicians do the engineers' "detective work" so that the engineers can devote more time to research and development.

Large agricultural machinery companies may employ agricultural equipment technicians to supervise production, assembly, and plant operations.

Most manufacturers market their products through regional sales organizations to individual dealers. Technicians may serve as sales representatives of regional sales offices, where they are assigned a number of dealers in a given territory and sell agricultural equipment directly to them. They may also conduct sales-training programs for the dealers to help them become more effective salespeople.

These technicians are also qualified to work in sales positions within dealerships, either as equipment sales workers or parts clerks. They are required to perform equipment demonstrations for customers. They also appraise the value of used equipment for trade-in allowances. Technicians in these positions may advance to sales or parts manager positions.

Some technicians involved in sales become *systems specialists,* who work for equipment dealerships, assisting farmers in the planning and installation of various kinds of mechanized systems, such as irrigation or materials-handling systems, grain bins, or drying systems.

In the service area, technicians may work as *field service representatives,* forming a liaison between the companies they represent and the dealers. They assist the dealers in product warranty work, diagnose ser

vice problems, and give seminars or workshops on new service information and techniques.

These types of service technicians may begin their careers as specialists in certain kinds of repairs. *Hydraulic specialists,* for instance, maintain and repair the component parts of hydraulic systems in tractors and other agricultural machines. *Diesel specialists* rebuild, calibrate, and test diesel pumps, injectors, and other diesel engine components.

Many service technicians work as *service managers* or *parts department managers.* Service managers assign duties to the repair workers, diagnose machinery problems, estimate repair costs for customers, and manage the repair shop.

Parts department managers in equipment dealerships maintain inventories of all the parts that may be requested either by customers or by the service departments of the dealership. They deal directly with customers, parts suppliers, and dealership managers and must have good sales and purchasing skills. They also must be effective business managers.

Technicians working on the farm have various responsibilities, the most important of which is keeping machinery in top working condition during the growing season. During off-season periods they may overhaul or modify equipment or simply keep the machinery in good working order for the next season.

Some technicians find employment as *on-farm machinery managers,* usually working on large farms servicing or supervising the servicing of all automated equipment. They also monitor the field operation of all machines and keep complete records of costs, utilization, and repair procedures relating to the maintenance of each piece of mechanical equipment.

Requirements

The work of the agricultural equipment technician is similar to that of an engineer. Technicians must have a knowledge of physical science and engineering principles and enough mathematical background to work with these principles. They must have a working knowledge of farm crops, machinery, and all agricultural-related products.

A high school diploma is necessary for anyone planning further education in the agricultural equipment technology field. The high school curriculum should include as much mathematics as is available, four years of English and language skills, social sciences, natural sciences, mechanical drawing, shop work, and any other pre-engineering or practical mechanics courses that the school offers.

Vocational agriculture courses are extremely useful to help future technicians understand the needs and problems of the farmers with whom they will be working. Many people educated in urban areas without access to such programs at the high school level attend two-year agricultural technician programs in community or technical colleges, technical institutes, or four-year colleges. Through these routes they are able to find highly rewarding careers in this field.

Because agricultural equipment technicians may work in either sales or engineering positions, their high school and postsecondary education should be oriented toward both fields.

Postsecondary education for the agricultural equipment technician should include courses in general agriculture, agricultural power and equipment, practical engineering, hydraulics, agricultural-equipment business methods, electrical equipment, engineering, social science, economics, and sales techniques. On-the-job experience during the summer is invaluable and frequently is included as part of the regular curriculum in these programs. Students are placed on farms, functioning as technicians-in-training. They also may work in farm equipment dealerships where their time is divided between the sales, parts, and service departments. Occupational experience, one of the most important phases of the postsecondary training program, gives students an opportunity to discover which field best suits them and which phase of the business they prefer. Upon completion of this program, most technical and community colleges award an associate degree.

Typical agricultural equipment technology courses offered the first year of a two-year program include communications; drawing, sketching, and diagramming; agricultural machinery; technical physics and mathematics; diesel and gasoline engines; hydraulics; technical reporting; and business organization.

Second-year courses may include equipment selling, distributing, and servicing; hydraulic equipment and air conditioning; principles of farm mechanization, computers, and automatic controls; materials handling; power unit testing and diagnosis; advanced agricultural equipment; and agricultural business management and accounting.

It is still possible to enter this career by starting as an inexperienced worker in a machinery manufacturer's plant or on a farm and learning machine technician skills on the job. However, this approach is becoming increasingly difficult due to the complexity of modern machinery. Because of this, some formal classroom training is usually necessary, and many people find it difficult to complete even part-time study of the field's theory and science while also working a full-time job.

Opportunities for Experience & Exploration

People who reside in farming regions have many ways to explore the agricultural equipment field. However, even those who live in towns or cities can explore and become acquainted with this career.

Vocational agriculture education programs in high schools can be found in most rural settings, many suburban setting, and even in some urban schools. The teaching staff and counselors in these schools can provide considerable information about this career.

Light industrial machinery is now used in almost every industry. It is always helpful to watch machinery being used and to talk with people who own, operate, and repair it.

Summer and part-time work on a farm, in an agricultural equipment manufacturing plant, or in an equipment sales and service business offers opportunities to work on or near agricultural and light industrial machinery. Such a job may provide a clearer idea about the various activities, challenges, rewards, and possible limitations of this career.

Methods of Entering

The demand for qualified agricultural equipment technicians exceeds the supply. Operators and managers of large, well-equipped farms and farm equipment companies in need of employees keep in touch with colleges offering agricultural equipment programs. Students who do well during their occupational experience period usually have an excellent chance of going to work for the same employer after graduation. Many colleges have an interview day on which personnel representatives of manufacturers, distributors, farm owners or managers, and dealers are invited to recruit students completing technician programs. In general, any student who does well in a training program can expect employment immediately upon graduation.

A moderate percentage of students in agricultural technician programs are sons, daughters, or other close relatives of farm owners and operators. They are often assured immediate employment when they return full time to their family farm in which they may have an ownership interest. These enterprising students have prepared themselves to be future owners and operators of farms in the best possible way to assure success.

Advancement

Opportunities for advancement and self-employment are excellent for those with the initiative to keep abreast of continuing developments in the farm equipment field. Technicians often attend company schools in sales and service or take advanced evening courses in colleges.

Employment Outlook

Employment for agricultural equipment technicians is expected to decline through the year 2006. Farmland today is increasingly being consolidated into fewer and larger farms. As a result, farmers will need to purchase a smaller amount of equipment that is newer, more efficient, and, that is, conversely, less prone to frequent service or breakdown. This complex, specialized machinery will require trained technical workers to design, produce, test, sell, and service them. Trained workers also are needed to instruct the final owners in their proper repair, operation, and maintenance. Most openings in this field will result from workers retiring or leaving the field for other reasons.

In addition, the agricultural industry is adopting advanced computer and electronic technology. Computer skills are becoming more and more useful in this field. Precision farming will also require specialized training as agricultural equipment becomes hooked up to satellite systems.

As agriculture becomes more technical, the agricultural equipment technician will assume an increasingly vital role in helping farmers solve problems that interfere with efficient production. These opportunities exist not only in the United States, but also worldwide. As agricultural economies everywhere become mechanized, inventive technicians with training in modern business principles should find expanding employment opportunities abroad. The best opportunities—as always—will be for those technicians who pursue formal training in diesel mechanics or farm equipment repair.

Earnings

According to the *1998-99 Occupational Outlook Handbook,* agricultural equipment technicians earn salaries that range from $13,312 to more than $21,736 per year for those who have grad-

uated from a two-year technical or community college. With further training and experience, technicians may earn much larger salaries, often ranging from $30,000 to $40,560. Those working on farms often receive room and board as a supplement to their annual salary. The salary that technicians eventually receive depends, as do most salaries, on individual ability, initiative, and the supply of skilled technicians in the field of work or locality.

In addition to their salaries, most technicians receive fringe benefits such as health and retirement packages, paid vacations, and other benefits similar to those received by engineering technicians. Technicians employed in sales are usually paid a commission in addition to their base salary.

Conditions of Work

Working conditions vary according to the type of field chosen. The technician who is a part of a large farming operation will work indoors or outdoors depending on the season and the tasks that need to be done. Planning machine overhauls and the directing of such work usually are done in enclosed spaces equipped for such work. As implied by its name, field servicing and repairs are done outdoors in the field.

Some agricultural equipment sales representatives work in their own or nearby communities, while others must travel extensively.

Technicians in agricultural equipment research, development, and production usually work under typical factory conditions: some work in an office or laboratory; others in a manufacturing plant; or, in some cases, field testing and demonstration are performed where the machinery will be used.

For technicians who assemble, adjust, modify, or test equipment and for those who provide customer service, application studies, and maintenance services, the surroundings may be similar to large automobile service centers.

In all cases, safety precautions must be a constant concern. Appropriate clothing, an acute awareness of one's environment, and careful lifting or hoisting of heavy machinery must be standard procedure. While safety practices have improved greatly over the years, certain risks do exist. Heavy lifting may cause injury, and burns and cuts are always possible. The surroundings may be noisy and grimy. Some work is performed in cramped or awkward physical positions. Gasoline fumes and odors from oil products are a constant factor. Most technicians ordinarily work a forty-

hour week, but emergency repairs may require working overtime.

Sources of Additional Information

■■Agricultural and Industrial Manufacturers Representatives
Association
5818 Reeds Road
Mission, KS 66202
Tel: 913-262-0317

■■National FFA Organization
PO Box 15160
Alexandria, VA 22309-0160
Tel: 703-360-3600

■■U.S. Department of Agriculture
Higher Education Program
14th Street and Independence, SW
Washington, DC 20250
Tel: 202-720-2791

Air-Conditioning, Refrigeration, and Heating Technicians

Definition

Air-conditioning, refrigeration, and heating technicians work on systems that control the temperature, humidity, and air quality of enclosed environments. They help design, manufacture, install, and maintain climate-control equipment. They provide people with heating and air-conditioning in such structures as shops, hospitals, malls, theaters, factories, restaurants, offices, and apartment buildings, and private homes. They may work to provide temperature-sensitive products such as computers, foods, medicines, and precision instruments with climate-controlled environments. They may also provide comfortable environments or refrigeration in such modes of transportation as ships, trucks, planes, and trains.

Nature of the Work

Many industries today depend on carefully controlled temperature and humidity conditions while manufacturing, transporting, or storing their products. Many common foods are readily available only because of extensive refrigeration. Less obviously, numerous chemicals, drugs, explosives, oil, and other products our society needs must be produced using refrigeration processes. For example, some room-sized computer systems need to be kept at a certain temperature and humidity; spacecraft must be able to withstand great heat while exposed to the rays of the sun and great cold when the moon or earth blocks the sun, and at the same time maintain a steady internal environment; the air in tractor trailer cabs must be regulated so that truck drivers can spend long hours behind the wheel in maximum comfort and safety. Each of these applications represents a different segment of a large and very diverse industry.

Air-conditioning, refrigeration, and heating technicians may work in installation and maintenance (which includes service and repairs), sales, or manufacturing. The majority of techni-

School Subjects
Mathematics
Shop (Trade/Vo-tech education)

Personal Interests
Building things
Figuring out how things work

Work Environment
Indoors and outdoors
Primarily multiple locations

Minimum Education Level
High school diploma
Apprenticeship

Salary Range
$15,000 to
$27,872 to
$46,124

Certification or Licensing
Required

Outlook
About as fast as the average

DOT
637

GOE
05.05.09

NOC
7313

cians who work in installation and maintenance work for heating and cooling contractors; manufacturers of air-conditioning, refrigeration, and heating equipment; dealers and distributors; or utility companies.

Technicians who assemble and install air-conditioning, refrigeration, and heating systems and equipment work from blueprints. Experienced technicians read blueprints as they would read detailed maps or patterns that show them how to assemble components and how the components should be installed into the structure. Because structure sizes and climate-control specifications vary, technicians have to pay close attention to blueprint details. While working from the blueprints, technicians use algebra and geometry to calculate the sizes and contours of duct work as they assemble it.

Air-conditioning, refrigeration, and heating technicians work with a variety of hardware, tools, and components. For example, in joining pipes and duct work for an air-conditioning system, technicians may use soldering, welding, or brazing equipment, as well as sleeves, couplings, and elbow joints. Technicians handle and assemble such components as motors, thermometers, burners, compressors, pumps, and fans. They must join these parts together when building climate-control units and then connect this equipment to the duct work, refrigerant lines, and power source.

As a final step in assembly and installation, technicians run tests on equipment to ensure that it functions properly. If the equipment is malfunctioning, technicians must investigate in order to diagnose the problem and determine a solution. At this time, they will adjust thermostats, reseal piping, and replace parts as needed. They retest the equipment to determine whether the problem has been remedied, and they continue to modify and test it until everything checks out as functioning properly.

Some technicians may specialize on only one type of cooling, heating, or refrigeration equipment. For example, *window air-conditioning unit installer-servicers* work on window units only. *Air-conditioning and refrigeration technicians* install and service central air-conditioning systems and a variety of refrigeration equipment. Air-conditioning installations may range from small wall units, either water- or air-cooled, to large central plant systems. Commercial refrigeration equipment may include display cases, walk-in coolers, and frozen-food units such as those in supermarkets, restaurants, and food processing plants.

Other technicians are *furnace installers,* also called *heating-equipment installers.* Following blueprints and other specifications, they install oil, gas, electric, solid-fuel (such as coal), and multi-fuel heating systems. They move the new furnace into place and

attach fuel supply lines, air ducts, pumps, and other components. Then they connect the electrical wiring and thermostatic controls and, finally, check the unit for proper operation.

Technicians who work in maintenance perform routine service to keep systems operating efficiently and respond to service calls for repairs. They perform tests and diagnose problems on equipment that has been installed in the past. They calibrate controls, add fluids, change parts, clean components, and test the system for proper operation. For example, in performing a routine service call on a furnace, technicians will adjust blowers and burners, replace filters, clean ducts, and check thermometers and other controls.

Technicians who maintain oil- and gas-burning equipment are called *oil-burner mechanics* and *gas-burner mechanics,* or *gas-appliance servicers.* They usually perform more extensive maintenance work during the warm weather, when the heating system can be shut down. Usually during the summer, technicians replace oil and air filters; vacuum vents, ducts, and other parts that accumulate soot and ash; and adjust the burner so that it achieves maximum operating efficiency. Gas-burner mechanics may also repair other gas appliances such as cooking stoves, clothes dryers, water heaters, outdoor lights, and grills.

Other air-conditioning, refrigeration, and heating technicians who specialize in a limited range of equipment include *evaporative cooler installers, hot-air furnace installer-and-repairers, solar-energy system installers and helpers,* and *air and hydronic balancing technicians.*

In their work on refrigerant lines and air ducts, air-conditioning, refrigeration, and heating technicians use a variety of hand and power tools, including hammers, wrenches, metal snips, electric drills, pipe cutters and benders, and acetylene torches. To check electrical circuits, burners, and other components, technicians work with volt-ohmmeters, manometers, and other testing devices.

Sometimes part of the installation and repair work done on cooling and heating systems is done by other craft workers, especially on large jobs where workers are covered by union contracts. For example, the duct work on a large air-conditioning system might be done by sheet-metal workers, the electrical work by electricians, and the installation of piping, condensers, and other components by pipefitters.

Rather than working directly with the building, installation, and maintenance of equipment, some technicians work in equipment sales. These technicians are usually employed by manufacturers or dealers and distributors and are hired to explain the equipment and its operation to prospective customers. These technicians must have a thorough knowledge of their products. They may explain newly developed equipment, ideas, and principles or assist dealers and distributors in the layout and installation of unfamiliar components. Some technicians employed as sales representatives contact prospective buyers and help them plan air-conditioning, refrigeration, and heating systems. They help the client select appropriate equipment and estimate costs.

Other technicians work for manufacturers in engineering or research laboratories, performing many of the same assembling and testing duties as technicians who work for contractors. However, they perform these operations at the manufacturing site rather than traveling to work sites as most contractors' technicians do. Technicians aid engineers in research, equipment design, and equipment testing. Technicians in a research laboratory may plan the requirements for the various stages of fabricating, installing, and servicing climate-control and refrigeration systems; recommend appropriate equipment to meet specified needs; and calculate heating and cooling capacities of proposed equipment units. They also may conduct operational tests on experimental models and efficiency tests on new units coming off the production lines. They might also investigate the cause of breakdowns reported by customers, and determine the reasons and solutions.

Engineering-oriented technicians employed by manufacturers may perform tests of new equipment, or assist engineers in fundamental research and development, technical report writing, and application engineering. Other engineering technicians serve as liaison representatives, coordinating the design and production engineering for the development and manufacture of new products.

Technicians may also be employed by utility companies to help ensure that their customers' equipment is using energy efficiently and effectively. *Utility technicians,* often called *energy conservation technicians,* may conduct energy evaluations of customers' systems, compile energy surveys, and provide customer information.

Technicians may also work for consulting firms, such as engineering firms or building contractors who hire technicians to estimate costs, determine air-conditioning and heating load requirements, and prepare specifications for climate-control projects.

Some technicians also open up their own businesses, either as heating and cooling contractors or consultants specializing in sales, parts supply, service and installation.

Requirements

Persons interested in the air-conditioning, refrigeration, and heating field need to have average or above average intelligence, an aptitude for working with tools, manual dexterity and manipulation, and the desire to perform challenging work that requires a high level of competence and quality. Students who are interested in how things work, who enjoy taking things apart and putting them back together, and who enjoy troubleshooting for mechanical and electrical problems may enjoy a career in air-conditioning, refrigeration, and heating.

Because of the wide range of positions available for technicians, requirements vary. Technicians employed by manufacturers in research and engineering departments need more of an engineering aptitude than those technicians employed in installation and maintenance. Technicians planning to work with engineers in research and development activities need an acquaintance with the theory and principles of engineering, some mathematical background, and a tolerance for working with numbers. They need the ability to read blueprints, building drawings, and electrical diagrams. In many specialty areas within the industry, the rapidly changing pace requires technicians to be able to read, comprehend, and make use of current periodicals and publications in the field. They also must be able to write reports, both formal and informal, that include concise and complete descriptions of tests, experiments, and research. Technicians increasingly need good computer skills because more air-conditioning, refrigeration, and heating systems and components are being installed with microcomputer controls.

Technicians involved in installation and maintenance need many of the same skills as those needed by technicians working with engineers, with less emphasis on engineering theory and report writing. They need to understand air-conditioning, refrigeration, and heating theory; design and construction of equipment; and the basics of installation, maintenance, and repairs.

Technicians in sales need a strong base of technical knowledge, which in many cases is acquired from having worked in installation and maintenance or by working with research and design engineers. In addition, they need to be good communicators and have the ability to explain technical information in clear, easy-to-understand language to diverse groups of people.

In high school, students considering the air-conditioning, refrigeration, and heating technology field should take algebra, geometry, English composition, physics, computer applications and programming, and classes in industrial arts or shop. Helpful shop classes include mechanical drawing and blueprint reading, power and hand tools operations, and metalwork. Shop courses in electricity and electronics provide a strong introduction into understanding circuitry and wiring and teach students to read electrical diagrams. Classes in computer-aided design are also helpful, as are business courses.

A variety of postsecondary educational programs are available. Vocational-technical schools, private trade schools, and junior colleges offer both one- and two-year programs. Graduates of two-year programs usually receive an associate degree in science or in applied science. Certificates, rather than degrees, are awarded to those who complete one-year programs. Although no formal education is required, most employers prefer to hire graduates of two-year applications-oriented training programs. This kind of training includes a strong background in mathematical and engineering theory. However, the emphasis is on the practical uses of such theories, not on explorations of their origins and development, such as one finds in engineering programs.

Two-year programs include classes on the theory of air-conditioning, refrigeration, and heating; electrical circuits, components, controls, accessories, and design; servicing; troubleshooting; installation of engineering control units; refrigerant handling; and energy audits and testing. Classes in advanced algebra, trigonometry, physics, technical writing, and English may also be required.

For the most part, no special licensing or certification is required for air-conditioning, refrigeration, and heating technicians. However, all technicians who handle refrigerants must receive approved refrigerant recovery certification, which is a recent requirement of the Environmental Protection Agency and requires passing a special examination.

Voluntary certification through professional associations is also available. This certification is offered to students graduating from an air-conditioning, refrigeration, and heating program and to those workers who have been in the field for less than a year. Certification is obtained by passing examinations such as those administered through the Air-Conditioning and Refrigeration Institute and demonstrates that one meets industry-agreed standards of entry-level competency.

In some areas of the field—for example, those who work with design and research engineers—certifica-

tion is increasingly the norm and viewed as a basic indicator of competence. Even where there are no firm requirements, it generally is better to be qualified for whatever license or certification is available.

Some parts of the United States have local requirements for certification. It is possible that future state or federal requirements will be instituted for technicians working in certain phases of the environmental control industry.

In some jobs, technicians may be required to join a union.

Opportunities for Experience & Exploration

A student trying to decide on a career in air-conditioning, refrigeration, and heating technology may have to base the choice on a variety of indirect evidence. Part-time or summer work is usually not available to high school students because of their lack of the necessary skills and knowledge. It may be possible, however, to arrange field trips to service shops, companies that develop and produce heating and cooling equipment, or other firms concerned with the environmental control field. Such visits can give the student a firsthand overview of the day-to-day work. A visit with a local contractor or to a school that conducts an air-conditioning, refrigeration, and heating technology training program can also be very helpful. Some individuals have been exposed to the field while serving in the armed forces as *heating and cooling mechanics* and have pursued further training on returning to civilian life. Prospective technicians may also contact heating and refrigeration associations, such as those listed at the end of this article, for information about how to get started in this field.

An important way to test interest in the occupation is through relevant courses such as physics, mathematics, mechanical drawing, and shop work. Taking classes that provide opportunities to work with hand tools and basic shop equipment may help students discover if they have the aptitude for this type of work. Students who dislike the theoretical aspects of science are likely to be at a disadvantage, because technical training programs, and most jobs in the field, generally require understanding of air-conditioning, refrigeration, and heating theory.

Methods of Entering

Many students in two-year programs work during the summer between the first and second years at a job related to their area of training. Their employers may hire them on a part-time basis during the second year and make offers of full-time employment after graduation. Even if such a job offer cannot be made, the employer may be aware of other companies that are hiring and help the student with suggestions and recommendations, provided the student's work record is good.

Some schools make work experience part of the curriculum, particularly during the latter part of their program. This is a valuable way for students to gain practical experience in conjunction with classroom work.

It is not unusual for graduates of two-year programs to receive several offers of employment, either from contacts they have made themselves or from companies that routinely recruit new graduates. Representatives of larger companies often schedule interview periods at schools with two-year air-conditioning, refrigeration, and heating technician programs. Other, usually smaller, prospective employers may contact specific faculty advisors who in turn make students aware of opportunities that arise.

In addition to using their schools' job placement services, resourceful students can independently explore other leads by responding to want ads in local newspapers or by applying directly to local heating and cooling contractors; sales, installation, and service shops; or manufacturers of air-conditioning, refrigeration, and heating equipment. State employment offices may also post openings or provide job leads.

Finally, student membership in the local chapter of a trade association, such as one of those listed at the end of this article, will often result in good employment contacts.

Advancement

There is such a wide range of positions within this field that workers who gain the necessary skills and experience have the flexibility to choose between many different options and types of positions. As employees gain on-the-job work experience, they may decide to specialize in a particular aspect or type of work. They may be able to be promoted into positions requiring more responsibilities and skills through experience and demonstrated proficiency, but in some cases additional training is required.

Many workers continue to take courses throughout their careers to upgrade their skills and to learn new techniques and methods used within the industry. Training can take the form of a specific class offered by a manufacturer regarding specific equipment or it may be a more extensive program resulting in certification for a specific area or procedure. Skill improvement programs that offer advanced training in specialized areas are available through vocational-technical institutes and trade associations. Technicians with an interest in the engineering aspect of the industry may go back to school to get a bachelor of science degree in air-conditioning, refrigerant, and heating engineering or mechanical engineering.

Technicians increase their value to employers and themselves with continued training. For example, a technician employed by a manufacturer may progress to the position of sales manager, who acts as liaison with distributors and dealers, promoting and selling the manufacturer's products, or to field service representative, who solves unusual service problems of dealers and distributors in the area. Technicians working for dealers and distributors or contractors may advance to a service manager or supervisory position, overseeing other technicians who install and service equipment. Another possible specialization is mechanical design, which involves designing piping, duct work, controls, and the distribution systems for consulting engineers, mechanical contractors, manufacturers, and distributors. Technicians who do installation and maintenance may decide to move into sales or work for the research and development department of a manufacturing company.

Some technicians also open up their own businesses, becoming cooling and heating contractors, consultants, self-employed service technicians, or specializing in sales and parts distribution.

Employment Outlook

Employment in the air-conditioning, refrigeration, and heating field is expected to increase about as fast as the average for all occupations through the year 2006. Some openings will occur because experienced workers retire or transfer to other work. Other openings will be generated because of a demand for new climate-control systems for residences and industrial and commercial users. In addition, many existing systems are being upgraded to provide more efficient use of energy and to provide benefits not originally built into the system. There is a growing emphasis on improving indoor air quality, with more of a demand for climate-control systems that not only regulate temperature but can also provide moisture control and dehumidification, energy recovery, high-efficiency filtration, and airflow monitoring functions. There is an increasing awareness on making equipment more environmentally friendly, and with the implementation of the Clean Air Act Amendment of 1990, systems that use CFCs need to be retrofitted or replaced with new equipment.

Comfort is only one of the major reasons for environmental control. Conditioned atmosphere is a necessity in any precision industry where temperature and humidity can affect fine tolerances. As products and processes become more complex and more highly automated, the need for closely controlled conditions becomes increasingly important. For example, electronics manufacturers must keep the air bone-dry for many parts of their production processes to prevent damage to parts and to maintain nonconductivity. Pharmaceutical and food manufacturers rely on pure, dirt-free air. High-speed multicolor printing requires temperature control of rollers and moisture control for the paper racing through the presses. There is every reason to expect that these and other sophisticated industries will rely more in the coming years on precision control of room conditions. The actual amount of industry growth for these applications will hinge on the overall health of the nation's economy and the rate of manufacturing.

Technicians who are involved in maintenance and repair are not as affected by the economy as workers in some other jobs. Whereas in bad economic times a consumer may postpone building a new house or installing a new air-conditioning system, hospitals, restaurants, technical industries, and public buildings will still require skilled technicians to maintain their climate-control systems. Technicians who are versed in more than one aspect of the job have greater job flexibility and can count on fairly steady work despite any fluctuations in the economy.

Earnings

The earnings of air-conditioning, refrigeration, and heating technicians vary widely according to the level of training and experience, the nature of their work, type of employer, region of the country, and other factors. In private industry, the average beginning salary for air-conditioning, refrigeration, and heating technicians who have completed a two-year postsecondary school program is approximately $15,000. Salaries for nonsupervisory air-conditioning, refrigeration, and heating technicians, including those with several years' experience, usu-

ally fall between $27,872 and $46,124 and average around $37,000 a year.

Many employers offer medical insurance and paid vacation days, holidays, and sick days, although the actual benefits vary from employer to employer. Some companies also offer tuition assistance for additional training.

Conditions of Work

The working conditions for air-conditioning, refrigeration, and heating technicians vary considerably depending on the area of the industry in which they work. For the most part, the hours are regular, although certain jobs in production may involve shift work, and service technicians may have to be on call some evenings and weekends to handle emergency repairs.

Technicians who work in installation and service may work in a variety of environments ranging from industrial plants to construction sites and can include both indoor and outdoor work. Technicians may encounter extremes in temperature when servicing outdoor and rooftop equipment and cramped quarters when servicing indoor commercial and industrial equipment. They often have to lift heavy objects as well as stoop, crawl, and crouch when making repairs and installations. Working conditions can include dirt, grease, noise, and safety hazards. Hazards include falls from rooftops or scaffolds, electric shocks, burns, and handling refrigerants and compressed gases. With proper precautions and safety measures, however, the risk from these hazards can be minimized.

Technicians who work in laboratories usually work in the research and development departments of a manufacturing firm or an industrial plant. Technicians employed by distributors, dealers, and consulting engineers usually work in an office or similar surroundings and are subject to the same benefits and conditions as other office workers. Some technicians—for example, sales representatives or service managers—usually go out periodically to visit customers or installation and service sites.

Air-conditioning, refrigeration, and heating technicians work for a variety of companies and businesses. They may be employed by heating and cooling contractors, manufacturers of air-conditioning, refrigeration, and heating equipment, dealers and distributors, utility companies, or engineering consultants. Some large institutions such as hospitals, universities, factories, office complexes, and sports arenas employ technicians directly, maintaining their own climate-control staffs.

Sources of Additional Information

For information on careers, educational programs, and certification, please contact:

Air-Conditioning and Refrigeration Institute
4301 North Fairfax Drive, Suite 425
Arlington, VA 22203
Tel: 703-524-8800

National Association of Plumbing-Heating-Cooling Contractors
180 South Washington Street
PO Box 6808
Falls Church, VA 22040
Tel: 703-237-8100

Air Conditioning Contractors of America
1712 New Hampshire Avenue, NW
Washington, DC 20009
Tel: 202-483-9370

Refrigerating Engineers and Technicians Association
401 North Michigan Avenue
Chicago, IL 60611-4267
Tel: 312-644-6610

American Society of Heating, Refrigerating and Air-Conditioning Engineers
1791 Tullie Circle, NE
Atlanta, GA 30329
Tel: 404-636-8400

Aircraft Mechanics

Definition

Aircraft mechanics examine, service, repair, and overhaul aircraft and aircraft engines. They also repair, replace, and assemble parts of the airframe (the structural parts of the plane other than the power plant or engine).

Nature of the Work

The work of aircraft mechanics employed by the commercial airlines may be classified into two categories, that of *line maintenance mechanics* and *overhaul mechanics.*

Line maintenance mechanics are all-around craft workers who make repairs on all parts of the plane. Working at the airport, they make emergency and other necessary repairs in the time between when aircraft land and when they take off again. They may be told by the pilot, flight engineer, or head mechanic what repairs need to be made, or they may thoroughly inspect the plane themselves for oil leaks, cuts or dents in the surface and tires, or any malfunction in the radio, radar, and light equipment. In addition, their duties include changing oil, cleaning spark plugs, and replenishing the hydraulic and oxygen systems. They work as fast as safety permits so the aircraft can be put back into service quickly.

Overhaul mechanics keep the aircraft in top operating condition by performing scheduled maintenance, making repairs, and conducting inspections required by the Federal Aviation administration (FAA). Scheduled maintenance programs are based on the number of hours flown, calendar days, or a combination of these factors. Overhaul mechanics work at the airline's main overhaul base on either or both of the two major parts of the aircraft: the airframe, which includes wings, fuselage, tail assembly, landing gear, control cables, propeller assembly, and fuel and oil tanks; or the power plant, which

School Subjects
Computer science
Shop (Trade/Vo-tech education)

Personal Interests
Airplanes
Fixing things

Work Environment
Indoors and outdoors
One location with some travel

Minimum Education Level
High school diploma
Apprenticeship

Salary Range
$23,000 to
$35,000 to
$48,000+

Certification or Licensing
Recommended

Outlook
About as fast as the average

DOT
621

GOE
05.05.09

NOC
7315

may be a radial (internal combustion), turbojet, turboprop, or rocket engine.

Airframe mechanics work on parts of the aircraft other than the engine, inspecting the various components of the airframe for worn or defective parts. They check the sheet-metal surfaces, measure the tension of control cables, and check for rust, distortion, and cracks in the fuselage and wings. They consult manufacturers' manuals and the airline's maintenance manual for specifications and to determine whether repair or replacement is needed to correct defects or malfunctions. They also use specialized computer software to assist them in determining the need, extent, and nature of repairs. Airframe mechanics repair, replace, and assemble parts using a variety of tools, including power shears, sheet-metal breakers, arc and acetylene welding equipment, rivet guns, and air or electric drills.

Aircraft powerplant mechanics inspect, service, repair, and overhaul the engine of the aircraft. Looking through specially designed openings while working from ladders or scaffolds, they examine an engine's external appearance for such problems as cracked cylinders, oil leaks, or cracks or breaks in the turbine blades. They also listen to the engine in operation to detect sounds indicating malfunctioning components, such as sticking or burned valves. The test equipment used to check the engine's operation includes ignition analyzers, compression checkers, distributor timers, and ammeters.

If necessary, the mechanics remove the engine from the aircraft, using a hoist or a forklift truck, and take the engine apart. They use sensitive instruments to measure parts for wear and use X-ray and magnetic inspection equipment to check for invisible cracks. Worn or damaged parts such as carburetors, superchargers, and magnetos are replaced or repaired; then the mechanics reassemble and reinstall the engine.

Aircraft mechanics adjust and repair electrical wiring systems and aircraft accessories and instruments; inspect, service, and repair pneumatic and hydraulic systems; and handle various servicing tasks, such as flushing crankcases, cleaning screens, greasing moving parts, and checking brakes.

Mechanics may work on only one type of aircraft or on many different types, such as jets, propeller-driven planes, and helicopters. For greater efficiency, some specialize in one section, such as the electrical system, of a particular type of aircraft. Among the specialists, there are *airplane electricians; pneumatic testers* and *pressure sealer-and-testers; aircraft body repairers* and *bonded structures repairers,* such as *burnishers* and *bumpers;* and *air conditioning mechanics, aircraft rigging and controls mechanics, plumbing and hydraulics mechanics,* and *experimental-aircraft testing mechan-*

ics. Avionics technicians are mechanics who specialize in the aircraft's electronic systems. *Flight engineers* are mechanics who function as a member of a larger airplane's flight crew and perform inspections, maintenance, and minor repair before, during, and after airplane flights.

Mechanics who work for businesses that own their own aircraft usually handle all necessary repair and maintenance work. The planes, however, generally are small and the work less complex than in repair shops.

In small, independent repair shops, mechanics must inspect and repair many different types of aircraft. The airplanes may include small commuter planes run by an aviation company, private company planes and jets, private individually owned aircraft, and planes used for flying instruction.

Requirements

The first requirement for prospective aircraft mechanics is a high school diploma. Courses in mathematics, physics, chemistry, and mechanical drawing are particularly helpful because they teach the principles involved in the operation of an aircraft, and this knowledge is often necessary to making the repairs. Machine shop, auto mechanics, or electrical shop are important courses for gaining experience in many skills needed by aircraft mechanics.

FAA certification is necessary for certain types of aircraft mechanics and is usually required to advance beyond entry-level positions. Most mechanics who work on civilian aircraft have FAA authorization as airframe mechanics, powerplant mechanics, or aircraft inspectors. Airframe mechanics are qualified to work on the fuselage, wings, landing gear, and other structural parts of the aircraft; powerplant mechanics are qualified for work on the engine. Mechanics may qualify for both airframe and powerplant licensing, allowing them to work on any part of the plane. Combination airframe and powerplant mechanics with an inspector's certificate are permitted to certify inspection work done by other mechanics. Mechanics without certification must be supervised by certified mechanics.

FAA certification is granted only to aircraft mechanics with previous work experience: a minimum of eighteen months for an airframe or powerplant certificate and at least thirty months working with both engines and airframes for a combination certificate. To qualify for an inspector's certificate, mechanics must have held a combined airframe and powerplant certificate for at least three years. In addition, all applicants for certification must pass written and oral tests and demonstrate their ability to do the work authorized by the certificate.

At one time, mechanics were able to acquire their skills through on-the-job training. This is rare today. Now most mechanics learn the job either in the armed forces or in trade schools approved by the FAA. The trade schools provide training with the necessary tools and equipment in programs that range in length from two years to thirty months. In considering applicants for certification, the FAA sometimes accepts successful completion of such schooling in place of work experience, but the schools do not guarantee an FAA certificate.

The experience acquired by aircraft mechanics in the armed forces sometimes satisfies the work requirements for FAA certification, and veterans may be able to pass the exam with a limited amount of additional study. But jobs in the military service are usually too specialized to satisfy the FAA requirement for broad work experience. In that case, veterans applying for FAA approval will have to complete a training program at a trade school. Schools occasionally give some credit for material learned in the service. However, on the plus side, airlines are especially eager to hire aircraft mechanics with both military experience and a trade school education.

Aircraft mechanics must be able to work with precision and meet rigid standards. Their physical condition is also important. They need more than average strength for lifting heavy parts and tools, as well as agility for reaching and climbing. And they should not be afraid of heights, since they may work on top of the wings and fuselages of large jet planes.

In addition to education and certification, union membership may be a requirement for some jobs, particularly for mechanics employed by major airlines. The principal unions organizing aircraft mechanics are the International Association of Machinists and Aerospace Workers and the Transport Workers Union of America. In addition, some mechanics are represented by the International Brotherhood of Teamsters, Chauffeurs, Warehousemen and Helpers of America.

Opportunities for Experience & Exploration

To test their interest in the work of aircraft mechanics, students should take such courses as shop, mathematics, and applied physics. Working with electronic kits, tinkering with automobile engines, and assembling model airplanes are also good ways of gauging their ability to do the kinds of work performed by aircraft mechanics.

A guided tour of an airfield can give a brief overall view of this industry. Even better would be a part-time or summer job with an airline in an area such as the baggage department. Small airports may also offer job opportunities for part-time, summer, or replacement workers. Students may also earn a Student Pilot license at the age of sixteen and may gain more insight into the basic workings of an airplane that way. Kits for building ultralight craft are also available and may provide even more insight into the importance of proper maintenance and repair.

In addition, experience with aircraft in the armed forces or the Civil Air Patrol is an excellent way of acquiring some technical knowledge plus a feel for the occupation.

Methods of Entering

High school graduates who wish to become aircraft mechanics may enter this field by enrolling in an FAA-approved trade school. (Note that there are schools offering this training that do not have FAA approval. If you are in doubt, check with the FAA or with the Future Aviation Professionals of America.) These schools generally have placement services available for their graduates.

Another method is to make direct application to the employment offices of companies providing air transportation and services or the local offices of the state employment service, although airlines prefer to employ people who have already completed training. Many airports are managed by private fixed-base operators (FBO), which also operate the airport's repair and maintenance facilities. The field may also be entered through enlistment in the armed forces.

Advancement

Promotions depend in part on the size of the organization for which an aircraft mechanic works. The first promotion after beginning employment is usually based on merit and comes in the form of a salary increase. To advance further, many companies require the mechanic to have a combined airframe and powerplant certificate, or perhaps an aircraft inspector's certificate.

Advancement could take the following route: journeyworker mechanic, head mechanic or crew chief, inspector, head inspector, and shop supervisor. With additional training, a mechanic may advance to engineering, administrative, or executive positions. In larger airlines, mechanics may advance to become flight engineers, then copilots and pilots. With business training, some mechanics open their own repair shops.

Employment Outlook

The importance of aircraft mechanics to the aviation industry means that trained and skilled mechanics will always be in demand. Nevertheless, this career is expected to grow about as fast as the average through 2006. As the airline industry comes out of the recession of the early 1990s, airlines will be adding more flights and more planes to their fleets. If, as predicted, the number of airline passengers grows by 60 percent over the next decade, the airlines will likely add even more planes to the fleet and will need to expand their repair staff accordingly. In addition, a large number of mechanics are expected to retire over the next decade, and many others will either be promoted to other positions or leave the industry for other jobs. However, a number of factors may limit the growth of jobs in this field.

The recession and concurrent wave of corporate downsizing has resulted in a continued decrease in the amount of business travel, an important source of income for the airlines. Many corporations that formerly owned and operated their own aircraft have chosen to use the services of regional and other airlines for their business needs. Executive flights, an important segment of the general aviation industry, are also down. Defense spending has slowed dramatically since the end of the Cold War, and the military is hiring few mechanics as it closes down many of its bases. The numbers of planes and flights the military buys and makes each year is much lower than before, resulting in a reduced need for mechanics to service its fleet. Commercial employment growth will also be restricted by a greater use of automated equipment, inventory control, and modular systems that speed repairs and maintenance. Many small, often privately run airports are expected to close during the coming years, and this, too, will mean fewer aircraft mechanic jobs.

Competition for the higher-paying airline jobs will continue to remain extremely high, as more qualified people than are needed apply for fewer jobs. Cuts in the defense budget has also meant greater numbers of military personnel entering the commercial and general aviation industries. The phasing out of flight engi-

neer positions by many airlines may eventually make this position obsolete.

Qualified mechanics, particularly if they are willing to relocate, should find more opportunities in general aviation, where most employment opportunities are with small companies. The number of general aviation flights continues to increase as more and more people become interested in flying, and these flights already comprise the vast majority of all flights made each year. Government agencies and other services, such as police, fire, rescue and emergency, forest, traffic, and relief efforts, are making greater use of airplanes and helicopters than ever before. Many of these agencies operate their own aircraft fleets. Because the wages paid by small companies are usually low, there will be less competition for these jobs than for jobs with airlines and large private companies. Many openings will be created as experienced mechanics leave for better-paying jobs in larger companies. Positions for avionics technicians are expected to grow as more aircraft are outfitted with increasingly sophisticated electronic systems.

All aviation jobs are affected by changes in the economy. A recession results in fewer people traveling, fewer flights, fewer aircraft purchases, and more layoffs of workers. These people will generally be the first to be hired back when the economy picks up again.

Earnings

Although some aircraft mechanics, especially at the entry level and at small businesses, earn little more than the minimum wage, most aircraft mechanics in 1996, according to the U.S. Department of Labor, earned an average of $23,000. Average salaries for airlines mechanics are around $35,000 per year. Experienced mechanics can earn as much as $48,000 per year. Mechanics with airframe and powerplant certification earn more than those without it. Flight engineers average around $38,000 per year, while avionics technicians average around $27,000 per year. Overtime, night shift, and holiday pay differentials are usually available and can greatly increase a mechanic's annual earnings.

Most major airlines are covered by union agreements. Their mechanics generally earn more than those working for other employers. Contracts usually include health insurance and often life insurance and retirement plans as well. An attractive fringe benefit for airline mechanics and their immediate families is free or reduced fares on their own and many other airlines. Mechanics working for the federal government also benefit from the greater job security of civil service and government jobs.

Conditions of Work

Of the roughly 137,000 aircraft mechanics currently employed in the United States, well over half work for scheduled airlines. Each airline usually has one main overhaul base, where most of its mechanics are employed. These bases are found along the main airline routes or near large cities, including New York, Chicago, Los Angeles, Atlanta, San Francisco, and Miami.

About one-sixth of aircraft mechanics work for the federal government. Many of these mechanics are civilians employed at military aviation installations, while others work for the FAA, mainly in their headquarters in Oklahoma City. About one-fifth of all mechanics work for aircraft assembly firms. Most of the rest are general aviation mechanics employed by independent repair shops at airports around the country, by businesses that use their own planes for transporting employees or cargo, by certified supplemental airlines, or by crop-dusting and air-taxi firms.

Most aircraft mechanics work a five-day, forty-hour week. Their working hours, however, may be irregular and often include nights, weekends, and holidays, as airlines operate twenty-four hours a day. and extra work is required during holiday seasons.

When doing overhauling and major inspection work, aircraft mechanics generally work in hangars with adequate heat, ventilation, and light. If the hangars are full, however, or if repairs must be made quickly, they may work outdoors, sometimes in unpleasant weather. Outdoor work is frequent for line maintenance mechanics, who work at airports, because they must make minor repairs and preflight checks at the terminal to save time. To maintain flight schedules, or to keep from inconveniencing customers in general aviation, the mechanics often have to work under time pressure.

The work is physically strenuous and demanding. Mechanics often have to lift or pull as much as fifty pounds of weight. They may stand, lie, or kneel in awkward positions, sometimes in precarious places such as on a scaffold or ladder.

Noise and vibration are common when testing engines. Regardless of the stresses and strains, aircraft mechanics are expected to work quickly and with great precision.

Although the power tools and test equipment are provided by the employer, mechanics may be expected to furnish their own hand tools.

Sources of Additional Information

■ **Air Line Employees Association**
6520 South Cicero Avenue
Bedford Park, IL 60638
Tel: 708-563-9999

For information on careers in aircraft mechanics, please contact:

■ **Aeronautical Repair Station Association**
121 North Henry
Alexandria, VA 22314
Tel: 703-739-9543

■ **Future Aviation Professionals of America**
4959 Massachusetts Boulevard
Atlanta, GA 30337
Tel: 800-JET-JOBS

■ **Professional Aviation Maintenance Association**
636 Eye Street, NW, Suite 300
Washington, D.C. 20001-3736
Tel: 202-216-9220
WWW: http://www.pama.org

For information on manufacturing careers in general aviation, please contact:

■ **General Aviation Manufacturers Association**
1400 K Street, NW, Suite 801
Washington, DC, 20005
Tel: 202-393-1500

Airplane and Helicopter Pilots

Definition

Airplane and helicopter pilots perform many different kinds of flying jobs. In general, pilots operate an aircraft for the transportation of passengers, freight, mail, or for other commercial purposes.

Nature of the Work

The best known pilots are the commercial airline pilots who fly for the airlines. Responsible, skilled professionals, they are among the highest paid workers in the country. The typical pilot flight deck crew includes the *captain,* who is the pilot in command, and the *copilot,* or *first officer.* In larger aircraft, there may be a third member of the crew, called the *flight engineer,* or *second officer.* The captain of a flight is in complete command of the crew, the aircraft, and the passengers or cargo while they are on flight. In the air, the captain also has the force of law. The aircraft flown by airline pilots usually costs millions of dollars. It may hold thirty people or three hundred or be completely loaded with freight, depending on the airline and type of operations. The plane may be fitted with either turbojet, turboprop (which have propellers driven by jet engines), or reciprocating propeller engines. An aircraft may operate near the speed of sound and at altitudes as high as thirty-five thousand to forty thousand feet.

In addition to actually flying the aircraft, pilots must perform a variety of safety-related tasks. Before each flight, they must determine weather and flight conditions, ensure that sufficient fuel is on board to complete the flight safely, and verify the maintenance status of the aircraft. The captain briefs all crew members, including the flight attendants, about the flight. Pilots must also perform system operation checks to test the proper functioning of instrumentation, controls, and electronic and mechanical systems on the flight deck. Pilots coordinate their flight plan with airplane dispatchers and air traffic

School Subjects
Mathematics
Physics

Personal Interests
Airplanes
Travel

Work Environment
Primarily indoors
Primarily multiple locations

Minimum Education Level
High school diploma

Salary Range
$20,600 to
$76,800 to
$200,000

Certification or Licensing
Required

Outlook
About as fast as the average

DOT
196

GOE
05.04.01

NOC
2271

controllers. Flight plans include information about the airplane, the passenger or cargo load, and the air route the pilot is expected to take.

Once all preflight duties have been performed, the captain taxis the aircraft to the designated runway and prepares for takeoff. Takeoff speeds must be calculated based on the aircraft's weight. The aircraft systems, levers, and switches must be in proper position for takeoff. After takeoff, the pilots may engage an electrical device known as the autopilot. This device can be programmed to maintain the desired course and altitude. With or without the aid of the autopilot, pilots must constantly monitor the aircraft's systems.

Because pilots may encounter turbulence, emergencies, and other hazardous situations during a flight, good judgment and ability are extremely important. Pilots also receive periodic training and evaluation on their handling of in-flight abnormalities and emergencies and on their operation of the aircraft during challenging weather conditions. As a further safety measure, airline pilots are expected to adhere to disciplined checklist procedures in all areas of flight operations.

During a flight, pilots monitor aircraft systems, keep a watchful eye on local weather conditions, perform checklists, and maintain constant communication with the air traffic controllers along the flight route. The busiest times for pilots are during takeoff and landing. The weather conditions at the aircraft's destination must be obtained and analyzed. The aircraft must be maneuvered and properly configured to make a landing on the runway. When the cloud cover is low and visibility is poor, pilots rely solely on the instruments on the flight deck. These instruments include an altimeter and an artificial horizon. Pilots select the appropriate radio navigation frequencies and corresponding course for the ground-based radio and microwave signals that provide horizontal, and in some cases vertical, guidance to the landing runway.

After the pilots have safely landed the aircraft, the captain taxis it to the ramp or gate area where passengers and cargo will be off-loaded. Pilots then follow "afterlanding and shutdown" checklist procedures, and inform maintenance crews of any discrepancies or other problems noted during the flight.

Pilots must also keep detailed logs of their flight hours, both for payroll purposes and to comply with Federal Aviation Administration (FAA) regulations. Pilots with major airlines generally have few nonflying duties. Pilots with smaller airlines, charter services, and other air service companies may be responsible for loading the aircraft, refueling, keeping records, performing minor repairs and maintenance, and arranging for more major repairs.

Flight instructors are pilots who teach others how to fly. They may teach in classrooms or provide in-flight instruction, or both. Other pilots work as *examiners,* or *check pilots.* They may fly with experienced pilots as part of their periodic review; they may also give examinations to pilots applying for licenses.

The *chief pilot* directs the operation of the airline's flight department. This individual is in charge of training new pilots, preparing schedules and assigning flight personnel, reviewing their performance, and improving their morale and efficiency. Chief pilots make sure that all legal and governmental regulations affecting flight operations are observed, advise the airline during contract negotiations with the pilots' union, and handle a multitude of administrative details.

In addition to airline pilots, there are many *business pilots,* or *executive pilots,* who fly for large businesses that have their own planes or helicopters. The National Business Aircraft Association estimates that more than eighteen thousand firms either own or lease planes. These aircraft may be either single-engine or multi-engine planes, either new or bought from military agencies as surplus. They may be used to transport cargo or products or to carry airline executives on various business assignments. In some cases, planes owned by firms fly inspection routes to determine the condition of pipelines or electric power lines or to inspect large company holdings.

Between flights, the business pilot is occupied with the maintenance of the company's planes. Pilots who wish to fly for business firms need to know as much as possible about the mechanics of an aircraft. They may fly to remote areas in which maintenance service would be difficult to secure.

Agricultural pilots are involved in such duties as weed control, insect control, chemical dusting of crops, orchards, soil, forests and swamps, plant disease control, fertilization, and seeding. Agricultural aircraft pilots may plant small fish in streams or lakes, check the condition of crops, count the number of cattle in a herd or the number of animals of a given kind in a particular area, fight forest fires, feed either domestic or wild animals by dropping hay in snow-covered areas, and patrol power lines.

Agricultural aircraft pilots may combine two interests: farming and flying. The pilot who chooses this career should know about farms and farming. This person must be an expert pilot, able to fly at low altitudes carrying a heavy load. He or she must have a respect for the chemicals loaded on the plane and must know both their potential harm and benefits.

Although there are not many *test pilots,* their job is a very important one. Every airplane manufacturer employs several highly skilled people to test new planes. *Engineering test pilots* combine an engineering background with their ability as a pilot. They test new models of planes to ensure that these planes perform in the expected manner. If they do not, the model is not put into production until corrections are made. Because test pilots understand engineering problems, they are able to make specific suggestions about improvements or corrections in the new model.

Although there are still relatively few *helicopter pilots,* their numbers are expected to increase. Greater use is being made of this kind of aircraft, and pilots for them will be needed more in the future. Because airports that can accommodate jet planes are usually located far from the center of cities, helicopters are used for air-taxi service to take passengers to downtown locations or to other airports. They are also used for transporting mail relatively short distances between airports and post offices. Helicopters are also used in sightseeing, rescue service, conservation service, and in aerial photography.

Some pilots are employed in the following specialties: *photogrammetry pilots* fly planes or helicopters over designated areas and photograph the earth's surface for mapping and other purposes. *Facilities-flight-check pilots* fly specially equipped planes to test air navigational aids, air traffic controls, and communications equipment and to evaluate installation sites for such equipment. This testing is directed by a supervising pilot.

Requirements

All prospective pilots should complete high school. Most companies that employ pilots are requiring at least two years of college training. Many airline companies require applicants to be college graduates. Pilots leaving the military are in great demand by the airlines. Courses in engineering, meteorology, physics, and mathematics are helpful in preparing for a pilot's career. Flying can be learned in either military or civilian flying schools. There are approximately one thousand FAA-certified civilian flying schools, including some colleges and universities that offer degree credit for pilot training.

Sound physical and emotional health are essential requirements for aspiring pilots. Emotional stability is necessary because the safety of other people depends upon a pilot remaining calm and level-headed, no matter how trying the situation. Physical health is equally important. Vision and hearing must be perfect; coordination must be excellent; and heart rate and blood pressure must be normal.

To become a pilot, certain rigid training requirements must be met. Although obtaining a private pilot's license is not difficult, it may be quite difficult to obtain a commercial license. Any student who is sixteen or over and who can pass the rigid mandatory physical examination may apply for permission to take flying instruction. When the training is finished, a written examination must be taken. If prospective pilots pass the examination, they may apply for a private pilot's license. To qualify for it, a person must be at least seventeen years of age, must successfully fulfill a solo flying requirement of twenty hours or more, and must check out in instrument flying and cross-country flying. Student pilots are restricted from carrying passengers; private pilots may carry passengers but may not receive any payment or other compensation for the piloting activities.

All pilots and copilots must be licensed by the FAA before they can do any type of commercial flying. An applicant who is eighteen years old and has 250 hours of flying time can apply for a commercial airplane pilot's license. In applying for this license, a candidate must pass a rigid physical examination and a written test given by the FAA covering safe flight operations, federal aviation regulations, navigation principles, radio operation, and meteorology. The applicant also must submit proof that the minimum flight-time requirements have been completed and, in a practical test, demonstrate flying skill and technical competence to a check pilot. Before pilots or copilots receive an FAA license, they must also receive a rating for the kind of plane they can fly (single-engine, multi-engine, or seaplane) and for the specific type of plane, such as Boeing 707 or 747.

Most people hired by the scheduled airlines and some larger supplemental airlines begin as flight engineers. For this position, the airlines generally require that the applicant have five hundred to one thousand flying hours of experience. In addition, an instrument rating by the FAA and a restricted radio telephone operator's permit by the Federal Communications Commission (FCC) are required. All airline captains must have an air transport pilot license. Applicants for this license must be at least twenty-three years old and have a minimum of fifteen hundred hours of flight time, including night flying and instrument time. All pilots are subject to two-year flight reviews, regular six-month FAA flight checks, simulator tests, and medical exams. The FAA also makes unannounced spot check inspections of all pilots.

Pilots who work in special areas must have special training in these areas. The agricultural aircraft pilot, for example, should acquire special training in aerial application of dusts or fluids. Courses in this field are offered at approximately sixteen schools in the West, South, and Midwest, including such institutions as Texas A&M, Ohio State University, Oklahoma State, and the University of Mississippi, as well as private academies that specialize in this kind of instruction. Both jet pilots and helicopter pilots must have special training in their respective areas.

Opportunities for Experience & Exploration

High school students who are interested in flying may join an Air Scouts troop (Boy Scouts of America) or a high school aviation club. At sixteen years of age, they may start taking flying lessons. One of the most valuable experiences for high school students who want to be a pilot is to learn to be a ham radio operator. By so doing, they meet one of the qualifications for commercial flying.

Methods of Entering

A large percentage of commercial pilots have received their training in the armed forces. A military pilot who wants to apply for a commercial airplane pilot's license is required to pass only the Federal Aviation Regulations examination if application is made within a year after leaving the service.

Pilots possessing the necessary qualifications and license may apply directly to a commercial airline for a job. If accepted, they will go through a company orientation course, usually including both classroom instruction and practical training in company planes.

Those who are interested in becoming business pilots will do well to start their careers in mechanics. They may also have military flying experience, but the strongest recommendation for a business pilot's job is an Airframe and Powerplant (A and P) rating. They should also have at least five hundred hours flying time and have both commercial and instrument ratings on their license. They apply directly to the firm for which they would like to work.

Advancement

The flight engineer with a large commercial airline may spend two to seven years in that position before being promoted to copilot and another five to fifteen years before becoming captain. Many airlines no longer require flight engineers, and in this case, beginning pilots start out as copilots.

Seniority is the pilot's most important asset. If pilots leave one employer and go to another, they must start from the bottom again, no matter how much experience was gained with the first employer. The position of captain on a large airline is a high-seniority, high-prestige, and high-paying job. Pilots may also advance to the position of *check pilot*, testing other pilots for advanced ratings; *chief pilot*, supervising the work of other pilots; or to administrative or executive positions with a commercial airline (ground operations). They may also become self-employed, opening a flying business, such as a flight instruction, agricultural aviation, air-taxi, or charter service.

Employment Outlook

About 110,000 civilian pilots held jobs in 1996, accounting for a little over one-quarter of all pilots in the United States. Three-fifths of all pilots are employed by airlines. Many others teach flying at local airports or fly cargo and personnel for large companies that use their own aircraft. Pilots also perform air-taxi services, dust crops, inspect pipelines, or conduct sightseeing trips. Other pilots work for federal, state, or local governments or are self-employed.

The employment prospects of airline pilots look very good into the next century. The airline industry expects passenger travel to grow by as much as 60 percent, and airlines will be adding more planes and more flights to accommodate passengers and cargo. The outlook is less favorable, however, for business pilots. The recession of the early 1990s caused a decrease in the numbers of business and executive flights as more companies chose to fly with smaller and regional airlines rather than buy and operate their own planes and helicopters. The position of flight engineer is slowly being phased out as more and more airlines install computerized flight engineering systems.

Competition is expected to diminish as the many pilots who were hired during the boom of the 1960s reach mandatory retirement age. In addition, because the military has increased its benefits and incentives, many pilots choose to remain in the service, further reducing the supply of pilots for civilian work. These factors are expected to create a shortage of qualified pilots.

The aviation industry remains extremely sensitive to changes in the economy. When an economic downswing causes a decline in air travel, airline pilots may be given furlough. Business flying, flight instruction, and testing of new aircraft are also adversely affected by recessions.

Earnings

Airline pilots are among the highest paid workers in the country. In 1996, according to the U.S. Department of Labor, captains averaged $76,800 per year and earned as much as $200,000 per year. Copilots earned an average of $72,700 per year, and flight engineers earned an average of $51,500 per year. Salaries vary widely depending on a number of factors, including the specific airline, type of aircraft flown, number of years with a company, and level of experience. Airline pilots are also paid more for international and nighttime flights. Starting salaries with the airlines are approximately $20,000 per year. Pilots with smaller airlines and other pilots generally earn lower salaries. Pilots flying jet aircraft are usually paid more than pilots flying other types of aircraft. Chief flight instructors average $24,700 per year and range up to $72,000 per year. Chief pilots average $38,000 annually and can earn as much as $82,000 per year.

Pilots with the airlines receive life and health insurance and retirement benefits; if they fail their FAA physical exam during their career, they are eligible to receive disability benefits. Some airlines give pilots allowances for buying and cleaning their uniforms. Pilots and their families may usually fly free or at reduced fares on their own or on other airlines.

Conditions of Work

Airline pilots work with the best possible equipment and under highly favorable circumstances. Their job is glamorous, and they command a great deal of respect. Although many pilots regularly fly the same routes, no two flights are ever the same. FAA regulations limit airline pilots to no more than one hundred flying hours per month, and most work around seventy-five hours per month, with few nonflying duties. This is because the pilot's job may be extremely stressful. During flights, they must maintain constant concentration on a variety of factors. They must always be alert to changes in conditions and to any problems that may occur. They are often responsible for hundreds of lives besides their own, and they are always aware that flying contains an element of risk. During emergencies, they must react quickly, logically, and decisively. Pilots often work irregular hours, may be away from home a lot, and are subject to jet lag and other conditions associated with

flying. Pilots employed with smaller airlines may also be required to perform other, nonflying duties, which increase the number of hours they work each month.

The job of the agricultural aircraft pilot is more hazardous than that of the airline pilot. In addition to the normal dangers of flying, they also may work with toxic chemicals and sometimes fly under difficult circumstances. Often, they will not have an airfield from which to work, but will have to take off and land on a relatively smooth piece of farmland.

For other pilots who handle small planes, emergency equipment, and supply delivery or routes to remote and isolated areas, the hazards may be more evident. Dropping medical supplies in Somalia, flying relief supplies into war zones, or delivering mail to northern Alaska are more difficult tasks than most pilots face. Business pilot schedules may be highly irregular and they must be on call for a great portion of their off-duty time. Business pilots and most private and small plane pilots are also frequently called upon to perform maintenance and repairs.

Sources of Additional Information

■■■**Air Line Employees Association**
6520 South Cicero Avenue
Bedford Park, IL 60638
Tel: 708-563-9999

■■■**Airline Pilots Association**
537 Herndon Parkway
Washington, DC 20090
Tel: 202-797-4033

■■■**Air Transport Association of America**
1301 Pennsylvania Avenue, NW, Suite 1100
Washington, DC 20006
Tel: 202-626-4000

■■■**Federal Aviation Administration**
Flight Standards Division
Fitzgerald Federal Building
John F. Kennedy International Airport
Jamaica, NY 11430

■■■**Future Aviation Professionals of America**
4291 J. Memorial Drive
Atlanta, GA 30032
Tel: 800-JET-JOBS

Animal Breeders and Technicians

Definition

Animal breeders and technicians help breed, raise, and market a variety of farm animals: cattle, sheep, pigs, horses, mules, chickens, turkeys, geese, and ducks; and other more exotic animals, such as ostriches, alligators, and minks. Technicians who are primarily involved with the breeding and feeding of animals are sometimes referred to as *animal husbandry technicians.*

In general, animal breeders and technicians are concerned with the propagation, feeding, housing, health, production, and marketing of animals. These technicians work in many different settings and capacities: they may supervise unskilled farm workers, serve as field representatives assisting in the sales of animals or animal products to customers, serve as sales representatives for farm-product or farm-services vendors, or act as purchasing agents for food-processing and packaging firms. The diversity of employment available for well-trained and well-qualified animal breeders and technicians makes this career extremely flexible. As science progresses, opportunities for these technicians will become even broader.

Nature of the Work

Most animal breeders and technicians work as *livestock production technicians* with cattle, sheep, swine, or horses; or as *poultry production technicians,* with chickens, turkeys, geese, or ducks.

Most livestock production technicians find employment either on livestock farms or ranches or with the businesses that service these farms and ranches. On a farm or ranch, they may be involved in animal feed preparation. A typical entry-level job is the *scale and bin tender,* who weighs and records all feed grain entering, leaving, or being used in the feeding yards. This person also arranges for proper grain storage and keeps an accurate inventory of all animals and types of feed on hand.

School Subjects
Agriculture
Biology

Personal Interests
Animals
Science

Work Environment
Indoors and outdoors
Primarily multiple locations

Minimum Education Level
High school diploma

Salary Range
$15,000 to
$24,900 to
$26,000+

Certification or Licensing
None

Outlook
About as fast as the average

DOT
410

GOE
03.01.02

Another entry-level position is the *feed-mixing technician*, who weighs, mixes, and blends animal feed according to recommendations made by the *ration technician*.

The ration technician is an experienced livestock production technician who selects the most desirable feed and supplements to keep animals healthy and growing rapidly, while producing the best return for the money invested. The ration technician must know the nutritional needs of each type of livestock with which he or she works. Nutritional requirements change with factors such as age, pregnancy, season, and health, and the ration technician must know how to adjust the feed accordingly.

Experienced livestock production technicians interested in animal feeding may also be employed as *feed buyers* or *feed lot managers*. Feed buyers supply the most suitable and economical feed needed on a farm for each of its many operations.

Feed lot managers oversee the entire feed lot operation. They must be familiar with shipping, receiving, mixing of feeds, buying and selling of livestock, and the work of each employee.

Another farm position for livestock production technicians is the *disease prevention technician*. This technician protects animals from disease and parasites, administers disease prevention treatments such as dipping and vaccination, conducts frequent examinations, and treats livestock for cuts, wounds, and minor diseases.

Off-farm livestock production technicians work in a variety of different capacities. Once again, they may be involved with feed preparation. Since small producers of cattle, sheep, and hogs often do not have facilities to store, mix, or grind feed, they must rely on feed companies, which hire technicians to perform the various feed-related activities.

Livestock production technicians also sell, service, and sometimes install the mechanical equipment used in livestock production. These include trucks and tractors, mechanized feed mixers and feed carriers, and manure-turning machines.

Another off-farm occupation is the judge and purchaser of livestock. Technicians working in this area are usually employed by slaughterhouses or meat-packing companies, for which they inspect, grade, and weigh livestock to determine value and yield. They may also arrange for the transportation and sale of livestock.

Some off-farm livestock production technicians are employed as *veterinarians' assistants*. They assist in the care of animals under treatment, sterilize equipment, and administer medication under the direction of the veterinarian.

Technicians who work in bird production can be divided into seven areas. In breeding-flock production, technicians may work as *farm managers,* directing the operation of one or several farms. They may be *flock supervisors* with five or six assistants working directly with farmers under contract to produce hatching eggs. On pedigree breeding farms, technicians may oversee all the people who transport, feed, and care for the poultry. Technicians in breeding-flock production seek ways to improve efficiency in the use of time, materials, and labor; they also strive to make maximum effective use of data-processing equipment.

Technicians in n hatchery management operate and maintain the incubators and hatchers, where eggs develop as embryos. These technicians must be trained in incubation, sexing, grading, scheduling, and effectively using available technology.

The production and marketing of table eggs require poultry technicians to handle birds on pullet-growing farms and egg farms. Experienced poultry technicians often work as supervisors of flocks and manage those who provide the actual care of the flocks. Poultry technicians may also work in or supervise smaller, specialized production units that clean, grade, or package eggs for wholesale or retail trade.

The egg processing phase begins when the eggs leave the farm. *Egg processing technicians* handle egg pickup, trucking, delivery, and quality control. With experience, technicians in this area can work as supervisors and plant managers. These technicians need training in egg processing machinery and refrigeration equipment.

Technicians in poultry meat production oversee the production, management, and inspection of birds bred specifically for consumption as meat. Technicians may work directly with flocks or in supervisory positions.

Poultry meat processing and sales technicians supervise or carry out the task of picking up meat birds at the farms on schedule to keep processing plants operating efficiently. Technicians working as *plant supervisors* handle all phases of processing, including inspection for quality, grading, packaging, and marketing. They also operate machinery, as well as maintain and manage plant personnel.

Poultry technicians are also employed in the sales and service of poultry equipment, feed, and supplies.

Within these seven broad areas, a number of specific kinds of jobs are commonly performed by poultry technicians. Following are descriptions of some of these jobs, each appropriate for entry-level technicians.

Poultry graders certify the grade of dressed or ready-to-cook poultry in processing plants according to government standards.

Poultry husbandry technicians conduct research in breeding, feeding, and management of poultry. They examine selection and breeding practices in order to increase efficiency of production and to improve the quality of poultry products.

Poultry inspectors certify wholesomeness and acceptability of live, dressed, and ready-to-cook poultry in processing plants.

Egg candlers inspect eggs to determine quality and fitness for consumption or incubation according to prescribed standards. They check to see if eggs have been fertilized and if they are developing correctly.

Egg graders inspect, sort, and grade eggs according to size, shape, color, and weight.

Some poultry technicians also work as *field-contact technicians,* inspecting poultry farms for food processing companies. They ensure that growers maintain contract standards for feeding and housing birds and controlling disease. They tour barns, incubation units, and related facilities to observe sanitation and weather protection procedures. Field-contact technicians ensure that specific grains are administered according to schedules, inspect birds for evidence of disease, and weigh them to determine growth rates.

One area of animal production technology that merits special mention is that of artificial breeding. Three kinds of technicians working in this specialized area of animal production are the *artificial-breeding technician,* the *artificial-breeding laboratory technician,* and the *artificial insemination technician.*

Artificial breeding can be differentiated by the goal of the breeder: food (poultry and cattle), sport (horses and dogs), and science (mice, rabbits, monkeys, and any other animals used for research). Breeders work to create better, stronger breeds of animals or to maintain good existing breeds.

Artificial-breeding technicians collect and package semen for artificial insemination. They examine the semen under a microscope to determine density and motility of sperm cells, and they dilute the semen according to standard formulas. They transfer the semen to shipping and storage containers with identifying data such as the source, date taken, and quality. They also keep records related to all of their activities. In some cases they may also be responsible for inseminating the females.

Artificial-breeding laboratory technicians handle the artificial breeding of all kinds of animals, but most often these technicians specialize in the laboratory aspects of the activity. They measure purity, potency, and density of animal semen and add extenders and antibiotics to it. They keep records, clean and sterilize laboratory equipment, and perform experimental tests to develop improved methods of processing and preserving semen.

Artificial insemination technicians do exactly what their name implies—they collect semen from the male species of an animal and artificially inseminate the female. *Poultry inseminators* collect semen from roosters and fertilize hens' eggs. They examine the roosters' semen for quality and density, measure specified amounts of semen for loading into inseminating guns, inject semen into hens, and keep accurate records of all aspects of the operation. This area of animal production is expected to grow as poultry production expands.

Cattle breeders work in a similar way. Their aim is to mate males and females with preferred traits; for example, producing animals with lean meat and less fat. It is desirable to produce cows who give birth easily and are less susceptible to illness than the average cow. They are inseminated with a gun, much like hens, which allows for many animals to be bred from the sperm of one male. By repeating the process of artificial breeding for many generations, a more perfect animal can be produced.

Horse and *dog breeders* strive to create more physically and physiologically desirable animals. They want horses and dogs who perform well, move fast, and look beautiful. Longer legs and shinier coats are examples of desirable show traits for these animals.

Some breeders produce many small animals such as mice, rabbits, dogs, and cats. These animals are used in scientific research. For example, some laboratories raise thousands of mice to be used in experiments. These mice are shipped all over the world so that scientists can study them.

Animals raised for fur or skin also require extensive technological assistance. Mink farms, ostrich farms, and alligator farms are animal production industries that need husbandry, feeding, and health technicians. As the popularity of one species rises or falls, others replace it, and new animal specialists are needed.

Requirements

High school students seeking to enter this field will find that the more agricultural background they acquire in high school, the better prepared they will be. In addition, courses in mathematics, business, communications, chemistry, and mechanics are valuable. Nine months to two years at a technical school or a college diploma are the preferred credentials for animal breeders and technicians. For the student who has not graduated high school, the road to this career will be much more difficult, although not impossible. By working as a stable hand and gaining valuable practical experience, someone without a high school diploma might be able to move up. However, a high school diploma is almost always necessary to enter any technical education program beyond the high school level.

Many colleges now offer two- and four-year programs in animal science or animal husbandry where additional knowledge, skills, and specialized training may be acquired. Besides learning the scientific side of animal breeding, students also take business classes that help them see the field from an economic point of view and increase their chances of doing well if they end up in a sales or management position. Many students use their training to springboard into other animal-related careers, for example, from livestock sales to animal photography to advertising. Whether trained by experience, at an academic institution, or both, all new hires at major breeding companies usually are put through some type of training program.

Certification is not required but nearly all major companies have certification programs and the additional knowledge can only enhance earnings and opportunities.

Animal breeders and technicians also need the ability to speak well, to conduct meetings, and to work cooperatively with individuals as well as groups of people.

Opportunities for Experience & Exploration

Children of farm families have the greatest opportunity to decide whether this career appeals to them. For those who have not grown up on a farm, however, there are summer jobs available on livestock farms that will help them decide if this type of work is what they want. In addition, organizations such as 4-H Clubs and the National FFA Organization (Future Farmers of America) offer good opportunities for hearing about, visiting, and participating in farm activities.

For at-home experience, raising pets is a good introduction to the skills needed in basic animal maintenance. Learning how to care for, feed, and house a pet provides some basic knowledge of working with animals. In addition, interested students can learn more about this field by reading books on animals and their care.

Other opportunities that provide animal maintenance experience include volunteering to work at anti-cruelty society centers, animal shelters, veterinary offices, and pet breeders' businesses.

Methods of Entering

The most common ways of entering the field of animal breeding are through direct, on-the-job experience, by attending a two-year technical school or a four-year college, or some combination of the two.

Most available programs in animal production technology are relatively new, and many job placement procedures have not been developed to the fullest degree. However, many avenues are open, and employers recognize the importance of education at the technical level. Many junior colleges participate in a "learn-and-earn" program, in which the college and prospective employer jointly provide the student's training, both in the classroom and on-the-job work with livestock and other animals. Most technical programs offer placement services for graduates, and the demand for qualified people often exceeds the supply.

Advancement

Even when a good training or technical program is completed, the graduate often must begin work at a low level before advancing to positions with more responsibility. But the technical program graduate will advance much more rapidly to positions of major responsibility and greater financial reward than the untrained worker.

Those graduates willing to work hard and keep abreast of changes in their field may advance to livestock breeder, feedlot manager, supervisor, or artificial breeding distributor. If they have the necessary capital, they can own their own livestock ranches.

Employment Outlook

Continuing changes are expected in the next few years, in both the production and the marketing phases of the animal production industry. Because of the costs involved, it is almost impossible for a one-person operation to stay in business. As a result, cooperatives of consultants and corporations will become more prevalent with greater emphasis placed on specialization. This, in turn, will increase the demand for technical program graduates. Other factors, such as small profit margins, the demand for more uniform products, and an increasing foreign market, will result in a need for more specifically trained personnel. This is a new era of specialization in the animal production industry; graduates of animal production technology programs have an interesting and rewarding future ahead of them.

Earnings

Salaries vary widely depending on the kind of employer, the technicians' educational and agricultural background, the kind of animal the technicians work with, and the geographical areas in which they work. In general, the salaries of all agricultural technicians tend to be lower in the northeastern part of the nation and higher in California and some parts of the Midwest, such as Minnesota and Iowa. According to the National Association of Colleges and Employers, starting salaries for animal breeders with a bachelor's degree averaged $24,900 in 1997. Salaries for technicians are significantly lower, ranging from approximately $15,000 to $26,000 a year or more. In addition, many technicians receive food and housing benefits that can amount to several thousand dollars a year. Other fringe benefits vary according to type of employer but can include paid vacation time, health insurance, and pension benefits.

Conditions of Work

Working conditions vary from operation to operation, but certain factors always exist in varying degrees. Much of the work is done outside in all types of weather, and often requires long, irregular hours and work on Sundays and holidays. Salaries are usually commensurate with the hours worked, and there are usually slack seasons when time off is given to compensate any extra hours worked. But for people with a strong desire to work with animals, long working hours or other less desirable conditions are offset by the benefits of this career.

Animal breeders and technicians are often their own bosses and make their own decisions. While this can be considered an asset to those who value independence, prospective animal breeders and technicians must realize that self-discipline is the most valuable trait to possess for success.

Sources of Additional Information

■**National Congress of Animal Trainers and Breeders**
23675 West Chardon Road
Grayslake, IL 60030
Tel: 847-546-0717

■**American Society of Animal Science**
309 West Clark Street
Champaign, IL 61820
Tel: 217-356-3182

The following is a conglomerate of state and beef breed registry associations representing farmers, breeders, and feeders of beef cattle. It functions as the central agency for national public information distribution and legislative efforts and as the industry liaison for the beef cattle business. For more information, contact its national headquarters:

■**National Cattlemen's Association**
PO Box 3469
Englewood, CO 80155
Tel: 303-694-0305

■**National Grain and Feed Association**
725 15th Street, NW, Suite 500
Washington, DC 20005
Tel: 202-289-0873

■**U.S. Department of Agriculture**
Human Resources Division, Agricultural Research Service
6305 Ivy Lane
Greenbelt, MD 20770
WWW: http://www.ars.usda.gov/

■**Canadian Cattlemen's Association**
#215, 6715 8th Street, North East
Calgary, AB T2E 7H7 Canada
Tel: 403-275-8558

Animal Caretakers

Definition

Animal caretakers feed, water, nurture, and exercise animals. They monitor the animals' general health, as well as clean and repair cages. Caretakers who work in zoos are responsible for transferring animals needed, arranging exhibits, and setting temperature controls to ensure that the animals are comfortable. Those who work with veterinarians may help treat animals for illness or disease, administer medications, or assist during surgery. Animal caretakers who work in veterinary research are involved in medical testing procedures.

Nature of the Work

Animal caretakers, also referred to as *animal attendants,* perform daily duties that include feeding, grooming, cleaning, and exercising animals. Kennels, pet stores, animal shelters, laboratories, zoos, and veterinary facilities all employ caretakers.

Kennel workers and *shelter workers* generally care for small animals such as cats and dogs. They learn to recognize signs of illness like poor posture, lack of appetite, fatigue, or weakness. They check for sharp edges and other dangerous situations in cages or pens. They take animals to rooms for treatment as well as let them outdoors for exercise. Attendants in an animal shelter screen applicants for animal adoption as well as take care of animals brought in by control officers or other people.

Skilled animal shelter attendants have the unpleasant job of euthanizing (putting to death) animals who are injured, ill, or unwanted. They also administer necessary vaccinations to healthy animals.

Stable workers feed and water horses, saddle and unsaddle them, give them rubdowns, and walk them through cool-offs after riding. Other duties for stable workers include cleaning out stalls, grooming the horses, storing feed and supplies and, with experience, horse training.

School Subjects
Biology
Mathematics

Personal Interests
Animals
The Environment

Work Environment
Primarily indoors
Primarily one location

Minimum Education Level
High school diploma

Salary Range
$11,000 to
$18,500 to
$30,000

Certification or Licensing
Recommended

Outlook
Faster than the average

DOT
079

GOE
02.03.03

NOC
6483

Pet shop attendants feed and water animals and clean their cages. Sometimes they bathe cats and dogs and trim their nails. They inspect animals for sores or signs of illness that could spread to other animals. *Groomers* can be part of a pet shop or self-employed and are responsible for maintaining the appearance of animals, usually dogs. They bathe and clip dogs according to different breed standards.

Veterinary technicians have completed formal studies and work in veterinary offices, animal laboratories, and animal hospitals. They prepare animals for surgery and assist during medical procedures. They also keep records. *Veterinary assistants* assist veterinarians or veterinary technicians. They feed and bathe animals and administer medications as well.

Animal laboratory workers are employed wherever live animals are used for research, testing, or educational purposes. Lab workers have various classifications. Entry-level *assistant laboratory animal technicians* feed animals, clean cages, and help handle the animals. As they gain experience, laboratory animal technicians administer medications, perform lab tests, take specimens, and record daily findings.

Laboratory animal technologists supervise the lab workers. They assist in surgery and oversee the advanced care of animals.

Zookeepers work in zoos or aquariums. They prepare the animals' food and closely monitor the health of the animals. They are often involved with educational projects and other programs dedicated to preserving endangered species.

Requirements

Students preparing for animal caretaker careers need a high school diploma. While in high school, classes in mathematics, biology, and English, are recommended. Students can obtain valuable knowledge by taking animal science classes. Any knowledge about animal breeds and behavior is helpful, as well as a basic grasp of business and computer skills.

For some caretaking positions, such as in shelters, pet shops, and stables, training occurs on the job. One can also learn about the care of animals through volunteer work

A high school diploma is essential for continuing an education in animal caretaking. There are two-year colleges offering courses in animal health that lead to an associate's degree. This type of program offers courses in anatomy, physiology, chemistry, mathematics, clinical pharmacology, pathology, radiology,

animal care and handling, infectious diseases, biology, and current veterinary therapy. Students graduating from programs like this go to work in veterinary practices, humane societies, zoos and marine mammal parks, pharmaceutical companies, and laboratory research institutions. Veterinary technicians should make sure that the programs they select are accredited by the American Veterinary Medical Association.

For students interested in working in zoos, a bachelor's degree in zoology, biology, or an animal-related field is necessary. Experience as a volunteer or paid employee in a small zoo is often required.

Most importantly, animal caretakers should love animals and have great patience and compassion. An animal caretaker should also be self-motivated and hard-working, able to tackle mundane tasks with as much energy as given to exciting ones. A caretaker should also be able to take direction from others as well as being confident and organized.

Opportunities for Experience & Exploration

High school students interested in animal caretaking can volunteer to work in animal shelters, zoos, stables, or veterinary offices, depending on their interests. Volunteering provides hands-on experience and exposes students to a variety of opportunities in the animal care field.

Informational interviews with a shelter worker, veterinary assistant, or zookeeper about his or her job can be an exciting way to learn more about the field. People are usually interested in spending time talking with someone who demonstrates a serious desire to learn more about a job. Before setting up an informational interview, it is helpful to think about what you'd like to know about the job; for example, how the person entered the field, what the job entails, how to get more information. It is sometimes possible to "shadow" an animal care worker for a day, going around with him or her as tasks are performed, getting an idea of an average day on the job.

Even an informal visit to a shelter or zoo can allow you the opportunity to observe someone at work, or to ask a few quick questions. Career counseling centers usually have resource materials on this career as do public libraries and bookstores.

Methods of Entering

High school students who volunteer at shelters, zoos, or veterinary offices will be able to see whether or not a career as an animal caretaker is truly for them. Volunteer experience is always valuable on a resume or job application, as it demonstrates to prospective employers a serious interest in the job. Volunteers also have opportunities to get to know other people working in the field and to see the type of work they do.

Students who graduate from formal veterinary technology programs have access to their schools' placement office for help finding jobs. The majority of animal caretakers work in veterinary offices or boarding kennels, but there are also jobs in research laboratories, pharmaceutical companies, teaching hospitals, the armed forces, federal and state government agencies, and food production companies.

Advancement

Advancement depends on the job setting. Kennel workers may be promoted to kennel supervisor, assistant manager, or manager. Some animal caretakers go on to open their own kennels. Pet store caretakers may move into management positions. Laboratory assistants may advance to laboratory animal technicians, and then to technologists; however, for the technologist position, a bachelor's degree in the life sciences is required. Shelter caretakers may move into management positions or directing the shelters, or work as an animal control officer. Zookeepers can advance to oversee other keepers in one part of the zoo, then on to administrative positions if they have the necessary qualifications and desire.

Employment Outlook

The animal care field continues to expand. More and more people have pets, whether in city apartments or at houses in the suburbs. As long as the public's love affair with pets continues to grow, there will be a need for more veterinary care, boarding facilities, and grooming and pet shops. There is demand by animal owners for better animal treatment and veterinary care.

Many camps offer horseback riding, requiring people to care for the horses. There is also an increasing need for caretakers at public and private stables.

There is a high turnover rate among animal caretakers. Much of the work is seasonal or part-time, and most job opportunities are a result of the need to replace people leaving the field. Many entry-level positions require little training and offer flexible work schedules. This is ideal for students and others interested in short-term or part-time work.

Positions as animal caretakers in zoos, aquariums, and wildlife rehabilitation centers are the most sought after; aspiring animal caretakers will find few openings in these subfields.

Graduates of veterinary technology programs have the best employment prospects. Laboratory animal technicians and technologists also have good opportunities. Increasing concern for animal welfare means an increase in the need for capable certified laboratory workers.

Another area with favorable prospects is the kennel industry. As owners focus more on the business side of kennels, they will need managers to oversee the various services.

Earnings

Several factors determine salaries for animal caretakers: experience, work performed, level of education, and employer. Entry-level employees earn an average salary of about $11,000.

Dog groomers earn between $12,000 and $30,000 a year. Some groomers work for someone else and make a commission on each dog groomed. Others own their own shops and are able to earn more money.

The highest paid workers in the animal caretaking business are veterinary technicians, laboratory animal technologists, and zookeepers. Licensed veterinary technicians earn an average of $18,500 a year. Zookeepers start at minimum wage and eventually make between $12 and $15 per hour. According to a recent American Association of Zookeepers survey, southern states have a tendency to pay zookeepers less than any other states. The best wages for zookeepers are found in the Pacific Northwest, but the cost of living is higher there.

Many animal caretakers belong to unions and have fairly regulated pay. Examples of weekly earnings are as follows: clerks and kennel persons, $250; attendants, $300; animal care technicians, $320; veterinary technicians, $350.

Fringe benefits vary for animal caretakers. Many full-time workers receive paid vacations. Depending on the employer and the business, many full-time employees receive benefits such as health insurance and sick leave. Pet store employees or shelter workers are seldom given benefits aside from vacation time, often unpaid.

Fringe benefits vary for animal caretakers. Many full-time workers receive paid vacations. Depending on the employer and the business, many full-time employees receive benefits such as health insurance and sick leave. Pet store employees or shelter workers are seldom given benefits aside from vacation time, often unpaid.

Conditions of Work

Animal caretakers are people who love animals and therefore enjoy their work and find it satisfying. It is challenging to work with not only different types of animals, but individual animals. Dealing with the various personalities and quirks of dogs or pigs or elephants keeps attendants on their toes.

Although animal caretakers derive considerable pleasure from their work, there are unpleasant parts of the job. The work is sometimes hard, repetitious, and dirty. Animals constantly need to be fed, watered, and exercised, and to have their living spaces cleaned. The job may involve heavy lifting (moving bags of feed or cages). Workers must bend and stoop to clean animal quarters. Working closely with animals often requires working around strong or foul smells.

While those caretakers who work in pounds and veterinary facilities enjoy close relationships with many of the animals brought in, there are painful moments, too. As much as some animals are affectionate, there are those who bite and scratch. People who form attachments to the lovable, scruffy, or spirited animals they help may later have to watch those animals die.

Humane societies euthanize the animals they cannot place in homes.

Many animal care jobs require more than the traditional forty-hour week. Some shelter or veterinary employees arrive early to feed the animals and take care of their cages. At the end of the shift, if an animal still requires care, the caretaker must stay and attend to that animal. Holidays and weekends are not necessarily vacation times for employees, although certain employers have temporary or weekend help. Groomers and kennel workers stay late according to the needs of their employers.

Proper working attire for animal caretakers varies. Groomers wear comfortable clothes that can get dirty. Veterinary technicians and laboratory workers wear lab coats to protect their clothes. People who work in pet shops dress according to the owners' specifications. Those who work outside wear comfortable, casual clothes.

Sources of Additional Information

For information on careers in animal caretaking, accredited schools, and potential employers, please contact:

■ **American Association for Laboratory Science**
70 Timber Creek Drive
Cordova, TN 38018-4233
Tel: 901-754-8620
Email: info@aalas.org

For a free copy of its Programs in Veterinary Technology, *contact:*

■ **American Veterinary Medical Association**
1931 North Meacham Road
Schaumburg, IL 60173-4360
Tel: 847-925-8070

Animal Trainers

Definition

Animal trainers teach animals to obey commands, to compete in shows or races, and to perform tricks to entertain audiences. They also may teach dogs to protect property or act as guides for the visually impaired. Animal trainers may specialize with one type of animal or with several types.

Nature of the Work

Many animals are capable of being trained, including horses, elephants, cockatoos, and seals. The techniques used to train them are basically the same regardless of the type of animal. Animal trainers conduct programs consisting primarily of repetition and reward to teach animals to behave in a particular manner and to do it consistently. First, trainers evaluate an animal's temperament, ability, and aptitude to determine whether it is trainable and what methods would be most effective. Then, by painstakingly repeating routines many times, rewarding the animal whenever it does what is expected, they train it to obey or perform on command. In addition, animal trainers are responsible for the feeding, exercising, grooming, and general care of the animals, either handling the duties themselves or supervising other workers.

Trainers usually specialize in one type of animal and are identified by this type of animal. Some trainers organize and direct animal shows and may take part in animal acts. They also may rehearse animals for specific motion pictures, stage productions, or circus programs and sometimes cue animals during a performance.

Not all trainers prepare animals for the entertainment field, however. *Dog trainers*, for example, may work with dogs to be used in police work, training them to search for drugs or missing people. Some train guard dogs to protect private property;

School Subjects
Biology
Education

Personal Interests
Animals
Entertaining/Performing

Work Environment
Indoors and outdoors
One location with some travel

Minimum Education Level
Some postsecondary training

Salary Range
$10,000 to
$25,000 to
$100,000

Certification or Licensing
Required for certain positions

Outlook
Decline

others train guide dogs for the blind and may help dog and master function as a team.

Horse trainers specialize in training horses for riding or for harness. They talk to and handle a horse gently to accustom it to human contact, then gradually get it to accept a harness, bridle, saddle, and other riding gear. Trainers teach horses to respond to commands that are either spoken or given by use of the reins and legs. Draft horses are conditioned to draw equipment either alone or as part of a team. Show horses are given special training to qualify them to perform in competitions. Horse trainers sometimes have to retrain animals that have developed bad habits, such as bucking or biting. Besides feeding, exercising, and grooming, these trainers may make arrangements for breeding the horses and help mares deliver their foals.

A highly specialized occupation in the horse-training field is that of *racehorse trainers*, who must create individualized training plans for every horse in their care. By studying the animal's performance record and becoming familiar with its behavior during workouts, trainers can adapt their training methods to take advantage of each animal's peculiarities. Like other animal trainers, racehorse trainers oversee the exercising, grooming, and feeding of their charges. They also clock the running time during workouts to determine when a horse is ready for competitive racing. Racehorse trainers coach jockeys on how best to handle a particular horse during a race and may give owners advice on purchasing horses.

Requirements

Prospective animal trainers should like animals and have a genuine interest in working with them. Establishments that hire trainers often require previous animal-keeping or equestrian experience as proper care and feeding of animals is an essential part of a trainer's responsibilities. Racehorse trainers often begin as jockeys or grooms in training stables.

Although there are no formal education requirements to enter this field, animal trainers in zoos, circuses, and the entertainment field may be required to have some education in animal psychology in addition to their caretaking experience. Trainers of guide dogs for the blind prepare for their work in a three-year course of study at schools that train dogs and instruct their blind owners.

Most trainers begin their careers as keepers and gain on-the-job experience in evaluating the disposition, intelligence, and "trainability" of the animals they look after. At the same time, they learn to make friends with their charges, develop a rapport with them, and gain

their confidence. The caretaking experience is an important building block in the education and success of an animal trainer. Although previous training experience may give job applicants an advantage in being hired, they still will be expected to spend time caring for the animals before advancing to a trainer position.

Racehorse trainers must be licensed by the state in which they work. Otherwise, there are no special requirements for this occupation.

Opportunities for Experience & Exploration

Students wishing to enter this field would do well to learn as much as they can about animals, especially animal psychology, either through coursework or library study. Interviews with animal trainers and tours of their workplaces might be arranged to provide firsthand information about the practical aspects of this occupation.

Part-time or volunteer work in animal shelters, pet shops, or veterinary offices provides would-be trainers a chance to become accustomed to working with animals and to discover whether they have the aptitude for it. Experience can be acquired, too, in summer jobs as animal caretakers at zoos, aquariums, museums that feature live animal shows, amusement parks, and for those with a special interest in horse racing, stables or riding stables.

Methods of Entering

People who wish to become animal trainers generally start out as animal keepers or caretakers and rise to the position of trainer only after acquiring experience within the ranks of an organization. They enter the field by applying directly for a job as animal keeper, letting the employer or their supervisor know of their ambition so they will eventually be considered for promotion.

Students with some background in animal psychology and previous experience caring for a specific animal may find summer jobs as trainers at large amusement or theme parks, but these jobs are not plentiful, and application should be made early in the year.

Advancement

Most establishments have very small staffs of animal trainers, which means that the opportunities for advancement are limited. The progression is from animal keeper to animal trainer. A trainer who directs or supervises others may be designated head animal trainer or senior animal trainer.

Some animal trainers go into business for themselves and, if successful, hire other trainers to work for them. Others become agents for animal acts.

Employment Outlook

The demand for animal trainers is not great as most employers have little need for a large staff and tend to promote from within. This field is expected to decline through the year 2006. Applicants must be well qualified to overcome the heavy competition for available jobs. Some openings may be created as zoos and aquariums expand or provide more animal shows in an effort to increase revenue.

Earnings

Salaries of animal trainers can vary widely depending on specialty and place of employment. Salaries can range from $10,000 to $100,00 a year, depending on the type of training done. In the field of racehorse training, however, trainers are paid an average fee ranging from $35 to $50 a day for each horse, plus 10 percent of any money their horses win in races. Depending on the horse and the races it runs, this can exceed the average high-end earnings for a trainer. Show horse trainers may earn as much as $30,000 to $35,000 a year. Trainers in business for themselves set their own fees for teaching both horses and owners.

Conditions of Work

The working hours for animal trainers vary considerably, depending on type of animal, performance schedule, and whether travel is involved. For some trainers, such as those who work with show horses, the hours can be long and quite irregular.

Except in warm regions, animal shows are seasonal, running from April or May through mid-autumn. During this time, much of the work is conducted outdoors. In winter, trainers work indoors, preparing for warm-weather shows. Trainers of aquatic mammals, such as dolphins and seals, work in water and must feel comfortable in aquatic environments.

Working with certain animals requires physical strength; for example, that required to push or pull an elephant into position.

Trainers who work with wild animals need to exercise particular caution as there is always the danger of a previously docile animal becoming violent or agitated.

This occupation calls for an infinite amount of patience. Trainers must spend long hours repeating routines and rewarding their pupils for performing well, while never getting angry with them or punishing them when they fail to do what is expected. Trainers must be able to exhibit the authority to keep animals under control without raising their voices or using physical force. Calmness under stress is particularly important when dealing with wild animals.

Sources of Additional Information

American Zoo and Aquarium Association
7970-D Old Georgetown Road
Bethesda, MD 20814
Tel: 301-907-7777

Animal Caretakers Information
Humane Society of the U.S.
Companion Animals Division
2100 L Street, NW
Washington, DC 20037
Tel: 202-452-1100

Canadian Association of Zoological Parks and Aquariums
Calgary Zoo
PO Box 3036
Calgary, AB T2M 4R8 Canada
Tel: 403-232-9300

Assessors and Appraisers

Definition

Assessors and *appraisers* collect and interpret data to make judgments about the value, quality, and use of property. Assessors are government officials who evaluate property for the express purpose of determining how much the real estate owner should pay the city or county government in property taxes. Appraisers evaluate the market value of property to help people make decisions about purchases, sales, investments, mortgages, or loans.

Assessors are public servants who are either elected or appointed to office, while appraisers are employed by private businesses, such as accounting firms, real estate companies, and financial institutions, and by larger assessors' offices.

Nature of the Work

Property is divided into two distinct types: real property and personal property. Real property is land and the structures built upon the land, while personal property includes all other types of possessions.

Appraisers answer questions about the value, quality, and use of real property and personal property based on selective research into market areas, the application of analytical techniques, and professional judgment derived from experience. In evaluating real property, they analyze the supply and demand for different types of property, such as residential dwellings, office buildings, shopping centers, industrial sites, and farms, in order to estimate their values. Appraisers analyze construction, condition, and functional design. They review public records of sales, leases, previous assessments, and other transactions pertaining to land and buildings, to determine the market values, rents, and construction costs of similar properties. Appraisers collect information about neighborhoods such as availability of gas, electricity, power lines, and transportation. They also may interview people familiar with the prop-

School Subjects
English
(writing/literature)
Mathematics

Personal Interests
Figuring out how things work
Reading/Books

Work Environment
Indoors and outdoors
Primarily multiple locations

Minimum Education Level
Some postsecondary training

Salary Range
$12,600 to
$31,500 to
$75,000+

Certification or Licensing
Required

Outlook
More slowly than the average

DOT
188/191

GOE
11.06.03

erty, and they take into account the amount of money needed to make improvements on the property.

Appraisers also must consider such factors as location and changes that could influence the future value of the property. A residence worth $200,000 in the suburbs may be worth only a fraction of that in the inner city or in a remote rural area. But that same suburban residence may depreciate in value if an airport is scheduled to be built nearby. After conducting a thorough investigation, appraisers usually prepare a written report that documents their findings and conclusions.

Assessors, also called *valuer-generals* and *assessment commissioners,* perform all these appraising duties, and then go one step further to compute the amount of tax to be levied on property, using applicable tax tables. The primary responsibility of the assessor is to prepare an annual assessment roll, which lists all properties in a district and their assessed values.

To prepare the assessment roll, assessors and their staffs must first locate and identify all taxable property in the district. To do so, they prepare and maintain complete and accurate maps that show the size, shape, location, and legal description of each parcel of land. Next, they collect information about other features of parcels, such as zoning, soil characteristics, and availability of water, electricity, sewers, gas, and telephones. They describe any building and how land and buildings are used. This information is put in a parcel record.

They also analyze relationships between property characteristics and sales prices, rents, and construction costs to produce valuation models or formulas that are used to estimate the value of every property as of the legally required assessment date. For example, assessors try to estimate how much an additional bedroom adds to the value of a residence, how much an additional acre of land adds to the value of a farm, or how much competition from a new shopping center detracts the value of a downtown department store. Finally, assessors prepare and certify an assessment roll listing all properties, owners, and assessed values and notify owners of the assessed value of their properties. Because taxpayers have the right to contest their assessments, assessors must be prepared to defend their estimates and methods.

Most appraisers deal with land and buildings, but some evaluate other items of value. Specialized appraisers evaluate antiques, gems and jewelry, machinery, equipment, aircraft, boats, oil and gas reserves, and businesses. These appraisers are specially trained in their area of expertise, but generally perform the same functions as real property appraisers.

Art appraisers, for example, determine the authenticity and value of works of art, including paintings, sculptures, and antiques. They examine works for color values, style of brushstroke, and other characteristics to establish the age of the piece or to identify the artist. Art appraisers are well versed in art history, art materials, techniques of individual artists, and contemporary art markets, and they use that knowledge to assign values. Art appraisers may use complex methods such as X-rays and chemical tests to detect frauds.

Personal property assessors help the government levy taxes on owners of taxable personal property by preparing lists of personal property owned by businesses and, in a few areas, householders. In addition to listing the number of items, these assessors also estimate the value of taxable items.

Requirements

High school students who are interested in the fields of assessing or appraising should take courses in mathematics, civics, English, and—if available—accounting and computer science.

College students should enroll in mathematics, engineering, economics, business administration, architecture, computer science, and urban studies classes. A liberal arts degree provides a solid background, as do courses in finance, economics, statistics, mathematics, urban studies, computer science, public administration, business administration, or real estate and urban land economics. Appraisers choosing to specialize in a particular area should have a solid background in that field. For example, art appraisers should hold at least a bachelor's degree in art history.

Basic training in assessment and appraisal is offered by professional associations such as the International Association of Assessing Officers, the American Institute of Real Estate Appraisers, and the Society of Real Estate Appraisers.

Because all appraisals used for federally regulated real estate transactions must be conducted by licensed appraisers, most appraisers now obtain a state license. Interested students may contact the state regulatory agency to learn more about licensing requirements. In addition to a license, some states may require assessors who are government employees to pass civil service tests or other examinations before they can start work.

Good appraisers are good investigators and must be proficient at gathering data. They must be familiar with sources of information on such diverse topics as public records, construction materials, building trends, economic trends, and governmental regulations affecting use of property. They should know how to read survey drawings and blueprints and be able to identify features of building construction.

Appraisers must understand equity and mortgage finance, architectural function, demographic statistics, and business trends. They must be competent writers and able to communicate effectively with people. Many of these skills are learned on the job, but because appraising is a complex profession, candidates should have some college education, and, preferably, a college degree.

Opportunities for Experience & Exploration

Students interested in a career as an appraiser may find a part-time or summer position with an appraisal firm. Some firms also have jobs as appraiser assistants or trainees. Experience can also be obtained by working at county assessors' offices, financial institutions, or real estate brokers. To learn the particulars of building construction applicable to appraisers, students might consider applying to construction companies for summer jobs. To practice the methods used by appraisers, students may want to write detailed analysis of assets and shortcomings when choosing a college or buying a car.

Methods of Entering

After acquiring mathematical and technical knowledge in the classroom, people interested in appraising should apply to area appraisal firms, local county assessors, real estate brokers, or large accounting firms. Because assessing jobs are often civil service jobs, they may be listed with government employment agencies.

Advancement

Appraising is a dynamic field, affected yearly by new legislation and technology. To distinguish themselves in the business, top appraisers continue their education and pursue certification through the various national appraising organizations, such as the Appraisal Institute, the American Society of Appraisers, and the International Association of

Assessing Officers. Certified appraisers are entrusted with the most prestigious projects and can command the highest fees.

Employment Outlook

Employment of assessors and appraisers is expected to grow more slowly than the average for all occupations through the year 2006. Most job openings will result from the need to replace retiring workers. In general, assessors work in a fairly secure field. As long as governments levy property taxes, they will need assessors to provide them with information. The real estate industry, however, is influenced dramatically by the overall health of the economy, and appraisers in real estate can expect to benefit during periods of growth and experience slowdowns during recessions and depressions.

Earnings

Many variables affect the earnings of assessors and appraisers, but according to the U.S. Department of Labor, salaries in 1996 ranged from $12,600 for beginners to $75,000 and above for professionals with experience and additional credentials. Appraisers employed in the private sector tend to earn higher incomes than those in the public sector. Assessors' salaries generally increase as the population of the jurisdiction increases. Earnings at any level are enhanced by higher education and professional designations. Fringe benefits for both public and private employees usually include paid vacations and health insurance.

Conditions of Work

Appraisers and assessors have a variety of working conditions, from the comfortable offices where they write and edit appraisal reports to outdoor construction sites, which they visit in both the heat of summer and the bitter cold of winter. Many appraisers spend mornings at their desks and afternoons in the field. Experienced appraisers may need to travel out of state.

Appraisers and assessors who work for a government agency or financial institution usually work forty-hour weeks, with overtime as necessary. Independent appraisers can often set their own schedules. Assessors' offices might employ administrators, property appraisers, mappers, systems analysts, computer technicians, public relations specialists, word processors, and clerical workers. In small offices, one or two people might handle most tasks; in large offices, some with hundreds of employees, specialists are more common.

Appraising is a very people-oriented occupation. Appraisers must be unfailingly cordial, and they have to deal calmly and tactfully with people who challenge their decisions. Appraising can be a high-stress occupation because a considerable amount of money and important personal decisions ride on their calculations.

Sources of Additional Information

For information on education and professional designations, please contact:

■American Society of Appraisers
PO Box 17265
Washington, DC 20041
Tel: 703-478-2228

For information on professional designations, publications, education, careers, and scholarships, contact:

■Appraisal Institute
875 North Michigan Avenue, Suite 2400
Chicago, IL 60611
Tel: 312-335-4100

■The Appraisal Foundation
1029 Vermont Avenue, NW, Suite 900
Washington, DC 20005-3517

Automobile Collision Repairers

Definition

Automobile collision repairers repair, replace, and refinish (repaint) damaged body parts and components of automobiles, buses, and light trucks. They use hand tools and power tools to straighten bent frames and body sections, replace badly damaged parts, smooth out minor dents and creases, remove rust, fill small holes or dents, and repaint damaged surfaces. Some repairers give repair estimates.

Nature of the Work

The average person is very reliant on their cars. If an accident occurs, the first thing they want to know from a collision repairer is how long a repair will take. Since most drivers carry auto insurance as required by law, the first thing they need from a body repair shop is a cost estimate of the necessary repairs. Either the shop supervisor or *repair service estimator* prepares the estimate. They inspect the extent of the damage to determine if the vehicle can be repaired or must be replaced. They note the year, model, and make of the car to determine type and availability of parts. Based upon past experience with similar types of repair and general industry guidelines, estimates are calculated for parts and labor and then submitted to the customer's insurance company. And finally, based on the work load, the extent of the repairs required, and the availability of parts, an estimate is given of when the car will be ready for pick up.

One "walk around" a car will tell the collision repairer what needs to be investigated. Since a collision often involves "hidden" damage, supervisors write up repair orders with specific instructions so no work is missed or, in some cases, done extra. Repair orders often only indicate specific parts are to be repaired or replaced. Collision repairers generally work on a project by themselves with minimal supervision. In large, busy shops, repairers may be assisted by helpers or apprentices.

School Subjects
Computer science
Shop (Trade/Vo-tech education)

Personal Interests
Cars
Fixing things

Work Environment
Primarily indoors
Primarily one location

Minimum Education Level
Some postsecondary training
Apprenticeship

Salary Range
$12,948 to
$24,076 to
$39,000

Certification or Licensing
Recommended

Outlook
About as fast as the average

DOT
807

GOE
05.05.06

NOC
7322

Vehicle bodies are made from a wide array of materials, including steel, aluminum, metal alloys, fiberglass, and plastic, with each material requiring a different technique of repair. Most repairers can work with all of these materials, but as car manufacturers produce vehicles with an increasing proportion of lightweight fiberglass, aluminum, and plastic parts, more repairers specialize in repairing these specific materials.

Collision repairers frequently must remove car seats, accessories, electrical components, hydraulic windows, dashboards, and trim to get to the parts that need repair. If the frame or a body section of the vehicle has been bent or twisted, frame repairers and straighteners can sometimes restore it to its original alignment and shape. This is done by chaining or clamping it to an alignment machine, which uses hydraulic pressure to pull the damaged metal into position. Repairers use specialty measuring equipment to set all components, such as engine parts, wheels, headlights, and body parts, at manufacturer's specifications.

After the frame is straightened, dents in the metal body can be corrected in several different ways, depending on how deep they are. If any part is too badly damaged to repair, the collision repairers remove it with hand tools, a pneumatic metal-cutting gun, or acetylene torch, then weld on a replacement part. Some dents can be pushed out with hydraulic jacks, pneumatic hammers, prying bars, and other hand tools. To smooth small dents and creases, collision repairers may position small anvils, called dolly blocks, against one side of the dented metal. They then hit the opposite side of the metal with various specially designed hammers. Tiny pits and dimples are removed with pick hammers and punches. Dents that cannot be corrected with this treatment may be filled with solder or a puttylike material that becomes hard like metal after it cures. When the filler has hardened, the collision repairers file, grind, and sand the surface smooth in the correct contour and prepare it for painting. In many shops the final sanding and painting are done by other specialists, who may be called *automotive painters*.

Since more than the body is usually damaged in a major automobile accident, repairers have other components to repair. Advanced vehicle systems on new cars such as anti-lock brakes, air bags, and other "passive restraint systems" require special training to repair. Steering and suspension, electrical components, and glass are often damaged and require repair, removal, or replacement.

Automotive painting is a highly skilled, labor-intensive job that requires a fine eye and attention to detail for the result to match the pre-accident condition.

Some paint jobs require that less than the whole vehicle be painted. In this case, the painter must mix pigments to match the original color. This can be difficult if the original paint is faded.

Requirements

In today's competitive job market you will need a high school diploma to land a job that offers growth possibilities, a good salary, and challenges; this includes jobs in the automobile service industry. Employers today prefer to hire only those who have completed some kind of formal training program in automobile mechanics—usually a minimum of two years. A wide variety of such programs are offered today at community colleges, vocational schools, independent organizations, and manufacturers.

As automotive technology changes, the materials and methods involved in repair work change. With new high-strength steels, aluminum, and plastics becoming ever more common in newer vehicles and posing new challenges in vehicle repair, repairers will need special training to detect the many "hidden" problems that occur beyond the impact spot. Postsecondary training programs provide students with the necessary, up-to-date skills needed for repairing today's vehicles.

There is a big demand in the automotive service industry for well-educated, highly skilled entry-level persons to join the job force. Technology demands more from the technician than it did ten years ago. In addition to automotive and shop classes, high school students should take mathematics, English, and computer classes. Adjustments and repairs to many car components require the technician to make numerous computations, for which good mathematics skills are essential. For today's technician to stay competitive, he or she has a lot of reading to do. English classes will prepare the technician with the necessary skills to read and comprehend the many volumes of repair manuals and trade journals he or she will need to remain informed and up-to-date. In addition, computers are common in most collision repair shops. They keep track of customer histories, parts, and often detail repair procedures. Use of computers in repair shops will only increase in the future.

Entry-level technicians in the industry can demonstrate their qualifications through certification by the National Automotive Technicians Education Foundation (NATEF), an affiliation of the National Institute for Automotive Service Excellence (ASE). Certification is voluntary, but assures students that the program they enroll in meets the standards employers expect from their entry-level employees. Many trade and vocational schools throughout the country have affiliation with NATEF. To remain certified, repairers must take the examination again within five years. Another industry-recognized standard of training is provided by the Inter-Industry Conference on Auto Collision Repair (I-CAR). I-CAR provides training for students and experienced technicians alike in the areas of advanced vehicle systems, aluminum repair and welding, complete collision repair, electronics for collision repair, finish matching, and other specialty fields.

Automobile collision repairers are responsible for providing their own hand tools at an investment approximately $6,000 to $20,000 or more, depending upon the technician's specialty. It is the employer's responsibility to provide the larger power tools and other test equipment. Skill in handling both hand and power tools is essential for any repairer. Since each collision repair job is unique and presents a different challenge, repairers often must be resourceful in their method of repair.

While union membership is not a requirement for collision repairers, many belong to the International Association of Machinists and Aerospace Workers; the International Union, United Automobile, Aerospace and Agricultural Implement Workers of America; the Sheet Metal Workers International Association; or the International Brotherhood of Teamsters, Chauffeurs, Warehousemen and Helpers of America. Most collision repairers who are union members work for large automobile dealers, trucking companies, and bus lines.

Opportunities for Experience & Exploration

Many community colleges and park districts offer general auto maintenance, mechanics, and body repair workshops where students can get additional practice working on real cars and learn from experienced instructors.

Trade magazines are an excellent source for learning what's new in the industry, and students should be able to find a good selection at most public libraries. In addition, many public television stations broadcast automobile maintenance and repair programs that can be of help to beginners to see how various types of cars differ.

Taking high school auto mechanics and shop courses are excellent ways to get started learning about this field. These courses can help students assess their mechanical aptitude and familiarize them with basic auto components and structure. Students will learn the proper use of many different tools used for specific automobile system and body repairs. Industrial arts courses are also a good choice as they prepare students by introducing them to the tools and skills repairers need, specifically in welding and metal cutting.

And, of course, working on cars as a hobby provides invaluable firsthand experience in repair work. A part-time job in a repair shop or dealership allows a feel for the general atmosphere and the kind of problems repairers face on the job, as well as provide a chance to learn from those already in the business.

Methods of Entering

The best way to start out in the field of automobile collision repair is, first, to attend one of the many postsecondary training programs available throughout the country and, second, to obtain accreditation.

Trade and technical schools usually provide job placement assistance for their graduates. Schools often have contacts with local employers who seek highly skilled entry-level employees. Often, employers post job opening at nearby trade schools with accredited programs.

Although postsecondary training programs are considered the best way to enter the field, some repairers learn the trade on the job as apprentices. Their training consists of working for several years under the guidance of experienced repairers. Fewer employers today are willing to hire apprentices because of the time and cost it takes to train them, but since there currently is a shortage of high quality entry-level collision repair technicians, many employers will continue to hire apprentices who can demonstrate good mechanical aptitude and a willingness to learn. Those who do learn their skills on the job will inevitably require some formal training if they wish to advance and stay in-step with the changing industry.

Internship programs sponsored by car manufacturers or independent organizations provide students with excellent opportunities to actually work with prospective employers. Internships can also provide students with valuable contacts who will be able to refer the student to future employers and provide a recommendation to potential employers once they have completed their training. Many students may even be hired by the company at which they interned.

Advancement

Like NATEF training programs, currently employed collision repairers may be certified by the National Institute for Automotive Service Excellence (ASE). Although certification is voluntary, it is a widely recognized standard of achievement for automobile collision repairers and the way many advance. The more certification a technician has, the more his or her worth to the employer the greater likelihood of advancement.

Certification is available in four specialty areas: structural analysis and damage repair, nonstructural analysis and damage repair, mechanical and electrical components, and painting and refinishing. Those who have passed all the exams are certified as master body/paint technicians. To maintain their certification, technicians must retake the examination for their specialties every five years. Many employers will only hire accredited technicians, and they base the technician's salary on the level of the technician's accreditation.

With today's complex automobile components and new materials requiring hundreds of hours of study and practice to master, employers encourage their employees to advance in responsibility by learning new systems and repair procedures. A repair shop's reputation will only go as far as its employees are skilled. Those with good communications and planning skills may advance to shop supervisor or service manager at larger repair shops or dealerships. Those who have mastered collision repair may go on to teaching at postsecondary schools or work for certification agencies.

Employment Outlook

With an estimated 189 million vehicles in operation today, collision repair technicians should feel confident that a good percentage of those will require repair because of accidents. With new model automobiles becoming increasingly high-tech, skilled and highly trained technicians will be in particular demand. Although less skilled workers will face tough competition, openings will exist for them because of the current lack of skilled entry-level applicants. The industry predicts it will need to replace 20 percent of its workforce by the end of the decade because of workers who retire and those who leave the field because they cannot keep up with the changing technology.

The number of automobiles sold in the United States has risen steadily since 1993. With more automobiles on the roads, more accidents will occur, and thus the demand for qualified collision repair technicians will increase. Many new vehicles will be fairly small, lightweight, and easily damaged in collisions. More vehicles today are made with plastics, new alloys, and aluminum parts that are difficult to work with after they are damaged.

The automobile collision repair business is not greatly affected by changes in economic conditions. Major body damage must be repaired to keep a vehicle in safe operating condition. During an economic downturn, however, people tend to postpone minor repairs until their budgets can accommodate the expense. Nevertheless, body repairers are seldom laid off. Instead, when business is bad, employers hire fewer new workers. During a recession, inexperienced workers face strong competition for entry-level jobs. People with formal training in repair work and automobile mechanics are likely to have the best job prospects in such times.

Earnings

Salary ranges of collision repair technicians vary depending upon level of experience, type of shop, and geographic location. According to the U.S. Department of Labor, the average technician with certification and postsecondary training earned about $24,000 in 1996. Less experienced technicians earned an average $13,000.

Since most repairers work on an hourly basis and frequently work overtime, their salaries can vary significantly depending on the number of hours they work. Managers of repair shops earn between $34,000 and $39,000. In many repair shops and dealerships, technicians can earn more by working on commission. They typically earn 40 to 50 percent of the labor costs charged to customers. Employers often guarantee a minimum level of pay in addition to commissions.

Benefits packages vary from business to business. Most repair technicians can expect health insurance and a paid vacation from employers. Other benefits may include dental and eye care, life and disability insurance, and a pension plan. Employers usually cover a technician's work clothes and may pay a percentage of the cost of hand tools they purchase. An increasing number of employers pay all or most of an employee's certification training, dependent on the employee passing the test. A technician's salary can increase through yearly bonuses or profit sharing if the business does well during the year.

Conditions of Work

Automobile repair shops are usually well ventilated to reduce dust and dangerous fumes. Collision repair work is generally noisy, dusty, and dirty. Because repairers weld and handle hot or jagged pieces of metal and broken glass, they wear safety glasses, masks, and protective gloves.

Minor hand and back injuries are the most common problems of technicians. When reaching in hard-to-get-at places or loosening tight bolts, technicians often bruise, cut, or burn their hands. With caution and experience most technicians learn to avoid hand injuries.

Working for long periods in cramped or bent positions often results in a stiff back or neck. Technicians also lift many heavy objects that can cause injury if not handled carefully; however, this is becoming less of a problem with new cars as automakers design smaller and lighter parts for better fuel economy.

Some technicians experience allergic reactions to the solvents and oils frequently used in cleaning, maintenance, and repair. Automotive painters wear respirators and other protective gear, and they work in specially ventilated rooms to keep from being exposed to paint fumes and other hazardous chemicals. Painters may need to stand for hours at a time as they work.

By following safety procedures and learning how to avoid typical problem situations, repairers can minimize the risks involved in this job. Likewise, shops must comply with strict safety procedures to help employees avoid accident or injury.

Collision repairers are often under pressure to complete the job quickly. Most repairers work between forty- and forty-eight-hour weeks but may be required to work longer hours when the shop is busy or for emergencies.

Sources of Additional Information

For more information on the automotive industry, please contact:

Automotive Service Industry Association (ASIA)
25 Northwest Point
Elk Grove Village, IL 60007
Tel: 847-228-1310

For more information on training and accreditation, please contact:

Inter-Industry Conference on Auto Collision Repair (I-CAR)
3701 Algonquin Road, Suite 400
Rolling Meadows, IL 60008
Tel: 800-1CAR USA

Motor and Equipment Manufacturers Association (MEMA)
PO Box 13966
10 Laboratory Drive
Research Triangle Park, NC 27709
Tel: 919-549-4800

National Automobile Dealers Association (NADA)
8400 Westpark Drive
McLean, VA 22102
Tel: 703-821-7000

National Automotive Technicians Education Foundation (NATEF)
13505 Dulles Technology Drive
Herndon, VA 22071-3415
Tel: 703-713-0100

For information on certification, please contact:

National Institute for Automotive Service Excellence (ASE)
13505 Dulles Technology Drive, Suite 2
Herndon, VA 22071-3415
Tel: 703-713-3800

Automobile Sales Workers

Definition

Automobile sales workers provide customers with information about new or used automobiles, and they prepare payment, financing, and insurance papers for customers who have purchased a vehicle. They prospect new customers by mail, telephone, or through personal contacts. To stay informed about their products, sales workers regularly attend information and training sessions about the vehicles they sell.

Nature of the Work

The automobile sales worker's main task is to inform customers on everything there is to know about a particular vehicle and in doing so to convincingly assure the customer that they are getting a fair deal, in fact, the best deal. Since the sticker price on new cars is only a starting point to be bargained down, and since most customers come to dealerships already knowing which car they would like to buy, sales workers spend much of their time negotiating the final selling price. Currently there is a trend in automobile dealerships to tone down sales techniques and give the customer more "breathing room," more pressure-free time to decide on their auto purchase.

Most dealerships have special sales forces for new cars, used cars, trucks, recreational vehicles, and leasing operations. In each specialty sales workers learn all aspects of the product they must sell. They may attend information and training seminars sponsored by manufacturers. New car sales workers, especially, are constantly learning new car features. Sales workers inform customers about a car's performance, fuel economy, safety features, and luxuries or accessories. They are able to talk about innovations over previous models, engine and mechanical specifications, ease of handling, and ergonomic dashboard designs. Good sales workers also keep track of competing models' features.

School Subjects
Business
Speech

Personal Interests
Cars
Selling/Making a deal

Work Environment
Primarily indoors
Primarily one location

Minimum Education Level
High school diploma

Salary Range
$20,000 to
$30,836 to
$45,000+

Certification or Licensing
Voluntary

Outlook
About as fast as the average

DOT
273

GOE
08.02.01

NOC
6421

In many ways, used car sales workers have a more daunting mass of information to keep track of. Whereas new car sales workers concentrate on the most current features of an automobile, used car sales workers must keep track of all features from several model years. Good used car dealers can look at a car and note immediately the make, model, and year of a car. Because of popular two and three year leasing options, the used car market has increased by nearly fifty percent in the last ten years.

Successful sales workers are generally good readers of a person's character. They can determine exactly what it is a customer is looking for in a new car. They must be friendly and understanding of customers' needs in order to put them at ease (due to the amount of money involved, car buying is an unpleasant task for most people). They are careful not to over-sell the car by providing the customers with information they may not care about or understand, thus confusing them. For example, if a customer only cares about style, sales workers will not impress upon him all of the wonderful intricacies of a new high-tech engine design—unless he feels this will help sell the car.

Sales workers greet customers and ask if they have any questions about a particular model. It's very important for sales workers to have immediate and confident answers to all questions about the vehicles they're selling. When a sell is difficult, they occasionally use psychological methods, or subtle "prodding," to influence customers. Some sales workers use aggressive selling methods and pressure the customer to purchase the car. Although recent trends are turning away from the pressure-sell, competition will keep these types of selling methods prevalent in the industry, albeit at a slightly toned-down level.

Customers usually make more than one visit to a dealership before purchasing a new or used car. Because one sales worker "works" the customer on the first visit—forming quasi-friendships and learning the customer's personality—he will usually stay with that customer until the sale is made or lost. To be certain he is at the dealership when the customer returns, and so he doesn't lose the sale to another sales worker, he will schedule times for the customer to come in and talk more about the car. Sales workers may make follow-up phone calls to make special offers or remind customers of certain features that make a particular model better than the competition, or they may send mailings for the same purpose.

In addition to providing the customer with information about the car, sales workers discuss financing packages, leasing options, and warranty. When the sale is made, they go over the contract with the customer and obtain a signature. Frequently the exact model with all of the features the customer requested is not in the dealership, and the sales worker must place an order with the manufacturer or distributor. When purchasing a new or used vehicle many customers trade in their old vehicle. Sales workers appraise the trade-in and offer a price.

At some dealerships sales workers also do public relations and marketing work. They establish promotions to get customers into their showrooms, print flyers to distribute in the local community, and make television advertisements. In order to keep their name in the back (or front) of the customer's mind, they may send past customers birthday and holiday cards or similar "courtesies." Most of the larger dealerships also have an auto maintenance and repair service department. Sales workers may help customers establish a periodic maintenance schedule or suggest repair work.

Computers are used at a growing number of dealerships. Customers use computers to answer questions they may have, consult price indexes, check on ready availability of parts, and even compare the car they're interested in with the competitions' equivalent. Although computers can't replace human interaction and sell the car to customers who need reassurances, they do help the customer feel more informed and more "in control" when buying a car.

Requirements

In today's competitive job market you will need a high school diploma to land a job that offers growth possibilities, a good salary, and challenges; and this includes jobs in the automobile sales industry. Employers prefer to hire entry-level employees who have had some previous experience in automotive services or in retail sales. They look for candidates who have good verbal, business, mathematics, electronics, and computer skills. A number of automotive sales and services courses and degrees are offered today at community colleges, vocational schools, independent organizations, and manufacturers. Sales workers should possess a valid driver's license and have a good driving record.

Because thorough knowledge of automobiles, from how they work, to how they drive, to how they are manufactured, is essential for a successful sales worker, automotive maintenance classes in high school are an excellent place to begin a foundation of auto knowledge. Classes in English, speech, drama, and psychology will help students achieve the excellent speaking skills they will need to make a good sale and gain customer confidence and respect. Classes in business and mathematics will teach students to manage and prioritize their work load, prepare goals, and work confidently with customer financing packages. As computers become increasingly prevalent in every aspect of the industry, students should take as many computer classes as they can. Students who can speak a second language are at an advantage, especially in major cities with large minority populations.

Sales workers must be enthusiastic, well organized, self-starters who thrive in a competitive environment. They must show a excitement and authority about each type of car they sell and convince customers, without being too "pushy" (though some pressure on the customer usually helps make the sale), that the car they're interested in is the "right" car, at the fairest price. Sales workers must be able to read a customer's personality and know when to be outgoing and when to pull back and be more reserved. A neat, professional appearance is also very important for sales workers.

Those who seek management-level positions will have a distinct advantage if they possess a college degree, preferably in business or marketing, but other degrees, whether they be in English, economics, or psychology, are no less important, so long as applicants have good management skills and can sell cars.

By completing the Certified Automotive Merchandiser (CAM) program offered by the National Automobile Dealers Association (NADA), students seeking entry-level positions gain a significant advantage. Certification assures employers that you have the basic skills they require. The course is offered through Northwood University's Michigan campus or through their correspondence courses. Other schools offer degrees in automotive marketing and automotive aftermarket management which prepare students to take high-level management positions. Even with a two- or four-year degree in hand, many dealerships may not begin new hires directly as managers, but first start them out as a sales worker.

Opportunities for Experience & Exploration

Automobile trade magazines and books, as well as selling technique and business books, provide an excellent source of further information. Local and state automobile and truck dealer associations can also provide you with information on career possibilities in automobile and truck sales. Your local Yellow Pages has a listing under "associations" for dealer organizations in your area.

Students interested in automobile sales work might first stop by their local dealer and ask about training programs and job requirements at their dealership. On a busy day at any dealership there will be several sales workers on the floor selling cars. Students can witness the basic selling process by going to dealer-

ships and unobtrusively watching and listening as sales workers talk with customers. Many dealerships hire students part-time to wash and clean cars. This is a good way to see the types of challenges and pressures automobile sales workers experience every day.

Although it may take a special kind of sales skill, or a different approach to selling a $30,000 vehicle over $50 shoes, any type of retail sales job that requires frequent interaction with customers will prepare students for a job as an automobile sales worker.

Methods of Entering

Generally, those just out of high school are not going to land a job as an automobile sales worker—older customers do not feel comfortable making such a large investment through a teenager. Employers prefer to see some previous automotive service experience with certification, such as ASE certification, or postsecondary training in automotive selling, such as NADA's Certified Automotive Merchandiser program. Dealerships will hire those with proven sales skill in a different field for sales worker positions and give them on-the-job training.

Employers frequently post job opening at schools that provide postsecondary education in business administration or automotive marketing. Certified automotive technicians or body repairers who think they will eventually like to break into a sales job should look for employment at dealership service centers where they will have frequent contact with sales workers and make connections with dealership managers and owners, as well as become so familiar with one or more models of a manufacturer's cars that they will make well informed, knowledgeable sales workers.

Some dealerships will hire young workers with little experience in automobile services but who can demonstrate proven skills in sales and a willingness to learn. These workers will learn on-the-job. They may first be given administrative tasks. Eventually they will accompany experienced sales workers on the showroom floor and learn "hands-on." After about a year, the workers will sell on their own, and managers will evaluate their selling skills in sales meetings and suggest ways of improving.

Advancement

The longer a sales worker stays with a dealership, the larger his client base grows and the more cars he sells. Advancement for many sales workers is increased earnings, and customer loyalty is the best way to earn it. As positions open, sales workers with proven management skills go on to be assistant and general managers. Managers with excellent sales skill and good client base may open a new franchise dealership or their own independent dealership.

The Society of Automotive Sales Professionals (SASP), a division of NADA, provides sales workers with advancement possibilities. Once a sales worker has completed a certification process and has six months minimum sales experience, he is eligible to participate in SASP seminars that stress improving the new car buying process by improving a sales worker's professional image.

Employment Outlook

Automobile dealerships are one of the businesses most severely affected by economic recession. The automotive industry has enjoyed growth since 1993; and continued expansion is predicted. In 1995, the average dealership saw a 5.7 percent increase in total gross sales dollars over 1994—a figure many dealers considered disappointing. For the sales worker, growth, in any percentage, is good news, as they are the so-called "front-line professionals" in the industry who are responsible for representing the dealerships and manufacturers and for getting their cars out on the streets. In 1994 there were 199,400 new and used vehicle sales workers employed at franchised dealerships throughout the nation.

The automobile sales worker faces many future challenges. A shift in customer buying preferences and experience is forcing sales workers to re-evaluate their selling methods. Information readily available on the Internet helps customers shop for the most competitive financing or leasing package and read reviews on car and truck models that interest them. Transactions are still brokered at the dealer, but once consumers become more familiar with the Internet, many will shop and buy exclusively from home.

Another trend threatening dealers is the automotive superstores, such as CarMax and CarChoice, where customers have a large inventory to select from at a base price and get information and ask questions about a car not from a sales worker, but from a computer. Sales workers are still needed to finalize the sale, but their traditional role at the dealership is lessened.

Earnings

Earnings for automobile sales workers vary depending on location, size, and method of salary. Previously most dealerships paid their sales workers either straight commission or salary plus commission. This forced the sales worker to become extremely aggressive in his selling strategy, and often too aggressive for many customers. With a new trend toward pressure-free selling, sales workers are earning a straight salary. Bonus and profit sharing can still increase their annual earnings. The average salary for sales workers is $30,836, according to the U.S. Bureau of Labor Statistics. Those who work on a straight commission basis can earn considerably more; however, their earnings are minimal during slow periods.

Benefits vary by dealership, but often include health insurance and a paid vacation. An increasing number of employers will pay all or most of an employee's certification training, if he or she passes the test.

Conditions of Work

Sales workers for new car dealerships work in pleasant indoor showrooms. Most used car dealerships keep the majority of their cars in outdoor lots where sales workers may spend much of their day. Upon final arrangements for a sale, they work in comfortable office spaces at a desk. Suits are the standard attire. During slow periods, when competition amongst dealers is fierce, sales workers often work under pressure. They must not allow "lost" sales to discourage their work. The typical workweek is between forty and fifty hours, although if business is good, a sales worker will work more. Since most customers shop for cars on the weekends and in the evenings, work hours are irregular.

Sources of Additional Information

For information on accreditation and testing, contact:

■**National Automobile Dealers Association (NADA)**
Communications/Public Relations Department
8400 Westpark Drive
McLean, VA 22102-3591
Tel: 703-821-7000

For information on certification, contact:

■**National Institute for Automotive Service Excellence**
13505 Dulles Technology Drive, Suite 2
Herndon, VA 22071-3415
Tel: 703-713-3800

Automobile Service Technicians

Definition

Automobile service technicians maintain and repair cars, vans, small trucks, and other vehicles. Using both hand tools and specialized diagnostic test equipment, they pinpoint problems and make the necessary repairs or adjustments. In addition to performing complex and difficult repairs, technicians perform a number of routine maintenance procedures, such as oil changes, tire rotation, and battery replacement. Technicians interact frequently with customers to explain repair procedures and discuss maintenance needs.

Nature of the Work

Many automobile service technicians feel that the most exciting part of their work is troubleshooting—locating the source of a problem and successfully fixing it. Diagnosing mechanical, electrical, and computer-related troubles requires a broad knowledge of how cars work, the ability to make accurate observations, and the patience to logically determine what went wrong. Technicians agree that it frequently is more difficult to find the problem than it is to fix it. With experience, knowing where to look for problems becomes second nature.

Generally, there are two types of automobile service technicians: generalists and specialists. Generalists work under a broad umbrella of repair and service duties. They have proficiency in several kinds of light repairs and maintenance of many different types of automobiles. Their work, for the most part, is routine and basic. Specialists concentrate in one or two areas and learn to master them for many different car makes and models. Today, in light of the sophisticated technology common in new cars, there is an increasing demand for specialists. Automotive systems are not as easy or as standard as they used to be, and now require many hours of experience to

School Subjects
Business
Shop (Trade/Vo-tech education)

Personal Interests
Figuring out how things work
Fixing things

Work Environment
Primarily indoors
Primarily one location

Minimum Education Level
High school diploma

Salary Range
$13,000 to
$24,856 to
$45,000

Certification or Licensing
Voluntary

Outlook
About as fast as the average

DOT
273

GOE
08.02.01

NOC
6421

master. To gain a broad knowledge in auto maintenance and repair, specialists usually begin as generalists.

When a car does not operate properly, the owner
brings it to a service technician and describes the
problem. At a dealership or larger shop, the customer
may talk with a *repair service estimator,* who writes
down the customer's description of the problem and
relays it to the service technician. The technician may
test-drive the car or use diagnostic equipment, such
as motor analyzers, spark plug testers, or compression gauges, to determine the problem. If a customer
explains that the car's automatic transmission does
not shift gears at the right times, the technician must
know how the functioning of the transmission
depends on the engine vacuum, the throttle pressure,
and, more common in newer cars, the onboard computer. Each factor must be thoroughly checked. With
each test, clues help the technician pinpoint the cause
of the malfunction. After successfully diagnosing the
problem, the technician makes the necessary adjustments or repairs. If a part is too badly damaged or
worn to be repaired, he or she replaces it after first
consulting the car owner, explaining the problem, and
estimating the cost.

Normal use of an automobile inevitably causes wear
and deterioration of parts. *Generalist automobile technicians* handle many of the routine maintenance tasks
to help keep a car in optimal operating condition. They
change oil, lubricate parts, and adjust or replace components of any of the car's systems that might cause a
malfunction, including belts, hoses, spark plugs,
brakes, filters, and transmission and coolant fluids.

Technicians who specialize in the service of specific
parts usually work in large shops with multiple departments, car diagnostic centers, franchised auto service
shops, or small independent shops that concentrate
on a particular type of repair work.

Tune-up technicians evaluate and correct engine
performance and fuel economy. They use diagnostic
equipment and other computerized devices to locate
malfunctions in fuel, ignition, and emissions-control
systems. They adjust ignition timing and valves and
may replace spark plugs, points, triggering assemblies
in electronic ignitions, and other components to
ensure maximum engine efficiency.

Electrical-systems technicians have been in greater
demand in recent years. They service and repair the
complex electrical and computer circuitry common
in today's automobile. They use both sophisticated
diagnostic equipment and simpler devices such as
ammeters, ohmmeters, and voltmeters to locate
system malfunctions. As well as possessing excellent

electrical skills, electrical-systems technicians require
basic mechanical aptitude to get at electrical and computer circuitry located throughout the automobile .

Front-end technicians are concerned with suspension and steering systems. They inspect, repair, and
replace front-end parts such as springs and shock
absorbers and linkage parts such as tie rods and ball
joints. They also align and balance wheels.

Brake repairers work on drum and disk braking systems, parking brakes, and their hydraulic systems.
They inspect, adjust, remove, repair, and reinstall such
items as brake shoes, disk pads, drums, rotors, wheel
and master cylinders, and hydraulic fluid lines. Some
specialize in both brake and front-end work.

Transmission technicians adjust, repair, and maintain gear trains, couplings, hydraulic pumps, valve
bodies, clutch assemblies, and other parts of automatic transmission systems. Transmissions have
become complex and highly sophisticated mechanisms in newer model automobiles. Technicians
require special training to learn how they function.

Automobile-radiator mechanics clean radiators,
using caustic solutions. They locate and solder leaks
and install new radiator cores. In addition, some radiator mechanics repair car heaters and air conditioners and solder leaks in gas tanks.

As more automobiles rely on a variety of electronic
components, technicians have become more proficient in the basics of electronics, even if they are not
electronic specialists. Electronic controls and instruments are located in nearly all the systems of today's
cars. Many previously mechanical functions in automobiles are being replaced by electronics, significantly
altering the way repairs are performed. Diagnosing
and correcting problems with electronic components
often involves the use of specialty tools and computers.

Automobile service technicians use an array of tools
in their everyday work, ranging from simple hand tools
to computerized diagnostic equipment. Technicians
supply their own hand tools at an investment of $6,000
to $25,000 or more, depending upon the technician's
specialty. It is usually the employer's responsibility to
furnish the larger power tools, engine analyzers, and
other test equipment.

To maintain and increase their skills and to keep up
with new technology, automobile technicians must
regularly read service and repair manuals, shop bulletins, and other publications. They must also be willing to take part in training programs given by
manufacturers or at vocational schools. Those who
have voluntary certification must periodically retake
exams to keep their credentials.

Requirements

In today's competitive job market aspiring automobile service technicians need a high school diploma to land a job that offers growth possibilities, a good salary, and challenges. There is a big demand in the automotive service industry to fill entry-level positions with well-trained, highly skilled persons. Technology demands more from the technician than it did ten years ago. Employers today prefer to hire only those who have completed some kind of formal training program in automobile mechanics—usually a minimum of two years. A wide variety of such programs are offered at community colleges, vocational schools, independent organizations, and manufacturers.

In high school, students should take automotive and shop classes, mathematics, English, and computer classes. Adjustments and repairs to many car components require the technician to make numerous computations, for which good mathematical skills will be essential. Good reading skills are also valuable as a technician must do a lot of reading to stay competitive in today's job market. English classes will prepare the technician to handle the many volumes of repair manuals and trade journals he or she will need to remain informed. Computer skills are also vital as computers are now common in most repair shops. They keep track of customers' histories and parts, and often detail repair procedures. Use of computers in repair shops will only increase in the future.

Many community colleges and vocational schools around the country offer accredited postsecondary education. Postsecondary training programs prepare students through a blend of classroom instruction and hands-on practical experience. They range in length from six months to two years or more, depending on the type of program. Shorter programs usually involve intensive study. Longer programs typically alternate classroom courses with periods of work experience. Some two-year programs include courses on applied mathematics, reading and writing skills, and business practices and lead to an associate's degree.

Some programs are conducted in association with automobile manufacturers. Students combine work experience with hands-on classroom study of up-to-date equipment and new cars provided by manufacturers. In other programs students alternate time in the classroom with internships in dealerships or service departments. These students may take up to four years to finish their training, but they become familiar with the latest technology and also earn a modest salary.

One recognized indicator of quality for entry-level technicians is certification by the National Automotive Technicians Education Foundation (NATEF), an affiliate of the National Institute for Automotive Service Excellence (ASE). NATEF's goals are to develop, encourage, and improve automotive technical education for students seeking entry-level positions as automobile service technicians. NATEF certifies many postsecondary programs for training throughout the country. Certification is available in the areas of automatic transmission/transaxle, brakes, electrical systems, engine performance, engine repair, heating and air conditioning, manual drive train and axles, and suspension and steering. Certification assures students that the program they enroll in meets the standards employers expect from their entry-level employees.

Automobile service technicians must be patient and thorough in their work—a shoddy repair job may put the driver's life at risk. They must have excellent troubleshooting skills and be able to logically deduce the cause of system malfunctions.

Opportunities for Experience & Exploration

Many community centers offer general auto maintenance and mechanics workshops where students can practice working on real cars and learn from instructors. Trade magazines are excellent sources for learning what's new in the industry and can be found at most public libraries or large bookstores. Many public television stations broadcast automobile maintenance and repair programs that can be of help to beginners to see how various types of cars differ.

High school auto mechanics and shop courses can help teach students mechanical aptitude and basic auto maintenance. Students learn the proper use of many different tools as they apply to specific auto components. Working on cars as a hobby provides valuable firsthand experience in the work of a technician. An afterschool or weekend part-time job in a repair shop or dealership can give a feel for the general atmosphere and kinds of problems technicians face on the job. Experience with vehicle repair work in the armed forces is another way many people pursue their interests in this field.

Methods of Entering

The best way to start out in this field is to attend one of the many postsecondary training programs available throughout the country and obtain accreditation. Trade and technical schools usually provide job placement assistance for their graduates. Schools often have contacts with local employers who need to hire well-trained people. Frequently employers post job openings at nearby trade schools that have accredited programs.

Although postsecondary training programs are considered a better way to learn, a decreasing number of technicians learn the trade on the job as apprentices. Their training consists of working for several years under the guidance of experienced mechanics. Trainees usually begin as helpers, lubrication workers, or service station attendants who gradually acquire the skills and knowledge necessary for the typical service or repair tasks technicians encounter. Fewer employers today are willing to hire apprentices due to the time and cost it takes to train them. Those who do learn their skills on the job will inevitably require some formal training if they wish to advance and stay in step with the changing industry.

Intern programs sponsored by car manufacturers or independent organizations provide students with excellent opportunities to actually work with prospective employers. Internships can provide students with valuable contacts who will be able to recommend future employers once they have completed their training. Many students may even be hired by the company at which they interned.

Advancement

Currently employed technicians may be certified by the National Institute for Automotive Service Excellence (ASE). Although certification is voluntary, it is a widely recognized standard of achievement for automobile technicians and is highly valued by many employers. Certification also provides the means and opportunity to advance. To maintain their certification, technicians must retake the examination for their specialties every five years. Many employers only hire ASE-accredited technicians and base salaries on the level of the technicians' accreditation.

With today's complex automobile components requiring hundreds of hours of study and practice to master, more repair shops prefer to hire specialists. Generalist automobile technicians advance as they gain experience and become specialists. Other technicians advance to diesel repair, where the pay may be higher. Those with good communications and planning skills may advance to shop foreman or service manager at large repair shops or to sales workers at dealerships. Master mechanics (technicians certified in all eight specialty areas) with good business skills often go into business for themselves and open their own shops. Some master mechanics may go on to teach at technical and vocational schools or at community colleges.

Employment Outlook

With an estimated 189 million vehicles in operation today, automobile service technicians should feel confident that a good percentage will require servicing and repair. Skilled and highly trained technicians will be in particular demand. Less skilled workers will face tough competition. The automotive service industry predicts it will need to replace 20 percent of its workforce by the end of the decade due to retirees and people who cannot keep up with the changing technology.

One concern for technicians is the automobile industry's trend toward developing the "maintenance-free" car. Manufactures are producing high-end cars that require no servicing for their first 100,000 miles. In addition, many new cars are equipped with onboard diagnostics (OBD) that detect both wear and failure for many of the car's components, eliminating the need for technicians to perform extensive diagnostic tests. Also, parts that are replaced before they completely wear out prevent further damage from occurring to connected parts that are affected by a malfunction or breakdown. Although this will reduce troubleshooting time and the number of overall repairs, the components that need repair will be more costly and require a more experienced (and hence, more expensive) technician to service.

Fluctuations in the economy have little effect on employment in this field; automobile service technicians generally enjoy the security of steady work. When the economy is bad, people tend to service and repair their cars rather than buy new ones. Conversely, when the economy is good, more people are apt to service their cars regularly and purchase new cars.

Most new jobs for technicians will be at independent service dealers, specialty shops, and franchised new car dealers. Because of the increase of specialty shops, fewer gasoline service stations will hire technicians, and many will eliminate repair services completely. Other opportunities will be available at companies or institutions with private fleets (e.g., cab, delivery, and rental companies, and government agencies and police departments).

Earnings

Salary ranges of automobile service technicians vary depending upon the level of experience, type of shop the technician works in, and geographic location. Technicians with certification earn on average $24,800 per year. Less experienced technicians earn on average $13,000 per year. Since most technicians work on an hourly basis and frequently work overtime, their salaries can vary significantly. Managers of service and repair shops earn between $34,000 and $45,000. In many repair shops and dealerships, technicians can earn higher incomes by working on commission. Typically they earn 40 to 50 percent of the labor costs charged to customers. Employers often guarantee a minimum level of pay in addition to commissions. Some mechanics are members of labor union, which negotiate standard pay scales throughout the country.

Benefit packages vary from business to business. Most technicians can expect health insurance and paid vacations. Additional benefits may include dental, life, and disability insurance and a pension plan. Employers usually cover a technician's work clothes and may pay a percentage of hand tools purchased. An increasing number of employers pay all or most of an employee's certification training, if he or she passes the test. A technician's salary can increase through yearly bonuses or profit sharing if the business does well in the course of a year.

Conditions of Work

Depending on the size of the shop and whether it's an independent or franchised repair shop, dealership, or government or private business, automobile technicians work with anywhere from two to twenty other technicians. Most shops are well lighted and well ventilated. They can frequently be noisy with running cars and power tools.

Minor hand and back injuries are the most common problems of technicians. When reaching in hard-to-get-at places or loosening tight bolts, technicians often bruise, cut, or burn their hands. With caution and experience most technicians learn to avoid hand injuries. Working for long periods of time in cramped or bent positions often results in a stiff back or neck. Technicians also lift many heavy objects that can cause injury if not handled carefully; however, this is becoming less of a problem with new cars, as automakers design smaller and lighter parts to improve fuel economy. Some technicians may experience allergic reactions to solvents and oils used in cleaning, maintenance, and repair. Shops must comply with strict safety procedures to help employees avoid accidents and injuries.

Most technicians work between forty and forty-eight hours a week but may be required to work longer hours when the shop is busy. Some technicians make emergency repairs to stranded, roadside automobiles.

Sources of Additional Information

For information on accreditation and testing and for general information on the American automobile industry, please contact:

American Automobile Manufacturers Association
1401 H Street, NW, Suite 900
Washington, DC 20005
Tel: 202-326-5500

For more information on the automotive parts industry, please contact:

Automotive Service Industry Association (ASIA)
25 Northwest Point
Elk Grove Village, IL 60007-1035
Tel: 847-228-1310

Automotive Warehouse Distributors Association (AWDA)
9140 Ward Parkway
Kansas City, MO 64114
Tel: 816-444-3500

Motor and Equipment Manufacturers Association (MEMA)
PO Box 13966
10 Laboratory Drive
Research Triangle Park, NC 27709
Tel: 919-549-4800

National Automobile Dealers Association (NADA)
8400 Westpark Drive
McLean, VA 22102
Tel: 703-821-7000

■■National Automotive Technicians Education Foundation
(NATEF)
13505 Dulles Technology Drive
Herndon, VA 22071-3415
Tel: 703-904-0100

For information on certification, contact:

■■National Institute for Automotive Service Excellence
13505 Dulles Technology Drive, Suite 2
Herndon, VA 22071-3415
Tel: 703-713-3800

Barbers, Stylists, and Cosmetologists

Definition

Barbers perform the personal services of coloring, bleaching, cutting, trimming, and shampooing hair and of trimming and shaping beards and mustaches.

Cosmetologists, often called *beauty operators, beauticians,* or *hairdressers,* work to improve and maintain the personal appearance of their clients. They cut, style, and dye hair, perform facials, apply makeup, and do manicures.

Nature of the Work

In general, the duties of the barber are well defined. Barbers tint, bleach, cut, trim, shape, style, and shampoo hair. They give shaves, facials, scalp treatments, and massages and advise customers on grooming habits and cosmetic aids. They also trim and style beards and mustaches and perform other related personal services for customers.

Barbers use certain tools in their services with trained skill, such as scissors, clippers, razors, combs, brushes, hot towels, tweezers, and razor sharpeners. The barber's tools and working surroundings must be kept in an antiseptic and sterile condition.

In their training, barbers learn some aspects of human physiology and anatomy, including the bone structure of the head and elementary facts about the nervous system. Barbers either cut hair as the customers request or they decide how to cut it by studying the contours of the head, the quality and texture of the hair, and the personal features of the customer. A successful barber recognizes that each customer is an individual and no two possess the same types of personal and physical characteristics.

Barbers may be employed in shops that have as few as one or two operators, or as many as ten or more employees. Some barbers work in combination barber-and-beauty shops, while others are employed in shops in hotels, hospitals, and resort areas. Those who operate their own shops must also take care

School Subjects
Business
Health

Personal Interests
Business management
Helping people: personal service

Work Environment
Primarily indoors
Primarily one location

Minimum Education Level
Postsecondary training
Apprenticeship

Salary Range
$13,000 to
$20,200 to
$31,000+

Certification or Licensing
Required

Outlook
About as fast as the average

DOT
330, 332

of the details of business operations. Bills must be paid, orders placed, invoices and supplies checked, equipment serviced, and records and books kept. The selection, hiring, and termination of other workers are also the owner's responsibilities. Barbershop employees may include manicurists, shoe shine attendants, assistant barbers, and custodial help. Like other responsible business people, barber shop owners are likely to be asked to participate in civic and community projects and activities.

Cosmetologists perform personal grooming services for customers that may include styling, cutting, trimming, straightening, permanent waving, coloring, tinting, bleaching, and shampooing hair. Cosmetologists may also give facials, massages, manicures, pedicures, and scalp treatments and may shape and tint eyelashes and eyebrows. They sometimes do makeup analysis, suggest cosmetic aids, and advise customers on what products to use and how to use them for the best results. Many specialize as *hairstylists*. Through advanced training, cosmetologists may specialize in some aspect of their work, such as permanent waving, cutting hair, or setting only the more difficult, high-fashion hairstyles. In small shops the cosmetologist's job duties may also include making appointments for customers, cleaning equipment, and sterilizing instruments.

Cosmetologists use certain tools and equipment in their work, such as scissors, razors, brushes, clippers, cosmetic aids, massage and manicure equipment, hair dryers, towels, and reclining chairs. Most of the equipment and tools are provided by the shop owners.

In some shops, *manicurists* tend to customers' nails, filing and polishing them and trimming the cuticles. Cosmetologists work in close personal contact with the public. They may have customers at any age level. Some even specialize in children's haircuts.

The work of barbers and that of cosmetologists are closely related, and both barbers and cosmetologists perform their services in the same type of surroundings. Although some beauty shops may be decorated to appeal more to a female clientele, many men now prefer to have their hair cut and styled by cosmetologists. Cosmetologists are employed in privately owned shops throughout the country, many of them small businesses. They may also be employed in beauty shops in large department stores, drugstores, hospitals, nursing homes, and hotels. Cosmetologists may be employed to demonstrate hairstyles and cosmetic products in various retail stores, fashion centers, photographic centers, and television studios. With advanced training, some cosmetologists may qualify to teach in beauty culture colleges and vocational training schools.

Cosmetologists serving the public must have pleasant, friendly, yet professional attitudes, as well as skill, ability, and an interest in their craft. These qualities are necessary to building a following of steady customers. The nature of the work demands that cosmetologists be aware of the psychological aspects of dealing with all types of customers.

Although many of the services performed by cosmetologists are repetitive in nature, the individual personalities of the clients add to the interest, satisfaction, and challenge of the occupation. With each new client, cosmetologists are presented with a fresh challenge; they must continually strive for creativity and artistic flair in their jobs through hairstyling, fashion creation, and makeup work for clients.

Requirements

The educational and training requirements for barbers vary among the states. Some states require potential barbers to have the minimum of an eighth-grade education; other states require a high school education. Nearly all states now require barbers to be licensed or certified by a state board of examiners. To obtain a license or certification in almost any state, the individual must pass a practical examination demonstrating skills and abilities and a written test reflecting knowledge of the trade. The great majority of states will not examine anyone younger than sixteen or eighteen who applies for a license. Applicants must also be able to obtain health certificates, and in almost every state they must be graduates of a barber school that is state-approved.

In most states barbers must first be licensed as barber apprentices. After a specified period of employment (usually one to two years), the apprentice may take another written and practical examination to qualify for a license as a journeyman barber. When barbers move from one state to another, they must satisfy the license requirements of the state to which they are moving. Some states will recognize the license from another state, in which case the barber does not need to be retested.

Training opportunities are available in about four hundred private barber colleges and public vocational training schools. Training periods are generally six months to one year. Most training institutions require approximately 1,000 to 2,000 hours of formal instruction, including courses in hygiene, anatomy, sanitation, and skin and scalp diseases. Other course work includes lectures, demonstrations, and practice in the art of barbering and the use and care of tools and equipment. Some schools instruct their students in business management and practices, the psychology of sales and advertising, professional ethics, and unionism. Some states have schools that offer advanced coursework for barbers who wish to specialize in such techniques as hair coloring or styling. Students should be careful to select barber schools that have training programs that meet at least the minimum requirements of their state. Some schools require students to purchase their basic barbering instruments at a cost of about $450.

A barber needs certain aptitudes to be successful. Finger dexterity is important because it is needed in all aspects of a barber's work. Hand-eye coordination is equally necessary.

A pleasant demeanor and an outgoing personality are very important to the successful barber. Clients look for a tactful, courteous, and friendly barber who is skillful and seems to enjoy the work and working with clients. A barber needs to present a neat, clean, and well-groomed appearance. Most people place a great deal of importance on how their hair looks, and when they do not like a cut or style, they may become angry or upset. It is crucial that a barber be aware of the high expectations placed on this work and do everything to prevent disappointment and frustration. The barber can accomplish this first by listening carefully to what the client wants and observing the specific characteristics of the client's hair and then by explaining his recommendations to the client. Frequently, a client will ask for a particular style or cut that is unsuitable for his features or perhaps the style simply won't work on his type of hair. The barber needs to be able to deal patiently but firmly with such a client, so that he understands perfectly that the end result may not achieve the desired effect.

Almost all cosmetologists learn their craft at an accredited school. The National Association of Cosmetology Schools estimates that more than 3,900 public and private training schools for cosmetologists operate across the country.

As with barbers, most states require that cosmetologists have either a minimum eighth-grade education or a high school diploma.

The majority of private schools offer training programs lasting six to nine months; in some states, however, courses require from twelve to fifteen months for completion. Public training school programs may cover a span of two or three years equal to the last three years of high school, because academic subjects are also a part of the curriculum.

Courses at cosmetology schools may include lectures, demonstrations, and practical work. Classroom training can include such subjects as anatomy, elementary physiology, hygiene, sanitation, applied chemistry, shop planning, applied electricity, and business basics. In practical training, students usually practice their techniques on mannequins with wigs, and on each other. As students gain experience, they may work on customers who come to the training clinics for their lower prices.

The cost of beauty culture training programs varies among schools. It is determined by such factors as the adequacy of the school's physical plant, training facilities, staff, location, and length of formal training. Tuition may also be affected by the requirements of the state board of examiners.

Cosmetologists in all states must obtain a license. In some states applicants must first pass an examination to qualify as a junior cosmetologist. After passing this exam and practicing for one year, they are eligible to take a second exam for senior cosmetologist. Fees for license examinations and yearly renewals are different in every state.

The number of hours of formal course training that students must have before they can apply for a cosmetologist's license with a state board of examiners varies among the states. States may require from 1,000 hours (six months) to 2,500 hours (fifteen months) of combined practical and classroom training. Some states allow applicants to complete this requirement in apprenticeship programs. These programs, however, are gradually decreasing in number as state boards of examiners realize that applicants need more formal and technical training.

Applicants must meet other criteria to be eligible to take the state board examinations for licenses. In the majority of states, the minimum age requirement is sixteen. Because standards and requirements vary from state to state, students are urged to contact the licensing board of the state in which they plan to be employed to verify the requirements.

Opportunities for Experience & Exploration

Those who are interested in becoming barbers may explore this occupation in a number of different ways. Students may visit barber colleges and talk to members of the administration, teachers, and students and request permission to visit a class in barbering instruction. Potential students may observe and talk with licensed barbers who are practicing the trade. They may wish to seek summer employment in barbershops as clean-up and errand workers so that they can observe firsthand the work of the barber.

The occupation of cosmetologist may be explored by visiting various training institutions, such as public training high schools and private beauty colleges. Some schools may permit potential students to visit and observe training classes. Watching and talking with licensed cosmetologists may provide additional information. There is little opportunity to explore this occupation through part-time work experience; however, some individuals may obtain summer or weekend jobs as general shop helpers.

Methods of Entering

Barbering jobs are most frequently obtained by either applying in person or enlisting the aid of barbering unions. The largest union for barbers is the United Food and Commercial Workers International Union. Nearly all barber colleges assist their graduates in locating employment opportunities. Applicants also use the placement services of state or private employment agencies. Newspaper advertisements and personal references are good sources for job opportunities. Some salons have their own training programs from which they hire new employees.

Cosmetologists secure their first jobs in various ways. The majority of beauty colleges and private and public vocational training schools aid their graduates in locating job opportunities. Many schools have formal placement services.

Applicants may also apply directly to beauty shops in which they would like to work. Applicants may hear about openings through newspaper advertisements or through city or state employment services.

Advancement

Barbers usually begin as licensed barber apprentices. Through experience and study, apprentices advance to journeymen barbers. Within small barbershops there is very little opportunity for advancement to the assignment of the "first chair," except by seniority and skill. The first chair is most often the chair nearest the shop entrance. Barbers can change their place of employment and move to bigger, more attractive, and better-equipped shops.

Many barbers aspire to be self-employed and own their own shop. There are many things to consider when contemplating going into business on one's own.

It is usually essential to obtain experience and financial capital before seeking to own a shop. The cost of equipping a one-chair shop can be very high. Owning a large shop or even a chain of barber shops is yet another aspiration for the very ambitious.

Most cosmetologists begin their careers as general beauticians performing a variety of services. In some states a person must begin as a junior operator; after a year of experience at this level, the individual is eligible to take an examination to become licensed as a senior cosmetologist. Some pursue advanced educational training to become specialized in one aspect of beauty culture, such as hairstyling or coloring.

Through skill, training, and seniority, a hairdresser may advance to a position as shop manager. After they have built a loyal clientele, some people may aspire to open their own shop. Cosmetologists may also advance by moving to beauty shops that are located in more affluent areas.

After some years of practical experience and, in many cases, additional academic training, some cosmetologists may become teachers in schools of beauty culture. These opportunities, however, are usually open only to those who possess exceptional skills and abilities.

Cosmetologists may find that their background in beauty culture can help them move into different fields. They may move into jobs such as representatives of cosmetic companies or equipment firms, beauty editors for magazines, makeup artists and stylists for motion picture and television studios, or inspectors on state licensing examination boards. Other related job opportunities include *body makeup artists,* who work with photographers and models, and *mortuary beauticians.*

Employment Outlook

Approximately 59,000 persons were employed as barbers in the United States in 1996. About three out of four own their own shops, while one out of every three works part-time.

Future employment opportunities for barbers are not as predictable as those for other occupations. Most openings that present themselves will be to replace barbers who leave the trade for other work, retire, or die.

Employment may rise slightly in the coming years as new shopping centers open and suburban areas continue to grow with the expanding population. Barbers who specialize in unisex hairstyling will increase their business opportunities greatly, since men as well as women patronize full-service salons in greater numbers. The competent and well-trained barber should find employment without too much difficulty, but it may not always be in the geographic locality or shop desired.

Most job opportunities through the year 2006 will be for cosmetologists. The market for cosmetologists is expanding as the general population increases, more shops are opened in suburban shopping centers, and working women seek out cosmetic services more frequently. Good employment opportunities are becoming increasingly available to the part-time cosmetologist.

An estimated 586,000 people were employed as cosmetologists and hairstylists in 1996. The number of male workers in this field is increasing steadily. Currently, the demand for cosmetologists far outnumbers the supply.

Earnings

Salaries vary based on a number of factors, including size and location of the business, number of hours worked, and the level of competition from other shops and salons. According to a January 1998 report from the Economic Research Institute, barbers and stylists with less than fifteen years experience earned roughly $16,100 a year; those with fifteen to twenty-nine years of experience, 20,200 annually; and those with thirty or more years experience in the industry, approximately $27,900 annually. Hairstylists and some barbers who own their own shops have incomes of $31,000 a year or more. Most barbers work on a commission basis, receiving from 50 to 70 percent of what they are paid by customers. Others work for set salaries plus a percentage commission. Only a small number of barbers work for a salary without commission.

Tips from customers are considered an important factor in determining a barber's salary. The amount to be earned in tips is unpredictable and depends on the locale of employment, the personality and skill of the barber, individual shop policies, and the income levels of the customers.

Paid vacations, medical insurance, and death benefits are available to some employees, especially those who belong to a union.

Salaries of cosmetologists depend on a number of factors, such as experience, ability, speed of performance, income levels of the shop's clientele, shop location (suburban or urban), and the salary arrangement between the worker and the salon. Most cosmetologists are employed on a commission basis, while others receive a base salary plus 40 percent to 50 per-

cent commission. Tips are also an important factor in the cosmetologist's earnings.

Considering all of these factors, it is difficult to quote exact salary figures for all cosmetologists. Estimated salaries for experienced operators in the late 1990s range from $20,000 to $25,000. Beginning cosmetologists with average skill earn from $13,000 to $14,000. In exclusive city salons, expert operators, specialists, and top hairstylists earn much more.

Cosmetologists may receive fringe benefits that include group health and life insurance and one- to two-week paid vacations. The availability of fringe benefits varies widely, depending on the employer. Furthermore, these benefits, except for paid vacations, are usually available only to those employed by beauty salon chains and large establishments such as department stores and nursing homes.

Conditions of Work

Barbers usually work a five- or six-day week, which averages approximately forty to fifty hours. Weekends and days preceding holiday seasons may be unusually busy workdays. Some employers allow barbers to have extra days off during slack periods.

Barbers work in shops that must, by law, meet and maintain strict state sanitation codes. Shops are usually comfortably heated, ventilated, and well-lighted. Barbers are usually assigned a chair position and their own work area in a shop. They are required to be on their feet most of their working hours, but little walking is involved. In general, they work in a small space.

Hazards of the trade include nicks and cuts from scissors and razors, minor burns when care is not used in handling hot towels, and occasional skin irritations arising from the constant use of grooming aids that contain chemicals. Some of the chemicals used in hair dyes can be quite abrasive, and plastic gloves are usually required for handling and contact. The nature of the work requires the barber to repeat the same activities and services over and over. A barber must like the work and be interested in people in order to find the job satisfying.

Most cosmetologists work a forty-hour week, although some may work forty-four to forty-eight hours weekly. Working hours usually include Saturdays and, very frequently, evening appointments. Some cosmetologists work according to a shift schedule. Holiday seasons and special community events may result in increased business, which would involve overtime work.

The nature of the cosmetologist's job requires standing for most of the workday. The continual use of water, shampoos, lotions, and other solutions with chemical contents may cause skin irritations. Like barbers, cosmetologists wear gloves when working with dyes or chemicals.

Cosmetologists usually work in attractive, well-lighted, and comfortably ventilated shops. The level of supervision varies from shop to shop and depends upon the employer's attitude, type of shop, and the cosmetologist's level of skill and experience.

Cosmetologists work in such close, personal contact with the public and need to have an even temperament, pleasant disposition, and patience.

Sources of Additional Information

■ **Hair International/Associated Master Barbers and Beauticians of America**
PO Box 273
124-B East Main Street
Palmyra, PA 17078
Tel: 717-838-0795

■ **National Association of Barber Styling Schools**
304 South 11th Street
Lincoln, NE 68508
Tel: 402-474-4244

■ **National Accreditation Commission of Cosmetology Arts and Sciences**
901 North Stuart Street, Suite 900
Alexandria, VA 22203
Tel: 703-527-7600

■ **National Cosmetology Association**
3510 Olive Street
St. Louis, MO 63103
Tel: 314-534-7980

■ **Canadian Cosmetics Careers Association, Inc.**
26 Ferrah Street
Unionville, ON L3R 1N5 Canada
Tel: 905-470-1966

Billing Clerks

Definition

Billing clerks produce and process bills and collect payments from customers. They enter transactions in business ledgers or spreadsheets, write and send invoices, and verify purchase orders. They are responsible for posting items in accounts payable or receivable, calculating customer charges, and verifying the company's rates for certain products and services. Billing clerks must make sure that all entries are accurate and up-to-date. At the end of the fiscal year they may work with auditors to clarify billing procedures and answer questions about specific accounts.

Nature of the Work

Billing clerks are responsible for keeping records and up-to-date accounts of all business transactions. They type and send bills for services or products and update files to reflect payments; they also review incoming invoices to ensure that the requested products have been delivered and that the billing statements are accurate and paid on time.

Billing clerks set up shipping and receiving dates. They check customer orders before shipping to make sure they are complete and that all costs, shipping charges, taxes, and credits are included. Billing clerks are also troubleshooters. They contact suppliers or customers when payments are past due or incorrect and help solve the minor problems that invariably occur in the course of business transactions.

Billing clerks enter all transaction information onto the firm's account ledger. This ledger lists all the company's transactions such as items bought or sold as well as the credit terms and payment and receiving dates. As payments come in, the billing clerk applies credit to customer accounts and applies any applicable discounts. All correspondence is carefully filed for future reference. Nearly all of this work is currently done using spreadsheets and computer databases.

School Subjects
Business
Mathematics

Personal Interests
Computers
Writing

Work Environment
Primarily indoors
Primarily one location

Minimum Education Level
High school diploma

Salary Range
$17,400 to
$20,000 to
$24,000

Certification or Licensing
None

Outlook
About as fast as the average

DOT
214

GOE
07.02.04

NOC
4131

The specific duties of billing clerks vary according to the nature of the business in which they work. In an insurance company, the transaction sheet will reflect when and how much customers must pay on their insurance bills. Billing clerks in hospitals compile itemized charges, calculate insurance benefits, and process insurance claims. In accounting, law, and consulting firms, they calculate billable hours and work completed.

Billing clerks are also often responsible for preparing summary statements of financial status, profit-and-loss statements, and payroll lists and deductions. These reports are submitted periodically to company management, who can then gauge the company's financial performance. Clerks may also write company checks, compute federal tax reports, and tabulate personnel profit shares.

Billing clerks may have a specific role within a company. These areas of specialization include:

Invoice-control clerks, who post items in accounts payable or receivable ledgers and verify the accuracy of billing data; *passenger rate clerks,* who compute fare information for business trips and then provide this information to business personnel; *COD (cash-on-delivery) clerks,* who calculate and record the amount of money collected on COD delivery routes; *interline clerks,* who compute and pay freight charges for airlines or other transportation agencies that carry freight or passengers as part of a business transaction; *settlement clerks,* who compute and pay shippers for materials forwarded to a company; *billing-control clerks,* who compute and pay utility companies for services provided; *rate reviewers,* who compile data relating to utility costs for management officials; *services clerks,* who compute and pay tariff charges for boats or ships used to transport materials; *foreign clerks,* who compute duties, tariffs, and price conversions of exported and imported products; *billing-machine operators,* who mechanically prepare bills and statements; *deposit-refund clerks who* prepare bills for utility customers; *raters,* who calculate premiums to be paid by customers of insurance companies; and *telegraph-service raters,* who compute costs for sending telegrams.

Billing clerks may work in one specific area or they may be responsible for several areas.

Requirements

A high school diploma is usually sufficient for a beginning billing clerk, although business courses in computer operations and bookkeeping are also helpful. English, communications, and business writing skills are also important. Some companies test their applicants on math, typing and computer skills, and others offer on-the-job training.

High school students should take courses in English, mathematics, and business-related courses such as computer operations and bookkeeping. Community colleges, junior colleges, and vocational schools often offer business education courses that provide additional training.

Prospective billing clerks should have excellent mathematical and organizational skills, be detail-oriented, and be able to concentrate on repetitive tasks for long periods of time. In addition, they should be dependable, honest, and trustworthy in dealing with confidential financial matters.

Opportunities for Experience & Exploration

Students can gain experience in this field by taking on clerical or bookkeeping responsibilities with a school club, student government, or other extracurricular activities. High school students interested in the field can work in retail operations, either part time or during the summer. Working at the cash register or even pricing products as a stockperson is a good introductory experience. It also may be possible to gain some experience by volunteering to help maintain the bookkeeping records for local groups, such as churches and small businesses.

Methods of Entering

Employers of billing clerks include hospitals, insurance companies, and other large businesses. High school job placement and guidance offices can help graduates find employment opportunities or establish job contacts. Specific jobs may also be found through classified newspaper advertisements.

Most companies provide on-the-job training for entry-level billing clerks in order to explain to them company procedures and policies and to teach them the basic tasks of their job. During the first month, billing clerks work with experienced personnel.

Advancement

Billing clerks usually begin by handling routine tasks such as recording transactions. With experience, they may advance to more complex assignments, which include computer training in databases and spreadsheets, and assume a greater responsibility for the work as a whole. With additional training and education, billing clerks can be promoted to positions as bookkeepers, accountants, or auditors. Billing clerks with strong leadership and management skills can advance to group manager or supervisor.

There is a high turnover rate in this field, which increases the chance of promotion for employees with ability and initiative.

Employment Outlook

Approximately 437,000 billing clerks were employed in 1996. About 40 percent of them work in banks, insurance companies, and health services. Approximately 20 percent work in wholesale and retail, while others are employed in manufacturing, transportation, communications, and the utilities industry. The federal government should continue to be a good source of job opportunities, and numerous openings will develop in private companies.

The number of jobs available for billing clerks is expected to grow as fast as the average for all occupations through the year 2006. As the volume and complexity of business transactions continue to increase, there will be ample opportunities for billing clerks. Many job openings will result as current workers transfer to other fields, or leave the workforce for other reasons. Technological advancements will speed up operations or replace tasks performed by some billing clerks. Computers and specialized billing software are replacing traditional billing machines, allowing clerks to calculate and prepare bills in one step. Electronic billing and payment will eventually become the norm.

More complex computer applications will demand employees with greater technical expertise. Billing, cost, and rate clerks will replace billing machine operators. In smaller companies, accounting clerks will make use of billing software, making billing clerks obsolete. The number of part-time positions will increase and turnover will remain high.

Earnings

Beginning billing clerks earn an average annual salary of $17,400, depending on the size and geographic location of the company and the employee's skills. Experienced clerks can earn $24,000 per year. Full-time workers also receive paid vacation, health insurance, and other benefits.

Conditions of Work

Like most office workers, billing clerks usually work in modern office environments and average thirty-seven to forty hours a week. Billing clerks spend most of their time behind a desk, and their work can be routine and repetitive. Working long hours in front of a computer can often cause eye strain, backaches, and headaches, although efforts are being made to reduce physical problems with ergonomically correct equipment. Billing clerks should enjoy systematic and orderly work and have a keen eye for numerical detail. While much of the work is solitary, billing clerks often interact with accountants and management and may work under close supervision.

Sources of Additional Information

Career information is available from local business schools and from:

Office of Professional Employees International Union
265 West 14th Street, Suite 610
New York, NY 10011
Tel: 212-675-3210

Biomedical Equipment Technicians

Definition

Biomedical equipment technicians handle the complex medical equipment and instruments found in hospitals, clinics, and research facilities. This equipment is used for medical therapy and diagnosis and includes heart-lung machines, artificial-kidney machines, patient monitors, chemical analyzers, and other electrical, electronic, mechanical, or pneumatic devices.

The technician's main duties are to inspect, maintain, repair, and install this equipment. They disassemble equipment to locate malfunctioning components, repair or replace defective parts, and reassemble the equipment, adjusting and calibrating it to ensure that it operates according to manufacturers' specifications. Other duties of biomedical equipment technicians include modifying equipment according to the directions of medical or supervisory personnel, arranging with equipment manufacturers for necessary equipment repair, and safety-testing equipment to ensure that patients, equipment operators, and other staff members are safe from electrical or mechanical hazards. Biomedical equipment technicians work with hand tools, power tools, measuring devices, and manufacturers' manuals.

Technicians may work for equipment manufacturers as salespeople or as service technicians, or for a health care facility specializing in the repair or maintenance of specific equipment such as that used in radiology, nuclear medicine, or patient monitoring.

Nature of the Work

Biomedical equipment technicians are an important link between technology and medicine. They repair, calibrate, maintain, and operate the biomedical equipment working under the supervision of researchers, biomedical engineers, physicians, surgeons, and other professional health care providers.

School Subjects
Biology
Shop (Trade/Vo-tech education)

Personal Interests
Fixing things
Helping people: physical health/medicine

Work Environment
Primarily indoors
Primarily one location

Minimum Education Level
Associate's degree

Salary Range
$19,000 to
$24,000 to
$46,000

Certification or Licensing
Recommended

Outlook
About as fast as the average

DOT
019

GOE
05.05.11

Biomedical equipment technicians may work with thousands of different kinds of equipment. Some of the most frequently encountered are the following: patient monitors; heart-lung machines; kidney machines; blood-gas analyzers; spectrophotometers; X-ray units; radiation monitors; defibrillators; anesthesia apparatus; pacemakers; blood pressure transducers; spirometers; sterilizers; diathermy equipment; patient-care computers; ultrasound machines; and diagnostic scanning machines such as the CT (computed tomography) scan machine, PETT (positive emission transaxial tomography) scanner, and MRI (magnetic resonance imagery) machines.

Repairing faulty instruments is one of the chief functions of biomedical equipment technicians. They investigate equipment problems, determine the extent of malfunctions, make repairs on instruments that have had minor breakdowns, and expedite the repair of instruments with major breakdowns, for instance, by writing an analysis of the problem for the factory. In doing this work, technicians rely on manufacturers' diagrams, maintenance manuals, and standard and specialized test instruments, such as oscilloscopes and pressure gauges.

Installing equipment is another important function of biomedical equipment technicians. They inspect and test new equipment to make sure it complies with performance and safety standards as described in the manufacturer's manuals and diagrams, and as noted on the purchase order. Technicians may also check on proper installation of the equipment or, in some cases, install it themselves. To ensure safe operations, technicians need a thorough knowledge of the regulations related to the proper grounding of equipment, and they need to actively carry out all steps and procedures to ensure safety.

Maintenance is the third major area of responsibility for biomedical equipment technicians. In doing this work, technicians try to catch problems before they become more serious. To this end, they take apart and reassemble devices, test circuits, clean and oil moving parts, and replace worn parts. They also keep complete records of all machine repairs, maintenance checks, and expenses.

In all three of these areas, a large part of the technician's work consists of consulting with physicians, administrators, engineers, and other related professionals. For example, they may be called upon to assist hospital administrators as they make decisions about the repair, replacement, or purchase of new equipment. They consult with medical and research staffs to determine that equipment is functioning safely and properly. They also consult with medical and engineering staffs when called upon to modify or develop equipment. In all of these activities, they use their knowledge of electronics, medical terminology, human anatomy and physiology, chemistry, and physics.

In addition, biomedical equipment technicians are involved in a range of other related duties. Some biomedical equipment technicians maintain inventories of all instruments in the hospital, their condition, location, and operator. They reorder parts and components, assist in providing people with emergency instruments, restore unsafe or defective instruments to working order, and check for safety regulation compliance.

Other biomedical equipment technicians may help physicians, surgeons, nurses, and researchers conduct procedures and experiments. In addition, they must be able to explain to staff members how to operate these machines, the conditions under which certain apparatus may or may not be used, how to solve small operating problems, and how to monitor and maintain equipment.

In many hospitals, technicians are assigned to a particular service, such as pediatrics, surgery, or renal medicine. These technicians become specialists in certain types of equipment. However, unlike electrocardiograph technicians or dialysis technicians, who specialize in one kind of equipment, for the most part biomedical equipment technicians must be thoroughly familiar with a large variety of instruments. They might be called upon to prepare an artificial kidney or to work with a blood-gas analyzer. Biomedical equipment technicians also maintain pulmonary function machines. These machines are used in clinics for ambulatory patients, hospital laboratories, departments of medicine for diagnosis and treatment, and for the rehabilitation of cardiopulmonary patients.

While most biomedical equipment technicians are trained in electronics technology, there is also a need for technicians trained in plastics to work on the development of artificial organs and for people trained in glass blowing to help make the precision parts for specialized equipment.

Many biomedical equipment technicians work for medical instrument manufacturers. These technicians consult and assist in the construction of new machinery, helping to make decisions concerning materials and construction methods used in the manufacture of the equipment.

Requirements

Biomedical equipment technicians require post–secondary education, usually a two-year program leading to an associate's degree. While still in high school, prospective technicians should take courses in chemistry, biology, and physics;

these courses will provide a helpful background for further study. Courses in English, mathematics, electronics, shop, and drafting will also help prepare students for further education and for work as technicians.

Biomedical equipment technology is a relatively new program in two-year colleges. Some schools refer to these programs as medical electronics technology or biomedical engineering technology. During the course of these programs, students receive instruction in anatomy, physiology, electrical and electronic fundamentals, chemistry, physics, biomedical equipment construction and design, safety in health care facilities, medical equipment troubleshooting, and communications skills. In addition to the classroom work, programs often provide students with practical experience in repairing and servicing equipment in a clinical or laboratory setting under the supervision of an experienced equipment technician. In this way, students learn about electrical components and circuits, the design and construction of common pieces of machinery, and computer technology as it applies to biomedical equipment.

By studying various pieces of equipment, technicians learn a problem-solving technique that applies not only to the equipment studied, but also to equipment they have not yet seen and even to equipment that has not yet been invented. Part of this problem-solving technique includes learning how and where to locate sources of information.

Some biomedical equipment technicians receive their training in the armed forces. During the course of an enlistment period of four years or less, military personnel can receive training that prepares them for entry-level or sometimes advanced-level positions later in the civilian workforce.

The Association for the Advancement of Medical Instrumentation, affiliated with the International Certification Commission for Clinical Engineering and Biomedical Technology, issues a certificate for biomedical equipment technicians based on a written examination and educational preparation. This program provides an opportunity for technicians to demonstrate that they have attained an overall knowledge of the field, and many employers prefer to hire technicians with this certificate. In some cases, the educational requirements for certification may be waived for technicians with appropriate employment experience.

Biomedical equipment technicians need mechanical ability and should enjoy working with tools. Because this job demands quick decision-making and prompt repairs, technicians should work well under pressure. They should also be extremely precise and accurate in their work and have good communications skills.

Opportunities for Experience & Exploration

It is difficult for interested high school students to gain any direct experience in biomedical equipment technology. The first opportunities for students generally come in the clinical and laboratory phases of their training programs. Students can, however, visit their school and community libraries to seek out books written about careers in medical technology. They can also join a hobby club devoted to chemistry, biology, radio equipment, or electronics.

Perhaps the best way to learn more about this job is to set up, with the help of teachers or guidance counselors, a visit to a local health care facility or arrange for a biomedical technician to speak to interested students, either on site or at a career exploration seminar hosted by the school. It would also be highly desirable for interested students to visit a school offering a program in biomedical equipment technology and discuss career plans with an admissions counselor.

Methods of Entering

Most schools offering programs in biomedical equipment technology work closely with local hospitals and industries, and school placement officers are usually informed about openings when they become available. In some cases, recruiters may visit a school periodically to conduct interviews. Also, many schools place students in part-time hospital jobs to help them gain practical experience. Students are often able to return to these hospitals for full-time employment after graduation.

Another effective method of finding employment is to write directly to hospitals, research institutes, or biomedical equipment manufacturers. Other good sources of leads for job openings include state employment offices and newspaper want ads.

Advancement

With experience, biomedical equipment technicians can expect to work with less supervision, and in some cases they may find themselves supervising other, less experienced technicians. They may advance to positions in which they serve as instructors, assist in research, or have administrative duties. Although many supervisory positions are open to biomedical equipment technicians, some positions are not available without additional education. In large metropolitan hospitals, for instance, the minimum educational requirement for biomedical engineers, who do much of the supervising of biomedical equipment technicians, is a bachelor's degree; many engineers have a master's degree as well.

Employment Outlook

Because of the increasing use of medical electronic devices and other sophisticated biomedical equipment, the demand for skilled and trained biomedical equipment technicians is predicted to grow about as fast as the average for all other occupations through the year 2006.

In hospitals the need for more biomedical equipment technicians exists not only because of the increasing use of biomedical equipment but also because hospital administrators realize that these technicians can help hold down costs. Biomedical equipment technicians do this through their preventive maintenance checks and by taking over some routine activities of engineers and administrators, thus releasing those professionals for activities that only they can perform. Through the coming decades, cost containment will remain a high priority for hospital administrators, and as long as biomedical equipment technicians can contribute to that effort, the demand for them should remain strong.

For the many biomedical equipment technicians who work for companies that build, sell, lease, or service biomedical equipment, job opportunities also should continue to grow.

The federal government also employs biomedical equipment technicians in its hospitals, research institutes, and the military. Employment in these areas will depend largely on levels of government spending. In the research area, spending levels may vary; however, in the health care delivery area, spending should remain high for the foreseeable future.

Earnings

Salaries for biomedical equipment technicians vary in different institutions and localities and according to the experience, training, certification, and type of work done by the technician. In general, entry-level salaries range from $19,000 to $24,000 for technicians working in hospitals and from $20,000 to $23,800 for technicians working for manufacturers or governmental agencies. Experienced technicians earn approximately $24,000 to $36,000 when working in a hospital and approximately $25,000 to $36,000 when working for a manufacturer. Senior technicians earn approximately $46,000 or more a year.

Conditions of Work

Working conditions for biomedical equipment technicians vary according to employer and type of work done. Hospital employees generally work a forty-hour week; their schedules may sometimes include weekends and holidays, or some may be on call for emergencies. Technicians working for equipment manufacturers may have to do extensive traveling to install or service equipment. The physical surroundings in which biomedical equipment technicians work may vary from day to day. On some days, technicians may work in a lab or treatment room with patients and staff; on others, they may consult with engineers, administrators, or other staff members and other entire days may be spent at a workbench repairing equipment.

Sources of Additional Information

■**Society of Biomedical Equipment Technicians**
3330 Washington Boulevard, Suite 400
Arlington, VA 22201-4890
Tel: 800-332-2264

Bodyguards

Definition

Bodyguards protect their clients from injury, kidnapping, harassment, or other types of harm. They may guard a politician during a political campaign, a business executive on a worldwide trip, a movie star going to the Academy Awards, or anyone else who wants personal protection. Bodyguards may be employed by a government agency, a private security firm, or directly by an individual.

Bodyguards work in potentially dangerous situations and must be trained to anticipate and respond to emergencies. They may carry weapons. Bodyguards combine the ability to react quickly and expertly in a tense or dangerous situation with the ability to predict, prevent, or avoid many of these situations.

Nature of the Work

Although a bodyguard's ultimate responsibility is relatively straightforward—that is, to protect a client from danger—there are a wide variety of tasks involved in this assignment. Bodyguards are part personal aide and part police officer. As a personal aide, a bodyguard helps plan and implement schedules; as a police officer, he or she protects the client at a public or private event.

Bodyguards face possible danger whenever they are on duty. When there was an attempted assassination of President Ronald Reagan in March 1981, for example, his Secret Service bodyguards quickly shielded the president as gunshots were fired. Bodyguards may have to sacrifice their own security in defense of those they are hired to protect. Of course, bodyguards are not just sitting targets. They are trained how to react in any situation, life-threatening or not. Skilled bodyguards do all they can to minimize danger to those they are protecting, as well as to themselves. As a result of their careful preparation,

School Subjects
Physical education
Psychology

Personal Interests
Helping people: personal service
Travel

Work Environment
Indoors and outdoors
Primarily multiple locations

Minimum Education Level
High school diploma

Salary Range
$21,500 to $41,000 to $135,000

Certification or Licensing
None

Outlook
Faster than the average

DOT
372

GOE
04.02.02

NOC
6651

bodyguards carry out most assignments in a relatively uneventful fashion.

By keeping a watchful eye on their clients, bodyguards are able to avoid many possible problems. In many cases, people are not actually out to harm a client but are simply interested in meeting an important person. Bodyguards learn not to overreact to these encounters, and in most cases a polite warning eliminates any potential problem.

When a client hires a bodyguard for a specific event, the bodyguard will determine how many additional people may be needed to provide adequate protection. The client's schedule and travel arrangements will be coordinated for maximum security and, if the client is appearing at a public event, the bodyguard will familiarize himself with the location, especially the exits and secured areas, in case the client needs sudden and immediate protection from danger.

Bodyguards often work in tandem with other security people as part of a large security operation. For example, bodyguards may help develop a plan to safeguard a major politician who is giving a speech, while security guards will develop a plan to safeguard the building where the speech will take place. All security personnel meet to discuss overall arrangements to ensure that specific details are worked out. Typically, one person will coordinate the security operations.

Bodyguards are hired to protect their clients, and activities that infringe on this job must be avoided. At a presidential dinner, for example, a bodyguard must keep an eye on their client and not become engaged in idle chatter with guests. Bodyguards should not confuse the power and excitement of an assignment with self-importance. Indeed, it is the person who can remain calm in the midst of an exciting event and can sense possible danger when all eyes are elsewhere that can makes a skillful bodyguard.

Requirements

Since bodyguards must be prepared for any possibility, the more skilled and knowledgeable they are in a variety of areas, the better the protection they can offer someone. Bodyguards often begin their careers as police officers, where they learn the necessary skills of crowd control, use of weapons, and emergency response. Some people may also receive training in the armed forces and in this way develop the skills necessary to protect themselves and others.

Generally, bodyguards will receive some higher education (including a college degree), although this is not always necessary. A well-educated person can often be the most responsive to rapidly changing situations, and, of course, work in crowd psychology,

law, and criminal justice can help a bodyguard better understand the demands of the job. On-the-job experience with different types of people in stressful situations is an integral part of the training.

Since many bodyguards are former police officers, bodyguards generally must be above the minimum age for police officers. This minimum age varies from eighteen to twenty-one, depending on the city or state. If a bodyguard comes from the police ranks, that person must also have passed a thorough physical exam. Many bodyguards also begin their careers as security guards or as other types of security personnel, for which they receive special training. Other bodyguards come from a military background.

Excellent physical fitness is a requirement for a bodyguard. Despite a popular image of bodyguards as big and tough men, extreme physical strength is not an absolute requirement, and many women have made successful careers as bodyguards. It is much more important that a bodyguard combines intelligence, sensitivity, and bravery with the ability to act quickly and decisively.

Many bodyguards receive training in martial arts, and increasingly they are incorporating a study of counterintelligence operations, electronic security devices, and surveillance techniques. Often, bodyguards will have training in first aid. Many bodyguards are also trained in specialized defensive driving techniques that enable them to maintain better control of a vehicle in emergency situations.

Bodyguards who travel overseas must be well versed in the language and culture of the host country. Good verbal skills are vital, and a bodyguard must be able to communicate directions to people at all times. A bodyguard must also be aware of what to expect in any situation. That is why an understanding of the customs of a certain area can help the bodyguard perceive unusual events and be alert for possible problems. Similarly, the legal use, registration, and licensing of weapons differs from country to country, and the bodyguard who travels overseas needs to be aware of and familiar with the regulations governing weapons in whichever country he or she is working.

Since bodyguards often work with important people and around sensitive information, they may be required to take a lie detector test before they begin work. Background checks of their work and personal histories may also be required. Bodyguards who work as permanent employees of a client must also exercise discretion and maintain confidentiality.

Bodyguards should obviously have a keen eye for detail and be able to spot trouble long before it happens. This ability to anticipate problems is crucial. A good bodyguard should rarely have to stop a kidnapping attempt as it occurs, for example, but rather prevent the attempt from happening through a combination of careful planning and skilled observation. If action is needed, however, the response must be swift and effective.

Opportunities for Experience & Exploration

Because bodyguards must be mature and highly skilled, it is difficult to obtain real opportunities to explore this career while still in high school. Nevertheless, there are chances to take classes and talk to people to get a feel for the demands of the profession. Classes in criminal justice should give an indication of the challenges involved with protecting people. Talking to a police officer who works part time as a bodyguard is another good way of learning about opportunities in this field. Many police departments hire high school students as police trainees or interns, providing an excellent introduction to careers in security and law enforcement.

Without the requisite skills and experience, it is difficult to get summer work as a bodyguard. It may be possible, however, to work in some other capacity at a security firm that hires bodyguards and in this way interact with bodyguards and learn more about the day-to-day rewards and challenges of the profession.

Methods of Entering

Many people begin a career as a bodyguard on a part-time basis, often taking on assignments while off duty as a police officer. The reason most people start part time is that the police training they receive is ideal preparation for work as a bodyguard. In addition to the excellent training a police officer receives, the officer is often in a good spot to receive job offers. Someone looking for a bodyguard may call the local police station and ask if there are officers willing to take on an assignment. Then, as a person acquires greater experience in being a bodyguard and more and more community members know of the person's skills and availability, additional work becomes available. That person may then work full time as a bodyguard or continue on a part-time basis.

Military service may also provide the background and skills for entry into this field. Many bodyguards enter this career after service in one of the special forces, such as the Green Berets or the Navy SEALs, or after experience in the Military Police. Other bodyguards enter this field through a career with private security companies and often begin training while employed as security guards. Careers with the Secret Service, the Federal Bureau of Investigation, or other governmental police and intelligence agencies may also provide the necessary background for a career as a bodyguard. In fact, a successful history with one of these respected agencies is one of the best magnets for potential employers.

Advancement

Those who enter the field as part-time bodyguards may soon find full-time work. As bodyguards develop their skills and reputation, they may be hired by a private security firm or a governmental agency. They may be given additional training in intelligence operations, surveillance techniques, and the use of sophisticated firearms.

Some bodyguards find opportunities as personal protection and security consultants. These consultants work for private companies, evaluating personal security operations and recommending changes. They may begin their own security services companies or advance to supervisory and director's positions within an existing company.

Employment Outlook

Career opportunities for bodyguards are likely to increase faster than the average through the year 2006 as more and more people look to bodyguards for protection. The threat of kidnapping and terrorism is always present for politicians, celebrities, business leaders, and others who enjoy wide recognition, and these individuals will take steps to safeguard themselves and their families by hiring bodyguards. As more and more companies enter the global economy, their business will take their executives to more areas of social and political unrest, and companies will need to increase their efforts for protecting their employees.

Governmental agencies will continue to hire bodyguards, but much of the growth in employment will take place in the private sector. Many bodyguards will find work with private security companies. Some estimates suggest that employment in private security may nearly double over the next decade.

Those with the most skill and experience will enjoy the best employment prospects. While the majority of bodyguards continue to be men, the increasing use of advanced security technologies will open up more and more opportunities for women.

Earnings

Many bodyguards begin their careers on a part-time basis and earn between $25 and $50 per hour for routine assignments. These assignments might last several hours. Earnings for full-time bodyguards vary enormously but generally fall within the range of $21,500 and $135,000 per year, with an average of $41,000 per year. A bodyguard's earnings depend on his or her experience, the notoriety or prestige of the client, the type of assignment, and whether the bodyguard is employed directly by the client or through a security agency. Highly dangerous, sensitive, or classified assignments generally pay higher than more routine protective assignments. Training in special skills such as electronic surveillance also brings higher wages.

Bodyguards employed by private security firms may receive health and life insurance benefits and other benefits. Benefits vary for those employed by private clients. Bodyguards who work as part of a government agency receive health and life insurance, vacation, holiday, and sick leave pay, and a pension plan. Self-employed bodyguards must provide their own insurance.

Conditions of Work

A bodyguard goes wherever the client goes. This means that the job can be physically demanding. Bodyguards must also have the strength and coordination to take actions to protect the client if the situation warrants it. A bodyguard must be able to act swiftly and decisively to thwart any attempt to harm a client. Bodyguards must be able to risk their own safety to protect their clients. They should be comfortable handling firearms and using physical means of restraining people.

Since bodyguards must accompany their clients at all times, there is no set work schedule. Bodyguards often work highly irregular hours, such as late evenings followed by morning assignments. It is also not unusual to work weekends, since this is when many high-profile clients make public appearances. Travel is a frequent component of the job.

Sources of Additional Information

■ **International Bodyguard Association**
458 West Kenwood
Brighton, TN 38011
Tel: 901-837-1915
Email: 103222.2541@compuserve.com

■ **American Society for Industrial Security**
1655 North Fort Myer Drive
Arlington, VA 22209
Tel: 703-522-5800

Boilermakers and Boilermaker Mechanics

Definition

Boilermakers and *boilermaker mechanics* construct, assemble, and repair boilers, vats, tanks, and other large metal vessels that are designed to hold liquids and gases. Following blueprints, they lay out, cut, fit, bolt, weld, and rivet together heavy metal plates, boiler tubes, and castings. Boilermaker mechanics maintain and repair boilers and other vessels made by boilermakers.

Nature of the Work

Some boilermakers and mechanics work at or near the site where the boiler, tank, or vat is installed. Such sites include petroleum refineries, schools and other institutions with large heating plants, factories where boilers are used to generate power to run machines, factories that make and store products such as chemicals or beer in large tanks, and atomic energy plants. Others work in shops or factories where boilers and other large vessels are manufactured.

Boilermakers who do layout work usually work in a shop or factory. These workers follow drawings, blueprints, and patterns to mark pieces of metal plate and tubing to indicate how the metal will be cut and shaped by other workers into the sections of vessels. Once the sections are fabricated, other workers at the shop, called fitters, temporarily put together the plates and the framework of the vessels. They check the drawings and other specifications and bolt or tack-weld pieces together to be sure that the parts fit properly.

In doing the final assembly at the site, boilermakers first refer to blueprints and mark off dimensions on the base that has been prepared for the finished vessel. They use measuring devices, straightedges, and transits. They attach rigging equipment, such as hoists, jacks, and rollers, to any prefabricated sections of the vessel that are so large they must be lifted into place with cranes. After crane operators move the sections

---

School Subjects
Mathematics
Shop (Trade/Vo-tech education)

Personal Interests
Building things
Fixing things

Work Environment
Primarily indoors
Primarily multiple locations

Minimum Education Level
High school diploma
Apprenticeship

Salary Range
$16,000 to
$31,720 to
$45,760

Certification or Licensing
None

Outlook
Decline

DOT
805

GOE
05.05.06

NOC
7262

close to the correct position, the boilermakers fine-tune the alignment of the parts. They use levels and check plumb lines and then secure the sections in place with wedges and turnbuckles. With cutting torches, files, and grinders, they remove irregularities and precisely adjust the fit and finally weld and rivet the sections together. They may also attach other tubing, valves, gauges, or other parts to the vessel and then test the container for leaks and defects.

Boilermakers also work in shipbuilding and in repairing the hulls, bulkheads, and decks of iron ships. In a typical repair, boilermakers first remove damaged metal plates by drilling out rivets and cutting off rivet heads with a chipping hammer. Then they take measurements of the damaged plates or make wooden patterns of them so that new plates can be made. They install the new plates, reaming and aligning rivet holes, then fastening on the plates by driving in rivets. Sometimes similar work is done on ships' boilers, condensers, evaporators, loaders, gratings, and stacks.

Boilermaker mechanics maintain and repair boilers and other vessels. They routinely clean or direct others to clean boilers, and they inspect fittings, valves, tubes, controls, and other parts. When necessary, they check the vessels to identify specific weaknesses or sources of trouble. They may update components such as burners and boiler tubes to make them as efficient as possible. They may dismantle the units to replace worn or defective parts, using hand and power tools, gas torches, and welding equipment. Sometimes repairs require that they use metalworking machinery such as power shears and presses to cut and shape parts to specification. They strengthen joints and supports, and they put patches on weak areas of metal plates. Like fabrication and installation work, all repairs must be done in compliance with state and local safety codes.

Requirements

A high school diploma is required for applicants to the boilermaking trade. In the past, people have become boilermakers through on-the-job training, but apprenticeships are now strongly recommended.

Formal apprenticeships usually last four years. An apprentice receives on-the-job practical training while working as a helper under the supervision of an experienced boilermaker. In addition to working, trainees attend classes in the technical aspects of the trade. Apprentices study subjects such as blueprint reading, layout, welding techniques, mechanical drawing, the physics and chemistry of various metals, and applied mathematics. While on the job, apprentices practice the knowledge they have acquired in the classroom.

They develop such skills as using rigging and hoisting equipment, welding, riveting, and installing auxiliary devices and tubes onto vessels.

Mechanical aptitude and manual dexterity are important characteristics for prospective boilermakers. Because the work can be very strenuous, stamina is needed for jobs that require a great deal of bending, stooping, squatting, or reaching. Before they begin work, boilermakers may need to pass a physical examination showing that they are in good enough health to do the work safely. On the job, they must be able to work well despite noisy surroundings, odors, working at heights or in small enclosed spaces, and other discomforts and dangers. It is also important that they be cautious and careful in their work and that they closely follow safety rules.

Opportunities for Experience & Exploration

It may be possible to observe boilermakers or workers who use similar skills as they work on construction projects or repair and maintenance jobs. For example, welders and equipment operators lifting heavy objects with elaborate rigging can sometimes be seen working at sites where large buildings are being erected. High school shop courses, such as blueprint reading and metalworking, can give students an idea of some of the activities of boilermakers. With the help of shop teachers or guidance counselors, students may be able to arrange to talk with people working in the trade. Information may also be obtained by contacting the local union-management committee in charge of apprenticeships for boilermakers.

Methods of Entering

Public employment offices, local union offices, and any businesses that employ boilermakers can provide information on apprenticeships. There are a limited number of apprenticeships available in boilermaking; only the best applicants are accepted, and there may be a waiting period before the apprenticeship starts.

Sometimes workers begin as helpers in repair shops and enter formal apprenticeships later. These helper jobs are often advertised in newspapers. Vocational and technical schools and sometimes high schools with metal shop courses may also help their graduates locate such positions. Other good approaches are to apply directly to employers and to contact the local office of the state employment service.

Advancement

Upon completing their training program, apprentices qualify as journeymen boilermakers. With experience and the right kind of leadership abilities, boilermakers may be able to advance to supervisory positions.

In fabrication shops, layout workers and fitters who start as helpers can learn the skills they need in about two years. In time, they may move up to become shop supervisors or they may decide to become boilermakers who work on-site to assemble vessels.

Employment Outlook

The number of boilermakers is expected to decrease somewhat through the year 2006. One reason for this is the current trend of repairing and retrofitting, rather than replacing, boilers. In addition, smaller boilers are currently being used that require less on-site assembly. Finally, the automation of production technologies and the increasing use of imported boilers will cut down on the need for boilermakers.

During economic downturns, boilermakers, including layout workers and fitters, may be laid off because many industries stop expanding their operations and install very few new boilers. On the other hand, boilermaker mechanics are less affected by downturns because they work more on maintaining and repairing existing equipment, which requires their services regardless of economic conditions.

Despite the decline in new jobs, there will continue to be many openings for boilermakers every year as experienced workers leave the field. Workers who have completed apprenticeships will have the best opportunities for good jobs.

Earnings

According to the limited data available through the U.S. Department of Labor, the median wage for boilermakers in 1996 was $610 per week for those working full time. According to the International Brotherhood of Boilermakers, journeymen boilermakers earned $22 per hour in 1996.

Apprentices start at about 60 percent of journeymen wages, or about $13 an hour. Earnings vary according to the part of the country where boilermakers work, the industry that employs them, and their level of skill and experience. Pay rates are usually highest for boilermakers doing installation work in the construction industry and lower for those in manufacturing industries, although workers in construction may not be employed as steadily. Workers in the Northeast, the Great Lakes area, and cities in the Far West tend to earn the highest wages.

Boilermakers tend to make more than boilermaker mechanics. Among employees in boiler-fabrication shops, layout workers generally earn more and fitters earn less. Both layout workers and fitters normally work indoors, and as a result their earnings are not limited by seasonal variations in weather.

Most boilermakers are members of unions, and union contracts set their wages and benefits. The largest union is the International Brotherhood of Boilermakers, Iron Ship Builders, Blacksmiths, Forgers and Helpers. Other boilermakers are members of the Industrial Union of Marine and Shipbuilding Workers of America; the Oil, Chemical, and Atomic Workers International Union; the United Steelworkers of America; the International Association of Machinists and Aerospace Workers; and the United Automobile, Aerospace, and Agricultural Implement Workers of America. Among the fringe benefits established under union contracts are health insurance, pension plans, and paid vacation time.

Conditions of Work

Boilermaking tends to be more hazardous than many other occupations. Boilermakers often work with dangerous tools and equipment; they must manage heavy materials; and they may climb to heights to do installation or repair work. Despite great progress in preventing accidents, the rate of on-the-job injuries for boilermakers remains higher than the average for all manufacturing industries. Employer and union safety programs and standards set by the federal government's Occupational Safety and Health Administration are helping to control dangerous conditions and reduce accidents.

The work often requires physical exertion and may be carried on in extremely hot, poorly ventilated, noisy, and damp places. At times it is necessary to work in cramped quarters inside boilers, vats, or tanks. At other times, the workers must handle materials and equipment several stories above ground level. Sometimes installation workers work on jobs that require them to remain away from home for considerable periods of time.

To protect against injury, boilermakers and mechanics use a variety of special clothing and equipment such as hard hats, safety glasses and shoes, harnesses, and respirators. A forty-hour week is average, but in some jobs, deadlines may require overtime work.

Sources of Additional Information

For information on the careers of boilermaker and mechanic, contact:

American Boiler Manufacturing Association
950 North Glebe, Suite 160
Arlington, VA 22203-1824

International Brotherhood of Boilermakers, Iron Ship Builders, Blacksmiths, Forgers and Helpers
753 State Avenue, Suite 570
Kansas City, KS 66101
Tel: 913-371-2640

Bookkeeping and Accounting Clerks

Definition

Bookkeeping and *accounting clerks* record financial transactions for government, business, and other organizations. They compute, classify, record, and verify numerical data in order to develop and maintain accurate financial records.

Nature of the Work

Bookkeeping workers keep systematic records and current accounts of financial transactions for businesses, institutions, industries, charities, and other organizations. The bookkeeping records of a firm or business are a vital part of its operational procedures because these records reflect the assets and the liabilities, as well as the profits and losses, of the operation.

Bookkeepers record these business transactions daily in spreadsheets on computer databases, and accounting clerks often input the information. The practice of posting accounting records directly onto ledger sheets, in journals, or on other types of written accounting forms is decreasing as computerized recordkeeping becomes more widespread. In small businesses, bookkeepers sort and record all the sales slips, bills, check stubs, inventory lists, and requisition lists. They compile figures for cash receipts, accounts payable and receivable, and profits and losses.

Accounting clerks handle the clerical accounting work; they enter and verify transaction data and compute and record various charges. They may also monitor loans and accounts payable and receivable. More advanced clerks may reconcile billing vouchers, while senior workers review invoices and statements.

Accountants set up bookkeeping systems and use bookkeepers' balance sheets to prepare periodic summary statements of financial transactions. Management relies heavily on these bookkeeping records to interpret the organization's over-

School Subjects
Business
Mathematics

Personal Interests
Computers
Reading/Books

Work Environment
Primarily indoors
Primarily one location

Minimum Education Level
High school diploma

Salary Range
$15,160 to
$24,700 to
$30,000

Certification or Licensing
None

Outlook
Decline

DOT
216

GOE
07.02.02

NOC
1231

all performance and uses them to make important business decisions. The records are also necessary to file income tax reports and prepare quarterly reports for stockholders.

Bookkeeping and accounting clerks work in retail and wholesale businesses, manufacturing firms, hospitals, schools, charities, and other types of institutional agencies. Many clerks are classified as *financial institution bookkeeping and accounting clerks, insurance firm bookkeeping and accounting clerks, hotel bookkeeping and accounting clerks,* and *railroad bookkeeping and accounting clerks.*

General bookkeepers and *general-ledger bookkeepers* are usually employed in smaller business operations. They may perform all the analysis, maintain the financial records, and complete any other tasks that are involved in keeping a full set of bookkeeping records. These employees may have other general office duties such as mailing statements, answering telephone calls, and filing materials. *Audit clerks* verify figures and may be responsible for sending them on to an *audit clerk supervisor.*

In large companies, an accountant may supervise a department of bookkeepers who have more specialized work. *Billing and rate clerks* and *fixed capital clerks* may post items in accounts payable or receivable ledgers, make out bills and invoices, or verify the company's rates for certain products and services. *Account information clerks* prepare reports, compile payroll lists and deductions, write company checks, and compute federal tax reports or personnel profit shares. Large companies may employ workers to organize, record, and compute many other types of financial information.

In large business organizations, bookkeepers and accountants may be classified by grades, such as Bookkeeper I or II. The job classification determines their responsibilities.

Requirements

Employers require bookkeepers to have at least a high school diploma and look for people with backgrounds in business mathematics, business writing, typing, and computer training. Students should pay particular attention to developing sound English and communication skills along with mathematical abilities.

Some employers prefer people who have completed a junior college curriculum or those who have attended a post–high school business training program. In many instances, employers offer on-the-job

training for various types of entry-level positions. In some areas, work-study programs are available in which schools, in cooperation with businesses, offer part-time, practical on-the-job training combined with academic study. These programs often help students find immediate employment in similar work after graduation. Local business schools may also offer evening courses.

There are no special certification or licensing requirements for bookkeeping and accounting clerk positions. Many of these workers belong to unions. Larger unions include the Office and Professional Employees International Union; the International Union of Electronics, Electrical, Salaried, Machine, and Furniture Workers; and the American Federation of State, County, and Municipal Employees. Depending on the place of business, clerks may also be represented by the same union as other manufacturing employees.

Bookkeepers need strong mathematical skills and organizational abilities, and they have to be able to concentrate on detailed work. The work is quite sedentary and often tedious, and bookkeepers should not mind long hours behind a desk. They should be methodical, accurate, and orderly and enjoy working on detailed tasks. Employers look for honest, discreet, and trustworthy individuals when placing their business in someone else's hands.

Opportunities for Experience & Exploration

High school students interested in bookkeeping can gain experience by participating in work-study programs or by obtaining part-time or summer work in beginning bookkeeping jobs or related office work. Any retail experience dealing with cash management, pricing, or customer service is also valuable.

Students can also volunteer to manage the books for extracurricular student groups. Managing income or cash flow or acting as a club treasurer for student government is an excellent way to gain experience in maintaining financial records.

Students can also visit local small businesses to observe their work and talk to representatives of schools that offer business training courses.

Methods of Entering

High school students may find jobs or establish contacts with businesses that are interested in interviewing graduates through their guidance or placement offices. A work-study program or internship may result in a full-time job offer. Business schools and junior colleges generally provide assistance to their graduates in locating employment.

Applicants may locate job opportunities by applying directly to firms or responding to ads in newspaper classified sections. State employment agencies and private employment bureaus can also assist in the job search process.

Advancement

Bookkeeping workers generally begin their employment by performing routine tasks such as the simple recording of transactions. Beginners may start as entry-level clerks, cashiers, bookkeeping machine operators, office assistants, or typists. With experience, they may advance to more complex assignments that include computer training in databases and spreadsheets and assume a greater responsibility for the work as a whole.

With experience and education, clerks become department heads or office managers. Further advancement to positions such as office or division manager, department head, accountant, or auditor is possible with a college degree and years of experience. There is a high turnover rate in this field, which increases the promotion opportunities for employees with ability and initiative.

Employment Outlook

In 1996, more than 2,250,000 people worked in bookkeeping jobs. However, employment of bookkeeping and accounting clerks is expected to decline through the year 2006. While the economy will grow and the demand for accounting services will increase, automation of office functions will continue and improve overall productivity. Information is currently being sent over local area networks, and clerks no longer need to reenter data. Excellent computer skills are vital to securing a job.

Virtually all new positions for bookkeeping and accounting clerks will be created in small, rapidly growing organizations. Large organizations are likely to continue to consolidate departments to eliminate duplicate work functions, reducing demand for workers. Despite lack of growth, there will be numerous replacement job openings since the turnover rate in this occupation is high. Offices are centralizing their operations, setting up one center to manage all accounting needs in a single location. As more companies trim back their workforces, opportunities for temporary work should continue to grow.

Earnings

According to the most recent U.S. Department of Labor figures available, bookkeepers and accounting clerks earned an average of $475 per week in 1993, or $24,700 a year. The average starting salary for accounting clerks in government jobs is $15,160. Those with one or two years of college generally earn higher starting wages. Experienced workers earn an average of $21,300. Top paying jobs average $30,000.

Conditions of Work

The majority of office workers, including bookkeeping workers, usually work a forty-hour week, although some employees may work a thirty-five- to thirty-seven-hour week. Employees usually receive six to eight paid holidays yearly and one-week paid vacation after six to twelve months of service. Paid vacations may increase to four weeks or more, depending on length of service and place of employment. Fringe benefits may include health and life insurance, sick leave, and retirement plans.

Bookkeeping and accounting clerks usually work in typical office settings. They are more likely to have a cubicle than an office. While the work pace is steady, it can also be routine and repetitive, especially in large companies where the employee is often assigned only one or two specialized job duties.

Attention to numerical details can be physically demanding, and the work can produce eyestrain and nervousness. While bookkeepers usually work with other people and sometimes under close supervision, they can expect to spend most of their day behind a desk; this may seem confining to people who need more variety and stimulation in their work. In addition, the constant attention to detail and the need for accuracy can place considerable responsibility on the worker and cause much stress.

Sources of Additional Information

■Foundation for Accounting Education
530 Fifth Avenue, 5th Floor
New York, NY 10036
Tel: 800-537-3635

■Institute of Management Accountants
10 Paragon Drive
Montvale, NJ 07645
Tel: 800-638-4427

■National Society of Public Accountants
1010 North Fairfax Street
Alexandria, VA 22314
Tel: 703-549-6400

Border Patrol Officers

Definition

Border patrol officers patrol more than 6,000 miles of border between the United States and Canada and between the United States and Mexico, as well as the coastal areas of the Gulf of Mexico and Florida. It is their duty to enforce laws regulating the entry of aliens and products into the United States. They are employed by the Immigration and Naturalization Service (INS) of the United States Justice Department.

Nature of the Work

Border patrol officers are federal law enforcement officers. The laws that they are hired to enforce deal with immigration and customs. U.S. immigration law states that people wishing to enter the United States must apply to the government for permission to do so. Those who want to work, study, or vacation in the United States must have appropriate visas. Those who want to move here and stay must apply for citizenship. Customs laws regulate materials, crops, and goods entering the United States. To ensure that foreigners follow these rules, border patrol officers are stationed at every border entry point of the United States.

Members of the border patrol cover the border on foot, on horseback, in cars or jeeps, in motor boats, and in airplanes. They track people near the borders to detect those who attempt to enter the country illegally. They may question people who live or work near the border to help identify illegal aliens. When border patrol officers find violators of U.S. immigration laws they are authorized to apprehend and detain the violators. They may deport, or return to their country, illegal aliens or arrest anyone who is assisting foreigners to enter the country illegally.

Border patrol officers work with local and state law enforcement agencies in discharging their duties. Although the uniformed patrol is directed from Washington, DC, the patrol

School Subjects
Foreign language (Spanish)
Government

Personal Interests
Current Events
Law

Work Environment
Indoors and outdoors
One location with some travel

Minimum Education Level
High school diploma

Salary Range
$29,000 to
$43,000 to
$56,000

Certification or Licensing
None

Outlook
Faster than the average

DOT
375

GOE
04.02.03

must have a good working relationship with officials in all of the border states. Local and state agencies can be very helpful to border patrol officers, primarily because these agencies are aware of the peculiarities of the terrain in their area, and they are familiar with the operating procedures of potential aliens or drug smugglers.

Border patrol officers work 24 hours a day along the borders with Mexico and Canada. During the night they may use night-vision goggles to spot trespassers. In rugged areas that are difficult to patrol on foot or on horseback, helicopters are used for greater coverage. At regular border crossing points, officers check all incoming vehicles for people or materials hidden in car trunks or truck compartments.

The prevention of drug smuggling has become a major part of the border patrol officer's work. The increase in drug traffic from Central and South America has led to increased efforts by the INS to control the border with Mexico. Drug-sniffing dogs have been added to the patrol's arsenal. Work for these officers has become more dangerous in recent years, and all border patrol officers are specially trained in the use of firearms.

Some employees of the INS may specialize in areas of immigration or customs. *Immigration inspectors* enforce laws pertaining to border crossing. They work at airports, seaports, and border crossing points and may question people arriving in the United States by boats, trains, or airplanes. They arrest violators of entry or immigration laws.

Customs officers work to prevent the import of contraband, or illegal merchandise. Most of their work is involved with illegal narcotics. Customs officers search the cargo of ships and airplanes; baggage in cars, trucks, trains, or buses; and mail. They work with travelers as well as with the crews of ships or airplanes. If they discover evidence of drug smuggling or other customs violations, they are responsible for apprehending the offenders.

Occasionally border patrol officers may also be called upon to help local law enforcement groups in their work. This may involve searching for lost hikers or travelers in rugged wilderness areas of the northern or southern United States.

Requirements

The minimum educational requirement for anyone wishing to train as a border patrol officer is a high school diploma, although a bachelor's degree is preferred. Knowledge of Spanish and other languages is also helpful.

Border patrol officers must be U.S. citizens. Test scores on an entrance exam admit potential patrol officers to the training program. Good character references are important, and civil service tests are also sometimes required.

Opportunities for Experience & Exploration

Because of the nature of border patrol work, students entering the field will not be able to receive direct experience. Courses in immigration law, Spanish, and criminal justice are helpful, however, as is a good sense of direction, geography, and experience hiking in and knowledge of wilderness areas. Also, since the job can be very demanding physically, stamina and strength may be built up through a program of exercise.

School and local libraries may have books containing information on criminal justice and law enforcement. The National Border Patrol Council, which is an association of INS employees, publishes a monthly newsletter called *The Educator.* Copies may be obtained by contacting the council at the address listed at the end of this article.

Methods of Entering

Prospective border patrol officers must pass an entrance exam before being accepted into a sixteen-week training course at the Federal Law Enforcement Training Center in Glynco, Georgia. The course teaches the basics of the immigration laws the officers will uphold. They undergo physical training and instruction in law enforcement and the safe use of firearms. Border patrol officer trainees are also taught Spanish as part of their training.

Once they complete the course, they will be stationed along the Mexican border. Border patrol officers take orders from their sector chiefs. Border patrol officers generally enter at the GS-5 or GS-7 levels, depending on the level of their education. Entry at the GS-7 level is generally restricted as part of the Outstanding Scholar's Program, which requires a grade-point average of 3.5 or higher during specified periods of an applicant's college career.

Advancement

After their first year, all border patrol officers advance to the GS-9 journeymen level. From there, they may compete for positions at the GS-11 level. With experience and training, border patrol officers can advance to other positions. They may become immigration inspectors or examiners, deportation officers, or special agents. Some border patrol officers may concentrate on the prevention of drug smuggling. They may advance to become plainclothes investigators who spend months or even years cracking a smuggling ring. They may lead criminal investigations into an alien's background, especially if there is suspicion of drug involvement. Others may prefer the immigration area and work checking passports and visas at border crossings. Border patrol officers may also advance to supervisory positions.

With experience, some border patrol officers leave the front lines and work in the service areas of the INS. They may interview people who wish to become naturalized citizens or administer examinations or interviews. Many of the higher echelon jobs for border patrol officers require fluency in Spanish. Advancement within the border patrol comes with satisfactory work. To rise to the supervisory positions, however, border patrol officers must be able to work competitively. These positions are earned based on the agency's needs as well as on merit.

Employment Outlook

Employment for border patrol officers is expected to increase faster than the average for all other occupations through the year 2006. There has been growing public support of drug prevention activities, including the prevention of drug smuggling. The public support of the war on drugs has enabled the INS to continue to increase its surveillance of U.S. borders. In addition, growing concerns over the level of illegal immigration has created demands for more border patrol officers.

Earnings

Border patrol officers begin at either the GS-5 or GS-7 grade, depending on their level of education. In 1997 these grades paid approximately $29,000 and $34,000 per year respectively. GS-9 or journeymen salaries paid approximately $43,000 per year. The highest nonsupervisory grade for a border patrol officer is GS-11, which paid approximately $56,000 in 1997. Officers in certain cities, such as New York, Los Angeles, Boston, San Francisco, Chicago, Washington, DC, and others are entitled to receive additional locality pay. Locality pay generally adds approximately 16 percent to the base salary. Law enforcement officials employed by the federal government are also entitled to additional pay of 25 percent of their base salary. Overtime and pay differentials for night, weekend, and holiday work can also greatly increase an officer's salary.

As federal workers, border patrol officers enjoy generous benefits, including health and life insurance, pension plans, and paid holidays, sick leave, and vacations.

Conditions of Work

The work of a border patrol officer can be tiring and stressful. The hours are irregular, since officers must cover the borders continuously. Most border patrol officers spend more time outdoors in jeeps, cars, helicopters, or on horseback than they do in offices. Still, there is a great deal of paperwork to process on each person detained, usually requiring several hours. The work may be dangerous, and many decisions must be made quickly. Border patrol officers must confront many people throughout their shift, remaining alert for potential illegal entry into the United States. Many people who attempt to enter the United States illegally have undergone extreme risk and hardship, and border patrol officers just as frequently encounter emotionally poignant situations as hostile, violent ones. For example, it can be very difficult to return to their country illegal aliens who have suffered the extremes of heat and discomfort by crowding into the back of a hot, airless truck in order to enter the United States. Border patrol officers must be able to cope with the stress and trauma of such situations. Finally, most of those who attempt to enter the country illegally will do so again and again. Even as agents prevent one group from entering the country, elsewhere several other groups of illegal aliens may be successfully crossing the border. Border patrol officers must be able to work at enforcing what may, at times, seem a futile and frustrating task.

Despite the difficulty of the job, it can be very rewarding. Border patrol officers perform a necessary function and know they are contributing to the health of their society.

Sources of Additional Information

■ **Immigration and Naturalization Service**
4422 North Fairfax Drive
Arlington, VA 22203
Tel: 800-755-0777
WWW: http://www.ins.usdoj.gov/

Information about entrance requirements, training, and career opportunities for all government jobs can be obtained from the U.S. Office of Personnel Management. Write them or use their telephone system, Career America Connection Line, or email address to access bulletins, job lists, or qualifying screening exams.

■ **U.S. Office of Personnel Management**
USA Jobs Line
Theodore Roosevelt Federal Building
1900 E Street, NW, Room 1416
Washington, DC 20415-0001
Tel: 202-606-1221
Email: ESProSrv@opm.gov
WWW: opm.gov/employ

Broadcast Technicians

Definition

Broadcast technicians, also referred to as *broadcast engineers*, or *broadcast operators*, operate and maintain the electronic equipment used to record and transmit the audio for radio signals and the audio and visual images for television signals to the public. They may work in a broadcasting station or assist in broadcasting directly from an outside site as a field technician.

Nature of the Work

Broadcast technicians are responsible for the transmission of radio and television programming, including live and recorded broadcasts. Broadcasts are usually transmitted directly from the station; however, technicians are capable of transmitting signals on location from specially designed, mobile equipment. The specific tasks of the broadcast technician depend on the size of the television or radio station. In small stations technicians have a wide variety of responsibilities. Larger stations are able to hire a greater number of technicians and specifically delegate responsibilities to each technician. In both small and large stations, however, technicians are responsible for the operation, installation, repair, and thorough knowledge of the equipment.

The *chief engineer* in both radio and television is the head of the entire technical operation and must orchestrate the activities of all the technicians to ensure smooth programming. He or she is also responsible for the budget and must keep abreast of new broadcast communications technology.

Larger stations also have an *assistant chief engineer* who manages the daily activities of the technical crew, controls the maintenance of the electronic equipment, and ensures the performance standards of the station.

Maintenance technicians are directly responsible for the installation, adjustment, and repair of the electronic equipment.

School Subjects
Computer science
Mathematics

Personal Interests
Computers
Film and Television

Work Environment
Indoors and outdoors
Primarily multiple locations

Minimum Education Level
Some postsecondary training

Salary Range
$16,422 to
$30,251 to
$91,051

Certification or Licensing
Recommended

Outlook
About as fast as the average

DOT
194

GOE
01.02.03

NOC
5224

Video technicians usually work in television stations to ensure the quality, brightness, and content of the visual images being recorded and broadcast. They are involved in several different aspects of broadcasting and videotaping television programs. Technicians who are mostly involved with broadcasting programs are often called *video-control technicians.* In live broadcasts using more than one camera, they operate electronic equipment that selects which picture goes to the transmitter for broadcast. They also monitor on-air programs to ensure good picture quality. Technicians mainly involved with taping programs are often called videotape-recording technicians. They record performances on videotape using video cameras and tape-recording equipment, then splice together separate scenes into a finished program; they can create special effects by manipulating recording and rerecording equipment.

The introduction of robotic cameras, six-foot-tall cameras that stand on two legs, created a need for a new kind of technician called a *video-robo technician.* Video-robo technicians operate the cameras from a control room computer, using joysticks and a video panel to tilt and focus each camera. With the help of new technology, one person can now effectively perform the work of two or three camera operators. Technicians may work with producers, directors, and reporters to put together videotaped material from various sources. These include networks, mobile camera units, and studio productions. Depending on their employer, technicians may be involved in any number of activities related to editing videotapes into a complete program.

Requirements

Broadcast technicians must have both an aptitude for working with highly technical electronic and computer equipment and minute attention to detail to be successful in the field. Preparation for a career in broadcast technology should include a strong background in math, science, electronics, and computer programming and possibly include courses in microwave technology, engineering, and physics.

To obtain an entry-level position, a high school diploma is required and technical school training is desirable. Positions that are more advanced require a bachelor's degree in broadcast communications or a related field. To become a chief engineer, students should aim for a bachelor's degree in electronics or electrical engineering. Because field technicians also act as announcers on occasion, speech courses and experience in a school radio station as an announcer can be helpful. Seeking education beyond a bache-

lor's degree will further the possibilities for advancement, although it is not required. FCC licenses and permits are no longer required of broadcast technicians. However, certification from the Society of Broadcast Engineers (SBE) is desirable, and certified engineers consistently earn higher salaries than uncertified engineers. The SBE offers an education scholarship and accepts student members; members receive a newsletter and have access to their job line. SBE also has a Web site.

Opportunities for Experience & Exploration

Experience is necessary to begin a career as a broadcast technician, and volunteering at a local broadcasting station is an excellent way to gain experience. Many schools have clubs for persons interested in broadcasting that sponsor trips to broadcasting facilities, schedule lectures, and provide a place where students can meet others with similar interests. Local television station technicians are usually willing to share their experience with interested young people. They can be a helpful source of informal career guidance. Visits or tours can be arranged by school officials, which allow students to see technicians involved in their work. Most colleges and universities also have radio and television stations where students can gain experience with broadcasting equipment.

Exposure to broadcasting technology also may be obtained through building and operating an amateur, or ham, radio and experimenting with electronic kits. Dexterity and an understanding of home-operated broadcasting equipment will aid in promoting success in education and work experience within the field of broadcasting.

Methods of Entering

In many towns and cities there are public-access cable television stations and public radio stations where high school students interested in broadcasting and broadcast technology can obtain an internship. An entry-level technician should be flexible about job location; most begin their careers at small stations and with experience may advance to larger-market stations.

Advancement

Entry-level technicians deal exclusively with the operation and maintenance of their assigned equipment; in contrast, a more advanced broadcast technician directs the activities of entry-level technicians and makes judgments on the quality, strength, and subject of the material being broadcast.

After several years of experience, a broadcast technician may advance to assistant chief engineer. In this capacity, he or she may direct the daily activities of all of the broadcasting technicians in the station as well as the field technicians broadcasting on location. Advancement to chief engineer usually requires at least a college degree in engineering and many years of experience. A firm grasp of management skills, budget planning, and a thorough knowledge of all aspects of broadcast technology are the requirements to become the chief engineer of a radio or television station.

Employment Outlook

Broadcasting technology is rapidly advancing in both radio and television broadcasting; manual broadcasting equipment is being replaced with automated equipment and reducing the number of broadcasting technicians needed to operate the equipment. As technological advances are made, most broadcasting equipment will shift to automated, computer-controlled equipment. The need for maintenance of the equipment will remain, as will the need for coordination of programming.

Earnings

Larger stations usually pay higher wages than smaller stations, and television stations tend to pay more than radio stations. According to a National Association of Broadcasters and Broadcast Cable Financial Management Association survey, radio station technicians averaged $30,251 a year in 1996. The salary for chief engineers averaged $46,602 a year (with ranges of $34,714 in the smallest markets to $46,602 in the largest). In television stations in 1996, a technician's salary averaged $24,260 a year (with ranges of $16,422 to $45,158) and a chief engineer's $53,655 annually (with ranges of $38,178 in the smallest markets to $91,051 in the largest).

Conditions of Work

Most technicians work in a broadcasting station that is modern and comfortable. The hours can vary; because most broadcasting stations operate twenty-four hours a day, seven days a week, there are technicians who must work at night, on weekends, and on holidays. Transmitter technicians usually work behind the scenes with little public contact. They work closely with their equipment and as members of a small crew of experts whose closely coordinated efforts produce smooth-running programs. Constant close attention to detail and to making split-second decisions can cause tension. Since broadcasts also occur outside of the broadcasting station on location sites, field technicians may work anywhere and in all kinds of weather.

Sources of Additional Information

For information on its summer internship, please contact:

■**Association of Independent Television Stations**
1320 19th Street, NW, Suite 300
Washington, DC 20036
Tel: 202-887-1970
WWW: http://www.cep.org

For a list of schools offering degrees in broadcasting, write to:

■**Broadcast Education Association**
1771 N Street, NW
Washington, DC 20036-2891
Tel: 202-429-5354
WWW: http://www.beaweb.org

For college programs and union information, write to:

■**National Association of Broadcast Employees and Technicians**
501 3rd Street, NW, 8th Floor
Washington, DC 20001
Tel: 202-434-1254
WWW: http://www.union.nabetcwa.org

For a booklet on careers in cable, write to:

■■■**National Cable Television Association**
1724 Massachusetts Avenue, NW
Washington, DC 20036
Tel: 202-775-3669
WWW: http://www.ncta.com

For scholarship and internship information, write to:

■■■**Radio-Television News Directors Association**
1000 Connecticut Avenue, NW, Suite 615
Washington, DC 20036
Tel: 202-659-6510
Email: rtnda@rtnda.org
WWW: http://www.rtnda.org/rtnda/

For scholarship and membership information, please contact:

■■■**Society of Broadcast Engineers**
8445 Keystone Crossing, Suite 140
Indianapolis, IN 46240
Tel: 317-253-1640
WWW: http://www.sbe.org

Cable Television Technicians

Definition

Cable television technicians inspect, maintain, and repair antennas, cables, and amplifying equipment used in cable television transmission.

Nature of the Work

Cable television technicians perform a wide range of duties in a variety of settings. Television cables usually follow the routes of telephone cables, running along poles in rural and suburban areas and through tunnels in cities. Working in tunnels and underground cable passageways, technicians inspect cables for evidence of damage and corrosion. Using diagrams and blueprints, they trace cables to locate sites of signal breakdown. They may also work at pole-mounted amplifiers, where they analyze the strength of incoming television signals, using field-strength meters and miniature television receivers to evaluate reception. At customers' homes, they service the terminal boxes, explain the workings of the cable system, answer questions, or respond to complaints that may indicate cable or equipment problems. When major problems arise, they repair or replace damaged or faulty cable systems.

Cable television technicians use various electrical measuring instruments (voltmeters, field-strength meters) to diagnose causes of transmission problems. They also use electricians' hand tools (including screwdrivers, pliers, etc.) to dismantle, repair, or replace faulty sections of cable or disabled equipment, such as amplifying equipment used to boost the signal at intervals along the cable system.

Some cable television technicians may perform a specific type of work, rather than a full range of tasks. Following are some of the specialized positions held by cable television technicians.

Trunk technicians, or *line technicians,* perform routine maintenance and fix electronic problems on the trunk line, which connects the feeder lines in the street to the headend. They also fix electronic failures in the feeder amplifiers. Amplifiers increase the strength of the electronic signal for clear reception to everyone and are spaced throughout the cable system. Some trunk technicians install both underground and aboveground cables. Using a sweep analyzer, they check signals in all parts of the cable television system to make sure all parts are operating correctly.

Headend technicians and *microwave technicians* check that the equipment providing input to the cable television system is working properly. The headend, or control center of a cable television system, is where incoming signals are amplified, converted, processed, and combined into a common cable. These technicians check antennas, preamplifiers, frequency converters, processors, demodulators, modulators, and other related equipment using power meters, frequency counters, and waveform monitors. In some companies, the headend technician works with satellite receiving stations and related equipment. This person may be the *chief technician* in some companies. Many electronics technicians work as headend technicians and microwave technicians.

Service technicians respond to problems with subscribers' cable reception. They work on amplifiers, poles, and lines, in addition to making calls to subscribers' homes. They check the lines and connections that go into a home and those inside it, troubleshoot problems, and repair faulty equipment.

Bench technicians work in a cable television system's repair facility. They examine malfunctioning equipment that is brought into the shop, diagnose the problem, and repair it. They may also repair and calibrate test equipment. Some bench technicians are electronics technicians.

Technical supervisors oversee the technicians who work in the field and provide on-the-job training to technicians. Duties vary, but can include dealing with contractors and coordinating with outside agencies such as utilities companies, municipalities, and large customers.

Chief technicians and *lead technicians* are among the most highly skilled of the technical staff. Many chief technicians do not work in the field except for emergency situations or complex situations requiring their special expertise. Chief technicians provide technical information to technicians in the field and may supervise the technical staff. They may work with satellite receiving equipment. These positions are usually held by senior staff personnel and require a strong background in electronics.

An important aspect of the work of cable television technicians involves implementing regular programs of preventive maintenance on the cable system. Technicians inspect connections, insulation, and the performance of amplifying equipment, using measuring instruments and viewing the transmitted signals on television monitors.

Requirements

Aspiring cable television technicians should take high school mathematics courses at least through plane geometry and have a solid knowledge of shop math. They should have sufficient language skills in order to read technical manuals and instructions and to follow detailed maintenance procedures. Although training beyond high school is not required, many employers prefer to hire applicants with an electronics background or people who have had some technical training. Technical training in electronics technology or communications technology is available through both one- and two-year programs at community colleges, trade schools, and technical institutes. Two-year programs provide hands-on training and include courses that cover the basics of electrical wiring and electronics, broadcasting theory and practice, blueprint and schematic diagram reading, and physics.

Certification in special skills can be obtained through one-year certification programs. Certification classes in specialized technology, such as digital technology, digital compression, and fiber optics, prepare students to work with the more advanced technologies commonly used in many cable television systems. Because cable technology is evolving so rapidly, students who learn new technology have better chances at employment and, once hired, better chances for advancement. All workers are encouraged to continue training throughout their careers to learn new technology, new equipment, and new methods.

Professional associations, such as the Society of Cable Telecommunications Engineers (SCTE), also offer training programs and certification in areas such as broadband communications technology. Examinations for certification are offered in different areas of cable technology including video and audio signals and systems, signal processing centers, terminal devices, and data networking and architecture.

A driver's license and a good driving record are needed for those workers who will be driving a company vehicle.

Cable television technicians need a mechanical aptitude, physical agility, the ability to work at heights or in confined spaces, and the capacity to work as part of a team. Acute vision, with no color-perception deficiency, is needed as it is essential for analyzing cable reception. In addition, it is helpful to feel at ease in using electrical equipment and electricians' tools.

Cable television technicians have much public contact and must have strong interpersonal skills and be able to deal with people from diverse backgrounds. They must be able to project a helpful, courteous, pleasant image. They may need to explain cable system operations and costs to customers, answer questions, and analyze customer descriptions of problems so repairs and other work can be done. The ability to communicate well with others is essential.

Opportunities for Experience & Exploration

Because of the special training required, rarely are any part-time or summer technician jobs available for high school students. However, educational seminars are offered by local cable television personnel across the country; these are available to interested student groups and can be arranged through a school guidance counselor or teacher. These presentations provide valuable career information and an opportunity to speak with cable technicians and their employers about the field. For more information about these seminars, contact the Society of Cable Telecommunications Engineers for the name and address of the nearest local chapter.

Those interested in this career can explore electronics or related activities, such as building a short-wave radio set or repairing radios and televisions, and participate in science clubs that emphasize electronics.

Methods of Entering

Two ways to enter this field are to enter as an unskilled installer and move up after receiving on-the-job training or to complete an electronics or telecommunications program in a technical school or through SCTE and start work as an electronics technician or cable television technician. Many times recruiters from various companies visit technical schools or have job fairs in which they interview students for positions that they start once they complete their training. Students can also check with their schools' job placement services for postings by employers or to get leads on companies that are hiring.

State employment offices and classified ads are other good sources of job leads. Interested persons also can apply directly to a cable television company or contractor.

Advancement

Most companies provide on-the-job training, including classes in basic technical and troubleshooting skills, basic electronics, and electronics in reference to the cable television business, parts of the cable television system, installation, and safety practices. Students who have already received technical training usually are able to advance into more highly skilled positions quicker than those who require extensive training. Many cable television technicians start out as installers or repairers and then move into technical positions, such as line technician, service technician, and bench technician. Workers with a strong industrial background, advanced training in electronics, and several years of experience can advance to supervisory and administrative positions such as technical supervisor, headend technician, chief technician, lead technician, and plant manager.

Workers also can advance to the position of chief engineer with additional training. Chief engineers are responsible for cable systems design, equipment planning, specification of standards for equipment and material, layout for cable communications networks, and technical advice to technicians and system operating managers. A degree in electrical engineering or related field is required to be a chief engineer.

It is helpful for technicians desiring to advance to demonstrate strong mechanical aptitudes, technical proficiency, interpersonal skills, and leadership abilities.

Employment Outlook

Employment opportuniites for cable television techs will be about as fast as average through the year 2006. Since most of the country is now wired for cable, the emphasis is no longer on installing the systems, but rather on maintaining and upgrading them. Some cable television companies have been replacing existing cables with fiber optic cable or hybrid fiber/coax systems that provide better reception and are much more maintenance-free. Many job openings will result from current workers retiring from the work force. Few prerequisite job skills, coupled with opportunity to earn good salaries, will create strong competition for jobs.

Both telephone companies and cable television companies are expected to invest heavily in capital expenditures in order to build new telecommunications networks that will allow telephone and cable television transmission over the same cables. Cable television companies are also spending billions of dollars on new products, such as advanced set-top converters, that will allow for many new services. Increased spending and advanced technology are stimulating new construction and product development, which could result in increased opportunities for technicians.

Earnings

Earnings for cable television technicians vary based on experience and geographic location. In 1996, according to the U.S. Department of Labor, the average annual salary for technicians was around $36,500. Trainees and entry-level technicians made considerably less, starting at about $18,000. Workers in the South and Southeast tend to make less than workers in the Northeast and California.

Companies offer a variety of benefit packages, which can include any of the following: paid holidays, vacations, and sick days; personal days; medical, dental, and life insurance; profit-sharing plans; 401(k) plans; retirement and pension plans; and educational assistance programs. Many cable television technicians belong to unions.

Conditions of Work

The work is moderately heavy, involving occasional lifting of up to fifty pounds. A large part of the cable television technician's time is spent on ladders and poles or in confined or underground spaces. These activities require care and precision. As with all maintenance work around conductors, there is some danger of electrical shock. The coaxial cables used to transmit television signals are from one-half to over one inch in diameter. Cables have to be manipulated into position for splicing, which involves medium to heavy physical work.

Normal working hours are a five-day, forty-hour week, although technicians may often need to work evenings or weekends to make necessary repairs. Some technicians work in shifts, working four ten-hour days a week. Many technicians, especially line technicians, are on call twenty-four hours a day and carry pagers. They may be called in for special repairs or in emergency situations.

Bench technicians and most supervisory technicians work inside, but most other technicians work in the field. Their work takes them to a variety of neighborhoods, and technicians may travel from an upscale neighborhood to a lower-economic neighborhood in the same day. Technicians need to feel comfortable in diverse environments and be able to interact well with people from varying backgrounds.

Technicians working in the field work in all kinds of weather. Their work involves extensive driving. Most companies provide a company vehicle, tools, equipment, and sometimes uniforms.

Sources of Additional Information

For information on careers, educational programs, educational seminars, and certification, please contact:

■ **Society of Cable Telecommunications Engineers**
669 Exton Commons
Exton, PA 19341
Tel: 800-542-5040

For information on careers, please contact:

■ **National Cable Television Association**
1724 Massachusetts Avenue, NW
Washington, DC 20036
Tel: 202-775-3550

■ **Women in Cable and Telecommunications**
230 West Monroe, Suite 730
Chicago, IL 60606
Tel: 312-634-2330

Cardiovascular Technologists

Definition

Cardiovascular technologists assist physicians in diagnosing and treating heart and blood vessel ailments. Depending on their specialty, they operate electrocardiograph machines, perform Holter monitor and stress testing, and assist in cardiac catheterization procedures and ultrasound testing. These tasks help the physicians diagnose heart disease and monitor progress during treatment.

Nature of the Work

Technologists who assist physicians in the diagnosis and treatment of heart disease are known as cardiovascular technologists. (Cardio means heart; vascular refers to the blood vessel/circulatory system.) They include *electrocardiograph (EKG) technologists, Holter monitoring and stress test technologists, cardiology technologists, vascular technologists and echocardiographers* (both ultrasound technologists), *cardiac monitor technicians,* and others. The services of EKG technicians/technologists may be required throughout the hospital, such as in the cancer wards or emergency room; there may be a separate department for these EKG professionals. Increasingly, however, hospitals are centralizing cardiovascular services under one full cardiovascular "service line" overseen by the same administrator.

In addition to cardiovascular technologists, the cardiovascular team at a hospital also may include radiology (X-ray) technologists, nuclear medicine technologists, nurses, physician assistants, respiratory technologists, and respiratory therapists. For their part, the cardiovascular technologists contribute by performing one or more of a wide range of procedures in cardiovascular medicine, including invasive (enters a body cavity or interrupts normal body functions), noninvasive, peripheral vascular or echocardiography (ultrasound) procedures. In most facilities they use equipment that is among the most advanced in the medical field; drug therapies also may be used

School Subjects
Anatomy and Physiology
Health

Personal Interests
Helping people: emotionally
Helping people: physical health/medicine

Work Environment
Primarily indoors
Primarily one location

Minimum Education Level
Some postsecondary training

Salary Range
$15,200 to
$20,200 to
$33,600

Certification or Licensing
Voluntary

Outlook
More slowly than the average, except cardiology technologists (Faster than the average)

DOT
078

GOE
10.02.02

as part of the diagnostic imaging procedures or in addition to them. Technologists' services may be required when the patient's condition is first being explored, before surgery, during surgery (cardiology technologists primarily), or during rehabilitation of the patient. Some of the work is performed on an outpatient basis.

Depending on their specific area of skill, some cardiovascular technologists are employed in nonhospital health care facilities. For example, EKG technologists may work for clinics, mobile medical services, or private doctors' offices. Their equipment can go just about anywhere. The same is true for the ultrasound technologists.

Some of the specific duties of cardiovascular technologists are described in the following paragraphs. Exact titles of these technologists often vary from medical facility to medical facility because there is no standardized naming system.

Electrocardiograph technologists, or EKG technologists, use an electrocardiograph (EKG) machine to detect the electronic impulses that come from a patient's heart during and between a heartbeat. The EKG machine then records these signals on a paper graph called an electrocardiogram. The electronic impulses recorded by the EKG machine can tell the physician about the action of the heart during and between the individual heartbeats. This in turn reveals important information about the condition of the heart, including irregular heartbeats or the presence of blocked arteries, which the physician can use to diagnose heart disease, monitor progress during treatment, or check the patient's condition after recovery.

To use an EKG machine, the technologist attaches electrodes (small, disklike devices about the size of a silver dollar) to the patient's chest. Wires attached to the electrodes lead to the EKG machine. Up to twelve leads or more may be attached. To get a better reading from the electrodes, the technologist may first apply an adhesive gel to the patient's skin that helps to conduct the electrical impulses. The technologist then operates controls on the EKG machine or (more commonly) enters commands for the machine into a computer. The electrodes pick up the electronic signals from the heart and transmit them to the EKG machine. The machine registers and makes a printout of the signals, with a stylus (pen) recording their pattern on a long roll of graph paper.

During the test, the technologist may move the electrodes in order to get readings of electrical activity in different parts of the heart muscle. Since EKG equipment can be sensitive to electrical impulses from other sources, such as other parts of the patient's body or equipment in the room where the EKG test is being done, the technologist must watch for false readings.

After the test, the EKG technologist takes the electrocardiogram off the machine, edits it or makes notes on it, and sends it to the physician (usually a cardiologist, or heart specialist). Physicians may have computer assistance to help them use and interpret the electrocardiogram; special software is available to assist them with their diagnoses.

EKG technologists do not have to repair EKG machines, but they do have to keep an eye on them and know when they are malfunctioning so they can call someone for repairs. They also may keep the machines stocked with paper.

Of all the cardiovascular technical positions, EKG technicians/technologists are the most numerous. They comprised about half of all cardiovascular technologists in 1996 (about 16,000 of a total of 32,000). Holter monitoring and stress testing may be performed by Holter monitor technologists or stress test technologists, respectively, or may be additional duties of some EKG technologists. In Holter monitoring, electrodes are fastened to the patient's chest and a small, portable monitor is strapped to the patient's body, such as at the waist. The small monitor contains a magnetic tape or cassette that records the heart during activity—as the patient moves, sits, stands, sleeps, etc. The patient is required to wear the Holter monitor for up to twenty-four to forty-eight hours while he or she goes about normal daily activities. When the patient returns to the hospital, the technologist removes the magnetic tape or cassette from the monitor and puts it in a scanner to produce audio (sound) and visual representations of heart activity. (Hearing how the heart sounds during activity helps physicians diagnose a possible heart condition.) The technologist reviews and analyzes the information revealed in the tape. Finally, the technologist may print out the parts of the tape that show abnormal heart patterns or make a full tape for the physician.

Stress tests record the heart's activity during physical activity. In one type of stress test, the technologist connects the patient to the EKG machine, attaching electrodes to the patient's arms, legs, and chest, and obtains a reading of the patient's resting heart activity and blood pressure. Then, the patient is asked to walk on a treadmill for a designated period of time while the technologist and the physician monitor the heart. The treadmill speed is increased so that the technologist physician can see what happens when the heart is put under higher levels of exertion.

Cardiology technologists specialize in providing support for cardiac catheterization (tubing) procedures. These procedures are classified as invasive because they require the physician and attending technologists to enter a body cavity or interrupt normal body functions. In one cardiac catheterization procedure—an angiogram—a catheter (tube) is inserted into the heart (usually by way of a blood vessel in the leg) in order to diagnose the condition of the heart blood vessels, such as whether there is a blockage. In another procedure, known as angioplasty, a catheter with a balloon at the end is inserted into an artery to widen it. Angioplasties are being performed with increasing frequency: approximately 300,000 in 1990, to approximately 6,000 in 1983. Cardiology technologists also perform a variety of other procedures.

Unlike some of the other cardiovascular technologists, cardiology technologists actually assist in surgical procedures. They may help secure the patient to the table, set up a 35mm video camera or other imaging device under the instructions of the physician (to produce images that assist the physician in guiding the catheter through the cardiovascular system), enter information about the surgical procedure (as it is taking place) into a computer, and provide other support. After the procedure, the technologist may process the angiographic film for use by the physician. Cardiology technologists may also assist during open-heart surgery by preparing and monitoring the patient and may participate in placement or monitoring of pacemakers.

This is a specialty that is growing in importance in cardiology care. In 1991, more than 1,300 hospitals had a cardiac catheterization lab and the numbers are expected to significantly expand, according to the American Academy of Medical Administrators.

Vascular technologists and echocardiographers are specialists in noninvasive cardiovascular procedures and use ultrasound equipment to obtain and record information about the condition of the heart. Ultrasound equipment is used to send out sound waves to the part of the body being studied; when the sound waves hit the part being studied, they send back an echo to the ultrasound machine. The echoes are "read" by the machine, which creates an image on a monitor, permitting the technologist to get an instant "image" of the part's condition.

Vascular technologists are specialists in the use of ultrasound equipment to study blood flow and circulation problems. Echocardiographers are specialists in the use of ultrasound equipment to evaluate the heart and its structures, such as the valves.

Cardiac monitor technicians are similar to and sometimes perform some of the same duties as EKG technologists. Usually working in the intensive care unit (ICU) or cardio-care unit of the hospital, cardiac monitor technicians keep watch over the patient-monitoring screens to detect any sign that a patient's heart is not beating as it should.

Cardiac monitor technicians begin their shift by reviewing the patient's records to familiarize themselves with what the patient's normal heart rhythms should be, what the current pattern is, and what types of problems have been observed. Throughout the shift, the cardiac monitor technician watches for heart rhythm irregularities that need prompt medical attention. Should there be any, he or she notifies a nurse or doctor immediately so that appropriate care can be given.

In addition to these positions, other cardiovascular technologists specialize in a particular aspect of health care. For example, a *cardiopulmonary technologist* specializes in procedures for diagnosing problems with the heart and lungs. He or she may conduct electrocardiograph, phonocardiograph (sound recordings of the heart's valves and of the blood passing through them), echocardiograph, stress testing, as well as respiratory test procedures.

Cardiopulmonary technologists also may assist on cardiac catheterization procedures, measuring and recording information about the the patient's cardiovascular and pulmonary systems during the procedure and alerting the cardiac catheterization team of any problems.

Nuclear medicine technologists, who use radioactive isotopes in diagnosis, treatment, or studies, assist in the diagnosis or treatment of cardiology problems. Radiology, respiratory, and exercise technicians and therapists also may assist in patient diagnosis, treatment, and/or rehabilitation.

Requirements

In the past, many EKG operators were trained on the job by an EKG supervisor. This still may be true for some EKG technician positions. Increasingly however, EKG technologists get postsecondary schooling before they are hired. Holter monitoring and stress testing may be part of the student's EKG schooling, or they may be learned through additional training. Ultrasound and cardiology technologists tend to have the most postsecondary schooling (up to a four-year bachelor's degree), and have the most extensive academic/experience requirements for credentialing purposes.

People can enter these positions without having had previous health care experience. However, it certainly doesn't hurt to have had some previous exposure to the business or even training in related areas. People with academic training or professional experience in nursing, radiology science, or respiratory science, for example, may be able to move into cardiology technology if they wish.

At a minimum, cardiovascular technologists need a high school diploma or equivalent to enter the field. Although no specific high school classes will directly prepare one to be a technologist, learning how to learn and getting a good grounding in basic high school subjects are important to all technologist positions.

During high school, students should take English, health, biology, and typing. They also might consider courses in social sciences to help them understand the social and psychological needs of patients.

As a rule of thumb, medical employers value post-secondary schooling that gives students actual hands-on experience with patients, in addition to classroom training. At many of the schools that train cardiovascular technologists, students work with patients in a variety of health care settings and train on more than one brand of equipment.

Some employers still train EKG technicians are still simply trained on the job by a physician or EKG department manager. Training generally lasts from one to six months. Trainee learn how to operate the EKG machine, produce and edit the electrocardiogram, and other related tasks.

Some vocational, technical, and junior colleges have one- or two-year training programs in EKG technology, Holter monitoring, or stress testing, or all three; otherwise, EKG technologists may obtain training in Holter and stress procedures after they've already started working, either on the job or through an additional six months or more of schooling. Formal academic programs give technologists more preparation in the subject than is available with most on-the-job training and allow them to earn a certificate (one-year programs) or associate's degree (two-year programs). The American Medical Association's Allied Health Directory has listings of accredited EKG programs.

Ultrasound technologists usually need a high school diploma or equivalent plus one, two, or four years of postsecondary schooling in a trade school, technical school, or community college. Vascular technologists also may be trained on the job. Again, a list of accredited programs can be found in the AMA's Allied Health Directory; also, a directory of training opportunities in sonography is available from the Society of Diagnostic Medical Sonographers.

Cardiology technologists tend to have the highest academic requirements of all; for example, a four-year bachelor of science degree or two-year associate's degree, or a certificate of completion from a hospital, trade, or technical cardiovascular program for training of varying length. A two-year program at a junior or community college might include one year of core classes (e.g. mathematics, biology, chemistry, and anatomy) and one year of specialized classes in cardiology procedures.

Cardiac monitor technicians need a high school diploma or equivalent, with additional educational requirements similar to those of EKG technicians.

Cardiology is a cutting-edge area of medicine, with constant advancements, and medical equipment relating to the heart is continually being updated. Therefore, keeping up with new developments is vital. In addition, technologists who add to their qualifications through taking part in continuing education tend to earn more money and have more employment opportunities. Major professional societies encourage and provide the opportunities for professionals to continue their education.

Right now, certification or licensing for cardiovascular technologists is voluntary, but the move to state licensing is expected in the near future. Many credentialing bodies for cardiovascular and pulmonary positions exist, including American Registry of Diagnostic Medical Sonographers (ARDMS), Cardiovascular Credentialing International (CCI), and others, and there are more than a dozen possible credentials for cardiovascular technologists. For example, sonographers can take an exam from the ARDMS to receive credentialing in sonography. Their credentials may be registered diagnostic medical sonographer, registered diagnostic cardiac sonographer, or registered vascular technologist.

Credentialing requirements for cardiology technologists or ultrasound technologists may include test taking plus formal academic and on-the-job requirements. Professional experience or academic training in a related field—nursing, radiology science, respiratory science, etc.—may be acceptable as part of these formal academic and professional requirements. As with continuing education, certification is a sign of interest and dedication to the field and is generally favorably regarded by potential employers.

Opportunities for Experience & Exploration

Prospective cardiovascular technologists will find it difficult to gain any direct experience on a part-time basis in electrocardiography. Their first experience with the work generally comes during their on-the-job training sessions. They may, however, be able to gain some exposure to patient-care activities in general by signing up for volunteer work at a local hospital. In addition, they can arrange to visit a hospital, clinic, or physician's office where electrocardiographs are taken. In this way, they may be able to watch a technician at work or at least talk to a technician about what the work is like.

Methods of Entering

Because most cardiovascular technologists receive their initial training on their first job, great care should be taken in finding this first employer. Students should pay close attention not only to the pay and working conditions, but also to the kind of on-the-job training that is provided for each prospective position. High school vocational counselors may be able to tell job seekers which hospitals have good reputations for EKG training programs. Applying directly to hospitals is a common way of entering the field. Information also can be gained by reading the classified ads in the newspaper and from talking with friends and relatives who work in hospitals.

For students who graduate from one- to two-year training programs, finding a first job should be easier. First, employers are always eager to hire people who are already trained. Second, these graduates can be less concerned about the training programs offered by their employers. Third, they should find that their teachers and guidance counselors can be excellent sources of information about job possibilities in the area. If the training program includes practical experience, graduates may find that the hospital in which they trained or worked before graduation would be willing to hire them after graduation.

Advancement

Opportunities for advancement are best for cardiovascular technologists who learn to do or assist with more complex procedures, such as stress testing, Holter monitoring, echocardiography, and cardiac catheterization. With proper training and experience, these technicians may eventually become cardiovascular technologists, echocardiography technologists, cardiopulmonary technicians, cardiology technologists, or other specialty technicians or technologists.

In addition to these kinds of specialty positions, experienced technicians may also be able to advance to various supervisory and training posts.

Employment Outlook

Openings for EKG technicians are expected to decline through the year 2006; although there is an increased demand for EKGs, the equipment and procedures are currently much more efficient than they used to be. One technician can perform far more tests each day than was previously possible, and, because of this, fewer technicians are required. In addition, newer equipment is easier to use, allowing employers to train other personnel, such as respiratory therapists or registered nurses, in its operation. In 1996, there were approximately 16,000 EKG technicians.

Employment of cardiology technologists, on the other hand, is expected to grow faster than the average through the year 2006. Again, growth will be primarily due to the increasing numbers of older people in our population. Most job openings for cardiovascular technologists will be to replace those technicians who are promoted, transferred, or retired.

Earnings

Beginning cardiovascular technologists can expect to receive starting salaries of approximately $15,200 a year, according to the U.S. Department of Labor. Average pay for all EKG technicians was $20,200 in 1996. Experienced technologists earn considerably more, with an average salary of $33,600.

Those with formal training earn more than those who trained on the job, and those who are able to perform more sophisticated tests, such as Holter monitoring and stress testing, are paid more than those who perform only the basic electrocardiograph tests.

EKG technicians working in hospitals receive the same fringe benefits as other hospital workers, including medical insurance, paid vacations, and sick leave. In some cases benefits also include educational assistance, retirement plans, and uniform allowances.

Conditions of Work

Cardiovascular technologists usually work in clean, quiet, well-lighted surroundings. They generally work five-day, forty-hour weeks, although technicians working in small hospitals may be on twenty-four-hour call for emergencies, and all technicians in hospitals, large or small, can expect to do occasional evening or weekend work. With the growing emphasis in health care on cost containment, more jobs are likely to develop in various outpatient settings, so in the future it is likely that cardiovascular technologists will work more often in clinics, cardiologists' offices, HMOs, and other nonhospital locations.

Cardiovascular technologists generally work with patients who either are ill or who have reason to fear they might be ill. With this in mind, there are opportunities for the technicians to do these people some good, but there is also a chance of causing some unintentional harm as well: a well-conducted test can reduce anxieties or make a physician's job easier; a misplaced electrode or an error in recordkeeping could cause an incorrect diagnosis. Technicians need to be able to cope with these responsibilities and consistently conduct their work in the best interests of their patients.

Part of the technician's job includes putting patients at ease about the procedure they are to undergo. Toward that end, technicians should be pleasant, patient, alert, and able to understand and sympathize with the feelings of others. In explaining the nature of the procedure to patients, cardiovascular technicians should be able to do so in a calm, reassuring, and confident manner.

Inevitably, some patients will try to get information about their medical situation from the technician. In cases like this, technicians need to be both tactful and firm in explaining that they are only making the electrocardiogram; the interpretation is for the physician to make.

Another large part of a technician's job involves getting along well with other members of the hospital staff. This task is sometimes made more difficult by the fact that in most hospitals there is a formal, often rigid, status structure, and cardiovascular technologists may find themselves in a relatively low position in that structure. In emergency situations or at other moments of frustration, cardiovascular technologists may find themselves dealt with brusquely or angrily. Technicians should not take outbursts or rude treatment personally, but instead should respond with stability and maturity.

Sources of Additional Information

American Society of Cardiovascular Professionals/Society of Cardiovascular Management (ASCP/SCM)
120 Falcon Drive, Unit 3
Fredericksburg, VA 22408
Tel: 540-891-0079

For information on credentials, please contact:

Cardiovascular Credentialing International (CCI)
4456 Corporation Lane, Suite 110
Virginia Beach, VA 23462
Tel: 800-326-0268

Carpenters

Definition

Carpenters cut, shape, level, and fasten together pieces of wood and other construction materials, such as wallboard, plywood, and insulation. Many carpenters work on constructing, remodeling, or repairing houses and other kinds of buildings. Other carpenters work at construction sites where roads, bridges, docks, boats, mining tunnels, and wooden vats are built. A carpenter may specialize in building the rough framing of a structure, and thus be considered a *rough carpenter,* or he or she may specialize in the finishing details of a structure, such as the trim around doors and windows, and thus be considered a *finish carpenter.*

Nature of the Work

Carpenters are the largest group of workers in the building trades. There are about a million carpenters in the United States today. About 80 percent of them work for contractors involved in building, repairing, and remodeling buildings and other structures. Manufacturing firms, schools, stores, and government bodies employ most other carpenters. One third are self-employed.

Carpenters do two basic kinds of work: rough carpentry and finish carpentry. Rough carpenters construct and install temporary structures and supports, wooden structures used in industrial settings, as well as parts of buildings that are usually covered up when the rooms are finished. Among the structures built by such carpenters are scaffolds for other workers to stand on, chutes used as channels for wet concrete, forms for concrete foundations, and timber structures that support machinery. In buildings, they may put up the frame, install rafters, joists, subflooring, wall sheathing, prefabricated wall panels and windows, and many other components.

Finish carpenters install hardwood flooring, staircases, shelves, cabinets, trim on windows and doors, and other woodwork and hardware that make the building look complete,

School Subjects
Mathematics
Shop (Trade/Vo-tech education)

Personal Interests
Building things
Fixing things

Work Environment
Indoors and outdoors
Primarily multiple locations

Minimum Education Level
High school diploma
Apprenticeship

Salary Range
$13,800 to
$24,700 to
$45,400

Certification or Licensing
None

Outlook
More slowly than the average

DOT
860

GOE
05.05.02

NOC
7271

inside and outside. Finish carpentry requires especially careful, precise workmanship as the result must have a good appearance in addition to being sturdy. Many carpenters who are employed by building contractors do both rough and finish work on buildings.

Although they do many different tasks in different settings, carpenters generally follow approximately the same basic steps. First they look over blueprints or plans for information (or get instructions from a supervisor) about the dimensions of the structure to be built and the type of materials to be used. Sometimes local building codes determine how a structure should be built, so carpenters need to know about such regulations. Using rulers, framing squares, chalk lines, and other measuring and marking equipment, they lay out how the work will be done. Using hand and power tools, they cut and shape the wood, plywood, fiberglass, plastic, or other materials. Then they nail, screw, glue, or staple the pieces together. Finally, they use levels, plumb bobs, rulers, and squares to check their work, and they make any necessary adjustments. Sometimes carpenters work with prefabricated units for components such as wall panels or stairs. Installing these is, in many ways, a much less complicated task, because much less layout, cutting, and assembly work is needed.

Carpenters who work outside of the building construction field may do a variety of installation and maintenance jobs, such as repairing furniture, changing locks, and installing ceiling tiles or exterior siding on buildings. Other carpenters specialize in building, repairing, or modifying ships, wooden boats, wooden railroad trestles, timber framing in mine shafts, woodwork inside railcars, storage tanks and vats, or stage sets in theaters.

Requirements

Carpenters can acquire the skills of their trade in various ways, through formal training programs and through informal on-the-job training. Of the different ways to learn, an apprenticeship is considered the best as it provides a more thorough and complete foundation for a career as a carpenter than other kinds of training. However, the limited number of available apprenticeships means that not all carpenters can learn their trade this way.

Many carpenters pick up skills informally on the job while they work as carpenter's helpers. Usually employers prefer applicants who have completed high school. They begin with little or no training and gradually learn as they work under the supervision of experienced carpenters. The skills that helpers develop depend on the jobs that their employers contract to do. Working for a small contracting company, a beginner may learn about relatively few kinds of carpentry tasks. On the other hand, a large contracting company may offer a wider variety of learning opportunities. Becoming a skilled carpenter by this method can take much longer than an apprenticeship, and the completeness of the training varies. Some people who are waiting for an apprenticeship to become available work as helpers to gain experience in the field.

Some people first learn about carpentry while serving in the U.S. armed forces. Other carpenters learn skills in vocational educational programs offered in trade schools and through correspondence courses. Vocational programs can be very good, especially as a supplement to other practical training. But without additional hands-on instruction, vocational school graduates may not be well-enough prepared to get many jobs in the field because some programs do not provide sufficient opportunity for students to practice and perfect their carpentry skills.

Apprenticeships usually last three to four years. They are administered by employer groups and local chapters of labor unions that organize carpenters. Applicants for apprenticeships must meet the specific requirements of local apprenticeship committees. Typically, applicants must be at least seventeen years old, have a high school diploma, and show that they have some aptitude for carpentry.

Apprenticeships combine on-the-job work experience with classroom instruction in a planned, systematic program. Initially, apprentices work at such simple tasks as building concrete forms, doing rough framing, and nailing subflooring. Toward the end of their training apprentices may work on finishing trimwork, fitting hardware, hanging doors, and building stairs. In the course of this experience, they become familiar with the tools, materials, techniques, and equipment of the trade, and they learn how to do layout, framing, finishing, and other basic carpentry jobs.

The work experience is supplemented by about 144 hours of classroom instruction per year. Some of this instruction concerns the correct use and maintenance of tools, safety practices, first aid, building code requirements, and the properties of different construction materials. Other subjects apprentices study include the principles of layout, blueprint reading, shop mathematics, and sketching. Both on the job and in the classroom, carpenters learn how to work effectively with members of other skilled building trades.

A good high school background for prospective carpenters would include carpentry and woodworking courses, as well as other shop classes, applied mathematics, mechanical drawing, and blueprint reading.

Carpenters need to have manual dexterity, good eye-hand coordination, and a good sense of balance. They need to be in good physical condition as the work involves a great deal of physical activity. Stamina is much more important than physical strength. On the job, carpenters may have to climb, stoop, kneel, crouch, and reach.

Opportunities for Experience & Exploration

High school students may begin finding out about the work that carpenters do by taking courses such as wood shop, applied mathematics, drafting, and other industrial arts. Simple projects such as building birdhouses or shelving at home can also help people gauge their abilities and interest in the field. In addition, summer employment at a construction site can provide students with a useful overview of the work performed in the construction industry and perhaps the opportunity to talk with carpenters on the job.

Methods of Entering

Two important ways of starting out in carpentry are participating in an apprenticeship program and gradually gaining experience and skills on the job. Information about apprenticeships can be obtained by contacting the local office of the state employment service, area contractors that hire carpenters, or the local offices of the United Brotherhood of Carpenters and Joiners of America, a union that cooperates in sponsoring apprenticeships. Helper jobs that can be filled by beginners without special training in carpentry may be advertised in newspaper classified ads or with the state employment service. Another possibility is contacting potential employers directly.

Advancement

After they have completed and met all the requirements of their apprenticeship training, former apprentices are considered journeymen carpenters. After they have gained enough experience, journeymen carpenters may be promoted to positions where they are responsible for supervising the work of other carpenters. If their background includes exposure to a broad range of construction activities, they may eventually advance to positions as general construction supervisors. Carpenters who are skillful at mathematical computations and have a good knowledge of the construction business may become estimators. Some carpenters go into business for themselves, doing repair or construction work as independent contractors.

Employment Outlook

Overall, the outlook for carpenters through the year 2006 is slower than the average for other occupational fields. Total employment of carpenters is expected to increase moderately as new construction and renovations of existing structures continue. But at any given time, building activity and thus job opportunities will be better in some geographic areas than in others, reflecting regional and local variations in economic conditions.

Even if construction activity is strong in coming years, several factors will contribute to a slower rate of employment growth than at times in the past. One factor affecting growth is the trend toward increasing the use of prefabricated building components, which are more quickly and easily installed than parts made by traditional construction methods. The use of prefabricated materials is likely to mean that fewer skilled carpenters will be needed. In addition, many new lightweight, cordless tools, such as nailers and drills, are making the work of carpenters easier and faster and thus tending to reduce the total number of workers needed.

Job turnover is relatively high in the carpentry field. Many people prefer to switch to another occupation after working for awhile because they find their skills are too limited to get the best jobs or they don't like the work. As a result, every year thousands of job openings become available. Carpenters with good all-around skills, such as those who have completed apprenticeships, will have the best chances of being hired for the most desirable positions.

Nonetheless, carpenters should expect periods of unemployment. The number of available jobs is always related to various factors, such as economic stability, government spending, and interest rates. During an economic downturn, fewer building projects are started. Carpenters need to plan for the possibility of major ups and downs in their income.

Earnings

In 1996, according to the U.S. Department of Labor, the majority of carpenters who did not own their own businesses earned between $17,900 and $34,300 per year. Some made as little as $13,800, while a few earned around 45,000 or more.

Starting pay for apprentices is approximately 50 percent of the experienced worker's pay scale. It is increased periodically so that by the last phase of training the pay of apprentices is 85 to 90 percent of the journeyman carpenter's rate. Fringe benefits, such as health insurance, pension funds, and paid vacations, are available to most workers in this field and vary with local union contracts.

Conditions of Work

Carpenters may work either indoors or outdoors. If they are engaged in rough carpentry, they probably do most of their work outdoors. They may have to work on high scaffolding or in a basement making cement forms. A construction site can be noisy, dusty, hot, cold, or muddy. Carpenters often must be physically active throughout the day, constantly standing, stooping, climbing, and reaching. Some of the possible hazards of the job include being hit by falling objects, falling off a ladder, straining muscles, and getting cuts and scrapes on fingers and hands. Carpenters who follow recommended safety practices and procedures can minimize these hazards.

Work in the construction industry involves changing from one job location to another, and from time to time being laid off because of poor weather, or shortages of materials, or simply lack of jobs. Workers in this field must thus be able to arrange their finances so that they can make it through sometimes long periods of unemployment. Most carpenters belong to the United Brotherhood of Carpenters and Joiners of America.

Sources of Additional Information

Associated General Contractors of America
1957 E Street, NW
Washington, DC 20006
Tel: 202-393-2040

Home Builders Institute
National Association of Homebuilders
15th and M Streets, NW
Washington, DC 20005
Tel: 202-822-0200

Ontario Carpentry Contractors Association
#305, 1 Greensboro Drive
Rexdale, ON M9W 1C8 Canada
Tel: 416-248-6213

United Brotherhood of Carpenters and Joiners of America
101 Constitution Avenue, NW
Washington, DC 20001
Tel: 202-546-6206

Caterers

Definition

Caterers plan, coordinate, and supervise food service at parties and other social functions. Working with their clients, they purchase appropriate supplies, plan menus, supervise food preparation, direct serving of food and refreshments, and ensure the overall smooth functioning of the event. As entrepreneurs, they are also responsible for budgeting, bookkeeping, and other administrative tasks.

Nature of the Work

A caterer is a chef, purchasing agent, personnel director, and accountant. Often a caterer will also play the role of host, allowing clients to enjoy their own party. A caterer's responsibilities vary depending on the size of the catering firm and the specific needs of individual clients. While preparing quality food is a concern no matter what the size of the party, larger events require far more planning and coordination. For example, a large catering firm may organize and plan a formal event for a thousand people, including planning and preparing a seven-course meal, decorating the hall with flowers and wall hangings, employing twenty or more wait staff to serve food, and arranging the entertainment. The catering firm will also set up the tables and chairs and provide the necessary linen, silverware, and dishes. A catering company may organize fifty or so such events a month or only several a year. A smaller catering organization may concentrate on simpler events, such as preparing food for an informal buffet for fifteen people.

Caterers not only service individual clients, but also industrial clients. A caterer may supervise a company cafeteria or plan food service for an airline or cruise ship. These caterers often take over full-time supervision of food operations, including ordering food and other supplies, supervising personnel and food preparation, and overseeing the maintenance of equipment.

School Subjects
Business
Family and consumer science

Personal Interests
Business management
Food/Cooking

Work Environment
Primarily indoors
Primarily multiple locations

Minimum Education Level
Some postsecondary training
Apprenticeship

Salary Range
$15,000 to
$30,000 to
$75,000+

Certification or Licensing
Required

Outlook
Faster than the average

DOT
319

GOE
09.05.02

NOC
7414

A caterer needs to be flexible in his or her approach to food preparation, that is, able to prepare food both on- and off-premises as required by logistical considerations and the wishes of the client. If the caterer is handling a large banquet in a hotel or other location, for example the caterer will usually prepare the food on-premises, using kitchen and storage facilities as needed. The caterer might also work in a client's kitchen for an event in a private home. In both cases, the caterer must visit the site of the function well before the actual event to determine how and where the food will be prepared. Caterers may also prepare food off-premises, working either in their own kitchens or in a mobile kitchen.

Working with the client is obviously a very important aspect of the caterer's job. Clients always want their affairs to be extra special, and the caterer's ability to present such items as a uniquely shaped wedding cake or to provide beautiful decorations will enhance the atmosphere and contribute to customer satisfaction. The caterer and the client work together to establish a budget, develop a menu, and determine the desired atmosphere. Many caterers have their own special recipes, and they are always on the lookout for quality fruits, vegetables, and meats. Caterers should have an eye for detail and be able to make fancy hors d'oeuvres and eye-catching fruit and vegetable displays.

Although caterers can usually prepare a variety of dishes, they may have a specialty, such as Cajun or Italian cuisine. Caterers may also have a special serving style, such as serving food in Renaissance period dress, that sets them apart from other caterers. Developing a reputation by specializing in a certain area is an especially effective marketing technique.

The caterer is a coordinator, working with suppliers, food servers, and the client to ensure an event comes off as planned. The caterer must be in frequent contact with all parties involved in the affair, making sure, for example, that the food is delivered on time, the flowers are fresh, and the entertainment shows up and performs as promised.

Good management skills are extremely important. The caterer must know how much food and other supplies to order, what equipment will be needed, how many staff to hire, and be able to coordinate the various activities to ensure a smooth-running event. Purchasing proper supplies entails knowledge of a variety of food products, their suppliers, and the contacts needed to get the right product at the best possible price.

Caterers with a large operation may appoint a manager to oversee an event. The manager will take care of the ordering, planning, and supervising responsibilities, and may even work with the client.

As entrepreneurs, caterers have many important day-to-day administrative responsibilities, such as overseeing the budgeting and bookkeeping of the operation. The caterer must make sure that the business continues to make a profit while keeping its prices competitive. Caterers must know how to figure costs and other budgetary considerations, plan inventories, buy food, and ensure compliance with health regulations.

Caterer helpers may prepare and serve hors d'oeuvres and other food and refreshments at social functions under the supervision of the head caterer. They also help arrange tables and decorations and then assist in the cleanup.

Requirements

Although there are no specific educational or professional requirements for this field, a professional caterer should combine the ability to understand proper food preparation with the ability to manage a food service operation. Many people develop these skills through on-the-job training, beginning as a caterer's helper or a restaurant worker.

As the catering field has grown more competitive, many successful caterers are choosing to get a college degree in business administration, family and consumer science (home economics), nutrition, or a related field. Others get their training through the various vocational schools and community colleges that offer apprenticeships and other forms of professional training for those interested in becoming caterers.

High school students interested in becoming caterers should take courses in mathematics, business administration, and home economics. They also should take courses in English and communications. A college program should include coursework in nutrition, health, and business management.

Most states require caterers to be licensed, and inspectors may make periodic visits to catering operations to ensure that local health and safety regulations are being maintained in food preparation, handling, and storage.

As a measure of professional status, many caterers become certified through the National Association of Catering Executives (NACE). To qualify for this certification, caterers must meet certain educational and professional requirements as well as pass a written examination. Further information on the certification process, as well as general career information, is available from NACE at the address given at the end of this article.

Certification is also offered by the International Food Service Executives Association (IFSEA). Contact the IFSEA at the address listed at the end of this article.

Opportunities for Experience & Exploration

An aspiring caterer can get part-time work in a restaurant as a waitperson or as an assistant banquet manager at a hotel. With some experience and training, it might even be possible to work as a manager with a large catering company. High school students may work in the school cafeteria or they may establish their own small catering service by working at parties for friends and relatives.

Methods of Entering

Some caterers enter the profession as a matter of chance after helping a friend or relative prepare a large banquet or volunteering to coordinate a group function. Most caterers, however, begin their careers after graduating from college with a degree in a program such as home economics, or finishing a culinary training program at a vocational school or community college.

Qualified people may begin work as a manager for a large catering firm or as a manager for a hotel or country club or banquet service. An individual will most likely start a catering business only with extensive experience and sufficient finances to purchase equipment and other start-up costs.

Advancement

As with most service-oriented businesses, the success of a caterer depends on the quality of work and a good reputation. Well-known caterers can expand their businesses, often growing from a small business to a larger operation. This may mean hiring assistants and buying more equipment in order to be able to serve a larger variety of clientele. Caterers who initially worked out of their own home kitchens may get an office or relocate to another area in order to take advantage of better catering opportunities. Sometimes successful caterers use their skills and reputations to secure full-time positions in large hotels or restaurants as banquet coordinators and planners. Independent caterers may also secure contracts with industrial clients, such as airlines, hospitals, schools, and companies, to staff their cafeterias or supply food and beverages. They may also be employed by such companies to manage their food operations.

Employment Outlook

Because of the strong food service industry in the United States, employment opportunities in catering should continue to grow through the year 2006. Opportunities will be good for firms that handle weddings, bar and bat mitzvahs, business functions, and other events.

Competition is keen as many hotels and restaurants branch out to offer catering services. Like all service industries, catering is sensitive to the economy, and a downturn in the economy may limit catering opportunities. Despite the competition and fluctuating economic conditions, highly skilled and motivated caterers should be in demand throughout the country, especially in and around large metropolitan areas.

Earnings

Earnings vary widely depending on the size and location of the catering operation and the skill and motivation of the individual entrepreneur. Many caterers charge according to the number of guests attending a function. In many cases, the larger the event, the larger the profit. Earnings are also influenced by whether a caterer works full time or only part time. Even very successful caterers often remain at it part-time, working full time at another job either because they enjoy their other job or to protect themselves against a possible downturn in the economy.

Full-time caterers can earn between $15,000 and $60,000 per year, depending on skill, reputation, and experience. An extremely successful caterer can easily earn more than $75,000 annually. A part-time caterer may earn $7,000 to $15,000 per year, subject to the same variables as the full-time caterer. Because most caterers are self-employed, vacations and other benefits are usually not part of the wage structure.

A caterer who works as a manager for a company cafeteria or other industrial client may earn between $18,000 and $35,000 per year, with vacation, health insurance, and other benefits usually included.

Conditions of Work

A caterer often works long hours planning and preparing for an event, and the day of the event might easily be a fourteen-hour workday from setup to cleanup.

There is a lot of variety in the type of work a caterer does. The caterer must work closely with a variety of clients and be able to adapt to last minute changes.

Caterers often spend long hours on their feet, and although the work can be physically and mentally demanding, caterers usually enjoy a great deal of work flexibility. As entrepreneurs, they can usually take time off when necessary. Caterers often work more than sixty hours a week during busy seasons, with most of the work on weekends and evenings, when events tend to be scheduled.

Caterers must be able to plan ahead, work gracefully under pressure, and have the ability to adapt to last minute mishaps. Attention to detail is critical, as is the ability to work long hours under demanding situations. Caterers must be able to direct a large staff of kitchen workers and waitpersons and be able to interact well with clients, guests, and employees.

Sources of Additional Information

Career, certification, and scholarship information is available from:

International Food Service Executives Association
1100 South State Road #7, Suite 103
Margate, FL 33068
Tel: 305-977-0767
WWW: http://www.ifsea.org/

Mobile Industrial Caterers Association
1240 North Jefferson Street, Suite G
Anaheim, CA 92807
Tel: 714-632-6800

Information on certification and other career information is available from:

National Association of Catering Executives
60 Revere Street, Suite 500
Northbrook, IL 60062
Tel: 847-480-9080

Cement Masons

Definition

Cement masons are skilled workers who place and finish the concrete surfaces in many different kinds of construction projects ranging from small patios and sidewalks to highways, dams, and airport runways.

Nature of the Work

The principal work of cement masons, also known as *concrete masons,* is to put into place and then smooth and finish concrete surfaces in a variety of different construction projects. Sometimes they add colors to the concrete to change its appearance or chemicals to speed up or slow down the time that the concrete takes to harden. They use various tools to create specified surface textures on fresh concrete before it sets. They may also fabricate beams, columns, or panels of concrete. Most cement masons are employed by concrete contractors or general contractors to help build roads, shopping malls, factories, and many other structures. A small number of masons are employed by manufacturers of concrete products.

Cement masons must know their materials well. They must be able to judge how long different concrete mixtures will take to set up and how factors such as heat, cold, and wind will affect the curing, or hardening, of the cement. They need to be able to recognize these effects by examining and touching the concrete. They need to know about the strengths of different kinds of concrete and how different surface appearances are produced.

In addition to understanding the materials they work with, cement masons must also be familiar with blueprint reading, applied mathematics, building code regulations, and the procedures involved in estimating costs and quantities of materials.

On a construction job, the preparation of the site where the concrete will be poured is very important. Cement masons

School Subjects
Mathematics
Shop (Trade/Vo-tech education)

Personal Interests
Building things
Fixing things

Work Environment
Primarily outdoors
Primarily multiple locations

Minimum Education Level
High school diploma
Apprenticeship

Salary Range
$14,800 to
$33,800 to
$42,700

Certification or Licensing
None

Outlook
More slowly than the average

DOT
844

GOE
05.05.01

NOC
7282

begin by setting up the forms that will hold the wet concrete until it hardens into the desired shape. The forms must be properly aligned and must allow for concrete of the correct dimensions, as specified in the original design. In some structures, reinforcing steel rods or mesh are set into place after the forms are put in position. The cement masons then pour or direct the pouring of the concrete into the forms so that it flows smoothly rather than drops unevenly. The cement masons or their helpers spread and tamp the fresh concrete into place. Then the masons level the surface by moving a straightedge back and forth across the top of the forms.

Using a bull float, which is a large wooden trowel, cement masons begin the smoothing operation. This process covers up the larger particles in the wet concrete and brings to the surface the fine cement paste in the mixture. On projects where curved edges are desired, cement masons may use an edger or radius tool, guiding it around the edge between the form and the concrete. They may make grooves or joints at intervals in the surface to help control cracking.

The process continues with more finishing work, either done by hand with a small metal trowel or with a power trowel. This smoothing gets out most remaining irregularities on the surface. On driveways, sidewalks, and similar projects, cement masons may use a brush or broom on the concrete to attain a nonslip surface texture. Or they may embed pebbles in the surface. Afterward, the concrete must cure to reach its proper strength, a process that can take up to a week.

On structures such as walls or columns with exposed surfaces when the forms are removed, cement masons must leave a smooth and uniform finish. To achieve this, they may rub down high spots with an abrasive material, chip out rough or defective spots with a chisel and hammer, and fill low areas with cement paste. They may finish off the exposed surface with a coating of a cement mixture to create an even, pleasing appearance.

Cement masons use a variety of hand and power tools, ranging from simple chisels, hammers, trowels, edgers, and leveling devices to pneumatic chisels, concrete mixers, and troweling machines. Smaller projects such as sidewalks and patios may be done by hand. But on large-scale projects such as highways, power-operated floats and finishing equipment are necessary. Although power equipment can speed many tasks, on most projects there are corners or other inaccessible areas that require hand work.

There are various specialists whose jobs involve covering, leveling, and smoothing cement and concrete surfaces. Among them are *concrete-stone finishers,* who work with ornamental stone and concrete surfaces; *concrete rubbers,* who polish concrete surfaces; and *nozzle cement sprayers,* who use spray equipment to apply cement mixtures to surfaces.

Poured concrete wall technicians are another occupational group whose activities are related to those of cement masons. These workers use surveying instruments to mark construction sites for excavation and to set up and true (that is, align correctly) concrete forms. They direct the pouring of concrete to form walls of buildings, and, after removing the forms, they may waterproof lower walls and lay drainage tile to promote drainage away from the building. Unlike cement masons, however, poured concrete wall technicians generally have at least two years of technical training in such subjects as surveying and construction methods.

Requirements

Cement masons can learn their skills either on the job or in apprenticeship programs. Many people with no special skills or experience begin work in helper positions and gradually learn the trade informally over an unspecified number of years by working with experienced masons. However, apprenticeships are the recommended way to acquire the necessary skills, as they provide more balanced, in-depth training through programs that last two to three years.

Many cement masons who pick up skills on the job begin as construction laborers or cement mason helpers. In considering applicants for helper jobs, most employers prefer to hire people who are at least eighteen, who are in good physical condition, and who possess a driver's license. The ability to get along with coworkers is important, as most cement masons work in teams. Although a high school diploma may not be required, applicants who have taken high school shop courses, blueprint reading, and mechanical drawing may have an advantage. Trainees usually begin with easy tasks such as edging and jointing, then progress to more difficult work such as final finishing of surfaces.

Apprenticeships are usually jointly sponsored by local contractors and unions. Applicants for apprenticeship programs sometimes must be approved by the local joint labor–management apprenticeship committee. They may have to take a written test and pass a physical examination. Training consists of a combination of planned work experience and classroom instruction. On the job, apprentices learn about handling the tools and materials of the trade, about layout work and finishing techniques, and about job safety. Classroom instruction involves at least 144 hours each year in such related subjects as mathematics, blueprint reading, architectural drawing, procedures for estimating materials and costs, and local building regulations.

Opportunities for Experience & Exploration

High school students can learn more about their aptitude for this kind of work by taking courses such as general mathematics, drafting, and various shop classes. In addition, summer employment as part of a construction crew can provide valuable firsthand experience. Some people are introduced to the building construction trades, including the work of cement masons, while they are serving in the military, especially with the Army Engineering Corps.

Methods of Entering

People who want to become cement masons can enter this field either through formal apprenticeship training programs or by obtaining a job that offers the opportunity for on-the-job training. For information about becoming an apprentice cement mason, it is possible to contact local cement contractors, the offices of the state employment service, or the area headquarters of one of the unions that organize cement masons. Many cement masons are members of either the Operative Plasterers and Cement Masons International Association or the International Union of Bricklayers and Allied Craftsmen.

People who wish to become on-the-job trainees can contact contractors in the area who may be hiring helpers. They may also want to follow up on job leads from the state employment service or newspaper classified ads.

Advancement

After they have gained some skills and become efficient workers in their trade, cement masons may specialize in one phase of the work. They may become, for example, lip-curb finishers, expansion joint finishers, or concrete paving-finishing machine operators.

Experienced masons with good judgment, planning skills, and the ability to deal with people may advance to supervisory positions. Supervisors with a broad understanding of the other construction trades may eventually become job superintendents, who are in charge of the whole range of activities at the job site. Cement masons may also become estimators for concrete contractors, calculating materials requirements and labor costs. Only a few cement masons decide to open their own contracting businesses, usually doing small projects like sidewalks and patios.

Employment Outlook

Employment opportunities for cement masons are expected to increase more slowly than the average for all occupations through the year 2006. Construction activity is expected to expand during this period, and concrete will be a very important building material. Cement masons will be in demand to help build roads, bridges, buildings, and many other structures. Yet, the productivity of cement masons will be improved considerably by the introduction of better equipment, tools, and materials. That is, fewer cement masons will be needed to do the same amount of work. The net effect will be that employment in this occupation will not keep up with the increasing use of concrete in construction.

Nonetheless, many new openings will arise every year as experienced workers move into other occupations or leave the labor force. In areas where the local economy is thriving and there are plenty of building projects, there may be occasional shortages of cement masons. At other times, even skilled masons may experience periods of unemployment due to downturns in the economy and declining levels of construction activity.

Earnings

The earnings of cement masons vary widely according to factors such as geographical location, whether they do much overtime work, how much bad weather or local economic conditions reduce the number of hours worked, and whether they are union members. Working overtime, usually at time-and-a-half rates, is frequently possible, because once concrete has been poured, the finishing operations must be completed quickly. Nonunion workers generally have lower wage rates than union workers.

In 1996, most cement masons earned between $19,500 and $33,800 per year, as reported by the U.S. Bureau of Labor Statistics. A few earned over $42,000, while some make as little as $14,800. Apprentices start at wages that are approximately 50 to 60 percent of a fully qualified mason's wage. They receive periodic raises, so that in the last phase of training, their wage is between 90 and 95 percent of the experienced worker's pay.

Conditions of Work

Cement masons do strenuous work, and they need to have good stamina. They stay active much of the time, especially when concrete has been poured and needs to be finished immediately. Many cement masons work outdoors. In general, concrete cannot be poured in cold or rainy weather, but temporary heated shelters are sometimes used to extend the time when work can be done. Masons work in a variety of locations, sometimes on the ground, sometimes on ladders and scaffolds. They may need to lift or push weights, and they often kneel, bend, and stoop. To protect their knees, many masons routinely wear kneepads. They may also wear water-repellent boots and protective clothing.

Common hazards on-the-job include falling off ladders, being hit by falling objects, muscle strains, and rough hands from contact with wet concrete. By exercising caution and following established job safety practices, cement masons can minimize their exposure to hazardous conditions.

Sources of Additional Information

Associated General Contractors of America
1957 E Street, NW
Washington, DC 20006
Tel: 202-393-2040
Email: 73264.15@compuserv.com
WWW: http://owlworld.compuserv.com/homepages/agc

Canadian Masonry Contractors Association
#201, 1013 Wilson Avenue
Downsview, ON M3K 1G1 Canada
Tel: 416-635-7179

International Union of Bricklayers and Allied Craftsmen
815 15th Street, NW, Suite 1001
Washington, DC 20005
Tel: 202-783-3788

Mason Contractors Association of America
1550 Spring Road, Suite 320
Oak Brook, IL 60521
Tel: 630-782-6767

Collection Workers

Definition

Collection workers—sometimes known as *bill collectors, collection correspondents,* or *collection agents*—are employed to persuade people to pay their overdue bills. Some work for collection agencies (which are hired by the business to which the money is owed), while others work for department stores, hospitals, banks, public utilities, and other businesses. Collection workers contact delinquent debtors, inform them of the delinquency, and either secure payment or arrange a new payment schedule. If all else fails, they might be forced to repossess property or turn the account over to an attorney for legal proceedings.

Nature of the Work

A collection worker's main job is to persuade people to pay bills that are past due. The procedure is generally the same in both collection firms and businesses that employ collection workers. The duties of the various workers may overlap, depending on the size and nature of the company.

When routine billing methods—monthly statements and notice letters—fail to secure payment, the collection worker receives a bad-debt file (usually on a computer tape downloaded to the agency's computer system). This file contains information about the debtor, the nature and amount of the unpaid bill, the last charge incurred, and the date of the last payment. The collection worker then contacts the debtor by phone or mail to request full or partial payment or, if necessary, to arrange a new payment schedule.

If the bill has not been paid because the customer believes it is incorrect, the merchandise purchased was faulty, or the service billed for was not performed, the collector takes appropriate steps to settle the matter. If after investigation the debt is still valid, the collector again tries to secure payment.

School Subjects
Psychology
Speech

Personal Interests
Computers
Helping people: personal service

Work Environment
Primarily indoors
Primarily one location

Minimum Education Level
High school diploma

Salary Range
$14,500 to $21,320 to $34,800

Certification or Licensing
None

Outlook
Faster than the average

DOT
241

GOE
07.04.02

NOC
1435

In cases where the customer has not paid because of a financial emergency or poor money management, a new payment schedule can be arranged. In instances where the customer goes to great or fraudulent lengths to avoid payment, the collector may recommend that the file be turned over to an attorney.

When all efforts to obtain payment fail, collection workers known as *repossessors* are assigned to locate the merchandise on which the debtor still owes money and return it to the seller. Such goods as furniture or appliances can be picked up in a truck. To reclaim automobiles and other motor vehicles, the repossessor might be forced to enter and start the vehicle with special tools if the buyer does not surrender the key.

In large agencies, some collection workers specialize as *skip tracers*. Skip tracers are assigned to locate debtors who skip out on their debts—that is, who move without notifying their creditors in order to evade payment of their bills. Skip tracers act like detectives, searching telephone directories and street listings and making inquiries at post offices in an effort to locate missing debtors. Increasingly such information can be found through computer databases (some agencies subscribe to a service to collect this information). Skip tracers also try to elicit information about a person's whereabouts by contacting former neighbors and employers, local merchants, friends, relatives, and references listed on the original credit application. They follow up every lead and prepare a report of the entire investigation.

In some small offices, collection workers perform clerical duties, such as reading and answering correspondence, filing, or posting amounts paid to people's accounts. They might offer financial advice to customers or contact them to inquire about their satisfaction with the handling of the account. In larger companies *credit and loan collection supervisors* might oversee the activities of several other collection workers.

Collection work can be emotionally taxing. It involves listening to a bill payer's problems and occasional verbal attacks directed at both the collector and the company. Some people physically threaten repossessors and other collection workers. Because debtors can be very emotional about money and credit problems, the job is potentially stressful.

Requirements

Because this is a people-oriented job, collection workers must have a pleasant manner and voice. Some spend much of their time on the telephone talking with people about overdue pay-

ments, which can be a delicate subject. They must be sympathetic and tactful, yet assertive and persuasive enough to overcome any reluctance on the part of the debtor to pay the overdue account. In addition, collectors must be alert, quick-witted, and imaginative to handle the unpredictable and potentially awkward situations that are encountered in this type of work.

A high school education is usually sufficient for this occupation. Courses in psychology and speech are particularly helpful. Collection procedures and telephone techniques are learned on the job in a training period spent under the guidance of a supervisor or an experienced collector. The legal restrictions on collection activities, such as when and how calls can be made, are also covered. The American Collectors Association conducts special seminars for its members to assist collectors in improving their collection and skip-tracing skills. A basic knowledge of legal proceedings is helpful for supervisors.

Opportunities for Experience & Exploration

The best way to explore collection work is to secure part-time or summer employment in a collection agency or credit office. Students might wish to interview a collection worker to obtain firsthand information about the practical aspects of this occupation.

Methods of Entering

The usual way of entering the field is to apply directly to an employer. The help wanted section of newspapers typically lists job openings, as do state employment services.

Advancement

Advancement opportunities are good, though limited. Workers with above-average ability can become supervisors or collection managers. A few become credit authorizers, credit managers, or bank loan officers. Some branch out to open their own collection agency.

Employment Outlook

In 1996, approximately twenty percent of collection workers were employed by commercial banks, finance companies, credit unions, and collection agencies, as well as in public utilities and retail and wholesale businesses. Jobs in this field are expected to grow faster than the national average for all occupations. The number of jobs for collection workers is expected to grow in part because of relaxed standards for credit cards. Credit card companies and retail stores are competing for customers by lowering the qualifications for obtaining a card and increasing the credit limits. As a result, more people will likely have trouble paying their bills.

Economic recessions also increase the amount of personal debt that goes unpaid. Therefore, unlike in many occupations, collection workers usually find that their employment and workloads increase during economic slumps.

Opportunities exist throughout the United States, especially in heavily populated urban areas. Companies that have branch offices in rural communities often locate their collection departments in nearby cities. Competition for positions will be strongest in large metropolitan banks, which generally offer higher salaries and better advancement opportunities.

Earnings

Collection workers might receive a salary plus a bonus or commission on the debt amounts they collect. Others work for a flat salary with no commissions. Since the pay system varies among different companies, incomes vary substantially. While the available information is limited, it appears that in 1996 beginning collectors earned between $14,500 and $24,000 a year. Those with experience can earn as much as $34,800 a year depending on how much they are able to collect from debtors. The median annual income for all bill collectors is approximately $21,300.

Conditions of Work

Most collectors work in pleasant offices, sit at a desk, and spend a great deal of time on the telephone. Because of the large quantity of work done over the phone, many companies use phone headsets and program-operated dialing systems.

Rarely does a collector have to make a personal visit to a customer. Repossession proceedings are undertaken only in extreme cases. The legal aspects must be understood when repossession is required.

Collection workers put in forty hours a week but often stagger their schedules. They might start late in the morning and work into the evening, or they might take a weekday off and work on Saturday. Evening and weekend work is common because debtors are often home during these times.

Sources of Additional Information

■American Collectors Association
PO Box 39106
Minneapolis, MN 55439-0106
Tel: 612-926-6547

Communications Equipment Technicians

Definition

Communications equipment technicians work with telecommunications equipment, which is used to transmit voices and data across long distances. As part of their job, communications equipment technicians install, test, maintain, troubleshoot, and repair a wide variety of equipment used for communications. This does not include, however, equipment that handles entertainment broadcast to the public via radio or television signals. Most communications equipment technicians work in telephone company offices or on customers' premises.

Nature of the Work

Although specific duties vary, most communications equipment technicians share some basic kinds of activities. They work with electrical measuring and testing devices and hand tools; read blueprints, circuit diagrams, and electrical schematics (diagrams); and consult technical manuals. The following paragraphs describe just a few of the many technicians who work in this complex industry.

Central office equipment installers, also called *equipment installation technicians,* are specialists in setting up and taking down the switching and dialing equipment located in telephone company central offices. They install equipment in newly established offices, update existing equipment, add on to facilities that are being expanded, and remove old, outdated apparatus.

Central office repairers, also called *switching equipment technicians* or *central office technicians,* work on the switching equipment that automatically connects lines when customers dial calls. They analyze defects and malfunctions in equipment, make fine adjustments, and test and repair switches and relays. These workers use various special tools, gauges, meters, and ordinary hand tools.

School Subjects
Mathematics
Shop (Trade/Vo-tech education)

Personal Interests
Figuring out how things work
Fixing things

Work Environment
Primarily indoors
Primarily multiple locations

Minimum Education Level
High school diploma

Salary Range
$25,000 to
$31,304 to
$42,000

Certification or Licensing
Required for certain positions

Outlook
More slowly than the average

DOT
822

GOE
05.05.05

NOC
7246

PBX systems technicians or *switching equipment technicians* work on PBXs, or private branch exchanges, which are direct lines that businesses install to bypass phone company lines. PBX systems can handle both voice and data communications and can provide specialized services like electronic mail and automatic routing of calls at the lowest possible cost.

PBX installers install these systems. They may assemble customized switchboards for customers. *PBX repairers* maintain and repair PBX systems and associated equipment. In addition, they may work on mobile radiophones and microwave transmission devices.

Maintenance administrators test customers' lines within the central office to find causes and locations of malfunctions reported by customers. They report the nature of the trouble to maintenance crews and coordinate their activities to clear up the trouble. Some maintenance administrators work in cable television company offices, diagnosing subscribers' problems with cable television signals and dispatching repairers if necessary. They use highly automated testboards and other equipment to analyze circuits. They enter data into computer files and interpret computer output about trouble areas in the system.

Many workers in this group are concerned with other kinds of communications equipment that are not part of telephone systems. Among these are *radio repairers and mechanics,* who install and repair radio transmitters and receivers. Sometimes they work on other electronics equipment at microwave and fiber optics installations. *Submarine cable equipment technicians* work on the machines and equipment used to send messages through underwater cables. Working in cable offices and stations, they check and adjust transmitters and printers and repair or replace faulty parts. *Office electricians* maintain submarine cable circuits and rearrange connections to ensure that cable service is not interrupted. *Avionics technicians* work on electronic components in aircraft communication, navigation, and flight control systems. *Signal maintainers* or *track switch maintainers* work on railroads. They install, inspect, and maintain the signals, track switches, gate crossings, and communications systems throughout rail networks. *Instrument repairers* work in repair shops, where they repair, test, and modify a variety of communications equipment.

Requirements

Communications equipment technicians need strong mechanical and electrical aptitudes, manual dexterity, problem-solving abilities, and the ability to work without a lot of direct supervision.

Most employers require applicants to have a high school diploma. In high school, students should take computer courses, algebra, geometry, English, physics, and shop. Useful shop courses are those that introduce students to principles of electricity and electronics, basic machine repair, reading blueprints and engineering drawings, and using hand tools.

Many telecommunications employers prefer to hire technicians who have already learned most of the necessary skills, either through service in the military or from a postsecondary training program, such as those available in community and junior colleges or technical schools. Programs in telecommunications technology, electronics, electrical, or electromechanical technology, or even computer maintenance or related subjects may be appropriate for people who want to become communications equipment technicians. Most programs last two years, although certification in specific areas often can be obtained through a one-year program. Useful classes are those that provide practical knowledge about electricity and electronics and teach the use of hand tools, electronic testing equipment, and computer data terminals. Classes in digital and fiber optic technology are also beneficial.

Applicants for entry-level positions may have to pass tests of their knowledge, general mechanical aptitude, and manual dexterity. Once hired, employees often go through company training programs. They may study practical and theoretical aspects of electricity, electronics, and mathematics that they will need to know for their work. Experienced workers also may attend training sessions from time to time. They need to keep their knowledge up-to-date as new technology in the rapidly changing telecommunications field affects the way they do their jobs.

Some communications equipment technicians must be able to identify the different color-coded wires in telephone equipment, so they cannot be color-blind.

Some workers in this field must obtain a license. Federal Communications Commission (FCC) regulations require that anyone who works with radio transmitting equipment must have a restricted radiotelephone operator's license. In order to receive a license, applicants need to pass a written test on radio laws and operating procedures and take a Morse Code examination. Effective February 1, 1999, a Global Maritime Distress and Safety System (GMDSS) license will be required rather than a restricted radiotelephone operator's license.

Opportunities for Experience & Exploration

In high school, students can begin to find out about the work of communications equipment technicians by taking whatever electronics, computer, and electrical shop courses are available, and also other shop courses that help them become familiar with using various tools. Teachers or guidance counselors may be able to help interested students arrange a visit to a telephone company central office where they can see telephone equipment and observe workers on the job. It may be possible to obtain a part-time or summer helper job at a business that sells and repairs electronics equipment. Such a job could provide the opportunity to talk to workers whose skills are like those needed by many communications equipment technicians. Serving in the armed forces in a communications section can also provide a way to learn about this field and gain some useful experience.

Methods of Entering

People who are interested in becoming communications equipment technicians can apply directly to the employment office of the local telephone company. Many times it is necessary for newly hired workers to take a position in a different part of the company until an opening as a technician becomes available. However, telephone companies have been reducing the number of technicians they need in recent years, and competition for these positions is especially stiff.

Long-distance telephone companies and manufacturers of telephone and other electronic communications equipment also employ these workers, and job seekers can apply directly to such companies. Information on job openings in this field may be available through the offices of the state employment service and through classified advertisements in newspapers. Because many communications equipment technicians are members of unions such as the Communications Workers of America and the International Brotherhood of Electrical Workers, job seekers can contact their local offices for job leads and assistance. Students who attend a technical program may be able to find out about openings at local companies through their schools' job placement services or through contacts with teachers and administrators.

Advancement

The advancement possibilities for communications equipment technicians depend on the area of the telecommunications industry in which they work. Because of changes in equipment and technology, workers who hope to advance will need to have received recent training or update their skills through additional training. This training may be offered through employers or can be obtained through technical institutes or telecommunications associations.

Advancement opportunities in telephone companies may be limited because of the fact that many telephone companies are reducing their workforces and will have less need for certain types of workers in the future. This will result in fewer positions to move into and increased competition for more advanced positions. However, some workers may be able to advance to supervisory or administrative positions.

Many workers can advance through education resulting in an associate's or bachelor's degree. Workers who have completed two- or four-year programs in electrical or telecommunications engineering programs have the best opportunity to advance and can become engineering assistants, engineers, or telecommunications specialists.

Employment Outlook

Employment of communications equipment technicians has been declining significantly and is expected to grow slower than the average for all occupations through the year 2006. This is because some areas of the telecommunications industry, and the telephone industry in particular, are in the process of being completely transformed by new technology. Maintenance and repair work on the new equipment will require fewer workers than the industry has employed in the past. New technology relies on transmission through telecommunications networks rather than central-office switching equipment. There are far fewer mechanical devices that break, wear out, and need to be periodically cleaned and lubricated. These networks contain self-diagnosing features that detect problems and, in some cases, route operations around a trouble spot until repairs can be made. When problems occur, it is usually possible simply to replace parts rather than repair them. Also, the consolidation and merger of telephone companies will further decrease the number of available positions.

It will be very difficult for new workers to gain employment as communications equipment technicians. Competition for existing positions will be keen and workers with formal training and experience stand the best chance of obtaining available jobs.

Earnings

In 1996, according to the Bureau of Labor Statistics, the average annual salary for communications equipment technicians was $31,304. Earnings of communications equipment technicians vary, with some employers paying more than others. Most workers in this group who are employed by telephone companies are union members, and their earnings are set by contracts between the union and the company. Many currently employed communications equipment technicians have several years of experience and are at the higher end of the pay scale.

Most workers in this field receive extra pay for hours worked at night, on weekends, or over forty hours a week. Benefits vary, but generally include paid vacations, paid holidays, sick leaves, and health insurance. In addition, some companies offer pension and retirement plans.

Conditions of Work

Communications equipment technicians usually work forty hours a week. Some work shifts at night, on weekends, or on holidays, because telecommunications systems must give uninterrupted service and trouble can occur at any time.

Central telephone offices are clean, well lighted, and well ventilated. The telephone industry's safety record is among the best.

Sources of Additional Information

For a copy of Phonefacts, *contact:*

■United States Telephone Association
1401 H Street, NW, Suite 600
Washington, DC 20005-2136
Tel: 202-326-7300

For information on the telephone industry, contact:

■Communications Workers of America
501 Third Street, NW
Washington, DC 20001
Tel: 202-434-1100

■International Brotherhood of Electrical Workers
1125 15th Street, NW
Washington, DC 20005
Tel: 202-833-7000

For information on educational programs in wireless technology (cellular, PCS, and satellite), contact:

■Personal Communications Industry Association
1501 Duke Street
Alexandria, VA 22314
Tel: 202-467-4770
WWW: http://www.pcia.com/newaves.htm

For information on licensing requirements and testing sites, contact:

■Federal Communications Commission
1919 M Street, NW
Washington, DC 20544
Tel: 202-418-0200
WWW: http://www.fcc/gov

Computer and Office Machine Service Technicians

Definition

Computer and office machine service technicians install, calibrate, maintain, troubleshoot, and repair equipment such as computers, printers, copy machines, adding machines, typewriters, fax machines, mail sorters, VCRs, and monitors. Their primary duty is to diagnose problems caused by mechanical and electronic malfunctions and ensure that computers and machines are running properly at all times.

Nature of the Work

Businesses use computers and office machines in order to perform normal business tasks more efficiently and accurately. Like other machines such as dishwashers or cars, computers and office machines require careful installation and regular preventive maintenance to run properly. And, like other machines, computers and office machines sometimes function poorly or break down entirely. Computer or machine "down time" can be extremely expensive for many companies, and a great nuisance to others. Computer and office machine service technicians are responsible for ensuring that machines function well at all times.

Most technicians, or servicers as they are sometimes called, perform the same basic duties: they install, calibrate, clean, maintain, troubleshoot, and repair machines. Servicers differ primarily in regard to the particular kinds of machines they are trained to work on and the nature and scope of their employer.

Service technicians who work in specialized repair shops are usually experts in fixing one or two types of machines. For example, a servicer might specialize in working on color laser printers or color copiers. Or he or she might be trained to work on communications technology products such as fax machines and modems. Other repair specialties include mail-processing equipment servicers and cash register servicers.

As the use of computers, computer peripherals, and computerized office machinery expands at a rapid pace, some technicians are finding they can make more money and have better job security if they are well trained in the installation, maintenance, and repair of these kinds of machines. Many large computer companies, whether manufacturers, servicers, or retailers, provide service contracts with the purchase of their products. They hire *computer service technicians* to fulfill service contract obligations. Computer service technicians provide a wide range of services. They install and set up computer equipment when it first arrives at the client's office. Later, they follow up installation with a series of preventative maintenance calls to make sure the computers are performing well. In addition, some technicians are always on call in case of emergency breakdown problems. Relying on their background knowledge of the product and diagnostic tests using special instruments, they are able to diagnose the nature and extent of the problem and repair the machines relatively quickly. They are usually trained in replacing semiconductor chips, circuit boards, and other hardware components. If they are unable to fix the computer on-site, they bring it back to their employer's service area.

Some technicians are employed in the maintenance department of large companies. Since there are typically many different kinds of machines in such companies, these technicians generally have a very good working knowledge of mechanical as well as electronic equipment. They receive extra training on specific equipment the business uses most often. In addition, they participate in training seminars conducted by the manufacturers of new equipment the business buys or leases.

Field service technicians usually work for specialty repair shops, machine manufacturers, or product-specific service companies. They are technicians who travel to the customer's workplace to do maintenance and repairs. They often follow a predetermined schedule for machine maintenance. For example, they might change the toner, clean the optic parts, and make mechanical adjustments to copiers and printers. They also have to make time each day to respond to incoming requests for emergency service. Even though supervisors prioritize maintenance and repair calls, field service technicians often have a hectic schedule involving a variety and large number of duties. In addition to performing the service, technicians are required to keep detailed written explanations of all service provided so that future problems can be dealt with more effectively.

When machines require service that is too complicated or messy to be dealt with in the customer's office, they are brought back to the repair shop or company service center to be worked on by *bench servicers*. Bench servicers are technicians that work primarily at their employer's location.

Some very experienced servicers open their own repair shops. These entrepreneurs often find it necessary to service a wide range of products in order to be successful, particularly when competition is tight. To further supplement their incomes, they might start selling certain products and offering service contracts on them. Business owners have the added responsibility of normal business duties, such as bookkeeping and advertising.

Requirements

Computer and office machine service technicians must have a strong technical background and an aptitude for learning about new technologies, good communications skills, and superior manual dexterity skills. A high school diploma is the minimum requirement for pursuing a career in this field. Traditional high school courses such as mathematics, physical sciences, and other laboratory-based sciences can provide a strong foundation for understanding basic mechanical and electronic principles. English and speech classes can help boost both written and verbal communications skills.

More specialized courses offered at the high school level, such as electronics, electricity, automotive/engine repair, or computer applications provide the opportunity to increase understanding of how machines work and gain hands-on experience with them. Any other courses or clubs that make use of flow charts, schematic reading, or audiovisual equipment can also be beneficial.

Since technology changes so quickly, some postsecondary education is recommended for newcomers to this field. Educational requirements vary across employers. Small repair shops, for example, might only require in-depth knowledge and some experience, which an individual could obtain on his or her own. Large corporations or computer companies, however, usually require at least one or two years of courses in mechanics or electronics from a city college or technical/vocational school.

Individuals interested in computer and peripheral repair should choose courses involving the nuts and bolts of computer technology (not just computer software applications), such as microelectronics and computer design. Some technical schools already offer a two-year degree in computer technology. While some office machine service technicians can find employment without a two-year degree, a computer-related two-year degree is required for technicians seeking to specialize in computer repair. The additional educational requirements include courses in elementary computer programming and the physics of heat and light.

Certification is not required by most employers of service technicians, but voluntary certification programs do exist through the International Society of Certified Electronics Technicians and the Institute for Certification of Computing Professionals. Individuals can take exams in order to be certified in fields such as computer, industrial, and commercial equipment. Although not required, voluntary certification can give an individual an edge if job competition is tight.

Regardless of educational background, service technicians receive heavy doses of on-the-job training aimed at familiarizing employees with the machines most often used by the company or its customers. Training programs vary greatly in duration and intensity. Some are self-study while others are conducted in classrooms. Most include both theoretical and more practical, hands-on sessions.

Computer and office machine technicians have to be motivated to keep up with modern computer and office machine technology. Machines rapidly become obsolete, and so does the service technician's training. As soon as new equipment is installed, service technicians must demonstrate the intellectual agility to learn how to handle problems that might arise.

Opportunities for Experience & Exploration

Students interested in a career in computer and office machine service should investigate the possibility of spending a day at a local technical school attending mechanics or electronics courses. This experience might help students develop a better feel for the specific content of the career and determine their interest level in it.

Students should also seek the help of a guidance counselor in arranging an on-the-job visit with a working service technician. In this way, students can see firsthand what the ins and outs of a typical day in this career might be. In addition, they might volunteer to tinker around with household machines, such as VCRs or car engines, to test their manual aptitude for such maintenance and repair. Students might decide to take related courses in high school and even at technical schools during summer vacations.

Methods of Entering

Graduates of city colleges or technical/vocational schools often find their first positions through the school's placement center. Employers regularly work directly with placement officers in order to find the best qualified service technicians. Other qualified individuals can identify potential employers by reading the classified ads. They can then write, call, or visit these companies in order to obtain an interview. Voluntary certification, as previously discussed, can boost an individual's chances of obtaining an interview. Prospective servicers should ask friends and family to watch for related job openings in their companies. Individuals already working as servicers can also be good sources of information about job openings.

Experience is an extremely important qualification to have in the job-hunting process. Prospective service technicians should try to gain experience in small, local repair shops by working after school, on weekends, or during summer vacations. Another way to expand technical experience is by volunteering to repair friends' and relatives' household appliances. These kinds of experience round out job applicants' qualifications and make them more attractive to employers.

Advancement

The field of computer and office machine service offers a variety of advancement opportunities, particularly because of the tremendous growth in computer products. Service technicians usually start working on relatively simple maintenance and repair tasks. Over time, they start working on more complicated projects.

Experienced service technicians may advance to positions of increased responsibility. They become supervisors of service crews or managers of service departments or small service companies. This type of promotion is usually reserved for individuals with strong communications skills; supervisors and managers talk at length with both servicers and customers, each of whom understand the products at very different levels. Supervisors and managers also have strong organizational and prioritizing skills and generally have had service experience in a wide range of areas.

Another advancement route a service technician may take is to become a sales representative for the manufacturer of a company whose product he or she has had extensive experience with. Technicians develop hands-on knowledge of particular machines and are thus often in the best position to advise potential buyers about important purchasing decisions.

Some entrepreneurial-minded servicers might open their own repair business, which can be risky but can also provide many rewards. Unless they fill a certain market niche, technicians usually find it necessary to service a wide range of computers and office machines.

Employment Outlook

Demand for computer service technicians is expected to increase much faster than average through the year 2006. Employment of office machine repairers is expected to grow about as fast as the average for all occupations through the year 2006.

While demand for computer and office machine service technicians will be higher than the national average, it is predicted that employment growth will not match the expected increase in the amount of equipment produced. This is a result of the increased reliability of the equipment, as well as the ease of its repair.

Large corporations with in-house repair departments will increase their demand for well-rounded servicers, those who can maintain and repair computers as well as office machines. Computer companies and service contractors will look for people with strong computer backgrounds in education or professional experience.

The key for individuals interested in this field: keep up with technology and be flexible.

Earnings

According to the Bureau of Labor Statistics, in 1996, average annual earnings for electronic equipment repairers ranged from a low of $17,108 to $50,908 for technicians who generally have many years of experience. Office machine repairers earned average salaries of $30,264 per year in 1996, according to the *1998-99 Occupational Outlook Handbook*. Technicians who develop expertise in certain machinery or product lines may make even more. Within this range, servicers who specialize in computers and computer-related equipment tend to make the most money in this field. Simply put, the highest salaries go to those who work on the most complicated machines.

Service technicians who work for computer companies or large corporations usually enjoy benefits such as health care, sick leave, and paid vacations. The benefits of employees of smaller businesses vary with the employer. In addition, some service technicians have the opportunity to earn bonuses by selling service contracts or for consistently high performance.

Conditions of Work

Working conditions are generally quite good for computer and office machine service technicians since most equipment is located in air-conditioned, well-lighted, and comfortable environments. Some of the bigger machinery, such as mail sorters or check-processing units, can be noisy, however. Some maintenance and repair work can be messy, involving grease and oil. In these cases, servicers wear work uniforms, often provided by employers, or their own casual clothes. The most strenuous labor usually involves moving the bigger machines around during installation or major repairs and overhauls. In some instances, servicers are required to work around extremely high voltages and are required to know related safety procedures and regulations. Field servicers often travel from one location to another to perform their duties, usually by car. Others work primarily in their employers' service centers.

Many service technicians work during regular business hours. In certain service departments, servicers take turns being on call during off-hours in case of requests for emergency service. When major installation and repair projects are being completed, some servicers may be required to work overtime. On-call hours and overtime are compensated, either by extra paid vacation or increased hourly wages.

Sources of Additional Information

For information about certification in the field of computer and office machine service, contact:

■ **Institute for the Certification of Computing Professionals**
2200 East Devon Avenue, Suite 247
Des Plaines, IL 60018
Tel: 847-229-4227

International Society of Certified Electronics Technicians
2708 West Berry Street, Suite 3
Fort Worth, TX 76109-2356
Tel: 817-921-9101
WWW: http://www.iscet.mainland.cc.tx.us

*For information about computer and office machine
service careers, accredited schools, and employers,
contact:*

Association for Computing Machinery
11 West 42nd Street, 3rd Floor
New York, NY 10036
Tel: 800-342-6626
Email: acmhelp@acm.org
WWW: http://info.acm.org/

Electronics Technicians Association, International
602 North Jackson Street
Greencastle, IN 46135
Tel: 317-653-8262
WWW: http://serv2.fwi.com/~n9pdt

Construction Inspectors

Definition

Construction inspectors work for federal, state, and local governments. Their job is to examine the construction, alteration, or repair of highways, streets, sewer and water systems, dams, bridges, buildings, and other structures to ensure that they comply with the building codes and ordinances, zoning regulations, and contract specifications.

Nature of the Work

This occupation is made up of four broad categories of specialization: building, electrical, mechanical, and public works. *Building inspectors* examine the structural quality of buildings. They check the plans before construction, visit the work site a number of times during construction, and make a final inspection when the project is completed. Some building inspectors specialize in areas such as structural steel or reinforced concrete buildings.

Electrical inspectors visit work sites to inspect the installation of electrical systems and equipment. They check wiring, lighting, generators, and sound and security systems. They may also inspect the wiring for elevators, heating and air-conditioning systems, kitchen appliances, and other electrical installations.

Mechanical inspectors inspect plumbing systems and the mechanical components of heating and air-conditioning equipment and kitchen appliances. They also examine gas tanks, piping, and gas-fired appliances. Some mechanical inspectors specialize in elevators, plumbing, or boilers.

Elevator inspectors inspect both the mechanical and the electrical features of lifting and conveying devices, such as elevators, escalators, and moving sidewalks. They also test their speed, load allowances, brakes, and safety devices.

Plumbing inspectors inspect plumbing installations, water supply systems, drainage and sewer systems, water heater

School Subjects
Mathematics
Shop (Trade/Vo-tech education)

Personal Interests
Building things
Fixing things

Work Environment
Indoors and outdoors
Primarily multiple locations

Minimum Education Level
High school diploma

Salary Range
$21,600 to
$33,700 to
$55,800

Certification or Licensing
Recommended

Outlook
As fast as the average

DOT
182

GOE
05.03.06

NOC
2264

installations, fire sprinkler systems, and air and gas piping systems; they also examine building sites for soil type to determine water table level, seepage rate, and other conditions.

Heating and refrigeration inspectors examine heating, ventilating, air-conditioning, and refrigeration installations in new buildings and approve alteration plans for those elements in existing buildings.

Public works inspectors make sure that government construction of water and sewer systems, highways, streets, bridges, and dams conforms to contract specifications. They visit work sites to inspect excavations, mixing and pouring of concrete, and asphalt paving. They also keep records of the amount of work performed and the materials used so that proper payment can be made. These inspectors may specialize in highways, reinforced concrete, or ditches.

Construction inspectors use measuring devices and other test equipment, take photographs, keep a daily log of their work, and write reports. If any detail of a project does not comply with the various codes, ordinances, or contract specifications, or if construction is being done without proper permits, the inspectors have the authority to issue a stop-work order.

Requirements

People interested in construction inspection must be high school graduates who have taken courses in drafting, algebra, geometry, and English. Employers prefer graduates of an apprenticeship program or a community or junior college or people with at least two years toward an engineering or architectural degree. Required courses include construction technology, blueprint reading, technical math, English, and building inspection.

Most construction inspectors have several years' experience either as a construction contractor or supervisor, or as a craft or trade worker such as a carpenter, electrician, plumber, or pipefitter. This experience shows a knowledge of construction materials and practices, which is necessary in inspections.

Construction inspectors receive most of their training on the job. The first few weeks are spent under the supervision of an experienced inspector. Then the new inspector is put to work on a simple project, such as a residence, and is gradually advanced to more complex types of construction.

Some states require certification for employment. Inspectors can earn a certificate by passing examinations on construction techniques, materials, and code requirements. The exams are offered by three model code organizations: International Conference of Building Officials; Building Officials and Code Administra-

tors International, Inc.; and Southern Building Code Congress International, Inc.

Construction inspectors are expected to have a valid driver's license as they must be able to travel to and from the construction sites. They must also pass a civil service exam.

Opportunities for Experience & Exploration

Field trips to construction sites and interviews with contractors or building trade officials are good ways to gain practical information about what it is like to work in the industry and how best to prepare for it.

Summer jobs at a construction site provide an overview of the work involved in a building project. Students may also seek part-time jobs with a general contracting company, with a specialized contractor (such as a plumbing or electrical contractor), or as a carpenter's helper. Jobs in certain supply houses will help students become familiar with construction materials.

Methods of Entering

People without postsecondary education usually enter the construction industry as a trainee or apprentice. Information about apprenticeships and training programs may be obtained from local contractors, building trade unions, or school vocational counselors. Graduates of technical schools or colleges of construction and engineering may expect to start work as an engineering aide, drafter, estimator, or assistant engineer. Jobs may be found through school placement offices, employment agencies, and unions or by applying directly to contracting company personnel offices. Application may also be made directly to the employment offices of the federal, state, or local government.

Advancement

An engineering degree is usually required to become a supervisory inspector.

The federal, state, and large city governments provide formal training programs for their construction inspectors to keep them abreast of new building code developments and to broaden their knowledge of construction materials, practices, and inspection techniques. Inspectors for small agencies can upgrade their skills by attending state-conducted training programs or taking college or correspondence courses.

Employment Outlook

In 1996, federal, state, and local governments employed approximately 66,000 construction and building inspectors in the United States; more than half of these inspectors work in municipal and county building departments. Large inspection staffs are employed by cities and suburbs that are experiencing rapid growth. Federal inspectors may work for such agencies as the Department of Defense or the Departments of Housing and Urban Development, Agriculture, and the Interior.

The demand for government construction inspectors is expected to grow as fast as the average for all occupations through the year 2006. There will likely be increased construction activity, as well as a rising concern for public safety and improved quality of construction. Some responsibilities handled by inspectors will be assumed by engineers, construction managers, and maintenance supervisors. The level of new construction fluctuates with the economy, but maintenance and renovation continue during the downswings, so inspectors are rarely laid off.

Earnings

In 1996, inspectors made an average of $33,700 a year, according to the U.S. Department of Labor. Salaries ranged between $21,600 and $55,800. Building inspectors earn slightly more than other inspectors. Salaries are slightly higher in the North and West than in the South and are considerably higher in large metropolitan areas.

Conditions of Work

Construction inspectors work both indoors and outdoors, dividing their time between their offices and the work sites. Inspection sites are dirty and cluttered with tools, machinery, and debris. Although the work is not considered hazardous, inspectors must climb ladders and stairs and crawl under buildings.

The hours are usually regular, but when there is an accident at a site, the inspector has to remain on the job until reports have been completed. The work is steady year-round, not seasonal as are some other construction occupations. In slow construction periods, the inspectors are kept busy examining the renovation of older buildings.

Sources of Additional Information

■Building Officials and Code Administrators International, Inc.
4051 West Flossmoor Road
Country Club Hills, IL 60478
Tel: 708-799-2300
WWW: http://www.bocai.org

■Canadian Construction Association
65 Albert Street, 10th Floor
Ottawa, ON K1P 6A4 Canada
Tel: 613-236-9455

■International Conference of Building Officials
5360 South Workman Mill Road
Whittier, CA 90601-2298
Tel: 310-699-0541
WWW: http://www.icbo.org

■Southern Building Code Congress International, Inc.
900 Montclair Road
Birmingham, AL 35213
Tel: 205-591-1853

Cooks, Chefs, and Bakers

Definition

Cooks, chefs, and *bakers* are employed in the preparation and cooking of food, usually in large quantities, in hotels, restaurants, cafeterias, and other establishments and institutions.

Nature of the Work

Cooks and chefs are primarily responsible for the preparation and cooking of foods. Chefs usually supervise the work of cooks; however, the skills required and the job duties performed by each may vary depending upon the size and type of establishment.

Cooks and chefs begin by planning menus in advance. They estimate the amount of food that will be required for a specified period of time, order it from various suppliers, and check it for quantity and quality when it arrives. Following recipes or their own instincts, they measure and mix ingredients for soups, salads, gravies, sauces, casseroles, and desserts. They prepare meats, poultry, fish, vegetables, and other foods for baking, roasting, broiling, and steaming. They may use blenders, mixers, grinders, slicers, or tenderizers to prepare the food; and ovens, broilers, grills, roasters, or steam kettles to cook it. During the mixing and cooking, cooks and chefs rely on their judgment and experience to add seasonings; they constantly taste and smell food being cooked and must know when it is cooked properly. To fill orders, they carve meat, arrange food portions on serving plates, and add appropriate gravies, sauces, or garnishes.

Some larger establishments employ specialized cooks, such as *banquet cooks, pastry cooks,* and *broiler cooks.* The *Garde Manger* designs and prepares buffets, and *pantry cooks* prepare cold dishes for lunch and dinner. Other specialists are *raw shellfish preparers* and *carvers.*

In smaller establishments without specialized cooks or kitchen helpers, the general cooks may have to do some of the

School Subjects
Family and Consumer Science
Mathematics

Personal Interests
Food/Cooking

Work Environment
Primarily indoors
Primarily one location

Minimum Education Level
Some postsecondary training
Apprenticeship

Salary Range
$12,480 to
$16,640 to
$38,000+

Certification or Licensing
Required for certain positions

Outlook
About as fast as the average

DOT
313, 315

preliminary work themselves, such as washing, peeling, cutting, and shredding vegetables and fruits; cutting, trimming, and boning meat; cleaning and preparing poultry, fish, and shellfish; and baking bread, rolls, cakes, and pastries.

Commercial cookery is usually done in large quantities, and many cooks, including *school cafeteria cooks* and *mess cooks,* are trained in "quantity cookery" methods. Numerous establishments today are noted for their specialties in foods, and some cooks work exclusively in the preparation and cooking of exotic dishes, very elaborate meals, or some particular creation of their own for which they have become famous. Restaurants that feature national cuisines may employ *international and regional cuisine specialty cooks.*

In the larger commercial kitchens, chefs may be responsible for the work of a number of cooks, each preparing and cooking food in specialized areas. They may, for example, employ expert cooks who specialize in frying, baking, roasting, broiling, or sauce cookery. Cooks are often titled by the kinds of specialized cooking they do, such as fry, vegetable, or pastry. Chefs have the major responsibility for supervising the overall preparation and cooking of the food.

Other duties of chefs may include training cooks on the job, planning menus, pricing food for menus, and purchasing food. Chefs may be responsible for determining portion weights to be prepared and served. Among their other duties they may supervise the work of all members of the kitchen staff. The kitchen staff may assist by washing, cleaning, and preparing foods for cooking; cleaning utensils, dishes, and silverware; and assisting in many ways with the overall order and cleanliness of the kitchen. Most chefs spend part of their time striving to create new recipes that will win the praise of customers and build their reputations as experts. Many, like *pastry chefs* and *ice-cream chefs* focus their attention on particular kinds of food.

Expert chefs who have a number of years of experience behind them may be employed as *executive chefs.* These chefs do little cooking or food preparation. Their main responsibilities are management and supervision. Executive chefs interview, hire, and dismiss all kitchen personnel, and they are sometimes responsible for the dining room waiters, waitresses, and other employees as well. These chefs consult with the restaurant manager regarding the profit and loss of the food service and ways to increase business and cut costs. A part of their time is spent inspecting equipment. Executive chefs are in charge of all food services for special functions such as banquets and parties, and many hours are spent in the coordination of the work for these activities. They may supervise the special chefs and assist them in planning elaborate arrangements and creations in food preparation. Executive chefs may be assisted by *sous chefs.*

Smaller restaurants may employ only one or two cooks and kitchen helpers to assist them. Cooks and helpers work together to prepare all the food for cooking and keep the kitchen clean. Because smaller restaurants and public eating places usually offer standard menus with little variation, the cook's job becomes standardized. Such establishments may employ *specialty cooks, barbecue cooks, pizza bakers, food order expediters, kitchen food assemblers,* or *counter supply workers.* In some restaurants food is cooked as it is ordered; cooks preparing food in this manner are known as *short-order cooks.*

Regardless of the duties performed, cooks and chefs are largely responsible for the reputation and monetary profit or loss of the eating establishment in which they are employed.

Bakers perform work similar to that of cooks and chefs as they prepare breads, rolls, muffins, biscuits, pies, cakes, cookies, and pastries. Bakers may be supervised by a *head baker.* In large establishments, *second bakers* may supervise other bakers who work with a particular type of baked goods. Bakers are often assisted by *baker helpers.*

Requirements

The occupation of chef, cook, or baker has specific training requirements. Many cooks start out as kitchen helpers and acquire their skills on the job, but the trend today is to obtain training through high schools, vocational schools, or community colleges. Professional associations and trade unions sometimes offer apprenticeship programs; one example is the three-year apprenticeship program administered by the local offices of the American Culinary Federation in cooperation with local employers and community colleges or vocational schools. Some large hotels and restaurants have their own training programs for new employees. The armed forces also offer good training and experience.

The amount of training required varies with the position. It takes only a short time to become an assistant or a fry cook, for example, but it requires many years of training and experience to acquire the skills necessary to become an executive chef or cook in a fine restaurant.

Although a high school diploma is not required, it is an asset to job applicants. For those planning a career as a chef or head cook, courses in business mathematics and business administration are useful.

Culinary students spend most of their time learning to prepare food through hands-on practice. At the same time, they learn how to use and care for kitchen equipment. Training programs often include courses in menu planning, determining portion size, food cost control, purchasing food supplies in quantity, selecting and storing food, and using leftovers. Students also learn hotel and restaurant sanitation and public health rules for handling food. Courses offered by private vocational schools, professional associations, and university programs often emphasize training in supervisory and management skills.

A successful chef or cook should have a keen interest in food preparation and cooking and have a desire to experiment in developing new recipes and new food combinations. Cooks, chefs, and bakers should be able to work as part of a team and to work under pressure during rush hours, in close quarters and with a certain amount of noise and confusion. These employees need a mild temperament and patience to contend with the public daily and also to work closely with many other kinds of employees.

Immaculate personal cleanliness and good health are necessities in this trade. Applicants should possess physical stamina and be without serious physical impairments because of the mobility and activity the work requires. These employees spend many working hours standing, walking, and moving about.

Chefs, cooks, and bakers must possess a keen sense of taste and smell. Hand and finger agility, hand-eye coordination, and a good memory are helpful. An artistic flair and creative talents in working with food are definitely strengths in this trade.

The principal union for cooks and chefs is the Hotel Employees and Restaurant Employees International Union (AFL-CIO).

To protect the public's health, chefs, cooks, and bakers are required by law in most states to possess a health certificate and to be examined periodically. These examinations, usually given by the state board of health, make certain that the individual is free from communicable diseases and skin infections.

Opportunities for Experience & Exploration

You may explore your interest in cooking by getting part-time or summer jobs in a fast food or other restaurant, or in an institutional kitchen as a sandwich or salad maker, soda-fountain attendant, kitchen helper, or waitperson where you can observe the work of chefs and cooks.

Practicing and experimenting with cooking at home and in high school home economics courses is another way of testing your interest in becoming a cook, chef, or baker.

Methods of Entering

Apprenticeship programs are one method of entering the trade. These programs usually offer the beginner sound basic training and a regular salary. Upon completion of the apprenticeship, cooks may be hired full time in their place of training or assisted in finding employment with another establishment. Cooks are hired as chefs only after they have acquired a number of years of experience. Cooks who have been formally trained through public or private trade or vocational schools or in culinary institutes may be able to take advantage of school placement services.

In many cases, a cook begins as a kitchen helper or cook's helper and, through experience gained in on-the-job training, is able to move into the job of cook. To do this, the person sometimes starts out in a small restaurant, perhaps as a short-order cook, grill cook, or sandwich or salad maker, and transfers to larger establishments as he or she gains experience.

School cafeteria workers who want to become cooks may have an opportunity to receive food-services training. Many school districts, with the cooperation of school food-services divisions of the state departments of education, provide on-the-job training and sometimes summer workshops for interested cafeteria employees. Similar programs are offered by some community colleges, state departments of education, and school associations. Cafeteria workers who have completed these training programs are often selected to fill positions as cooks.

Job opportunities may be located through employment bureaus, trade associations, unions, contacts with friends, newspaper want ads, or local offices of the state employment service. Another method is to apply directly to restaurants or hotels. Small restaurants, school cafeterias, and other eating places with simple food preparation will provide the greatest number of starting jobs for cooks. Job applicants who have had courses in commercial food preparation will have an advantage in large restaurants and hotels, where hiring standards are often high.

Advancement

Advancement depends on the skill, training, experience, originality, and ambition of the individual. It also depends somewhat on the general business climate and employment trends.

Cooks with experience can advance by moving to other places of employment for higher wages or to establishments looking for someone with a specialized skill in preparing a particular kind of food. Cooks who have a number of years of successful job experience may find chef positions open to them; however, in some cases it may take ten or fifteen years to obtain such a position, depending on personal qualifications and other employment factors.

Expert cooks who have obtained supervisory responsibilities as head cooks or chefs may advance to positions as executive chefs or to other types of managerial work. Some go into business for themselves as caterers or restaurant owners; others may become instructors in vocational programs in high schools, colleges, or other academic institutions.

Employment Outlook

In 1996, approximately 3,400,000 cooks, chefs, and bakers worked in the United States. Most work in restaurants and other retail eating establishments, but many work in hotels, schools, colleges, airports, and hospitals. Still others are employed by government agencies, factories, private clubs, and other organizations.

The employment of chefs, cooks, and bakers will experience about as fast as the average growth through 2006, compared with all other occupations. Openings will be plentiful as the industry expands in response to the increased population (especially the growing 55-and-over segment) and the strong economy. As people earn higher incomes and have more leisure time, they dine out more often and take more vacations. The families of working women will also dine out frequently as a convenience. There is also a high degree of turnover in this field because of the minimal training and education requirements. Many job openings occur annually as older, experienced workers retire, die, or transfer to other occupations.

Earnings

The salaries earned by chefs and cooks are widely divergent and depend on many factors, such as the size, type, and location of the establishment, and the skill, experience, training, and specialization of the worker. Salaries are usually pretty standard among the same type of establishment. For example, restaurants and diners serving inexpensive meals and a sandwich-type menu generally pay cooks less than establishments with medium-priced or expensive menus. The highest wages are earned in large, well-known restaurants and hotels in urban areas.

According to a survey by the National Restaurant Association, the median salary for cooks in 1995 was about $14,560, with most earning between $12,480 and $16,640. The median salary for bread and pastry bakers is $13,520, with most earning between $12,480 and $16,120. Fast food workers generally earn the minimum wage. Cooks and chefs in famous restaurants, of course, earn much more; many executive chefs may be paid $38,000 a year or more.

Chefs and cooks usually receive their meals free during working hours and are furnished with any necessary job uniforms.

Conditions of Work

Working conditions vary with the place of employment. Many kitchens are modern, well lighted, well equipped, and air-conditioned, but some older, smaller eating places may be only marginally equipped. The work of cooks can be strenuous, with long hours of standing, lifting heavy pots, and working near hot ovens and ranges. Possible hazards include falls, cuts, and burns, although serious injury is uncommon. Even in the most modern kitchens, cooks, chefs, and bakers usually work amid considerable noise from the operation of equipment and machinery.

Experienced cooks may work with little or no supervision, depending on the size of the food service and the place of employment. Less experienced cooks may work under much more direct supervision from expert cooks or chefs.

Chefs, cooks, and bakers may work a forty- or forty-eight-hour week, depending on the type of food service offered and certain union agreements. Some food establishments are open twenty-four hours a day, while others may be open from the very early morning until late in the evening. Establishments open long hours may have two or three work shifts, with some chefs and cooks working day schedules while others work evenings.

All food-service workers may have to work overtime hours, depending on the amount of business and rush-hour trade. These employees work many weekends and holidays, although they may have a day off every week or rotate with other employees to have alternate weekends free. Many cooks are required to work early morning or late evening shifts. For example, doughnuts, breads, and muffins for breakfast service must be baked by 6:00 or 7:00 AM, which requires bakers to begin work at 2:00 or 3:00 AM. Some people will find it very difficult to adjust to working such late and irregular hours.

Sources of Additional Information

For a directory of accredited schools offering programs in culinary art, contact:

Accrediting Commission of Career Schools and Colleges of Technology
2101 Wilson Boulevard, Suite 302
Arlington, VA 22201

American Culinary Federation
10 SanBartola Drive
St. Augustine, FL 32085
Tel: 904-824-4468
Email: acf@aug.com
WWW: http://www.acfchefs.org

American Institute of Baking
1213 Bakers Way, PO Box 3999
Manhattan, KS 66505-3999
Tel: 785-537-4750
Email: information@aibonline.org

Bakery Council of Canada
885 Don Mills Road, Suite 301
Don Mills, ON M3C 1V9 Canada
Tel: 416-510-8041

British Columbia Chefs Association
PO Box 2007
Vancouver, BC V6B 3P8 Canada
Tel: 604-538-4547

Chefs de Cuisine Association of America
155 East 55th Street, Suite 302B
New York, NY 10022
Tel: 212-832-4939

Culinary Institute of America
433 Albany Post Road
Hyde Park, NY 12538-1499
Tel: 914-452-9600
WWW: http://www.ciachef.edu

Educational Foundation of the National Restaurant Association
250 South Wacker Drive, Suite 1400
Chicago, IL 60606
Tel: 312-715-1010
WWW: http://www.restaurant.org

Educational Institute of the American Hotel and Motel National Association
PO Box 1240
East Lansing, MI 48826
Tel: 517-353-5500
WWW: http://www.ei-ahma.org

Corrections Officers

Definition

Corrections officers guard people who have been arrested and are awaiting trial or who have been tried, convicted, and sentenced to serve time in a penal institution. They search prisoners and their cells for weapons, drugs, and other contraband; inspect windows, doors, locks, and gates for signs of tampering; observe the conduct and behavior of inmates to prevent disturbances or escapes; and make verbal or written reports to superior officers. Corrections officers assign work to inmates and supervise their activities. They guard prisoners who are being transported between jails, courthouses, mental institutions, or other destinations, and supervise prisoners receiving visitors. When necessary, these workers use weapons or force to maintain discipline and order.

Nature of the Work

The corrections officer is concerned with the safekeeping of persons who have been arrested and are awaiting trial or who have been tried, found guilty, and are serving time in a correctional institution. Corrections officers maintain order in accordance with an institution's policies, regulations, and procedures.

To prevent disturbances or escapes, corrections officers carefully observe the conduct and behavior of the inmates at all times. They watch for forbidden activities and infractions of the rules, as well as for poor attitudes or unsatisfactory adjustment to prison life on the part of the inmates. They try to settle disputes before violence can erupt. They may search the prisoners or their living quarters for weapons or drugs and inspect locks, bars on windows and doors, and gates for any evidence of tampering. The inmates are under guard constantly while eating, sleeping, exercising, bathing, and working. They are counted periodically to be sure all are present. Some officers are stationed on towers and at gates to prevent escapes. All rule violations and anything out of the ordinary are reported to a

---

School Subjects
Physical education
Psychology

Personal Interests
Helping people: protection
Law

Work Environment
Primarily indoors
Primarily one location

Minimum Education Level
High school diploma

Salary Range
$20,200 to
$33,540 to
$50,000

Certification or Licensing
Voluntary

Outlook
Much faster than the average

DOT
372

GOE
04.01.01

NOC
6462

superior officer such as a *chief jailer.* In case of a major disturbance, corrections officers may use weapons or force to restore order.

Corrections officers give work assignments to prisoners, supervise them as they carry out their duties, and instruct them in unfamiliar tasks. Corrections officers are responsible for the physical needs of the prisoners, such as providing or obtaining meals and medical aid. They assure the health and safety of the inmates by checking the cells for unsanitary conditions and fire hazards.

These workers may escort inmates from their cells to the prison's visiting room, medical office, or chapel. Certain officers, called *patrol conductors,* guard prisoners who are being transported between courthouses, prisons, mental institutions, or other destinations, either by van, car, or public transportation. Officers at a penal institution may also screen visitors at the entrance and accompany them to other areas within the facility. From time to time, they may inspect mail addressed to prisoners, checking for contraband, help investigate crimes committed within the prison, or aid in the search for escapees.

Some *police officers* specialize in guarding juvenile offenders being held at a police station house or detention room pending a hearing, transfer to a correctional institution, or return to their parents. They often investigate the background of first offenders to check for a criminal history or to make a recommendation to the magistrate regarding disposition of the case. Lost or runaway children are also placed in the care of these officers until their parents or guardians can be located.

Immigration guards guard aliens held by the immigration service awaiting investigation, deportation, or release. *Gate tenders* check the identification of all persons entering and leaving the penal institution.

In most correctional institutions, psychologists and social workers are employed to counsel inmates with mental and emotional problems. It is an important part of a corrections officer's job, however, to supplement this with informal counseling. Officers may help inmates adjust to prison life, prepare for return to civilian life, and avoid committing crimes in the future. On a more immediate level, they may arrange for an inmate to visit the library, help inmates get in touch with their families, suggest where to look for a job after release from prison, or discuss personal problems. In some institutions, corrections officers may lead more formal group counseling sessions. As they fulfill more rehabilitative roles, corrections officers are increasingly required to possess a college-level education in psychology, criminology, or related areas of study.

Corrections officers keep a daily record of their activities and make regular reports, either verbal or written, to their supervisors. These reports concern the behavior of the inmates and the quality and quantity of work they do, as well as any disturbances, rule violations, and unusual occurrences that may have taken place.

Head corrections officers supervise and coordinate other corrections officers. They perform roll call and assign duties to the officers, direct the activities of groups of inmates, arrange the release and transfer of prisoners in accordance with the instructions on a court order, maintain security and investigate disturbances among the inmates, maintain prison records and prepare reports, and review and evaluate the performance of their subordinates.

In small communities, corrections officers (who are sometimes called *jailers*) may also act as deputy sheriffs or police officers when they are not occupied with guard duties.

Requirements

Candidates for the occupation of corrections officer generally must be at least eighteen to twenty-one years of age and have a high school diploma or its equivalent. Individuals with less than a high school education may be considered for employment if they have qualifying work experience. Probation and parole experience are considered related work experience. Many states and correctional facilities prefer or require officers with postsecondary training in psychology, criminology, or related areas of study. Military experience or related work experiences is also required by some state governments. On the federal level, applicants should have at least two years of college or two years of work or military experience. Other requirements include good health and physical strength, and many states have set minimum height, vision, and hearing standards. Sound judgment and the ability to think and act quickly are important qualities for this occupation. All candidates must have a clean arrest record.

Training for corrections officers ranges from the special academy instruction provided by the federal government and some states to the informal, on-the-job training furnished by most states and local governments. The Federal Bureau of Prisons operates a training center in Glynco, Georgia, where new hires generally undergo a three-week program of basic corrections education. Training academies have programs that last from four to eight weeks and instruct trainees on institutional policies, regulations, and procedures; the behavior and custody of inmates; security measures; and report writing. Training in self-defense, the use of firearms and other weapons, and emergency medical techniques is often provided. On-the-job trainees spend two to six months or more under the supervision of an experienced officer. During that period of time, they receive in-house training while gaining actual experience. Periodically, corrections officers may be given additional training as new ideas and procedures in criminal justice are developed.

Some states require applicants to have one or two years of previous experience in corrections or related police work. A few states require passing a written examination. Corrections officers who work for the federal government and most state governments are covered by civil service systems or merit boards and may be required to pass a competitive exam for employment. Many states require random or comprehensive drug testing of their officers, either during hiring procedures or while employed at the facility.

Opportunities for Experience & Exploration

Because of age requirements and the nature of the work, there are no opportunities for high school students to gain actual experience while still in school. Where the minimum age requirement is twenty-one, prospective corrections officers may prepare for employment by taking college courses in criminal justice or police science. Enrollment in a two- or four-year college degree program in a related field is encouraged. Military service may also offer experience and training in corrections. Social work is another way to gain experience. Students may also look into obtaining a civilian job as a clerk or other worker for the police department or other protective service organization. Related part-time, volunteer, or summer work may also be available in psychiatric hospitals and other institutions providing physical and emotional counseling and services.

The ability to speak foreign languages is often a plus when applying for corrections jobs. Many on-line services also have forums for corrections officers and other public safety employees, and these may provide opportunities to read about and communicate with people active in this career.

Methods of Entering

To apply for a job as a corrections officer, contact federal or state civil service commissions, state departments of correction, or local correctional facilities and ask for information about entrance requirements, training, and job opportunities. Private contractors and other companies are also a growing source of employment opportunities. Many officers enter this field from social work areas and parole and probation positions.

Advancement

With additional education and training, experienced officers may qualify for promotion to head corrections officer or advancement to some other supervisory or administrative position, and eventually may become *prison directors*. Some officers transfer to related fields, such as law, law enforcement, or probation and parole.

Employment Outlook

The prison population has more than doubled in the last ten years, and this growth is expected to be sustained for the near future. The increasing number of prisoners means there will be a strong need for new corrections officers. Of the more than 320,000 corrections officers employed in the United States, roughly 60 percent work in state-run correctional facilities such as prisons, prison camps, and reformatories. Most of the rest are employed at city and county jails or other institutions, while a few thousand work for the federal government. An increasing number are employed by private corrections contractors.

Employment in this field is expected to increase much faster than the average for all jobs. It is estimated that another 120,000 jobs will be created through the year 2006. The ongoing war on illegal drugs, new tough-on-crime legislation, and increasing mandatory sentencing policies will create a need for more prison beds and more corrections officers. The extremely crowded conditions in today's correctional institutions have created a need for more corrections officers to guard the inmates more closely and relieve the tensions. A greater number of officers will also be required as a result of the expansion or new construction of facilities. As prison sentences become longer through mandatory minimum sentences set by state law, the number of prisons needed will increase. In addition, many job openings will occur from a characteristically high turnover rate, as well as from the need to fill vacancies caused by the death or retirement of older workers. Traditionally, correction agencies have difficulty attracting qualified employees due to job location and salary considerations.

Because security must be maintained at correctional facilities at all times, corrections officers can depend on steady employment. They are not usually affected by poor economic conditions or changes in government spending. Corrections officers are rarely laid off, even when budgets need to be trimmed. Instead, because of high turnovers, staffs can be cut quickly simply by not replacing those officers who leave.

Most jobs will be found in relatively large institutions located near metropolitan areas, although opportunities for corrections officers exist in jails and other smaller facilities throughout the country. The increasing use of private companies and privately run prisons may limit somewhat the growth of jobs in this field as these companies are more likely to keep a close eye on the bottom line. Use of new technologies, such as surveillance equipment, automatic gates, and other devices, may also allow institutions to employ fewer officers.

Earnings

There is a wide variation in wages for corrections officers, depending on which level of government employs them. According to a 1996 national survey in *Correction Compendium,* beginning corrections officers received an average of $20,200. The average salary for all corrections officers was $33,540, but salaries range widely from one state to another. In southern California, for example, corrections officers started at $17,300, while Rhode Island corrections officers could earn $41,000 or more.

Beginning corrections officers at the federal level are generally rated GS-6, with a salary range of $21,000 to $28,000 depending on the location of service. Sergeants and other supervisors generally start at $41,000. The average for all federal corrections officers and sergeants is $30,000 per year, and supervisors average more than $50,000. Overtime, night shift, weekend, and holiday pay differentials are generally available at most institutions.

Benefits may include health, disability, and life insurance; uniforms or a cash allowance to buy their own; and sometimes meals and housing. Officers who work for the federal government and for most state governments are covered by civil service systems or merit boards. Some corrections officers also receive retirement and pension plans, and retirement is often available after twenty years of service.

Conditions of Work

Because prison security must be maintained around the clock, work schedules for corrections officers may include nights, weekends, and holidays. The workweek, however, generally consists of five, eight-hour days, except during emergencies, when many officers work overtime.

Corrections officers may work indoors or outdoors, depending on their duties. Conditions can vary even within an institution: some areas are well lighted, ventilated, and temperature-controlled, while others are overcrowded, hot, and noisy. Officers who work outdoors, of course, are subject to all kinds of weather. Correctional institutions occasionally present unpredictable or even hazardous situations. If violence erupts among the inmates, corrections officers may be in danger of injury or death. Although this risk is higher than for most other occupations, corrections work is usually routine.

Corrections officers need physical and emotional strength to cope with the stress inherent in dealing with criminals, many of whom may be dangerous or incapable of change. A correctional officer has to remain alert and aware of the surroundings, prisoners' movements and attitudes, and any potential for danger or violence. Such continual, heightened levels of alertness often create psychological stress for some workers. Most institutions have stress-reduction programs or seminars for their employees, but if not, insurance usually covers some form of therapy for work-related stress.

Sources of Additional Information

■ **The American Correctional Association**
4380 Forbes Boulevard
Lanham, MD 20706
Tel: 301-918-1800

■ **The American Probation and Parole Association**
c/o Council of State Governments
Iron Works Pike
PO Box 11910
Lexington, KY 40578
Tel: 606-244-8203
Email: appa@csg.org

■ **The International Association of Correctional Officers**
Box 53, 1333 South Wabash Avenue
Chicago, IL 60605
Tel: 312-996-5401

Court Reporters

Definition

Court reporters record the testimony given at hearings, trials, depositions, and other legal proceedings. They use stenotype machines to take shorthand notes of public testimony, judicial opinions, sentences of the court, and other courtroom matters. Most court reporters transcribe the notes of the proceedings by using computer-aided transcription systems that print out regular, legible copies of the proceedings.

Nature of the Work

Court reporters are responsible for accurately recording all testimony by witnesses, lawyers, judges, and other participants at legal proceedings. Court reporters use symbols or shorthand forms of complete words in order to record what is said as quickly as it is spoken. People in court may speak at a rate of between 250 and 300 words a minute, and court reporters must record this testimony word for word.

The tool used by court reporters to record these proceedings is called a stenotype machine. The stenotype machine, which resembles a small typewriter, has twenty-four keys on its keyboard, each of which will print a single symbol. Unlike a typewriter, however, the operator of a stenotype machine can press more than one key at a time to print different combinations of symbols. Each symbol or combination represents a different sound, word, or phrase. As testimony is given, the reporter strikes one or more keys to create a phonetic representation of the testimony on a strip of paper, as well as on a computer disk inside the stenotype machine. The court reporter later uses a computer to translate and transcribe the testimony into legible, full-page documents or stores them for reference.

Accurate recording of a trial is vital because the court reporter's record becomes the official transcript for the entire proceeding. In our legal system, court transcripts can be used

School Subjects
English (writing/literature)
Government

Personal Interests
Computers
Foreign language
Law

Work Environment
Primarily indoors
Primarily one location

Minimum Education Level
Some postsecondary training

Salary Range
$15,000 to $56,160 to $70,000+

Certification or Licensing
Required

Outlook
About as fast as the average

DOT
202

GOE
07.05.03

NOC
1244

after the trial for many important purposes. If a legal case is appealed, for example, the court reporter's transcript will become the foundation for any further legal action. The appellate judge will refer to the court reporter's transcript to see what happened in the trial and how the evidence was presented.

Because of the importance of accuracy, a court reporter who misses a word or phrase must interrupt the proceedings to have the words repeated. By the same token, the court reporter may be asked by the judge to read aloud a portion of recorded testimony during the trial to refresh everyone's memory. Court reporters must pay close attention to all the proceedings and be able to hear and understand everything. Sometimes it may be difficult to understand a particular witness or attorney due to poor diction, a strong accent, or a soft speaking voice. Nevertheless, the court reporter cannot be shy about stopping the trial and asking for clarification.

Court reporters must be adept at recording testimony on a wide range of legal issues, from medical malpractice to income tax evasion. In some cases, court reporters may record testimony at a murder trial or a child-custody case. Witnessing tense situations and following complicated arguments are unavoidable parts of the job. The court reporter must be able to remain detached from the drama that unfolds in court while faithfully recording all that is said.

Computers play a large role in helping court reporters fulfill their job responsibilities. Computer programs help convert the symbols and words of a stenotype machine into standard English. This process requires the use of a specially constructed stenotype machine to record the symbols so that they can be fed into the computer. Not only is the computer-based system very efficient and accurate, it also saves time, because the computer can print out a transcript of the trial more quickly than the court reporter can type a transcript on a typewriter or word processor. These transcripts may then be used promptly by a judge or jury before rendering a decision, or after a trial for review purposes.

Many court reporters are employed by city, county, state, or federal courts. Others work for themselves as freelancers or as employees of freelance reporting agencies. These freelance reporters are hired by attorneys to record the pretrial statements, or depositions, of experts and other witnesses. When people want transcripts of other important discussions, freelance reporters may be called on to record what is said at business meetings, large conventions, or similar events.

A new application of court-reporting skills and technology is in the field of television captioning. Using specialized computer-aided transcription systems, reporters can produce captions for live television events, including sporting events and national and local news, for the benefit of hearing-impaired viewers.

Requirements

Court reporters must have a high school diploma or its equivalent. Those interested in this profession should take English and other law or business-related courses in high school. Comprehensive training in grammar and spelling is a must. Training in Latin can also be a great benefit as it increases a court reporter's understanding of the many medical and legal terms that arise during court proceedings. Knowledge of other foreign languages can also be helpful as court reporters often transcribe the testimony of non-English speakers with the aid of court-appointed translators.

Court reporters are required to complete a specialized training program in shorthand reporting. These programs usually last between two and four years and include instruction on how to enter at least 225 words a minute on a stenotype machine. Other topics include computer operations, transcription methods, English grammar, and the principles of law. For court cases involving medical issues, students must also take courses on human anatomy and physiology. Basic medical and legal terms are also explained.

Two- and four-year degree programs in shorthand reporting are offered by over 350 community colleges, private business schools, and four-year colleges. The National Court Reporters Association has approved about 112 of these programs.

Opportunities for Experience & Exploration

Persons interested in pursuing a career as a court reporter are encouraged to talk with professionals already working in the field to learn more about its rewards and responsibilities. Attending actual court sessions is also informative.

Methods of Entering

After completing the required training, court reporters usually work for a freelance reporting company that provides court reporters for business meetings and courtroom proceedings on a temporary basis. Job placement counselors at schools offering training programs often are helpful in locating employment opportunities. Qualified reporters can also contact these freelance reporting companies on their own. Occasionally a court reporter will be hired directly out of school as a courtroom official, but ordinarily only those with several years of experience are hired for full-time judiciary work.

Advancement

Skilled court reporters may be promoted to a larger court system or to an otherwise more demanding position, with an accompanying increase in pay and prestige. Those working for a free-lance company may be hired permanently by a city, county, state, or federal court. Those with experience working in a government position may choose to become a freelance court reporter and thereby have greater job flexibility and perhaps earn more money. Those with the necessary training, experience, and business skills may decide to open their own freelance reporting company.

Employment Outlook

Employment opportunities for skilled court reporters should remain stable through the year 2006. The rising number of criminal court cases and civil lawsuits will cause both state and federal court systems to expand. Though many court proceedings are now videotaped, there still is a need for written transcipts of these cases. Job openings for reporters will also arise due to retirement or attrition, and will be greatest in and around large metropolitan areas.

As always, job prospects will be best for those with the most training and experience. Applicants certified by the National Court Reporters Association will have an edge.

Earnings

Earnings vary depending on the skill, speed, and experience of the court reporter, as well as his or her geographic location. Court reporters just out of school may earn between $15,000 and $25,000 a year. Those who are employed by large court systems generally earn more than their counterparts in smaller communities. Experienced court reporters earned an average salary of $56,160 in 1995, according to the National Court Reporters Association. Court reporters with considerable experience and ability may earn $70,000 a year or more.

Court reporters who work in small communities or as freelancers may not be able to work full-time. Free-lancers are usually not paid a yearly salary but rather earn their wages based on the number of transcript pages they produce. Successful court reporters with jobs in business environments may earn more than those in courtroom settings, but such positions carry less job security.

Those working for the government or full-time for private companies usually receive health insurance and other benefits, such as paid vacations and retirement pensions. Freelancers may or may not receive health insurance or other benefits, depending on the policies of their agencies.

Conditions of Work

Offices and courtrooms are usually pleasant places to work. Under normal conditions, a court reporter can expect to work between 37 and 40 hours per week. During lengthy trials or other complicated proceedings, court reporters often work much longer hours. They must be on hand before and after the court is actually in session and must wait while a jury is deliberating. A court reporter often must be willing to work irregular hours, including some evenings. Court reporters must be able to spend long hours transcribing testimony with complete accuracy. There may be some travel involved, especially for freelance reporters.

Court reporters must be familiar with a wide range of medical and legal terms and must be assertive enough to ask for clarification if a term or phrase goes by without the reporter understanding it. Court reporters must be as unbiased as possible and accurately record what is said, not what they believe to be true. Patience and perfectionism are vital characteristics, as is the ability to work closely with judges and other court officials.

Sources of Additional Information

Career and certification information is available from:

National Court Reporters Association
8224 Old Courthouse Road
Vienna, VA 22182
Tel: 703-556-6272
Email: 72123.3102@compuserve.com
WWW: http://www.verbatimreporters.com

Customs Officials

Definition

Customs officials are federal workers who are employed by the United States Customs Service (an arm of the Treasury Department) to enforce laws governing imports and exports and to combat smuggling and revenue fraud. The U.S. Customs Service generates revenue for the government by assessing and collecting duties and excise taxes on imported merchandise. Amid a whirl of international travel and commercial activity, customs officials process travelers, baggage, cargo, and mail, as well as administer certain navigation laws. Stationed in the United States and overseas at airports, seaports, and all crossings, as well as at points along the Canadian and Mexican borders, customs officials examine, count, weigh, gauge, measure, and sample commercial and non-commercial cargoes entering and leaving the United States. It is their job to determine whether or not goods are admissible and, if so, how much tax or "duty" should be assessed on them. To prevent smuggling, fraud, and cargo theft, customs officials also check the individual baggage declarations of international travelers and oversee the unloading of all types of commercial shipments.

Nature of the Work

Like shrewd detectives, customs officials enforce U.S. Customs Service laws by controlling imports and exports and by combatting smuggling and revenue frauds. They make sure that people, ships, planes, and trains—anything used to import or export cargo—comply with all entrance and clearance requirements at borders and ports. *Customs inspectors* carefully and thoroughly examine cargo to make sure that it matches the description on a ship's or aircraft's manifest. They inspect baggage and personal items worn or carried by travelers entering or leaving the United States by ship, plane, or automobile. Inspectors are authorized to go aboard a ship or plane to determine the exact nature of the

School Subjects
Government
Foreign language

Personal Interests
Helping people: personal service
Law

Work Environment
Primarily indoors
Primarily one location

Minimum Education Level
High school diploma

Salary Range
$24,200 to
$40,020 to
$50,000+

Certification or Licensing
None

Outlook
More slowly than the average

DOT
168

GOE
04.01.02

NOC
1236

cargo being transported. In the course of a single day they review cargo manifests, inspect cargo containers, and supervise unloading activities to prevent smuggling, fraud, or cargo thefts. They may have to weigh and measure imports to see that commerce laws are being followed and to protect American distributors in cases where restricted trademarked merchandise is being brought into the country. In this way, they can protect the interests of American companies.

Customs inspectors examine crew and passenger lists, sometimes in cooperation with the police, who may be searching for criminals. They are authorized to search suspicious individuals and to arrest them if necessary. They are also allowed to conduct body searches of suspected individuals to check for contraband. They check health clearances and ship's documents in an effort to prevent the spread of disease that may require quarantine.

Individual baggage declarations of international travelers also come under their scrutiny. Inspectors who have baggage examination duty at points of entry into the United States classify purchases made abroad and, if necessary, assess and collect duties. All international travelers are allowed to bring home certain quantities of foreign purchases, such as perfume, clothing, tobacco, and liquor, without paying taxes. However, they must declare the amount and value of their purchases on a customs form. If they have made purchases above the duty-free limits, they must pay taxes. Customs inspectors are prepared to advise tourists about U.S. Customs regulations and allow them to change their customs declarations if necessary and pay the duty before baggage inspection. Inspectors must be alert and observant to detect undeclared items. If any are discovered, it is up to the inspector to decide whether an oversight or deliberate fraud has occurred. Sometimes the contraband is held and a U.S. Customs hearing is scheduled to decide the case. A person who is caught trying to avoid paying duty is fined. When customs violations occur, inspectors must file detailed reports and often later appear as witnesses in court.

Customs officials often work with other government agents and are sometimes required to be armed. They cooperate with special agents for the Federal Bureau of Investigation (FBI), the Drug Enforcement Administration (DEA), the U.S. Immigration and Naturalization Service (INS), the Food and Drug Administration (FDA), and public health officials and agricultural quarantine inspectors.

Business magnates, ships' captains, and importers are among those with whom customs inspectors have daily contact as they review manifests, examine cargo, and control shipments transferred under bond to ports throughout the United States.

Some of the specialized fields for customs officials are as follows:

Customs patrol officers conduct surveillance at points of entry into the United States to prohibit smuggling and detect customs violations. They try to catch people illegally transporting smuggled merchandise and contraband such as narcotics, watches, jewelry, and weapons, as well as fruits, plants, and meat that may be infested with pests and diseases. Armed and equipped with two-way communication devices, they function much like police officers. On the waterfront, customs patrol officers monitor piers, ships, and crew members and are constantly on the lookout for items being thrown from the ship to small boats nearby. Customs patrol officers provide security at entrance and exit facilities of piers and airports, make sure all baggage is checked, and maintain security at loading, exit, and entrance areas of customs buildings and during the transfer of legal drug shipments to prevent hijackings or theft.

Using informers and other sources, they gather intelligence information about illegal activities. When probable cause exists, they are authorized to take possible violators into custody, using physical force or weapons if necessary. They assist other customs personnel in developing or testing new enforcement techniques and equipment.

Customs pilots, who must have a current Federal Aviation Administration (FAA) commercial pilot's license, conduct air surveillance of illegal traffic crossing U.S. borders by air, land, or sea. They apprehend, arrest, and search violators and prepare reports used to prosecute the criminals. They are stationed along the Canadian and Mexican borders as well as along coastal areas, flying single- and multi-engine planes or helicopters.

Canine enforcement officers train and use dogs to prevent smuggling of all controlled substances as defined by customs laws. These controlled substances include marijuana, narcotics, and dangerous drugs. After undergoing an intensive twelve-week basic training course in the Detector Dog Training Center, where each officer is paired with a dog and assigned to a post, canine enforcement officers work in cooperation with customs inspectors, customs patrol officers, and special agents to find and seize contraband and arrest smugglers. Currently, most canine enforcement officers are used at entry points along the border with Mexico.

Import specialists become technical experts in a particular line of merchandise, such as wine or electronic equipment. They keep up-to-date on their area of specialization by going to trade shows and importers' places of business. Merchandise for delivery to commercial importers is examined, classified, and appraised by these specialists, who must enforce import quotas and trademark laws. They use import quotas and current market values to determine the unit value of the merchandise in order to calculate the amount of money due the government in tariffs. Import specialists routinely question importers, check their lists, and make sure the merchandise matches the description and the list. If they find a violation, they call for a formal inquiry by customs special agents. Import specialists regularly deal with problems of fraud and violations of copyright and trademark laws. If the importer meets federal requirements, the import specialist issues a permit that authorizes the release of merchandise for delivery. If not, the goods might be seized and sold at public auction. These specialists encourage international trade by authorizing the lowest allowable duties on merchandise.

Customs chemists form a subgroup of import specialists who protect the health and safety of Americans. They analyze imported merchandise for textile fibers, lead content, and narcotics. In many cases, the duty collected on imported products depends on the chemist's analysis and subsequent report. Customs chemists often serve as expert witnesses in court. The customs laboratories in Boston, New York, Baltimore, Savannah, New Orleans, Los Angeles, San Francisco, Chicago, Washington, DC, and San Juan, Puerto Rico, have specialized instruments that can analyze materials for their chemical components. These machines can determine such things as the amount of sucrose in a beverage, the fiber content of a textile product, the lead oxide content of fine crystal, or the presence of toxic chemicals and prohibited additives.

Special agents are plainclothes investigators who make sure that the government obtains revenue on imports and that contraband and controlled substances do not enter or leave the country illegally. They investigate smuggling, criminal fraud, and major cargo thefts. Special agents target professional criminals as well as ordinary tourists who give false information on baggage declarations. Often working undercover, they cooperate with customs inspectors and the FBI. Allowed special powers of entry, search, seizure, and arrest, special agents have the broadest powers of search of any law enforcement personnel in the United States. For instance, special agents do not need probable cause or a warrant to justify search or seizure near a border or port of entry. However, in the interior of the United States probable cause but not a warrant is necessary to conduct a search.

Requirements

Applicants to the U.S. Customs Service must be U.S. citizens and at least twenty-one years of age. They must have earned at least a high school diploma, but applicants with college degrees are preferred. Applicants are required to have three years of general work experience involving contact with the public or four years of college.

Applicants must be in good physical condition, possess emotional and mental stability, and demonstrate the ability to correctly apply regulations or instructional material and make clear, concise oral or written reports.

Like all federal employees, applicants to the U.S. Customs Service must pass a physical examination and undergo a security check. They must also pass a federally administered standardized test, called the Professional and Administrative Career Examination (PACE). Entrance-level appointments are at grades GS-5 and GS-7, depending on the level of education or work experience.

Special agents must establish an eligible rating on the Treasury Enforcement Examination (TEA), a test that measures investigative aptitude, successfully complete an oral interview, pass a personal background investigation, and be in excellent physical condition. Although they receive extensive training, these agents need to have two years of specialized criminal investigative or comparable experience. Applicants with the necessary specialized law-enforcement experience or education should establish eligibility on the Mid-Level Register for appointment grades GS-9, 11, and 12.

Opportunities for Experience & Exploration

High school students have several ways to learn about the various positions available at the U.S. Customs Service. They can talk with people employed as customs inspectors, consult their high school counselors, or contact local labor union organizations and offices for additional information.

Information on federal government jobs is available from offices of the state employment service, area offices of the U.S. Office of Personnel Management, and Federal Job Information Centers throughout the country.

Methods of Entering

Applicants may enter the various occupations of the U.S. Customs Service by applying to take the appropriate civil service examinations. Interested applicants should note the age, citizenship, and experience requirements previously described and realize that they will undergo a background check and a drug test. If hired, applicants will receive exacting, on-the-job training.

Advancement

All customs agents have the opportunity to advance through a special system of promotion from within. Although they enter at the GS-5 or GS-7 level, after one year they may compete for promotion to supervisory positions or simply to positions at a higher grade level in the agency. The journeyperson level is grade GS-9. Supervisory positions at GS-11 and above are available on a competitive basis. After attaining permanent status (i.e., serving for one year on probation), customs patrol officers may compete to become special agents. Entry-level appointments for customs chemists are made at GS-5. However, applicants with an advanced degree and/or professional experience in the sciences should qualify for higher-graded positions. Advancement potential exists for the journeyperson level at GS-11 and to specialist, supervisory, and management positions at grades GS-12 and above.

Employment Outlook

Employment as a customs official is steady work that is not affected by changes in the economy. Even with the increased emphasis on law enforcement, including the detection of illegally imported drugs and pornography and the prevention of exports of sensitive high-technology items, the outlook for steady employment in the U.S. Customs Service is likely to grow slower than the average through the year 2006. Many of the job openings will result from the need to replace retiring inspectors.

Earnings

The federal government employs approximately 75,000 customs workers. Beginning salaries for all types of government inspectors in 1996 ranged from $24,200 to $29,600. The average annual salary for experienced customs inspectors was $40,020 in 1997, according to the *1998-99 Occupational Outlook Handbook*. Customs officials in supervisory positions may earn $50,000 or more a year.

Federal employees in certain cities receive locality pay in addition to their salaries in order to offset the higher cost of living in those areas. Locality pay generally adds an extra 16 percent to the base salary. Certain customs officials are also entitled to receive Law Enforcement Availability Pay, which adds another 25 percent to their salaries. All federal workers receive annual cost-of-living salary increases. Federal workers enjoy generous benefits, including health and life insurance, pension plans, and holiday, sick leave, and vacation pay.

Conditions of Work

The customs territory of the United States is divided into nine regions that include the fifty states, the District of Columbia, Puerto Rico, and the U.S. Virgin Islands. In these regions there are nearly three hundred ports of entry along land and sea borders. Customs inspectors may be assigned to any of these ports or to overseas work at airports, seaports, waterfronts, border stations, customs houses, or the U.S. Customs Service Headquarters in Washington, DC. They are able to request an assignment in s certain locality and usually receive it when possible.

A typical work schedule is eight hours a day, five days a week, but customs employees often work overtime or long into the night. United States entry and exit points must be supervised twenty-four hours a day, which means that workers rotate night shifts and weekend duty. Customs inspectors and patrol officers are sometimes assigned to one-person border points at remote locations where they may perform immigration and agricultural inspections in addition to regular duties. They often risk physical injury from criminals violating customs regulations.

Sources of Additional Information

U.S. Customs Service
Office of Human Resources
1301 Constitution Avenue, NW
Washington, DC 20229
Tel: 202-927-6724

Dairy Products Manufacturing Workers

Definition

Dairy products manufacturing workers set up, operate, and tend continuous-flow or vat-type equipment to process milk, cream, butter, cheese, ice cream, and other dairy products following specified methods and formulas.

Nature of the Work

Dairy products manufacturing workers handle a wide variety of machines that process milk, manufacture dairy products, and prepare the products for shipping. Workers are usually classified by the type of machine they operate. Workers at some plants handle more than one type of machine.

Whole milk is delivered to a dairy processing plant from farms in large containers or in special tank trucks. The milk is stored in large vats until *dairy-processing-equipment operators* are ready to use it. First, the operator connects the vats to processing equipment with pipes, assembling whatever valves, bowls, plates, disks, impeller shafts, and other parts are needed to prepare the equipment for operation. Then the operator turns valves to pump a sterilizing solution and rinse water throughout the pipes and equipment. While keeping an eye on temperature and pressure gauges, the operator opens other valves to pump the whole milk into a centrifuge where it is spun at high speed to separate the cream from the skim milk. The milk is also pumped through a homogenizer to produce a specified emulsion (consistency that results from the distribution of fat through the milk) and, last, through a filter to remove any sediment. All this is done through continuous-flow machines.

The next step for the equipment operator is pasteurization, or the killing of bacteria that exist in the milk. The milk is heated by pumping steam or hot water through pipes in the pasteurization equipment. When it has been at the specified

School Subjects
Agriculture
Biology

Personal Interests
Fixing things
Food/Cooking

Work Environment
Primarily indoors
Primarily one location

Minimum Education Level
High school diploma

Salary Range
$15,000 to
$27,500 to
$40,000+

Certification or Licensing
Required

Outlook
Decline

DOT
52

GOE
06.04.10

NOC
2221

temperature for the correct time, a refrigerant is pumped through refrigerator coils in the equipment, which quickly brings the milk temperature down. Once the milk has been pasteurized, it is either bottled in glass, paper, or plastic containers, or it is pumped to other storage tanks for further processing. The dairy-processing-equipment operator may also add to the milk specified amounts of liquid or powdered ingredients, such as vitamins, lactic culture, stabilizer, or neutralizer, to make products such as buttermilk, yogurt, chocolate milk, or ice cream mix. The batch of milk is tested for acidity at various stages of this process, and each time the operator records the time, temperature, pressure, and volume readings for the milk. The operator may clean the equipment before processing the next batch of whole milk.

Processed milk includes a lot of nonfat dry milk, which is far easier to ship and store than fresh milk. Dry milk is made in a gas-fired drier tended by a *drier operator.* The drier operator first turns on the equipment's drier mechanism, vacuum pump, and circulating fan and adjusts the flow controls. Once the proper drier temperature is reached, a pump sprays liquid milk into the heated vacuum chamber where milk droplets dry to powder and fall to the bottom of the chamber. The drier operator tests the dried powder for the proper moisture content and the chamber walls for burnt scale, which indicates excessive temperatures and appears as undesirable sediment when the milk is reconstituted. *Milk-powder grinders* operate equipment that mills and sifts the milk powder, ensuring a uniform texture.

For centuries, butter was made by hand in butter churns in which cream was agitated with a plunger until pieces of butter congealed and separated from the milk. Modern butter-making machines perform the same basic operation on a much larger scale. After sterilizing the machine, the *butter maker* starts a pump that admits a measured amount of pasteurized cream into the churn. The butter maker activates the churn and, as the cream is agitated by paddles, monitors the gradual separation of the butter from the milk. Once the process is complete, the milk is pumped out and stored, and the butter is sprayed with chlorinated water to remove excess remaining milk. With testing apparatus, the butter maker determines the butter's moisture and salt content and adjusts the consistency by adding or removing water. Finally, the butter maker examines the color and smells and tastes the butter to grade it according to predetermined standards.

In addition to the churn method, butter can also be produced by the butter-chilling method. In this process, the butter maker pasteurizes and separates cream to obtain butter oil. The butter oil is tested in a standardizing vat for its levels of butter fat, moisture,

salt content, and acidity. The butter maker adds appropriate amounts of water, alkali, and coloring to the butter oil and starts an agitator to mix the ingredients. The resulting mix is chilled in a vat at a specified temperature until it congeals into butter.

Cheesemakers cook milk and other ingredients according to formulas to make cheese. The cheesemaker first fills a cooking vat with milk of a prescribed butterfat content, heats the milk to a specified temperature, and dumps in measured amounts of dye and starter culture. The mixture is agitated and tested for acidity as because the level of acidity affects the rate at which enzymes coagulate milk proteins and make cheese. When a certain level of acidity has been reached, the cheesemaker adds a measured amount of rennet, a substance containing milk-curdling enzymes. The milk is left alone to coagulate into curd, the thick, protein-rich part of milk used to make cheese. The cheesemaker later releases the whey, the watery portion of the milk, by pulling curd knives through the curd or using a hand scoop. Then the curd is agitated in the vat and cooked for a period of time, with the cheesemaker squeezing and stretching samples of curd by hand and adjusting the cooking time to achieve the desired firmness or texture. Once this is done, the cheesemaker or a *cheesemaker helper* drains the whey from the curd, adds ingredients such as seasonings, and then molds, packs, cuts, piles, mills, and presses the curd into specified shapes. To make certain types of cheese, the curd may be immersed in brine, rolled in dry salt, pierced or smeared with a culture solution to develop mold growth, or placed on shelves to be cured. Later, the cheesemaker samples the cheese for its taste, smell, look, and feel. Sampling and grading is also done by *cheese graders,* experts in cheeses who are required to have a state or federal license.

The distinctive qualities of various kinds of cheeses depend on a number of factors, including the kind and condition of the milk, the cheesemaking process, and the method and duration of curing. For example, cottage cheese is made by approximately the method described above. However, the *cottage cheese maker* at the last cooking stage starts the temperature low and slowly increases it. When the curd reaches the proper consistency, the cottage cheese maker stops the cooking process and drains off the whey. This method accounts for cottage cheese's loose consistency. Cottage cheese and other soft cheeses are not cured like hard cheeses and are meant for immediate consumption.

Process cheese products are made by blending and cooking different cheeses, cheese curd, or other ingredients such as cream, vegetable shortening, sodium citrate, and disodium phosphate. The *process cheese cooker* dumps the various ingredients into a vat and cooks them at a prescribed temperature. When the mixture reaches a certain consistency, the cooker pulls a lever to drain the cheese into a hopper or bucket. The process cheese may be pumped through a machine that makes its texture finer. Unheated cheese or curd may be mixed with other ingredients to make cold pack cheese or cream cheese. Other cheese workers include *casting-machine operators,* who tend the machines that form, cool, and cut the process cheese into slices of a specified size and weight, and *grated-cheese makers,* who handle the grinding, drying, and cooling equipment that makes grated cheese.

Ice cream is usually made from milk fat, nonfat milk solids, sweeteners, stabilizer (usually gelatin), and flavorings such as syrup, nuts, and fruit. Ice cream can be made in individual batches by *batch freezers* or in continuous-mix equipment by *freezer operators.* In the second method, the freezer operator measures the dry and liquid ingredients, such as the milk, coloring, flavoring, or fruit puree, and dumps them into the flavor vat. The mix is blended, pumped into freezer barrels, and injected with air. In the freezer barrel, the mix is agitated and scraped from the freezer walls while it slowly hardens. The operator then releases the ice cream through a valve outlet that may inject flavored syrup for rippled ice cream. The ice cream is transferred to a filling machine that pumps it into cartons, cones, cups, or molds for pies, rolls, and tarts. Other workers may process the ice cream into its various types, such as cones, varicolored packs, and special shapes. These workers include *decorators, novelty makers, flavor room workers,* and *sandwich-machine operators.*

Newly hired inexperienced workers in a dairy processing plant may start out as *dairy helpers,* cheesemaker helpers, or *cheese making laborers.* Beginning workers may do any of a wide variety of support tasks, such as scrubbing and sterilizing bottles and equipment, attaching pipes and fittings to machines, packing cartons, weighing containers, and moving stock. If they prove to be reliable, workers may be given more responsibility and assigned tasks such as filling tanks with milk or ingredients, examining canned milk for dirt or odor, monitoring machinery, cutting and wrapping butter and cheese, or filling cartons or bags with powdered milk. In time, workers may be trained to operate and repair any of the specialized processing machines found in the factory.

The raw milk at a dairy processing plant is supplied by *dairy farmers,* who raise and tend milk-producing livestock, usually cows. Dairy farmers often own their own farms, breed their own cows, and use special equipment to milk the cows, often twice a day. Many also perform other farm-related tasks, including growing crops. Assisting the dairy farmer is often the *dairy herd supervisor,* who takes milk samples from cows and tests the milk samples for information such as the amount of fat, protein, and other solids present in the milk. The dairy herd supervisor helps the farmer make certain that each cow in the herd is healthy and that the milk they produce will be fit for human consumption. Dairy herd supervisors do not generally work for one dairy farmer, but rather may oversee the milk production at a number of farms.

Requirements

Most dairy products manufacturing workers learn their skills from company training sessions and on-the-job experience. Employers prefer to hire workers with at least a high school education. Courses that can provide helpful background for work in this field include mathematics, biology, and chemistry. Machine shop classes can also be useful for the experience gained in handling and repairing heavy machinery. People interested in becoming cheesemakers may find it necessary to obtain a college degree in a food technology or food science program. Dairy herd supervisors, in addition to a two-year or four-year food technology or food science degree, should try to gain experience working on a dairy farm.

To assure that consumers are receiving safe, healthful dairy foods, many dairy products manufacturing workers must be licensed by a state board of health or other local government unit. Licensing is intended to guarantee workers' knowledge of health laws, their skills in handling equipment, and their ability to grade the quality of various goods according to established standards. Some workers, such as cheese graders, may need to be licensed by the federal government as well.

Opportunities for Experience & Exploration

People who think they may be interested in working in the dairy products manufacturing industry may be able to find summer jobs as helpers in dairy processing plants. Assisting or at least observing equipment operators, cheesemakers, butter makers, and other workers as they work is a good way to learn about this field. High school students may also find part-time or summer employment at dairy farms.

Methods of Entering

The best place to find information about job openings may be at the personnel offices of local dairy processing plants. Other good sources of information include newspaper classified ads and the offices of the state employment service. Those with associate's or bachelor's degrees in food technology, food science, or a related program can apply directly to dairy processing plants; many schools offering such programs provide job placement assistance. Many dairy farmers begin their careers by working on their own family farms.

Advancement

After gaining some experience, dairy products manufacturing workers may advance to become shift supervisors or production supervisors. Advancement is usually limited to those with at least an associate's or bachelor's degree in a food technology, food science, or related course of study. Formal training in related fields is necessary in order to move up to such positions as laboratory technician, plant engineer, or plant manager.

Workers who wish to change industries may find that many of their skills can be transferred to other types of food processing. With further training and education, they may eventually become dairy plant inspectors or technicians employed by local or state health departments.

Employment Outlook

The demand for American dairy products will probably remain high in the foreseeable future. Among the products that have grown in popularity in recent years are cheeses, ice cream, and lowfat milk. Despite this demand, employment in the dairy products manufacturing industry is expected to decline through the year 2006. Improvements in technology and increased automation are two important factors contributing to this trend. However, because the milk industry is rarely affected by recessions or other economic difficulties and trends facing other industries, employment remains relatively stable and this industry suffers fewer layoffs than others. Because of continuing advances in the technology of dairy manufacturing and food science, the demand for laboratory technicians, plant engineers, and other technical staff is expected to remain strong.

Earnings

Earnings of dairy products manufacturing workers vary widely according to the responsibilities of the worker, geographical location, and other factors. Entry-level and unskilled workers can expect to begin at salaries around $15,000 per year. Dairy production workers with experience averaged approximately $27,500 per year in 1995—the most recent statistics available. The overall average earnings for dairy production workers also varies according to the type of product produced by the plant. Workers processing fluid milk earned an average of $28,700 per year, while those at cheese processing plants averaged about $24,400 per year. Cheesemakers and others with food technology degrees may earn as much as $40,000 per year or more. Production supervisors, plant engineers, and plant managers can earn $30,000 per year or more. Annual income for dairy farmers can vary widely, from as low as $10,000 per year to $90,000 per year and more; most dairy farmers own their own business and are responsible for its upkeep, as well as paying employees' salaries. Dairy herd supervisors are paid based on the number of herd they test. Starting supervisors earn between $18,700 and $25,000, while experienced supervisors may earn $30,000 per year. The most experienced and highly-trained supervisors can earn as much as $35,000 per year. Most dairy products workers are eligible for overtime pay for hours worked over forty hours in a week. Benefits vary according to the company and its location, but sometimes include health insurance and vacation and sick pay.

Conditions of Work

Because of the strict health codes and sanitary standards to which they must adhere, dairy plants are generally clean, well-ventilated workplaces, equipped with modern, well-maintained machines. When workplace safety rules are followed, dairy processing plants are not hazardous places to work.

Workers in this industry generally report for work as early as six AM, with shifts ending around three in the afternoon. Dairy farmers and others may start work as early as four or five in the morning. People involved in the agriculture industry often work very long hours, often more than twelve hours per day. Many dairy products manufacturing workers stand during most of their workday. In some positions the work is very repetitive. Although the milk itself is generally transported from tank to tank via pipelines, some workers have to lift and carry other heavy items, such as cartons of flavoring, emulsifier, chemical additives, and finished products like cheese. To clean vats and other equipment, some workers have to get inside storage tanks and spray the walls with hot water, chemicals, or live steam.

Sources of Additional Information

American Dairy Association
O'Hare International Centre
10255 West Higgins Road, Suite 900
Rosemont, IL 60018-2000
Tel: 847-803-2000

American Dairy Science Association
309 West Clark Street
Champaign, IL 61820-4690
Tel: 217-356-3182

Dairy Producers Co-operative Ltd.
PO Box 560
Regina, SK S4P 3A5 Canada

International Dairy-Deli-Bakery Association
PO Box 5528
313 Price Place, Suite 202
Madison, WI 53705
Tel: 608-238-7908

Milk Industry Foundation
1250 H Street, NW, Suite 900
Washington, DC 20005
Tel: 202-737-4332

Data Entry Clerks

Definition

Data entry clerks transfer information from paper documents to a computer system. They use either a typewriter-like (alphanumeric) keyboard or a ten-key (numerals only) pad to enter data into the system. In this way, the data is converted into a form the computer can easily read and process.

Nature of the Work

Data entry clerks are responsible for entering data into computer systems so that the information can be processed at various times to produce important business documents such as sales reports, billing invoices, mailing lists, and many others. Specific job responsibilities vary according to the type of computer system being used and the nature of the employer. For example, a data entry clerk may enter financial information for use at a bank, merchandising information for use at a store, or scientific information for use at a research laboratory.

From a source document such as a financial statement, data entry clerks type in information in either alphabetic, numeric, or symbolic code. The information is entered using a keyboard, either the regular typewriter-like computer keyboard or a more customized key pad developed for a certain industry or business. The entry machine converts the coded information into either electronic impulses or a series of holes in a tape that the computer can read and process electronically. Newer, more sophisticated computers have eliminated the need for magnetic tapes, however, and rely exclusively on computer files. Some data entry work does not involve inputting actual information but rather entering special instructions that tell the computer what functions to perform and when.

In small companies, data entry clerks may combine data entry responsibilities with general office work. Because of staff limitations, they may have to know and operate several types

School Subjects
Business
Computer science

Personal Interests
Computers
Figuring out how things work

Work Environment
Primarily indoors
Primarily one location

Minimum Education Level
High school diploma

Salary Range
$15,500 to
$18,100 to
$21,500

Certification or Licensing
None

Outlook
Decline

DOT
203

GOE
07.06.01

NOC
1422

of computer systems. Larger companies tend to assign data entry clerks to one type of entry machinery. For example, data entry clerks in a check or credit processing center might be assigned solely to changing client addresses on the company database or entering payment amounts from individual checks.

Some data entry clerks are responsible for setting up their entry machines according to the type of input data. Clerks who handle vast amounts of financial data, for example, set their machines to automatically record a series of numbers as dollar amounts or transaction dates without having to input dollar signs or hyphens. The special set-ups reduce the number of strokes a data entry clerk has to perform in order to finish one transaction, thereby increasing his or her productivity. Some data entry clerks may be responsible for loading the appropriate tape or other material into their machines and selecting the correct coding system (that is, the alphabetic, numeric, or symbolic representations).

Accuracy is an essential element of all data entry work. If a customer pays one hundred dollars toward a credit card bill but the clerk records only a ten dollar payment, the company will experience problems down the line. Therefore, most companies have an extensive series of accuracy checks and error tests designed to detect as many errors as possible. Some tests are computerized, checking entries against expected information for the type of work or is scanned in directly from source documents. Data entry clerks must always verify their own work as well. They consistently check their computer screens for obvious typographical errors and systematically refer back to the source documents to ensure that they entered the information correctly. Sometimes *verifier operators* are employed specifically to perform accuracy tests of previously processed information. Such tests may be random or complete, depending on the nature and scope of the work. When verifier operators find mistakes, they correct them and later prepare accuracy reports for each data entry clerk.

Data typists and *keypunch operators* used to prepare data for computer input by punching data into special coding cards or paper tapes. The cards were punched on machines that resembled typewriters. When tapes were used, the work was done on machines such as bookkeeping or adding machines that had special attachments to perforate paper tape. The use of cards and tape is decreasing substantially as electronic databases become more flexible, fast, and efficient. Consequently, most data typists and keypunch operators working today are basically doing data entry work at terminals similar to that of other data entry clerks.

Data-coder operators examine the information in the source material to determine what codes and symbols should be used to enter it into the computer. They may write the operating instructions for the data entry staff and assist the system programmer in testing and revising computer programs designed to process data entry work. Data-coder operators might also assist programmers in preparing detailed flow-charts of how the information is being stored and used in the computer system and in designing coded computer instructions to fulfill business needs.

Terminal operators also use coding systems to input information from the source document into a series of alphabetic or numeric signals that can be read by the computer. After checking their work for accuracy, they send the data to the computer system via telephone lines or other remote-transmission methods if they do not input directly into the computer network.

Requirements

A high school diploma is usually required for data entry work. In a few cases, some college training is desirable. Most data entry clerks receive on-the-job training pertaining specifically to the computer system and input procedures used by the employer. Data entry clerks should be able to quickly scan documents and type the information they read before they begin their first job. High school students interested in becoming data entry clerks should take English, typing, and other business courses that focus on the operation of office machinery.

Many aspiring data entry clerks now complete data processing courses that instruct students on proper inputting methods and other skills needed for the job. Technical schools, community colleges, business schools, and some adult education programs offer courses related to data processing. These courses are generally between six months and two years in duration. Secretarial or business schools may also offer data entry courses.

Most companies test prospective employees to evaluate their typing skills in terms of both speed and accuracy. Competency in general mathematics and spelling is frequently reviewed as well. Data entry clerks must be accurate and highly productive, capable of inputting several hundred pieces of information per hour, and they must be comfortable with the high degree of routine and repetition involved in their daily tasks. As computers continue to change, data entry clerks must always be ready to learn new methods and techniques of input.

Opportunities for Experience & Exploration

High school students interested in pursuing a career in data entry should discuss the field with individuals who are already employed as clerks. A visit to an office that uses data processing systems may provide a good opportunity to learn more about the rewards and drawbacks of this position. Secretarial work or similar office work may also be helpful in understanding what data entry work involves. At home or school, interested students can practice typing by using a computer or typewriter or by entering data for various club or group activities.

Methods of Entering

Many people entering the field have already completed an educational program at a technical school or other institution that provides data processing training. Job placement counselors at these schools are often very helpful in locating employment opportunities for qualified applicants.

Local and state employment offices as well as classified advertisements list job openings. Individuals may also make direct contact with area employers who maintain large data processing departments as there tends to be a rather high turnover in this field.

Major employers of data entry clerks include insurance companies, utilities, banks, credit or check clearinghouses, mail-order catalogs, temporary employment agencies, and manufacturing firms. The federal government operates its own training program for data entry clerks. Applications for such positions may be made through the Office of Personnel Management.

Advancement

Data entry positions are considered entry-level jobs, and as such, data entry itself does not offer tremendous potential for growth. Data entry clerks may be promoted to working on more complicated machines or systems, but the work is basically the same. Better opportunities arise when data entry clerks use their computer experience and training to springboard to higher-level positions. For example, skilled data entry clerks may be promoted to supervisory positions where they are responsible for overseeing the data processing department or a team of clerks. Duties might include ensuring high accuracy and productivity rates.

Employment Outlook

Because of improvements in data-processing technology that enable businesses to process greater volumes of information with fewer workers, employment opportunities for data entry clerks are expected to decline through the year 2006. Jobs are becoming limited, for example, because many computer systems can now send information directly to another computer system without the need for a data entry clerk to input the information a second time. In addition, the widespread use of personal computers, which permit numerous employees to enter data directly, will also diminish the need for skilled entry personnel. Computer scanners, which read hand- and typewritten information directly from source documents are slowly making data entry clerks obsolete. Data entry clerks must continually improve and upgrade their skills in order to stay competitive. Despite these advances in technology, the need for data entry clerks will continue in some businesses.

Even though there will be a slowdown in new job openings for data entry clerks, the computer processing field as a whole will remain very strong, and continued employment opportunities should arise due to retirement, job promotions, and attrition. Those with the most advanced skills and the ability to adapt to the changing needs of the computer processing field will stand the best chance for continued employment. Job opportunities will be greatest in and around large metropolitan areas where most banks, insurance and utilities companies, and government agencies are located.

Knowledge of different computer systems and general computer science enhance a data entry clerk's desirability among employers. The ability to work on different systems, particularly specialty systems such as page layout programs and typesetting programs, offers the clerk greater job flexibility. Voice recognition techniques, where text and data are entered by simply speaking to a computer, are being improved and will soon be in wide use.

Earnings

According to the Bureau of Statistics, in 1996 beginning data entry clerks earned between $15,500 and $18,000 annually, depending on their employer, the complexity of their job duties, and their level of training. Experienced clerks earned up to $21,500, with those working in manufacturing and utilities companies earning slightly more than their counterparts in banking and other service industries. Similarly, incomes tend to vary by region, with salaries in the Western United States being the highest. Salaries for federal and local government employees are comparable to those earned in the private sector. Full-time and some part-time employees can expect benefits such as medical insurance, sick leave, and paid vacation.

Conditions of Work

Most data entry clerks work a thirty-seven- to forty-hour workweek, with part-time positions becoming increasingly popular. Data entry workstations are usually located in comfortable, well-lighted areas. Data entry clerks must be able to work side by side with other employees and, in most cases, under close supervision. The work is routine, repetitious, and fast-paced and demands the constant, concentrated use of eyes and hands.

The continuous need for accuracy may be stressful to an individual unaccustomed to such working conditions. Duties may require lifting, reaching, and moving boxes of cards, tape, or other materials. Data entry personnel sit for long hours at a time. Long exposure to video screens at close range may strain the eyes, and constant use of the hands for typing may lead to nerve or muscle problems, such as carpal tunnel syndrome in the hands and arms.

Sources of Additional Information

For more information on the data entry field, contact:

Association for Computing Machinery
11 West 42nd Street, 3rd Floor
New York, NY 10036
Tel: 212-869-7440

For a brochure about careers in data processing and information about any of the 300 student chapters of DPMA, contact:

Data Processing Management Association
505 Busse Highway
Park Ridge, IL 60068
Tel: 847-825-8124
WWW: http://negaduck.cc.vt.edu/dpma/

Data Processing Management Association of Canada
2 Whitehall Boulevard
Winnipeg, MB R2C 0Y2 Canada

Dental Assistants

Definition

Dental assistants perform a variety of duties in the dental office, including helping the dentist examine and treat patients and completing laboratory and office work. They assist the dentist by preparing patients for dental exams, handing the dentist the proper instruments, taking and processing X-rays, preparing materials for making impressions and restorations, and instructing patients in oral health care. They also perform administrative and clerical tasks so that the office runs smoothly and the dentist's time is available for working with patients.

Nature of the Work

Dental assistants help dentists as they examine and treat patients. They usually greet patients, escort them to the examining room, and prepare them by covering their clothing with paper or cloth bibs. They also adjust the headrest of the examination chair and raise the chair to the proper height. Many dental assistants take X-rays of patients' teeth and process the film for the dentist to examine. They also obtain patients' dental records from the office files, so the dentist can review them before the examination.

During dental examinations and operations, dental assistants hand the dentist instruments as they are needed and use suction devices to keep the patient's mouth dry. When the examination or procedure is completed, assistants may give the patient after-care instructions for the teeth and mouth. They also provide instructions on infection-control procedures, preventing plaque buildup, and keeping teeth and gums clean and healthy between office visits.

Dental assistants also help with a variety of other clinical tasks. When a dentist needs a cast of a patient's teeth or mouth—used for diagnosing and planning the correction of dental problems—assistants may mix the necessary materials necessary. They may also pour, trim, and polish these study casts.

School Subjects
Anatomy and Physiology
Health

Personal Interests
Helping people: physical health/medicine

Work Environment
Primarily indoors
Primarily one location

Minimum Education Level
High school diploma

Salary Range
$14,700 to
$23,500 to
$26,800

Certification or Licensing
Recommended

Outlook
Much faster than the average

DOT
079

GOE
10.03.02

NOC
3411

Some assistants prepare materials for making dental restorations, and many polish and clean patients' dentures. Some may perform the necessary laboratory work to make temporary dental replacements.

State laws determine which clinical tasks a dental assistant is able to perform. Dental assistants are not the same as dental hygienists, who are licensed to perform a wider variety of clinical tasks such as scaling and polishing teeth. Some states allow dental assistants to apply medications to teeth and gums, isolate individual teeth for treatment using rubber dams, and remove excess cement after cavities have been filled. In some states dental assistants can actually put fillings in patients' mouths. Dental assistants may also check patients' vital signs, update and check medical histories, and help the dentist with any medical emergencies that arise during dental procedures.

Many dental assistants also perform clerical and administrative tasks. These include receptionist duties, scheduling appointments, managing patient records, keeping dental supply inventories, preparing bills for services rendered, collecting payments, and issuing receipts. Dental assistants often act as business managers who perform all nonclinical responsibilities such as hiring and firing auxiliary help, scheduling employees, and overseeing office accounting.

Requirements

Most dental assistant positions are entry level. They usually require little or no experience and no education beyond high school. High school students who wish to work as dental assistants should take courses in general science, biology, health, chemistry, and business management. Typing is also an important skill for dental assistants.

Dental assistants commonly acquire their skills on the job. Many, however, go on to receive training after high school at trade schools, technical institutes, and community and junior colleges that offer dental assisting programs. The armed forces also trains some dental assistants.

Students who complete two-year college programs receive associate's degrees, while those who complete one-year trade and technical school programs earn a certificate or diploma. Entrance requirements to these programs require a high school diploma and good grades in high school science, typing, and English. Some postsecondary schools require an interview or written examination, and some require that applicants pass physical and dental examinations. About 240 of these programs are accredited by the American Dental Association's Commission on Dental Accreditation. Some four- to six-month nonaccredited courses in dental assisting are also available from private vocational schools. The University of Kentucky College of Dentistry offers a correspondence course for assistants who cannot participate full time in an accredited, formal program. The course generally takes two years to complete and is equivalent to one year of full-time formal study.

Accredited programs instruct students in dental assisting skills and theory through classes, lectures, and laboratory and preclinical experience. Students take courses in English, speech, and psychology as well as in the biomedical sciences, including anatomy, microbiology, and nutrition. Courses in dental science cover subjects such as oral anatomy and pathology, and dental radiography. Students also gain practical experience in chairside assisting and office management by working in dental schools and local dental clinics that are affiliated with their program. Graduates of such programs may be assigned a greater variety of tasks initially and may receive higher starting salaries than those with high school diplomas alone.

Dental assistants may wish to obtain certification from the Dental Assisting National Board, but this is usually not required for employment. Certified dental assistant (CDA) accreditation shows that an assistant meets certain standards of professional competence. To take the certification examination, assistants must be high school graduates who have taken a course in cardiopulmonary resuscitation and must have either a diploma from a formal training program accredited by the Commission on Dental Accreditation or two years of full-time work experience with a recommendation from the dentist for whom the work was done.

In twenty-one states dental assistants are allowed to take X-rays (under a dentist's direction) only after completing a precise training program and passing a test. Completing the program for CDA certification fulfills this requirement. To keep their CDA credentials, however, assistants must either prove their skills through retesting or acquire further education.

Dental assistants need a clean, well-groomed appearance and a pleasant personality. Manual dexterity and the ability to follow directions are also important.

Opportunities for Experience & Exploration

Students in formal training programs receive dental assisting experience as part of their training. High school students can learn more about the field by talking with assistants in local dentists' offices. The American Dental Assistants Association, through the ADA SELECT program, can put students in contact with dental assistants in their areas. Part-time, summer, and temporary clerical work may also be available in dentists' offices.

Methods of Entering

High school guidance counselors, family dentists, dental schools, dental placement agencies, and dental associations may provide applicants with leads about job openings. Students in formal training programs often learn of jobs through school placement services.

Most dentists work in private practice, so that's where a dental assistant is most likely to find a job. An office may have a single dentist or it may be a group practice with several dentists, assistants, and hygienists. Other places to work include dental schools, hospitals, public health departments, and U.S. Veterans and Public Health Service hospitals.

Advancement

Dental assistants may advance in their field by moving to larger offices or clinics, where they can take on more responsibility and earn more money. In small offices they may receive higher pay by upgrading their skills through education. Specialists in the dental field, who typically earn higher salaries than general dentists, often pay higher salaries to their assistants.

Further educational training is required for advancing to positions in dental assisting education. Dental assistants who wish to become dental hygienists must enroll in a dental hygiene program. Because many of these programs do not allow students to apply dental assisting courses toward graduation, dental assistants who think they would like to move into hygienist positions should plan their training carefully.

In some cases, dental assistants move into sales jobs with companies that sell dental industry supplies and materials. Other areas that are open to dental assistants include office management, placement services, and insurance companies.

Employment Outlook

According to the U.S. Department of Labor, employment for dental assistants is expected to grow much faster than average for all occupations through 2006, with about fifty percent more jobs expected to open in the field. Advances in dental care now allow the general population to maintain better dental health as well as keep their natural teeth longer. Thus, more people will seek dental services for preventative care and cosmetic improvements.

Recent graduates are more likely to hire assistants as compared to older dentists. Dental assistants can handle routine jobs, allowing dentists to perform more difficult and profitable procedures.

Also, as dentists increase their knowledge of innovative techniques such as implantology and periodontal therapy, they generally delegate more routine tasks to assistants so they can make the best use of their time and increase profits. Job openings will also be created through attrition as other assistants leave the field or change jobs.

Earnings

Dental assistants' salaries are determined by specific responsibilities, type of office they work in, and the geographic location of their employer. According to the American Dental Association's 1996 Survey of Dental Practice, the average earnings of full-time dental assistants working for general dentists were between $14,700 and $23,500 a year. Dental assistants working for specialists, such as orthodontists or pediatric dentists, earn slightly more.

About 25 percent of dental assistants work part time. Some offices offer benefits packages such as paid vacations and insurance coverage.

Conditions of Work

Dental assistants work in offices that are generally clean, modern, quiet, and pleasant. They are also well lighted and well ventilated. In small offices, dental assistants may work solely with dentists, while in larger offices and clinics they may work with dentists, other dental assistants, dental hygienists, and laboratory technicians.

Although dental assistants may sit at desks to do office work, they spend a large part of the day beside the dentist's chair where they can reach instruments and materials.

About one-third of all dental assistants work forty-hour weeks, sometimes including Saturday hours. About one-half work between thirty-one and thirty-eight hours a week. The remainder work less, but some part-time workers work in more than one dental office.

Taking X-rays poses some risk because regular doses of radiation can be harmful to the body. However, all dental offices must have lead shielding and safety procedures that minimize the risk of exposure to radioactivity.

Sources of Additional Information

For information on dental assisting careers, accredited schools, scholarships, and possible employers, please contact the following organizations:

American Association of Dental Examiners
211 East Chicago Avenue, Suite 760
Chicago, IL 60611
Tel: 312-440-7464

American Association of Dental Schools
1625 Massachusetts Avenue, NW
Washington, DC 20036
Tel: 202-667-9433
Email: aads@aads.jhu.edu

American Dental Assistants Association
203 North LaSalle Street, Suite 1320
Chicago, IL 60601
Tel: 312-541-1320

American Dental Association
211 East Chicago Avenue
Chicago, IL 60611
Tel: 312-440-2500
WWW: http://www.ada.org/prac/careers/dc-menu.html

Dental Assisting National Board, Inc.
216 East Ontario Street
Chicago, IL 60611
Tel: 312-642-3368

National Association of Dental Assistants
900 South Washington Street, Suite G13
Falls Church, VA 22046
Tel: 703-237-8616

Dental Hygienists

Definition

Dental hygienists perform clinical tasks, serve as oral health educators in private dental offices, work in public health agencies, and promote good oral health by educating adults and children. Their main responsibility is to perform oral prophylaxis, a process of cleaning teeth by using sharp dental instruments, such as scalers and prophy angles. With these instruments, they remove stains and calcium deposits, polish teeth, and massage gums.

Nature of the Work

In clinical settings, hygienists help prevent gum diseases and cavities by removing deposits from teeth and applying sealants and fluoride to prevent tooth decay. They remove tartar, stains, and plaque from teeth, take X rays and other diagnostic tests, place and remove temporary fillings, take health histories, remove sutures, polish amalgam restorations, and examine head, neck, and oral regions for disease.

The focus of their work is providing oral prophylaxis, a process of cleaning teeth using sharp dental instruments such as scalers and prophy angles. With these special instruments, they remove stains and calcium deposits, polish teeth, and massage gums.

Their tools include hand and rotary instruments to clean teeth, syringes with needles to administer local anesthetic (such as Novocain), teeth models to explain home care procedures, and X-ray machines to take pictures of the oral cavity that the dentist uses to detect signs of decay or oral disease.

A hygienist also provides nutritional counseling and screens patients for oral cancer and high blood pressure. More extensive dental procedures are done by dentists. The hygienist is also trained and licensed to take and develop X-rays. Other responsibilities depend on the employer.

School Subjects
Anatomy and Physiology
Health

Personal Interests
Helping people: physical health/medicine
Science

Work Environment
Primarily indoors
Primarily one location

Minimum Education Level
Associate's degree

Salary Range
$15,200 to $24,000 to $39,400

Certification or Licensing
Required

Outlook
Much faster than the average

DOT
078

GOE
10.02.02

NOC
3222

Private dentists might require that the dental hygienist mix compounds for filling cavities, sterilize instruments, assist in surgical work, or even carry out clerical tasks such as making appointments and filling in insurance forms. The hygienist might well fill the duties of receptionist or office manager, functioning in many ways to assist the dentist in carrying out the day's schedule.

Although some of these tasks might also be done by a dental assistant, only the dental hygienist is licensed by the state to clean teeth. Licensed hygienists submit charts of each patient's teeth, noting possible decay or disease. The dentist studies these in making further diagnoses.

The school hygienist cleans and examines the teeth of students in a number of schools. The hygienist also gives classroom instruction on correct brushing and flossing of teeth, the importance of good dental care, and the effects of good nutrition. Dental records of students are kept, and parents must be notified of any need for further treatment.

Dental hygienists may be employed by local, state, or federal public health agencies. These hygienists carry out an educational program for adults and children, as well as oral prophylaxis, in public health clinics, schools, and other public facilities. A few dental hygienists may assist in research projects. For those with further education, teaching in a dental hygiene school may be possible.

Like all dental professionals, hygienists must be aware of federal, state, and local laws that govern hygiene practice. In particular, hygienists must know the types of infection control and protective gear that, by law, must be worn in the dental office to protect workers from infection. Dental hygienists, for example, must wear gloves, protective eyewear, and a mask during examinations. As with most health care workers, hygienists must be immunized against contagious diseases, such as hepatitis.

Dental hygienists are required by their state and encouraged by professional organizations to continue learning about trends in dental care, procedures, and regulations by taking continuing education courses. These may be held at large dental society meetings, colleges and universities, or in more intimate settings, such as a nearby dental office.

Requirements

The minimum requirement for admission to a dental hygiene school is graduation from high school. While in high school, students should follow a college preparatory program. Two types of postsecondary training are available to the prospective dental hygienist. One is a four-year college program offering a bachelor's degree. More common is a two-year program leading to a dental hygiene certification. The bachelor's degree is often preferred by employers, and more schools are likely to require completion of such a degree program in the future. In 1997, there were about 230 accredited schools in the United States that offer one or both of these courses.

Aptitude tests sponsored by the American Dental Hygienists' Association are frequently required by dental hygiene schools to help applicants determine whether they will succeed in this field. Skill in handling delicate instruments, a sensitive touch, and depth perception are important attributes that are tested. The hygienist should be neat, clean, and personable.

Classroom work emphasizes general and dental sciences and liberal arts. Lectures are usually combined with laboratory work and clinical experience.

Dental hygienists, after graduation from accredited schools, must pass state licensing examinations, both written and clinical. The American Dental Association Joint Commission on National Dental Examinations administers the written part of the examination. This test is accepted by all states and the District of Columbia. The clinical part of the examination is administered by state or regional testing agencies.

Opportunities for Experience & Exploration

Work as a dental assistant can be a stepping-stone to a dental hygienist's career. As a dental assistant, one could closely observe the work of a dental hygienist. The individual could then assess personal aptitude for this work, discuss any questions with other hygienists, and enroll in a dental hygiene school where experience as a dental assistant would certainly be helpful. A high school student may be able to find part-time or summer work as a dental assistant or clerical worker in a dentist's office. A prospective dental hygiene student also may be able to arrange to observe a dental hygienist working in a school or a dentist's office or visit an accredited dental hygiene school. The aptitude testing program required by most dental hygiene schools helps students assess their future abilities as dental hygienists.

Methods of Entering

Once dental hygienists have passed the National Board exams and a licensing exam in a particular state, they must decide on an area of work, such as a private dentist's office, school system, or public health agency. Hospitals, industrial plants, and the armed forces employ a small number of dental hygienists. Most dental hygiene schools maintain placement services for the assistance of their graduates, and finding a satisfactory position is usually not too difficult.

Advancement

Opportunities for advancement, other than increases in salary and benefits that accompany experience in the field, usually require additional study and training. Educational advancement may lead to a position as an administrator, teacher, or director in a dental health program or to a more advanced field of practice. With further education and training, some hygienists may choose to go on to become dentists.

Employment Outlook

Dental hygenists are projected to be one of the twenty fastest growing occupations, according to the U.S. Department of Labor. About fifty percent more dental hygiene positions are expected to be created between 1996 and 2006. The demand for dental hygienists is expected to grow as younger generations who grew up receiving better dental care keep their teeth longer.

Population growth, increased public awareness of proper oral home care, and the availability of dental insurance should result in the creation of more dental hygiene jobs. Moreover, as the population ages, there will be a special demand for hygienists to work with older people, especially those who live in nursing homes.

Because of increased awareness about caring for animals in captivity, hygienists are also among a small number of dental professionals who volunteer to help care for animals' teeth and perform annual examinations. Dental professionals are not licensed to treat animals, however, and must work under the supervision of veterinarians.

Earnings

The dental hygienist's income is influenced by such factors as education, experience, locale, and type of employer. Most dental hygienists who work in private dental offices are salaried employees though some are paid a commission for work performed or a combination of salary and commission. According to the U.S. Department of Labor, in 1996 the average earnings of full-time hygienists ranged between $24,000 and $39,500 a year. The average hourly wage for full-time hygienists was $20.40; the average for part-time hygienists was $24.50. Beginning hygienists earned an average of $15,200 to $17,500 a year. Salaries in large metropolitan areas are generally somewhat higher than in small cities and towns. In addition, dental hygienists in research, education, or administration may earn higher salaries. A salaried dental hygienist in a private office typically receives a paid two- or three-week vacation. Part-time or commissioned dental hygienists in private offices usually have no paid vacation.

Conditions of Work

Working conditions for dental hygienists are pleasant, with well-lighted, modern, and adequately equipped facilities. Hygienists usually sits while working. State and federal regulations require that hygienists wear masks, protective eyewear, and gloves. Most hygienists don't wear any jewelry, such as earrings or a wedding band. They are required by new government infection control procedures to leave their work clothes at work, so many dentists offices now have laundry facilities to launder work clothes according to government guidelines. They must also follow proper sterilizing techniques on equipment and instruments to guard against passing infection or disease.

Approximately 50 percent of all hygienists work full time, about thirty-five to forty hours a week. It is common practice among part-time and full-time hygienists to work in more than one office because many dentists schedule a hygienist to come in only two or three days a week. Hygienists frequently piece together part-time positions at several dental offices and substitute for other hygienists who take days off. About 88 percent of hygienists see eight or more patients daily, and 68 percent work in only one practice. Many private offices are open on Saturday. Government employees work hours regulated by the particular agency.

Sources of Additional Information

■**American Association of Dental Examiners**
211 East Chicago Avenue, Suite 760
Chicago, IL 60611
Tel: 312-440-7464

■**American Association of Dental Schools**
1625 Massachusetts Avenue, NW
Washington, DC 20036
Tel: 202-667-9433
Email: aads@aads.jhu.edu

■**American Dental Association**
211 East Chicago Avenue
Chicago, IL 60611
Tel: 312-440-2500
WWW: http://www.ada.org/prac/careers/dc-menu.html

■**American Dental Hygienists' Association**
444 North Michigan Avenue, Suite 3400
Chicago, IL 60611
Tel: 312-440-8929
WWW: http://www.adha.org

■**National Dental Hygienists' Association**
5506 Connecticut Avenue, NW, Suite 24-25
Washington, DC 20015
Tel: 202-244-7555

Dental Laboratory Technicians

Definition

Dental laboratory technicians are skilled craftspeople who make and repair dental appliances, such as dentures, inlays, bridges, crowns, and braces, according to dentists' and orthodontists' written prescriptions. They work with plastics, ceramics, and metals, using models made from impressions taken by the dentist of a patient's mouth or teeth. Some dental laboratory technicians, especially those who work for smaller dental laboratories, perform the whole range of laboratory activities, while many others specialize in only one area. Some specialties include making orthodontic appliances, such as braces for straightening teeth; applying layers of porcelain paste or acrylic resin over a metal framework to form crowns, bridges, and tooth facings; making and repairing wire frames and retainers for teeth used in partial dentures; and making and repairing full and partial dentures. Job titles often reflect a specialization. For example, technicians who make porcelain and acrylic restorations are *dental ceramicists.*

Nature of the Work

Dental laboratory technicians often find that their talents and preferences lead them toward one particular type of work in their field. The broad areas of specialization open to them include full and partial dentures, crowns and bridges, ceramics, and orthodontics.

Complete dentures, also called false teeth or plates, are worn by people who have had all their teeth removed on the upper or lower jaw, or both jaws. Applying their knowledge of oral anatomy and restoration, technicians who specialize in making dentures carefully position teeth in a wax model for the best occlusion (how the upper and lower teeth fit together when the mouth is closed), then build up wax over the denture model. After the denture is cast in place, they clean and buff the product, using a bench lathe equipped with polishing

School Subjects
Biology
Health

Personal Interests
Helping people: physical health/medicine
Science

Work Environment
Primarily indoors
Primarily one location

Minimum Education Level
Associate's degree

Salary Range
$15,000 to
$22,250 to
$31,000+

Certification or Licensing
Required

Outlook
More slowly than the average

DOT
078

GOE
10.02.02

NOC
3222

wheels. When repairing dentures they may cast plaster models of replacement parts and match the new tooth's color and shape to the natural or adjacent teeth. They cast reproductions of gums, fill cracks in dentures, and rebuild linings using acrylics and plastics. They may also bend and solder wire made of gold, platinum, and other metals and sometimes fabricate wire using a centrifugal casting machine.

Partial dentures, often called partials, restore missing teeth for patients who have some teeth remaining on the jaw. The materials and techniques in their manufacture are similar to those for full dentures. In addition, wire clasps are mounted to anchor the partial denture to the remaining teeth yet allow it to be removed for cleaning.

Crown and bridge specialists restore the missing parts of a natural tooth to recreate it in its original form. These appliances, made of plastics and metal, are sometimes called fixed bridgework because they are permanently cemented to the natural part of the tooth and are not removable. Technicians in this area are skilled at melting and casting metals. Waxing (building up wax around the setup before casting) and polishing the finished appliance are also among their responsibilities.

Some dental laboratory technicians are porcelain specialists, known as *dental ceramicists*. They fabricate natural-looking replacements to fit over natural teeth or to replace missing ones. Many patients concerned with personal appearance seek porcelain crowns, especially on front teeth. The ability to match color exactly and delicately shape teeth is thus crucial for these technicians. To create crowns, bridges, and tooth facings, dental ceramicists apply multiple layers of mineral powders or acrylic resins to a metal base and fuse the materials in an oven. The process is repeated until the result conforms exactly to specifications. Ceramicists must know and understand all phases of dental technology and possess natural creative abilities. Because they require the highest level of knowledge and talent, ceramicists are generally the best paid of dental technicians.

Orthodontics, the final area of specialization for dental laboratory technicians, involves bending wire into intricate shapes and soldering wires into complex positions. *Orthodontic technicians* shape, grind, polish, carve, and assemble metal and plastic appliances. Although tooth-straightening devices such as retainers, positioners, and tooth bands are not considered permanent, they may have to stay in place for long periods of time.

Dental laboratory technicians may work in a general or full-service laboratory, a category that includes nearly half of all dental laboratories. Or they may find employment with a laboratory that performs specialized services. Most specialized laboratories are concerned with the various uses of a particular material. For example, one specializing in acrylics is likely to make complete and partial dentures; another laboratory that does gold work will make gold inlays and bridges.

The lab's size may be related to the kinds of tasks its technical employees perform. Some large commercial laboratories may have staffs of two hundred or more, allowing for a high degree of specialization. On the other hand, technicians working in a one- or two-person private laboratory may be called on to do a wide range of jobs.

Requirements

The basic educational requirement for a dental laboratory technician is a high school diploma. Useful high school courses include chemistry, shop, mechanical drawing, art, and ceramics. Any other course or activity that allows students to learn about metallurgy or the chemistry of plastics would be very helpful.

Inevitably, these technicians must learn much of their job by working under the supervision of experienced technicians. Three to four years of on-the-job training in a dental laboratory is the method of career entry used by some technicians. They start as trainees doing simple jobs such as mixing plaster and pouring it into molds. As they gradually gain experience, they are assigned more complex tasks.

Increasing numbers of technicians enroll in a formal training program that leads to an associate's degree in applied science. A typical two-year curriculum might include courses in denture construction, processing and repairing dentures, tooth construction, waxing and casting inlays, and constructing crowns. In addition, the student may be expected to take courses such as biochemistry, English, business mathematics, and American government.

Although newly graduated technicians still need several years of work experience to refine their practical skills, these graduates benefit from a program combining academic courses with laboratory instruction. Exposure to a wide range of skills and materials pays off in the long run for most graduates. Employers often prefer to hire new employees with this type of formal academic training.

Technicians with appropriate training and experience can become certified dental technicians, thus earning the right to place the initials CDT after their names. Although certification is not mandatory for employment, many employers regard it as the best evidence of competence.

Certification is conducted by the National Board for Certification in Dental Laboratory Technology. For initial certification, candidates must pass a basic written and practical examination in at least one of the five laboratory specialties: complete dentures, partial dentures, crowns and bridges, ceramics, and orthodontics.

Certification requirements also include five years' experience in the field. The time that a dental laboratory technician has spent in an approved dental laboratory technology training program may count toward the total requirement. Every year certified dental technicians must meet specific continuing education requirements in order to maintain certification status.

Although membership is not required, dental laboratory technicians may choose to belong to various professional organizations. The most prominent among these are the National Association of Dental Laboratories and the American Dental Association. Local meetings bring together technicians and laboratory owners to share ideas of common interest and information about job opportunities.

Successful dental laboratory technicians possess the precision, patience, and dexterity of a skilled artisan. They must be able to carry out written and sometimes verbal instructions to the letter because each dental fixture has to be constructed according to very specific designs provided by the dentist. Good eyesight and good color discrimination, as well as the ability to do delicate work with one's fingers are very important. Although it is by no means a requirement, prospective dental laboratory technicians will profit from experience building model airplanes or cars, and other such work that involves mixing and molding various materials.

Opportunities for Experience & Exploration

High school students with an interest in dental laboratory technology can seek out courses and activities that allow exploration of ceramics, metal casting and soldering, molding, and the related skills practiced by dental laboratory technicians. In addition, a local dentist or school guidance counselor may be able to recommend a technician or laboratory in the area that the student might visit in order to get a firsthand idea of the work involved.

Part-time or summer jobs as laboratory helpers may be available to high school students. Such positions usually consist of picking up and delivering work to dentists' offices, but they may also provide a chance for the student to observe and assist practicing dental laboratory technicians. Students in dental laboratory technology training programs often have part-time jobs that develop into full-time technician positions upon graduation.

Methods of Entering

Newly graduated dental laboratory technicians seeking employment can apply directly to dentists' offices and laboratories as well as to private and state employment agencies. The best way for students to locate vacancies is through their schools' placement offices.

Local chapters of professional associations are a good way to make contacts and keep up with new developments and employment openings. Sometimes more experienced dental technicians can get leads by inquiring at dental supply houses. Their sales workers are in constant contact with dentists and laboratories in the area and often know something about staffing needs.

In general, entry-level jobs are likely to include training and routine tasks that allow the technician to become familiar with the laboratory's operations. In a very large commercial laboratory, for instance, newcomers may be assigned to various departments. At the plaster bench they may make and trim models; some technicians may do routine minor repairs of dentures and other appliances; others may polish dentures. As their skills develop, beginning dental laboratory technicians gradually take on more complicated tasks.

Advancement

The best way to advance is to develop individual skills. Technicians can expect advancement as they become expert in a specialized type of work. Depending on skill, experience, and education, some technicians become supervisors or managers in commercial laboratories. Such promotions often depend on the employee having an associate's degree, so many technicians who began their careers with on-the-job training eventually return for formal education.

Technicians interested in advancing can find out about new methods and update their skills in many ways: professional organizations provide a variety of learning opportunities; materials manufacturers also offer courses, often free of charge, in the use of their products—outstanding technicians may be hired as instructors in these courses.

Some dental laboratory technicians, seeking variety and new outlets for their creativity, develop sideline activities that require similar skills and materials. Fine jewelry making, for example, is a natural career development for some technicians. Some technicians become teachers in training programs; others become sales representatives for dental products manufacturers.

Many technicians aspire to own and operate an independent laboratory. This requires a broad understanding of dental laboratory work, a well-developed business sense, and a considerable investment. Nonetheless, most of today's commercial laboratory owners have worked as laboratory technicians themselves.

Employment Outlook

The outlook for employment of dental laboratory technicians is mixed. Job opportunities are favorable, especially for those with strong experience and exceptional ability. Public awareness of dental health and appearance has increased substantially in recent years. At the same time, the number of people covered by dental insurance plans is rising. People in older age groups, who utilize a large share of dental appliances, are becoming a larger segment of the population. In addition, the climate in future years should be good for entrepreneurial technicians establishing new commercial laboratories because increased workloads for most dentists have increased the demand for laboratory services. However, the occupation as a whole is expected to grow slower than the average through the year 2006, largely due to the improved dental care of the general population. Fluoridation of drinking water and greater emphasis on dental care has reduced the need for dental prosthetics.

Earnings

There is limited information available about salaries of dental laboratory technicians. Recent graduates of two-year programs earn about $15,000 per year; with two to five years of experience, dental technicians earn $18,200. The overall average salary for dental laboratory technicians is probably around $22,250 a year. Technicians with proven abilities and special skills earn more.

Generally technicians specializing in ceramics or gold earn the most, often over $33,000 a year. Man-

agers and supervisors in large laboratories and self-employed technicians also exceed the average earnings.

Conditions of Work

Most dental laboratory technicians work in well-lighted, calm, pleasant, and quiet surroundings. Technicians usually have their own workbenches and equipment.

The normal workweek for technicians employed in commercial laboratories is forty hours. Sometimes technicians face deadline pressure, although dentists' requirements are usually flexible enough to allow for special problems or difficult jobs. Many laboratories must operate on weekends, and in areas where there is a shortage of technicians, it may be necessary to work overtime, with wages adjusted accordingly. Self-employed technicians or those in very small laboratories may have irregular or longer hours.

Technicians usually work by themselves, concentrating on details of the pieces they are making or repairing. While the work does not demand great physical strength, it does require deft handling of materials and tools. Technicians usually have little contact with people other than their immediate coworkers and the dentists whose instructions they follow. Work is often brought in and out by messengers or by mail.

Successful dental laboratory technicians enjoy detailed work, are good at following instructions, and take pride in perfection. They should enjoy working independently but still be able to coordinate their activities with other workers in the same laboratory when necessary.

Sources of Additional Information

■**American Dental Association**
Department of Career Guidance
211 East Chicago Avenue
Chicago, IL 60611
Tel: 312-440-2500
WWW: http://www.ada.org/prac/careers/dc-menu.html

For information on certification, please contact:

■**National Association of Dental Laboratories**
555 East Braddock Road
Alexandria, VA 22314
Tel: 703-683-5263

Detectives

Definition

Detectives are almost always plain-clothes investigators who gather difficult-to-obtain information on criminal activity and other subjects. They conduct interviews and surveillance, locate missing persons and criminal suspects, examine records, and write detailed reports. Some make arrests and take part in raids.

Nature of the Work

The job of a *police detective* begins after a crime has been committed. Uniformed police officers are usually the first to be dispatched to the scene of a crime, however, and it is police officers who are generally required to make out the initial crime report. This report is often the material with which a detective begins an investigation.

Detectives may also receive help early on from other members of the police department. Evidence technicians are sometimes sent immediately to the scene of a crime to comb the area for physical evidence. This step is important because most crime scenes contain physical evidence that could link a suspect to the crime. Fingerprints are the most common physical piece of evidence, but other clues, such as broken locks, broken glass, and footprints, as well as blood, skin, or hair traces, are also useful. If there is a suspect on the scene, torn clothing or any scratches, cuts, and bruises are noted. Physical evidence may then be tested by specially trained crime lab technicians.

It is after this initial stage that the case is assigned to a police detective. Police detectives may be assigned as many as two or three cases a day, and having thirty cases to handle at one time is not unusual. Because there is only a limited amount of time, an important part of a detective's work is to determine which cases have the greatest chance of being solved. The most serious offenses or those in which there is considerable evidence and obvious leads tend to receive the highest priority. All cases,

School Subjects
Government
Psychology

Personal Interests
Helping people: personal service
Law

Work Environment
Indoors and outdoors
One location with some travel

Minimum Education Level
High school diploma

Salary Range
$22,500 to
$41,200 to
$64,500

Certification or Licensing
Required

Outlook
About as fast as the average

DOT
375

GOE
02.04.01

NOC
6261

however, are given at least a routine follow-up investigation.

Police detectives have numerous means of gathering additional information. For example, they contact and interview victims and witnesses, familiarize themselves with the scene of the crime and places where a suspect may spend time, and conduct surveillance operations. Detectives sometimes have informers who provide important leads. Because a detective must often work undercover, ordinary clothes, not a police uniform, are worn. Also helpful are existing police files on other crimes, on known criminals, and on people suspected of criminal activity. If sufficient evidence has been collected, the police detective will arrest the suspect, sometimes with the help of uniformed police officers.

Once the suspect is in custody, it is the job of the police detective to conduct an interrogation. Questioning the suspect may reveal new evidence and help determine whether the suspect was involved in other unsolved crimes. Before finishing the case, the detective must write a detailed written report. Detectives are sometimes required to present evidence at the trial of the suspect.

Narcotics squad detectives, officially called *DEA (Drug Enforcement Administration) special agents,* have similar duties as police detectives, but their focus is on violators of the federal government's Controlled Substances Act. Among the duties of a narcotics squad detective are investigating major drug cases, conducting surveillance, operating undercover in drug activities, and apprehending suspects. They also confiscate drug supplies and assets gained by drug trafficking, write detailed reports, and testify in court.

Criminal investigation is just one area in which private investigators are involved. Some specialize, for example, in finding missing persons, while others may investigate insurance fraud, gather information on the background of persons involved in divorce or child custody cases, provide lie detection tests, debug offices and telephones, or offer security services. Cameras, video equipment, tape recorders, and lock picks are used in compliance with legal restrictions to obtain necessary information.

Some private investigators work for themselves, but many others work for detective agencies or businesses. Clients include private individuals, corporations concerned with theft, insurance companies suspicious of fraud, and lawyers who want information for a case. Whoever the client, the private investigator is usually expected to provide a detailed report of the activities and results of the investigation.

Requirements

Because detectives work on a wide variety of cases, high school students interested in this field are encouraged take a diverse course load. English, American history, business law, government, psychology, sociology, chemistry, and physics are suggested, as are courses in journalism, computers, and a foreign language. The ability to type is often needed.

To become a police detective, one must first have experience as a police officer. Hiring requirements for police officers vary, but most departments require at least a high school diploma. In some departments a college degree may be necessary for some or all police positions. Many colleges and universities offer courses or programs in police science, criminal justice, or law enforcement. Newly hired police officers are generally sent to a police academy for job training.

After gaining substantial experience in the department—usually about three to five years—and demonstrating the skills required for detective work, police officers may be promoted to a position as a detective. In some police departments, candidates must first take a qualifying exam. For new detectives there is usually a training program, which may last from a few weeks to several months.

In almost all large cities the hiring of police officers must follow local civil service regulations. In such cases a candidate generally must be at least twenty-one years old, a U.S. citizen, and within the locally prescribed height and weight limits. Other requirements include 20/20 corrected vision and good hearing. A background check is often done.

The civil service board usually gives both a written and physical examination. The written test is intended to measure a candidate's mental aptitude for police work, while the physical examination focuses on strength, dexterity, and agility.

Narcotics squad detectives are required to have a college degree, usually with at least a B average. Only U.S. citizens between the ages of twenty-one and thirty-four are considered. Candidates must be in excellent shape and have an uncorrected vision no worse than 20/200 in both eyes (corrected to at least 20/40 in one and 20/20 in the other). All candidates are required to undergo an extensive background check. Experience in the military, law enforcement, a foreign language, navigation and aviation, computers, electronics, or accounting is helpful.

Private detective agencies usually do not hire individuals without previous experience. A large number of private investigators are former police officers. Those with no law enforcement experience who want to become private investigators can enroll in special private investigation schools, although they do not guarantee qualification for employment. These schools teach skills essential to detective work, such as how to lift and develop fingerprints, pick locks, test for human blood, investigate robberies, identify weapons, and take pictures. The length of these programs and their admissions requirements vary considerably. Some are correspondence programs, while others offer classroom instruction and an internship at a detective agency. A college degree is an admissions requirement at some private investigation schools. Experience can also be gained by taking classes in law enforcement, police science, or criminal justice at a college or university.

Licensing for private investigators varies from state to state, but in general applicants must pass a written examination and file a bond. Depending on the state, applicants may also need to have a minimum amount of experience, either as a police officer or as an apprentice under a licensed private investigator. An additional license is sometimes required for carrying a gun.

Among the most important personal characteristics helpful for detectives are an inquisitive mind, good observation skills, a keen memory, and well-developed oral and written communication skills. The large amount of physical activity requires that detectives be in good shape. An excellent moral character is especially important.

Opportunities for Experience & Exploration

There are few means of exploring the field of detective work, and actual experience in the field prior to employment is unlikely. Some police departments, however, do hire teenagers for positions as police trainees and interns. Students and others interested in becoming a detective are advised to talk with a school guidance counselor, their local police department, local private detective agencies, a private investigation school, or a college or university offering police science, criminal justice, or law enforcement courses. In addition, the FBI operates an Honors Internships Program for undergraduate and graduate students that exposes interns to a variety of investigative techniques.

Methods of Entering

Those interested in becoming a detective should contact local police departments, the civil service office or examining board, or private detective agencies in their area to determine hiring practices and any special requirements. Newspapers may list available jobs. Those who earn a college degree in police science, criminal justice, or law enforcement may benefit from the institution's placement or guidance office. Some police academies accept candidates not sponsored by a police department, and for some people this may be the best way to enter police work. To apply for a position as a narcotics squad detective, contact the local office of the U.S. Drug Enforcement Administration or the national office in Washington, DC.

Advancement

Advancement within a police department may depend on several factors, such as job performance, length of service, formal education and training courses, and special examinations. Large city police departments, divided into separate divisions with their own administrations, often provide greater advancement possibilities.

Because of the high dropout rate for private investigators, those who manage to stay in the field for more than five years have an excellent chance for advancement. Supervisory and management positions exist, and some private investigators start their own agencies.

Employment Outlook

In 1996, police, detectives, and special agents held a total of 704,000 positions nationwide. A large percentage of these work for police departments or other government agencies, such as the U.S. Drug Enforcement Administration. Ten percent of all police and detectives were employed by state police agencies; various federal agencies employed about 27 percent

The employment outlook for police detectives is expected to be as fast as the average through the year 2006. The number of new jobs will depend greatly on the level of government spending for law enforcement initiatives. As a rule, detectives enjoy one of the lowest turnovers of all occupations. Still, many openings will likely result from police detectives retiring or leaving their department for other reasons. Job openings for narcotics squad detectives are expected to continue attracting a large number of applicants.

The outlook for private investigators is expected to be high, although it is important to keep in mind that law enforcement or comparable experience is often required for employment. The use of private investigators by insurance firms, restaurants, hotels, and other businesses is on the rise. An area of particular growth is the investigation of the various forms of computer fraud.

Earnings

According to 1996 statistics given by the U.S. Department of Labor, salaries of police detectives ranged from $22,500 to nearly $64,500 depending on location. Compensation generally increases considerably with experience. Police departments generally offer better than average benefits, including health insurance, paid vacation, sick days, and pension plans. Starting salaries of narcotics squad detectives generally range from $21,000 to $26,000 depending on the candidate's previous experience.

Special agents working for the FBI start at base salary of $33,800 a year with potential to earn $66,000 or more a year. Federal special agents are eligible to administratively uncontrolled overtime (AUO), equal to about 25 percent of their salary, which can boost their final yearly earnings. Federal employees, as a rule, are given exceptional benefit packages.

Conditions of Work

The working conditions of a detective are diverse. Almost all work out of an office, where they may consult with colleagues, interview witnesses, read documents, or contact people on the telephone. Their assignments bring detectives to a wide range of environments. Interviews at homes or businesses may be necessary. Traveling is also common. Rarely do jobs expose a detective to possible physical harm or death, but detectives are more likely than most people to place themselves in a dangerous situation.

Schedules for detectives are often irregular, and overtime, as well as working at night and on the weekend, may be necessary. At some police departments and detective agencies, overtime is compensated with additional pay or time off.

Although the work of a detective is portrayed as exciting in popular culture, the job has its share of monotonous and discouraging moments. For example, detectives may need to sit in a car for many hours waiting for a suspect to leave a building entrance only to find that the suspect is not there. Even so, the great variety of cases usually makes the work interesting.

Sources of Additional Information

International Security and Detective Alliance (ISDA)
PO Box 6303
Corpus Christi, TX 78466-6303
Tel: 512-888-6164

International Association of Chiefs of Police
515 North Washington Street, 4th Floor
Alexandria, VA 22314
Tel: 703-836-6767

National Association of Investigative Specialists (NAIS)
PO Box 33244
Austin, TX 78764
Tel: 512-719-3595

American Federation of Police
3801 Biscayne Boulevard
Miami, FL 33137
Tel: 305-573-9819

Drug Enforcement Administration (DEA)
Washington, DC 20537
Tel: 202-401-7834

Diagnostic Medical Sonographers

Definition

Diagnostic medical sonographers, or *sonographers,* use advanced technology in the form of high frequency sound waves similar to sonar to produce two-dimensional, gray-scale images of the internal body for analysis by radiologists and other physicians.

Nature of the Work

Sonographers work on the orders of a physician or radiologist. They are responsible for the proper set up and selection of the ultrasound equipment for each specific exam. They explain the procedure to the patient, recording any additional information that may be of later use to the physician. Sonographers instruct and assist the patient into the proper physical position so that the test may begin.

When the patient is properly aligned, the sonographer applies a gel to the skin that improves the diagnostic image. The sonographer selects the transducer, a microphone-shaped device that directs high frequency sound waves into the area to be imaged, and adjusts equipment controls according to the proper depth of field and specific organ or structure to be examined. The transducer is moved as the sonographer monitors the sound wave display screen in order to ensure that a quality ultrasonic image is being produced. Sonographers must master the location and visualization of human anatomy to be able to clearly differentiate between healthy and pathological areas.

When a clear image is obtained, the sonographer activates equipment that records individual photographic views or sequences as real-time images of the affected area. These images are recorded on computer disk, magnetic tape, strip printout, film, or videotape. The sonographer removes the film after recording and prepares it for analysis by the physician. In order to be able to discuss the procedure with the physician, if

---

School Subjects
Anatomy and Physiology
Chemistry

Personal Interests
Computers
Helping people: physical health/medicine

Work Environment
Primarily indoors
Primarily one location

Minimum Education Level
Associate's degree

Salary Range
$23,500 to
$35,000 to
$41,600

Certification or Licensing
Board certification required by many employers

Outlook
Faster than the average

DOT
078

GOE
02.04.01

NOC
3216

asked, the sonographer may also record any further data or observations that occurred during the exam.

Other duties include updating patient records, monitoring and adjusting of sonographic equipment to maintain accuracy, and, after considerable experience, preparing work schedules and evaluating potential equipment purchases.

Requirements

Instruction in diagnostic medical sonography is offered by hospitals, colleges, universities, technical schools, and the armed forces in the form of hospital certificates, two-year associate's, and four-year bachelor's degree programs. Educational programs consist of classroom and laboratory instruction, as well as hands-on experience in the form of internships in a hospital ultrasound department. Areas of study include patient care and medical ethics, general and cross-sectional anatomy, physiology and pathophysiology, applications and limitations of ultrasound, and image evaluation.

High school students interested in a career in sonography should take courses in mathematics, biology, physics, anatomy and physiology, and, especially, chemistry. Speech and technical writing courses will also provide strong communication skills.

After completing their degrees, sonographers may register with the American Registry of Diagnostic Medical Sonographers (ARDMS). Registration allows qualified sonographers to take the National Boards to gain certification, which, although optional, is frequently required by employers. Other licensing requirements may exist at the state level but vary greatly.

On a personal level, prospective sonographers need to be technically adept and detail and precision minded. They need to enjoy helping others and working with a variety of professionals as part of a team. They must be able to follow physician instructions, while maintaining a creative approach to imaging as they complete each procedure. Sonographers need to cultivate a professional demeanor, while still expressing empathy, patience, and understanding in order to reassure patients. This professionalism is also necessary because, in many instances, tragedy, such as cancer, untreatable disease, or fetal death is revealed during imaging procedures. As a result, sonographers must be able to skillfully deflect questions better left to the radiologist or the attending physician. Clear communication, both verbal and written, is a plus for those who are part of a health care team.

Students should also be aware of continuing education requirements that exist to keep sonographers at the forefront of current technology and diagnostic theory. They are required to maintain certification through continuing education classes, which vary from state to state. This continuing education, offered by hospitals and ultrasound equipment companies, usually occurs after regular work hours have ended.

Opportunities for Experience & Exploration

Although it is impossible for students to gain direct experience in sonography without proper education and certification, students can gain insight into duties and responsibilities by speaking directly to an experienced sonographer. Students can visit a hospital, health maintenance organization, or other locations to view the equipment and facilities used and to watch professionals at work. Interested students may also consider contacting teachers at schools of diagnostic medical sonography or touring their educational facilities. Guidance counselors or science teachers may also be able to arrange a presentation by a sonographer.

Methods of Entering

Those interested in becoming diagnostic medical sonographers must complete a sonographic educational program such as one offered by teaching hospitals, colleges and universities, technical schools, and the armed forces. Students should be sure to enroll in an accredited educational program as those who complete such a program stand the best chances for employment. Prospective sonographers can contact the American Medical Association (AMA) for a list of accredited sonography programs.

Voluntary registration with the American Registry of Diagnostic Medical Sonographers (ARDMS) is key to gaining employment. Most employers require registration with ARDMS. Other methods of entering the field include responding to job listings in sonography publications, registering with employment agencies specializing in the health care field, contacting headhunters, or applying to the personnel officers of health care employers. While hospitals are the main employers of sonographers, increasing employment opportunities exist in nursing homes, HMOs, imaging centers, private physicians' offices, research laboratories, educational institutions, and industry.

Advancement

Many advancement areas are open to sonographers who have considerable experience, and most importantly, advanced education. Sonographers with a bachelor's degree stand the best chance to gain additional duties or responsibilities. Technical programs, teaching hospitals, colleges, universities, and, sometimes, in-house training programs can provide this further training. Highly trained and experienced sonographers can rise to the position of chief technologist, administrator, or clinical supervisor, overseeing sonography departments, choosing new equipment, and creating work schedules. Others may become sonography instructors, teaching ultrasound technology in hospitals, universities, and other educational settings. Other sonographers may gravitate toward marketing, working as ultrasound equipment sales representatives and selling ultrasound technology to medical clients. Sonographers involved in sales may market ultrasound technology for nonmedical uses to the plastics, steel, or other industries. Sonographers may also work as machinery demonstrators, traveling at the behest of manufacturers to train others in the use of new or updated equipment.

Sonographers may pursue advanced education in conjunction with or in addition to their sonography training. Sonographers may become certified in computer tomography, magnetic resonance imaging, nuclear medicine technology, radiation therapy, and cardiac catheterization. Others may become diagnostic cardiac sonographers or focus on specialty areas such as obstetrics/gynecology, neurosonography, peripheral vascular doppler, and ophthalmology.

Employment Outlook

The use of diagnostic medical sonography, like many other imaging fields, will continue to grow because of its safe, nonradioactive imaging and its success in detecting life-threatening diseases and in analyzing previously nonimageable internal organs. Sonography will play an increasing role in the fields of obstetrics/gynecology and cardiology. Furthermore, the aging population will create high demand for qualified technologists to operate diagnostic machinery. Demand for qualified diagnostic medical sonographers exceeds the current supply in some areas of the country, especially rural communities, small towns, and some retirement areas. Those flexible about location and compensation will enjoy the best opportunities in current and future job markets.

A few important factors may slow growth. The health care industry is currently in a state of transition because of public and governmental debate concerning Medicare, universal health care, and the role of third-party payers in the system. Also, some procedures may prove too costly for insurance companies or governmental programs to cover. Hospital sonography departments will also be affected by this debate and continue to downsize. Some procedures will be done only on weekends, weeknights, or on an outpatient basis, possibly affecting employment opportunities, hours, and salaries of future sonographers. Conversely, nursing homes, HMOs, mobile imaging centers, and private physicians' groups will offer new employment opportunities to highly skilled sonographers.

Anyone considering a career in sonography should be aware that there is considerable competition for the most lucrative jobs. Those flexible in regard to hours, salary, and location and who possess advanced education stand to prosper in future job markets. Those complementing their sonographic skills with training in other imaging areas, such as magnetic resonance imaging, computer tomography, nuclear medicine technology, or other specialties, will best be able to meet the changing requirements and rising competition of future job markets.

Earnings

According to the American Society of Radiologic Technologists (ASRT), starting sonographers can expect to earn from $23,500 to $28,500 per year. Those with experience will earn between $30,500 and $34,000 per year. Senior diagnostic medical sonographers with superior expertise, experience, and managerial duties can earn up to $41,600 yearly. Pay scales vary based on experience, educational level, and type and location of employer, with urban employers offering higher compensation than rural areas and small towns. The ASRT also reports that the most financially lucrative areas for sonography in the United States are the Northeast and Pacific regions. Beyond base salaries, sonographers can expect to enjoy many fringe benefits, including paid vacation, sick and personal days, and health and dental insurance.

Conditions of Work

A variety of work settings exist for sonographers, from health maintenance organizations to mobile imaging centers to clinical research labs or industry. In health care settings, diagnostic medical sonographers may work in departments of obstetrics/gynecology, cardiology, neurology, and others. The typical workplace for sonographers is clean, indoors, well lighted, quiet, and professional. Most sonographers work at one location, although mobile imaging sonographers and sales representatives can expect a considerable amount of travel.

The typical sonographer is constantly busy, seeing as many as twenty-five patients in the course of an eight-hour day. Overtime may also be required by some employers. The types of examinations vary by institution, but frequent areas include fetal ultrasounds, gynecological (i.e., uterus, ovaries), and abdominal (i.e., gallbladder, liver, and kidney) tests. Prospective sonographers should be aware of the sometime repetitive nature of the job and the long hours usually spent standing . Daily duties may be both physically and mentally taxing. Although not exposed to harmful radiation, sonographers may nevertheless be exposed to communicable diseases and hazardous materials from invasive procedures. Universal safety standards exist to ensure the safety of the sonographer.

Sources of Additional Information

For information regarding the examination to become a registered diagnostic medical sonographer, write or call:

■ **American Registry of Diagnostic Medical Sonographers (ARDMS)**
2368 Victory Parkway, Suite 510
Cincinnati, OH 45206-2810
Tel: 800-541-9754
WWW: http://www.ardms.org

For information regarding a career in sonography or to subscribe to the Journal of Diagnostic Medical Sonography, *write or call:*

■ **Society of Diagnostic Medical Sonographers**
12770 Coit Road, Suite 508
Dallas, TX 75251
Tel: 214-239-7367
WWW: http://www.sdms.org

For information regarding certified programs of sonography, call or write:

■ **American Medical Association (AMA)**
515 North State Street
Chicago, IL 60610
Tel: 312-464-4818

To receive Ultrasound in Medicine and Biology, *a publication geared toward diagnostic imagers, call or write:*

■ **Elsevier Science Publishing Company, Inc.**
655 Avenue of the Americas
New York, New York 10010-5107
Tel: 212-633-3750

Dialysis Technicians

Definition

Dialysis technicians, also called *nephrology technicians* or *renal dialysis technicians,* set up and operate hemodialysis artificial kidney machines for patients with chronic renal failure (CRF). CRF is a condition where the kidneys cease to function normally. Many people, especially diabetics or people who suffer from undetected high blood pressure, develop this condition. These patients require hemodialysis to sustain life. In hemodialysis the patient's blood is circulated through the dialysis machine, which filters out impurities, wastes, and excess fluids from the blood. The cleaned blood is then returned to the body. Dialysis technicians also maintain and repair this equipment as well as help educate the patient and family about dialysis.

Nature of the Work

Dialysis technicians work in hospitals, nursing homes, dialysis centers, and patients' homes. The National Association of Nephrology Technicians/Technologists (NANT) recognizes three types of dialysis technicians. These are the patient-care technician, the biomedical/equipment technician, and the dialyzer reprocessing (reuse) technician.

Dialysis patient-care technicians are responsible for preparing the patient for dialysis, monitoring the procedure, and responding to any emergencies that occur during the treatment. Before dialysis, the technician measures the patient's vital signs (including weight, pulse, blood pressure, and temperature) and obtains blood samples and specimens as required. The technician then inserts tubes into access routes, such as a vein or a catheter, which will exchange blood between the patient and the artificial kidney machine throughout the dialysis session.

While monitoring the process of dialysis, the technician must be attentive, precise, and alert. He or she measures and

School Subjects
Anatomy and Physiology
Biology
Chemistry

Personal Interests
Helping people: emotionally
Helping people: physical health/medicine

Work Environment
Primarily indoors
Primarily one location

Minimum Education Level
High school diploma

Salary Range
$12,500 to
$18,000 to
$40,000

Certification or Licensing
Required in some states

Outlook
About as fast as the average

DOT
078

GOE
10.02.02

NOC
3212

adjusts blood-flow rates as well as checks and rechecks the patient's vital signs. All of this information is carefully recorded in a log. In addition, the technician must respond to any alarms that occur during the procedure and make appropriate adjustments to the dialysis machine. Should an emergency occur during the session, the technician must be able to administer cardiopulmonary resuscitation (CPR) or other life-saving techniques.

Biomedical equipment technicians are responsible for maintaining and repairing the dialysis machines. *Dialyzer reuse technicians* care for the dialyzers—the apparatus through which the blood is filtered. Each one must be cleaned and bleached after use, then sterilized by filling it with formaldehyde overnight so that it is ready to be used again for the patient's next treatment. To prevent contamination, a dialyzer may only be reused with the same patient, so accurate records must be kept. Some dialysis units reuse plastic tubing as well; this, too, must be carefully sterilized.

While most hemodialysis takes place in a hospital or special dialysis centers, the use of dialysis in the patient's home is becoming more common. In these cases, technicians travel to patients' homes to carry out the dialysis procedures or to instruct family members in assisting with the process.

In many dialysis facilities the duties described above overlap. The dialysis technician's role is determined by a number of factors: the dialysis facility's management plan, the facility's leadership and staff, the technician's skills and background, the unit's equipment and facilities, and the long-term care plans for patients. However, all dialysis technicians work under the supervision of physicians or registered nurses.

Requirements

Interested high school students should study biology, chemistry, mathematics, health, and communications. Although there is a movement toward providing more formal academic training in the field of renal dialysis, presently only a few two-year dialysis preparatory programs exist in technical schools and junior colleges. Many people entering the field have some type of experience in a patient-care setting or college training in biology, chemistry, or health-related fields. By far, the majority of technicians learn their skills through on-the-job training at the first hospital or dialysis center they are employed. Therefore, a potential technician should be extremely inquisitive, willing to learn, and able to work as a team member.

The ability to talk easily with patients and their families is essential. Kidney patients, especially those who are just beginning dialysis, are confronting a major—and permanent—life change. The technician must be able to help them deal with the emotional as well as the physical effects of their condition. Good interpersonal skills are crucial, not only in the technician-patient relationship, but in working closely with other technicians and health care professionals as well.

A good head for mathematics and familiarity with the metric system are required. Technicians must be able to calibrate machines and calculate the correct amounts and proportions of solutions to be used as well as quickly determine any necessary changes if there are indications that a patient is not responding to the treatment appropriately.

Because the slightest mistake can have deadly consequences, a technician must be thorough and detail oriented. Since the technician is responsible for the lives of patients, he or she must be mature, able to respond to stressful situations calmly, and think quickly in an emergency.

In most states, dialysis technicians are not required to be registered, certified, or licensed. California and New Mexico are the only states that require certification. In some states, technicians are required to pass a test before they can work with patients.

The Board of Nephrology Examiners—Nursing and Technology (BONENT) and the National Nephrology Technology Certification Board (NNTCB) offer a voluntary program of certification for nurses and technicians. The program's purposes are to identify safe, competent practitioners, to promote excellence in the quality of care available to kidney patients, and encourage study and advance the science of nursing and technological fields in nephrology. These organizations hope that eventually all dialysis technicians will be certified.

Technicians who wish to become certified must be high school graduates. They must either have a minimum of one year of experience and be currently working in a dialysis facility or successful completion of an accredited dialysis course. The certification examination contains questions related to anatomy and physiology, principles of dialysis, treatment and technology related to the care of patients with end-stage renal disease, and general medical knowledge. Certified technicians use the letters CHT (certified hemodialysis technician) after their names. Recertification is required every four years. To be recertified, dialysis technicians must continue working in the field and present evidence of having completed career-related continuing education.

Opportunities for Experience & Exploration

Volunteering in a hospital, nursing home, dialysis center, or other patient-care facility can give students a taste of what it is like to care for patients. Students will soon discover whether they have the necessary disposition to help patients heal both physically and emotionally. Most hospitals have volunteer programs that are open to high school students.

Students interested in the requirements for becoming a dialysis technician may obtain job descriptions from NANT and BONENT. Those whose interest lies specifically in the area of nursing may want to contact the American Nephrology Nurses' Association (ANNA). Also, several journals, such as *Contemporary Dialysis and Nephrology, Dialysis and Transplantation,* and *Nephrology News and Issues* discuss the professional concerns and development of dialysis technicians.

Until there are a greater number of organized and accredited training programs, those who are interested in the career of the dialysis technician must seek information about educational opportunities from local sources such as high school guidance centers, public libraries, and occupational counselors at technical and community colleges. Specific information is best obtained from dialysis centers, dialysis units of local hospitals, home health care agencies, medical societies, schools of nursing, or individual nephrologists.

Methods of Entering

The best way to enter this field is through a formal training program in a hospital or other training facility. A well-qualified high school graduate may also contact his or her local hospital and dialysis center to determine the possibility of on-the-job training. Some hospitals pay trainees as they learn.

Other ways to enter this field are through schools of nurse assisting, practical nursing, or nursing programs for emergency medical technicians. The length of time required for a person to progress through the dialysis training program and advance to higher levels of responsibility should be shorter if he or she first completes a related training program. Most dialysis centers offer a regular program of in-service training for their employees.

Advancement

Dialysis technicians who have gained knowledge, skills, and experience advance to positions of greater responsibility within their units and can work more independently. They may also work in supervisory positions. The NANT guidelines encourage a distinction between technicians and technologists, with the latter having additional training and broader responsibilities. Some technologists conduct biochemical analysis or research studies to improve equipment. Not all dialysis units make this distinction.

A technician looking for career advancement in the patient-care sector may elect to enter nurses' training; many states require that supervisory personnel in this field are registered nurses. Social, psychological, and counseling services appeal to others who find their greatest satisfaction in interacting with patients and their families.

Someone interested in advancement in the area of machine technology may elect to return to college and become a biomedical equipment technician. Biomedical equipment technicians may go on to managerial positions in this field. Dialysis technicians technicians also go into industrial engineering or consulting firms.

Employment Outlook

There should continue to be a need for dialysis technicians in the future. The number of patients receiving dialysis in the United States doubled in the ten years from 1978 to 1988, and it continues to grow. These patients will need dialysis on a daily basis unless they undergo a kidney transplant. By the year 2000, approximately 20 percent of the American population will be over sixty years old. Many of these people will need treatment for end-stage renal disease. If the current trend continues, the number of people with kidney disease will steadily increase. The survival of these patients depends on the continuation of dialysis programs. This means that dialysis technicians will continue to be needed to provide treatment and related services.

Technicians make up the largest proportion of the dialysis team, since they can care for only a limited number of patients at a time (the ratio of patient-care technicians to nurses is generally about four to one). There is also a high turnover rate in the field of dialysis technicians, creating many new job openings. Lastly, there is a shortage of trained dialysis technicians in most localities.

A factor that may decrease employment demand is the further development of procedures that may remove the need for dialysis treatments in health care facilities. For instance, if the percentage and number of individuals able to participate in home dialysis increase, the staffing requirements and number of dialysis facilities would be affected. Similarly, the growing use of peritoneal dialysis threatens the need for dialysis technicians. In this process the membrane used is the peritoneum (the lining of the abdomen), and the dialysis process takes place within, rather than outside, the patient's body. An increase in the number of kidney transplants could also slow the future demand for dialysis technicians. The number of kidney transplants increased nearly fourfold between 1978 and 1988, and this trend may continue as it costs much less to treat a patient with a kidney transplant than with dialysis. However, there are limited numbers of kidneys available for transplants, and until researchers discover a cure for kidney disease, dialysis technicians will be needed to administer treatment.

Earnings

Dialysis technicians can earn between $12,500 and $35,000 per year, depending on their job performance, responsibilities, locality and length of service. Some employers pay higher wages to certified technicians than to those who are not certified. Technicians who rise to management positions can earn from $35,000 to $40,000, and those who go into industrial engineering or consulting firms may do even better.

Technicians receive the customary benefits of vacation, sick leave or personal time, and health insurance. Many hospitals or health care centers not only offer in-service training but pay tuition and other education costs as an incentive to further self-development and career advancement.

Conditions of Work

Dialysis technicians most often work in a hospital or special dialysis centers. The work environment is usually a clean and comfortable patient-care setting. Some technicians are qualified to administer dialysis in patients' homes, and their jobs may require some local travel. Patients who use

dialysis at home need education, assistance, and monitoring. Also, technicians may have to take care of patients when trained family members cannot.

A dialysis technician works a forty-hour week. Patients who work full-time or part-time often arrange to take their dialysis treatments at times that least interfere with their normal activities, therefore some evening and weekend shifts may be required. Flextime is common in some units, offering four- and even three-day workweeks. Technicians in hospitals may be on call nights or weekends to serve in emergencies.

The spread of hepatitis and the growing risk of HIV infection have necessitated extra precautions in the field of hemodialysis, as in all fields whose procedures involve possible contact with human blood. All technicians must observe universal precautions, which include the wearing of a protective apron, foot covers, gloves, and a full face shield.

The work of a technician can also be physically strenuous, especially if the patient is very ill. However, the equipment is mobile and easily moved.

Because the field of renal dialysis is constantly evolving, technicians must keep themselves up to date with technological advances and incorporate new technology as it becomes available. One advantage of being a certified technician is that organizations such as NANT, BONENT, and ANNA provide journals and offer educational seminars to members.

It can be upsetting to work with people who are ill, and a cheerful disposition and pleasant manner will help ease the patient's anxiety. Although the daily tasks of a dialysis technician can be monotonous, the patients and staff are a diverse group of people. Patients come from all walks of life, all ages, and all levels of society. There is also a great satisfaction in helping critically ill patients stay alive and active. Some patients are carried through a temporary crisis by dialysis treatments and return to normal after a period of time. Other patients may be best treated by kidney transplants. But while they wait for a suitable donated kidney, their lives depend on dialysis treatment.

Sources of Additional Information

The following are organizations that provide information on careers in renal technology, training programs, certification, and employers:

■ **Board of Nephrology Examiners—Nursing and Technology (BONENT)**
PO Box 15945-282
Lenexa, KS 66285
Tel: 913-541-9077

American Nephrology Nurses Association (ANNA)
East Holly Avenue, Box 56
Pitman, NJ 08071-0056
Tel: 800-203-5561
WWW: http://www.inurse.com/

National Association of Nephrology Technicians/Technologists (NANT)
PO Box 2307
Dayton, OH 45401-2307
Tel: 513-223-9765

National Nephrology Technology Certification Board (NNTCB)
PO Box 2307
Dayton, OH 45401-2307
Tel: 513-223-9765

National Kidney Foundation, Inc.
30 East 33rd Street
New York, NY 10016
Tel: 212-889-2210 or 800-622-9010

Diesel Technicians

Definition

Diesel technicians repair and maintain diesel engines that power trucks, buses, locomotives, ships, construction and roadbuilding equipment, farm equipment, and some automobiles. They may also maintain and repair nonengine components, such as brakes, electrical systems, and heat and air conditioning.

Nature of the Work

Most diesel technicians work on the engines of heavy trucks, such as those used in hauling freight over long distances or in heavy industries such as construction and mining. Many are employed by companies that maintain their own fleet of vehicles. The diesel technician's main task is preventive maintenance to assure against breakdowns, but they also make engine repairs when necessary. Diesel technicians frequently perform maintenance on other nonengine components, such as brake systems, electronics, transmissions, and suspensions.

Through periodic maintenance, diesel technicians keep vehicles or engines in good operating condition. They run through a checklist of standard maintenance tasks, such as changing oil and filters, checking cooling systems, and inspecting brakes and wheel bearings for wear. They make the appropriate repairs or adjustments and replace parts that are worn. Fuel injection units, fuel pumps, pistons, crankshafts, bushings, and bearings must be regularly removed, reconditioned, or replaced.

As more diesel engines rely on a variety of electronic components, technicians have become more proficient in the basics of electronics. Previously technical functions in diesel equipment (both engine and nonengine parts) are being replaced by electronics, significantly altering the way technicians perform maintenance and repairs. Technicians may need addi-

School Subjects
Computer science
Shop (Trade/Vo-tech education)

Personal Interests
Figuring out how things work
Fixing things

Work Environment
Primarily indoors
Primarily one location

Minimum Education Level
Some postsecondary training
Apprenticeship

Salary Range
$21,060 to
$28,340 to
$42,432+

Certification or Licensing
Recommended

Outlook
More slowly than the average

DOT
625

GOE
05.05.09

NOC
7312

tional training when using tools and computers to diagnose and correct problems with electronic parts.

Diesel engines are scheduled for periodic rebuilding usually every eighteen months or 100,000 miles. Technicians rely upon extensive records they keep on each engine to determine the extent of the rebuild. Records detail the maintenance and repair history that helps technicians determine repair needs and predict and prevent future breakdowns. Technicians use various specialty instruments to make precision measurements and diagnostics of each engine component. Micrometers and various gauges test for engine wear. Ohmmeters, ammeters, and voltmeters test electrical components. Dynamometers and oscilloscopes test overall engine operations.

Engine rebuilds usually require several technicians, each specializing in a particular area. They use ordinary hand tools such as ratchets and sockets, screwdrivers, wrenches and pliers; power tools such as pneumatic wrenches; welding and flame-cutting equipment; and machine tools like lathes and boring machines. Technicians supply their own hand tools at an investment of $6,000 to $25,000 or more, depending upon their specialty. It is the employer's responsibility to furnish the larger power tools, engine analyzers, and other diagnostic equipment.

In addition to trucks and buses, diesel technicians also service and repair construction equipment such as cranes, bulldozers, earth moving equipment, and road construction equipment. The variations in transmissions, gear systems, electronics, and other engine components of various types of diesel engines may require that technicians take additional training.

To maintain and increase their skills and to keep up with new technology, diesel technicians must regularly read service and repair manuals, industry bulletins, and other publications. They must also be willing to take part in training programs given by manufacturers or at vocational schools. Those who have certification must periodically retake exams to keep their credentials. Frequent changes in technology demand that technicians keep up-to-date with the latest training.

Requirements

A high school diploma is the minimum requirement to land a job that offers growth possibilities, a good salary, and challenges. In addition to automotive and shop classes, high school students should take mathematics, English, and computer classes. Adjustments and repairs to many car components require the technician to make numerous computations, for which good mathematical skills will be essential. Technicians must be vora-

cious readers in order to stay competitive; there are many must-read volumes of repair manuals and trade journals. Computer skills are also important as computers are common in most repair shops.

Employers prefer to hire only those who have completed some kind of formal training program in diesel mechanics, or in some cases automobile mechanics—usually a minimum of two years' education in either case. A wide variety of such programs are offered at community colleges, vocational schools, independent organizations, and manufacturers. Most accredited programs last two years and include periods of internship. Some programs are conducted in association with truck and heavy equipment manufacturers. Students combine work experience with hands-on classroom study of up-to-date equipment provided by manufacturers. In other programs students alternate time in the classroom with internships at manufacturers. Although these students may take up to four years to finish their training, they become familiar with the latest technology and also earn modest salaries.

One indicator of quality for entry-level technicians recognized by everyone in the industry is certification by the National Automotive Technicians Education Foundation (NATEF), an affiliation of the National Institute for Automotive Service Excellence (ASE). NATEF offers certification through many secondary and postsecondary training programs throughout the country. Enrolling in a certified program assures students that the program t meets the standards employers expect from their entry-level employees.

Diesel technicians must be patient and thorough in their work. They require excellent troubleshooting skills and must be able to logically deduce the cause of system malfunctions. Diesel technicians also need a Class A driver's license.

Opportunities for Experience & Exploration

Many community centers offer general auto maintenance and technicians workshops where students can get additional practice working on real cars and learn from instructors. Trade magazines are an excellent source for learning what's new in the industry and can be found at libraries, some larger bookstores, or through associations. Many public television stations broadcast automobile maintenance and repair programs that can be of help to beginners to see how various types of cars and components differ.

High school auto technicians and shop courses can help teach students technical aptitude and basic auto maintenance. Students learn the proper use of many different tools as applicable to specific auto components. Working on cars or, if available, diesel engines as a hobby provides valuable firsthand experience in the work of a diesel technician. An after-school and weekend part-time job in a repair shop or dealership can prepare students for the atmosphere and challenges a technician faces on the job. The armed forces provide opportunities to learn heavy equipment diesel repair in addition to providing students with an excellent foundation to pursue a job as a diesel technician after they complete their term of service.

Many diesel technicians began their exploration on automobiles—spare diesel engines are hard to come by for those who are just trying to learn and experiment. Diesel engines are very similar to gasoline engines except for their ignition systems and size. Besides being larger, diesel engines are distinguished by the absence of common gasoline engine components such as spark plugs, ignition wires, coils, and distributors. Diesel technicians use the same hand tools as automobile technicians, however, and in this way learning technical aptitude on automobiles will be important for the student who wishes to eventually learn to work on diesel engines. Diesel technicians, however, do use different diagnostic equipment than automobile technicians.

Methods of Entering

The best way to begin a career as a diesel technician is to enroll in a postsecondary training program and obtain accreditation. Trade and technical schools nearly always provide job placement assistance for their graduates. Such schools usually have contacts with local employers who need to hire well-trained people. Often employers post job openings at nearby trade schools that have accreditation programs.

Although postsecondary training programs are considered a better way to learn, some technicians learn the trade on the job as apprentices. Their training consists of working for several years under the guidance of experienced technicians. Trainees usually begin as helpers, lubrication workers, or service station attendants and gradually acquire the skills and knowledge necessary for many service or repair tasks. However, fewer employers today are willing to hire apprentices because of the time and cost it takes to train them. Those who do learn their skills on the job inevitably require some formal training if they wish to advance and stay in step with the changing industry.

Despite employers' preference to hire trained, accredited workers, demand is expected to exceed the number of postsecondary graduates through the year 2005, thus keeping apprentice options open for the near future. An apprenticeship is an excellent way to gain hands-on experience.

Intern programs sponsored by truck manufacturers or independent organizations provide students with opportunities to actually work with prospective employers. Internships can provide students with valuable contacts who will be able to recommend future employers once students have completed their classroom training. Many students may even be hired by the company in which they interned.

Advancement

Like NATEF training programs, currently employed technicians may be certified by the National Institute for Automotive Service Excellence (ASE) in medium and heavy truck repair. Certification is available in gasoline engines, diesel engines, drive train, brakes, suspension and steering, preventive maintenance inspection, and electrical systems. Although certification is voluntary, it is a widely recognized standard of achievement for diesel technicians and the way many advance. The more certification a technician has, the more his or her worth to an employer, and the higher he or she advances. Those who pass all seven exams earn the status of master truck technician. To maintain their certification, technicians must retake the examination for their specialties every five years. Some employers will only hire ASE-accredited technicians and base starting salary on the level of the technician's accreditation.

With today's complex diesel engine and truck components requiring hundreds of hours of study and practice to master, more employers prefer to hire certified technicians. Certification assures the employer that the employee is skilled in the latest repair procedures and is familiar with the most current diesel technology. Those with good communications and planning skills may advance to shop supervisor or service manager at larger repair shops or companies that keep large fleets. Others, with good business skills, go into business for themselves and open their own shops or work as freelance technicians. Some master technicians may teach at technical and vocational schools or at community colleges.

Employment Outlook

With diesel technology getting better (smaller, smarter, and less noisy), more light trucks and other vehicles and equipment are switching to diesel engines. Diesel engines already are more fuel-efficient than gasoline engines. This increase in diesel powered vehicles, together with a trend toward increased cargo transportation via trucks, will open jobs for highly skilled diesel technicians. Less skilled workers will face tough competition. It is expected that this field will grow slower than the average for all occupations through the year 2006. Many positions will open due to workers retiring from the workforce.

Diesel technicians enjoy good job security. Fluctuations in the economy have little effect on employment in this field. When the economy is bad, people service and repair their trucks and equipment rather than replace them. Conversely, when the economy is good more people are apt to service their trucks and equipment regularly as well as buy new trucks and equipment.

The most jobs for diesel technicians will open up at trucking companies who hire technicians to maintain and repair their fleets. Construction companies are also expected to require an increase in diesel technicians to maintain their heavy machinery, such as cranes, earthmovers, and other diesel powered equipment.

Earnings

Diesel technicians' earnings vary depending upon their region, industry (trucking, construction, railroad), and other factors. Technicians in the West and Midwest tend to earn more than those in other regions, although these distinctions are gradually disappearing. Diesel technicians who work at hourly rates can make significantly more money through overtime pay. Technicians who work for companies that must operate around the clock, such as bus lines, may work at night, on weekends, or on holidays and receive extra pay for this work. Some industries are subject to seasonal variations in employment levels, such as construction. Entry-level positions for skilled, accredited technicians generally pay about $21,000 per year. The median salary for an experienced diesel technician is about $28,340 a year, according to 1996 statistics given by the U.S. Department of Labor.

Technicians employed by firms that maintain their own fleets, such as trucking companies, can have earnings that average over $32,000 per year, at a forty-hour week. Those who put in longer hours or work during periods when they are eligible for extra pay may make substantially more. Some technicians also work on commission. Among technicians who service company vehicles, the best paid are usually those employed in the transportation industry. Technicians employed by companies in the manufacturing, wholesale, and retail trades and service industries have average hourly earnings that may be as much as 10 percent lower than transportation diesel technicians. Diesel technicians working for construction companies during peak summer building seasons earn up to $1,000 a week.

Many diesel technicians are members of labor unions, and their wage rates are established by contracts between the union and their employer. Benefits packages vary from business to business. Technicians can expect health insurance and paid vacation from most employers. Other benefits may include dental and eye care, life and disability insurance, and a pension plan. Employers usually cover a technician's work clothes and may pay a percentage of hand tools purchases. An increasing number of employers pay all or most of an employee's certification training if he or she passes the test. A technician's salary can increase by yearly bonuses or profit sharing if the business does well in the course of a year.

Conditions of Work

Depending on the size of the shop and whether it's a trucking or construction company, government or private business, diesel technicians work with anywhere from two to twenty other technicians. Most shops are well lighted and well ventilated. They can be frequently noisy due to running trucks and equipment. Hoses are attached to exhaust pipes and led outside to avoid carbon monoxide poisoning.

Minor hand and back injuries are the most common problem for diesel technicians. When reaching in hard-to-get-at places or loosening tight bolts, technicians often bruise, cut, or burn their hands. With caution and experience most technicians learn to avoid hand injuries. Working for long periods of time in cramped or bent positions often results in a stiff back or neck. Technicians also lift many heavy objects that can cause injury if not handled cautiously; however, most shops have small cranes or hoists to lift the heaviest objects. Some may experience allergic reactions to the variety of solvents and oils frequently used in cleaning, maintenance, and repair. Shops must comply with strict safety procedures to help employees avoid accidents. Most technicians work between forty- and fifty-hour workweeks, but may be required to work longer hours when the shop is busy or during emergencies. Some technicians make emergency repairs to stranded, roadside trucks or to construction equipment.

Sources of Additional Information

Automotive Service Industry Association (ASIA)
25 Northwest Point
Elk Grove Village, IL 60007-1035
Tel: 847-228-1310

For information on accreditation and testing, please contact:

Inter-Industry Conference on Auto Collision Repair (I-CAR)
3701 Algonquin Road, Suite 400
Rolling Meadows, IL 60008
Tel: 800-ICAR USA

For more information on the automotive parts industry please contact:

Motor and Equipment Manufacturers Association (MEMA)
PO Box 13966
10 Laboratory Drive
Research Triangle Park, NC 27709
Tel: 919-549-4800

National Automobile Dealers Association (NADA)
8400 Westpark Drive
McLean, VA 22102
Tel: 703-821-7000

National Automotive Technicians Education Foundation (NATEF)
13505 Dulles Technology Drive
Herndon, VA 22071-3415
Tel: 703-904-0100

National Institute for Automotive Service Excellence (ASE)
13505 Dulles Technology Drive, Suite 2
Herndon, VA 22071-3415
Tel: 703-713-3800

Pittsburgh Diesel Institute
111 Business Route. 60
Moon Township, PA 15108
Tel: 800-875-5963

Disc Jockeys

Definition

Disc jockeys, or *DJ's,* play recorded music on radio or during parties, dances, and special events. On the radio they intersperse the music with a variety of advertising material and informal commentary. They may also perform such public services as announcing the time, the weather forecast, or important news. Interviewing guests and making public service announcements may also be part of the DJ's job.

Nature of the Work

Disc jockeys serve as a bridge between the music itself and the listener. They also perform such public services as announcing the time, the weather forecast, or important news. Working at a radio station can be a lonely job, since often the disc jockey is the only person in the studio. But because their job is to maintain the good spirits of their audience and attract new listeners, disc jockeys must possess the ability to sound relaxed and cheerful.

Unlike the more conventional radio or television announcer, the DJ is not bound by a written script. Except for commercial announcements, which must be read as written, the disc jockey's statements are usually spontaneous. Disc jockeys are not always free to play what they want, though; at some radio stations, especially the larger ones, the program director or the music director makes the decisions about the music that will be played. And while some stations may encourage their disc jockeys to talk, others emphasize music over commentary and restrict the amount of a DJ's ad-libbing.

Disc jockeys should be levelheaded and able to react calmly even in the face of a crisis. Many unexpected circumstances can arise that demand the skill of quick thinking. For example, if guests who are to appear on a program either do not arrive or become too nervous to go on the air, the disc jockey must fill the air time. He or she must also smooth over a breakdown in equipment or some other technical difficulty.

School Subjects
Speech

Personal Interests
Current Events
Entertaining/Performing
Music

Work Environment
Primarily indoors
Primarily one location

Minimum Education Level
Some postsecondary
training

Salary Range
$7,100 to
$31,251 to
$102,676

Certification or Licensing
None

Outlook
More slowly than the
average

DOT
159

GOE
01.03.03

NOC
5231

Many disc jockeys have become well-known public personalities in broadcasting; they may participate in community activities and public events.

Disc jockeys who work at parties and other special events usually work on a part-time basis. A DJ who works for a supplying company receives training, equipment, music, and job assignments from the company. Self-employed DJs must provide everything they need themselves. Party DJs have more contact with people than radio DJs, so they must be personable and patient with clients.

Requirements

Disc jockeys should have good diction and knowledge of English usage and correct pronunciation. Voice quality matters, but it is not as important as personality. Although there are no formal educational requirements for becoming a disc jockey, many large stations prefer applicants with some college education. Some schools train students for broadcasting, but such training will not necessarily improve the chances of an applicant's getting a job at a radio station. Students interested in becoming a disc jockey and advancing to other broadcasting positions should attend a school that will train them to become an announcer. There are some private broadcasting schools that offer good courses, but others are poor; students should get references from the school or the local Better Business Bureau before taking classes.

Candidates may also apply for any job at a radio station and work their way up. Competition for disc jockey positions is strong. Although there may not be any specific training program required by prospective employers, station officials pay particular attention to taped auditions of the applicant. Companies that hire DJs for parties will often train them; experience is not always necessary if the applicant has a suitable personality.

Union membership may be required for employment with larger stations, and is a necessity with the networks. The largest talent union is the American Federation of Television and Radio Artists (AFTRA).

Opportunities for Experience & Exploration

Students who think they may be interested in becoming disc jockeys might seek a summer job at a radio station. Although they will probably not have any opportunity to broadcast, they may be able to judge whether or not that kind of work might appeals to them as a career.

Any chance to speak or to perform before an audience should be welcomed by the prospective disc jockey. Appearing as a speaker or a performer can show aspirants whether or not they have the necessary stage presence for a career on the air.

Many colleges and universities have their own radio stations and offer courses in radio. Students gain valuable experience working at college-owned stations. Some radio stations offer students financial assistance and on-the-job training in the form of internships and co-op work programs, as well as scholarships and fellowships.

Methods of Entering

One way to enter this field is to apply for an entry-level job rather than a job as a disc jockey. It is also advisable to start at a small local station. As opportunities arise, DJs commonly move from one station to another.

An announcer is employed only after an audition. Audition material should be selected carefully to show the prospective employer the range of the applicant's abilities. A prospective DJ should practice talking aloud, alone, then make a tape of him- or herself with five to seven minutes of material to send to radio stations. The tape should include a news story, two sixty-second commercials, and a sample of the applicant introducing and coming out of a record. (Tapes should not include the whole song, just the first and final few seconds, with the aspiring DJ introducing and finishing the music; this is called "telescoping.") In addition to presenting prepared materials, applicants may also be asked to read material that they have not seen previously. This may be a commercial, news release, dramatic selection, or poem.

Advancement

Most successful disc jockeys advance from small stations to large ones. The typical experienced disc jockey will have held several jobs at different types of stations.

Some disc jockeys get into other types of radio or television work. More people are employed in sales, promotion, and planning than in performing and they are often paid more than disc jockeys.

Employment Outlook

Competition for entry-level employment as a radio disc jockey during the coming years will be strong because the broadcasting industry always attracts more applicants than needed to fill its available openings. Opportunities for experienced broadcasting personnel will continue to become available as a result of increased licensing of new radio stations. Small radio stations tend to hire applicants with little experience; such jobs usually offer low pay. Most larger stations look for disc jockeys that can attract and keep a large audience.

Work for party DJs will continue to be available, but it is not usually full time.

Earnings

The range of salaries for disc jockeys is a rather wide one. In a 1996 survey conducted by the National Association of Broadcasters, average annual salaries for disc jockeys ranged from $7,100 for late night talent to $102,676 for morning drive talent. Median salary for this occupation is $31,251.

Salaries are higher in the larger markets. Employees of larger market stations belong to unions and receive higher salaries than their nonunion counterparts. DJs who work at parties and special events earn $100 or more for a single event, which may last three to six hours.

Conditions of Work

Work in radio stations is usually very pleasant. Almost all stations are housed in modern facilities. Temperature and dust control are important factors in the proper maintenance of technical electronic equipment, and people who work around such machinery benefit from the precautions taken to preserve it.

The work can be demanding. It requires that every activity or comment on the air begin and end exactly on time. This can be difficult, especially when the disc jockey has to handle news, commercials, music, weather, and guests within a certain time frame. It takes a lot of skill to work the controls, watch the clock, select music, talk with a caller or guest, read reports, and entertain the audience; often several of these tasks must be performed simultaneously. A disc jockey must be able to plan ahead and stay alert so that when one song ends he or she is ready with the next song or with a scheduled commercial.

Because radio audiences listen to disc jockeys who play the music they like and talk about the things that interest them, disc jockeys must always be aware of pleasing their audience. If listeners begin switching stations, ratings go down and disc jockeys can lose their jobs.

Disc jockeys do not always have job security; if the owner or manager of a radio station changes, the disc jockey may lose his or her job. The current consolidation of radio stations to form larger, cost-efficient stations has caused some employees, including disc jockeys, to lose their jobs.

Disc jockeys usually work a forty-hour week, but they may work irregular hours. They may have to report for work at a very early hour in the morning. Sometimes they will be free during the regular working hours of others, but will have to work late into the night. Some radio stations operate on a twenty-four-hour basis. All-night announcers may be alone in the station during their working hours.

The disc jockey who stays with a station for a period of time becomes a well-known personality in the community. Such celebrities are sought after as participants in community activities and may be recognized on the street.

Disc jockeys who work at parties and other events work in a variety of settings. They generally have more freedom to choose music selections but little opportunity to ad-lib. Their work is primarily on evenings and weekends.

Sources of Additional Information

For a list of schools offering degrees in broadcasting, contact:

■ **Broadcast Education Association**
1771 N Street, NW
Washington, DC 20036-2891
Tel: 202-429-5355
WWW: http://www.beaweb.org/main.html

For college programs and union information, contact:

■ **National Association of Broadcast Employees and Technicians**
501 3rd Street, NW, 8th Floor
Washington, DC 20001
Tel: 202-434-1254

Dispensing Opticians

Definition

Dispensing opticians measure and fit clients with prescription eyeglasses and contact lenses. They help clients with the selection of appropriate frames and order all necessary ophthalmic laboratory work.

Nature of the Work

Dispensing opticians must be familiar with methods, materials, and operations employed in the optical industry. Their tasks include ensuring that the eyeglasses are made according to the optometrist's prescription, determining exactly where the lenses should be placed in relation to the pupils of the eyes, assisting the customer in selecting appropriate frames, preparing work orders for the optical laboratory mechanic, and sometimes selling optical goods.

Opticians should be good at dealing with people and with handling administrative tasks. They work with the customer to determine which type of frames are best suited to the person's needs. Considerations include the customer's habits, facial characteristics, comfort, and the thickness of the corrective lenses.

The dispensing optician prepares work orders for the ophthalmic laboratory so the technicians can grind the lenses and insert them into the frames. Opticians are responsible for recording lens prescriptions, lens size, and the style and color of the frames.

After the lenses return from the lab, the optician makes sure the glasses fit the customer correctly. The optician will use small hand tools and precision instruments to make minor adjustments to the frames. Most dispensing opticians work with prescription eyeglasses, but some work with contact lenses. Opticians must exercise great precision, skill, and patience in fitting contact lenses. They measure the curvature of the cornea, and, following the optometrist's prescription, prepare complete specifications for the optical mechanic who

School Subjects
Biology
Mathematics

Personal Interests
Building things
Helping people: personal service

Work Environment
Primarily indoors
Primarily one location

Minimum Education Level
High school diploma,
Apprenticeship

Salary Range
$15,000 to
$27,432 to
$35,000

Certification or Licensing
Required for certain positions

Outlook
About as fast as the average

DOT
299

GOE
05.10.01

NOC
3231

manufactures the lens. They must teach the customer how to remove, adjust to, and care for the lenses, a process that can take several weeks.

Requirements

A high school diploma is necessary to enter an apprenticeship or other training program in opticianry. High school students should take courses such as basic anatomy, algebra, geometry, and physics. Mechanical drawing course work is also helpful.

Although many dispensing opticians learn their skills on the job, there has been a recent trend toward a technical training program to provide the background necessary to be successful in this field. Employers prefer to hire graduates of two-year college programs in opticianry. These associate's degree holders are able to advance more rapidly than those who complete an apprenticeship program. Two-year optician programs are offered at community colleges, trade schools, and a few colleges and universities. Twenty-three programs that awarded two-year associate degrees in optometric technology or ophthalmic dispensing were accredited by the Commission on Opticianry Accreditation in 1997. These programs offer courses on mechanical optics, geometric optics, ophthalmic dispensing procedures, contact lens practice, business concepts, communications, mathematics, and laboratory work in grinding and polishing procedures. There are also shorter courses in optometric technology—some less than one year in length.

Some dispensing opticians complete an apprenticeship program offered by optical dispensing companies. Larger companies usually conduct a more formal program, while smaller businesses may have more informal programs. These on-the-job programs include some of the same subjects as those covered in the two-year associate's degree program and may take two to four years to complete. Some specialized training programs may be offered by contact lens manufacturers and professional societies. These are generally shorter and usually cover a particular area of technical training, such as contact lens fitting.

More than twenty states currently require licensing of dispensing opticians. Licensing sometimes requires meeting certain educational standards and passing a written examination. Some states require a practical, hands-on examination. To find out more about licensing procedures, contact the licensing board of the state or states you would work in.

Professional credentials may also include voluntary certification. Certification is offered by the American Board of Opticianry and the National Contact Lens Examiners. Certification must be renewed every three years through continuing education courses. Addresses for these two organizations can be found at the end of this chapter.

Some states may permit dispensing opticians to fit contact lenses without certification, providing they have additional training.

Opportunities for Experience & Exploration

Part-time or summer employment in an optical shop is an excellent way of gaining an insight into the skills and temperament needed to excel in this field. A high school student can also explore opportunities in the field through discussions with professionals already working as dispensing opticians.

Methods of Entering

Since the usual ways of entering the field are either through completion of a two-year associate's degree or through completion of an apprenticeship program, students can use the services of their school's placement office or they can apply directly to optical stores.

Advancement

Skilled dispensing opticians can expect to advance to supervisory or managerial positions in a retail optical store or become sales representatives for manufacturers of eyeglasses or lenses. Some open their own stores. A few opticians, with additional college training, become optometrists.

Employment Outlook

The demand for dispensing opticians is expected to increase as fast as the average through the year 2006. One reason is an increase in the number of middle-aged and elderly people in the population Both age demographics need more eye care than other segments of the population. Educational programs such as vision screening have made the public more aware of eye problems, therefore increasing the need for dispensing opticians. Insurance programs cover more optical needs, which means more clients can afford optical care. Employment opportunities should be especially good in larger urban areas because of the greater number of retail optical stores. Those with an associate's degree in opticianry should be most successful in their job search.

Earnings

Beginning salaries average between $15,000 and $20,000 per year for dispensing opticians just entering the field. Experienced workers can make between $18,000 and $35,000. A survey in the April 1997 *Eyecare Business* magazine reports that dispensing opticians earn an average annual salary of $27,432. Supervisors earn about 20 percent more than skilled workers, depending on experience, skill, and responsibility. Dispensing opticians who own their own stores can earn much more.

Most dispensing opticians are eligible for paid vacation and sick leave, as well as health and dental insurance.

Conditions of Work

The majority of dispensing opticians work in retail shops or department showrooms. The work requires little physical exertion and is usually performed in a quiet, well-lighted environment. Customer contact is a big portion of the job. Some laboratory work may be required, especially if a dispensing optician works with a larger outfit that makes eyeglasses on the premises. The wearing of safety goggles and other precautions are necessary in a laboratory environment.

Dispensing opticians should expect to work forty hours a week, although overtime is not unusual. They should be prepared to work evenings and weekends, especially if they work for a large retail establishment.

Sources of Additional Information

For a list of home-study programs, seminars, and review materials, contact:

National Academy of Opticianry
10111 Martin Luther King, Jr., Highway, Suite 112
Bowie, MD 20720-4299
Tel: 301-577-4828
WWW: http://www.nao.org

For more information about a career as a dispensing optician, contact:

Opticians Association of America
10341 Democracy Lane
Fairfax, VA 22030-2521
Tel: 703-691-8355
WWW: http://www.opticians.org

For a list of accredited programs and general career information, contact:

Commission on Opticianry Accreditation
10341 Democracy Lane
Fairfax, VA 22030-2521
Tel: 703-352-8028
WWW: http://www.nao.org/coa.htm

Drafters

Definition

The *drafter* prepares working plans and detail drawings of products or structures from the rough sketches, specifications, and calculations of engineers, architects, and designers. These drawings are used in engineering or manufacturing processes to reproduce exactly the product or structure according to the specified dimensions. The drafter uses knowledge of various machines, engineering practices, mathematics, building materials, and other physical sciences to complete the drawings.

Nature of the Work

The drafter prepares detailed plans and specification drawings from the ideas, notes, or rough sketches of scientists, engineers, architects, and designers. Sometimes drawings are developed after a visit to a project in the field or as the result of a discussion with one or more people involved in the job. The drawings, which usually provide a number of different views of the object, must be exact and accurate. They vary greatly in size depending on the type of drawing. Some assembly drawings, often called layouts, are twenty-five to thirty feet long, while others are very small. Drawings must contain enough detail, whatever their size, so that the part, object, or building can be constructed from them. Such drawings usually include information concerning the quality of materials to be used, their cost, and the processes to be followed in carrying out the job. In developing drawings made to scale of the object to be built, drafters use a variety of instruments, such as protractors, compasses, triangles, squares, drawing pens, and pencils.

Drafters are often classified according to the type of work they do or the level of responsibility. *Senior drafters* use the preliminary information and ideas provided by engineers and architects to make design layouts. They may have the title of *chief drafter* and assign work to other drafters and supervise their activities. *Detailers* make complete drawings, giving dimensions, material, and any other necessary information of each part shown on the layout. *Checkers* carefully examine drawings to check for errors in computing or in recording dimensions and specifications. *Tracers,* who are usually *assistant drafters,* make corrections and prepare drawings for reproduction by tracing them on transparent cloth, paper, or plastic film.

Drafters may also specialize in a particular field of work, such as mechanical, electrical, electronic, aeronautical, structural, or architectural drafting.

Although the nature of the work of drafters is not too different from one specialization to another, there is a considerable variation in the type of object with which they deal.

Commercial drafters do all-around drafting, such as plans for building sites, layouts of offices and factories, and drawings of charts, forms, and records. *Computer-assisted drafters* use computers to make drawings and layouts for such fields as aeronautics, architecture, or electronics.

Civil drafters make construction drawings for roads and highways, river and harbor improvements, flood control, drainage, and other civil engineering projects. *Structural drafters* draw plans for bridge trusses, plate girders, roof trusses, trestle bridges, and other structures that use structural reinforcing steel, concrete, masonry, and other structural materials.

Cartographic drafters prepare maps of geographic areas to show natural and constructed features, political boundaries, and other features. *Topographical drafters* draft and correct maps from original sources, such as other maps, surveying notes, and aerial photographs.

Architectural drafters draw plans of buildings, including artistic and structural features. *Landscape drafters* make detailed drawings from sketches furnished by landscape architects.

Heating and ventilating drafters draft plans for heating, air-conditioning, ventilating, and sometimes refrigeration equipment. *Plumbing drafters* draw diagrams for the installation of plumbing equipment.

Mechanical drafters make working drawings of machinery, automobiles, power plants, or any mechanical device. *Castings drafters* prepare detailed drawings of castings, which are objects formed in a mold. *Tool design drafters* draft manufacturing plans for all kinds of tools. *Patent drafters* make drawings of mechanical devices for use by lawyers to obtain patent rights for their clients.

Electrical drafters make schematics and wiring diagrams to be used by construction crews working on equipment and wiring in power plants, communication centers, buildings, or electrical distribution systems.

Electronics drafters draw schematics and wiring diagrams for television cameras and TV sets, radio transmitters and receivers, computers, radiation detectors, and other electronic equipment.

Electromechanisms design drafters draft designs of electromechanical equipment such as aircraft engines, data processing systems, gyroscopes, automatic materials handling and processing machinery, or biomedical equipment. *Electromechanical drafters* draw wiring diagrams, layouts, and mechanical details for the electrical components and systems of a mechanical process or device.

Aeronautical drafters prepare engineering drawings for planes, missiles, and spacecraft. *Automotive design drafters* and *automotive design layout drafters* both turn out working layouts and master drawings of components, assemblies, and systems of automobiles and other vehicles. Automotive design drafters make original designs from specifications, and automotive design layout drafters make drawings based on prior layouts or sketches.

Marine drafters draft the structural and mechanical features of ships, docks, and marine buildings and equipment. Projects range from petroleum drilling platforms to nuclear submarines.

Geological drafters make diagrams and maps of geological formations and locations of mineral, oil, and gas deposits. *Geophysical drafters* draw maps and diagrams based on data from petroleum prospecting instruments such as seismographs, gravity meters, and magnetometers. *Directional survey drafters* plot boreholes for oil and gas wells. *Oil and gas drafters* draft plans for the construction and operation of oil fields, refineries, and pipeline systems.

A design team working on electrical or gas power plants and substations may be headed by a *chief design drafter,* who oversees architectural, electrical, mechanical, and structural drafters. *Estimators* and drafters draw specifications and instructions for installing voltage transformers, cables, and other electrical equipment that delivers electric power to consumers.

Requirements

Interested high school students should take science and mathematics courses, mechanical drawing (minimum of one to two years), and wood, metal, or electric shop. They also should take English and social studies classes.

Preparation beyond high school should include courses in the physical sciences, mathematics, drawing, sketching and drafting techniques, and in other technical areas is essential for certain types of beginning positions and for advancement to positions of greater salary and more responsibility. This training is available through apprenticeships, junior colleges, or technical institute programs. Apprenticeship programs usually run three to four years. During this period, the apprentice works on the job and is required to take related classroom work in theory and practice.

Students interested in drafting should have a good sense of space perception (ability to visualize objects in two or three dimensions), form perception (ability to compare and discriminate between shapes, lines, and forms and shadings), and coordinated eye-finger-hand movements.

Opportunities for Experience & Exploration

High school programs provide several opportunities for gaining experience in drafting. Mechanical drawing is a good course to take. There are also many hobbies and leisure time activities, such as woodworking, building models, and repairing and remodeling projects, that require the preparation of drawings or use of blueprints. After the completion of some courses in mechanical drawing, it may be possible to locate a part-time or summer job in drafting.

Methods of Entering

Beginning drafters should have graduated from a postsecondary programs at a technical institute or junior college. School placement offices can assist graduates in finding their first jobs. Applicants for government positions may need to take a civil service examination. Those wishing to enter the field through an apprenticeship program can obtain information from a school counselor, a mechanical drawing or shop instructor, a local union, or from the local, state, or national apprenticeship training representatives.

Beginning or inexperienced drafters often start as tracers. Students with some formal postsecondary technical training often qualify for positions as junior drafters who revise detail drawings and gradually assume assignments of a more complex drawing nature.

Advancement

With additional experience and skill, beginning drafters become checkers, detailers, design drafters, or senior drafters. Movement from one to another of these job classifications is not restricted; each business modifies work assignments based on its own needs.

Drafters often move into related positions. Some typical positions include technical report writers, sales engineers, engineering assistants, production foremen, and installation technicians.

Employment Outlook

In 1996, there were 310,000 drafters employed in business, industry, and government positions, according to the U.S. Department's Bureau of Labor Statistics. About 32 percent work for engineering and architectural companies; 29 percent work for manufacturers of machinery, electrical equipment, fabricated metals, and other durable goods. Other industries that employ drafters include construction, communications, transportation, utilities, and government agencies, most of them at the state and local levels. The majority of federal government drafters work for the Department of Defense. About 5,000 drafters were self employed.

Employment of drafters is expected to change little through the year 2006 despite the anticipated expansion of technological and scientific processes. New products and processes of more complex design will require more drafting services, as will the general growth of industry. However, the increased use of computer-aided design (CAD) systems is expected to offset some of the demand, particularly for lower-level drafters who do routine work. CAD equipment can produce more and better variations of a design, which could stimulate additional activity in the field and create opportunities for drafters who are willing to learn and switch to the new techniques. Applicants with at least two years of CAD experience, and training with a sound drafting program have the best chances for success.

Employment trends for drafters fluctuate with the economy. During recessions, fewer buildings and manufactured products are designed, which could reduce the need for drafters in architectural, engineering, and manufacturing firms.

Earnings

In private industry, the average starting salary for drafters is about $19,000. Experienced drafters earn between $23,000 and $41,000, with the average salary approximately $31,500. Senior drafters can make up to $50,750.

Conditions of Work

The drafter usually works in a well-lighted, air-conditioned, quiet room. This may be a central drafting room where drafters work side by side at large, tilted drawing tables. Some drafters work in an individual department, like engineering, research, or development, where they work alone or with other drafters and with engineers, designers, or scientists. Occasionally, drafters may need to visit other departments or construction sites to consult with engineers or to gain firsthand information.

Most drafters work a forty-hour week with little overtime. Drafters work at drawing tables for long periods of time at arrangements that require undivided concentration, close eyework, and very precise and accurate computations and drawings. There is generally little pressure, but occasionally last-minute design changes or a rush order may create tension or require overtime.

Sources of Additional Information

■ **American Design Drafting Association**
PO Box 799
Rockville, MD 20848
Tel: 301-460-6875

■ **International Federation of Professional and Technical Engineers**
8701 Georgia Avenue, Suite 701
Silver Spring, MD 20910
Tel: 301-565-9016

■ **Manitoba Society of Certified Engineering Technicians and Technologists**
602-1661 Portage Avenue
Winnipeg, MB R3J 3T7 Canada
Tel: 204-783-0088
Email: cttam@mts.net

■ **National Association of Trade and Technical Schools**
PO Box 2006
Department BL
Annapolis Junction, MD 20701

Drywall Installers and Finishers

Definition

Drywall installers and *drywall finishers* plan and carry out the installation of drywall panels on interior wall and ceiling surfaces of residential, commercial, and industrial buildings.

Nature of the Work

Drywall panels are manufactured in standard sizes, such as four feet by twelve feet or four feet by eight feet. With such large sizes, the panels are heavy and awkward to handle and often must be cut into pieces. The pieces must be fitted together and applied over the entire surface of walls, ceilings, soffits, shafts, and partitions, including any odd-shaped and small areas, such as those above or below windows.

Installers begin by measuring the wall or ceiling areas and marking the drywall panels with chalk lines and markers. Using a straightedge and utility knife, they score the board along the cutting lines and break off the excess. With a keyhole saw, they cut openings for electric outlets, vents, air-conditioning units, and plumbing fixtures. Then they fit the pieces into place. They may fasten the pieces directly to the building's inside frame with adhesives, and they secure the drywall permanently with screws or nails.

Often the drywall is attached to a metal framework or furring grid that the drywall installers put up to support the drywall. When such a framework is used, installers must first study blueprints to plan the work procedures and determine materials, tools, and assistance they will require. They measure, mark, and cut metal runners and studs and bolt them together to make floor-to-ceiling frames. Furring is anchored in the ceiling to form rectangular spaces for ceiling drywall panels. Then the drywall is fitted into place and screwed to the framework.

Because of the weight of drywall, installers are often assisted by helpers. Large ceiling panels may have to be raised with a

School Subjects
Mathematics
Shop (Trade/Vo-tech education)

Personal Interests
Building things
Drawing/Painting

Work Environment
Primarily indoors
Primarily multiple locations

Minimum Education Level
High school diploma
Apprenticeship

Salary Range
$10,600 to
$22,300 to
$45,200

Certification or Licensing
None

Outlook
More slowly than the average

DOT
840

GOE
05.05.04

NOC
7284

special lift. After the drywall is in place, drywall installers may measure, cut, assemble, and install prefabricated metal pieces around windows and doors and in other vulnerable places to protect drywall edges. They may also fit and hang doors and install door hardware such as locks, as well as decorative trim around windows, doorways, and vents.

Drywall finishers, or *tapers*, seal and conceal the joints where drywall panels come together and prepare the walls for painting or papering. Either by hand or with an electric mixer, they prepare a quick-drying sealing material called joint compound, then spread the paste into and over the joints with a special trowel or spatula. While the paste is still wet, the finishers press perforated paper tape over the joint and smooth it to imbed it in the joint compound and cover the joint line. On large commercial projects, this pasting-and-taping operation is accomplished in one step with an automatic applicator. When the sealer is dry, the finishers spread another two coats of cementing material over the tape and blend it into the wall to completely conceal the joint. Any cracks, holes, or imperfections in the walls or ceiling are also filled with joint compound, and nail and screw heads are covered. After a final sanding of the patched areas, the surfaces are ready to be painted or papered. Drywall finishers may apply textured surfaces to walls and ceilings with trowels, brushes, rollers, or spray guns.

Requirements

Most employers prefer applicants who have completed high school, although many hire workers who are not graduates. High school courses in carpentry provide a good background, and mathematics is also important. Drywall workers should be in good physical condition.

Most drywall installers and finishers are trained on the job, beginning as helpers aiding experienced workers. Installer helpers carry materials, hold panels, and clean up. They learn how to measure, cut, and install panels. Finisher helpers tape joints and seal nail holes and scratches. In a short time, they learn to install corner guards and to conceal openings around pipes. After they have become skilled workers, both kinds of helpers complete their training by learning how to estimate the costs of installing and finishing drywall.

Some drywall workers learn the trade through apprenticeship programs, which combine classroom study with on-the-job training. A major union in this field, the United Brotherhood of Carpenters and Joiners of America, offers four-year apprenticeships in carpentry that include instruction in drywall installation. A similar four-year program for nonunion workers is conducted by local affiliates of the Associated Builders and Contractors and the National Association of Home Builders. A two-year apprenticeship for finishers is run by the International Brotherhood of Painters and Allied Trades. Union membership is not a requirement for all drywall workers. Some installers belong to the United Brotherhood of Carpenters and Joiners of America, and some finishers are members of the International Brotherhood of Painters and Allied Trades.

Opportunities for Experience & Exploration

It may be possible for students to visit a job site and observe installers and finishers at work. Part-time or summer employment as a helper to drywall workers, carpenters, or painters or even as a laborer on a construction job is a good way to get some practical experience in this field.

Methods of Entering

People who want to work in this field can start out as on-the-job trainees or as apprentices. Those who plan to learn the trade as they work may apply directly to contracting companies for entry-level jobs as helpers. Good places to look for job openings include the offices of the state employment service, the classified ads section in local newspapers, and the local offices of the major unions in the field. Information about apprenticeship possibilities may be obtained from local contractors or local unions.

Advancement

Opportunities for advancement are good for people who stay in the trade. Experienced workers who show leadership abilities and good judgment may be promoted to supervisors of work crews. Sometimes they become cost estimators for contractors. Other workers open their own drywall contracting business.

Employment Outlook

Through the year 2006, employment of drywall installers and finishers will grow more slowly than the average for all other occupations. Most jobs will be created by replacement needs, since turnover for this occupation tends to be quite high. Drywall will continue to be used in many kinds of building construction, and it is expected that the level of construction activity will generally remain steady.

Jobs will be located throughout the country, although they will be more plentiful in metropolitan areas where contractors have enough business to hire full-time drywall workers. In small towns, carpenters often handle drywall installation, and painters may do finishing work. Like other construction trades workers, drywall installers and finishers may go through periods of unemployment or part-time employment when the local economy is in a downturn and construction activity slows.

Earnings

The annual earnings of drywall workers vary widely. The majority of workers have earnings that fall roughly between $22,000 and $45,000, with some making significantly less, according to 1996 U.S. Department of Labor statistics. Apprentices generally receive about half the rate earned by journeymen workers.

Some drywallers are paid according to the hours they work; the pay of others is based on how much work they complete. For example, a contractor might pay installers and finishers five to six cents for every square foot of panel installed. The average worker is capable of installing thirty-five to forty panels a day, with each panel measuring four feet by twelve feet.

Drywall workers usually work a standard workweek of thirty-five to forty hours. Construction schedules sometimes require installers and finishers to work longer hours or during evenings or on weekends. Workers who are paid by the hour receive extra pay at these times.

Conditions of Work

Drywall installation and finishing can be strenuous work. The large panels are difficult to handle and frequently require more than one person to maneuver them into position. Workers must spend long hours on their feet, often bending and kneeling. To work high up on walls or on ceilings, workers must stand on stilts, ladders, or scaffolding, risking falls unless they use caution. Another possible hazard is injury from power tools such as saws and nailers. Because sanding creates a lot of dust, finishers wear protective masks and safety glasses.

Drywall installation and finishing is indoor work that can be done in any season of the year. Unlike workers in some construction occupations, drywall workers seldom lose time because of adverse weather conditions.

Sources of Additional Information

International Joint Painting, Decorating, and Drywall Apprenticeship and Manpower Training Fund
1750 New York Avenue, NW, 8th Floor
Washington, DC 20006
Tel: 202-783-7770

Electricians

Definition

Electricians design, lay out, assemble, install, test, and repair electrical fixtures, apparatus, and wiring used in a wide range of electrical, telecommunications, and data communications systems that provide light, heat, refrigeration, air-conditioning, power, and communications.

Nature of the Work

Many electricians specialize in either construction or maintenance work, although some work in both fields. Electricians in construction are usually employed by electrical contractors. Other *construction electricians* work for building contractors or industrial plants, public utilities, state highway commissions, or other large organizations that employ workers directly to build or remodel their properties. A few are self-employed.

Maintenance electricians, also known as *electrical repairers,* may work in large factories, office buildings, small plants, or wherever existing electrical facilities and machinery need regular servicing to keep them in good working order. Many maintenance electricians work in manufacturing industries, such as those that produce automobiles, aircraft, ships, steel, chemicals, and industrial machinery. Some are employed by hospitals, municipalities, housing complexes, or shopping centers to do maintenance, repair, and sometimes installation work. Some work for or operate businesses that contract to repair and update wiring in residences and commercial buildings.

When installing electrical systems, electricians may follow blueprints and specifications or they may be told verbally what is needed. They may prepare sketches showing the intended location of wiring and equipment. Once the plan is clear, they measure, cut, assemble, and install plastic-covered wire or electrical conduit, which is a tube or channel through which heavier grades of electrical wire or cable are run. They strip insulation from wires, splice and solder wires together,

School Subjects
Mathematics
Physics

Personal Interests
Computers
Fixing things

Work Environment
Primarily indoors
Primarily multiple locations

Minimum Education Level
High school diploma
Apprenticeship

Salary Range
$17,600 to
$32,200 to
$52,900

Certification or Licensing
Required for certain positions

Outlook
More slowly than the average

DOT
003

GOE
05.01.01

NOC
2241

and tape or cap the ends. They attach cables and wiring to the incoming electrical service and to various fixtures and machines that use electricity. They install switches, circuit breakers, relays, transformers, grounding leads, signal devices, and other electrical components. After the installation is complete, they test circuits for continuity and safety, adjusting the setup as needed.

Electricians must work according to the National Electrical Code (NEC) and state and local building and electrical codes (electrical codes are standards that electrical systems must meet to ensure safe, reliable functioning). In doing their work, electricians should always try to use materials efficiently, plan for future access to the area for service and maintenance on the system, and avoid hazardous and unsightly wiring arrangements, making their work as neat and orderly as possible.

Electricians use a variety of equipment ranging from simple hand tools such as screwdrivers, pliers, wrenches, and hacksaws to power tools such as drills, hydraulic benders for metal conduit, and electric soldering guns. They also use testing devices such as oscilloscopes, ammeters, and test lamps. Construction electricians often supply their own hand tools. Experienced workers may have hundreds of dollars invested in tools.

Maintenance electricians do many of the same kinds of tasks, but their activities are usually aimed at preventing trouble before it occurs. They periodically inspect equipment and carry out routine service procedures, often according to a predetermined schedule. They repair or replace worn or defective parts and keep management informed about the reliability of the electrical systems. If any breakdowns occur, maintenance electricians return the equipment to full functioning as soon as possible so that the expense and inconvenience are minimal.

A growing number of electricians are involved in activities other than constructing and maintaining electrical systems in buildings. Many are employed to install computer wiring and equipment, telephone wiring, or the coaxial and fiber optics cables used in telecommunications and computer equipment. Electricians also work in power plants, where electric power is generated; in machine shops, where electric motors are repaired and rebuilt; aboard ships, fixing communications and navigation systems; at locations that need large lighting and power installations, such as airports and mines; and in numerous other settings.

Requirements

Some electricians still learn their trade the same way electrical workers did many years ago—informally on the job, while employed as helpers to skilled workers. Especially if that experience is supplemented with vocational or technical school courses, correspondence courses, or training received in the military, electrical helpers may in time become well-qualified craft workers in some area of the field.

However, it is generally accepted that apprenticeship programs provide the best all-around training in this trade. Apprenticeships combine a series of planned, structured, supervised job experiences with classroom instruction in related subjects. Many programs are designed to give apprentices a variety of experiences by having them work for several electrical contractors doing different kinds of jobs. Typically, apprenticeships last four to five years. Completion of an apprenticeship is usually a significant advantage in getting the better jobs in the field.

Applicants for apprenticeships generally need to be high school graduates, at least eighteen years of age, in good health, and with at least average physical strength. Although local requirements vary, many applicants are required to take tests to determine their aptitude for the work.

All prospective electricians, whether they intend to enter an apprenticeship or learn informally on the job, ought to have a high school background that includes such courses as applied mathematics and science, shop classes that teach the use of various tools, and mechanical drawing. Electronics courses are especially important for those who plan to become maintenance electricians. Good color vision is necessary, because electricians need to be able to distinguish color-coded wires. Agility and manual dexterity are also desirable characteristics.

Most apprenticeship programs are developed and conducted by state and national contractor associations such as the Independent Electrical Contractors, Inc. and the union locals of the International Brotherhood of Electrical Workers. Some programs are conducted as cooperative efforts between such groups and local community colleges and training organizations. In either situation, the apprenticeship program is usually managed by a training committee. An agreement regarding in-class and on-the-job training is usually established between the committee and each apprentice.

Usually apprenticeships involve at least 144 hours of classroom work each year, covering such subjects as electrical theory, electronics, blueprint reading, mathematics, electrical code requirements, and first aid. On the job, apprentices learn how to safely use and care for tools, equipment, and materials commonly encountered in the trade. Over the years of the program, they spend about 8,000 hours working under the supervision of experienced electricians. They begin with simple tasks, such as drilling holes and setting up conduit. As they acquire skills and knowledge, they progress to more difficult tasks, such as diagramming electrical systems and connecting and testing wiring and electrical components.

Many electricians find that after they are working in the field, they still need to take courses to keep abreast of new developments. Unions and employers may sponsor classes introducing new methods and materials or explaining changes in electrical code requirements. By taking skill-improvement courses, electricians may also improve their chances for advancement to better-paying positions.

Electricians may or may not belong to a union. While many electricians belong to such organizations as the International Brotherhood of Electrical Workers; the International Union of Electronic, Electrical, Salaried, Machine, and Furniture Workers; the International Association of Machinists and Aerospace Workers; and other unions, an increasing number of electricians are opting to affiliate with independent (nonunion) electrical contractors.

Some states and municipalities require that electricians be licensed. To obtain a license, electricians usually must pass a written examination on electrical theory, NEC requirements, and local building and electrical codes.

Opportunities for Experience & Exploration

High school students can get an idea about their aptitude for and interest in tasks that come up regularly in the work of electricians by taking such courses as metal and electrical shop, drafting, electronics, and mathematics. Hobbies such as repairing radios, building electronics kits, or working with model electric trains involve skills similar to those needed by electricians. In addition to sampling related activities like these, prospective electricians may benefit by arranging to talk with an electrician about his or her job. With the help of a teacher or guidance counselor, it may be possible to contact a local electrical contracting firm and locate someone willing to give an insider's description of the occupation.

Methods of Entering

People seeking to enter this field may either begin working as helpers with little background in the field, or they may enter an apprenticeship program. Leads for helper jobs may be located by contacting electrical contractors directly and by checking the usual sources for jobs listings, like the local offices of the state employment service and newspaper classified advertising sections. Students in trade and vocational school courses may be able to find job openings through the placement office of their school.

People who want to become apprentices may start by contacting the union local of the International Brotherhood of Electrical Workers, the local chapter of the Independent Electrical Contractors, Inc., or the local apprenticeship training committee. Information on apprenticeship possibilities can also be obtained through the state employment service.

Advancement

The advancement possibilities for skilled, experienced electricians depend partly on their field of activity. Those who work in construction may become supervisors, job site superintendents, or estimators for electrical contractors. Some electricians are able to establish their own contracting businesses, although in many areas contractors must obtain a special license. Another possibility for some electricians is to move, for example, from construction to maintenance work or into jobs in the shipbuilding, automobile, or aircraft industry.

Employment Outlook

Through the year 2006, job opportunities for skilled electricians are expected to be good, although the Bureau of Labor Statistics predicts slower than average growth for electricians as a whole.

The growth in this field will be principally related to overall increased levels in construction of buildings for residential and commercial purposes. In addition, growth will be driven by the ever-increasing use of electrical and electronic devices and equipment. Electricians will be called on to upgrade old wiring and to install and maintain more extensive wiring systems than have been necessary in the past. In particular, the increased use of sophisticated telecommunications and data-processing equipment and automated manufacturing systems is expected to lead to many job opportunities for electricians.

While the overall outlook for this occupational field is good, the availability of jobs will vary over time and from place to place. Construction activity fluctuates depending on the state of the local and national economy. Thus, during economic slowdowns, opportunities for construction electricians may not be plentiful. People working in this field need to be prepared for periods of unemployment between construction projects. Openings for apprentices also decline during economic downturns. Maintenance electricians are usually less vulnerable to periodic unemployment because they are more likely to work for one employer that needs electrical services on a steady basis. But if they work in an industry where the economy causes big fluctuations in the level of activity, like automobile manufacturing, they may be laid off during recessions.

Not many electricians switch completely out of their job field because of the time that must be invested in training and the relatively good pay for skilled workers. Nonetheless, many of the job openings that occur each year develop as electricians move into other occupations or leave the labor force altogether. During the coming years, enough electricians are expected to retire that a national shortage of well-qualified workers could develop if training programs don't attract more applicants who can eventually take the place of the retirees.

Earnings

The earnings of electricians vary widely depending on such factors as the industry in which they are employed, their geographic location, union membership, and other factors. In general, the majority of electricians who were employed full-time in 1996 had annual earnings that ranged from $24,300 to $42,300 or more, as reported by the U.S. Bureau of Labor Statistics. One national survey reported that the average wages for electricians who are union members are at least $33,700 a year. Another

study has showed that maintenance electricians in metropolitan areas have earnings that average approximately $34,000 a year. Electricians in the West and Midwest tend to make more than those in the Northeast and South.

Wages rates for many electricians are set by agreements between unions and employers. In addition to their regular earnings, electricians may receive fringe benefits such as employer contributions to health insurance and pension plans, paid vacation and sick days, and supplemental unemployment compensation plans.

Wages of apprentices often start at about 30 to 50 percent of the skilled worker's rate and increase every six months until the last period of the apprenticeship, when the pay approaches that of fully qualified electricians.

Conditions of Work

Electricians usually work indoors, although some must do tasks outdoors or in buildings that are still under construction. The standard workweek is approximately forty hours. In many jobs overtime may be required. Maintenance electricians often have to work some weekend, holiday, or night hours because they must service equipment that operates all the time.

Electricians often spend long periods on their feet, sometimes on ladders or scaffolds or in awkward or uncomfortable places. The work can be strenuous. Electricians may have to put up with noise and dirt on the job. They may risk injuries such as falls off ladders, electrical shocks, and cuts and bruises. By following established safety practices, most of these hazards can be avoided.

Sources of Additional Information

For a general brochure on electrical apprenticeship, contact:

National Joint Apprenticeship Training Committee for the Electrical Industry
16201 Trade Zone Avenue, Suite 105
Upper Marlboro, MD 20774

For information on its electrical apprenticeship curriculum and a list of chapter offices, contact:

■ **Independent Electrical Contractors, Inc.**
507 Wythe Street
Alexandria, VA 22314
Tel: 703-549-7351

For a list of local unions in your area, contact:

■ **International Brotherhood of Electrical Workers**
1125 15th Street, NW
Washington, DC 20005

■ **International Society of Certified Electronics Technicians**
2708 West Berry Street, Suite 3
Fort Worth, TX 76109-2356
Tel: 817-921-9101
WWW: http://www.iscet.org

■ **National Electrical Contractors Association**
3 Bethesda Metro Center, Suite 1100
Bethesda, MD 20814

Electrologists

Definition

Electrologists remove unwanted hair from the skin of patients by using sterilized probes that deaden the hair root with small charges of electricity and tiny forceps to remove the loosened hair.

Nature of the Work

Electrologists, who usually conduct business in a professional office, salon, or medical clinic, work with only one patron at a time. This enables them to focus their complete attention and concentration on the delicate treatment they are performing. Since electrolysis can sometimes be uncomfortable, it reassures patrons to know that the practitioner's complete focus is on them and their needs.

The first step in the treatment is the cleansing of the area of skin that will be worked on. Rubbing alcohol or an antiseptic is often used for this purpose. Once the skin is cleansed, hair removal can begin. Electrologists use a round-tipped probe to enter the opening of the skin fold, also known as the hair follicle. The probe also penetrates the papilla, which is the organ beneath the hair root. The electrologist sets the proper amount and duration of the electrical current in advance and presses gently on a floor pedal to distribute that current through the probe. The electrical current helps deaden the tissue, after which the hair can be lifted out gently with a pair of tweezers or forceps.

Electrologists can remove hair from almost any area of the body. The most common areas they treat are the arms, legs, chest, and portions of the face such as upper or lower lip, chin, or cheek. Electrologists should not remove hair from inside the ears or nose or from the eyelids. They should also have the written consent of a physician to remove hair from a mole or birthmark and legitimate malpractice insurance coverage.

Electrologists determine the extent of treatments that will be necessary for complete removal of the unwanted hair. They

School Subjects
Biology
Health

Personal Interests
Helping people: personal service
Science

Work Environment
Primarily indoors
Primarily one location

Minimum Education Level
Some postsecondary education

Salary Range
$15,000 to
$25,000 to
$50,000

Certification or Licensing
Required

Outlook
About as fast as the average

DOT
824

GOE
05.05.05

NOC
7241

may schedule weekly appointments that last fifteen, thirty, forty-five, or even sixty minutes. The length of the individual appointments depends on both the amount of hair to be removed and the thickness and depth of the hair. If a patient is very sensitive to the treatments, the electrologist may set up shorter appointments.

Electrolysis is mainly performed for aesthetic reasons. As is the case with cosmetic surgery, the procedure can be fairly expensive. The electrologist should first consult with a patient to determine what is desired and why and then discuss the cost of the procedure.

Requirements

Students with high school diplomas or equivalency certificates may enroll in trade schools or professional schools that offer electrolysis training. In these programs students study microbiology, dermatology, neurology, and electricity. They also learn about proper sterilization and sanitation procedures to avoid infections or injury. Cell composition, the endocrine system, the vascular pulmonary system, and basic anatomy may also be covered.

Although the training offered is designed to educate students about the theory of electrolysis and its relation to the skin and tissue, the greater part of the training is of a practical nature. Many training hours are spent learning the purpose and function of the different types of equipment. In addition, hands-on experience with patrons needing different treatments gives students confidence in operating equipment and working with patients.

Programs may be offered on a full-time or part-time basis. Although tuition varies, some schools offer financial assistance or payment plans to make their programs more affordable. Sometimes lab and materials fees are charged. Applicants should determine whether the school is accredited or associated with any professional organizations. Licensing requirements of the various states may also affect the length and depth of training that the schools offer.

States that require licensing offer examinations through the state health department. The examination usually covers various topics in the areas of health and cosmetology. Students should become familiar with their state's licensing requirements prior to beginning their training so they can be sure their education provides them with everything necessary to practice.

Electrologists have many professional organizations that provide information on new equipment, special seminars, and networking and employment opportunities. The American Electrolysis Association, the International Guild of Professional Electrologists, and the Society of Clinical and Medical Electrologists offer useful information for beginning practitioners and guidelines for certification and advanced study.

Electrologists help people feel good about themselves by improving aspects of their physical appearance. They feel a sense of accomplishment for helping patients through the various stages of their treatment. They may sometimes feel the anxiety of a patient who is impatient or unrealistic about the results or is nervous about the process. Because electrologists perform personal and sometimes uncomfortable treatments, it is important that they be patient and caring and develop an empathetic working style.

Opportunities for Experience & Exploration

Students interested in finding out more about the field of electrology may wish to contact local trade schools for information. Also, some two-year colleges that offer coursework in medical-technician careers may be able to supply literature on programs and training in electrology.

Cosmetology schools, which are located in many different areas of the country, may also prove helpful for investigating this profession. Some schools and training programs allow interested students to speak with faculty and guidance counselors for further information.

Methods of Entering

Many newly licensed electrologists begin as assistants to a practicing professional. They may handle extra patients when the office is overbooked or have new patients referred to them. In this way, beginning electrologists can build a clientele without having to cover the costs of equipment and supplies themselves.

Some electrologists may open their own business in a medical office complex and receive referrals from their neighboring health care professionals. Others may be employed by clinics or hospitals before deciding to get their own office space.

Advancement

Electrologists usually advance through building up the various aspects of their practices. As an electrologist becomes more experienced and gains a reputation, he or she often attracts more new patients and repeat clients. Some electrologists who work as part of a clinic staff may open their own office in a more visible and accessible location or office complex.

Employment Outlook

A moderate increase in employment opportunities is expected to continue for electrologists. Many hospitals and clinics strive to develop new services and technologies, which can result in more jobs for electrologists. In addition, there is a trend among allied health professionals toward large group practices to pool resources and offset joint costs, such as common supplies, support staff, and so on. This may make it more feasible for beginning electrologists to open their own practices right out of school.

Earnings

Because electrologists schedule patient treatments that vary in length, their fees are often based on quarter-hour appointments. Rates for a fifteen-minute treatment may begin at $20 in some cities, while electrologists in large urban regions may begin at $30. Treatments lasting thirty or sixty minutes in large cities may begin at $50 and $100, respectively. Although rates in smaller towns are often less, these electrologists still earn a competitive wage for their work. Experienced electrologists can earn between $15,000 and $50,000 per year. Electrologists who are employed by a medical clinic or salon may have to contribute a portion of their fees to help cover office space, utilities, and support staff like receptionists and bookkeepers.

Conditions of Work

Whether the electrologist works in a professional office, a salon, a medical clinic, or a private shop, the nature of the work requires the environment to be clean, comfortable, and professional. Because electrologists perform delicate work, they may operate in spaces that are quiet to allow for greater concentration. Sometimes music is played in the background to help put patients at ease.

A neat appearance is important, so electrologists often wear uniforms or lab coats. As well as being comfortable and practical for the electrologist, a medical uniform may also reassure and comfort the patient.

Sources of Additional Information

The AEA sponsors the International Board of Electrologist Certification (IBEC), an additional credential for licensing. For information regarding the IBEC and for a directory of accredited schools and state requirements relating to electrology, send a stamped, self-addressed envelope to:

■**American Electrology Association (AEA)**
106 Oak Ridge Road
Trumbull, CT 06611
Tel: 203-374-6667

■**International Guild of Professional Electrologists**
202 Boulevard, Suite B
High Point, NC 27262
Tel: 910-841-6631

■**National Commission for Electrologist Certification**
132 Great Road, Suite 200
Stow, MA 01775
Tel: 508-461-0313

■**Society of Clinical and Medical Electrologists**
132 Great Road, Suite 200
Stow, MA 01775
Tel: 508-461-0313

Electroneurodiagnostic Technologists

Definition

Electroneurodiagnostic technologists, sometimes called *EEG technologists* or *END technologists,* operate electronic instruments called electroencephalographs. These instruments measure and record the brain's electrical activity. The information gathered is used by physicians (usually neurologists) to diagnose and determine the effects of certain diseases and injuries, including brain tumors, cerebral vascular strokes, Alzheimer's disease, epilepsy, some metabolic disorders, and brain injuries caused by accidents or infectious diseases.

Nature of the Work

The basic principle behind electroencephalography (EEG) is that electrical impulses emitted by the brain, often called brain waves, vary according to the brain's age, activity, and condition. Research has established that certain brain conditions correspond to certain brain waves. Therefore, testing EEG can aid the neurologist (a physician specially trained in the study of the brain) in making a diagnosis of a person's illness or injury.

The EEG technologist's first task with a new patient is to take a simplified medical history. This entails asking questions and recording answers about his or her past health status and present illness. These answers provide the technologist with necessary information about the patient's condition. They also provides an opportunity to help the patient relax before the test.

The technologist then applies electrodes to the patient's head. Often, technologists must choose the best combination of instrument controls and placement of electrodes to produce the kind of tracing that has been requested. In some cases, a physician will give special instructions to the technologist regarding the placement of electrodes.

Once in place, the electrodes are connected to the recording equipment. Here, a bank of sensitive electronic amplifiers

School Subjects
Anatomy and Physiology
Biology

Personal Interests
Computers
Helping people: physical health/medicine

Work Environment
Primarily indoors
Primarily one location

Minimum Education Level
High school diploma

Salary Range
$16,000 to
$26,800 to
$46,000

Certification or Licensing
Voluntary

Outlook
Much faster than the average

DOT
078

GOE
10.03.01

NOC
3218

transmits information. Tracings from each electrode are made on a moving strip of paper or recorded on optical disks in response to the amplified impulses coming from the brain. The resulting graph is a recording of the patient's brain waves.

EEG technologists are not responsible for interpreting the tracings (that is the job of the neurologist); however, they must be able to recognize abnormal brain activity and any readings on the tracing that are coming from somewhere other than the brain, such as readings of eye movement or nearby electrical equipment.

Technologists can make recording changes to better present the abnormal findings for physician interpretation. Stray readings are known as artifacts. Technologists must be able to determine what kinds of artifacts should be expected for an individual patient on the basis of his or her medical history or present illness. They should also be sensitive to these artifacts and be able to identify them if they occur.

Technologists must be able to detect faulty recordings made by technologist error or by machine malfunctions. When mechanical problems occur, technologists should notify their supervisors so that the machine can be repaired by technologist supervisors or trained equipment technicians.

Throughout the procedure, electroneurodiagnostic technicians observe the patient's behavior and make detailed notes about any aspect of the behavior that might be of use to the physician in interpreting the tracing. They also keep watch on the patient's brain, heart, and breathing functions for any signs that the patient is in any immediate danger.

During the testing, the patient may be either asleep or awake. In some cases, the physician may want recordings taken in both states. Sometimes drugs or special procedures are prescribed by the physician to simulate a specific kind of condition. Administering the drugs or procedures is often the technologist's responsibility.

EEG technologists need a basic understanding of any medical emergencies that can occur during this procedure. By being prepared, they can react properly if one of these emergencies should arise. For instance, if a patient suffers an epileptic seizure, technologists must know what to do. They must be flexible and able to handle medical crises should they arise.

EEG technologists may also handle other specialized electroencephalograms. For example, in a procedure called ambulatory monitoring, both heart and brain activity are tracked over a twenty-four-hour period by a small recording device on the patient's side. In evoked potential testing, a special machine is used to measure the brain's response to specific types of stimulus. And electroencephalograms are increasingly used on a routine basis in the operating room to monitor patients during major surgery.

Besides conducting various kinds of electroencephalograms, EEG technologists also maintain the machine, perform minor repairs (major repairs require specially trained repairers), schedule appointments, and order supplies. In some cases they may have some supervisory responsibilities; however, most supervision is done by registered electroencephalographic technologists.

Requirements

Prospective EEG technologists should plan to get a high school diploma, as it is usually a requirement for entry into any kind of EEG technologist training program, whether in school or on the job. In general, students will find it helpful to have three years of mathematics, including algebra, and three years of science, including biology, chemistry, and physics. In addition, students should take courses in English, especially those that help improve their communications skills, and in social sciences so that they can better understand the social and psychological needs of their patients.

There are two main types of postsecondary training available for EEG technologists: on-the-job training and formal classroom training. Many technologists who are currently working received on-the-job training; however, EEG equipment is becoming so sophisticated that many employers prefer to hire EEG technologists with prior formal training.

On-the-job training generally lasts from a few months to one year, depending on the employer's special requirements. Trainees learn how to handle the equipment and carry out procedures by observing and receiving instruction from senior electroencephalographic technicians or technologists.

Formal training consists of both practice in the clinical laboratory and instruction in the classroom. The classroom instruction usually focuses on basic subjects such as human anatomy, physiology, neuroanatomy, clinical neurology, neuropsychiatry, clinical and internal medicine, psychology, electronics, and instrumentation. The postsecondary programs usually last from one to two years and are offered by hospitals, medical centers, and community or technical colleges.

Students who have completed one year of on-the-job training or who have graduated from a formal training program may apply for registration.

The American Board of Registration of Electroencephalographic and Evoked Potential Technologists (ABRET) registers technologists at one level of experience and education—that is, as a registered electroencephalographic technologist (REEGT). Technicians who have been in the field for at least one year can earn this registration by passing an exam.

Although registration is not required for employment, it is an acknowledgment of the technologist's training and does make advancement easier. Registration may also provide a salary increase.

EEG technologists need good vision and manual dexterity, an aptitude for working with mechanical and electronic equipment, and the ability to get along well with patients, their families, and members of the hospital staff.

Opportunities for Experience & Exploration

Prospective EEG technologists will find it difficult to gain any direct experience on a part-time basis in electroencephalography. Their first direct experience with the work will generally come during their on-the-job training sessions or in the practical-experience portion of their formal training. They may, however, be able to gain some exposure to patient-care activities in general by signing up for volunteer work at a local hospital. In addition, they could arrange to visit a hospital, clinic, or doctor's office where electroencephalograms are taken. In this way, they may be able to watch technicians at work or talk to them about what the work is like.

Methods of Entering

Technologists often obtain permanent employment in the hospital where they received their on-the-job or work-study training.

Prospective technologists can also find employment through classified ads in newspapers and by contacting the personnel offices of hospitals, medical centers, clinics, and government agencies that employ EEG technologists.

Advancement

Opportunities for advancement are good for registered electroneurodiagnostic technologists. EEG technologists who do not take this step will find their opportunities for advancement severely limited.

Usually, technologists are assigned to conduct more difficult or specialized electroencephalograms. They also supervise other electroencephalographic technicians, arrange work schedules, and teach techniques to new trainees. They may also establish procedures, manage a laboratory, keep records, schedule appointments, and order supplies.

EEG technologists may advance to *chief electroencephalographic technologist* and thus take on even more responsibilities in laboratory management and in teaching new personnel and students. Chief electroencephalographic technologists generally work under the direction of an electroencephalographer, neurologist, or neurosurgeon.

Employment Outlook

The total number of people employed as electroneurodiagnostic technologists is expected to grow much faster than the average for other occupations at least through the year 2006. This is a reflection of the increasing number of neurodiagnostic tests performed in surgery, diagnosing and monitoring patients, and research on the human brain. Though most jobs are currently in hospitals, positions will grow fastest in neurologists' offices and clinics.

Earnings

Starting salaries are approximately $16,000 a year. Experienced EEG technologists average approximately $26,499 a year and may earn as much as $35,000 to $46,000 a year. Salaries for registered EEG technologists tend to be $6,000 to $10,000 a year higher than nonregistered technologists with equivalent experience.

The highest salaries for EEG technologists tend to go to those who work as laboratory supervisors, teachers in training programs, and program directors in schools of electroencephalographic technology.

Electroencephalographic technicians working in hospitals receive the same fringe benefits as other hospital workers. These benefits usually include hospitalization insurance, paid vacations, and sick leave. In some cases the benefits may also include educational assistance, pension plans, and uniform allowances.

Conditions of Work

EEG technologists usually work five-day, forty-hour workweeks, with only occasional overtime required. Some hospitals require them to be on call for emergencies during weekends, evenings, and holidays. Technologists doing sleep studies may work most of their hours at night. EEG technologists work in clean, well-lighted surroundings.

EEG technologists generally work with people who are ill and may be frightened or emotionally disturbed. Successful technologists are the ones who like people, can quickly recognize what others may be feeling, and gear their treatment to the patient's needs. They need to be able to realize that some patients will be very ill; others may be in the process of dying. Work as an EEG technologist can be unpredictable and challenging.

Most EEG technologists work in hospitals, where they work closely with other staff members. This task is sometimes made more difficult by the fact that in most hospitals there is a formal, often rigid, status structure, and EEG technologists often find themselves in a relatively low position in that structure. In emergency situations or at other moments of frustration, EEG technologists can find themselves dealt with brusquely or angrily. Technologists should try not to take these outbursts or rude treatments personally, but instead should respond with stability and maturity. Depending on where the EEG technologist works, the pace can be fast and demanding.

Sources of Additional Information

■American Board of Registration of Electroencephalographic and Evoked Potential Technologists
PO Box 916633
Longwood, FL 32791-6633
Tel: 407-788-6308

■American Society of Electroneurodiagnostic Technologists, Inc.
204 West 7th
Carroll, IA 51401
Tel: 712-792-2978

For information and an application to start the EEG or Evoked Potential examination process, contact:

■Professional Testing Corporation
1211 Avenue of the Americas, 15th Floor
New York, NY 10036
Tel: 212-852-0400

Electronics Engineering Technicians

Definition

Electronics engineering technicians work with electronics engineers to design, develop, and manufacture industrial and consumer electronic equipment, including sonar, radar, and navigational equipment, and computers, radios, televisions, stereos, and calculators. They are involved in fabricating, operating, testing, troubleshooting, repairing, and maintaining equipment. Those involved in the development of new electronic equipment help make changes or modifications in circuitry or other design elements.

Other electronics technicians inspect newly installed equipment or instruct and supervise lower-grade technicians' installation, assembly, or repair activities.

As part of their normal duties, all electronics engineering technicians set up testing equipment, conduct tests, and analyze the results; they also prepare reports, sketches, graphs, and schematic drawings to describe electronics systems and their characteristics. Their work involves the use of a variety of hand and machine tools, including such equipment as bench lathes and drills.

Depending on their area of specialization, electronics technicians may be designated by such titles as *computer laboratory technicians, development instrumentation technicians, electronic communications technicians, nuclear reactor electronics technicians, engineering development technicians,* or *systems testing laboratory technicians.*

Nature of the Work

Most electronics technicians work in one of three broad areas of electronics: product development, manufacturing and production, and service and maintenance. Technicians involved with service and maintenance are known as *electronics sales and service technicians.* For information on this area, see the article *Electronics Sales and Service Technicians.*

School Subjects
Mathematics
Physics

Personal Interests
Figuring out how things work
Fixing things

Work Environment
Primarily indoors
Primarily one location

Minimum Education Level
High school diploma

Salary Range
$18,000 to
$37,000 to
$54,800+

Certification or Licensing
Voluntary

Outlook
As fast as the average

DOT
003

GOE
05.01.01

NOC
2241

In the product-development area, electronics technicians, or *electronics development technicians*, work directly with engineers or as part of a research team. Engineers draw up blueprints for a new product, and technicians build a prototype according to specifications. Using hand tools and small machine tools, they construct complex parts, components, and subassemblies.

After the prototype is completed, technicians work with engineers to test the product and make necessary modifications. They conduct physical and electrical tests to test the product's performance in various stressful conditions; for example, they test to see how a component will react in extreme heat and cold. Tests are run using complicated instruments and equipment, and detailed, accurate records are kept of the tests performed.

Electronics technicians in the product-development field may make suggestions for improvements in the design of a device. They may also have to construct, install, modify, or repair laboratory test equipment.

Electronics drafting is a field of electronics technology closely related to product development. *Electronics drafters*, or *computer-aided design drafters*, convert rough sketches and written or verbal information provided by engineers and scientists into easily understandable schematic, layout, or wiring diagrams to be used in manufacturing the product. These drafters may also prepare a list of components and equipment needed for producing the final product, as well as bills for materials.

Another closely related field is cost estimating. *Cost-estimating technicians* review new product proposals in order to determine the approximate total cost to produce a product. They estimate the costs for all labor, equipment, and materials needed to manufacture the product. The sales department uses these figures to determine at what price a product can be sold and whether production is economically feasible.

In the manufacturing and production phase, electronics technicians, or *electronics manufacturing and production technicians*, work in a wide variety of capacities, generally with the day-to-day handling of production problems, schedules, and costs. These technicians deal with any problems arising from the production process. They install, maintain, and repair assembly or test line machinery. In quality control, they inspect and test products at various stages in the production process. When a problem is discovered, they are involved in determining the nature and extent of it and in suggesting remedies.

Those involved in quality control inspect and test the products at various stages of completion. They also maintain and calibrate test equipment used in all phases of the manufacturing. They determine the causes for rejection of parts or equipment by assembly-line inspectors and then analyze field and manufacturing reports of product failures.

These technicians may make specific recommendations to their supervisor to eliminate the causes of rejects and may even suggest design, manufacturing, and process changes and establish quality-acceptance levels. They may interpret quality-control standards to the manufacturing supervisors. And they may establish and maintain quality limits on items purchased from other manufacturers, thus ensuring the quality of parts used in the equipment being assembled.

Another area of electronics technology is that of technical writing and editing. *Technical writers* and *technical editors* compile, write, and edit a wide variety of technical information. This includes instructional leaflets, operating manuals, books, and installation and service manuals having to do with the products of the company. To do this, they must confer with design and development engineers, production personnel, salespeople, drafters, and others to obtain the necessary information to prepare the text, drawings, diagrams, parts, lists, and illustrations. They must understand thoroughly how and why the equipment works to be able to tell the customer how to use it and the service technician how to install and service it.

At times, they may help prepare technical reports and proposals and write technical articles for engineering societies, management, and other associations. Their job is to produce the means (through printed word and pictures) by which the customer can get the most value out of the purchased equipment.

Requirements

A high school diploma is necessary for anyone wishing to build a career as an electronics engineering technician. While in high school, interested students should take algebra, geometry, physics, chemistry, computer science, English, and communications classes. Courses in electronics and introductory electricity are also helpful as are shop courses and courses in mechanical drawing.

Most employers prefer to hire graduates of two-year, postsecondary training programs. These programs provide a solid foundation in the basics of electronics and supply enough general background in science as well as other career-related fields such as business and economics to aid the student in advancing to positions of greater responsibility.

Two-year programs in electronics technology are available at community colleges and technical institutes. Completion of these programs results in an associate's degree. Programs vary quite a bit, but in general, a typical first-year curriculum includes courses in physics for electronics, technical mathematics, communications, AC/DC circuit analysis, electronic amplifiers, transistors, and instruments and measurements.

Typical second-year courses include physics, applied electronics, computer information systems, electronic drafting, electronic instruments and measurements, communications circuits and systems, digital electronics, technical writing, and control circuits and systems.

Students unable to attend a technical institute or community college should not overlook opportunities provided by the military. The military provides extensive training in electronics and other related fields. In addition, some major companies, particularly utilities, hire people straight out of high school and train them through in-house programs. Other companies promote people to technicians' positions from lower-level positions, provided they attend educational workshops and classes sponsored by the company.

Certification as an electronics technician is generally not mandatory, although it is required for anyone who works with radio transmitting equipment. These technicians are required by the Federal Communications Commission (FCC) to have a restricted radiotelephone operator's license, which involves passing written tests on radio laws, operating procedures, and the Morse Code. Effective February 1, 1999, a Global Maritime Distress and Safety System (GMDSS) license will be required rather than the restricted radiotelephone operator's license.

Voluntary certification as a certified electronics technician (CET) is obtained by many technicians. This certification is regarded as a demonstration of professional dedication, determination, and know-how. CET certification is available through professional associations (see addresses at the end of this article) and is awarded to those who successfully complete a written, multiple-choice examination. The associate-level CET test is designed for technicians with less than four years of experience. After four years of experience or education, a technician can take another CET examination in order to earn a journeyman-level CET certification. Additional certificates are available based on proficiency and experience in different areas.

Prospective electronics technicians should have an interest in and an aptitude for mathematics and science and should enjoy using tools and scientific equipment; on the personal side, they should be patient, methodical, persistent, and able to get along with a variety of different kinds of people. Because technology changes so rapidly, technicians will need to pursue additional training throughout their careers. People planning to work in electronics need to have the ability and desire to learn quickly, an inquisitive mind, and the willingness to read and study materials to keep up-to-date.

Opportunities for Experience & Exploration

Students interested in a career as an electronics engineering technician can gain relevant experience by taking shop courses, belonging to electronics or radio clubs in school, and assembling electronic equipment with commercial kits.

Anyone considering a career as an electronics technician should take every opportunity to discuss the field with people working in it. It is advisable to visit a variety of different kinds of electronics facilities—service shops, manufacturing plants, and research laboratories—either through individual visits or through field trips organized by teachers or guidance counselors. These visits will provide a realistic idea of the opportunities in the different areas of the electronics industry. It is also suggested that students take an introductory course in basic electricity or electronics to test their aptitude, skills, and interest. Students who are enrolled in a community college or technical school may be able to secure off-quarter or part-time internships with local employers through their schools' job placement offices. Internships are valuable ways to gain experience while still in school.

Methods of Entering

Students may find their first full-time position through their schools' job placement offices. These offices tend to develop very good working relationships with area employers and can offer students excellent interviewing opportunities.

Another way to obtain employment is through direct contact with a particular company. It is best to write to the personnel department and include a resume summarizing one's education and experience. If the company has an appropriate opening, a company representative will schedule an interview for the prospective employee. There are also many excellent public and commercial employment organizations that can help graduates obtain a job appropriate to their training and experience. In addition, the classified ads in most metropolitan Sunday newspapers list a number of job openings with companies in the area.

Professional associations compile information on job openings and publish job lists. For example, the International Society of Certified Electronics Technicians (ISCET) publishes a monthly job list, titled *Career Opportunities in Electronics,* which lists job openings around the country. Information about job openings can also be found in trade magazines on electronics.

Advancement

Advancement possibilities in the field of electronics can be almost unlimited. Technicians usually begin work under the direct and constant supervision of an experienced technician, scientist, or engineer. As they gain experience or additional education, they are given more responsible assignments, often carrying out particular work programs under only very general supervision.

From there technicians may move into supervisory positions; those with exceptional ability can sometimes qualify for professional positions after receiving additional academic training.

The following short paragraphs describe some of the positions to which electronics technicians can advance.

Electronics technician supervisors work on more complex projects than electronics technicians. They supervise other technicians and may also have administrative duties, such as making the employee work schedule, assigning laboratory projects to various technicians, overseeing the training progress of new employees, and keeping the workplace clean, organized, and well stocked. In general, they tend to have more direct contact with project managers and project engineers.

Engineering technicians are senior technicians or engineering assistants who work as part of a team of engineers and technicians in research and development of new products. Additional education, resulting in a bachelor of science degree in engineering, is required for this position.

Production test supervisors make detailed analysis of production assembly lines in order to determine where production tests should be placed along the line and the nature and goal of the test. They may be responsible for designing the equipment set up used in production testing.

Quality control supervisors determine the scope of a product sampling and the kinds of tests to be run on production units. They translate specifications into testing procedures.

Workers who want to advance to engineering positions can become electrical or electronics engineers through additional education. A bachelor of science degree in engineering is required.

All electronics technicians will need to pursue additional training throughout their careers in order to keep up-to-date with new technologies and techniques. Many employers offer continuing education in the form of in-house workshops or outside seminars. Professional associations also offer seminars and classes on newer technologies and skill building.

Employment Outlook

There is good reason to believe that the electronics industry will be one of the most important industries in the United States through the year 2006. New and exciting consumer products such as large screen televisions, videocassette recorders, compact disc players, personal computers, and home appliances with solid-state controls are very popular and in high demand. Two areas showing high growth are computers and telecommunications products. Multimedia and interactive products are expanding rapidly, and many new products are expected in the coming years. In addition, increasing automation and computer-assisted manufacturing processes rely on advanced electronic technology.

All of these uses for electronics should continue to stimulate growth in the electronics industry. The U.S. Department of Labor estimates that opportunities for electronics engineering technicians will grow as fast as the average through the year 2006. Foreign competition, general economic conditions, and levels of government spending may impact certain areas of the field to some degree. This is an industry, however, that is becoming so central to our lives and for which there is still such growth potential that it seems unlikely that any single factor could substantially curb its growth and its need for specially trained personnel.

Prospective electronics technicians should begin paying attention to certain factors that might affect the area they are thinking of working in. For example, workers planning to work for the military or for a military contractor or subcontractor in radar technology need to keep an eye on federal legislation concerning military spending cuts or increases. The Department of Defense has cut orders for many of the products that it ordered in large quantities in the past. This is significantly impacting some areas of electronics production.

In some areas, the demand for workers is higher than the number of trained workers available. For example, there is a need for highly skilled electronics technicians for companies who produce electronics products with related telecommunications or computer technology. Electromedical and biomedical subfields, dealing with technical hospital machines, have also been identified as high-demand areas (see the articles *Biomedical Equipment Technicians* and *Biomedical Engineers*).

The electronics industry is undeniably indispensable to our lives, and although there will be fluctuations in growth for certain subfields, there will be a need for qualified personnel in another. The key to success for an electronics technician is to stay up-to-date with technology and to be professionally versatile. Building a career on a solid academic and hands-on foundation in basic electronics enables an electronics technician to remain competitive in the job market.

Earnings

Electronics engineering technicians who have completed a two-year postsecondary training program and are working in private industry earn starting salaries of approximately $18,000 a year, according to the U.S. Department of Labor. Average yearly earnings of all electronics engineering technicians are approximately $37,000. At the very top pay levels, technicians can earn $54,800 or more. Salaries vary depending on the worker's experience and education.

Electronics engineering technicians generally receive premium pay for overtime work on Sundays and holidays and for evening and night-shift work. Most employers offer benefit packages that include paid holidays, paid vacations, sick days, and health insurance. Companies may also offer pension and retirement plans, profit sharing, 401(k) plans, tuition assistance programs, and release time for additional education.

Conditions of Work

Because electronics equipment usually must be manufactured in a dust-free, climate-controlled environment, electronics engineering technicians can expect to work in modern, comfortable, well-lighted surroundings. Many electronics plants have been built in industrial parks with ample parking and little traffic congestion. Technicians who work with cable, MATV, satellites, and antennas work outside. Frequency of injuries in the electronics industry is far less than in most other industries, and injuries that do occur are usually not serious.

Most employees work a forty-hour workweek, although overtime is not unusual. Some technicians regularly average fifty to sixty hours a week.

Some workers in electronics manufacturing are covered by union agreements. The principal unions involved are the International Union of Electronics, Electrical, Salaried, Machine, and Furniture Workers; International Brotherhood of Electrical Workers; the International Association of Machinists and Aerospace Workers; and the United Electrical, Radio and Machine Workers of America.

Sources of Additional Information

For information on careers and educational programs, please contact:

Institute of Electrical and Electronics Engineers (IEEE)
1828 L Street, NW, Suite 1202
Washington, DC 20036-5104
Tel: 202-785-0017
WWW: http://www.ieee.org/usab

Electronic Industries Association
2500 Wilson Boulevard
Arlington, VA 22201-3834
Tel: 703-907-7670

For information on student chapters and certification, please contact:

International Society of Certified Electronics Technicians
2708 West Berry, Suite 3
Fort Worth, TX 76109-2356
Tel: 817-921-9101
WWW: http://www.iscet.org

For information on careers, educational programs, and certification, please contact:

Electronics Technicians Association, International
602 North Jackson
Greencastle, IN 46135
Tel: 317-653-8262
WWW: http://serv2.fwi.com/˜n9pdt

American Society of Certified Engineering Technicians
PO Box 1348
Flowery Branch, GA 30542
Tel: 770-967-9173

For information on student clubs, careers, and educational programs, please contact:

Junior Engineering Technical Society (JETS)
1420 King Street, Suite 405
Alexandria, VA 22314
Tel: 703-548-5387
Email: jets@nas.edu

Electronics Sales and Service Technicians

Definition

Electronics sales and service technicians assist consumers in their purchases of electronics equipment, for use in either their homes or businesses. This equipment typically includes televisions, audio and video equipment, computers, microwave ovens, and other kinds of home electronic devices. Technicians meet with potential customers to discuss their requirements, then discuss the various kinds of equipment available to meet those requirements. In order to meet special needs, technicians may show the customer how to modify existing equipment or else a new way to combine it with other equipment to provide what the customer wants. Once equipment has been selected, technicians supervise its installation and maintain the equipment in good working order. Technicians also make repairs when necessary and advise customers on the equipment's replacement when it is no longer practical to maintain. Some electronics sales and service technicians may work with electronic office equipment, such as photocopy machines, dictating machines, and fax (facsimile) machines.

Nature of the Work

The primary work of electronics sales and service technicians is to service and repair electronic home-entertainment equipment, including television sets, videocassette recorders, compact disc players, radios and audio recording equipment, personal computers and peripheral equipment, and such related electronic equipment as garage door openers, microwave ovens, kitchen appliances, home security systems, antennas, satellite reception equipment, electronic organs, and amplifying equipment for other electrified musical instruments.

Technicians service equipment that is working properly and diagnose and repair malfunctioning equipment. They usually begin by gathering information from customers about the problems they are having with their equipment. A preliminary inspection may reveal a loose connection or other simple problem, and the technician may be able to complete repairs quickly. In other cases, a problem may be more complicated and may require that the equipment be taken to a shop for more thorough testing and the installation of new components.

Electronics sales and service technicians are classified as inside or outside technicians. Some technicians work as both inside and outside technicians. Outside technicians make service calls on customers, gather information, and make preliminary examinations of malfunctioning equipment. They may also install new equipment. Inside, or bench, technicians work in shops where they make more thorough examinations of problems using testing equipment and hand tools such as pliers and socket wrenches to dismantle sets and make repairs. The testing equipment used includes devices such as voltage meters, oscilloscopes, signal generators, monitor testers, analyzers, and frequency counters.

Some of the tasks that inside and outside technicians perform include reading service manuals and wiring diagrams, operating testing equipment, replacing defective parts, installing solid-state electronic components, making adjustments in electronic controls, cutting and connecting wires, and soldering metal components together. Technicians also write reports about the service or repairs done and calculate bills for parts and labor costs.

The servicing of other kinds of electronic equipment, such as audio and videocassette recorders, requires special knowledge of their components. Electronics technicians learn about such special areas and keep up with new developments in electronics by attending short courses given by manufacturers at their factories, by a factory technician at local shops, or through professional associations.

Another area of specialization is computer service and repair. *Computer service technicians* specialize in installing, servicing, and repairing computers and related equipment such as printers. They need to be familiar with the many components and assemblies making up a computer and be able to advise people on the necessary equipment needed to upgrade systems. They may also advise consumers on compatible equipment they can add on to their existing equipment in order to allow new functions, such as modems that hook up to telephone lines and allow the use of fax machines.

Technicians involved with the sale of electronic equipment meet with potential customers to discuss and explain the kinds of equipment available to meet the specific needs of the customer. They describe the equipment's features, explain the manufacturer's specifications, and demonstrate how to use the equipment. For customers with special needs, they may recommend ways to either modify existing equipment or combine it with other equipment to provide what the customer wants. Once equipment has been selected, the technician may be involved, often in a supervisory capacity, with the installation and maintenance of the equipment. These technicians also make repairs when necessary and advise customers regarding replacement of equipment that is no longer practical to maintain.

Requirements

Persons interested in working as electronics sales and service technicians should have a mathematical aptitude, problem-solving ability, the ability to learn quickly, and the willingness to learn throughout one's career. In most cases, a high school diploma is required. In high school, students should take as many science and mathematics courses as possible. At minimum, they should take algebra, geometry, physics, and chemistry. Other useful classes are English, communications, applied mathematics, and shop classes. Shop classes that teach the basics of electricity and the use of hand tools and provide an introduction to electronic measurement devices and testing equipment are especially helpful. English and communications classes provide students with the language skills they will need to read electronics texts and manuals comfortably and express themselves well when making spoken and written proposals.

People interested in electronics should have training beyond high school in a technical institute or community college, studying electronics theory and repair of televisions, radios, and other electronic equipment. Different types of programs are available. Some programs, especially in vocational schools, concentrate on only one type of repair, such as television repair. Community colleges and technical schools offer both one- and two-year programs that provide more extensive training in electronics. One-year programs concentrate on electronics and related courses and result in certification in a specific area of study. Two-year programs include electronics courses and other more in-depth courses that result in an associate's degree. Most employers prefer to hire graduates of two-year programs.

Two-year programs in community colleges and technical schools may be found in programs such as electronics, electrical/electronics technology, or electronics technology. These programs are usually broad-based electronics programs geared to electronics technicians in general, rather than specifically to sales and service technicians.

Students enrolled in a one-year program may take classes such as electronic assembly techniques, electronic circuits, and technical mathematics. Students in two-year programs will study those topics plus take classes such as physics, computer information systems, electronic drafting, microprocessors, digital electronics, applied electronics, electronic instruments and measurements, and communication electronics. Many students also take technical writing. Other classes may focus on specific types of repairs, such as servicing computer monitors or video laser discs.

Students who are unable to attend a vocational school or technical institute may wish to consider opportunities provided by the military. The military offers extensive training in electronics to members of the armed forces and provides valuable practical experience.

In some cases, workers learn through an apprenticeship program, which combines on-the-job training with classroom instruction. This is not as common for electronics sales and service technicians as for other types of electronics technicians. Apprenticeships generally last four years.

Extensive on-the-job training is becoming much less common. Whereas shops formerly provided complete on-the-job instruction for untrained employees, they now usually limit such training to current employees—delivery drivers, antenna installers, and so forth—who show a basic understanding of electronics, an aptitude for careful work, and an interest in learning. Such opportunities usually occur in shops that place a higher value on practical experience than on theory. Even so, individuals in such programs will have to supplement their practical training with evening school or home study courses.

To be successful, technicians need to possess mechanical aptitude and a solid knowledge of practical electronics. They should be familiar with and able to use electrical hand tools and basic electronic and electrical testing equipment. Precision and accuracy are often required in adjusting electronic equipment. The physical requirements of their work are moderate, sometimes involving lifting and carrying television sets and other equipment. Technicians are often required to stand and bend for extended periods while working.

Technicians also need good interpersonal and communications skills as this type of work involves interacting with a wide variety of people. Technicians often work in customers' homes and should be able to meet and communicate clearly with strangers. The ability to extract useful information from customers about their equipment can be a great time-saver.

Because of the constantly changing technology of electronic devices, electronics sales and service technicians must be willing to keep growing and learning in their trade skills if they are to be successful. This may require going back to school to learn new technologies and equipment or taking classes through professional associations.

Some states require some electronics sales and service technicians to be licensed. Such licenses are obtained by passing tests in electronics and demonstrating proficiency with testing equipment. Prospective technicians should check with a training institution in their state to determine whether licensing is required.

Only a few technicians belong to labor unions. Most of those who belong are members of the International Brotherhood of Electrical Workers.

Technicians who work in the field or as outside technicians need a driver's license and good driving record. In most cases, employers provide a vehicle to drive to customers' homes and businesses, but some shops may require a technician to provide his or her own vehicle.

Opportunities for Experience & Exploration

Students interested in the electronics field have many opportunities to explore their interests and aptitudes for this type of work. Joining a science or electronics club and participating in competitions provide hands-on activities and experiences related to different facets of electronics. Students can build electronic kits, take apart radios and television sets, or test their repair abilities on discarded appliances. Reading electronics magazines is another way to explore the wide field of electronics and learn about specific types of technology, such as digital and telecommunications technologies.

Other ways to learn about the actual work that electronics sales and service technicians do is by talking with people working in the field. Local electronics sales and service technicians are usually willing to share their experience and knowledge with interested young people. Owners of stores or repair shops may be especially helpful with the business aspects of a career in this field. Summer employment as a helper or a delivery person can provide an opportunity to observe the day-to-day activities of technicians.

Interested persons can also request information from schools that offer training in electronics and other related fields to find out what kind of programs are available. Local chapters of the International

Brotherhood of Electrical Workers and local offices of the state employment service can also supply information about training opportunities as well as the employment outlook in a specific area.

Methods of Entering

Most people enter this field after completing some type of formal training program in a technical school or community college. Employers generally prefer to hire graduates of two-year programs in electronics or a related field. Students who are enrolled in a community college or technical institute may learn about job openings through their schools' job placement services. They may also hear about job openings or prospective employers through contacts they may have made during training and through teachers and school administrators.

Applicants may also apply directly to a company that hires these technicians, such as a service department of a large retail firm, a specialty shop that sells and repairs electronic equipment, or a shop that specializes in electronics repairs. Most companies provide some sort of on-the-job training, such as classes in repair techniques or assigning new workers to work with an experienced worker who trains them and supervises their work. In some cases, especially for workers who have not completed technical training, new workers require a year of shop supervision before they are able to work independently without the direction of a more experienced electronics technician.

Advancement

Advancement in this field depends to a large extent on the size and character of the technician's place of employment. Early advancement usually comes in the form of increased salary and less supervision as a recognition of the technician's increasing skill. In a small shop, the only other advancement possibility may be for the technician to go into business alone, if the community can support another retail store or repair shop.

Persons interested in working for themselves often are able to open up their own shops or work as freelance technicians. Freelance technicians usually operate out of their homes and perform the same services as other technicians.

In a larger store or shop, the electronics technician usually advances to a supervisory position, as a crew chief, sales supervisor, senior technician, or service or sales manager. This may involve not only scheduling and assigning work, but also training new employees and arranging refresher courses and factory training in new products for experienced electronics technicians.

Technicians with strong theoretical training in electronics may go on to become technical school instructors. They may also become service representatives for manufacturers. Those employed in stores or shops that handle a wide variety of electronics sales and service work may become involved in working on more complicated equipment, from radio-frequency heating equipment to electron microscopes and computer systems. This work may also lead to working with engineers in designing and testing new electronic equipment.

Because the work that electronics sales and service technicians do is similar to that done by industrial electronics technicians, technicians have the opportunity to transfer to the industrial electronics segment. Technicians may also become electrical or electronics engineers through additional education resulting in a bachelor of science degree in engineering.

Employment Outlook

Electronics service technicians held about 396,000 jobs in 1996; home electronics repairers accounted for 33,000 of this total, while computer and office machine repairers numbered 141,000. Employment of electronics sales and service technicians is expected to grow more slowly than the average of all other occupations through the year 2006. While production of televisions, radios, VCRs, compact disc players, large screen TVs, and satellite and cable equipment is rapidly increasing, continuing improvements in electronics technology will lower equipment prices and make repairs easier and less costly, therefore limiting demand for service technicians. Employment for technicians who specialize in computer repair will enjoy much faster than average growth through the year 2006 as computers and related technology play an even larger role in the world of work.

Employment for electronics sales technicians will grow about as fast as the average for all occupations through the year 2006. There is high turnover in this field and many opportunities will emerge as workers leave the field as a result of retirement, to enter other occupations, or for other reasons. There are numerous part-time positions available in this field, as well as temporary positions during peak selling seasons, such as Easter and Christmas.

Earnings

Salaries for electronics service technicians in 1996 ranged from $17,108 to $49,908, with a median average of $32,188, according to the Bureau of Labor Statistics. Office machine repairers earned an average annual salary of $30,264 in 1996. The median annual salary for electronics sales technicians was $21,996 in 1996. Self-employed technicians earn higher than average salaries, generally, but they also work longer hours.

Benefits vary depending on the type and size of employer, geographic location, and type of work done. Companies may offer any of the following benefits: paid vacations, paid holidays, health insurance, life insurance, retirement plans, educational assistance, 401(k) plans, and profit sharing.

Conditions of Work

The work of electronics sales and service technicians is performed indoors, in homes and shops, under generally comfortable conditions. Technicians working on cable and satellite equipment work outdoors. Actual working conditions vary based on the type of company one works for. A large retail store may have a lot more activity, noise, and customer contact than a quiet electronics repair shop that has few visitors. Technicians who work in specialty stores, such as musical equipment retailers, may work in noisy surroundings, with many types of music playing at the same time. Inside technicians and technicians involved in sales deal with retail consumers and need to be polite, courteous, and helpful to shoppers who may be rushed, pressured, or unsure of what they want.

Outside technicians may spend considerable time driving from call to call. Their work may take them to a variety of neighborhoods, and they need to feel comfortable with people from varying backgrounds.

All technicians risk occasional electrical shock, but this risk is minimized greatly by following proper safety precautions. Their work may involve lifting heavy items, working with delicate parts, and working in tight spaces. Depending on the type of repair, bending and stretching may be required.

Once they have completed their training, electronics sales and service technicians work with a minimum of supervision. They must, however, be able to

work carefully and accurately. Because the result of their work is often immediately evident to the owner of the equipment, service technicians must be able to handle criticism when they are not completely successful.

Self-employed technicians may operate out of their homes, where they keep a shop in the basement, garage, or a special workroom. Others operate small shops and hire workers to help run the shop or assist in repairs.

Sources of Additional Information

American Electronics Association
5201 Great America Parkway, Suite 520
Santa Clara, CA 95054
Tel: 408-987-4200
WWW: http://www.aeanet.org

Electronic Industries Association
2500 Wilson Boulevard
Arlington, VA 22201-3834
Tel: 703-907-7670

For information on careers, educational programs, and certification, please contact:

Electronics Technicians Association, International
602 North Jackson Street
Greencastle, IN 46135
Tel: 317-653-8262
WWW: http://www.serv2.fwi.com/n9pdt

For information on student chapters and certification, please contact:

International Society of Certified Electronics Technicians
2708 West Berry Street, Suite 3
Fort Worth, TX 76109-2356
Tel: 817-921-9101
WWW: http://www.iscet.mainland.cc.tx.us

For information on educational programs and certification, please contact:

American Society of Certified Engineering Technicians
PO Box 1348
Flowery Branch, GA 30542
Tel: 770-967-9173

Electroplating Workers

Definition

Electroplating is the process of plating, or coating, an article with a thin layer of metal by using a liquid solution of the metal and an electric current that causes the metal to deposit on the article's surface. Types of objects that are electroplated include automobile bumpers, grills, and trim; metal furniture; aircraft parts; electronic components; small appliances; and plumbing fixtures. Electroplating provides a protective surface and helps an object resist wear, corrosion, or abrasion. The various workers who carry out this process are known as *electroplaters* or *platers*.

Nature of the Work

To achieve a good result, electroplating workers often must closely control the composition and temperature of the liquid solution containing the plating metal and the amount of electric current that is run through the plating bath. Platers begin by checking a work order that specifies what parts of the product are to be plated, the type of plating to be used, how thick the metal is to be applied, and the time and amount of electric current that will be required for the plate to reach the desired thickness. Sometimes they are responsible for mixing and testing the strength of the plating bath.

The platers must prepare the object for the plating process. They put it through various cleaning and rinsing baths. They may have to measure, mark, and mask off with lacquer, rubber, or tape parts of the object that are to be left unplated. Then they put the article into the plating tank, suspending it in the plating solution from what amounts to the negative terminal of a battery. Sometimes they have to put together special racks to hold the product in position. A piece of the plating metal is suspended from the positive terminal.

Once the apparatus is ready, the platers operate the controls on a rectifier, which is a device that converts electricity from

School Subjects
Chemistry
Shop (Trade/Vo-tech education)

Personal Interests
Building things
Figuring out how things work

Work Environment
Primarily indoors
Primarily one location

Minimum Education Level
High school diploma

Salary Range
$16,000 to
$21,000 to
$32,000

Certification or Licensing
None

Outlook
Little change or more slowly than the average

DOT
50

GOE
06.02.21

NOC
9497

the usual alternating current to direct current. This makes electricity (that is, a stream of electrons) flow continuously from the negative terminal. Positively charged ions of the plating metal are drawn to the negative terminal, where they combine with some of the negatively charged electrons and deposit out as a thin metal layer on the object. In some plating operations, platers must pull the object out of the solution from time to time to monitor the development of the metal layer and then adjust the flow of current based on their observations.

When the desired result has been achieved, the article is removed from the tank, rinsed, and dried. The platers examine it for any defects and recheck the thickness of the plating with micrometers, calipers, or electronic devices. This examination may be done by *plating inspectors.*

Sometimes workers are designated according to a specific activity or the electroplating equipment they operate. *Barrel platers* operate machines that hold objects to be plated in perforated or mesh barrels that are immersed in plating tanks. *Electrogalvanizing-machine operators* and *zinc-plating-machine operators* run and maintain machines that coat steel strips and wire with zinc. *Production platers* operate and maintain automatic plating equipment. To prepare objects that do not conduct electricity, such as plastic items, *electroformers* coat the items with a conductive substance. Platers may be designated according to the metal they work with, such as *tin platers, cadmium platers,* and *gold platers. Anodizers* control equipment that provides a corrosion-resistant surface on aluminum objects. *Plating strippers* operate equipment with the positive and negative terminals reversed so that old plating is removed from objects.

The duties of platers vary according to the size of the shop in which they work. In some large shops, all major decisions are made by chemists and chemical engineers, and the platers do only routine plating work. In other shops, platers are responsible for the whole process, including ordering chemicals and other supplies, preparing and maintaining solutions, plating the products, and polishing finished objects. If they have helpers, platers may be called *plater supervisors,* while the assistants may be called *electroplating laborers.*

Today, a majority of electroplating workers are employed in independent shops that specialize in plating and polishing metals for other businesses and individuals. Other electroplaters work for large manufacturing firms that use plated parts in their products, such as the makers of plumbing fixtures, electric appliances, automobiles, kitchen utensils, wire products, and hardware items.

Many electroplating workers are members of unions, notably the Metal Polishers, Buffers, Platers and Allied Workers International Union. Other unions in this field are the International Union, United Automobile, Aerospace and Agricultural Implement Workers of America, and International Association of Machinists and Aerospace Workers.

Requirements

Many electroplaters start out as helpers with little or no prior training and learn the trade by working with skilled platers. Using this approach, it often takes at least four years to become a skilled plater. Platers may work with just one or two metals, because it takes too much time to learn the necessary techniques for more than that. Workers who know only one or two metals may have trouble transferring to other shops where different metals are used.

A high school education is usually required by most employers. A good background for people interested in becoming electroplaters includes high school courses in mathematics, science subjects such as chemistry and physics, electrical shop, metal shop, and blueprint reading. Classes such as these introduce some of the basic concepts underlying the industrial applications of electroplating as well as give students a hands-on sense of related technical fields.

The trend in this industry has been for plating processes to involve increasing complexity and engineering precision. Many employers now prefer to hire students who have had specialized training and technical education. Some community colleges and vocational schools presently offer courses in electroplating that are one to two years in length. In addition, some branches of the American Electroplaters and Surface Finishers Society conduct courses in electroplating.

Opportunities for Experience & Exploration

Participation in metalworking hobbies can familiarize a student with some of the basic properties of metal, which will provide a good foundation to determine one's interest in the field. However, there are few hobbies that actually utilize electroplating. To get more direct experience of this occupation, it may be possible to arrange a part-time or summer job in a shop where electroplating is done or at least to speak with workers in such a shop about their activities.

Methods of Entering

People who are seeking to enter this trade may apply directly to a shop specializing in electroplating or a manufacturing company with an electroplating department. Listings of local job openings are available through the state employment service and in the classified advertising section of newspapers. Students in technical programs are often able to get job leads through their schools' placement services.

Most workers begin in helper positions and learn as they work. Working under the supervision of a more experienced worker, trainees learn each phase of the plating process. As they gradually learn various steps of the process, they are given more responsibility and less supervision. Once they have acquired the basic skills, they are able to work on their own. Workers who have received some kind of technical training usually require less extensive on-the-job training.

Advancement

Many workers in electroplating shops work with only one type of metal. Taking technical classes to learn new techniques and how to work with other metals increases one's knowledge about electroplating and provides opportunities to move into areas requiring more responsibility and skill. In addition, it increases the number and types of electroplating shops one can find employment in, therefore providing greater job flexibility if one wants to move or transfer to a different shop. Some platers may be able to increase their pay levels by getting training in additional metal finishing methods. With increased knowledge and skill, workers can move into supervisory positions in which they coordinate and direct the activities of other workers.

Employment Outlook

In the late 1990s, according to the Bureau of Labor Statistics, there are approximately 78,000 electroplaters in the United States. This number is expected to remain about the same or slightly decline through the year 2006. Although there is expected to be a greater number of electroplated items produced, a growing trend to mechanize the processes related to electroplating will reduce the number of workers needed. For this reason, employment levels in this field will not grow at rates that match the growth in output of electroplated products.

Nonetheless, every year new job openings will occur, both for new positions and to replace workers who are transferring to other occupations or leaving the labor force altogether. Students who have completed a technical program in electroplating have the best opportunities at finding entry-level positions.

Earnings

Limited information available about this field indicates that the earnings of electroplaters vary widely depending on skills and experience, the type of work being done, geographical location, and other factors. On average, platers appear to make around $21,000 a year or more. Experienced workers may make up to $32,000 a year or more. Many electroplaters are paid according to wage scales that are established by agreements between unions and company management. In general, most companies offer paid vacations, holidays, and sick days and health insurance. Some companies offer tuition assistance programs, profit sharing, and 401(k) plans.

Helpers and entry-level workers without any technical training start at comparatively low wages and receive raises at regular intervals throughout their training until their earnings approach those of skilled electroplaters.

Conditions of Work

Job conditions are generally good for platers today. In most plants, improved ventilating systems have reduced the odor and humidity problems that used to be common. Many plants are completely modernized, with automated electroplating equipment. Although there are some hazards associated with using strong chemicals, good safety practices and protective clothing minimize the risk of injury. Electroplaters are on their feet most of their working day. They may have to lift and carry moderately heavy objects, but in most cases, mechanical devices are used for the heavy work.

Sources of Additional Information

For information on educational programs and scholarships, please contact:

American Electroplaters and Surface Finishers Society
12644 Research Parkway
Orlando, FL 32826
Tel: 407-281-6441

For information on electroplating and metal finishing, please contact:

National Association of Metal Finishers
401 North Michigan Avenue
Chicago, IL 60611-4267
Tel: 312-644-6610

Emergency Medical Technicians

Definition

Emergency medical technicians, often called *EMTs,* respond to medical emergencies to provide immediate treatment for ill or injured persons both on the scene and during transport to a medical facility. They function as part of an emergency medical team, and the range of medical services they perform varies according to their level of training and certification.

Nature of the Work

EMTs work in fire departments, private ambulance services, police departments, volunteer Emergency Medical Services (EMS) squads, hospitals, industrial plants, or other organizations that provide prehospital emergency care. The goals of this emergency care are to rapidly identify the nature of the emergency, stabilize the patient's condition, and initiate proper procedures at the scene and en route to a hospital. Unfortunately, well-intentioned emergency help from persons who are not trained can be disastrous, especially for automobile accident victims. Communities often take great pride in their emergency medical services, knowing that they are as well prepared as possible and that they can minimize the tragic consequences of mishandling emergencies.

EMTs are sent in an ambulance to the scene of an emergency by the dispatcher, who acts as a communications channel for all aspects of emergency medical services. The dispatcher may also be trained as an EMT. It typically is the dispatcher who receives the call for help, sends out the appropriate medical resource, serves as the continuing link between the emergency vehicle and medical facility throughout the situation, and relays any requests for special assistance at the scene.

EMTs, who often work in two-person teams, must be able to get to an emergency scene in any part of their geographic area quickly and safely. For the protection of the public and themselves, they must obey the traffic laws that apply to emergency

School Subjects
Biology
Health

Personal Interests
Helping people: personal service
Helping people: physical health/medicine

Work Environment
Indoors and outdoors
Primarily multiple locations

Minimum Education Level
Some postsecondary training

Salary Range
$18,000 to
$25,000 to
$35,000

Certification or Licensing
Required

Outlook
Faster than the average

DOT
079

GOE
10.03.02

NOC
3234

vehicles. They must be familiar with the roads and any special conditions affecting the choice of route, such as traffic, weather-related problems, and road construction.

Once at the scene, they must cope immediately and effectively with whatever awaits them. They may find victims who appear to have had heart attacks, are burned, trapped under fallen objects, lacerated, in childbirth, poisoned, or emotionally disturbed—in short, people with any urgent problem for which medical assistance is needed. Because people who have been involved with an emergency are sometimes very upset, EMTs often have to exercise skill in calming both victims and bystanders. They must do their work efficiently and in a reassuring manner.

EMTs are often the first qualified personnel to arrive on the scene, so they must make the initial evaluation of the nature and extent of the medical problem. The accuracy of this early assessment can be crucial. EMTs must be on the lookout for any clues, such as medical identification emblems, indicating that the victim has significant allergies, diabetes, epilepsy, or other conditions that may affect decisions about emergency treatment. EMTs must know what questions to ask bystanders or family members if they need more information about a patient.

Once they have evaluated the situation and the victim's condition, EMTs establish the priorities of required care. They administer emergency treatment under standing orders or in accordance with specific instructions received over the radio from a physician. For example, they may have to open breathing passages, perform cardiac resuscitation, treat shock, or restrain emotionally disturbed patients.

The particular procedures and treatments that EMTs may carry out depend partly on the level of certification they have achieved. A majority of EMTs have only basic certification, which is known as EMT-basic, or EMT-ambulance. EMT-basics can do such things as control bleeding, administer CPR, treat shock victims, apply bandages, and splint fractures. The second level of certification, the EMT-intermediate, allows EMTs to perform somewhat more advanced procedures, such as starting an I.V. A growing number of EMTs have attained the highest level of certification as Registered EMT-paramedics. There are over sixty thousand *paramedics* in the United States. EMT-paramedics are authorized to administer drugs intravenously and operate complicated life-support equipment—for example, an electric device (defibrillator) to shock a stopped heart into action.

When victims are trapped, EMTs must first assess the medical problem; only after administering suitable medical care and protection do EMTs remove the victims, using specialized equipment. EMTs may have

to radio requests for special assistance in order to free victims. During a longer extrication process, it may be necessary for EMTs to help police with crowd control. Sometimes freeing victims involves lifting and carrying them, climbing to high places, or dealing with other difficult or physically demanding situations.

Victims who must be transported to the hospital are put on stretchers or backboards, lifted into the ambulance, and secured for the ride. The choice of hospital is not always up to the EMTs, but when it is they must base the decision on their knowledge of the equipment and staffing needed by the patients. The receiving hospital's emergency department is informed by radio, either directly or through the dispatcher, of details such as the number of persons being transported and the nature of their medical problems. Meanwhile EMTs continue to monitor the patients and administer care as directed by the medical professional with whom they are maintaining radio contact. When necessary, EMTs also try to be sure that contact has been initiated with any utility companies, municipal repair crews, or other services that should be called to correct dangerous problems at the emergency scene, such as fallen power lines or tree limbs.

Once at the hospital, EMTs help the staff bring the victims into the emergency department and may assist with the first steps of in-hospital care. They supply whatever information they can, verbally and in writing, for the hospital's records. In the case of a victim's death, they complete the necessary procedures to ensure that the deceased's property is safeguarded.

After the patient has been delivered to the hospital, EMTs check in with their dispatchers and then prepare the vehicle for another emergency call. This includes replacing used linens and blankets; replenishing supplies of drugs, oxygen, and so forth; sending out equipment to be sterilized; and taking inventory of the contents of the vehicle to ensure adequate supplies. In the case of any special kind of contamination, such as certain contagious diseases or radioactivity, EMTs report the situation to the proper authorities and follow procedures for decontamination.

In addition, EMTs make sure that the ambulance is clean and in good running condition. At least once during the shift, they check the gas, oil, battery, siren, brakes, radio, and other systems.

Requirements

While still in high school, interested students should take courses in health and science, driver education, and English. To be admitted to a basic training program, applicants usually must be at least eighteen years old and have a high school diploma and valid driver's license. Exact requirements vary slightly in different states and in different training courses. Many EMTs first become interested in the field while in the U.S. armed forces, where they may have received training as medics.

The standard basic training program for EMTs was designed by the U.S. Department of Transportation. It is taught in hospitals, community colleges, and police, fire, and health departments across the country. It is approximately 110 hours in length and constitutes the minimum mandatory requirement to become an EMT. In this course, students are taught how to manage common emergencies such as bleeding, cardiac arrest, fractures, and airway obstruction. They also learn how to use equipment such as stretchers, backboards, fracture kits, and oxygen delivery systems.

Successful completion of the basic EMT course opens several opportunities for further training. Among these are a two-day course on removing trapped victims and a five-day course on driving emergency vehicles. Another, somewhat longer course, trains dispatchers. Completion of these recognized training courses may be required for EMTs to be eligible for certain jobs in some areas. In addition, EMTs who have graduated from the basic program may work toward meeting further requirements to become registered at one of the two higher levels recognized by the National Registry of Emergency Medical Technicians: EMT-intermediate and EMT-paramedic.

All fifty states have some certification requirement. Certification is only open to those who have completed the standard basic training course. In some states, EMTs meet the certification requirement by meeting the requirements for basic registration with the National Registry of Emergency Medical Technicians. Some states offer new EMTs the choice of the National Registry examination or the state's own certification examination. A majority of states accept national registration in place of their own examination for EMTs who relocate to their states.

At present, the National Registry of Emergency Medical Technicians recognizes three levels of competency. Although it is not always essential for EMTs to become registered with one of these three ratings, EMTs can expect better prospects for good jobs as they attain higher levels of registration. As time passes, registration requirements may increase, and a larger proportion of EMTs are expected to become registered voluntarily.

Candidates for the basic level of registration, known as EMT-basic, must have completed the standard Department of Transportation training program (or their state's equivalent), have six months' experience, and pass both a state-approved practical examination and a written examination.

Since 1980, the National Registry has recognized the EMT-intermediate level of competency. This registration requires all candidates to have current registration at the basic EMT level. They must also have a certain amount of experience and pass both a written test and a practical examination that assess knowledge and skills above those of basic registered EMTs, but below those of the highest-rated registrants.

EMT-paramedics (or EMT-Ps), the EMTs with the highest levels of registration, must be already registered at least at the basic level. They must have completed a special EMT-paramedic training program, have six months' experience as an EMT-paramedic, and pass both a written and practical examination. Because their training is much more comprehensive and specialized than other EMTs, EMT-ps are prepared to make more physician-like observations and judgments.

The training programs for EMT-paramedics are currently accredited by the Committee on Allied Health Education and Accreditation of the American Medical Association. They last approximately nine months, although exact course length depends largely on the availability of actual emergency care incidents in which students can gain supervised practical experience. Training is very broad in scope and includes classroom instruction and in-hospital clinical practice, in addition to a field internship.

Once they have attained registration, EMTs must reregister every two years. To reregister, they need to meet certain experience and continuing education requirements. Refresher courses are available to help EMTs stay abreast of new techniques and equipment.

Anyone who is considering becoming an EMT should have a desire to serve people and be emotionally stable and clearheaded. It is important that workers in this field project an impression of confidence and efficiency to both victims and bystanders. Moreover, they must back up the impression of competence with genuine levelheadedness and sufficient calmness to let them consistently exercise good judgment in times of stress. They must be efficient, neither wasting time nor working too fast to do a good job. A strong desire to help people, even when it involves difficult work, is essential.

Prospective EMTs also need to have an interest in the health field, and they need to be in good physical condition. Other requirements include manual dexterity and motor coordination; the ability to lift and carry up to 125 pounds; good visual acuity, with lenses for correction permitted; accurate color vision, enabling safe driving and immediate detection of diagnostic signs; and competence in giving and receiving verbal and written communication.

Opportunities for Experience & Exploration

Students in high school usually have little opportunity for direct experience with the emergency medical field. They may be able to arrange to talk with local EMTs who work for the fire or police department or for a voluntary agency that provides emergency ambulance service to the community. It may be possible to learn a great deal about the health-services field through a part-time, summer, or volunteer job in a hospital or clinic. Such service jobs can provide a chance to observe and talk to staff members concerned with emergency medical services.

High school health courses are a useful introduction to some of the concepts and terminology that EMTs use. Students may also be able to take a first-aid class or training in cardiopulmonary resuscitation. Organizations such as the Red Cross can provide information on local training courses available.

Methods of Entering

A good source of employment leads for a recent graduate of the basic EMT training program is the school or agency that provided the training. EMTs can also apply directly to local ambulance services, hospitals, fire and police departments, and private and public employment agencies.

In some areas, new EMT graduates may face stiff competition if they are seeking full-time paid employment. Although these EMTs may sometimes qualify for positions with fire and police departments, they are generally more likely to be successful in pursuing positions with private companies.

Volunteer work is another option for EMTs. Volunteer EMTs, who are likely to average eight to twelve hours of work per week, do not face the same competition as those who are seeking full-time work. Beginning EMTs, without prior work experience in the health field, may therefore find it advantageous to start their careers as part-time volunteers. As they gain training and experience, they can work toward registration, which may open new job opportunities.

Flexibility about the location of a job may help new EMTs gain a foothold on the career ladder. In some areas, salaried positions are hard to find because of a strong tradition of volunteer ambulance services. In other areas, the demand for EMTs is much greater. Therefore, if an EMT is willing to relocate to an area where the demand is higher, he or she should have a better chance of finding employment.

Advancement

With experience, EMTs can gain more responsibility while retaining the same job. However, more significant advancement is possible if an EMT moves up through the progression of ratings recognized by the NREMT. These ratings acknowledge increasing qualifications, making higher paying jobs and more responsibility easier to obtain.

An avenue of advancement for some EMTs leads to holding an administrative job, such as supervisor, director, operations manager, or trainer. Communications, safety and risk management, and quality control are other administrative areas that are receiving increasing attention. Another avenue of advancement might be further training in a different area of the health care field. Some EMTs eventually move out of the health care field entirely and into medical sales, where their familiarity with equipment and terminology can make them valuable employees.

Employment Outlook

The employment outlook for paid EMTs depends partly on the community in which they are seeking employment. Many communities perceive the advantages of high-quality emergency medical services and are willing and able to raise tax dollars to support them. In these communities, which are often larger, the employment outlook should remain favorable. Volunteer services are being phased out in these areas, and well-equipped emergency services operated by salaried EMTs are replacing them.

In some communities, however, particularly smaller ones, the employment outlook is not so favorable. Maintaining a high-quality emergency medical services delivery system can be expensive, and financial strains on some local governments could inhibit the growth of these services. In addition, cutbacks in federal aid to local communities and an overall national effort to contain medical expenditures may lead health care planners to look for ways of controlling or reducing community-based health-related costs. Under such economic conditions, communities may not be able to support the level of emergency medical services that they would otherwise like to, and the employment prospects for EMTs may remain limited.

One general factor that impacts the EMT's employment outlook is the growing number of municipalities that are contracting with private ambulance companies to provide emergency medical services to the community. If this trend continues, job opportunities with private companies should increase.

Another important factor affecting the outlook is that the proportion of older people, who use most emergency medical services, is growing in many communities, placing more demands on the emergency medical services delivery system and increasing the need for EMTs. Many states are starting to give EMTs more responsibility, such as performing primary care on the scene. Turnover is quite high for this occupation due to stressful working conditions, modest salary in the private sector, and the limited growth potential.

Earnings

Earnings of EMTs depend on the type of employer and individual level of training and experience. Those working in the public sector, for police and fire departments, usually receive a higher wage than those in the private sector, working for ambulance companies and hospitals. Salary levels typically rise with increasing levels of skill, training, and certification.

According to a salary survey in the 1996 *Journal of Emergency Medical Services,* the average salary is $25,000 for those classified as EMT-basic, and $30,400 for EMT-paramedic. To show the disparity in pay between employers, the average pay for an experienced EMT-basic at a private ambulance service is $18,600; at a fire department, it is $29,800.

Benefits vary widely depending on the employer, but generally include paid holidays and vacations, health insurance, and pension plans.

Conditions of Work

EMTs must work under all kinds of conditions, both indoors and outdoors, and sometimes in very trying circumstances. They must do their work regardless of extreme weather conditions and are often required do fairly strenuous physical tasks such as lifting, climbing, and kneeling. They consistently deal with situations that many people would find upsetting and traumatic, such as death, accidents, and serious injury.

EMTs usually work irregular hours, including some nights, weekends, and holidays. Those working for fire departments often put in fifty-six hours a week, while EMTs employed in hospitals, private firms, and police departments typically work a forty-hour week. Volunteer EMTs work much shorter hours. Because the working conditions are so stressful and emotionally exhausting, many EMTs find that they must have a high degree of commitment to the job.

An additional stress factor faced by EMTs is concern over contracting AIDS or other infectious diseases from bleeding patients. The actual risk of exposure is quite small, and emergency medical programs have implemented procedures to protect EMTs from exposure to the greatest possible degree; however, some risk of exposure does exist, and prospective EMTs should be aware of this factor as they consider the career.

In spite of the intensity of their often-demanding job, many EMTs derive enormous satisfaction from knowing that they are able to render such a vital service to the victims of sudden illness or injury.

Sources of Additional Information

For information on EMT education and careers, contact:

National Association of Emergency Medical Technicians
408 Monroe
Clinton, MS 39056
Tel: 614-888-8920

American Ambulance Association
3800 Auburn Boulevard, Suite C
Sacramento, CA 95821
Tel: 916-483-3827

For information on testing for EMT certification, contact:

National Registry of Emergency Medical Technicians
Box 29233
6610 Busch Boulevard
Columbus, OH 43229
Tel: 614-888-4484

American Medical Association
Division of Allied Health Education and Accreditation
515 North State Street
Chicago, IL 60610
Tel: 312-464-5000

Farm Equipment Mechanics

Definition

Farm equipment mechanics maintain, adjust, repair, and overhaul equipment and vehicles used in planting, cultivating, harvesting, moving, processing, and storing plant and animal farm products. Among the specialized machines with which they work are tractors, harvesters, combines, pumps, tilling equipment, silo fillers, hay balers, and sprinkler irrigation systems. They work for farm equipment repair shops, farm equipment dealerships, and on large farms that have their own shops.

Nature of the Work

The success of today's large-scale farming operations depends on the reliability of many complex machines. It is the responsibility of farm equipment mechanics to keep the machines in good working order and repair or overhaul them when they break down.

When farm equipment is not working properly, farm equipment mechanics begin by diagnosing the problem. They use intricate testing devices to identify what is wrong. A compression tester, for example, can determine whether cylinder valves leak or piston rings are worn, and a dynamometer can measure engine performance. Mechanics also examine the machine, observing and listening to it in operation and looking for clues like leaks, loose parts, and irregular steering, braking, and gear shifting. It may be necessary to dismantle whole systems in the machine to diagnose and correct malfunctions.

When the problem is located, the broken, worn-out, or faulty components are repaired or replaced, depending on the extent of their defect. The machine or piece of equipment is reassembled, adjusted, lubricated, and tested to be sure it is again operating at its full capacity.

Farm equipment mechanics use many tools in their work. Besides hand tools such as wrenches, pliers, and screwdrivers and precision instruments such as micrometers and torque

School Subjects
Agriculture
Shop (Trade/Vo-tech education)

Personal Interests
Figuring out how things work
Fixing things

Work Environment
Indoors and outdoors
Primarily multiple locations

Minimum Education Level
High school diploma
Apprenticeship

Salary Range
$13,300 to
$21,700 to
$40,500

Certification or Licensing
None

Outlook
Decline

DOT
620

GOE
05.05.09

NOC
7312

wrenches, they may use welding equipment, power grinders and saws, and other power tools. In addition, they sometimes do major repairs using machine tools such as drill presses, lathes, and milling and wood-working machines.

As farm equipment becomes more complex, mechanics are expected to have strong backgrounds in electronics. For instance, newer tractors have large, electronically controlled engines and air-conditioned cabs, as well as transmissions with many speeds. Some even have complex stereo systems that sometimes need repair.

Much of the time, farmers can bring their equipment into a shop, where mechanics have all the necessary tools available. But during planting or harvesting seasons, when timing may be critical for the farmers, mechanics are expected to travel to farms for emergency repairs in order to get the equipment up and running with little delay.

Farmers usually bring movable equipment into a repair shop on a regular basis for preventive maintenance services such as adjusting and cleaning parts and tuning engines. Routine servicing not only ensures less emergency repairs for the mechanics, but it also assures farmers that the equipment will be ready when it is needed. Shops in the rural outskirts of metropolitan areas often handle maintenance and repairs on a variety of lawn and garden equipment, especially lawn mowers.

In large shops, mechanics may specialize in specific types of repairs. For example, some mechanics overhaul gasoline or diesel engines; others repair clutches and transmissions; still others concentrate on the air-conditioning units in the cabs of combines and large tractors. Some mechanics, called *farm-machinery set-up mechanics,* uncrate, assemble, adjust, and often deliver machinery to farm locations. Mechanics also do body work on tractors and other machines, repairing damaged sheet metal body parts.

Mechanics may work exclusively on certain types of equipment, such as hay balers or harvesters. Some mechanics work on equipment that is installed on farms. For example, *sprinkler-irrigation equipment mechanics* install and maintain self-propelled circle-irrigation systems, which are like giant motorized lawn sprinklers. *Dairy equipment repairers* inspect and repair dairy machinery and equipment such as milking machines, cream separators, and churns.

Most farm equipment mechanics work in the service departments of equipment dealerships. Others are employed by independent repair shops. A smaller number work on large farms that have their own shops.

Requirements

Most farm equipment mechanics learn on the job. They are hired as assistants and receive training from experienced mechanics. Employers almost always prefer to hire high school graduates, and increasingly they seek people who have completed training programs for mechanics, such as those offered at vocational and technical schools and community and junior colleges. These programs may last one to two years and cover such fields as the maintenance and repair of diesel and gasoline engines, hydraulic systems, welding, and electronics. Some high schools offer these courses as well.

Employers look for applicants with mechanical aptitude. A farm background is considered desirable but not essential. Farm mechanics must be able read blueprints and understand circuit diagrams in order to make repairs on electrical and electronic systems.

Some mechanics learn their trade through apprenticeship programs. These programs combine three to four years of on-the-job training with classroom study related to farm equipment repair and maintenance. Apprentices are usually chosen from among shop helpers.

Many people who become trainees in this field have prior experience in related occupations. They may have worked as farmers, farm laborers, heavy-equipment mechanics, automobile mechanics, or air-conditioning mechanics. Although people with this kind of related experience are likely to begin as helpers, their training period may be considerably shorter than the training for beginners with no such experience.

To stay up-to-date on technological changes that affect their work, mechanics and trainees may take special short-term courses conducted by equipment manufacturers. In these programs, which may last a few days, company service representatives explain the design and function of new models of equipment and teach mechanics how to maintain and repair them. Some employers help broaden their mechanics' skills by sending them to local vocational schools for special intensive courses in subjects such as air-conditioning repair, hydraulics or electronics.

Farm machinery is usually large and heavy. Mechanics need the strength to lift heavy machine parts such as transmissions. They also need manual dexterity to be able to handle tools and small components.

Farm equipment mechanics are usually expected to supply their own hand tools. After years of accumulating favorite tools, experienced mechanics may have collections that represent an investment of thousands of dollars. Employers generally provide all the large power tools and test equipment needed in the shop.

Opportunities for Experience & Exploration

High school students can prepare for work in this field by taking courses such as electrical shop, welding, mechanical drawing, and automobile mechanics. Prospective farm equipment mechanics may also take vocational school courses related to farm equipment to get a better idea of whether this is the field for them.

A practical knowledge of how farm machines work is very helpful for farm equipment mechanics. Living on a farm or working on a farm after school, on weekends, or during the summer is very helpful for the future farm equipment mechanic. If the prospective farm equipment mechanic is a city dweller, a part-time or summer job in a gasoline service station, automobile repair shop, or automotive supply house can at least introduce the basic tools, skills, and vocabulary used by mechanics.

Methods of Entering

People who are interested in becoming farm equipment mechanics usually apply directly to local farm equipment dealers or independent repair shops. Graduates of vocational schools can often get help finding jobs through their schools' placement service. State employment service offices are another source of job leads, as well as a source of information on any apprenticeships that may be available in the region.

Advancement

After they have gained some experience, farm equipment mechanics employed by equipment dealers may be promoted to such positions as shop supervisor, service manager, and eventually manager of the dealership. Some mechanics eventually decide to open their own repair shops (approximately one mechanic in ten is self-employed). Others become service representatives for farm equipment manufacturers. Additional formal education, such as completion of a two-year associate degree program in agricultural mechanics or a related field, may be required of service representatives.

Employment Outlook

The improved quality of farm equipment is but one factor contributing to the decline in demand for agricultural equipment technicians. The ongoing consolidation of existing farmland into larger farms and new farming techniques have influenced this occupation as well. The majority of job openings will result from current technicians leaving the workforce due to retirement or other reasons.

Agricultural equipment businesses now demand more expertise than ever before. A variety of complex specialized machines and mechanical devices are steadily being produced and modified to help farmers improve the quality and productivity of their labor. These machines require trained technical workers to design, produce, test, sell, and service them. Trained workers also are needed to instruct the final owners in their proper repair, operation, and maintenance.

In addition, the agricultural industry is adopting advanced computer and electronic technology. Computer skills are becoming more and more useful in this field. Precision farming will also require specialized training as agricultural equipment becomes hooked up to satellite systems.

As technology begins to play a larger role in agriculture, the agricultural equipment technician will assume an increasingly vital role in helping farmers solve problems that interfere with efficient production. These opportunities exist not only in the United States, but also worldwide. As agricultural economies everywhere become mechanized, inventive technicians with training in modern business principles will find expanding employment opportunities abroad.

Earnings

Starting salaries for agricultural equipment technicians ranged from approximately $13,300 to more than $21,700 per year for those who have graduated from a two-year technical or community college, according to 1996 U.S. Department of Labor statistics. With further training and experience, technicians may earn much larger salaries, often $40,500 or more. There is opportunity for overtime work, especially during busy planting and harvesting seasons. Those working on farms often receive room and board as a supplement to their annual salary. The salary that technicians eventually receive depends, as do most salaries, on individual ability, initiative, and the supply of skilled technicians in the field of work or locality.

In addition to their salaries, most technicians receive fringe benefits such as health and retirement packages, paid vacations, and other benefits similar to those received by engineering technicians. Technicians employed in sales are usually paid a commission in addition to their base salary.

Conditions of Work

Farm equipment mechanics are employed throughout the United States, with the greatest concentration in small cities and rural areas. Most independent repair shops employ fewer than five mechanics, while in dealers' service departments there may be ten or more mechanics on the payroll.

Farm equipment mechanics generally work indoors on equipment that has been brought into the shop. Most modern shops are properly ventilated, heated, and lighted. Some older shops may be less comfortable. During harvest seasons, mechanics may leave the shop frequently and travel many miles to farms, where they perform emergency repairs outdoors in any kind of weather. They may often work six to seven days a week, ten to twelve hours a day during this busy season.

In the event of an emergency repair, mechanics often work independently, with little supervision. They need to be self-reliant and able to solve problems under pressure. When a farm machine breaks down, the lost time can be very expensive for the farmer. Mechanics must be able to diagnose problems quickly and do repairs without delay.

Grease, gasoline, rust, and dirt are part of the farm equipment mechanic's life. Although safety precautions have improved in recent years, mechanics are often at risk of injury when lifting heavy equipment and parts with jacks or hoists. Other hazards they must routinely guard against include burns from hot engines, cuts from sharp pieces of metal, and exposure to toxic farm chemicals. Following good safety practices can reduce the risks of injury to a minimum.

Farm equipment mechanics should love machines. They should have a strong curiosity about what makes them run and be able to diagnose problems when they break down. Mechanics are an important cog in the machinery that runs the agricultural industry.

Sources of Additional Information

Canadian Farm and Industrial Equipment Institute
Suite 307 720 Guelph Line
Burlington, ON L7R 4E2 Canada
Tel: 905-632-8483

Equipment Manufacturers Institute
10 South Riverside Plaza
Chicago, IL 60606-3710
Tel: 312-321-1470

North American Equipment Dealers Association
10877 Watson Road
St. Louis, MO 63127-1081
Tel: 314-821-7220

Farmers, Independent Farm Operators, and Managers

Definition

Farmers either own or lease land on which they raise crops such as corn, wheat, tobacco, cotton, vegetables, or fruits; raise animals or poultry, mainly for food; or maintain herds of dairy cattle for the production of milk. Whereas some farmers may combine several of these activities, most specialize in one specific area. They are assisted by farm laborers, who are either hired workers or members of farm families and who perform various tasks. Farm operators work on large farms that they either own or lease, and they coordinate the work of laborers and the general and specific farm operations. Farm managers bring a knowledge of business and farm management to either their own farms or to those of others.

As increasingly complex technology continues to have an impact on the agricultural industry, farms are becoming larger. Most contemporary farms are thousands of acres in size and include massive animal and plant production operations. Subsistence farms that produce only enough to support the farmer's family are becoming increasingly rare.

Nature of the Work

There are probably as many different types of farmers as there are different types of plants and animals whose products are consumed by humans. In addition to *diversified crops farmers,* who grow different combinations of fruits, grains, and vegetables, and *general farmers,* who raise livestock as well as crops, there are *cash grain farmers,* who grow barley, corn, rice, soybeans, and wheat; *vegetable farmers; tree-fruit-and-nut crops farmers; field crops farmers,* who raise alfalfa, cotton, hops, peanuts, mint, sugarcane, and tobacco; *animal breeders; fur farmers; livestock ranchers; dairy farmers; poultry farmers; beekeepers; reptile farmers; fish farmers;* and even *worm growers.*

School Subjects
Agriculture
Business

Personal Interests
Animals
Plants/Gardening

Work Environment
Primarily outdoors
Primarily multiple locations

Minimum Education Level
High school diploma

Salary Range
$10,600 to
$25,200 to
$39,500+

Certification or Licensing
Voluntary

Outlook
Decline

DOT
421

GOE
03.01.01

NOC
8251

In addition to the different types of crop farmers, there are two different types of farming management careers: the farm operator and the farm manager.

The *farm operator* either owns his or her own farm or leases land from other farms. Farm operators' responsibilities vary depending on the type of farm they run, but in general they are responsible for making managerial decisions. They determine the best time to seed, fertilize, cultivate, spray, and harvest. They keep extensive financial and inventory records of the farm operations, which are currently done with the help of computer programs.

Farm operators perform tasks ranging from caring for livestock to erecting sheds. The size of the farm often determines what tasks the operators handle themselves. On very large farms, operators hire employees to perform tasks that an operator on a small farm would do him- or herself.

The *farm manager* has a wide range of duties. The owner of a large livestock farm may hire a farm manager to oversee a single activity, such as feeding the livestock. In other cases, a farm manager may oversee the entire operation of a small farm for an absentee owner. Farm management firms often employ highly skilled farm managers to manage specific operations on a small farm or to oversee tenant farm operations on several farms.

Whether farm operators or managers, the farmers' duties vary widely depending on what product they farm. A common type of farmer is the *crop farmer*. Following are a number of crops that the crop farmer might manage.

Corn farmers and *wheat farmers* begin the growing season by breaking up the soil with plows, then harrowing, pulverizing, and leveling it. Some of these tasks may be done after the harvest the previous year and others just before planting. Corn is usually planted around the middle of May with machines that place the corn seeds into dirt hills a few inches apart, making weed control easier. On the average, a crop is cultivated three times during a season. Corn is also used in the making of silage, a type of animal feed made by cutting the corn and allowing it to ferment in storage silos.

Wheat may be sown in the fall or spring, depending on the severity of the past winter and the variety of wheat being sown. Wheat is planted with a drill, close together, allowing greater cultivation and easier harvesting. The harvest for winter wheat occurs in early summer. Wheat farmers use combines to gather and thresh the wheat in one operation. The wheat is then stored in large grain storage elevators, which are owned by private individuals, companies, or farming cooperatives.

Cotton planting begins in March in the Southwest and somewhat later in the Southeast. Tobacco plants must be carefully protected from harsh weather conditions. The soil in which tobacco is grown must be thoroughly broken up, smoothed, and fertilized before planting, as tobacco is very hard on the soil.

The peanut crop can be managed like other types of farm crops. It is not nearly as sensitive to weather and disease nor does it require the great care of tobacco or cotton.

Specialty crops such as fruits and vegetables are subject to seasonal variations, so the farmer usually relies heavily on hired seasonal labor. This type of farmer uses more specialized equipment than do general farmers.

The mechanization of farming has not eliminated all the problems of raising crops. Judgment and experience are always important in making decisions. The *hay farmer,* for example, must determine the best time for mowing that will yield the best crop in terms of stem toughness and leaf loss. These decisions must be weighed against possible harsh weather conditions. To harvest hay, hay farmers use specialized equipment such as mowing machines and hay rakes that are usually drawn by tractors. The hay is pressed into bales by another machine for easier storage and then transported to storage facilities or to market.

Decisions about planting are just as crucial as those about harvesting. For example, potatoes need to be planted during a relatively short span of days in the spring. The fields must be tilled and ready for planting, and the farmer must estimate weather conditions so the seedlings will not freeze from late winter weather.

The crop specialty farmer uses elaborate irrigation systems to water crops during seasons of inadequate rainfall. Often these systems are portable as it is necessary to move the equipment from field to field.

Farms are strongly influenced by the weather, diseases, fluctuations in prices of domestic and foreign farm products, and, in some cases, federal farm programs. Farmers must carefully plan the combination of crops they will grow so that if the price of one crop drops they will have sufficient income from another to make up for it. Since prices change from month to month, farmers who plan ahead may be able to store their crops or keep their livestock to take advantage of better prices later in the year.

Farmers who raise and breed animals for milk or meat are called *livestock and cattle farmers*. There are various types of farmers that fall into this category.

Livestock farmers generally buy calves from ranchers who breed and raise them. They feed and fatten young cattle and often raise their own corn and hay to lower feeding costs. They need to be familiar with cattle diseases and proper methods of feeding. They provide their cattle with fenced pasturage and adequate shelter from rough weather. Some livestock farmers specialize in breeding stock for sale to ranchers and dairy farmers. These specialists maintain and improve purebred animals of a particular breed. Bulls and cows are then sold to ranchers and dairy farmers who want to improve their herds.

Sheep ranchers raise sheep primarily for their wool. Large herds are maintained on rangeland in the western states. Since large areas of land are needed, the sheep rancher must usually buy grazing rights on government-owned lands.

Although the *dairy farmers'* first concern is the production of high-grade milk, they also raise corn and grain to provide feed for their animals. Dairy farmers must be able to repair the many kinds of equipment essential to their business and know about diseases, sanitation, and methods of improving the quantity and quality of the milk.

Dairy animals must be milked every day, once in the morning and once at night. Records are kept of each cow's production of milk to ascertain which cows are profitable and which should be traded or sold for meat. After milking, when the cows are at pasture, the farmer cleans the stalls and barn by washing, sweeping, and sterilizing milking equipment with boiling water. This is extremely important because dairy cows easily contract diseases from unsanitary conditions, and this in turn may contaminate the milk. Dairy farmers must have their herds certified to be free of disease by the U.S. Department of Health.

The great majority of *poultry farmers* do not hatch their own chicks, but buy them from commercial hatcheries. The chicks are kept in brooder houses until they are seven or eight weeks old and are then transferred to open pens or shelters. After six months, the hens begin to lay eggs and roosters are culled from the flock to be sold for meat.

The primary duty of poultry farmers is to keep their flocks healthy. They provide shelter from the chickens' natural enemies and from extreme weather conditions. The shelters are kept extremely clean, because diseases can spread through a flock rapidly. The poultry farmer selects the food that best allows each chicken to grow or produce to its greatest potential while at the same time keeping costs down.

Raising chickens to be sold as broilers or fryers requires equipment to house them until they are six to thirteen weeks old. Farmers specializing in the production of eggs gather eggs at least twice a day and more often in very warm weather. The eggs then are stored in a cool place, inspected, graded, and packed for market.

The poultry farmer who specializes in producing broilers is usually not an independent producer but is under contract with a backer, who is often the operator of a slaughterhouse or the manufacturer of poultry feeds.

Fishers are considered farmers as well. Commercial fishing is an important component of the U.S. agricultural industry. Commercial fishers, both deep-sea and in-shore, catch or gather aquatic animal life for use as food for animals and humans. *Fish production technicians* work on fish farms to raise young fish in captivity for eventual use as food for animals or humans.

Beekeepers set up and manage bee hives and harvest and sell the excess honey that bees don't use as their own food. The sale of honey is less profitable than the business of cultivating bees for lease to farmers to help pollinate their crops.

Farmers and farm managers make a wide range of administrative decisions. In addition to their knowledge of crop production and animal science, they determine how to market the foods they produce. They keep an eye on the commodities markets to see which crops are most profitable. They take out loans to buy farm equipment or additional land for cultivation. They keep up with new methods of production and new markets. Farms today are large, complex businesses, complete with the requisite anxiety over cash flow, competition, markets, and production.

Requirements

Although there are no specific educational requirements for this field, every successful farmer, whether working with crops or animals, must have a knowledge of the principles of soil preparation and cultivation, disease control, and machinery maintenance, as well as a mastery of business practices and bookkeeping. Farmers must know their crops well enough to be able to choose the proper seeds for their particular soil and climate. They also need experience in evaluating crop growth and weather cycles. Livestock and dairy farmers should enjoy working with animals and have some background in animal science, breeding, and care.

High school courses that are valuable to the prospective farmer include algebra, geometry, biology, chemistry, accounting, and English. Extension courses should also be taken to keep abreast of developments in farm technology.

The state land-grant universities across the country were established to encourage agricultural research and to educate young people in the latest advancements in farming. They offer agricultural programs that award bachelor's degrees as well as shorter programs in specific areas. Some universities offer advanced studies in horticulture, animal science, agronomy, and agricultural economics. Most students in agricultural colleges are also required to take courses in farm management, business, finance, and economics.

Technical schools often have home-study courses, and evening courses are available in many areas for adult farmers. Two-year colleges often have programs leading to associate degrees in agriculture.

The American Society of Farm Managers and Rural Appraisers offers farm operators voluntary certification as an accredited farm manager (AFM). Certification requires several years experience working on a farm, an academic background—a bachelor's or preferably master's degree in a branch of agricultural science—and passing courses covering the business, financial, and legal aspects of farm management.

Farmers and farm operators need to keep updated on new farming methods throughout the world. They must be flexible and innovative enough to adapt to new technologies that will produce crops or raise livestock more efficiently. Farmers and operators should also have good mechanical aptitude and be able to work with a wide variety of tools and machinery.

Opportunities for Experience & Exploration

Few people enter farming as a career unless they grew up on or around a farm, but the opportunities for experience are plentiful from childhood on for those who want to make farming their career. For young people whose families do not own farms, there are many opportunities for part-time farmwork as a hired hand, especially during seasonal operations.

In addition, organizations such as the 4-H Club and Future Farmers of America offer good opportunities for learning about, visiting, and participating in farming activities. Agricultural colleges often have their own farms where students can gain actual experience in farm operations as well as classroom work.

Methods of Entering

It is becoming increasingly difficult for a person to purchase land for farming. The capital investment in a farm today is so great that it is almost impossible for anyone to start from scratch.

However, those who lack a family connection to farming or who do not have enough money to start their own farm can lease land from other farmers. Money for leasing land and equipment may be available from local banks or the Farmers Home Administration.

Because the capital outlay is so high, many wheat, corn, and specialty crop farmers often start as tenant farmers, renting land and equipment. They may also share the cash profits with the owner of the land. In this way, these tenants hope to gain both the experience and cash to purchase and manage their own farms.

Livestock farmers generally start by renting property and sometimes animals on a share-of-the-profits basis with the owner. Government lands, such as national parks, can be rented for pasture as well. Later, when the livestock farmer wants to own property, it is possible to borrow based on the estimated value of the leased land, buildings, and animals. Dairy farmers can begin in much the same way. However, loans are becoming more difficult to obtain. After several years of lenient loan policies, financial institutions in farm regions have tightened their requirements.

The best way to get into the poultry industry is to work part-time on a poultry farm during time off from school. Another possibility is to seek a job with a firm closely related to poultry farming, such as a feed or equipment dealer. This may lead to full-time work either on a farm or in a firm. Most poultry farms are actually owned by large firms such as feed producers.

Advancement

Farmers advance by buying their own farms or additional acreage to increase production and income. The same holds true for livestock, dairy, or poultry farmers. In farming, as in other fields, a person's success depends greatly on education, motivation, and keeping up with the latest developments.

Employment Outlook

Approximately 1,327,000 people are employed as farm owners or managers, with eighty five percent employed as farm workers of all kinds. It is expected that there will be a decrease in the number of people working as farmers and farm laborers over the next decade, although this decrease will occur at a slower rate than in the recent past. The majority of job openings will result from farmers leaving the workforce for economic or other reasons. Increases in automation and crop productivity will result in fewer people and less land required to produce the same amount of food. The surpluses that exist for many farm products make it even harder to earn a living by farming.

Large corporate farms are fast replacing the small farmer, who is being forced out of the industry by the spiraling costs of feed, grain, land, and equipment. The late 1970s and early 1980s were an especially hard time for farmers. Many small farmers were forced to give up farming; some lost farms that had been in their families for generations.

Aquaculture, or fish farming, is on the rise and may generate a different type of farming opportunity for motivated individuals.

Earnings

Farmers' incomes vary greatly from year to year, since the prices of farm products fluctuate according to weather conditions and the amount and quality of what all farmers were able to produce. A farm that shows a large profit one year may show a loss for the following year. Many farmers, especially those with small farms, earn incomes from non-farm activities that are several times larger than their farm incomes.

Farm incomes also vary greatly depending on the size and type of farm. In general, large farms generate more income than small farms. Exceptions include some specialty farms that produce low-volume but high-quality horticultural and fruit products.

Income for farm managers and operators varies substantially. According to the U.S. Department of Labor, salaries range from $10,600 to $25,200, although they can be as high as $39,500 per year. Large corporate farms may earn considerably more.

Conditions of Work

The farmer's daily life has its rewards and dangers. Machine-related injuries, exposure to the weather, and illnesses caused by allergies or animal-related diseases are just some of the hazards that farmers face on a regular basis. In addition, many farms are often isolated, away from many conveniences and necessities such as immediate medical attention.

Farming can be a difficult and frustrating career, but for many it is a satisfying way of life. The hours are long and the work is physically strenuous, but working outdoors and watching the fruits of one's labor grow before one's eyes can be very rewarding. The changing seasons bring variety to the day-to-day work. Farmers seldom work five eight-hour days a week. When harvesting time comes or the weather is right for planting or spraying, farmers work long hours to see that everything gets done. Even during the cold winter months they stay busy repairing machinery and buildings. Dairy farmers and other livestock farmers work seven days a week all year round.

Sources of Additional Information

American Farm Bureau Federation
225 Touhy Avenue
Park Ridge, IL 60068
Tel: 847-399-5700

American Society of Farm Managers and Rural Appraisers
950 South Cherry Street, Suite 508
Denver, CO 80222
Tel: 303-758-3513

National Council of Farmer Cooperatives
50 F Street, NW, Suite 900
Washington, DC 20001
Tel: 202-626-8700

National Farmers Union
250-C 2 Avenue South
Saskatoon, SK S7K 2M1 Canada

National Grange
1616 H Street, NW
Washington, DC 20006
Tel: 202-628-3507

U.S. Department of Agriculture
Higher Education Program
14th Street and Independence, SW
Washington, DC 20250
Tel: 202-720-2791

Fashion Designers

Definition

Fashion designers create or adapt original designs for clothing.

Nature of the Work

Fashion designers create designs for almost anything that is a part of the costume of men, women, or children. They may design both outer and inner garments or hats, purses, shoes, gloves, costume jewelry, scarves, or beachwear, or they may specialize in certain types of clothing such as bridal gowns or sportswear. People in this profession range from the few top haute couture designers who produce one-of-a-kind designs for high fashion houses that cater to a high-priced market, to the thousands of designers who work in the American garment industry creating fashions for mass production and sale to millions of Americans. The largest number of fashion designers are followers rather than originators of fashion, adapting styles to meet the price requirements of customers. Many fashion designers are self employed; some work on a freelance basis.

The designer's original idea for a garment is usually sketched. After a rough sketch is created, the designer begins to shape the pattern pieces that make the garment. The pieces are drawn to actual size on paper and cut out on a rough material, often muslin. The muslin pieces are sewn together and fitted on a model. The designer makes modifications in the pattern pieces or other features of the rough mock-up to complete the design. From the rough model, sample garments are made in the fabric that the designer intends to use.

Today's designers are greatly assisted by computer software. Computer-assisted designing and computer-assisted manufacturing (CAD/CAM) allow for thousands of fashion styles and colors to be stored in a computer and accessed at the touch of a button, largely eliminating the long process of gathering fabrics and styling them into samples.

School Subjects
Art
Family and Consumer Science

Personal Interests
Clothes
Drawing/Painting

Work Environment
Primarily indoors
One location with some travel

Minimum Education Level
Some postsecondary training

Salary Range
$14,500 to
$30,600 to
$67,600+

Certification or Licensing
None

Outlook
About as fast as the average

DOT
141

GOE
01.02.03

NOC
5243

Sample garments are displayed at a "showing," to which press representatives and buyers are invited and which designers supervise. Major designers may present large runway shows twice a year to leading retailers and the fashion press for potential publicity and sales. Selected garments are then mass-produced, displayed by fashion models, and shipped to stores where they are available for purchase.

In some companies, designers are involved in every step of the production of a selected line, from the original idea to the completed garments. Many designers prefer to supervise their own workrooms. Others work with supervisors to solve problems that arise in the production of the garments.

Most manufacturers produce new styles four times each year: spring and summer; fall and winter; "cruise," for people on vacations; and, "holiday," or special styles, for the winter holiday season. Designers generally are expected to create between 50 and 150 styles for each showing. Their work calendar differs from the actual time of year. They must be working on spring and summer designs during fall and winter and on fall and winter clothing during the summer.

Designers work cooperatively with the head of their manufacturing firm. They design a line that is consistent with the ideas of their employers. They also work cooperatively with those who do the actual production of the garments and must be able to estimate the cost of a garment. Some company designers produce designs and oversee a workroom staff, which may comprise a head designer, an assistant designer, and one or more sample makers. Designers in large firms may plan and direct the work of one or more assistant designers, select fabrics and trims, and help determine the pricing of the products they design.

Designers spend time in exploration and research, visiting textile manufacturing and sales establishments to learn of the latest fabrics and their uses and capabilities. They must know about fabric, weave, draping qualities, and strength of materials. A good understanding of textiles and their potentialities underlies much of designers' work. They browse through stores to see what fashion items are being bought by the public and which are passed by. They visit museums and art galleries to get ideas about color and design. They go to places where people congregate—theaters, sports events, business and professional meetings, and resorts—and meet with marketing and production workers, salespeople, and clients to discover what people are wearing and discuss ideas and styles.

Designers also keep abreast of changing styles. If the styles are too far ahead of public taste, customers will reject the designs. If, however, they cling to styles that have been successful in the past, they may find that the taste of buyers has surged ahead. In either case it may be equally disastrous for their employers.

There are many opportunities for specialization in fashion designing. The most common specialties are particular types of garments such as resort wear, bridalwear, or sports fashionwear. An interesting specialty in fashion designing is theatrical design, a relatively limited field but challenging to those who are interested in combining an interest in theater with a talent for clothing design.

Requirements

Fashion designing is a highly competitive business. The more well prepared an aspiring designer is, the broader the opportunities. Today, aspiring fashion designers not only need to be able to show their talent by quick-sketching a garment but also need to take formal courses in commercial fashion marketing and trade prediction. In fact, designers schooled in a total fashion course that includes marketing and other business skills are more favored by employers than a talented person with no working knowledge of business procedures. A college degree is recommended, although not required. Graduation from a fashion design school is highly desirable. Employers seek designers who have had courses in mathematics, business, design, sketching, art history, costume history, literature, pattern-making, clothing construction, and textiles.

Some colleges offer a four-year degree in fine arts with a major in fashion design. Many reputable schools of fashion design in the United States offer a two- or three-year program that does not lead to a degree but instead offers a diploma or certificate.

High school students who are interested in fashion designing should take as many courses as possible in art, clothing construction, and textiles. Those entering the fashion design field should also take computer-aided design courses as these tools are increasingly being used by designers to better visualize a final product, create prototypes, and reduce design production time and cost.

Prospective fashion designers must be artistically creative and imaginative with a flair for color and clothing coordination, a working knowledge of clothing construction, and an eye for trends. They must possess technical aptitudes, problem-solving skills, and the ability to conceptualize in two- and three-dimensions. Personal qualifications include self-motivation, team spirit, and the ability to handle pressure, deadlines, and long hours. This career also demands energy and a good head for business.

Opportunities for Experience & Exploration

The person who enjoys sewing and sews well may have taken the first step toward exploring a career in the fashion world. If the skills in garment construction are adequate, the next step may be an attempt at designing and making clothing. Art and design courses will help assess talent and ability as a creative artist.

Students who are able to obtain summer jobs in department or specialty stores can observe retailing practices and gain some practical insights into the merchandising aspects of the fashion world. They also can visit a garment manufacturer to see fashion employees at work.

Those who are interested in fashion design should take every opportunity to attend style shows, visit art galleries, observe clothing worn by fashion leaders, and browse through a variety of stores in which garments are sold. They should do extensive reading of the many books and magazines that are published about fashion, particularly *Women's Wear Daily,* which is the best known periodical of the garment industry.

Methods of Entering

Few people ever begin their careers as fashion designers. Frequently, well trained college graduates begin in positions as assistant designers and must prove that they have ability before they are entrusted with the responsible job of the designer. Many young people find that assistant designer jobs are difficult to locate, so they accept beginning jobs in the workroom where they spend time cutting or constructing garments. Fashion design school graduates may receive placement information from their school or college placement office.

Advancement

Advancement in fashion designing varies a great deal. There is much moving around from firm to firm, and vacancies frequently occur. Aspiring designers should create, collect, and continuously update a portfolio of their designs and continue to look for opportunities to show their work to employers. Beginners may work as cutting assistants or assist designers. From these entry-level positions, the fashion designer's career path may lead to positions as assistant technical designer, pattern company designer, designer, and head designer. Designers who have grown with a company may design less and take on more operational responsibilities.

Designers may choose to move into a business or merchandising position where they direct lines, set prices, supervise production, and work directly with buyers. After years of work, top designers may become partners in the design or apparel firms for which they work. Others may open their own retail clothing store. Those who continue as designers may want to work for firms that offer increasing design responsibility and fewer restrictions to become established as a house designer or eventually as an independent name designer.

Employment Outlook

Designers are the key people in the garment industry, yet relatively few of them are needed to make employment possible for thousands of people. It is estimated that there are more than 342,000 jobs held by designers and assistant designers in the United States. Some designers work only for the high-priced custom trade, some for the mass market, and some on exclusive designs, which will be made for only one person. Many designers are employed by manufacturers of paper patterns.

Good designers will always be needed, although not in great numbers. However, increasing populations and growing personal incomes are expected to spur demand for fashion designers. Fashion designers enjoy high pay and prestige, and those at the top of their profession rarely leave their positions. Therefore, opportunities for newcomers are limited. There always will be more people hoping to break into the field than there are jobs available. It takes a great deal of talent and perseverance to achieve success as a high-fashion designer. The employment outlook may be better in other fields, such as children's clothing. Openings are more readily available for assistant designers. Most openings will occur as workers leave the workforce for retirement or other reasons.

Earnings

According to the U.S. Department of Labor, entry positions averaged about $14,500 per year. For experienced designers, salaries may range between $19,700 and $46,200 a year. A few highly skilled and well-known designers in top firms have annual incomes of $67,600 or more. Top fashion designers who have successful lines of clothing can earn bonuses that bring their annual incomes into the millions of dollars. As designers become well known, they are usually offered a share of the ownership of the company for which they design. Their ownership percentage increases with their reputation.

Theatrical designers usually work on a contract basis. Although the remuneration for the total contract is usually good, there may be long periods of idleness between contracts. The annual incomes for theatrical designers usually are not as great as those of fashion designers, although while they are working they may be making more than $1,000 per week.

Conditions of Work

Fashion design is competitive and stressful, but often exciting and glamorous. Many designers work in cluttered and noisy surroundings. Their work environment may consist of a large room with long tables for cutting out patterns or garments. There may be only one or two other people working in the room, or there may be several others.

Many designers travel a great deal for showings and conferences. They may spend time in stores or shops looking at clothing that has been manufactured by competitors.

Most designers work a forty-hour week, but they may have to work more during rush periods. Styles previewed in spring and fall require a great amount of work during the weeks and months before a show. The work pace usually is hectic as pressure builds before collection showings.

Sources of Additional Information

International Association of Clothing Designers and Executives
475 Park Avenue, South, 17th Floor
New York, NY 10016
Tel: 212-685-6602

National Association of Schools of Art and Design
11250 Roger Bacon Drive, Suite 21
Reston, VA 22090
Tel: 703-437-0700

Financial Institution Tellers

Definition

Tellers are employees of banks and other financial institutions who handle certain types of customer account transactions. At the teller window, they receive and pay out money, record customer transactions, cash checks, sell traveler's checks, and perform other banking duties. Most people are familiar with commercial tellers who cash checks and handle deposits and withdrawals from customers. Many specialized tellers arc employed, too, especially in large financial institutions.

Nature of the Work

Tellers may perform a variety of duties in their jobs, but all of these duties involve accepting and disbursing funds to customers and keeping careful records of these transactions. *Commercial tellers*, or *paying and receiving* tellers, serve the public directly by accepting customers' deposits and providing them with receipts, paying out withdrawals and recording the transactions, cashing checks, exchanging money for customers to provide them with certain kinds of change or currency, and accepting savings account deposits. When cashing checks, tellers are responsible for checking the signatures to make sure they are valid, getting a valid identification of the person cashing the check, and, in some cases, verifying that the account against which the check is drawn has enough money to cover the amount.

Tellers make sure that deposit slips, deposit receipts, and the amount entered in passbooks are correctly recorded. They must be very cautious when counting amounts of money that they pay out or accept for deposit. Machines are often used to add and subtract, make change, print records and receipts for customers' records, post transactions on ledgers, and count coins. Almost all banks today are computerized. In some large institutions with many branches, tellers use a computer linked

School Subjects
Business
Mathematics

Personal Interests
Computers
Helping people: personal service

Work Environment
Primarily indoors
Primarily one location

Minimum Education Level
High school diploma

Salary Range
$11,900 to
$16,300 to
$24,800

Certification or Licensing
None

Outlook
Little or no change

DOT
211

GOE
07.03.01

NOC
1433

to the main office database to conduct transactions and verify customer balances.

At the beginning of every day, tellers are given cash drawers from the vault containing a certain amount of cash. During the day, they use this money to pay customers and add all deposited money. After their shift, tellers count the money in their cash drawers, add up the transactions they have conducted, and balance the day's accounts. If their calculations show a different amount from the money in their cash drawers, they double check their math and account sheets. Conscientious tellers are able to balance the day's accounts to the penny every day.

Tellers may be responsible for sorting checks and deposit slips, counting and wrapping money by hand or machine, filing new-account cards, and removing closed-account cards from the files. They give customers written information about the types of services and accounts available at the bank and answer any questions. They are supervised by *head tellers* and *teller supervisors*, who train them, arrange their schedules, and monitor their records of the day's transactions, helping to reconcile any discrepancies in balancing.

In large financial institutions, tellers may be identified by the specialized types of transactions that they handle. *Note tellers* are responsible for receiving and issuing receipts or payments on promissory notes and recording these transactions correctly. *Discount tellers* are responsible for issuing and collecting customers' notes. *Foreign banknote tellers* work in the exchange department, where they buy and sell foreign currency. When customers need to trade their foreign currency for U.S. currency, these tellers determine the current value of the foreign currency in dollars, count out the bills requested by the customer, and make change. These tellers may also sell foreign currency and traveler's checks for people traveling out of the country. *Collection and exchange tellers* accept payments in forms other than cash—contracts, mortgages, and bonds, for example.

Tellers may be employed by financial institutions other than banks. These institutions include savings and loan associations, personal finance companies, credit unions, government agencies, and large businesses operating credit offices. Although the particular duties may differ among institutions, the responsibilities and need for accuracy are the same. Tellers comprise the largest specialized occupational group of bank employees.

Requirements

Most banks and financial institutions require that applicants have at least a high school education. Many bank employees today have college educations or have taken specialized training courses offered by the banking industry. Many individuals who have earned a college education work as tellers to gain experience in this aspect of banking, anticipating promotions to higher positions within the bank. Aspiring bank tellers should take courses in high school on business arithmetic, business law, typing, computers, and business machines.

Training opportunities for this occupational group are numerous. Many business schools, junior colleges, and universities offer programs in business administration or special programs in banking. Many people apply for jobs in banking immediately after graduating from high school. They then continue to prepare for more advanced positions through their bank's specific training programs or by taking night courses offered by colleges or professional training associations.

The educational division of the American Banking Association—the American Institute of Banking—has a vast array of adult education classes in business fields and offers training courses in numerous parts of the country that enable people to earn standard or graduate certificates in bank training. Individuals may also enroll for correspondence study courses. Other educational institutions, such as the New York Institute of Finance and the Stonier Graduate School of Banking, offer opportunities for experienced bankers to study specialized areas of banking.

Desirable aptitudes for a bank teller are accuracy, speed, a good memory, the ability to work with figures, manual dexterity to handle money quickly, neatness, and orderliness. An essential prerequisite for tellers is that their honesty is above reproach, reflecting absolute trustworthiness. The work of the teller involves handling large sums of money. Therefore, bank tellers must be able to meet the standards established by bonding companies to be personally bonded as employees.

A prospective teller must be able to present a list of references that will attest to the person's good character and high standards of moral conduct. The teller must be able to work cooperatively with others and have a pleasant personality and friendly manner when working with the public. The nature of the teller's work and the bank's responsibility to its customers demand that all banking business be treated confidentially and not be discussed with anyone outside the workplace.

Tellers must always take the responsibilities of their work seriously. Carelessness is not tolerated in this occupation. A calm demeanor, emotional stability, and patience for routine tasks are positive assets for the teller, who sometimes must work under pressure during busy periods.

Opportunities for Experience & Exploration

Individuals may explore their interest in this occupation in numerous ways. Summer or part-time work is frequently available, depending on the locality. Students can work in clerical jobs, as messengers, or in other positions to observe the work of the tellers. Interested people may also visit banks and other financial institutions to talk with people employed in the field.

For those interested in working for a bank or financial institution, participating in school clubs and community activities will give them experience in working with people, handling money, and functioning as part of a team. Employers view these types of activities favorably when they consider applicants for teller positions.

Methods of Entering

Most tellers are promoted to teller positions from beginning jobs as bookkeeping or other general clerks. The skills and aptitudes people show in these beginning jobs, in addition to seniority, usually determine who will be promoted to a teller position. On the other hand, some applicants are able to obtain beginning jobs as tellers, especially in banks in large cities that offer on-the-job training programs.

Job opportunities can be found by applying in person to the institution for which you would like to work or which you have heard is hiring. Openings can also be found through newspaper help wanted ads, private or state employment agencies, or school placement services.

Advancement

Many banks and financial institutions follow a "promote-from-within" policy. Promotions are usually given on the basis of past job performance and consider the employee's seniority, ability, and general personal qualities. Tellers may be promoted to head teller or other supervisory positions such as department head. Some head tellers may be transferred from the main branch bank to a smaller branch and through experience and seniority be promoted to assistant branch manager or branch manager.

Employees who show initiative in their job responsibilities, pursue additional formal education and job training, and show their ability to assume leadership may in time be promoted to junior bank officer positions. These positions include such jobs as assistant cashier, assistant trust officer, and assistant departmental vice president. Such advancements reflect a recognition of the individual's potential for even greater future job responsibilities. Advancement to the higher echelons of the bank usually require a formal college or advanced degree.

Employment Outlook

In 1996, there were 545,000 bank tellers in the United States. Employment for tellers is predicted to experience little or no growth through the year 2006. In recent years, overexpansion by banks and competition from companies that offer banklike services have resulted in closings, mergers, and consolidations in the banking industry. Furthermore, the rate of employment for tellers is not expected to keep pace with overall employment growth in other banking occupations because of the increasing use of automatic teller machines and other technologies that increase teller efficiency or remove the need for tellers altogether.

Most employment opportunities will arise from the need to replace those workers who have left the field. This occupation provides a relatively large number of job openings due to its large size and high turnover rate. Demand for part-time tellers, especially during peak periods, is expected to be particularly strong. The field of banking offers a greater degree of job stability than some other fields as it is less likely to be affected by dips in the general economy.

Earnings

More than one-fourth of all tellers are employed part time. Yearly salaries and hourly wages paid to tellers vary across the country and are usually determined by the bank's size and geographic location and the employee's experience, responsibilities, formal education, specialized training, and ability. In 1996, tellers earned an average of about $16,300 a year. The highest-paid tellers earned about $24,800 a year, while those with fewer responsibilities in lower-paying areas of the country may earn as little as $11,900.

In most cases, fringe benefits for these workers are very good. Paid holidays may range from five to twelve days, depending on the bank's geographic location. Paid vacation periods vary, but many employees receive a two-week paid vacation after one year of service, three weeks after ten to fifteen years, and four weeks after twenty-five years. Group life, hospitalization, and surgical insurance plans are usually available, and employees frequently participate in shared employer–employee retirement plans. In some banks profit-sharing plans are open to employee enrollment. However, part-time employees are not eligible for basic benefits such as life and health insurance.

Conditions of Work

Most bank employees work a forty-hour week. Tellers may sometimes be required to work irregular hours or overtime. Many banks today stay open until 8:00 PM on Friday nights to accommodate the large number of workers who receive paychecks on that day. Part-time work for tellers is increasingly available.

Banks and financial institutions are usually pleasant and attractive places in which to work. Office equipment and furnishings are usually modern, and efforts are made to create a relaxed but efficient work atmosphere. Although tellers usually do not perform any physically strenuous work, they may have to stand at their stations for long periods of time. Dealing with customers may be tiring, especially during busy periods or when customers are difficult or demanding.

Sources of Additional Information

American Bankers Association
American Institute of Banking
1120 Connecticut Avenue, NW
Washington, DC 20036
Tel: 202-663-5221
WWW: http://www.aba.com/aba

Fish Production Technicians

Definition

Fish production technicians work in fish hatcheries and fish farms helping to raise young fish for eventual sale as human or animal food. Some fish are raised for sport fishing and are returned to the sea when they have reached maturity. Several kinds of fish can be successfully raised in captivity, among them trout, catfish, and salmon. Fish production technicians handle the day-to-day care of the fish and keep records of their activities.

Nature of the Work

The duties of fish production technicians vary depending on the type of hatchery or fish farm where they are employed. Some technicians work in hatcheries run by federal, state, or county governments to produce fish for release in open bodies of water. These fish are intended to be caught later by sport fishers. Other technicians work for privately owned commercial fish farms that raise fish to be sold as food for people or animals.

In both settings, fish production technicians carry out the day-to-day operations of the hatchery. For example, they monitor and record conditions in the tanks or ponds, feed the fish, clear the water of sick and dead fish, and maintain the equipment that circulates the water and regulates its temperature.

Fish production technicians are responsible for artificially breeding the fish. They first catch the fish in the holding pond and remove, or "strip," the eggs from the female fish and put them into a pail or other container. They do the same with the male fish, removing sperm or milt and putting it in the bucket with the eggs. The mixture of eggs and sperm is then stirred and rinsed and put in hatchery incubators with fertilized eggs. Technicians regulate water depth, flow, temperature, and velocity to ensure the optimum environment for incubation.

Workers must inspect the eggs periodically. They remove dead or unfertilized eggs with a syringe. When the fish hatch,

School Subjects
Agriculture
Chemistry

Personal Interests
Animals
The Environment

Work Environment
Indoors and outdoors
Primarily one location

Minimum Education Level
High school diploma

Salary Range
Minimum wage to
$20,000 to
$30,000

Certification or Licensing
None

Outlook
Faster than the average

DOT
446

GOE
03.04.03

NOC
2221

technicians move them to rearing tanks where they are fed by hand or by a blower that automatically scatters the food over a large area. Fish production technicians must also watch the fish for disease and add medicine to the food or water if the situation warrants. Later, mature fish are transferred to farm ponds or outdoor tanks.

Some fish production technicians work in laboratories at fish farms or hatcheries. Usually assisting biologists, they study methods to increase the production of healthy fish. Certain regulating factors such as the feed, the fish pond's size or depth, and the water's oxygen level and temperature can make a big difference in how fast the fish grow. These fish production technicians often learn to operate microscopes and measuring devices on the job. They keep records of their results so that they can be used to improve the production of the hatchery or fish farm.

Fish production technicians also perform the slippery task of attaching small tags to individual fish before releasing them into lakes or rivers. When the fish is caught, the tag is returned to the hatchery so that technicians can study the factors that affect fish health and survival. Technicians may also work with wild fish that were caught for use in laboratory research.

Fish raised for sport fishing must be moved from the hatchery to lakes or rivers when they reach maturity. They are usually transported in tank trucks. Fish production technicians often handle the loading and unloading of the fish from the trucks.

Requirements

A high school diploma is usually required for fish production technicians. For jobs that involve laboratory work, employers look for applicants with some post-high school training. Only a few community colleges and technical institutes offer two-year post-high school programs concerned with fish production. However, programs that include courses in biology, chemistry, and mathematics should provide suitable preparation for many technician jobs in fish hatcheries and farms. Government-run hatcheries and farms usually require two years of college education. Increasingly, many states require a bachelor's degree for employment.

While still in high school, students interested in this field should take courses in science, especially chemistry and biology, mathematics, and environmental studies.

Personal requirements for fish production technicians include patience in performing sometimes repetitious and exacting tasks and an ability to follow instructions. Good communications skills are a must in almost any profession.

Opportunities for Experience & Exploration

Those interested in becoming fish production technicians can visit fish farms or hatcheries near their homes to get a good picture of the everyday duties of a technician. High school counselors may be able to organize group tours or a presentation by a qualified fish production technician. Students may also join conservation organizations or volunteer in local conservation projects to gain general experience in the field.

Teenagers aged fifteen to eighteen may take advantage of a summer program run by the National Park Service, the U.S. Fish and Wildlife Service, and the U.S. Forest Service. Participants in the program work in an outdoor setting for at least eight weeks, gaining experience in a wide variety of duties and settings.

Methods of Entering

High school graduates can apply to nearby fish farms or hatcheries for employment opportunities. College students can access the job placement office for opportunities in fish production. State employment offices may have information regarding civil service opportunities in fish production.

There are many regions throughout the United States that offer good employment opportunities for fish production technicians. States such as Louisiana, Arkansas, and Mississippi offer excellent conditions for catfish farming. Shrimp farming—which requires a temperature of at least 68 degrees F—is concentrated in southern coastal states. Opportunities for those interested in raising trout exist in Idaho and Montana. Cultured shellfish and salmon are raised in the Pacific Northwest.

Some federal agencies that employ fish production technicians include U.S. Fish and Wildlife Service, National Marine Fisheries Service, the Environmental Protection Agency, the National Park Service, and the Forest Service.

There are many foreign opportunities for fish production technicians. Marine shrimp are raised in

China, Ecuador, and the Philippines. Salmon is raised quite successfully in Norway and Japan. Israel and the Philippines both have large freshwater fish farms.

Other employers of fish production technicians include bait farms, private hydropower companies, and tropical fish producers.

Advancement

Experienced fish production technicians may advance to supervisory positions or be given more demanding duties. Those who pursue advanced education and training may obtain high-paying positions with the federal government. Others may use their skills and experience to open their own fish farms or hatcheries.

Employment Outlook

Employment opportunities for fish production technicians are expected to be good through the year 2006. Federal controls over coastal fish harvests have limited commercial fisheries. Increasingly, commercial entities are focusing on fish farming and harvesting in the United States and in developing countries. Fish are much cheaper to raise than livestock.

Fish production technicians will also see growth in employment as a result of increasing interest in health and good eating habits. Fish are lower in cholesterol than meat and are also good sources of protein.

Earnings

Earnings for fish production technicians vary depending on the size and type of operation. Earnings may range from minimum wage to over $10 per hour. Federal or state fish production technicians—who raise fish for release back into the wild—earn salaries based on a civil service scale. Starting salaries in 1994 ranged from $19,400 (GS-5 grade) to $24,038 (GS-7 grade). Salaries depend on experience, education, and the skills the workers bring with them to the job. Fish production technicians who work for the federal government earn higher salaries and better benefits than those technicians employed by state and local governments.

Fish production technicians are also eligible to receive paid sick days and vacation, medical and dental insurance, and pension plans.

Conditions of Work

The career of a fish production technician is suitable for those interested in fish who would not be comfortable spending much of their time on the water as a fisher. Obviously, a fish production technician should be able to tolerate the smell of fish if he or she is planning a career working on a fish farm. Fish production technicians who work for federal or state government may have to wade in lakes or streams when introducing fish back into the environment. In addition, the fish production technician is expected to perform work that it is intricate and repetitive. Patience is needed.

Sources of Additional Information

■ The American Fisheries Society
5410 Grosvenor Lane, Suite 110
Bethesda, MD 20814-2199
Tel: 301-897-8616

■ National Fisheries Institute
1901 North Fort Myer Drive, Suite 700
Arlington, VA 22209
Tel: 703-524-8880
WWW: http://www.nfi.org/

■ National Marine Fisheries Service
Silver Spring Metro Building 3, Room 14555
1315 East-West Highway
Silver Spring, MD 20910

■ U.S. Department of Agriculture
Aquaculture Information Society
NAL Building, Room 111
Beltsville, MD 20705

■ Western Association of Fish and Wildlife Agencies
1416 Ninth Street, Twelfth Floor
Sacramento, CA 95814
Tel: 916-653-4711

Fishers

Definition

Fishers catch fish and other marine life by net, trap, and hook and then sell their catch to commercial food processors, restaurants, and retail and whole-sale fish markets. Fishers work both in the ocean and fresh water bodies. Some fishers run recreational charter fishing businesses: they rent power boats, provide fishing expertise, and take customers out on the water for sport fishing trips.

Nature of the Work

Now that large corporate fishing fleets dominate the fishing industry, most fishing is done from large commercial vessels that employ many fishers as crew. The *captain* plans and oversees the entire fishing operation. He or she decides which fish should be caught, where they will best be found, the method of capture, the duration of the trip, and how the catch will be sold. The captain also makes sure the sailing vessel is in suitable condition and hires and supervises *crew members*. The *first mate* is the captain's assistant. He or she must be familiar with navigation requirements and up to date on all the latest electronic devices used on fishing boats. The mate, under the supervision of the captain, oversees the fishing operations and the sailing responsibilities of the *deck-hands*. The *boatswain* is an experienced deckhand with some supervisory responsibilities. He or she directs the loading of equipment and supplies onto the vessel before it sets sail. The boatswain also operates and repairs much of the fishing gear. The deckhand does much of the actual fishing. Deckhand release and pull in nets and lines and extract the catch from the lines or nets. They wash, salt, ice, and store the fish. Deckhands also make sure that the deck is clean and clear at all times and that the vessel's engines and equipment are in working order.

Fishers are classified according to the type of equipment they use, the type of fish they catch, and where they go to catch

School Subjects
Business
Shop (Trade/Vo-tech education)

Personal Interests
Boating
Fixing things

Work Environment
Primarily outdoors
Primarily multiple locations

Minimum Education Level
High school diploma

Salary Range
$11,960 to
$20,280 to
$27,040

Certification or Licensing
None

Outlook
Decline

DOT
441

GOE
03.04.03

NOC
8262

them. Fishers work all over the country. Major fishing industries can be found in Maine, Maryland, Massachusetts, Louisiana, Florida, Texas, California, Oregon, Washington, and Alaska. The northeastern states are good for lobster and sardine fishing, while fishers in the Gulf states catch shrimp and oysters. Most *tuna fishers* work off the California coastline. U.S. vessels also travel into the Bering Sea for snow crab, halibut, pollock, and salmon and to the oceans off Africa and China for tuna.

Net fishers are usually deep sea fishers. They either work alone or as part of a crew, using many types of nets to catch fish. Some boats make only short day runs, while others go for weeks or months at a time, keeping their catches fresh in huge refrigeration units. While small boats may carry a few crew members, large tuna boats can carry as many as twenty-two and measure more than two hundred feet long.

After the boats leave port, they head for the fishing grounds—areas of the sea that are known to have fish. Crew members keep track of weather reports and fishing conditions over the radio. They scan for schools of fish using sonar and other electronic equipment. When they think they have located a school of fish, they lower the nets. *Purse seiners,* who mainly catch tuna, use a huge net—often a mile long and hundreds of feet deep. The net is weighted on the bottom and is held vertical by floats attached to the top. A smaller boat called a skiff, driven by a skiff operator, holds one end of the net while the fishing vessel circles around the school to surround it with the net. Once that is done, fishers close the bottom of the net by retracting steel cables that act like a drawstring, then pull in the net and haul the catch on board.

Net fishers are responsible for readying and repairing nets while the boat is moving to and from the fishing waters. The catch is often so heavy that they must use hydraulic pumps and conveyor belts to haul it in. Depending on the captain's orders, fish are cleaned and sorted before or after returning to shore. Large tuna boats that stay at sea for many weeks catch as many as twelve hundred tons of fish, which the fishers usually turn over to canneries upon their return.

Line fishers catch fish with poles, hooks, and lines. They work alone or in crews. They lay out lines and attach hooks, bait, and other equipment, depending on the type of fish they plan to catch. This process can take several hours. They then lower these lines into the water. To haul catches on board they use reels, winches, or their bare hands. They take the fish off the hooks, sometimes stunning them first by hitting them with clubs. They store their catch in the boat's hold or in boxes packed with ice. Some of these fishers use a gaff—a long pole with a hook on the end—to help

them catch fish and bring them aboard. Line fishers may also clean fish while their vessel heads to shore.

Because ships usually do not return to shore until bad weather, darkness, or the ship's hold is full of fish, net and line fishers will repeat their tasks several times a day.

Pot fishers trap crab, eel, and lobster using baited cages with funnel-shaped net openings. They fish near the shore or in inland waters off small boats. Pot fishing is done by lowering the cages into the water, pulling them in when the fish are trapped, and dumping the catch onto the deck. These fishers must measure each animal to make sure it is large enough under law to keep. Undersize fish are thrown back into the water. When catching lobster, fishers must sometimes insert pegs between the hinges of their claws to keep them from killing each other in the hold of the ship. Pot fishers often sell their catches live to processors who can, freeze, or sell them fresh. Because they are hardy animals, lobster and crab are often sold and shipped to various places while they are still alive.

Terrapin fishers trap terrapin turtles by stretching nets across marshes, creeks, or rivers and chasing the terrapins into the nets. They may pole a skiff around in grassy waters and catch terrapins with a hand net or wade in mud and catch them by hand. *Weir fishers* make traps out of brush or netting, chase the fish into them, and remove the catch with a purse seine or net. *Oyster fishers* harvest oysters from beds in bays or river estuaries, using tongs, grabs, and dredges. They create "sea farms" to grow their catches by creating an environment suitable for growing oysters and keeping natural predators out of the oysters' waters.

While most fishers are involved with commercial fishing, some captains and deckhands are primarily involved with recreational fishing. Typically a group of people charter a fishing vessel—for periods ranging from several hours to a few days—for sport fishing, socializing, and relaxation. The captain and crew are responsible for a safe voyage and will usually help the recreational fishers on board with their fishing.

Requirements

Fishers learn their skills through experience on the job. Certain academic courses, however, can help prepare workers for their first job. Some high schools, colleges, and technical schools in port cities offer useful courses in handling boats and fishing equipment, biology, meteorology, navigation, and marketing. Commercial fishing programs are offered by three trade schools: Bellingham Vocational Technical Institute in Washington, Southwest Oregon Community College in Oregon, and Willmar Community College in Minnesota. Additionally, the University of Rhode Island offers a bachelor's degree program in fishery technology. Instruction includes classwork and hands-on experience in the fishing industry.

Experienced fishers often take short-term courses offered by postsecondary schools. These programs provide information on electronic navigation and communications equipment and the latest improvements in fishing gear.

Captains and first mates on large fishing vessels of at least two hundred gross tons must be licensed. Captains of charter sport fishing boats must also be licensed, regardless of the size of the vessel. Crew members on certain fish processing vessels may require merchant mariner's documentation. These licenses and documents are issued by the U.S. Coast Guard. Individuals seeking certification must meet physical and academic requirements.

People who enjoy risk, independence, and hard work may enjoy commercial fishing. Fishers should be self-sufficient and able to cope with the everyday dangers of working with heavy equipment on wet decks and in stormy seas. Teamwork is essential when seas become rough or equipment breaks down, so fishers must stay calm in the face of trouble. Mechanical aptitude is also essential as fishers spend a good deal of time setting up, repairing, and maintaining equipment. Business acumen will benefit those fishers who want to be skippers of their own boats.

Opportunities for Experience & Exploration

In order to explore this field, students may try to obtain summer work on a small fishing boat or at a fishing port. Talking to fishers to find out more about their work is also helpful.

Methods of Entering

Many people find employment by entering their families' fishing businesses. Others seek deckhand jobs by applying to captains of commercial fishing vessels. These boats may be privately or corporately owned.

Advancement

Fishing has little formal structure within which workers can advance. Fishers can, however, increase their earnings and responsibilities by becoming more skilled at vessel and net operation and by exploring ways of becoming involved in all aspects of the fishing industry. Enterprising fishers who save enough money may be able to buy their own boats. Some run their own processing operations or catch seafood for their own restaurants. Advancement is limited only by the individual's own desire, drive, and skill. Owning one boat or a number of boats usually provides the highest profits for commercial fishers.

Employment Outlook

Once booming, fishing as an industry has experienced hard times in the past few decades. In 1996, fewer than 47,000 fishers worked in the United States. The employment outlook for fishers is expected to decline in the next decade. Pollution and overfishing in the past have affected this occupation. The industry is also affected by such variables as environmental law, ship maintenance costs, improvements in electronic and other fishing gear (which has limited the expansion in crew size), and the increasing use of "floating processors," which process "catches" on-board (further limiting employment opportunities). Recently, federal enforcement of a two-hundred-mile offshore boundary has reduced foreign competition for U.S. fishers. Sport fishing positions will continue to grow as the travel and recreation fields continue to expand. Some may find employment in the growing field of aquaculture, the commercial raising of fish and other water-based organisms.

Earnings

Earnings of fishers vary with the season, economy, abundance of fish, market demands, and workers' skills and willingness to stay out at sea. Few fishers receive a fixed wage. Instead, they usually earn percentages of the catch's receipts. In New England, ship owners can receive 50 percent of the catch's receipts. The captain may receive 10 percent, and the captain and crew share the remaining 40 percent. Year-round fishers can earn from $12,000 to $27,000 a year. Seasonal fishers earn less. Fishers with their own boats, and cannery owners, can earn substantially more. Many workers earn hourly rates ranging from minimum wage to around $8.00 an hour.

Some are paid according to the number of pounds of fish they catch.

Conditions of Work

Fishers work long hours under conditions that are often dangerous and difficult. Lookout watches—usually six hours long—are a regular duty for crew members, who must be prepared to perform this job day or night. Hauling fish on board takes great physical strength and endurance, and the work can be exhausting. Fishers work in all kinds of weather and sometimes spend months at sea in cramped quarters. Some fishers work all year, while others work only in certain seasons when certain fish can be caught.

Some fishers belong to unions. The crew members of vessels of the American Tunaboat Association are members of a union, and they receive pensions, health and welfare benefits, and liberal disability benefits if they are injured while working on a vessel.

Sources of Additional Information

■ **American Tunaboat Association**
One Tuna Lane
San Diego, CA 92101
Tel: 619-233-6405

For a list of schools that offer fishing and marine educational programs, contact:

■ **Marine Technology Society**
1828 L Street, NW, Suite 906
Washington, DC 20036-5104
Tel: 202-775-5966

For general information regarding fishing careers, contact:

■ **National Fisheries Institute**
1525 Wilson Boulevard, Suite 500
Arlington, VA 22209
Tel: 703-524-8880

Flight Attendants

Definition

Flight attendants are responsible for the safety and comfort of airline passengers from the initial boarding to the final disembarkment. They are trained to respond in the event of emergencics and passenger illness. Flight attendants are required on almost all national and international commercial flights.

Nature of the Work

Flight attendants perform a variety of preflight and in-flight duties. At least one hour before takeoff, they attend briefing session with the rest of the flight crew; carefully check flight supplies, emergency life jackets, oxygen masks, and other passenger safety equipment; and see that the passenger cabins are neat, orderly, and furnished with pillows and blankets. They also check the plane galley to see that food and beverages to be served are on board and that the galley is secure for takeoff.

Attendants welcome the passengers on the flight and check their tickets as they board the plane. They show the passengers where to store briefcases and other small parcels, direct them to their cabin section for seating, and help them put their coats and carry-on luggage in overhead compartments. They often give special attention to elderly or disabled passengers and those traveling with small children.

Before takeoff, a flight attendant speaks to the passengers as a group, usually over a loudspeaker. He or she welcomes the passengers and gives the names of the crew and flight attendants. The passengers also learn about weather, altitude, and safety information. As required by federal law, flight attendants demonstrate the use of lifesaving equipment and safety procedures and check to make sure all passenger seatbelts are fastened before takeoff.

Upon takeoff and landing and during any rough weather encountered during the flight, flight attendants routinely check to make sure passengers are wearing their safety belts properly and have their seats in an upright position. They may distribute reading materials to passengers and answer any questions regarding flight schedules, weather, or the geographic terrain over which the plane is passing. Sometimes they call attention to points of interest that can be seen from the plane. They observe passengers during the flight to ensure their personal comfort and assist anyone who becomes airsick or nervous.

During some flights, attendants serve prepared breakfasts, lunches, dinners, or between-meal refreshments. They are responsible for certain clerical duties, such as filling out passenger reports and issuing reboarding passes. They keep the passenger cabins neat and comfortable during flights. Attendants serving on international flights may provide customs and airport information and sometimes translate flight information or passenger instructions into a foreign language.

Most flight attendants work for commercial airlines. A small number, however, work on private airplanes owned and operated by corporations or private companies.

Requirements

Airline companies are very selective in accepting applicants for positions as flight attendants. These employees play a major role in promoting good public relations for the airlines. Attendants are in constant contact with the public, and the impressions they make and the quality of service they render represent a type of advertisement for the airline. Airlines are particularly interested in employing people who are intelligent, poised, resourceful, and able to work in a congenial and tactful manner with the public. Flight attendants must have excellent health, good vision, and the ability to speak clearly.

Flight attendants need to have at least a high school education. Applicants with additional college-level education are often given preference in employment. Business training and experience in working with the public are also considered assets. Attendants employed by international airlines are usually required to be able to converse in a foreign language. Airlines in the United States require flight attendants to be U.S. citizens, have permanent resident status, or have valid work visas. In general, applicants must be at least nineteen to twenty years old, although some airlines have higher minimum age requirements. They should be at least five feet, two inches tall in order to reach overhead compartments, and their weight should be in proportion to their height. Although most flight atten-

dants are women, the number of men in this field is increasing.

Most large airline companies maintain their own training schools for flight attendants. Training programs may last from four to six weeks. Some smaller airlines send their applicants to the schools run by the bigger airlines. A few colleges and schools offer flight attendant training, but these graduates may still be required to complete an airline's own training program.

Airline training programs usually include classes in company operations and schedules, flight regulations and duties, first aid, grooming, emergency operations and evacuation procedures, flight terminology, and other types of job-related instruction. Flight attendants also receive twelve to fourteen hours of additional emergency and passenger procedures training each year. Trainees for international flights are given instruction on customs and visa regulations and are taught procedures for terrorist attacks. Near the end of the training period, trainees are taken on practice flights, in which they perform their duties under supervision.

An on-the-job probationary period, usually six months, follows training school. During this time, experienced attendants pay close attention to the performance, aptitudes, and attitudes of the new attendants. After this period, new attendants serve as reserve personnel and fill in for attendants who are ill or on vacation. While on call, these reserve attendants must be available to work on short notice.

Young people who are interested in this occupation need to have a congenial temperament, a pleasant personality, and the desire to serve the public. They must have the ability to think clearly and logically, even in emergency situations, and they must be able to follow instructions working as team members of flight crews.

Opportunities for Experience & Exploration

Opportunities for experience in this occupation are almost nonexistent until an individual has completed flight training school. Interested persons may explore this occupation by talking with flight attendants or people in airline personnel offices. Airline companies and private training schools publish many brochures describing the work of flight attendants and send them out upon request.

Methods of Entering

Individuals who are interested in becoming flight attendants should apply directly to the personnel divisions of airline companies. The names and locations of these companies may be obtained by writing to the Air Transport Association of America. Addresses of airline personnel division offices can also be obtained from almost any airline office or ticket agency. Some major airlines have personnel recruiting teams that travel throughout the United States interviewing prospective flight attendants. Airline company offices can provide interested people with information regarding these recruitment visits, which are sometimes announced in newspaper advertisements in advance of the actual visit.

Advancement

A number of advancement opportunities are open to flight attendants. They may advance to positions as *first flight attendant* (sometimes known as the *flight purser*), *supervising flight attendant,* instructor, or airline recruitment representative. They may also have the opportunity to move up to *chief attendant* in a particular division or area. Although the rate of turnover in this field was once high, more people are making careers as flight attendants and competition for available supervisory jobs is very high.

Many flight attendants who no longer qualify for flight duty because of health or other factors move into other jobs with the airlines. These jobs may include reservation agent, ticket agent, or personnel recruiter. They may also work in the public relations, sales, air transportation, dispatch, or communications divisions. Trained flight attendants may also find similar employment in other transportation or hospitality industries such as luxury cruise ship lines.

Employment Outlook

Nearly 132,000 professionally trained flight attendants are employed in the United States. Commercial airlines employ the vast majority of all flight attendants, most of whom are stationed in the major cities that serve as their airlines' home base.

Employment opportunities for flight attendants are predicted to grow much faster than average in the next decade. More and more people are flying regularly today for business and pleasure, and some estimates predict that the number of flight passengers will increase significantly to accommodate the demand. To meet the needs of the traveling public, airline companies are using larger planes and adding more flights. Because federal regulations require at least one attendant on duty for every fifty passengers aboard a plane, this means there will be many more openings for flight attendants. A large number of jobs will result from current flight attendants leaving the workforce due to a variety of factors, including retirement.

Finding employment as a flight attendant is highly competitive. Even though the number of job openings is expected to grow, airlines receive thousands of applications each year. Students interested in this career will have a competitive advantage if they have at least two years of college and prior work experience in customer relations or public contact. Courses in business, psychology, sociology, geography, speech, communications, first aid and emergency medical techniques such as CPR, and knowledge of foreign languages and cultures will make the prospective flight attendant more attractive to the airlines.

Earnings

The average income of beginning flight attendants is approximately $12,800 a year. The average salary of all flight attendants was $19,000 per year in 1996, according to the U.S. Department of Labor. Senior flight attendants can earn $35,000 to $40,000 a year. Wage and work schedule requirements are established by union contract. Most flight attendants are members of the Transport Workers Union of America or the Association of Flight Attendants.

Flight attendants are limited to a specific number of flying hours. In general, they work approximately eighty hours of scheduled flying time and an additional thirty-five hours of ground duties each month. They receive extra compensation for overtime and night flights. Flight attendants on international flights customarily earn higher salaries than those on domestic flights. Most airlines give periodic salary increases until a maximum pay ceiling is reached. Flight assignments are often based on seniority, with the most senior flight attendants having their choice of flight times and destinations.

Airlines usually pay flight attendants in training either living expenses or a training salary. Companies usually pay flight attendants' expenses such as food, ground transportation, and overnight accommodations while they are on duty or away from home base. Some airlines may require first-year flight attendants to furnish their own uniforms; however, most companies supply the airline uniform.

Fringe benefits include paid sick leave and vacation time, free or reduced air travel rates for attendants and their families, and, in some cases, group hospitalization and life insurance plans and retirement benefits.

Conditions of Work

Flight attendants are usually assigned to a home base in a major city or large metropolitan area. These locations include New York, Chicago, Boston, Miami, Los Angeles, San Francisco, St. Louis, and other cities. Some airlines assign attendants on a rotation system to home bases, or they may give preference to the requests of those with rank and seniority on bids for certain home bases. Those with the longest records of service may be given the most desirable flights and schedules.

Flight attendants need to be flexible in their work schedules, mainly because commercial airlines maintain operations twenty-four hours a day throughout the entire year. They may be scheduled to work nights, weekends, and on holidays, and they may find some of their allotted time off occurs away from home between flights. They are often away from home for several days at a time. They work long days, but over a year's time, a flight attendant averages about 156 days off, compared with 96 days off for the average office worker.

The work performed by flight attendants may be physically demanding in some respects. For most of the flight, they are usually on their feet servicing passengers' needs, checking safety precautions, and, in many cases, serving meals and beverages. Working with the public all day can be draining. Flight atten-

dants are the most visible employee of the airline, and they must be courteous to everyone, even passengers who are annoying or demanding. The occupation is not considered a hazardous one; however, there is a certain degree of risk involved in any type of flight work. Flight attendants may suffer minor injuries as they perform their duties in a moving aircraft.

The combination of free time and the opportunity to travel are benefits that many flight attendants enjoy. For those who enjoy helping and working with people, being a flight attendant may be a rewarding career.

Sources of Additional Information

For information on educational and career opportunities, please contact:

Air Line Employees Association
6520 South Cicero Avenue
Bedford Park, IL 60638
Tel: 708-563-9999

Air Transport Association of America
1301 Pennsylvania Avenue, NW
Washington, DC 20004

Federal Aviation Administration
U.S. Department of Transportation
800 Independence Avenue, SW
Washington, DC 20591

Future Aviation Professionals of America
4959 Massachusetts Boulevard
Atlanta, GA 30337
Tel: 800-JET-JOBS

Floor Covering Installers

Definition

Floor covering installers include resilient floor layers, who install, replace, and repair shock-absorbing, sound-deadening, or decorative floor covering such as vinyl tile and sheet vinyl on finished interior floors of buildings, and carpet layers, who install carpets and rugs, especially wall-to-wall carpeting.

Nature of the Work

Installers' tasks vary somewhat according to whether they specialize in the installation of carpets or resilient floor coverings. Some installers do both types of coverings.

For both types of flooring, the preparation of the surface beneath the finish material is very important. The subfloor surface must be firm, dry, smooth, and free of loose dust and dirt. Installers may have to sweep, scrape, sand, or chip dirt and other irregularities from the floor, as well as fill cracks with a filler material. Sometimes a new surface of plywood or cement must be laid down before any floor covering can be installed.

Experienced installers must be able to gauge the moisture content of the subfloor and decide whether conditions are suitable for installing the covering. They should also know about the various adhesives that can be used, depending on conditions. Once the subfloor surface is prepared, installers consult blueprints or sketches and carefully measure the floor to determine where joints and seams will fall.

When the layout is clear, the installers, perhaps assisted by apprentices or helpers, measure and cut the floor covering to create sections of the proper size. They use a rule, straightedge, linoleum knife, and snips. They may also cut and lay in place on the subfloor a foundation material such as felt. Then they apply adhesive cement to the floor and cement the foundation in place. With chalk lines and dividers, installers lay out lines on the foundation material to guide them in installing the floor

School Subjects
Mathematics
Physics

Personal Interests
Airplanes
Figuring out how things work

Work Environment
Primarily indoors
Primarily multiple locations

Minimum Education Level
High school diploma

Salary Range
$11,560 to
$26,000 to
$45,448

Certification or Licensing
Required

Outlook
About as fast as the average

DOT
621

GOE
05.03.06

NOC
2271

covering. They trowel on adhesive cement and lay the floor covering in place, following the guidelines. Installers must be especially careful to align the pieces if there is any pattern in the flooring. They must also pay particular attention to fitting the pieces in odd-shaped areas around door openings, pipes, and posts. To make tight seams where sections of sheet covering must join, they overlap edges and cut through both layers with a knife. After the covering is laid in place, they often run a roller over it to smooth it and ensure good adhesion.

In installing wall-to-wall carpeting, carpet layers first measure the floor and plan the layout. They should allow for expected foot-traffic patterns so that the best appearance and longest wear will be obtained from the carpet. They also must locate seams where they will be least noticed.

When the layout is completed, installers make sure that the floor surface is in the proper condition and correct any imperfections that may show through the carpet. Some carpet can be tacked directly to certain kinds of floor, but in many buildings, including residences, installers often use the tackless strip method of laying carpet. A tackless strip is a thin strip of plywood with rows of steel pins projecting upward from it to grip carpeting firmly in place. Installers nail tackless strips around the border of the floor. Next, they cut and place padding in the open area of the floor.

Carpet often comes in twelve-foot widths, so some rooms require that sections of carpet be seamed together. If the carpet has not been precut and seamed in the floor covering firm's workroom, the installers must use a carpet knife to cut pieces to the correct sizes, then attach the pieces together. They may sew the seam with a curved needle or use a heat-activated adhesive tape and an electric heating tool like an iron.

When pieces are cut and ready, the installers position the carpet and stretch it with special tools so it fits evenly on the floor, with no lumps or rolls. They fasten it in place, either with the tackless strips or by tacking directly to the floor. Any excess material must be trimmed off so that the carpet meets the wall and door thresholds with a snug, exact fit.

Carpet installers use hand tools, including mallets, staple guns, pry bars, trowels, carpet knives, and shears; measuring and marking devices, such as tape measures, straightedges, and chalk lines; and power tools, such as stretchers.

Requirements

Floor covering installers can learn their skills on the job or through apprenticeship programs, which combine on-the-job training with classroom instruction.

A floor covering installer applies adhesive to a surface before placing the sheet vinyl on top of it. Most installers begin as helpers working for flooring installation contractors and learn informally on the job. When they are first hired, helpers are assigned simple tasks, such as tacking down strips. As they gain skills and experience, they are given more difficult work, such as measuring and cutting. Employers look for applicants who have manual dexterity and good eye-hand coordination. They may require that helpers have a high school education. High school courses that are good background for applicants include wood and metal shop classes, mechanical drawing, general mathematics, and geometry. Because installers work on the premises of the customer, they should have a neat appearance and a courteous manner. It may take an installer eighteen months to two years of informal on-the-job training to learn the basics of carpet laying or resilient floor laying.

Apprenticeship programs, which often last three to four years, usually provide much more complete training in all phases of installation. Some apprenticeships teach installation of both types of flooring, while others teach one or the other. Apprentices work under the supervision of experienced installers and typically attend classes in related subjects once a week.

Opportunities for Experience & Exploration

High school shop courses can introduce students to the hand tools and skills that floor covering installers use, and courses in applied mathematics can help students gauge their ability to do the kinds of computations that installers must do. A part-time or summer job as a helper working for a flooring installation contractor would be a good way to directly experience this work and might lead to full-time employment later. Even a do-it-yourself home improvement project installing vinyl floor tiles can provide a sample of the activities of these workers.

Methods of Entering

People who plan to start out as helpers in this field and learn their skills on the job can apply directly to floor covering contractors and retailers. For specific job leads, they may want to check the listings in newspaper classified ads or the local offices of the state employment service. Information on apprenticeships in the area may be available from contractors, the state employment service, or the local offices of unions to which some installers belong, such as the United Brotherhood of Carpenters and Joiners of America and the International Brotherhood of Painters and Allied Trades.

Advancement

Installers who work for large floor-laying firms may be promoted to positions in which they supervise crews of installers. Installers who are familiar with the business, who get along well with people, and can communicate effectively may move into sales jobs with retailers of flooring products. Or they may become estimators, workers who measure floors, compute areas, and figure costs using their knowledge of the materials and labor required for various kinds of installations.

With additional education and training, installers may go to work for manufacturers of floor covering materials, becoming, for example, manufacturers' representatives to retailers. Many installers decide to go into business for themselves as independent subcontractors.

Employment Outlook

In the late 1990s, there are more than 110,000 floor covering installers employed in the United States, including about 64,000 who work mainly or exclusively with carpets. Through the year 2006, employment of these workers is expected to increase at a rate that is about as fast as the average for all occupations. Installers will be needed to put down flooring in newly constructed buildings and to replace flooring in older buildings that are being refurbished. Even during economic downturns, when new construction levels drop drastically, the need to renovate existing buildings will mean some employment opportunities will continue to be available for installers. During coming years, most job opportunities that open up will probably occur when experienced workers leave the field for other occupations, retire, or die.

Carpeting continues to be a very popular floor covering, a sign that the demand for carpet installers will continue. Carpet can easily be installed on the plywood and concrete floors that are common in new buildings today. Modern carpet fibers, which are long-wearing, stain-resistant, and come in many colors and styles, are making carpeting increasingly attractive as a choice of floor cover.

Earnings

The earnings of floor covering installers vary depending on their geographic location, whether their wages are set by union contracts, and other factors. Installers in the West tend to be paid more than the national average, while those in the South make less than the average. Overall, experienced workers have earnings that average roughly $26,000 a year. According to the *1998-99 Occupational Outlook Handbook,* the median earnings in 1996 for carpet layers were somewhat lower at $24,752 a year. A few workers earned as much as $45,448 a year, while the lowest paid workers earned as little as $11,560 annually. Starting wages for apprentices and other trainees are usually about one-half the rate for experienced workers.

Most installers are paid by the hour, but some are paid by the number of yards of flooring they install, a system that can benefit installers who are particularly fast workers.

Conditions of Work

Although installers usually work in the daytime, some flooring replacement work is done at night or on weekends to minimize disruption of offices and stores during business hours. The standard work week is about forty hours. Installers usually receive overtime for weekend and holiday work. Self-employed installers may work very irregular hours.

Unlike most other construction trades, floor covering installation involves few hazards. The areas where installers work are usually indoors, well lighted, clean, and comfortable. Installers must bend, reach, and stretch often as they work. They sometimes get knee and back injuries, because they must constantly kneel as they work and they lift heavy rolls of floor covering.

Sources of Additional Information

■Floor Covering Installation Contractors Association
PO Box 948
Dalton, GA 30722-0948
Tel: 706-226-5488

■Carpet and Rug Institute
PO Box 2048
Dalton, GA 30722
Tel: 800-882-8846
WWW: http://www.carpet-rug.com

■Resilient Floor Covering Institute
966 Hungerford Drive, Suite 12-B
Rockville, MD 20850
Tel: 301-340-8580
WWW: http://www.buildernet.com/rcfi

Forestry Technicians

Definition

Forestry technicians work as members of a forest management team under the direction of a professional forester. They collect the data and information that are necessary in making decisions about resources and resource depletion. They also help plan, supervise, and conduct the operations necessary to maintain and protect forest growth, including harvesting, replanting, and marketing of forest products. Forestry technicians are knowledgeable in the inventory methods and management skills required to produce wood fiber and forest products. They help manage forests and wildlife areas and control fires, insects, and disease. Forestry technicians may also survey land, measure the output of forest products, and operate logging and log-handling equipment.

Nature of the Work

Forestry technicians carry out duties that require scientific training and skill, frequently doing work that was once performed by professional foresters. Most are employed in forest land management and administration; they may be involved in timber production, recreation, wildlife forage, water regulation, preservation for scientific studies and special uses, or a combination of these areas.

The day-to-day work of the forestry technician is based on a cycle of activities for managing and harvesting a forest. The first major step in the cycle is planting trees to replace those that have been cut down, harvested, or lost to disease or fire. Technicians tend and care for maturing trees by thinning them to obtain the best growth, spraying them with pesticides when necessary, and protecting them from fire or other damage. Periodic measuring or scaling of trees to determine the amount of lumber they will produce is necessary in planning for harvesting and marketing.

School Subjects
Geology
Geography

Personal Interests
The Environment
Plants/Gardening

Work Environment
Primarily outdoors
Primarily multiple
locations

Minimum Education Level
Associate's degree

Salary Range
$11,960 to
$23,140 to
$33,280

Certification or Licensing
Required for certain
positions

Outlook
Little or no change

DOT
452

GOE
03.02.02

NOC
2223

Harvesting and marketing the trees is the last step. In preparing for harvesting, access roads for logging machinery and trucks are planned, surveyed, and built, sometimes with the use of aerial photography. Technicians must understand the land surveys and be able to interpret aerial photographs. After harvesting is complete, the land is reconditioned and the cycle begins again.

The work of a forestry technician is more complicated than it was just a few decades ago. Equipment and methods used to detect, prevent, and fight tree diseases and parasites have developed rapidly, as has the machinery used for harvesting, with powerful log handlers and loaders now being commonly used.

A forestry technician's work includes many different kinds of activities. In addition to the various duties required for each step of the tree-growing cycle, each forest area is managed with a particular objective, which affect the specific duties of the technician. If the plan is to produce large saw-logs, for example, the planting, thinning, and care are different from those used to produce pulp wood. Because the management plan for each area differs, technicians often have responsibilities that require different skills.

Many forestry technicians are employed by private industry, where they "cruise" timber (measure the volume of standing trees), measure logs to find their lumber content, survey logging roads, prepare maps and charts, and mark trees for cutting or thinning.

Forestry technicians employed by the federal government may specialize in a specific area of forestry and progress through the ranks via a limited scope of activities. More often, however, they work as assistants to professional foresters in research connected with watershed management, timber management, wildlife management, forest genetics, fire control, disease and insect control, recreational development, and other matters. Many communities also now employ forestry technicians in the management of their municipal watersheds and in their parks and recreation development programs.

Following are descriptions of specialized positions that are held by forestry technicians. These positions may be found with federal or state agencies or the private forestry industry. Each requires a different mix of skills and abilities.

Information and education technicians write news releases and act as public relations specialists in nature centers.

Survey assistants locate and mark boundary lines. They also assist in the clearing of forests and construction of logging roads, prepare maps of surveys, and work on land appraisal and acquisition problems for private, state, and federal employers.

Biological aides work in forest insect and disease prevention and control. They record and analyze data, run experiments under supervision, and prepare maps to show damage done to forests by parasites.

Technical research assistants gather and analyze field data to assist scientists in basic and applied research problems that relate to timber, watershed, and wildlife management.

Sawmill buyers purchase high-grade logs for milling and furniture manufacture.

Pulp buyers purchase pulp logs for use in paper mills and other pulp and paper companies.

Lumber inspectors and/or graders grade and calculate the volume of hardwood and softwood lumber at mills or in retail and wholesale yards.

Tree-nursery management assistants help operate and manage tree nurseries. They keep records, hire temporary personnel, and supervise tree production during planting season. These technicians may also run seed tests and analyze data, operate and maintain equipment, and help supervise forest planting-stock production.

Wildlife technicians conduct field work for various game commissions and federal agencies engaged in fish and game preservation and management. They capture, tag, and track animals with radio collars to establish territories and animal survival records. Wildlife technicians also help take wildlife censuses and maintain daily crew records.

Requirements

The best way to enter this field is to graduate from a formal training program after high school. Almost all technical forestry programs require a high school diploma. Entrance requirements to most technical programs include two courses in college-preparatory mathematics and one course in physics. Courses in chemistry, biology, earth sciences, English, and writing are also recommended.

Whether attending a technical institute or a junior or community college, prospective technicians usually take a two-year program that leads to an associate's degree. More than fifty schools offer such programs; twenty-five of them have been recognized by the Society of American Foresters as meeting their standards.

Since forestry technicians must learn both scientific theory and applied science practices, the technical program is a demanding one. It requires organized classroom study and considerable time in the laboratory or field as well. Students must learn about forests, the kinds of trees and plants that grow in a forest, and how they relate to or affect other plants. Two formal fields of study in this area are silvics and dendrology. When this knowledge is directed at managing forests, it is called silviculture. Technicians also learn about measuring and calculating the amount of lumber in a tree. This is called mensuration, or forest measurements.

Students in forestry technician programs take mathematics appropriate to forestry, communications, botany, engineering, and technical forestry courses. The specific type of forestry courses taken vary depending upon the climate in a given locale and the nature of local forestry practice.

A typical first year's study in a two-year forestry program might include the following courses or the equivalent: elementary forest surveying, communication skills, technical mathematics, dendrology (tree identification), botany of forests, forest orientation, technical reporting, elementary forest measurements, applied silviculture, forest soils, computer applications, and elementary business management.

A typical second year's courses might include the following or the equivalent: personnel management, forest business methods, timber harvesting, advanced forest surveying and map drafting, outdoor recreation and environmental control, wildlife ecology, elements of social science, forest products utilization, forest protection, forest insect and disease control, forest fire control, advanced forest measurements, and aerial photographic interpretation.

Since student technicians also need practical experience working in a forest to learn many of the aspects of their jobs, almost all forestry technician programs require actual work experience in forested areas. Some schools arrange summer jobs for students between the first and second years of study. Many forestry technician programs also own or use a small sawmill where students can learn the basic elements of sawmill operation.

A special feature of some programs is a second-year seminar that includes visits to tree nurseries, sawmills, paper mills, veneer mills, wallboard manufacturing plants, and furniture factories. These visits help students understand how forest products are processed, used, measured, and classified by levels of quality. They also give students a better understanding of different types of companies that employ forestry technicians.

In some states, forestry technicians need to be licensed to perform certain duties. For example, those working with pesticides or chemicals must be trained and licensed in their use. Technicians who make surveys of land for legal public property records are also required to hold a license.

Forestry technicians must have a genuine enthusiasm for outdoor work. Because the job is often tough and physically demanding, technicians should have good health and stamina. In dealing with dangerous

or emergency situations, such as forest fires, it is necessary that technicians be able to think clearly and act calmly and efficiently.

It is of great importance that technicians be able to work without supervision. Often working in rural and remote areas, they may be isolated from a supervisor and other workers for days or weeks at a time. Those who choose this career must be self-sufficient, resourceful, and able to tolerate solitude.

Despite the remoteness of most forestry work, effective communications skills are extremely important. Technicians must deal with other workers, members of the public who use the forest for recreation, and conservationists who protect fish, game, and plant life. Technicians may also supervise and coordinate the activities of laborers and field workers. Communications skills also are needed to prepare oral and written reports.

Forestry technicians must be able to apply both theoretical knowledge and specialized occupational skills. They need to be familiar with certain principles of engineering, biology, mathematics, and statistics and know how to operate a computer.

Opportunities for Experience & Exploration

High school guidance counselors can provide materials and information on forestry careers. Community and technical colleges also have career information centers or other services that can provide information.

Interested individuals may visit a park or public land area and talk with forestry technicians about the specifics of their jobs. It may be possible to obtain a summer or part-time job in forestry-related work, such as when unskilled workers are needed for timber harvesting, clearing, or planting operations. State forestry departments, federal agencies, private companies, or environmental groups are all potential sources of summer or part-time work.

Methods of Entering

Graduates of technical forestry programs have the best prospects for entering this profession. Although a two-year degree is not a requirement, it is much more difficult to find a job without one.

Technicians who have graduated from a college program may learn about employment leads from their school placement services, instructors, or guidance staff members. Students who have worked in forestry part time or during the summers are frequently hired on a permanent basis after graduation.

Graduates of technical programs may also be employed by private firms or government agencies. Government agencies that hire forestry technicians include the Forest Service, Bureau of Land Management, Soil Conservation Service, and National Park Service. In addition, municipal governments and city managers increasingly are hiring forestry technicians. Most forestry technicians, however, work in private industry. In most cases, applying directly to promising agencies or companies is advised.

Advancement

Forestry technicians can advance in a number of different ways. Technicians who are federal employees advance to higher grades and better salaries after attaining a certain number of years of experience. Some advancement opportunities require additional schooling. For example, a forestry technician who wants to become a forester needs to complete a four-year degree program. Other forestry technicians advance by moving into research work. Following are potential positions to which a technician can advance to.

Timber cruisers supervise crews in the measurement of trees for volume computations. They keep records, run statistical analysis of volumes, and mark timber for sale. They recommend logging methods and use aerial photographs to locate future timber harvesting areas.

Forest-fire control technicians maintain fire control supplies in a central area and report fires by radio-telephone. They recruit, train, and supervise forest-fire wardens and crews, sometimes dispatching and serving as crew leaders in fire suppression. They also conduct investigations into the causes of fires. They also educate communities in fire prevention.

Refuge managers supervise work crews in game and fish management. They help plant food plots for wildlife and other plants for habitat improvement. They patrol restricted areas, conduct census studies, and make maps.

Sawmill managers supervise sawmills, oversee crew and production schedules, and keep payroll records.

Kiln operators supervise and control the kiln schedules for correct drying of lumber. They run drying tests and submit reports on loads of drying lumber.

Forest recreation technicians supervise the operation and maintenance of outdoor recreation facilities.

They are responsible not only for tactful enforcement of rules but also for fire watches.

Assistant logging superintendents control harvesting and loading operations for timber sales. They help maintain safety, keep payroll and supply records, and write technical reports for superintendents.

Forestry consultants fill an increasingly important role in forestry by providing forestry services to people whose property or business do not require a permanent, full-time forester.

Experienced forestry technicians may also build rewarding careers in research. *Research technicians* perform many varied functions, such as obtaining data for computer analysis, helping develop new chemical fire retardants, and designing machines to prepare forest soils for planting. Research technicians work for private industries, large cities, or state and federal government agencies.

Employment Outlook

Forestry-related employment is expected to grow more slowly than the average through the year 2006. As a result, competition in the field will be high, and technicians with good preparation in forestry technology and machinery management will have an advantage over less prepared applicants in the job market.

One promising area of future employment for forestry technicians is in the area of forest recreation, which includes hunting and fishing. Ever-increasing numbers of people are enjoying the forests. These resources must be managed for the protection of the users, as well as of the resources themselves, and such management requires the expertise of foresters and forestry technicians.

In addition, new uses for wood and wood products are continually being found. Meeting this growing demand requires an increasing supply of timber and pulp. Forestry technicians who specialize in land management and the various aspects of logging and sawmill work will play a valuable role in assuring this supply. Research technicians who help find improved methods of planting, growing, and timber and pulp production will be needed in greater numbers.

Overseas employment with oil, rubber, and timber companies is also a possible outlet for technicians who like to travel. Compensation for this type of work will continue to be quite good.

Earnings

Most forestry technicians begin their careers in private industry at an hourly wage, while those employed by a government agency are typically paid a monthly or annual salary. For beginning forestry technicians in government agencies, salaries are usually slightly lower than for those in private industry. However, the two sectors tend to offer comparable pay after a certain length of time.

Average starting salaries for forestry technicians who have graduated from a two-year technical program are $11,960 per year. Annual salaries of graduates with three to five years of experience in private industry ranged from about $16,000 to $27,300, according to 1996 U.S. Department of Labor statistics. Salaries of technicians who have advanced to supervisory positions or special consulting positions may be around $33,200 or more a year, depending on their specialization, the quality of their work, and their employer.

Benefits usually include paid holidays, vacation and sick days, and insurance and retirement plans, although these vary by employer. Some employers offer part or full tuition reimbursement for job-related schooling.

Conditions of Work

Working hours for forestry technicians are fairly normal. Most technicians work eight-hour days, five days a week. In case of fires or other unusual situations, however, longer hours may be necessary.

Some of the work is physically demanding. For many technicians, most of the working day is spent outdoors, even in unpleasant weather, in settings that are sparsely settled, primitive, and remote. Many forest areas do not have paved roads, and large areas have only a few roads or trails that are passable. In addition, technicians working in the field may occasionally have to deal with hazardous conditions such as forest fires. There is also the possibility of accidents and injury in logging and harvesting jobs and in sawmill operations. Technicians who work in laboratories or offices generally have well-lit, modern, and comfortable surroundings.

The twin purposes of forestry—wise management of the resources they offer and use of the recreational opportunities they offer—present challenges to forestry technicians. Many technicians find satisfaction in assisting in the conservation and improvement of the forest and in providing an essential public service.

Sources of Additional Information

For information on education and careers in forestry in the United States, contact the following:

American Forests
1516 P Street, NW
Washington, DC 20005
Tel: 202-667-3300
WWW: http://www.amfor.org

For information on technicians' careers in forestry consulting, contact:

Association of Consulting Foresters
5400 Grosvenor Lane, Suite 300
Bethesda, MD 20814
Tel: 301-530-6795
Email: acf@igc.apc.org

National Recreation and Park Association
2775 South Quincy Street, Suite 300
Arlington, VA 22206
Tel: 703-820-4940
Email: info@nrpa.org
WWW: http://www.nrpa.org/press/logo.htm

For a list of accredited educational programs, contact:

Society of American Foresters
5400 Grosvenor Lane
Bethesda, MD 20814
Tel: 301-897-8720

USDA Forest Service
PO Box 96090
Central Wing, 2nd Floor
Washington, DC 20090
Tel: 202-205-8333
WWW: http://www.fs.fed.us

Forge Shop Occupations

Definition

Forging is a process of shaping and conditioning metal by pressing, pounding, or squeezing it, with or without benefit of heat. Many workers in *forge shop occupations* set up and operate equipment in which hot metal that is to be shaped into something useful is held in place on a die, or metal form, and a second die is dropped or forced against the hot metal, pressing it into the desired shape.

Nature of the Work

Forging changes the properties of metals, increasing their strength. For this reason, forge shops produce items that must withstand heavy wear, including tools like wrenches, drill bits and parts for automobiles and aircraft. Forged products come in many sizes, from keys that can be carried in a pocket to the components of massive machinery used in industry.

The metal used in forgings is often steel, although forgings can be made with aluminum, copper, brass, bronze, and other nonferrous metals (metals containing no iron). Because nonferrous forgings resist corrosion and are strong but relatively light in weight, they are ideal in such uses as aircraft landing gear.

The techniques used in forging items are roughly the same for any metal and any size product. The metal is often, but not always, heated to a high temperature in a furnace until it is workable. It is placed between two metal dies and pounded or squeezed into shape by power hammers or presses, sometimes with tremendous force. Excess metal and rough edges are trimmed or ground away. The forgings may be heat-treated to harden or temper the metal, smoothed, polished, and otherwise finished, then inspected to ensure that they meet specifications.

The equipment of a forge shop includes various types of hammers, presses, dies, upsetters (presses that produce nails, screws, bolts, and other headed items), and furnaces. The

School Subjects
Mathematics
Shop (Trade/Vo-tech education)

Personal Interests
Building things
Sculpting

Work Environment
Primarily indoors
Primarily one location

Minimum Education Level
High school diploma
Apprenticeship

Salary Range
$17,000 to
$23,000 to
$30,000

Certification or Licensing
None

Outlook
Decline

DOT
612

GOE
06.02.02

NOC
9612

workers also use hand tools such as hammers, tongs, and punches to mold and shape forgings. Products are measured throughout the manufacturing process. Quality control systems, such as statistical process control, include electronic sensors on machines that take measurements at various steps of production. In addition, inspectors and press operators take periodic manual and visual inspections to test for tolerances and other specifications. Instruments such as gauges, rules, scales, and calipers are used.

Some of the major forge-shop production occupations are described in the following paragraphs.

Hammersmiths operate or direct the operation of power hammers equipped with open dies, which are flat dies, similar to a blacksmith's hammer. Hammersmiths may head a crew of four or more workers. They draw on their knowledge of forging and the physical properties of metal and follow blueprints, diagrams, and work orders to shape heated metal stock into forgings that meet exact specifications. After determining how the metal is to be positioned under the hammer and selecting the correct tools needed to produce the finished product, hammersmiths use rules and squares to align the dies in position and hand tools to bolt the dies onto the ram and anvil of the machine. The metal is heated in furnaces regulated by workers called *heaters.* When the color of the metal indicates that it has reached the proper temperature for forging, the hammersmith signals the heater to remove the metal from the furnace and directs another worker operating a crane to place it under the hammer. The hammersmith determines how much hammer force is needed and instructs the *hammer driver,* who regulates the action of the machine. Hammersmiths decide if and when the metal has to be reheated during the forging operation and after finishing use rules and calipers to verify the dimensions of the forging.

Hammer operators have duties similar to those of hammersmiths. They, too, may be assisted by heaters and other helpers. The major difference is that hammer operators forge metal parts with impression- or closed-die hammers rather than open-die hammers. Hammer operators who are highly skilled can turn out very intricate forgings. They regulate the action of the power hammering machine, causing the ram to strike the metal workpiece repeatedly, forcing it into the shape of the impression in the die. By moving the workpiece through a series of dies, the operator can attain progressively finer detail.

Press operators set up and operate power presses that use hydraulic pressure to slowly squeeze metal into desired shapes, rather than pounding the metal with drop hammers or power hammers. Using skills similar to those of hammersmiths and hammer operators, press operators set the dies with rules, squares, shims, feelers, and hand tools; determine when the metal has reached forging temperature; operate the controls that regulate machine pressure; and move the hot metal between the dies.

Upsetters operate another type of closed-die forging machine used to produce headed items, such as bolts and screws. After the dies and other parts of the machine are set up and the metal stock has been heated to the proper temperature, upsetters position the hot metal so that a horizontal ram on the machine squeezes the end of the metal into a cavity, where it expands to the desired shape. Upsetters may be assisted by heaters and several helpers.

Heaters are the workers who control the furnaces that heat the metal stock to proper temperatures for forging. The metal stock may be in bars, plates, rods, or other shapes. The furnaces, which operate on gas, oil, or electricity, are equipped with dials, gauges, and regulating knobs so that the heaters are able to maintain specific temperatures. Heaters use tongs or chain hoists to position the metal in the furnace and to transfer the heated metal to hammers or presses. They determine when the metal stock is ready for forging by observing its color or reading an instrument for measuring high temperatures called a pyrometer. Heaters generally work as members of hammer, press, or upsetter crews.

Inspectors examine completed forgings to determine if they meet the requirements set forth in specifications and blueprints. Using measuring instruments such as calipers, gauges, and rules, they check the size and shape of forged parts. They may test strength and hardness with special machines and electronic devices. Internal flaws may be detected using ultrasonic inspection equipment. A visual examination of the parts may reveal surface defects, such as scale, laps, and cracks. Inspectors report defects and their causes to supervisors. Based on their findings, they may shut down production to change the furnace temperature, modify the force of the hammer, realign the dies, or otherwise revise the production process.

Die sinkers are skilled workers who make the impression dies for hammers and presses used in forging. They begin by studying blueprints or drawings, then outline the item to be forged on two matching steel die blocks. They use a variety of machine tools, such as milling machines, electrical discharge machinery, and electrical chemical machinery, to form the impression cavities in the die blocks. The impressions are contoured and finished exactly to specifications with tools that include power grinders, scrapers, files, and emery cloths. Die sinkers inspect the finished die cavities, using templates and measuring instruments such as calipers, micrometers, and height gauges, and make a sample forging to check against the original specifications.

Many different workers may be required for cleaning and finishing forgings. Following are descriptions of some of these occupations:

Trimmers operate power presses equipped with trimming dies to remove excess metal from forgings. They may visually inspect parts or measure forgings with gauges to determine the amount of excess.

Grinders remove rough edges and smooth contoured surfaces of forgings and forging dies with a variety of abrasive tools, including files, grindstones, emery cloths, and power grinders and buffers. They are also required to inspect for flaws and smoothness both visually and by touch.

Sandblasters or *shotblasters* clean and polish forgings with blasts of compressed air mixed with abrasives such as sand, grit, or metal shot. Sandblasters load large metal parts on racks in an enclosed room, and with a nozzle attached to the air compression equipment direct the abrasive spray over the metal surfaces. Small parts may be cleaned in a container equipped with glove-fitted openings through which the blasters insert their arms to manipulate the parts under a nozzle. To protect themselves from injury, sandblasters wear protective suits and other equipment such as helmets, gloves, and hoods.

Picklers control equipment that cleans the forgings chemically. They remove surface scale by immersing the parts in a series of acid baths and rinses. Picklers are responsible for draining, cleaning, and refilling the tanks in their equipment and for maintaining the consistency of the cleaning solutions.

Heat treaters harden and temper metal forgings by heating and cooling them. After keeping forged items in a furnace at the correct temperature for a prescribed time, they may use a water, oil, or other bath to cool the objects, or they may let them cool in the furnace or in the air.

Requirements

Apprenticeship programs are available for occupations such as die setters, die sinkers, forge shop machinery repairers, press operators, and heat treaters and generally take one to four years to complete. Apprentices get practical experience by working under the supervision of skilled workers. The work experience is supplemented by classroom training in related subjects such as the properties of metals, power hammer and furnace operation, the use of hand tools, and blueprint reading.

Persons employed in forge shops need to have strong mechanical aptitudes, good mathematical and reading skills, and the ability to pay attention to fine details. A high school diploma is required, and many employers prefer to hire applicants who have had electronics training or training in quality control systems in a trade school, community college, or technical institute. In high school, students should take English, mathematics (especially geometry), mechanical drawing, blueprint reading, machine shop, and other shop courses. Students in two-year technical programs should study electronics or take programs in metallurgy, engineering, machinery, or computers.

Workers in forge shops today need to work with complex machinery and sophisticated quality control systems. The ability to read complex blueprints, an understanding of quality standards, and attention to detail and accuracy are crucial. Workers should also be in good physical condition. They need to be able to lift objects of up to fifty pounds, and they have to put up with working in a hot, noisy environment.

Union membership may be a requirement for some forge shop workers. Many workers belong to the International Brotherhood of Boilermakers, Iron Ship Builders, Blacksmiths, Forgers and Helpers. Others are members of the United Steelworkers of America; the International Union, United Automobile, Aerospace and Agricultural Implement Workers of America; and the International Association of Machinists and Aerospace Workers.

Opportunities for Experience & Exploration

High school and vocational school courses in electronics, machining, and metal shop can be valuable both as a way of testing interest in metalworking activities and as practical experience. Occasionally, students may be able to find part-time or summer jobs as helpers in shops where forging or other metalworking is done. Even if a job cannot be arranged, it may be possible to tour a local forge shop and observe workers in this field on the job.

Methods of Entering

People who want to work in a forge shop usually apply directly to the personnel departments of forge shops for jobs as helpers or heaters. Most forge shop workers start out as helpers or heaters on hammer or press crews and learn by working alongside more experienced employees. As they become more skillful, they are given more responsibility and more complicated tasks. Several years of training and experience may be necessary to become well qualified for skilled positions.

Job leads and information about apprenticeships may be obtained by contacting local offices of the state employment service or local offices of labor unions that organize these workers.

Advancement

Forge shop production workers who start out as helpers or heaters can advance to more skilled jobs after several years of training and experience. A helper may become, for example, a hammersmith, who relies on accumulated knowledge and directs a crew of workers. Skilled workers, with experience in many different areas of forge shop operations, can also advance to supervisory positions if they show leadership and management ability. Completion of college courses in engineering, metallurgy, electronics, and computers can also be helpful for those hoping to advance.

Employment Outlook

Forging is a very small industry. There are only a couple hundred companies in North America that have forging operations. Since the 1980s, employment in forge shops has declined and is expected to continue declining through the year 2006. Foreign competition, mechanization, and nonforging metalwork have been reducing the number of forge shop workers needed. Even though the demand for the total number of forged parts has been increasing in the 1990s, the increased use of automation has allowed for a greater number of parts to be made with fewer workers. Although some new jobs will be created to meet the increased demand for forged products, most openings will develop as experienced workers retire, change occupations, or otherwise leave the workforce. Automation and changing manufacturing processes require highly skilled workers, and applicants who have training in electronics, knowledge of quality control systems, and a strong academic background have the best chance of filling any positions that become available.

Fluctuations in the economy will continue to affect some forge shops. For example, many forged parts are used in the manufacture of automobiles. In an economic downturn, the sale of new cars drops considerably, resulting in a reduced demand for forged parts. Forge shops that supply automobile manufacturers, then, will have fewer jobs until car sales go up again. During periods when production is slow, forge shop workers may work fewer hours or be laid off.

Earnings

Production workers in iron and steel forging plants have earnings that average around $30,000 a year. Entry-level workers generally average between $17,000 and $20,000 a year.

The Economic Research Institute reports the following annual salaries in 1998 for various forge shop workers: die sinkers, $25,246; heat treaters, $22,460; grinders and trimmers, $21,356; press operators, $24,922; sand blasters, 22,500; shotblasters. $23,656.

Some companies are experimenting with pay systems based on profit sharing and productivity. Most forge shop workers receive paid holidays, paid vacations, and sick days, with medical insurance also being offered through employers.

Conditions of Work

Forge shops are noisy, hot, and dirty, and they present more hazards than most manufacturing plants. Many shops have installed equipment that minimizes the discomfort and dangers associated with forging. Heat deflectors and ventilating fans reduce heat and smoke. Improved machinery and shop practices help cut down the noise and vibration from hammers. Workers are given safety training and use protective equipment such as face shields, ear plugs and muffs, safety glasses, safety shoes, and helmets; and machines are equipped with safety guards. Cranes, remote control tongs, and conveyors are used to move very large objects, but workers may still have to lift and move heavy forgings and dies. The heat, noise, and heavy work require considerable stamina, endurance, and strength.

Sources of Additional Information

Forging Industry Association
25 Prospect Avenue, West, Suite 300
Cleveland, OH 44115-1040
Tel: 216-781-6260

Glaziers

Definition

Glaziers select, cut, fit, and install all types of glass and glass substitutes such as plastics. They may install windows, mirrors, shower doors, glass tabletops, display cases, skylights, special items such as preassembled stained glass and leaded glass window panels, and many other glass items.

Nature of the Work

Glaziers install different kinds of glass in different places. They put insulating glass where it is desirable to keep heat or sound on one side and laminated glass in doors and windows where safety is a concern. They install large structural glass panels on building exteriors to create walls that admit natural light. They install mirrors, storefronts, automobile windows, and sun-space additions to homes.

In most of these applications, the glass is precut to size in a shop or factory and comes to the work site mounted in a frame. Because glass is heavy and easily breakable, glaziers may need to use a hoist or a crane to move larger pieces into position. The glass is held with suction cups and gently guided into place.

When it is in place, glaziers often put the glass on a bed of putty or another kind of cement inside a metal or wooden frame and secure the glass with metal clips, metal or wooden molding, bolts, or other devices. They may put a rubber gasket around the outside edges to clamp the glass in place and make a moisture-proof seal. In windows, glaziers may pack a putty-like glazing compound into the joints at the edges of the glass in the molding that surrounds the open space. They trim off the excess compound with a glazing knife to make a neat appearance.

Sometimes glaziers must manually cut glass to size at a work site. They put uncut glass on a rack or cutting table and mea-

School Subjects
Mathematics
Shop (Trade/Vo-tech education)

Personal Interests
Building things
Figuring out how things work

Work Environment
Primarily indoors
Primarily multiple locations

Minimum Education Level
High school diploma
Apprenticeship

Salary Range
$13,800 to
$26,400 to
$50,336

Certification or Licensing
None

Outlook
About as fast as the average

DOT
865

GOE
05.10.01

NOC
7292

sure and mark the cutting line. They use a cutting tool such as a small, sharp wheel of hard metal, which cuts the glass when rolled firmly over the surface. After making a cut, they break off the excess by hand or with a notched tool.

In some situations, glaziers cut and fasten together pieces of metal. When installing storefront windows, for example, they cut the drain moldings and face moldings that fit around the opening. They screw the drain molding into position and place plate glass into position against the metal. Then they bolt the face molding around the edges and attach metal corner pieces. When installing glass doors, they fit hinges and bolt on handles, locks, and other hardware.

Some workers in glazing occupations specialize in other kinds of glass installations. Among these workers are *aircraft safety glass installers,* who cut and install laminated safety glass in airplane windows and windshields; *auto glass installers,* who replace pitted or broken windows and windshields in motor vehicles; *refrigerator glaziers,* who install the plate glass windows in refrigerator display cases and walk-in coolers; and *glass installers,* who work in planing mills where they fit glass into newly manufactured millwork products, such as doors, window sashes, china cabinets, and office partitions.

Requirements

The best way for glaziers to learn their trade is by completing an apprenticeship program. Apprenticeships last three to four years and combine on-the-job training with classroom instruction in related subjects. Apprenticeship programs are operated by the National Glass Association in cooperation with local committees representing unions and employers or local contractor groups.

Apprentices spend roughly 6,000 hours working under the supervision of experienced glaziers in planned programs that teach all aspects of the trade. Apprentices learn how to use tools and equipment; how to handle, measure, cut, and install glass, molding, and metal framing; and how to install glass doors. Their formal classroom instruction, about 144 hours each year of the apprenticeship, covers subjects such as glass manufacturing, selecting glass for specific purposes, estimating procedures, mathematics, blueprint reading, construction techniques, safety practices, and first aid.

Requirements for admission to apprenticeship programs are set by the local administrators of each program. Typically, applicants need to be high school graduates, at least seventeen years old, in good physical condition, with proven mechanical aptitude. Some previous high school or vocational school courses in

applied mathematics, shop, blueprint reading, and similar subjects are desirable as preparation for work in glazing occupations.

Many glaziers also learn their skills informally on the job. They are hired in helper positions and gradually pick up skills as they assist experienced workers. When they start, they are assigned simple tasks, like carrying glass; later they may get the opportunity to cut glass and do other more complex tasks. Glaziers who learn informally on the job often do not receive as thorough training as apprentices, and the training usually takes longer.

Although union membership is not necessarily a requirement for employment, many glaziers who work in construction are members of the International Brotherhood of Painters and Allied Trades.

Opportunities for Experience & Exploration

Prospective glaziers can get an indication of their abilities and interest in similar skilled activities by taking shop courses, blueprint reading, mechanical drawing, and mathematics. Hobbies that require manual dexterity, using a variety of hand tools, and attention to detail are also good experience. Working with stained glass, making decorative objects such as windowpanes, lampshades, and ornaments, is an excellent hobby for the prospective glazier.

For a more direct look at this career, students may be able to get a part-time or summer job as a helper at a construction site or in a glass shop. If this cannot be arranged, it may be possible to talk with someone employed in a glass shop or as a glazier in construction work to get an insider's view of the field.

Methods of Entering

People who would like to enter this field either as apprentices or on-the-job trainees can obtain more information about local opportunities by contacting area glazing contractors, the local offices of the state employment service, or local offices of the International Brotherhood of Painters and Allied Trades. Information about apprenticeships may also be available through the state apprenticeship agency. Job leads for helper positions may also be listed in newspaper classified ads.

Advancement

Experienced glaziers usually have only a few possible avenues for advancement. In some situations, they can move into supervisory positions, directing the work done by other glazing workers at construction sites or in shops or factories. Or they can become estimators, figuring the costs for labor and materials before jobs are done. Advancement for glaziers often consists of pay increases without changes in job activity.

Employment Outlook

There were 36,000 glaziers employed in 1996. Through the year 2006, employment in this occupational field is expected to increase at a rate that is about the same as the average for all occupations. During this period, there will probably be an overall increase in the construction of new buildings that involve substantial glazing, as well as a growing need to update older buildings. Glass will most likely continue to be popular for both its good looks and its practical advantages, and further improvements in glass and glass products may well make glass still more desirable as a construction material.

Nonetheless, glaziers who work in construction should realize that there will be variations from time to time and place to place in the opportunities available to them. They should expect to go through periods of unemployment, and they must plan for these times. During economic downturns, construction activity is significantly reduced, and jobs for construction craftworkers, including glaziers, become scarce. Also, construction jobs are almost always of limited length, and workers may be unemployed between projects. On the other hand, when the level of construction activity is high in a region, there may be more jobs available than there are skilled workers to fill them. In general, jobs will be most abundant in and near cities, where most glazing contractors and glass shops are located.

In addition to newly created jobs, many openings will develop every year as experienced workers move to other occupations or leave the labor force altogether.

Earnings

Earnings of glaziers vary substantially in different parts of the country. A recent study suggested that annual earnings can average from about $13,800 to about $50,300, depending on geographical location and experience. In another sampling of wages, the *Engineering News Record* reported that in 1997 hourly wages of union workers averaged $31.92, including fringe benefits, and ranged from $21.68 (in New Orleans) to $47.77 (in New York City). However, bad weather, periods of unemployment, and other factors can mean that the number of hours glaziers work, and thus their real earnings, are considerably lower than the high hourly figures suggest.

Glaziers who work under union contracts usually make more money than workers who are not union members. Wages for apprentices usually start at about 50 percent of the skilled glazier's rate and increase periodically throughout the training period.

Conditions of Work

Most glaziers work in construction, renovation, and repair of buildings and are employed by construction companies, glass suppliers, or glazing contractors. Working on buildings may require them to be outdoors, sometimes in unpleasant weather. Bad weather can also cause the shutdown of job activities, limiting the hours glaziers work and thus also limiting their pay. Glaziers typically work forty-hour weeks and receive compensation for overtime.

Glaziers in construction often have to work at great heights, on scaffolding, or in buildings that are not yet completed. On the job, they must frequently bend, kneel, lift objects, and move about. The hazards they need to guard against include cuts from broken glass, falls from heights, and muscle strains caused by using improper techniques to lift heavy pieces of glass.

Glaziers who are employed by construction companies, glass suppliers, or glazing contractors may have to drive trucks that carry glass and tools to and from job sites.

Sources of Additional Information

Glazing Contractors Association
840 Weston Street
Coquitlam, BC V3J 529 Canada
604-931-2725

International Brotherhood of Painters and Allied Trades
United Nations Building
1750 New York Avenue, NW
Washington, DC 20006
Tel: 202-637-0700

Graphic Designers

Definition

Graphic designers are practical artists whose creations are intended to express ideas, convey information, or draw attention to a product. They design a wide variety of materials including advertisements, displays, packaging, signs, computer graphics and games, book and magazine covers and interiors, animated characters, and company logos to fit the needs and preferences of their various clients.

Nature of the Work

Graphic designers are not primarily fine artists, although they may be highly skilled at drawing or painting. Most designs commissioned to graphic designers involve both artwork and copy (that is, words). Thus, the designer must not only be familiar with the wide range of art media (photography, drawing, painting, collage, etc.) and styles, but he or she must also be familiar with a wide range of typefaces and know how to manipulate them for the right effect. Because design tends to change in a similar way to fashion, designers must keep up-to-date with the latest trends and hot looks. At the same time, they must be well grounded in more traditional, classic designs.

Graphic designers can work as in-house designers for a particular company, as staff designers for a graphic design firm, or as freelance designers working for themselves. Some designers specialize in designing advertising materials or packaging; others focus on "corporate identity" materials such as company stationery and logos; others work mainly for publishers designing book and magazine covers and page layouts; others work in the area of computer graphics, creating still or animated graphics for computer software, videos, or motion pictures. A highly specialized type of graphic designer, the environmental graphic designer, designs large outdoor signs. Some graphic designers design exclusively on the computer,

School Subjects
Art
Computer science

Personal Interests
Computers
Drawing

Work Environment
Primarily indoors
Primarily one location

Minimum Education Level
Some postsecondary training

Salary Range
$15,000 to
$27,100 to
$43,000+

Certification or Licensing
None

Outlook
Faster than the average

DOT
141

GOE
01.02.03

NOC
5241

while others may use both the computer and traditional hand drawings or paintings, depending on the project's needs and requirements.

Whatever the specialty and whatever their medium, all graphic designers take a similar approach to a project, whether it is for an entirely new design or for a variation on an existing one. Graphic designers begin by determining as best they can the needs and preferences of the clients and the potential users, buyers, or viewers.

In the case of a graphic designer working on a company logo, for example, he or she will likely meet with company representatives to discuss such points as how and where the company is going to use the logo and what size, color, and shape preferences company executives might have. Project budgets must be carefully respected: a design that may be perfect in every way but that is too costly to reproduce is basically useless. Graphic designers may need to compare their ideas with similar ones from other companies and analyze the image they project. Thus they must have a good knowledge of how various colors, shapes, and layouts affect the viewer psychologically.

After a plan has been conceived and the details worked out, the graphic designer does some preliminary designs (generally two or three) to present to the client for approval. The client may reject the preliminary design entirely and request a new design, or he or she may ask the designer to make alterations to the existing design. The designer then goes "back to the drawing board" to attempt a new design or make the requested changes. This process continues until the client approves the design.

Once a design has been approved, the graphic designer prepares the design for professional reproduction, that is, printing. The printer may require a "mechanical," in which the artwork and copy are arranged on a white board just as it is to be photographed, or the designer may be asked to submit an electronic copy of the design. Either way, designers must have a good understanding of the printing process, including color separation, paper properties, and halftone (i.e., photographs) reproduction.

Requirements

As with all artists, graphic designers need a degree of artistic talent, creativity, and imagination. They must be sensitive to beauty and have an eye for detail and a strong sense of color, balance, and proportion. To a great extent, these qualities are natural, but they can be developed through training, both on the job and in professional schools, colleges, and universities.

More and more graphic designers need solid computer skills and working knowledge of several of the common drawing, image editing, and page layout programs. Graphic design on the computer is more commonly done on a Macintosh system than on a PC system; however many designers have both types of computers.

More graphic designers are recognizing the value of formal training, and at least two out of three people entering the field today have a college degree or some college education. Over one hundred colleges and art schools offer graphic design programs that are accredited by the National Association of Schools of Art and Design. At many schools, graphic design students must take a year of basic art and design courses before being accepted into the bachelor's degree program. In addition, applicants to the bachelor's degree programs in graphic arts may be asked to submit samples of their work to prove artistic ability. Many schools and employers depend on samples, or portfolios, to evaluate the applicant's skills in graphic design. Many programs increasingly emphasize the importance of using computers for design work. Computer proficiency among graphic designers will be very important in the years to come. Interested individuals should select an academic program that incorporates computer training into the curriculum, or train themselves on their own.

A bachelor of fine arts program at a four-year college or university may include courses such as principles of design, art and art history, painting, sculpture, mechanical and architectural drawing, architecture, computerized design, basic engineering, fashion designing and sketching, garment construction, and textiles. Such degrees are desirable but not always necessary for obtaining a position as a graphic designer.

With or without specialized education, graphic designers seeking employment should have a good portfolio containing samples of their best work. The graphic designer's portfolio is extremely important and can make a difference when an employer must choose between two otherwise equally qualified candidates.

A period of on-the-job training is expected for all beginning designers. The length of time it takes to become fully qualified as a graphic designer may run from one to three years, depending on prior education and experience as well as innate talent.

Opportunities for Experience & Exploration

High school students interested in a career in graphic design have a number of ways to find out whether they have the talent, ambition, and perseverance to succeed in the field. Students should take as many art and design courses as possible while still in high school. They should also take any computer courses available in order to become proficient at working on computers. In addition, to get an insider's view of various design occupations, they could enlist the help of art teachers or school guidance counselors to make arrangements to tour design companies and interview designers.

While studying, students interested in graphic design can get practical experience by participating in school and community projects that call for design talents. These might include such activities as building sets for plays, setting up exhibits, planning seasonal and holiday displays, and preparing programs and other printed materials. For those interested in publication design, work on the school newspaper is invaluable.

Part-time and summer jobs offer would-be designers an excellent way to become familiar with the day-to-day requirements of a particular design occupation and to gain some basic related experience. Possible places of employment include design studios, design departments in advertising agencies and manufacturing companies, department and furniture stores, flower shops, workshops that produce ornamental items, and museums. Museums also use a number of volunteer workers. Inexperienced people are often employed as sales, clerical, or general helpers; those with a little more education and experience may qualify for jobs in which they have a chance to develop actual design skills and build portfolios of completed design projects.

Methods of Entering

The best way to enter the field of graphic design is to have a strong portfolio. Potential employers rely on portfolios to evaluate talent and how that talent might be used to fit the company's special needs. Beginning graphic designers can assemble a portfolio from work completed at school, in art classes, and in part-time or freelance jobs. The portfolio should continually be updated to reflect the designer's growing skills, so it will always be ready for possible job changes.

Job interviews may be obtained by applying directly to companies that employ designers. Many colleges and professional schools have placement services to help their graduates find positions, and sometimes it is possible to get a referral from a previous part-time employer or volunteer coordinator.

Advancement

As part of their on-the-job training, beginning graphic designers generally are given the simpler tasks and work under direct supervision. As they gain experience, they move up to more complex work with increasingly less supervision.

Experienced graphic designers, especially those with leadership capabilities, may be promoted to *chief designer, design department head,* or other supervisory positions.

Computer graphic designers can move into other computer-related positions with additional education. Some may become interested in graphics programming in order to further improve computer design capabilities. Others may want to become involved with multimedia and interactive graphics. Video games, touch-screen displays in stores, and even laser light shows are all products of *multimedia graphic designers.*

When designers develop personal styles that are in high demand in the marketplace, they sometimes go into business for themselves. Freelance design work can be erratic, however, so usually only the most experienced designers who have an established client base can count on consistent full-time work.

Employment Outlook

Employment opportunities look very good for qualified graphic designers through the year 2006, especially for those involved with computer graphics. The design field in general is expected to grow at a faster than average rate for all other occupations, according to the *1998-99 Occupational Outlook Handbook.*

As computer graphic technology continues to advance, there will be a need for well-trained computer graphic designers. Companies who have always used graphics will expect their designers to perform work on computers. Companies for whom graphic design was before too time consuming or costly are now sprucing up company newsletters and magazines, among other things, and need computer graphic designers to do it.

Because the design field is a popular one, appealing to many talented individuals, competition is expected to be strong in all areas. Beginners and designers with only average talent or without formal education and technical skills may encounter some difficulty in securing employment.

About one-third of all graphic designers are self-employed, a higher proportion than is found in most other occupations. Salaried designers work in many different industries, including the wholesale and retail trade (department stores, furniture and home furnishings stores, apparel stores, florist shops); manufacturing industries (machinery, motor vehicles and aircraft, metal products, instruments, apparel, textiles, printing and publishing); service industries (business services, engineering, architecture); construction firms; and government agencies. Public relations and publicity firms, advertising agencies, commercial printers and mail-order houses all have graphic design departments. The demand for graphic artists is also influenced partly by the level of government funding available from such entities as the National Endowment for the Arts.

Earnings

The range of annual salaries for graphic designers is quite broad. Many earn as little as $15,000, while others receive more than $43,000. Salaries depend primarily on the nature and scope of the employer, with computer graphic designers earning wages on the high end of the range.

Self-employed designers can earn a lot one year and substantially more or less the next. Their earnings depend on individual talent and business ability, but, in general, are higher than those of salaried designers, although like any self-employed individual, they must pay their own insurance costs and taxes and are not compensated for vacation or sick days.

Salaried designers who advance to the position of design manager or design director earn about $60,000 a year and, at the level of corporate vice-president, make $70,000 and up. The owner of a consulting firm can make $85,000 or more.

Graphic designers who work for large corporations receive full benefits, including health insurance, paid vacation, and sick leave.

Conditions of Work

Most graphic designers work regular hours in clean, comfortable, pleasant offices or studios. Conditions vary depending on the design specialty.

Some graphic designers work in small establishments with few employees; others, in large organizations with large design departments. Some deal mostly with their coworkers; others may have a lot of public contact. Freelance designers are paid by the assignment. To maintain a steady income, they must constantly strive to please their clients and to find new ones.

Computer graphic designers may have to work long, irregular hours in order to complete an especially ambitious project.

Sources of Additional Information

■American Center for Design
233 East Ontario, Suite 500
Chicago, IL 60611
Tel: 312-787-2018

For more information about careers in graphic design, contact:

■American Institute of Graphic Arts
164 Fifth Avenue
New York, NY 10160-1652
Tel: 800-548-1634
Email: aiganatl@aol.com

■National Association of Schools of Art and Design
11250 Roger Bacon Drive, Suite 21
Reston, VA 22090
Tel: 703-437-0700

■Society for Environmental Graphic Design
1 Story Street
Cambridge, MA 02138
Tel: 617-868-3381

■Society of Publication Designers
60 East 42nd Street, Suite 721
New York, NY 10165
Tel: 212-983-8585

■Urban Art International
PO Box 868
Tiburon, CA 94920
Tel: 415-435-5767
WWW: http://www.imagesite.com

Hazardous Waste Management Specialists

Definition

The title *hazardous waste management specialist* is an umbrella term referring to those who have knowledge of specific aspects of hazardous waste management. For instance, they may be experts in the properties of hazardous waste or they may have an in-depth understanding of the way an environment will react to the introduction of hazardous waste. In general, their job entails studying ongoing hazardous waste projects to determine best treatment options, calculate economic and environmental impact of alternative procedures, and recommend guidelines for reporting incidents and regulating sites.

Nature of the Work

The Environmental Protection Agency (EPA) defines hazardous waste as any substance that is harmful to health or environment. Four criteria determine whether waste is hazardous: toxicity, ignitability, corrosivity, and reactivity. By "waste" the EPA refers to the lack of usefulness of the substance. For example, even though the millions of gallons of crude oil spilled in the Exxon Valdez disaster were a valuable commodity, once they were uselessly afloat off the Alaskan coast they were considered waste. If potential waste can be used for some purpose—recycled into material for some other end product—then it is not considered a waste. One job of a hazardous waste management specialist might be the development of processes that utilize potential waste.

Specialists also play a variety of other roles. Many specialties are connected with the management of hazardous waste cleanup sites. Because for many years hazardous waste was simply dumped anywhere, contaminated sites exist everywhere. Before hazardous waste laws such as SARA and Superfund were passed, for example, a paint manufacturer might have innocently dumped mounds of garbage containing toxic

School Subjects
Biology
Chemistry

Personal Interests
The Environment
Science

Work Environment
Indoors and outdoors
Primarily multiple
locations

Minimum Education Level
Associate's degree

Salary Range
$25,000 to
$56,000 to
$80,000+

Certification or Licensing
Required for certain
positions

Outlook
Faster than the average

DOT
168

GOE
11.10.03

NOC
2263

substances into a nearby field. Today, that dump may be leaking hazardous substances into the surrounding groundwater, which nearby communities need for drinking water. Specialists study the site and determine what hazardous substances are involved, how bad the damage is, and what can be done to remove the waste and restore the site. They suggest strategies for the cleanup within legal, economic, and other constraints. Once the cleanup is under way, teams of specialists help ensure the waste is removed and the site properly restored. Some specialists supervise hazardous waste management technicians who do the sampling, monitoring, and testing at suspect sites.

Specialists who work for emergency response companies help stop accidental spills and leaks of hazardous waste, such as those that can occur when a tank truck containing gasoline is involved in an accident. Specialists working for hospitals or other producers of medical wastes help determine how to safely dispose of such wastes; working for research institutes or other small generators of radioactive materials, they advise employers about handling or storing materials.

Government-employed hazardous waste management specialists often perform general surveys of past and ongoing projects, assemble comparative cost analysis of different remedial procedures, and make recommendations for the regulation of new hazardous wastes. Government hazardous waste management specialists make detailed analysis of hazardous waste sites, known as Remedial Investigation and Feasibility Studies (RI/FS). Using data provided by technicians and other support personnel, these hazardous waste specialists weigh economic, environmental, legal, political, and social factors and devise a remediation (cleanup) plan that best suits a particular site. Some help develop hazardous waste management laws.

Other specialists work in pollution control and risk assessment for private companies. They help hazardous waste-producing firms limit their waste output, decrease the likelihood of emergency situations, maintain compliance with federal regulations, and even modify their processes to eliminate hazardous waste altogether. Some specialists work for several companies as independent consultants. Still other specialists are employed by citizen groups and environmental organizations to provide technical knowledge about environmental and safety hazards that may not warrant Superfund attention but still concern citizens who may be affected by them.

Requirements

High school students interested in preparing for careers as hazardous waste management specialists need to be strong in chemistry and other sciences such as biology and geology. Although some specialists enter this field with undergraduate degrees in engineering—environmental, chemical, or civil—it is not strictly necessary for the work involved. Many employers in this field train their employees with the help of technical institutes or community colleges with courses on hazardous waste disposal. A bachelor's degree in environmental resource management, chemistry, geology, or ecology also may be acceptable. Areas of expertise such as hydrology or subsurface hydrology may require a master's or doctoral degree.

Certification available to specialists is not universally recognized, and requirements for certification vary not only from state to state, but region to region, and year to year as well. After some years in the field, hazardous waste management professionals can gain certification through associations such as the National Environmental Health Association in Denver. Training for this certification can be obtained through job experience or coursework provided by a number of institutes and community colleges nationwide. Some employers pay for workshops run in-house by these institutes to update their employees on such topics as emergency response, Superfund regulations, and emerging technologies. Although certification is no required it lends weight to recommendations made by government-employed specialists and in general enhances a specialist's credibility.

The relative newness of this field, its dependence on political support, the varied nature of its duties, and its changing regulations and technologies all require a large degree of flexibility from hazardous waste management specialists. The ability to take into consideration the many economic, environmental, legal, and social aspects of each project is key, as are thoroughness and patience in completing the necessary work. Prospective employers look for job candidates with excellent communications skills, no matter what their specialty, as this position is so reliant on the shared information of numerous professionals.

Opportunities for Experience & Exploration

Those who would like to explore avenues of hazardous waste management can get involved in local chapters of citizen watchdog groups and become familiar with nearby Superfund sites. What is being done at those sites? Who is responsible for the cleanup? What effect does the site have on its community? The Citizens Clearinghouse for Hazardous Waste, founded by Love Canal resident Lois Marie Gibbs, may be able to provide information about current concerns of citizens (see listing at the end of this article).

Additionally, understanding the problems of hazardous waste management and the controversy surrounding some of the limitations of Superfund provide a more detailed picture of the specialist's job. There are numerous magazines published on hazardous waste management, including those addressing the different waste generators and involved professionals—for example, chemical manufacturers, oil industry representatives, engineers, and conservationists.

Outreach programs sponsored by the Army Corps of Engineers offer presentations to high schools in some areas and may be arranged with the help of science departments and placement office staff members.

Methods of Entering

Employers in this field prefer hazardous waste management applicants with hands-on experience. Volunteering is one good way to acquire this experience and gauge the field to find a suitable niche. Internships are available through the Environmental Careers Organization (ECO), local not-for-profit groups, and the EPA, among others. On-site experience at this level usually amounts to being a technician of sorts—running tests, preparing samples, and compiling data, but most employers prefer candidates with even this kind of experience over applicants who have never seen how their education applies to real situations.

Advancement

To advance, hazardous waste management specialists need to be proficient in several aspects of hazardous waste management and able to handle an entire hazardous waste site or group of similar sites. This involves supervising other specialists, engineers, laboratory chemists, and various support personnel, as well as being the party responsible for reporting to regulatory agencies. Other specialists may find positions in public relations fields or higher management levels. Still others may seek further formal education and advance upon completion of higher degrees of specialization.

Employment Outlook

ECO calls hazardous waste management a "hot" environmental career and seeks individuals with specific technical skills who can also see the big picture. As with some other highly skilled environmental professions, hazardous waste management is currently suffering from a lack of qualified professionals. The sheer enormity of the hazardous waste problem, with over 37,000 known sites and more expected to be identified in the near future, ensures that there will be cleanup jobs available as long as funding is available.

An Environmental Careers Survey recorded in *The Engineering News Record* cautions, "Though there's still a lot of hazardous waste to clean up, it's anyone's guess as to when it will be done." Despite this, the 1990s have seen a higher-than-average growth rate for hazardous waste management professionals—about 16 to 18 percent through 1996, according to *Environmental Business Journal*—and that trend is expected to continue for at least the next decade. ECO advises students to plan for changes in the field; whereas the current emphasis is on waste removal, neutralization, and disposal, future job markets will revolve around waste prevention. Keeping track of trends in the field while still in school will enable students to tailor their educations to the anticipated needs of the future job market.

Earnings

Hazardous waste management specialists who enter the field with no experience earn around $25,000 per year; those who have experience as an intern or technician start at around $32,000. Some 75 percent of hazardous waste workers are employed by the private sector, with middle-range salaries for those with five years of experience and a two-year degree averaging between $30,000 and $50,000 per year. Specialists with degrees in areas of high demand, such as toxicology or hydrology, can earn $80,000 or more, depending on seniority and certification levels.

Salaries do vary by region. According to a 1997 survey in *Environmental PROTECTION,* experienced hazardous waste management specialists in the West earned the lowest salaries at $54,185, while specialists employed in the South averaged the highest salaries at $56,352. Specialists also enjoy benefits such as full health plans, vacation time, and subsidized travel arrangements.

Conditions of Work

Hazardous waste management work is highly regulated and dependent on continued political support. A 1993 career survey in *Pollution Engineering* magazine reported that 71.9 percent of hazardous waste management workers feel government regulations are the major factor influencing their work. The complexity of the regulations often makes remediation work painstakingly slow, but also provides a measure of job security. High-publicity sites may bring considerable political and social pressure to bear on those responsible for their cleanup, especially if work appears to be moving very slowly. Competition for lucrative contracts can be fierce, and considerable effort must be made by employer and employee alike to stay abreast of changing technologies and legislation in order to be at the cutting edge of the field.

The job of a specialist may require on-site exposure to hazardous wastes, and protective clothing that can hamper work efforts is often necessary. However, individuals in this field report a sense of accomplishment, and satisfaction in the field is extremely high. For some, the new developments that are a major part of the job provide welcome change and challenges.

Sources of Additional Information

The following association provides certification for hazardous waste specialists:

■**National Environmental Health Association**
720 South Colorado Boulevard
Denver, CO 80222
Tel: 303-756-9090

The following is a national grassroots organization founded by Lois Marie Gibbs and other Love Canal activists which offers publications on environmental health and community organization:

■**Citizens Clearinghouse for Hazardous Waste (CCHW)**
PO Box 6806
Falls Church, VA 22040
Tel: 703-237-2249

For information on hazardous waste management training and degree programs nationwide, contact:

■**National Partnership for Environmental Technology in Education (PETE)**
6601 Owens Drive, Suite 235
Pleasanton, CA 94588
Tel: 510-225-0668

The following is a branch of the military that employs engineering professionals in hazardous waste management projects such as Superfund remediation sites:

■**The United States Army Corps of Engineers**
Massachusetts Avenue, NW
Washington, DC 20314-1000
Tel: 202-761-0010

Home Care Aides

Definition

Home care aides, also known as *homemaker-home health aides* or *home attendants,* serve elderly and infirm persons by visiting them in their homes and caring for them. Working under the supervision of nurses or social workers, they perform various household chores that clients are unable to perform for themselves, as well as attend to patients' personal needs. Although they work primarily with the elderly, home care aides also attend to clients with disabilities or those needing help with small children.

Nature of the Work

Home care aides enable elderly persons to stay in their own homes. For some clients, just a few visits a week are enough to help them look after themselves. Although physically demanding, the work is often emotionally rewarding. Home care aides may not have access to equipment and facilities such as those found in hospitals, but they also don't have the hospital's frantic pace. Home care aides are expected to take the time to get to know their clients and their individual needs. They perform their duties within the client's home environment, which often is a much better atmosphere than the impersonal rooms of a hospital.

In addition to the elderly, home care aides assist people of any age who are recovering at home following hospitalization. They also help children whose parents are ill, disabled, or neglectful. Aides may be trained to supply care to people suffering from specific illnesses such as AIDS, Alzheimer's disease, or cancer, or patients who are developmentally disabled and lack sufficient daily living skills.

Clients unable to feed themselves may depend on home care aides to shop for food, prepare their meals, feed them, and clean up after meals. Likewise, home care aides may assist clients in dressing and grooming, including washing, bathing, cleaning teeth and nails, and fixing the clients' hair.

School Subjects
Health
Psychology

Personal Interests
Helping people: personal service
Helping people: physical health/medicine

Work Environment
Primarily indoors
Primarily multiple locations

Minimum Education Level
High school diploma

Salary Range
$10,000 to
$14,830 to
$34,000

Certification or Licensing
Voluntary

Outlook
Much faster than the average

DOC
354

GOE
10.03.03

NOC
3413

Massages, alcohol rubs, whirlpool baths, and other therapies and treatments may be a part of a client's required care. Home care aides may work closely with a client's physician or home nurse in giving medications and dietary supplements and helping with exercises and other therapies. They may check pulses, temperatures, and respiration rates. Occasionally, they may change nonsterile dressings, use special equipment such as a hydraulic lift, or assist with braces or artificial limbs.

Home care aides working in home care agencies are supervised by a registered nurse, physical therapist, or social worker who assigns them specific duties. Aides report changes in patients' conditions to the supervisor or case manager.

Household chores are often another aspect of the home care aide's responsibilities. Light housekeeping such as changing and washing bed linens, doing the laundry and ironing, and dusting may be necessary. When a home care aide looks after the children of a disabled or neglectful parent, work may include making lunches for the children, helping them with their homework, or providing companionship and adult supervision in the evening.

Personal attention and comfort are important aspects of an aide's care. Home care aides can provide this support by reading to children, playing checkers, or visiting with an elderly client. Often just listening to clients' personal problems will help the client through the day. Because elderly people do not always have the means to venture out alone, a home care aide may accompany an ambulatory patient to the park for an afternoon stroll or to the physician's office for an appointment.

Requirements

Caring for people in their own homes can be physically demanding work. Lifting a client for baths and exercise, helping a client up and down stairs, performing housework, and aiding with physical therapy all require that an aide is in good physical condition. The aide does not have the equipment and facilities of a hospital to help them with their work, and this requires adaptability and ingenuity. Oftentimes they must make do with the resources available in an average home.

An even temperament and a willingness to serve others are important characteristics for home care aides. People in this occupation should be friendly, patient, sensitive to others' needs, and tactful. At times an aide will have to be stern in dealing with uncooperative patients or calm and understanding with those who are angry, confused, despondent, or in pain. Genuine warmth and respect for others are important attributes. Cheerfulness and a sense of humor can go a long way in establishing a good relationship with a client, and a good relationship can make working with the client much easier.

In states where certification is required, home care aides need special training. Most agencies will offer free training to prospective employees. Such training may include instruction on how to deal with depressed or reluctant patients, how to prepare easy and nutritious meals, and tips on housekeeping. Specific course work on health and sanitation may also be required.

Homemaker-home health aides must be willing to follow instructions and abide by the health plan created for each patient. Aides provide an important outreach service, supporting the care administered by the patient's physician, therapist, or social worker. They are not trained medical personnel, however, and must know the limits of their authority.

A Model Curriculum and Teaching Guide for the Instruction of the Homemaker-Home Health Aide was developed by the National Homecaring Council. The training set forth in this curriculum combines classroom study and hands-on experience, with sixty hours of class instruction supplemented by an additional fifteen hours of field work. It reflects the widespread desire to upgrade training for people in this field.

Many programs require only a high school diploma for entry-level positions. Previous or additional coursework in home economics, cooking, sewing, and meal planning are very helpful, as are courses that focus on family living and home nursing.

Health care agencies usually focus their training on first aid, hygiene, and the principals of health care. Cooking and nutrition, including meal preparation for patients with specific dietary needs, are often included in the program. Home care aides may take courses in psychology and child development as well as family living. Because of the need for hands-on work, aides usually learn how to bathe, dress, and feed patients, as well as how to help them walk upstairs or get up from bed. The more specific the skill required for certain patients, the more an agency is likely to have more comprehensive instruction.

Opportunities for Experience & Exploration

Home care aides are employed in many different areas. Interested students can learn more about the work by contacting local agencies and programs that provide home care services and requesting information on the organization's employment guidelines or training programs. Visiting the county or city health department and contacting the personnel director may provide useful information as well. Often, local organizations sponsor open houses to enlighten the community to the services they provide. This could serve as an excellent opportunity to meet the staff involved in hiring and program development and to learn about job opportunities. In addition, it may be possible to arrange to accompany a home care aide on a home visit.

Methods of Entering

Some social service agencies enlist the aid of volunteers. By contacting agencies and inquiring about such openings, aspiring home care aides can get an introduction to the type of work this profession requires. Also, many agencies or nursing care facilities offer free training to prospective employees.

Checking the local yellow pages for agencies that provide health care to the aged and disabled or family-service organizations can provide a list of employment prospects. Nursing homes, public and private health care facilities, and local chapters of the Red Cross and United Way are likely to hire entry-level employees. The National Homecaring Council can also supply information on reputable agencies and departments that employ home care aides.

Advancement

As home care aides develop their skills and deepen their experience, they may advance to management or supervisory positions. Those who find greater enjoyment working with clients may branch into more specialized care and pursue additional training. Additional experience and education often bring higher pay and increased responsibility.

Aides who wish to work in a clinic or hospital setting may return to school to complete a nursing degree. Other related occupations include social worker, therapist, and registered dietitian. Along with a desire for advancement, however, must come the willingness to meet additional education and experience requirements.

Employment Outlook

As government and private agencies develop more programs to assist the dependent, the need for home care aides will continue to grow. Because of the physical and emotional demands of the job, there is high turnover and, therefore, frequent job openings for home care aides.

Also, the number of people seventy years of age and older is expected to increase substantially, and many of them will require at least some home care. Rising health care costs are causing many insurance companies to consider alternatives to hospital treatment, so many insurance providers now cover home care services. In addition, hospitals and nursing homes are trying to balance the demand for their services and their limitations in staff and physical facilities. The availability of home care aides can allow such institutions as hospitals and nursing homes to offer quality care to more people.

Earnings

Earnings for home care aides are commensurate with salaries in related health care positions. Depending on the agency, considerable flexibility exists in working hours and patient load. For many aides who begin as part-time employees, the starting salary is usually the minimum hourly wage. For full-time aides with significant training or experience, earnings may be around $6.00 to $8.00 per hour. According to the U.S. Department of Labor, Medicare-certified aides earned an hourly average of $6.00 in 1996. Aides are usually paid only for the time worked in the home. They normally are not paid for travel time between jobs.

Conditions of Work

Health aides in a hospital or nursing home setting work at a much different pace and in a much different environment than the home care aide. With home care, aides can take the time to sit with their clients and get to know them. Aides spend a certain amount of time with each client and can perform their responsibilities without the frequent distractions and demands of a hospital. Home surroundings differ from situation to situation. Some homes are neat and pleasant, while others are untidy and depressing. Some patients are angry, abusive, depressed, or otherwise difficult; others are pleasant and cooperative.

Because home care aides usually have more than one patient, the hours an aide works can fluctuate based on the number of clients and types of services needed. Many clients may be ill or disabled. Some may be elderly and have no one else to assist them with light housekeeping or daily errands. These differences can dictate the type of responsibilities a home care aide has for each patient.

Vacation policies and benefits packages vary with the type and size of the employing agency. Many full-time home care aides receive one week of paid vacation following their first year of employment and often receive two weeks of paid vacation for each suc-cessive year. Full-time aides may also be eligible for health insurance and retirement benefits. Some agencies also offer holiday or overtime compensation.

Working with the infirm or disabled can be a rewarding experience, as aides enhance the quality of their clients' lives with their help and company. However, the personal strains—on the clients as well as the aides—can make the work challenging and occasionally frustrating. There can be difficult emotional demands that aides may find exhausting. Considerable physical activity is involved in this line of work, such as helping patients to walk, dress, or take care of themselves. Traveling from one home to another and running various errands for patients can also be tiring and time-consuming or can be a pleasant break.

Sources of Additional Information

For career and certification information, contact:

National Association for Home Care
228 7th Street, SE
Washington, DC 20003
Tel: 202-547-7424
WWW: http://www.nahc.org

Horticultural Technicians

Definition

Horticultural technicians cultivate and market plants and flowers that make human surroundings more beautiful. They work with flowers, shrubs, trees, and grass. A horticulturist researches and develops methods to improve the quality, yield, and disease resistance of fruits, vegetables, and plants. Horticultural technicians are engaged in the practical application of the horticulturist's research. They plant and care for ground cover and trees in parks, playgrounds, along public highways, and other areas. They also landscape public and private lands.

Nature of the Work

Horticultural technicians usually specialize in one or more of the following areas: floriculture (flowers), nursery operation (shrubs, hedges, and trees), turfgrass (grass), arboriculture (trees), and landscape development. This is a field that has many different components, some of which overlap. Careers in the area of grounds management are covered in more detail in the chapter Landscapers and Grounds Managers. In addition, the career of landscape architect is covered in a separate chapter.

The activities of floriculture technicians and of nursery-operation technicians are closely related. Both kinds of technicians work in nurseries or greenhouses to raise and sell plants. Floriculturalists specialize in flowers and nursery operators in plants, but in most cases the duties overlap. Nursery operators may include flowers among their products for sale, and floriculture technicians need to know something about the shrubs that produce ornamental flowers. In general, both floriculture and nursery-operation technicians must be able to determine correct soil conditions for specific plants, the proper rooting material for cuttings, and the best fertilizer for promoting growth. Both kinds of technicians may also be involved with the merchandising aspects of growing plants.

School Subjects
Biology
Chemistry

Personal Interests
The Environment
Plants/Gardening

Work Environment
Indoors and outdoors
Primarily one location

Minimum Education Level
Some postsecondary training

Salary Range
$10,400 to
$24,000 to
$50,000

Certification or Licensing
None

Outlook
About as fast as the average

DOT
040

GOE
02.02.02

NOC
2225

Technicians working in floriculture or nursery operations may become *horticultural-specialty growers*. These growers propagate and raise specialty products and crops such as flowers, ornamental plants, bulbs, rootstocks, sod, and vegetables, both in fields and under the environmentally controlled conditions of greenhouses and growing sheds. They work either indoors or out and carefully plan growing schedules, quantities, and utilization schemes to gain the highest quality and most profitable yield. Some of their duties include planting seeds, transplanting seedlings, inspecting crops for nutrient deficiencies, insects, diseases, and unwanted plant growth, removing substandard plants, and pruning other plants.

In greenhouses and growing sheds, horticultural-specialty growers monitor timing and metering devices that administer nutrients to the plants and flowers. They are also responsible for regulating humidity, ventilation, and carbon dioxide conditions, often using computer programs. They formulate schedules for the dispensing of herbicides, fungicides, and pesticides and explain and demonstrate growing techniques and procedures to other workers. When working with field crops, they may drive tractors or harvesters and be responsible for adjusting and repairing equipment. Horticultural-specialty growers may also hire personnel, work with vendors and customers, and handle recordkeeping.

Another position that both floriculture and nursery-operation technicians may hold is that of *plant propagator*. Plant propagators work in greenhouses and nurseries to initiate new kinds of plant growth. They develop and revise nutrient formulas to use with the new plants, select growth media and other kinds of materials to be used, and prepare the growing containers. They use such techniques as grafting, budding, layering, and rooting. Plant propagators also monitor temperature and humidity conditions and regulate systems of heaters, fans, and sprayers. They train and supervise coworkers, keep records, and prepare reports for supervisors.

Technicians may work as *plant diagnosticians*. Diagnosticians determine the problems that prevent plants from growing properly. They usually work in a greenhouse or nursery advising customers on how to best care for their plants and flowers.

The following short paragraphs describe some entry-level jobs that floriculture technicians may hold:

Floral designers create all kinds of floral settings, such as corsages, bouquets, wreaths, wedding decorations, and funeral pieces.

Wholesale florist assistants help prepare and market cut flowers and potted plants, grown either indoors or outdoors, for sale to wholesale customers.

Flower salespeople sell fresh flowers, potted plants, floral arrangements, ferns, greenery, and other flower products at the retail level.

Most entry-level technicians work as growers, propagators, or retail or wholesale salespeople. One specialty job for nursery-operation technicians is *storage manager*. Storage managers work only in large nurseries, where they put plants into temporary storage and take them out with minimum plant loss.

More experienced floriculture and nursery-operation technicians may work as *garden center managers, greenhouse managers, flower shop managers,* and *nursery managers.* These managers are responsible for the operation of a retail or wholesale outlet or a specific section of one. They maintain inventories, deal with customers and suppliers, hire, train, and supervise employees, direct advertising and promotion activities, and keep records and accounts. They are often aided by assistant managers who tend to be trained technicians with less experience.

Experienced floriculture or nursery-operation technicians also may work as *horticultural inspectors.* They usually work for state or federal government agencies to inspect plants, especially those that may be transported across state lines or those that are about to come into the United States. They look for insects and diseases, quarantine infested or sick plants, and see that forbidden plants are not brought across state or national borders.

With additional experience and education (usually a degree from a four-year institution), some floriculture and nursery-operation technicians go on to become *horticulturists,* either at a research facility or a large firm. Horticulturists conduct experiments and investigations into problems of breeding, production, storage, processing, and transit of fruits, nuts, berries, vegetables, flowers, bushes, and trees. They develop new plant varieties and determine methods of planting, spraying, cultivating, and harvesting.

Horticultural therapists teach horticultural techniques to the emotionally and mentally handicapped, senior citizens, inner-city youths, blind persons, and disabled individuals. The physical and emotional benefits of working with plants has been known for centuries, but only recently has this type of therapy received formal recognition from the psychiatric community. Horticultural therapists need backgrounds in horticulture, psychology, and education.

Horticultural technicians working in the area of turfgrass management are usually employed in one of three major areas: commercial lawn maintenance and construction; planning and maintaining public lands such as parks, highways, and playing fields; and related areas such as sod production, seed production, irrigation, transportation, and sales of other products and services.

In the private sector, *turfgrass technicians* may run their own businesses or work for someone else. In general, these businesses provide lawn care services to homeowners, corporations, colleges, and other large institutions with extensive grounds. These services include mowing, fertilization, insect, disease, and weed control, irrigation, installing new lawns, and renovating old lawns. They also may provide tree and snow removal services. Sometimes these businesses work with engineering and architectural firms that need help in planning turfgrass areas and preparing specifications.

In the public sector, turfgrass technicians usually work for local, county, state, or federal government agencies. They may be involved in planning turfgrass areas sturdy enough to stand up to hard use in parks or playing field, or they may help in the design of grassy areas along public highways.

A related area is sod production, which is the preparation of ready-made squares of grass to be used to establish new lawns and renovate old ones. Other employment opportunities include producing or selling seeds, fertilizers, insecticides, fungicides, herbicides, and other equipment and supplies needed by contractors, public agencies, and homeowners. Finally, technicians may work for private firms or public agencies to carry out research related to turfgrass management.

Following are descriptions of additional careers in turfgrass management:

Turfgrass maintenance supervisors work for turfgrass maintenance services. They supervise workers, help plan all of the operations that go into building or maintaining grounds and landscapes, and deal directly with customers. *Sod salespeople* recommend and sell various strains of sod to customers who plant, grow, or care for sod. They give advice to customers on problems such as insects, diseases, and weeds. *Estimators* judge the amount of materials, the labor needed, and the costs of constructing a lawn or other sod job. *Turfgrass research and development technicians* carry out research and development for local, state, or federal government agencies or for privately owned turfgrass seed companies. They record data, write reports, and handle other details associated with scientific research projects. *Commercial sod growers* are experienced technicians who may be self-employed or who grow sod for large individual growers or companies. *Turfgrass consultants* are experienced technicians who analyze turfgrass problems and recommend solutions, such as the type of turfgrass to use, the best schedule or techniques for mowing, and other maintenance and growing procedures.

Many horticultural technicians work in arboriculture. *Arboriculture technicians* plant, feed, prune, and provide pest control for trees. They are called upon to diagnose diseases that are infesting trees and to take corrective action. They must know about various tree species and where they thrive best. Technicians need to know when and how trees should be removed, what trees to plant, where and how to place them.

Horticultural technicians working in arboriculture are generally employed in one of two broad areas: in the private sector, either with their own small business or a company; or the public sector, working for a park system, botanical garden or arboretum, or other county, state, or federal agency, such as those responsible for public highways, buildings, or monuments.

In the private sector, self-employed arboriculture technicians may contract their services to private businesses. They may plant, feed, prune, and spray the trees found on the company grounds or in the landscaped areas of industrial parks. These technicians sometimes contract their services to a group of companies located in the same industrial park or neighborhood. Private companies may hire arboriculture technicians to keep trees healthy in order to prevent damage to power lines or to write instructional materials for customers and for company work crews.

In the public sector, arboriculture technicians may be employed by local, state, or federal agencies. They decide when and how trees should be removed and where new trees should be placed on public property. They may also work for park and parkway systems, public recreational agencies, and public school systems.

Many arboriculture technicians work as landscapers or grounds managers. For more information on careers in the field of arboriculture, see the chapter titled "Landscapers and Grounds Managers".

Arboretum and botanical garden superintendents supervise the entire operation of an arboretum or botanical garden. They decide what, when, and where to plant, and they determine the best methods for planting, spraying, and cultivating. They conduct or direct experiments and investigate new methods to improve various species of trees. They also hire, train, and supervise workers, plan work schedules, keep accounts, and buy equipment and materials.

Horticultural technicians working in the field of landscape development prepare sketches, develop planting plans, draw up lists of materials, and oversee or carry out the construction activities related to landscaping a piece of property.

Landscape-development technicians interested in landscape planning or design usually work for private companies that provide these services directly to customers. However, they may work for a city or county, designing landscapes for small parks, fire stations, playgrounds, parking lots, or streets. They consult with local officials and select planting materials on the basis of appearance, required upkeep, and cost.

Some landscape-development technicians find employment on the staff of a *landscape architect* who performs or supervises landscape construction, including construction walks, pools, walls, or larger structures.

Landscape-development technicians often start their own businesses. They usually require only a small investment, and expansion can occur in many directions. Some begin by taking on grounds maintenance for one or more small industrial plants. Others start a small nursery on the side. This may lead to design work for customers, and the technician may be asked to do the construction of the approved plan and to carry out maintenance afterwards.

Requirements

Horticultural technicians must possess an eye for aesthetic beauty and a love of nature, regardless of their field of specialty. In high school, prospective technicians should take courses in algebra, chemistry, biology, English, and geometry. If available, courses in horticulture, agriculture, and botany are excellent preparation for a career in this field.

Employers usually prefer graduates from a two-year college or institute, which grants an associate's degree in applied science. However, it is possible to obtain an entry-level job with a good high school background and practical experience.

Some positions require additional education, and some proprietors of businesses (such as nursery operators and landscape contractors) may need a license for their business.

Opportunities for Experience & Exploration

Students who enjoy mowing lawns, growing flowers, and tending gardens already have valuable experience for a career as a horticultural technician. Many nurseries and flower shops use temporary summer employees to work in various capacities. Interested students can also join garden clubs, visit local flower shops, and attend botanical shows. In addition, the American Association of Botanical Gardens and Arboreta (AABGA) offers internships in public gardens throughout the United States.

Methods of Entering

Summer and part-time jobs often lead to a full-time jobs with the same employer. Most institutes or colleges have job placement services for their students. Faculty members often are approached by prospective employers in search of future graduates. Applying directly to firms or governmental agencies is also an excellent way to obtain employment.

Advancement

Floriculture technicians may advance to *garden center, greenhouse,* or *flower shop manager.* A nursery-operation technician can become a *horticultural inspector,* a *sales-yard manager,* or a *nursery proprietor.* Arboriculture technicians find opportunities as *botanical garden superintendents, tree surgeons,* and *park supervisors.* Turfgrass technicians may advance to such positions as *grounds superintendent, commercial sod grower, consultant,* or *park/golf course supervisor.* In the field of landscape development, horticultural technicians may become *landscape designers, consultants, contractors,* or *landscape-construction supervisors.* With further education, they can become landscape architects.

In general, horticultural technicians can expect to advance to more responsible and better-paying positions as they gain experience, additional education, and training. To increase their chances for better positions, they should continue their education not only by learning on the job but also by taking short courses, attending seminars, and reading technical journals.

Many advancement opportunities in this field require technicians to start their own businesses. This requires some but not much money and the willingness to commit one's own financial resources to career development.

Employment Outlook

The broad field of ornamental horticulture will experience about as fast as the average growth for all occupations through the year 2006. An increasing population and the continuing development and redevelopment of urban, suburban, and rural areas for human needs have increased the demand for the services of horticultural technicians. Commercial establishments maintaining landscaped areas around their buildings, highways using more shrubs and bushes, and civic enthusiasm for parks and playgrounds all contribute and should continue to contribute to the need for trained people in this area. The need for research to curb the ongoing battle against pests and pollution will create more jobs in the future.

Earnings

There are a variety of careers available to horticultural technicians, and the salaries vary depending on the type of job and the educational level of the candidate. According to the U.S. Department of Labor, 1996 graduates of two-year technical programs can expect to receive starting salaries roughly in the $10,400 to $24,000 a year range, depending if they work seasonally or year-round. Managers, who usually have a bachelor's degree, earn between $38,000 and $50,000 per year for seasonal work.

Fringe benefits vary from employer to employer, but generally include hospitalization and other insurance coverage, retirement benefits, and educational assistance.

Conditions of Work

Horticultural technicians generally work a forty-hour week. Whether working indoors in a greenhouse or florist shop or outdoors in a park or on a golf course, they are surrounded by beauty. Arboriculture technicians, landscape developers, and turfgrass technicians spend a good deal of time outdoors and occasionally must work in bad weather Arboriculture may involve climbing trees and be physically demanding. Those who work in parks are often required to work weekends. As the population increases and cities become more crowded, people are becoming tremendously aware of the need for flowers, trees, parks, and gardens for aesthetic enjoyment and spiritual replenishment. Those who work in the field of horticulture contribute to the beautification of our cities and towns. Technicians working in this field almost always find fulfillment and satisfaction in both their environments and the products of their work—the flowers or plants they tend.

Sources of Additional Information

American Association of Botanical Gardens and Arboreta (AABGA)
786 Church Road
Wayne, PA 19087
Tel: 610-688-1120

American Institute of Biological Sciences
1444 I Street, NW, Suite 200
Washington, DC 20005
Tel: 202-628-1500

American Society for Horticultural Science
600 Cameron Street
Alexandria, VA 22314
Tel: 703-836-4606

For employment information on careers in horticulture or agriculture, contact:

U.S. Department of Agriculture
Human Resources Division, Agricultural Research Service
6305 Ivy Lane
Greenbelt, MD 20770
WWW: http://www.ars.usda.gov/

Industrial Engineering Technicians

Definition

Industrial engineering technicians assist industrial engineers in their duties: they collect and analyze data and make recommendations for the efficient use of personnel, materials, and machines to produce goods or to provide services. They may study the time, movements, and methods a worker uses to accomplish daily tasks in production, maintenance, or clerical areas.

Industrial engineering technicians prepare charts to illustrate work flow, floor layouts, materials handling, and machine utilization. They make statistical studies, analyze production costs, prepare layouts of machinery and equipment, help plan work flow and work assignments, and recommend revisions to revamp production methods or improve standards.

As part of their job, industrial engineering technicians often use equipment such as computers, timers, motion-picture cameras, and videotape recorders.

Nature of the Work

The type of work done by an industrial engineering technician depends on the location, size, and products of the company for which he or she works. Usually a technician's duties fall in one or more of the following areas: methods engineering, work measurement, production control, wage and job evaluation, quality control, or plant layout.

Industrial engineering technicians involved in methods engineering analyze new and existing products to determine the best way to make them at the lowest cost. In these analysis, methods engineering technicians recommend the best kinds of processing equipment to be used, determine how fast materials can be processed, develop flowcharts, and consider all materials-handling, movement, and storage aspects of the production.

The *materials-handling technician* studies the present methods of handling material, then compares and evaluates

School Subjects
Computer science
Mathematics

Personal Interests
Computers
Figuring out how things work

Work Environment
Primarily indoors
Primarily multiple locations

Minimum Education Level
Associate's degree

Salary Range
$20,200 to
$32,700 to
$54,800+

Certification or Licensing
Voluntary

Outlook
About as fast as the average

DOT
012

GOE
05.03.06

NOC
2233

alternatives. The technician then suggests changes that will reduce physical effort, make handling safer, and lower costs and damage to products.

Work measurement is a way to gauge the production rate of a given product and establish the amount of time required for all individual activities. *Work measurement technicians* study the production rate of a product and determine how much time is needed for all the activities involved. They do this by timing the motions necessary for a complete operation, analyzing films of workers, and consulting previously accumulated statistics collected in the factory.

One special kind of work measurement technician is the *time study technician,* who analyzes and determines elements of work, their order, and the time required to produce a part.

Control determination is the area of industrial engineering that regulates certain industrial functions, such as production, inventory, quality, cost, and budget. The technicians in production control often work in scheduling departments where they coordinate the many complex details to ensure product delivery to the customer on the requested date. To do this, *production control technicians* must know the products and assemblies to be made, the routes to be used through the plant, and the time required for the process. These technicians also issue orders to manufacture products, check machine loads, and maintain constant surveillance of the master schedules.

Production control technicians also work in dispatching offices where they issue orders to the production areas, watch department machine loads, report progress of products, and expedite necessary parts to avoid delays.

Inventory control technicians maintain inventories of raw materials, semifinished products, completed products, packaging materials, and supplies. They ensure an adequate supply of raw materials, watch for obsolete parts, and prevent damage or loss to products.

In quality control, technicians work with inspection departments to uphold the quality standards set by production engineers. They check all incoming materials and forecast the quality of obtainable materials. *Quality-control technicians* use various techniques to carry out their work and perform other duties that include part-drawing surveillance, checking of parts with inspection tools, identifying trouble, and providing corrective procedures.

Cost control technicians compare actual product costs with budgeted allowances. These technicians investigate cost discrepancies, offer corrective measures, and analyze results.

Budget technicians gather figures and facts and make graphs to determine break-even points. They present budgets to management and present the effects of production schedules on profitability.

Technicians working in the area of wage and job evaluation gather and organize material pertaining to the skill, manual effort, education, and other factors involved in the jobs of all hourly employees. They collect this information to help set salary ranges and establish job descriptions.

The technician most involved with plant facilities and design is the *plant layout technician.* This technician works with materials-handling personnel, supervisors, and management to help make alterations in manufacturing facilities. Plant layout technicians study old layouts, consider all present and future aspects of operations, and revise, consult, and then propose layouts to production and management personnel.

Requirements

Most employers prefer to hire graduates of two-year post-high school programs; therefore, prospective technicians should take classes that prepare them for further schooling. Helpful high school include algebra, geometry, calculus, chemistry, physics, trigonometry, mechanical drawing, metal shop, English, and communications.

Computers are fast becoming the most used tool in industrial engineering. Knowledge of technology is critical to a student considering a career in this field. Students should take all classes available in the computer sciences. Also recommended are courses in shop sketching, blueprint reading, graph making, and model making, if available.

"Industrial technology" usually refers to post–high school programs designed for prospective industrial engineering technicians. Most of these are two-year programs. Typical first-year courses include mathematics, orthographic and isometric sketching, blueprint reading, manufacturing processes, communications, technical reporting, introduction to numerical control, and introduction to computer-aided design (CAD).

Typical second-year courses include methods, operation, and safety engineering; industrial materials; statistics; quality control; computer control of industrial processes; plant layout and materials handling; process planning and manufacturing costs; production problems; psychology and human relations; and industrial organization and institutions.

No special license is required for industrial engineering technicians. To give recognition and encouragement to technicians, the National Institute for Certification in Engineering Technologies has established a certification program that some industrial engineering technicians may wish to participate in.

Government clearance may be required for certain high level and security positions within industries that perform defense and other sensitive work for the federal government.

Industrial engineering technicians should be adept at compiling and organizing data and be able to express themselves clearly and persuasively both orally and in writing.

Opportunities for Experience & Exploration

Opportunities to gain experience in high school are somewhat limited. Students, however, can obtain part-time work or summer jobs in industrial settings even if not specifically in the industrial engineering area. Although this work may consist of the most menial tasks, it offers firsthand experience and demonstrates interest to future employers. Part-time jobs often lead to permanent employment, and some companies offer tuition reimbursement for educational costs.

Insights into the industrial engineering field can also be gained in less direct ways. Professional associations regularly publish newsletters and other information relevant to the technician. Industrial firms frequently advertise or publish articles in professional journals or in business or general-interest magazines that discuss new innovations in plant layout, cost control, and plans for improved productivity. By finding and collecting these articles or advertisements, prospective technicians can acquaint themselves with and stay informed on developments in industrial engineering technology.

Methods of Entering

Many industrial engineering technicians find their first jobs through interviews with company recruiters who usually visit campuses during the last semester of the school year. In many cases, students are invited to visit the prospective employer's plant for further consultation and to become better acquainted with the area, product, and facilities. Some students find job opportunities through ads in local newspapers, local employment services, and leads provided by friends, relatives, or teachers.

For many students, the job placement office of their college or technical school is the best source of possible jobs. Local manufacturers or companies are in constant contact with these facilities; therefore, the student job center has the most current, up-to-date job listings. Employers also trust that these counselors are best suited to recommend or refer a qualified candidate for a job.

Advancement

As industrial engineering technicians gain additional experience, and especially if they pursue related advanced education, they become likely candidates for various advanced positions in this field.

Continuing education is fast becoming the most important aspect of achieving advancement, regardless of work experience. An industrial engineering technician who pursues a more advanced degree or course of study is likely to rise in the ranks of business or industry. Most employers encourage this course and many will pay for a valued worker to continue his or her education.

The typical path of advancement for industrial engineering technicians is to supervisory positions, to industrial engineer, and possibly to a chief industrial engineer position.

Some examples of advanced positions and their duties follow.

Production control managers supervise all production control employees, train new technicians, and coordinate manufacturing departments.

Production supervisors oversee the manufacturing personnel and compare departmental records of production, scrap, and expenditures with departmental allowances.

Plant layout engineers supervise all plant-layout department personnel, estimate costs, and confer directly with other department heads to obtain information needed by the layout department.

Managers of quality control supervise all inspection and quality control employees, select techniques used, teach employees new techniques, and meet with toolroom and production people when manufacturing tolerances and amount of scrap become a problem.

Chief industrial engineers supervise all industrial engineering employees, consult with all department heads, direct all departmental projects, set departmental budgets, estimate annual savings from their department's efforts, and submit annual reports of their group's activities and accomplishments.

Employment Outlook

The vast majority of industrial engineering technicians are employed in the manufacturing sector of the economy. Most economists foresee this occupation growing as fast as the average of all occupations through the year 2006. Not all areas of manufacturing, however, will be similarly affected; areas such as computer equipment, medical instruments and supplies, and many plastics products, will experience growth, while defense related jobs will see a decline.

Greater importance is being placed on controlling costs and increasing production. Continuing financial pressures will lead to a greater demand for increased industrial efficiency and hence for more well-trained industrial engineering technicians to assist in reducing and controlling manufacturing waste and inefficiency.

Changing and increasing numbers of environmental and safety regulations may lead companies to change some of their procedures and practices, and new technicians may be needed to assist in these changeovers.

Prospective technicians should remember that advances in technology and management techniques make industrial engineering a constantly changing field. Technicians will only be able to take best advantage of the increased need for their services if they are willing to continue their training and education throughout their careers. Graduates of two-year programs in engineering technology have the best outlook for employment.

Earnings

The salary range for entry-level industrial engineering technicians varies according to the product being manufactured, geographic location, and the education and skills of the technician. Most industrial engineering technicians earn between $25,000 and $32,700 a year. Some technicians, however, especially those at the very beginning of their careers, earn $20,200 a year or less, while some senior technicians with special skills and experience earn as much as $54,800 a year or more.

In addition to salary, most employers offer paid vacation time, holidays, insurance and pension plans, and tuition assistance for work-related courses.

Conditions of Work

Industrial engineering technicians generally work indoors. Depending on their jobs, they may work in the shop or office areas or in both. The type of plant facilities depends on the product. For example, an electronics plant producing small electronic products requiring very exacting tolerances has very clean working conditions.

Industrial engineering technicians often travel to other locations or areas. They may accompany engineers to technical conventions or on visits to other companies to gain insight on new or different methods of operation and production.

Continuing education plays a large role in the life of industrial engineering technicians. They may attend classes or seminars, keeping up to date with emerging technology and the methods of managing production efficiently.

Hours of work may vary and depend on factory shifts and hours of production. Industrial engineering technicians are often called upon to get jobs done quickly, meeting set deadlines in a limited amount of time.

Some hazards or risk of injury may exist, so industrial engineering technicians need to take necessary precautions while working in a factory or production environment.

Industrial engineering technicians occupy an intermediary role in the workplace. In terms of both training and responsibility, they fall somewhere between management and the hourly workers involved in production. Associating with so many different types of people requires good communications skills and a great deal of patience.

Sources of Additional Information

American Society of Certified Engineering Technicians (ASCET)
PO Box 1348
Flowery Branch, GA 30542
Tel: 404-967-9173

American Purchasing and Inventory Control Society (APICS)—The Educational Society for Resource Management
500 West Annandale Road
Falls Church, VA 22046
Tel: 703-237-8344

IEEE Industry Applications Society
c/o Institute of Electrical and Electronics Engineers
345 East 47th Street
New York, NY 10017
Tel: 212-705-7900

Institute of Industrial Engineers
25 Technology Park/Atlanta
Norcross, GA 30092
Tel: 404-449-0460

Junior Engineering Technical Society (JETS)
1420 King Street, Suite 405
Alexandria, VA 22314-2794
Tel: 703-548-5387
Email: jets@nas.edu

For information on certification, please contact:

National Institute for Certification in Engineering Technologies
1420 King Street
Alexandria, VA 22314-2715
Tel: 703-480-1730

Industrial Machinery Mechanics

Definition

Industrial machinery mechanics, often called *maintenance mechanics* or *industrial machinery repairers,* inspect, maintain, repair, and adjust machinery and equipment to ensure its proper operation in various industries.

Nature of the Work

The types of machinery on which industrial machinery mechanics work are as varied as the types of industries operating in the United States today. They are employed in metal stamping plants, printing plants, chemical and plastics plants—almost any type of large-scale industrial operation that can be imagined. The machinery in these plants must be maintained regularly. Breakdowns and delays with one machine can hinder a plant's entire operation, which is costly for the company.

Preventive maintenance is a major part of mechanics' jobs. They inspect the equipment, oil and grease moving components, and clean and repair parts. They also keep detailed maintenance records on the equipment they service. They often follow blueprints and engineering specifications to maintain and fix equipment.

When breakdowns occur, mechanics may partially or completely disassemble a machine to make the necessary repairs. They replace worn bearings, adjust clutches, and replace and repair defective parts. They may have to order replacement parts from the machinery's manufacturer. If no parts are available, they may have to make the necessary replacements, using milling machines, lathes, or other tooling equipment. After the machine is reassembled, they may have to make adjustments to its operational settings. They often work with the machine's regular operator to test it. When repairing electronically controlled machinery, mechanics may work closely with electronic repairers or electricians who maintain the machine's electronic parts.

School Subjects
Mathematics
Shop (Trade/Vo-tech education)

Personal Interests
Figuring out how things work
Fixing things

Work Environment
Primarily indoors
Primarily one location

Minimum Education Level
High school diploma
Apprenticeship

Salary Range
$17,160 to
$29,640 to
$48,360

Certification or Licensing
None

Outlook
More slowly than the average

DOT
626

GOE
05.05.09

NOC
7311

Often these mechanics can identify potential breakdowns and fix problems before any real damage or delays occur. They may notice that a machine is vibrating, rattling, or squeaking or they may see that the items produced by the machine are flawed. Many types of new machinery are built with programmed internal evaluation systems that check the accuracy and condition of equipment. This assists mechanics in their jobs, but it also makes them responsible for maintaining the check-up systems.

Industrial mechanics may use a wide range of tools when doing preventive maintenance or making repairs. For example, they may use a screwdriver and wrench to repair an engine or a hoist to lift a printing press off the ground. In addition, they may have to solder or weld equipment. They use both power and hand tools and precision measuring instruments. In some shops, mechanics troubleshoot for the entire plant's operations. Others may become experts in electronics, hydraulics, pneumatics, or other specialties.

Requirements

In the past, most industrial machinery mechanics learned the skills of the trade informally by spending several years as helpers in a particular factory. Currently, as machinery is becoming more complex, more formal training is necessary. Many mechanics are learning the trade through apprenticeship programs. Apprenticeship programs usually last four years and include both on-the-job and related classroom training. In addition to the use and care of machine and hand tools, apprentices learn the operation, lubrication, and adjustment of the machinery and equipment they will maintain. In class they learn shop mathematics, blueprint reading, safety, hydraulics, welding, and other subjects related to the trade.

Students may also obtain training through vocational or technical schools. Useful programs are those that offer machine shop courses or provide training in electronics and numerical control machine tools.

While most employers prefer to hire those who have completed high school, opportunities do exist for those without a diploma as long as they have had some kind of related training. High school courses in mechanical drawing, general mathematics, algebra, geometry, physics, computers, and electronics are important. Students interested in this field should also possess mechanical aptitude and manual dexterity. Good physical condition and agility are necessary because mechanics sometimes have to lift heavy objects, crawl under large machines, or climb to reach equipment located high above the factory floor.

These workers are responsible for valuable equipment and are often called upon to exercise considerable independent judgment. Because of technological advances, they should be willing to learn the requirements of new machines and production techniques. When a plant purchases new equipment, the equipment's manufacturer often trains plant employees in proper operation and maintenance. Technological change requires mechanics to have adaptability and an inquiring mind.

Industrial mechanics may be represented by one of several unions, depending on their industry and place of employment. These unions include the International Union, United Automobile, Aerospace and Agricultural Implement Workers of America; the United Steelworkers of America; the International Union of Electronic, Electrical, Salaried, Machine, and Furniture Workers; and the International Association of Machinists and Aerospace Workers.

Opportunities for Experience & Exploration

Students interested in this field should take as many shop courses as they can. Exploring and repairing machinery such as automobiles and home appliances will sharpen the skills of those who are mechanically inclined. Students may also land part-time work or summer jobs in an industrial plant that give them an opportunity to observe industrial repair work being done.

Methods of Entering

Jobs can be obtained by directly applying to a company that uses industrial equipment or machinery. The majority of mechanics work for manufacturing plants. These plants are found in a wide variety of industries, including the automotive, plastics, textile, electronics, packaging, food, beverage, and aerospace industries. Chances for job openings may be better at a large plant. New workers are generally assigned to work as helpers or trainees.

Prospective mechanics also may learn of job openings or apprenticeship programs through union locals that represent these types of workers. Private and state employment offices are another good source of job openings.

Advancement

Those who begin as helpers or trainees usually advance to journeyworkers in four years. Although opportunities for advancement beyond this rank are somewhat limited, industrial machinery mechanics who learn more complicated machinery and equipment can advance into higher-paying positions. The most highly skilled mechanics may be promoted to master mechanics. Those who demonstrate good leadership and interpersonal skills can become supervisors. Skilled mechanics also have the option of becoming machinists, numerical control tool programmers, tool and die makers, packaging machinery technicians, and robotics technicians. Some of these positions do require additional training, but the skills of a mechanic readily transfer to these areas.

Employment Outlook

Over five hundred thousand industrial machinery mechanics are employed throughout the United States. The U.S. Bureau of Labor Statistics predicts that through the year 2006, there will be slower than average growth in the number of industrial machinery mechanics needed. Some industries will have a greater need for mechanics than others. Areas that are experiencing some growth include the telecommunications, computer, and packaging machinery industries. Other industries, such as the automotive and metal fabricating industries, are experiencing periods of increased production fluctuating with slower activity. Many of the job openings will result from workers leaving the workforce.

Certain industries are extremely susceptible to economic factors and reduce production activities when sales don't keep up with inventories and production output. During these periods, companies may lay off workers, reduce hours, or even shut down operations during a shift or for a period of time. Mechanics are less likely to be laid off than other workers as they still need to maintain machines during slower production periods and often use temporary shutdowns to overhaul equipment. Nonetheless, employment opportunities are generally better at companies experiencing growth or stable levels of production.

Because machinery is becoming more complex and automated, mechanics need to be more highly skilled than in the past. Mechanics who stay up-to-date with new technologies, particularly those related to electronics and computers, will be best prepared to meet the needs of companies that use these workers.

Earnings

In 1996, according to the U.S. Department of Labor, the average annual earnings for industrial machinery mechanics was around $29,600. Apprentices generally earn much lower wages and earn incremental raises as they advance in their training. Earnings vary based on experience, skills, type of industry, and geographic location. For example, mechanics employed in the textile industry generally earn wages at the low end of the scale, with workers in the automotive, metalworking, and aircraft industries earning wages at the high end. Mechanics in the Midwest typically earn higher salaries than those in the South. Those working in union plants generally earn more than those in nonunion plants.

Most industrial machinery mechanics are provided with benefit packages, which can include paid holidays and vacations, medical, dental, and life insurance, pension plans, and 401(k) programs. Many mechanics are members of a union.

Conditions of Work

Industrial machinery mechanics work in all types of manufacturing plants, which may be either hot, noisy, and dirty or relatively quiet and clean. Mechanics frequently work with greasy and dirty equipment and need to be able to adapt to a variety of physical conditions. Because machinery is not always accessible, mechanics may have to work in stooped or cramped positions or on high ladders.

Although working around machinery poses some danger, with proper safety precautions this risk is minimized. Modern machinery includes many safety features and devices, and most plants follow good safety practices. Mechanics often wear protective clothing and equipment such as hard hats and safety belts, glasses, and shoes.

Mechanics work with little supervision and need to be able to work well with others. They need to be flexible and respond to changing priorities, which can result in interruptions that pull a mechanic off one job to repair a more urgent problem. Although the standard work week is forty hours, overtime is common. Because factories and other sites cannot afford breakdowns, industrial machinery mechanics may be called to the plant at night or on weekends for emergency repairs.

Sources of Additional Information

■■■**The Association for Manufacturing Technology**
7901 Westpark Drive
McLean, VA 22102-4269
Tel: 800-544-3597

■■■**International Union, United Automotive, Aerospace and Agricultural Implement Workers of America (UAW)**
Public Relations Department
8000 East Jefferson Avenue
Detroit, MI 48214
Tel: 313-926-5000

Instrumentation Technicians

Definition

Instrumentation technicians are involved in the field of measurement and control. They inspect, test, repair, and adjust instruments that detect, measure, and record changes in industrial environments.

Nature of the Work

Instrumentation technicians work with complex instruments that detect, measure, and record changes in industrial environments. As part of their duties, these technicians perform tests, develop new instruments, and install, repair, inspect, and maintain the instruments. Examples of such instruments include altimeters, pressure gauges, speedometers, and radiation detection devices.

Some instrumentation technicians operate the laboratory equipment that produces or records the effects of certain conditions on the test instruments, such as vibration, stress, temperature, humidity, pressure, altitude, and acceleration. Other technicians sketch, build, and modify electronic and mechanical fixtures, instruments, and related apparatus.

As part of their duties, technicians might verify the dimensions and functions of devices assembled by other technicians and craftworkers, plan test programs, and direct technical personnel in carrying out these tests. Instrumentation technicians also often perform mathematical calculations on instrument readings and test results to put them in usable form for preparing graphs and written reports.

Instrumentation technicians work with three major categories of instruments:

Pneumatic and electropneumatic equipment includes temperature and flow transmitters and receivers and devices that start or are started by such things as pressure springs, diaphragms, and bellows, which receive or transmit pneumatic or electropneumatic signals.

School Subjects
Mathematics
Physics

Personal Interests
Figuring out how things work
Fixing things

Work Environment
Primarily indoors
Primarily one location

Minimum Education Level
Associate's degree

Salary Range
$18,000 to
$38,000 to
$55,000

Certification or Licensing
Voluntary

Outlook
About as fast as the average

DOT
003

GOE
05.01.01

NOC
2243

Hydraulic instrumentation includes hydraulic valves, hydraulic valve operators, and electrohydraulic equipment.

Electrical and electronic equipment includes electrical sensing elements and transducers, electronic recorders, electronic telemetering systems, and electronic computers.

Instrumentation technicians are employed in many industries: aerospace, automotive, chemical, petroleum, food, metals, ceramics, pulp and paper, power, textiles, pharmaceutical, mining, metals, air and water pollution, biomedical instrumentation, and national defense systems.

In some industries, a technician will perform a whole range of duties working on equipment from each category, while in other industries a technician will be responsible for performing only one specific type of task. The different levels of responsibility depend also on the instrumentation technician's level of training and experience. With experience and further study, technicians can advance from routine mechanical functions to repair, troubleshoot, and assist in design.

The following paragraphs describe some of the different types of positions that instrumentation technicians may hold.

Mechanical instrumentation technicians handle routine mechanical functions, but must also be able to visualize functions or malfunctions of various mechanisms. They check out equipment before operation, calibrate it during operation, rebuild it using standard replacement parts, mount interconnecting equipment from blueprints, and perform routine repairs. They use simple tools, such as screwdrivers, wrenches, pliers, electrical drills, and soldering irons. The ability to read both instrumentation and electronic schematic diagrams is necessary.

Instrumentation repair technicians determine the causes of malfunctions and carry out needed repairs. Such repairs usually involve individual pieces of equipment, as distinguished from entire systems, and would include mechanisms, components, and circuits contained in the individual instruments. This job requires preparation, primarily laboratory-oriented, beyond that of mechanical instrumentation technicians.

Troubleshooting instrumentation technicians determine the cause of a problem and perform corrections in instruments and control systems. They make adjustments, calibrate equipment, set up tests, diagnose malfunctions, and revise existing systems. Their work is performed either on-site or at a workbench. Advanced training is required for this level of work, including training in mathematics, physics, and graphics.

Technicians who are involved in the design of instruments are *instrumentation design technicians*. These technicians work under the supervision of a design engineer. Using information prepared by engineers, they build models and prototypes of instruments and prepare sketches, working drawings, and diagrams. These technicians also test out new system designs, order parts, and make mock-ups of new systems.

Technicians in certain industries have more specialized duties and responsibilities. The following paragraphs describe a few of these types of instrument technicians.

Biomedical equipment technicians work with instruments used during medical procedures. They receive special training in the biomedical area in which their instruments are used. Like other technicians, they calibrate and repair instruments; however, they pay special attention to things such as electrical interference that can occur when more than one device or instrument is used. Biomedical equipment technicians also are concerned with the safety and welfare of both the patient and the medical technician using the equipment.

Calibration technicians, also known as *standards laboratory technicians*, work in the electronics industry and in aerospace and aircraft manufacturing. They test, calibrate, and repair the electrical, mechanical, and electronic instruments used to measure and record voltage, heat, magnetic resonance, and other factors. As part of their inspection of recording systems and measuring instruments, they measure parts for conformity to specifications using micrometers, calipers, and other precision instruments. They repair or replace parts, using jeweler's lathes, files, soldering irons, and other tools. They also help engineering personnel develop calibration standards, devise formulas to solve problems in measurement and calibration, and write procedures and practical guides for other calibration technicians. Calibration tools are now so refined that surfaces can be measured to one-thousandth of an inch.

Electromechanical technicians work with automated mechanical equipment controlled by electronic sensing devices. They assist mechanical engineers in the design and development of such equipment, analyze test results, and write reports. The technician follows blueprints, operates metalworking machines, and uses hand tools and precision measuring and testing devices to build instrument housings, install electrical equipment, and calibrate instruments and machinery. Technicians who specialize in the assembly of prototype instruments are known as *development technicians*. *Fabrication technicians* specialize in the assembly of production instruments.

Nuclear instrumentation technicians work with instruments at a nuclear power plant. These instruments control the various systems within the nuclear reactor, detect radiation, and sound alarms in case of equipment failure.

Some instrumentation technicians work in sales. *Instrument sales technicians* work for equipment manufacturing companies. They analyze customer needs for specific control instruments, outline specifications for equipment cost and function, and sometimes do emergency goodwill troubleshooting.

Requirements

The basic requirement for an entry-level job is completion of a two-year technical program or equivalent experience in a related field. Such equivalent experience may come from work in an electronics or manufacturing firm or any job that provides experience working with mechanical or electrical equipment.

In high school, students should take math and science courses, including algebra, geometry, physics, and chemistry. In addition, high school machine and electrical shop courses will help students become familiar with electrical, mechanical, and electronic technology. Classes in mechanical drawing and computer-aided drafting are also beneficial. Instrumentation technicians also need good writing and communications skills and should take English, composition, and speech classes.

Technical programs beyond high school can be found in junior or community colleges as well as technical schools. Programs are found in many different disciplines. In addition to programs in instrumentation technology, programs may be in electronics or in electrical, mechanical, biomedical, or nuclear technology.

Most programs allow technicians to develop hands-on and laboratory skills, as well as learn background theories. Classes are likely to include theoretical instruction in electronic circuitry and digital and microprocessing computers. Since instrumentation technicians use knowledge and techniques drawn from mathematics and physics, these subjects and learning experiences are part of a solid foundation in any program. Courses in basic electronics, electrical theory, graphics, and digital computers are also important. Technical writing is helpful as most technicians will need the ability to prepare technical reports. Industrial economics, applied psychology, and plant management are courses that will be very useful to instrumentation technicians who plan to advance in the field as customer service representatives or design technicians.

Instrumentation technicians who are graduates of qualified technical programs may become certified by the Institute for the Certification of Engineering Technicians, although this is not a required part of the job. Technicians are also eligible to become members of ISA, the International Society for Measurement and Control, and similar professional societies. Membership in such organizations is optional but encouraged as a means of keeping abreast of advancing technology.

Successful instrumentation technicians need mathematical and scientific aptitudes and the patience to methodically pursue complex questions. A tolerance for following prescribed procedures is essential, especially when undertaking assignments requiring a very precise, unchanging system of problem solving. Successful instrumentation technicians are able to provide solutions quickly and accurately even in stressful situations.

Opportunities for Experience & Exploration

Students interested in testing their abilities at and learning more about calibration work can build small electronic equipment and adapt or adjust it. Kits for building radios and other small appliances are available in some electronic shops. This gives some basic understanding of electronic components and applications.

Some communities and schools also have clubs for people interested in electronics. They may provide classes that teach basic skills in construction, repair, and adjustment of electrical and electronic products.

Model building, particularly in hard plastic and steel, gives a good understanding of how to adjust and fit parts together. It may also help build hand skills for those who want to work with precision instruments.

Visits to industrial laboratories, instrument shops, research laboratories, power installations, and manufacturing companies that rely on automated processes can provide a glimpse of the working environment and activities of instrumentation technicians. During such visits, it may be possible to speak with several technicians on the job about their work or with employers about possible openings in their company.

In addition, while still in high school it may be possible to obtain summer or part-time employment as a helper on an industrial maintenance crew. This helps students to evaluate their own manual dexterity and mechanical or technical aptitude and to observe working conditions in a particular industry.

Methods of Entering

Many companies recruit students who are about to graduate. Chemical and medical research companies especially need maintenance and operations technicians and usually recruit at schools where training in these areas is strong. Similarly, many industries in search of design technicians recruit at technical institutes and community colleges where the program is likely to meet their needs.

Students may also get assistance in their job searches through their schools' job placement services or learn about openings through ads in the newspapers. Prospective employees can also apply directly to a company in which they are interested.

Employers of instrumentation technicians include oil refineries, chemical and industrial laboratories, electronics firms, aircraft and aeronautical manufacturers, biomedical firms, and companies involved in space exploration and oceanographic research.

Advancement

Entry-level technicians perform maintenance and adjustment tasks to develop their skills with their employers' equipment. Those with superb academic records may, upon completion of an employer's basic program, start at an advanced level in sales or another area where a general understanding of the field is more important than specific laboratory skills. Technicians who show proficiency in instrumentation may advance to supervisory or specialized positions that require knowledge of a particular aspect of instrumentation.

Employment Outlook

Employment opportunities for instrumentation technicians will be favorable through the year 2006. Opportunities will be best for graduates of postsecondary technical training programs.

Most new developments in automated manufacturing techniques, including robotics and computer-controlled machinery, rely heavily on instrumentation devices. The emerging fields of air and water pollution control are other areas of growth. Scientists and technicians measure the amount of toxic substances in the air or test water with the use of instrumentation. Additionally, instrumentation is required to quickly evaluate toxic waste in land.

Oceanography, including the search for undersea deposits of oil and minerals, is another expanding field for instrumentation technology, as is medical diagnosis, including long-distance diagnosis by physicians through the use of sensors, computers, and telephone lines.

One important field of growth is the teaching profession. As demand rises for skilled technicians, qualified instructors with combined knowledge of theory and application will be needed. Opportunities already exist, not only in educational institutions but also in those industries that have internal training programs.

Earnings

Earnings for instrumentation technicians vary by region. Most entry-level technicians earn between $18,000 and $29,000 a year, with the average salary around $21,700. Experienced technicians may earn as much as $55,000 a year, with the average annual salary around $41,000.

Employee benefits vary but can include any of the following: paid vacations, paid holidays, sick leave, insurance benefits, 401(k) plans, profit sharing, pension plans, and tuition assistance programs.

Conditions of Work

Working conditions vary widely for instrumentation technicians. An oil refinery plant job is as different from space mission instrumentation work as a nuclear reactor instrumentation job is different from work in the surgical room of a hospital. All employment for these workers uses similar principles, however, and instrumentation technicians can master new areas of application by applying what they have learned previously. For technicians who would like to travel, the petroleum industry, in particular, provides employment opportunities in foreign lands.

Instrumentation technicians' tasks may range from routine to the highly complex and challenging. A calm, well-controlled approach to work is essential. Calibration and adjustment require the dexterity and control of a watchmaker. Consequently, a person who is easily excited or impatient is not well suited to this kind of employment.

Sources of Additional Information

For information on educational programs and certification, please contact:

Association for the Advancement of Medical Instrumentation
3330 Washington Boulevard, Suite 400
Arlington, VA 22201-4598
Tel: 800-332-2264

IEEE Instrumentation and Measurement Society
c/o Institute of Electrical and Electronics Engineers
345 East 47th Street
New York, NY 10017
Tel: 617-942-9283

For information on careers and student membership, please contact:

ISA, the International Society for Measurement and Control
PO Box 12277
67 Alexander Drive
Research Triangle Park, NC 27709
Tel: 919-549-8411
WWW: http://www.isa.org/

For information on careers and student clubs, please contact:

Junior Engineering Technical Society (JETS)
1420 King Street, Suite 405
Alexandria, VA 22314-2794
Tel: 703-548-5387
Email: jets@nas.edu

For information on certification, please contact:

National Institute for Certification in Engineering Technologies
1420 King Street
Alexandria, VA 22314-2794
Tel: 703-684-2835

Insurance Claims Representatives

Definition

Insurance claims representatives, or *claims adjusters,* investigate claims for personal, casualty, or property loss or damages. They determine the extent of the insurance company's liability and try to negotiate an out-of-court settlement with the claimant.

Nature of the Work

An insurance company's reputation and success is dependent upon its ability to quickly and effectively investigate claims, negotiate equitable settlements, and authorize prompt payments to policyholders. Claims representatives perform these duties.

Claims clerks review insurance forms for accuracy and completeness. Frequently, this involves calling or writing the insured party or other people involved to secure missing information. After placing this data in a claim file, the clerk reviews the insurance policy to determine coverage. Routine claims are transmitted for payment; if further investigation is needed, the clerk informs the claims supervisor.

In companies specializing in property and casualty insurance, claims adjusters may perform some or all of the duties of claims clerks. They can determine whether the policy covers the loss and amount claimed. Through investigation of physical evidence, the securing of testimony from relevant parties, including the claimant, witnesses, police, and, if necessary, hospital personnel, and the examination of reports, they promptly negotiate a settlement. Adjusters make sure that the settlement reflects the actual claimant losses while making certain the insurer is protected from invalid claims.

Adjusters may issue payment checks or submit their findings to claims examiners for payment. If litigation is necessary, adjusters recommend this action to legal counsel, and they may attend court hearings.

School Subjects
Business
Mathematics

Personal Interests
Computers
Travel

Work Environment
Indoors and outdoors
One location with some travel

Minimum Education Level
Bachelor's degree

Salary Range
$17,680 to
$22,800 to
$55,000

Certification or Licensing
Required

Outlook
Faster than the average

DOT
241

GOE
11.12.01

NOC
1233

Some claims adjusters do not specialize in one type of insurance, but most do. They act exclusively in one field, such as fire, marine, automobile, or product liability. A special classification is the claims agent for petroleum, who handles activities connected with the locating, drilling, and producing of oil or gas on private property. In states with "no fault" insurance, adjusters are not concerned with responsibilities, but they still must determine the amount of payment. To help settle automobile insurance claims, an automobile damage appraiser examines damaged cars and other vehicles, estimates the cost of labor and parts, and determines whether it is more practical to make the repairs on the damaged car or to pay the claimant the precollision market value of the vehicle.

For minor or routine claims, the trend among property and casualty insurers is to employ telephone or inside adjusters. They use the telephone and written correspondence to gather information, including loss estimates, from the claimant. Drive-in claim centers have developed to provide on-the-spot settlement for minor claims. After determining the loss, the adjuster issues a check immediately.

More complex claims are handled by outside adjusters. Outside adjusters spend more time in the field investigating the claim and gathering relevant information.

In life and health insurance companies, *claims examiners* perform all the functions of claims adjusters. Examiners in these companies, and in others where adjusters are employed, review settled claims to make sure the settlements and payments adhere to company procedures and policies. They report on any irregularities. In cases involving litigation, they confer with attorneys. Where large claims are involved, a senior examiner frequently handles the case.

Requirements

College graduates generally are preferred for insurance claims jobs, but persons with special experience may not need a degree. No specific college major is preferred, but certain ones may indicate a possible specialty. For example, an engineering degree would be valuable in industrial claims, and a legal background would be helpful in ones involving workers' compensation and product liability. In most companies, on-the-job training is usually provided.

Supplementary professional education is encouraged by insurance companies. A number of options are available. The Insurance Institute of America offers a series of courses culminating in a comprehensive examination. Passing the exam earns the examinee an Associate in Claims (AIC) designation. The College of Insurance in New York City offers a program leading to a professional certificate in insurance adjusting. In addition, life and health claims examining programs for people interested in working as claims examiners are offered by both the Life Office Management Association (LOMA) and the International Claim Association (ICA), both of which lead to a professional designation.

Claims representatives are in a people-oriented job. They must be able to communicate effectively to gain the respect and confidence of all involved parties. They should be mathematically adept and have a good memory. Knowledge of legal and medical terms and practice, as well as state and federal insurance laws and regulations, is required in this profession. Some companies require applicants to take aptitude tests designed to measure mathematical, analytical, and communications skills. Increasingly, an interest in and knowledge of computers are important.

Most states require licensing of claims representatives. The requirements for licensing vary and may include age restrictions, state residency, education in such classes as loss adjusting or insurance, character references, and written examinations.

Opportunities for Experience & Exploration

There are vast opportunities for career exploration, ranging from getting a job with an insurance company, to taking relevant coursework and interviewing people in the field.

Methods of Entering

A person can enter this occupation by applying directly to an employer, answering a newspaper ad, or using the local office of the U.S. Employment Service Office.

Advancement

Depending upon the individual, advancement prospects are good. As trainees demonstrate competence and advance in coursework, they are assigned higher and more difficult claims.

Promotions are possible to department supervisor in a field office or a managerial position in the home office. Sometimes claims workers transfer to underwriting and sales departments.

Employment Outlook

Growth for this field will be faster than the national average for all occupations through the year 2006. Most of the new jobs will be created as a result of increased insurance sales, resulting in a larger number of insurance claims, as well as of changes in the population, economics, trends in insurance settlement procedures, and opportunities arising from employees who change jobs or retire.

The predominance of the group most in need of protection, individuals between twenty-five and fifty-four, indicates the need for more claims jobs. Also, as the number of working women rises, so will their demand for increased insurance coverage. New and expanding businesses will require insurance for production plants and equipment, as well as employees.

Claims representatives who specialize in complex business insurance such as marine cargo, workers' compensation, and product and pollution liability insurance will be in demand. Insurance claims representatives will always be in demand since their work requires significant interpersonal contact, and does not lend itself to automation.

Earnings

According to the U.S. Department of Labor, claims representatives earned an average of about $22,800 a year in 1996. Adjusters are furnished a company car or reimbursed for business travel.

Claims examiners make about $31,000 a year; claims supervisors, $44,000; and claims managers, $55,000. Insurance companies have liberal vacation policies and employee-financed life and retirement programs.

Conditions of Work

Inside adjusters work in offices, as do clerks and examiners. They work thirty-five to forty hours a week and occasionally travel. They may work additional hours during peak claim periods or when quarterly or annual reports are due. Outside claims adjusters may travel extensively. An adjuster may be on call twenty-four hours a day.

Sources of Additional Information

General information about claims representative careers is available from many insurance companies, as well as the following:

Alliance of American Insurers
1501 Woodfield Road, Suite 400 West
Schaumburg, IL 60173
Tel: 847-330-8500

Information on health insurance adjusting can be obtained from:

Health Insurance Association of America
555 13th Street, NW, Suite 600 East
Washington, DC 20004
Tel: 202-824-1600

Insurance Information Institute
110 William Street
New York, NY 10038
Tel: 212-669-9200
WWW: http://www.iii.org

National Association of Independent Insurers
2600 River Road
Des Plaines, IL 60018
Tel: 847-297-7800
WWW: http://www.naii.org

Information on public insurance adjusting can be obtained from:

National Association of Public Insurance Adjusters
300 Water Street, Suite 400
Baltimore, MD 21202
Tel: 410-539-4141

Insurance Institute of Canada
18 King Street East, 6th Floor
Toronto, ON M5C 1C4 Canada
Tel: 416-362-8586

Interior Designers and Decorators

Definition

Interior designers and *decorators* evaluate, plan, and design the interior areas of residential, commercial, and industrial structures. They may advise clients on architectural requirements, space planning, and the function and purpose of the environment. They help the client select equipment and fixtures, and they supervise the coordination of colors and materials. The designer obtains estimates and costs within the client's budget and supervises the execution and installation of the project.

Nature of the Work

The terms "interior designer" and "interior decorator" are sometimes used interchangeably. However, there is an important distinction to be made between the two. Interior designers plan and create the overall design for interior spaces, and interior decorators focus on the decorative aspects of the design and furnishing of interiors. In other words, interior design includes interior decoration, but interior decoration does not encompass interior design.

Interior designers perform many different services, depending on the type of project and the client's requirements. They may design interiors for residences, hotels, hospitals, restaurants, schools and universities, office buildings, factories, or clubs. In addition to planning the interiors of new buildings, they also redesign existing interiors. A job may range from accomplishing a single detail in a private residence to designing and coordinating the entire interior arrangement of a huge building complex.

Interior designers begin by evaluating a project. They must consider the use to which the space will be put as well as the needs, desires, and tastes of the client. Their designs must suit both the project's functional requirements and the client's preferences. Often the designer works closely with the architect in planning the complete layout of rooms and use of space; the

School Subjects
Art
Mathematics

Personal Interests
Drawing
Photography

Work Environment
Primarily indoors
Primarily multiple locations

Minimum Education Level
Associate's degree

Salary Range
$14,500 to
$30,680 to
$67,600

Certification or Licensing
Recommended

Outlook
Faster than the average

DOT
141

GOE
01.02.03

NOC
5242

designer's plans must fit in with the architect's blueprints and other building requirements. This type of work is usually done in connection with the building or renovation of large buildings. Interior designers may design the furniture and accessories to be used on a project or they may plan from materials already available. They select and plan the arrangement of furniture, draperies, floor coverings, wallpaper and paint, and other decorations. The designer must consult and respect the tastes of clients and the amount of money they wish to spend. When the designer is working on a private home, the work becomes even more personal. The personalities, way of life, needs, and financial situation of the family must be considered in designing the interior.

Interior designers make a presentation to their clients that usually includes scaled floorplans, color charts, photographs of furnishings, and samples of materials for upholstery, draperies, and wall coverings, and often also includes color renderings or sketches. They will probably also provide a cost estimate of furnishings, materials, labor, transportation, and incidentals required to complete the installation.

Once plans are approved by the client, the interior designer assembles materials—drapery fabrics, upholstery fabrics, new furniture, paint and wallpaper—and supervises the work, often acting as agent for the client in contracting the services of craftworkers and specifying custom-made merchandise. Designers must be familiar with many materials used in interior furnishing. They must know when certain materials are suitable, how these will blend with other materials, and how they will wear. They must also be familiar with historical periods influencing design and have a knack for using and combining the best contributions of these designs of the past. Because designers supervise the work done from their plans, they also must know something about the work of painters, carpet layers, carpenters, cabinetmakers, and other craftworkers. They must also be able to buy materials and services at reasonable prices and still produce quality work. A reputation as an interior designer depends on all these things.

Some designers specialize in a particular aspect of interior design such as furniture, carpeting, or artwork. Others specialize in particular environments such as homes, offices, or transportation, including ships, aircraft, and trains.

Another job available for the interior designer is working in a large department or furniture store, advising customers on plans for decoration and suggesting purchases. These designers sell the store's merchandise through the decorating service. Such interior designers must be familiar with the materials they sell and decorating trends, and they should have a knowledge of historical periods in decorating.

Some designers work in large architectural firms designing interior environment, while others work in advertising or journalism. Some may find the design of theater, film, and television settings an interesting outlet for their talent and training. A few designers may become teachers or lecturers.

Many designers are fortunate enough to establish their own businesses. A few become consultants, but most designers sell all or some of the materials used in their work, such as drapery fabrics, furniture, carpeting, and other accessories. Whether such designers work alone or with assistants depends on the financial success and workload of the individual business.

Some designers renovate old buildings and research the styles in which the rooms were originally decorated and furnished. This may involve supervising the manufacture of furniture and accessories to be used. The design of interiors of ships and aircraft may also require supervising manufacturing.

Considerable paperwork is involved in interior design, much of it related to budgets and costs. The designer must determine quantities and make and obtain cost estimates. Orders must be placed and deliveries carefully checked. All of this requires an ability to attend to detail in the business aspect of interior design.

Requirements

Although formal training is not always necessary to find employment in the field of interior design, it is becoming increasingly important and is probably essential for advancement. Most architectural firms, department stores, and design firms accept only professionally trained people for beginning positions.

Professional schools offer two- or three-year certificates or diplomas in interior design. Colleges and universities award undergraduate degrees in four-year programs, and graduate study also is available. Studies include art history, architectural drawing and drafting, fine arts, furniture design, codes and standards of design, computer-aided design, and the types of materials primarily used, such as fibers, wood, metals, and plastics. Knowledge of lighting and electrical equipment, as well as furnishings, art pieces, and antiques, is important. Courses in business and management are useful, and learning research methods to keep up with government regulations and safety standards is essential. In addition, keeping up with product performance and new developments in materials and manufacture is part of the ongoing education of the interior designer.

Individuals with background in architecture or environmental planning, art historians, and others with qualifications in commercial or industrial design may also qualify for employment in interior design.

Interior designers need to be able to sense client needs that may not always be clear. At the same time, artistic taste and knowledge of current and enduring fashion trends is essential. Artistic talent involves an eye for color, proportion, balance, and detail, and the ability to visualize. Designers must be able to render an image clearly to the client and carry it out consistently. The designer must also be able to work well with suppliers, craftworkers, and others to ensure that the work is done to specifications and the clients' expectations.

In addition to formal education and on-the-job experience, membership in a professional society is an important achievement that may enhance job opportunities. Membership in the American Society of Interior Designers (ASID) generally requires a combination of six years of experience in the field and formal education. The successful completion of both a written and a design-problem examination earns a professional status in the organization. The design-problem test takes ten hours and includes lighting and electrical plans as well as space allocation and furnishing arrangement.

Opportunities for Experience & Exploration

One might first become interested in interior design through a high school course in home economics, or possibly because of a talent for art. Certain aptitude tests can help students determine whether their ability is sufficient for success as an interior designer.

Those interested in interior design may also be able to find a part-time or summer job in a department or furniture store to learn more about the materials used in interior decorating and to see the store's interior design service in action. Even general selling experience would be valuable.

Methods of Entering

Most of the large department stores and design firms with established reputations hire only trained interior designers. More often than not, these employers look for prospective employees with a good portfolio and a bachelor of fine arts degree. Many schools, however, offer apprenticeship or internship programs in cooperation with professional studios or offices of interior design. These programs make it possible for students to apply their academic training in an actual work environment prior to graduation.

After graduating from a two- or three-year training program, the beginning designer must be prepared to spend one to three years as an assistant to an experienced interior designer before achieving full professional status. This is the usual method of entering the field of interior design and achieving membership in a professional organization. Sometimes placement in an assistant job can be difficult; if so, experience may be gained as a sales clerk for interior furnishings, as a shopper for matching accessories or fabrics, or even as a receptionist or stockroom assistant. Any practical experience is valuable and may serve as a good stepping-stone to an entry-level designer's job.

Advancement

As designers gain experience, they can move into positions of greater responsibility and may eventually be promoted to heads of design departments, interior furnishings coordinators, or supervisors of other departments. People who work with furnishings in architectural firms often become more involved in product design and sales with manufacturers. Designers also can also establish their own business. Consulting is another common area of work for the established designer.

Competition for jobs is intense, and designers must possess a combination of talent, personality, and business sense to reach the top. Long years of training and experience are necessary before one can expect to make any real advancement, and income is only moderate—even for many experienced interior designers. A beginning designer must take a long-range career view, accept jobs that offer practical experience, and put up with long hours and occasionally difficult clients.

Employment Outlook

In 1996, there were over 340,00 workers employed in the designing field, primarily in large cities and metropolitan areas. About 40 percent of designers are self-employed. The majority worked for interior design firms, retail stores, and architectural firms.

Employment opportunities for designers with formal training and talent are expected to be faster than average for all occupations through the year 2006. It will be difficult, however, for those lacking experience to get ahead in the profession. The service offered by the interior designer is, of course, in many ways a luxury. Thus, in times of prosperity, there is a steady increase in jobs for interior designers; but when the economy slows down, job opportunities in this field decrease markedly.

Competition is strong in this field, especially in large cities. At present, there is a need for industrial interior designers in housing developments, hospital complexes, hotels, and other large building projects. Also, as the building of houses increases, more work will be available for residential designers.

Earnings

In the 1990s, beginning salaries for graduates of interior design schools range from about $14,500 to $20,000 a year. The median salary for experienced designers is around $30,680. The average salary is between $16,800 and $34,400 a year; however, the top 10 percent make more than $46,500. Established interior designers earn considerably more. Nationally recognized designers may earn $67,600 or more annually.

A wide range of earnings exists among designers in business for themselves. Income depends on such factors as amount of business, reputation, clients' financial status, and the designer's own knack for running a successful business. Even the earnings of designers employed by firms or stores vary because some receive salaries and a commission while others receive only a commission. The general practice of interior design firms is to charge fees for advisory services.

Conditions of Work

Working conditions for interior designers vary depending on where they are employed. They may spend the day in a department store office or working with the decorating materials sold by the firm and the clients who purchase them; they might be in a workroom supervising the making of draperies or consulting with other craftworkers who help them carry out decorating plans.

Whether designers are employed by a firm or operate their own business, a good deal of their time will be spent in clients' homes and businesses. While more and more offices are using the services of the interior designer, the larger part of the business still lies in the field of home design. Home designers work intimately with the customer, planning, selecting, receiving instructions, and sometimes subtly guiding the customer's tastes and choices in order to achieve an atmosphere that is both aesthetic and functional.

Hours for the interior designer can often be irregular, patterned to suit the client. Often deadlines must be met, and if there have been problems and delays on the job, the designer must work hard to complete the work on schedule. The more successful a designer becomes, the longer and more irregular the hours. The beginner works fairly regular hours.

The main objective of all the pressure endured by the interior designer is to please the customer and thus help establish a good reputation. Customers may at times be difficult. They may change their minds several times, forcing the designer to revise plans. But the work is interesting and provides a variety of activities.

Sources of Additional Information

American Society of Interior Designers
608 Massachusetts Avenue, NE
Washington, DC 20002
Tel: 202-546-3480

Foundation for Interior Design Education Research
60 Monroe Center, NW, Suite 300
Grand Rapids, MI 49503
Tel: 616-458-0400

Interior Design Educators Council
14252 Culver Drive, Suite A-311
Irvine, CA 92714

National Council for Interior Design Qualification
50 Main Street, 5th Floor
White Plains, NY 10606-1920
Tel: 914-948-9100
Email: ncidq@aol.com

Interior Designers of Canada
Ontario Design Center
260 King Street East, Suite 506
Toronto, ON M5A 1K3 Canada
Tel: 416-594-9310

Ironworkers

Definition

Ironworkers fabricate, assemble, and install structural and reinforcing metal products used in the construction of buildings and bridges. They also install steel walls, iron stairways, and other metal components of buildings; assemble large metal tanks for chemicals, water, and oil; and do similar structural work with other metals.

Nature of the Work

Structural ironworkers work as members of crews, usually a team of five people. They often work high above the ground as they raise, place, and join together different combinations of steel components, such as girders and columns, into completed structures or frameworks. At a construction site, they begin by setting up cranes and derricks that will be used to move structural steel, buckets of concrete, reinforcing steel bars, lumber, and other materials. This hoisting equipment is usually delivered to the site in sections that must be joined together.

Next the workers start laying out the steel building components. They follow blueprints and instructions from supervisors. Structural steel, reinforcing bars, and other parts are usually delivered to the site already cut to the correct size, with holes drilled for bolts, and numbered for easy identification. The workers at the site usually need only to bolt and weld the pieces together. They unload and identify the steel for assembly, stacking the pieces so they will be available when needed.

When it is time to lift a piece of steel into position, the workers fasten it to cables on the crane or derrick. One worker (called the *pusher* or *foreman*) hand signals to the *crane operator*; another (the *hook-on man*) applies the choker around the iron so that it is secure and has good balance; and another (the *tag line man*) hooks on to the iron being erected, using a line with a small iron hook to guide the iron to the *connectors*. The

School Subjects
Mathematics
Shop (Trade/Vo-tech education)

Personal Interests
Building things
Fixing things

Work Environment
Primarily outdoors
Primarily multiple locations

Minimum Education Level
High school diploma
Apprenticeship

Salary Range
$15,900 to
$31,096 to
$49,800+

Certification or Licensing
None

Outlook
More slowly than the average

DOT
801

connectors, up in the air where the steel is being erected, guide the steel into the approximate position, pushing, pulling, and prying if necessary. Then they position the steel more exactly by aligning the holes in it with the framework that is already in place. They secure it temporarily, holding it with drift pins or a special wrench. Before the steel is fastened in place, they verify its horizontal and vertical alignment, using plumb bobs, laser equipment, transits, and levels. Finally they bolt or weld the steel member permanently in place.

Ornamental ironworkers assemble and install metal stairways, floor gratings, ladders, railings, catwalks, window frames, fences, lampposts, and other metal structures that may be decorative as well as functional. Usually the metal is prefabricated and hoisted into place after the building framework is completed. The workers must align the metal pieces with the structure, then bolt, braze, or weld them securely in place.

Reinforcing ironworkers, or *rodmen,* set reinforcing metal bars or wire fabric into concrete forms before the concrete is poured, giving the cured concrete greater strength. Based on sketches, blueprints, or oral instructions from supervisors, the workers determine the number, size, shape, and intended location of the metal reinforcements. Although the metal is usually delivered to the site already shaped, the workers may have to shape it further. They may fasten bars together by using pliers to wrap wire around them. Sometimes they must cut the metal, using metal shears or acetylene torches. They may bend bars, by hand or using rod-bending machines, and they may weld bars together. Once the reinforcing metal is prepared, they set it in place in the concrete forms. For concrete floors, they must put supports under the metal to hold it off the deck. A concrete crew puts the wet concrete in place. As the concrete goes in, ironworkers may position wire fabric in place using hooked rods.

Ironworker riggers usually work on special rigging jobs where they use biber line, wire rope, chains and hooks, slings and guylines, hoisting equipment, anchorages, scaffolding, and skids and rollers to lift and move loads. These ironworkers must be able to tie special knots and hitches and make splices.

Other workers in this field include *tank setters,* who erect metal tanks used to store crude oil at oil fields. *Metal building assemblers* assemble prefabricated buildings. Following blueprints and specifications, they bolt the steel frames together, attach sheet-metal panels to the framework, cut openings, and install doors, windows, and ventilators. Some ironworkers work in fabricating shops away from the site where metal products will eventually be used. They lay out raw steel from mills and cut, bend, drill, and weld

pieces together in accordance with specifications for particular jobs.

Requirements

Ironworkers may learn their skills by completing an apprenticeship, or they may learn informally on the job. Apprenticeships are the preferred method, because apprentices usually receive more complete training in a shorter period of time. For either kind of training, workers need to be at least eighteen years old. A high school diploma is desirable and may be required. A good background for this kind of work would include high school courses in shop, mechanical drawing, blueprint reading, and applied mathematics.

Apprenticeships combine a planned on-the-job training program with classroom instruction in related subjects. They last three years and include at least 144 hours of classroom instruction each year. On the job, apprentices are supervised by skilled workers. They learn all the different aspects of the trade, including unloading and arranging materials at job sites, rigging steel for lifting with hoisting equipment, techniques for connecting steel to the building framework, use of measuring equipment to verify position, and welding. In the classroom, they learn such subjects as blueprint reading, mathematics for layout work, the basics of erecting and assembling structures, job safety practices, and the use and care of tools. Apprenticeships are usually run by joint committees representing local branches of contractors' associations and locals of the union to which these workers often belong, the International Association of Bridge, Structural and Ornamental Ironworkers.

Workers who learn informally on the job usually start as helpers to experienced workers. They begin with simple tasks, like carrying materials, and work up to the more difficult tasks, like fitting steel sections together. Unlike apprentices, they do not have the benefit of classroom instruction, but some employers have thorough training programs.

Ironworkers need to be agile, able to climb, stoop, crouch, reach, and kneel. They must be in good physical condition, have good eyesight, including depth perception, good coordination and balance, and, perhaps most importantly for ironworkers on skyscrapers, they should not be afraid of heights. In many jobs, they need strength enough to lift very heavy weights and stamina to keep active for much of the workday.

Opportunities for Experience & Exploration

High school students can begin to gauge their interest in this field by taking courses in mathematics, mechanical drawing, blueprint reading, and shop. A course that introduces welding would be especially useful, because that skill is often used by these workers. It is not easy to get a part-time or temporary job in this field. However, perhaps with the help of a teacher, it may be possible to visit a construction site where ironworkers are employed.

Methods of Entering

Those who would like to enter this field as apprentices should contact the local offices of the International Association of Bridge, Structural and Ornamental Ironworkers for details on applying for apprenticeship positions. Information about apprenticeships, as well as about job openings for nonapprentice helpers in this field, may be obtained through the local offices of the state employment service. Job seekers can also apply directly to local structural steel erection and reinforcing steel contractors and other contractors that may be hiring for helper positions.

Advancement

Skilled and experienced ironworkers may be considered for positions as supervisors, directing the activities of a crew of other ironworkers. With additional education, a good knowledge of other construction trades, and judgment and leadership qualities, workers may advance to become job superintendents. Experienced workers also can establish their own businesses.

Employment Outlook

In 1996, there were 770,000 workers employed as structural and reinforcing ironworkers. Through the year 2006, this field should grow slower than the average for all other occupations. This prediction is a result of the slow growth in industrial and commercial construction. Existing factories, power plants, highways and bridges will need rehabilitation work creating a few new jobs. Most job openings, however, will stem from the need to replace older workers who leave the field for various reasons.

Like workers in other construction trades, ironworkers can expect job opportunities to vary with economic conditions. When the overall economy is in a downturn, construction activity usually falls noticeably, and these workers may face long periods between construction projects. They may have to relocate to other areas to find steadier employment. Because construction usually picks up during the warm months, there are usually more jobs available during the spring and summer.

Earnings

In 1996, the U.S. Department of Labor reported annual earnings for ironworkers ranging from $15,900 to $50,000 or more, assuming they work full-time. Workers may lose hours during bad weather, and their earnings are reduced if they must be out of work between jobs. Overtime pay can boost earnings somewhat.

According to the *Engineering News Record*, apprentices start at 40 to 60 percent of the skilled worker's rate and receive periodic increases during their training.

Conditions of Work

Most ironworkers are employed by large construction companies located in large cities. Most of the work is done outdoors, in varying weather conditions. Although some of the job is done at great heights, workers do not go high above the ground during icy, wet, or very windy weather.

Because of the danger of falling, these workers always use safety nets, belts, scaffolding, or other safety equipment. They also must be constantly careful to avoid being hit by falling objects.

Sources of Additional Information

Associated General Contractors of America
1957 E Street, NW
Washington, DC 20006
Tel: 202-393-2040
WWW: http://www.laborers.agc.org

International Association of Bridge, Structural and Ornamental Ironworkers
1750 New York Avenue, NW
Washington, DC 20006
Tel: 202-383-4800

National Association of Reinforcing Steel Contractors
10382 Main Street, Suite 300
Fairfax, VA 22030
Tel: 703-591-1870

National Erectors Association
1501 Lee Highway, #202
Arlington, VA 22209
Tel: 703-524-3336

Jewelers and Jewelry Repairers

Definition

Jewelers fabricate, either from their own design or one by a design specialist, rings, necklaces, bracelets, and other jewelry out of gold, silver, or platinum. They also make repairs, alter ring sizes, reset stones, and refashion old jewelry. Restringing beads and stones, resetting clasp and hinges, and mending breaks in ceramic and metal pieces are aspects of the *jewelry repairer's* job.

A few jewelers are also *gemologists*, who examine, grade, and evaluate gems, or *gem cutters,* who cut, shape, and polish gemstones.

Nature of the Work

Jewelers may design, make, sell, or repair jewelry. Many jewelers do a combination of two or more of these skills. Designers conceive and sketch ideas for jewelry that they may make themselves or have made by another craftsperson. The materials of the jeweler and the jewelry repairer are usually precious and semiprecious or synthetic stones and gold, silver, and platinum. The jeweler begins by forming an article in wax or metal with carving tools and then places the wax model in a casting ring and pours plaster into the ring to form a mold. The mold is then inserted in a furnace to melt the wax. A metal model is cast from the plaster mold. The jeweler pours the precious molten metal into the mold or uses a centrifugal casting machine to cast the article. Final touches, such as cutting, filing, and polishing, complete the work.

Jewelers do most of their work sitting down. They use small hand and machine tools such as drills, files, saws, soldering irons, and jewelers' lathes. They often wear an eye "loupe," or magnifying glass. They are constantly using their hands and eyes and need to have good finger-hand dexterity.

Jewelers usually specialize in creating or making certain kinds of jewelry, or in a particular operation such as making,

School Subjects
Art
Shop (Trade/Vo-tech education)

Personal Interests
Fixing things
Sculpting

Work Environment
Primarily indoors
Primarily one location

Minimum Education Level
High school diploma
Apprenticeship

Salary Range
$10,400 to
$31,000 to
$50,000+

Certification or Licensing
None

Outlook
Decline

DOT
700

GOE
01.06.02

NOC
7344

polishing, or stone-setting models and tools. Specialists include *gem cutters, stone setters, fancy-wire drawers, locket, ring, hand chain makers,* and *sample makers.*

Experienced jewelers may become qualified to make and repair any kind of jewelry. Assembly line methods employing factory workers are used to produce costume jewelry and some types of precious jewelry, but the models and tools needed for factory production must be made by highly skilled jewelers. Some molds and models for manufacturing are designed and created using computer-aided design/manufacturing (CAD/CAM) systems. Costume jewelry is often made by a die stamping process. In general, the more precious the metals, the less automated the manufacturing process.

Jewelers and jewelry repairers are both self-employed and employed by manufacturing and retail establishments. Workers in a manufacturing plant include skilled, semiskilled, and unskilled positions. Skilled positions include jewelers, *ring makers, engravers, toolmakers, electroplaters,* and *stone cutters and setters.* Semiskilled positions include *polishers,* repairers, *toolsetters,* and *solders.* Unskilled workers are *press operators, carders,* and *linkers.*

Although some jewelers operate their own retail stores, an increasing number of jewelry stores are owned or managed by business persons who are not jewelers. In such instances, a jeweler or jewelry repairer may be employed by the owner, or the store may send its repairs to a trade shop operated by a jeweler who specializes in repair work. Jewelers who operate their own stores sell jewelry, watches, and, frequently, such merchandise as silverware, china, and glassware. Many retail jewelry stores are located in or near large cities, with the eastern section of the country providing most of the employment in jewelry manufacturing.

Other jobs in the jewelry business include *appraisers,* who examine jewelry and determine its value and quality; *sales staff,* who set up and care for jewelry displays, take inventory, and help customers; and *buyers,* who purchase jewelry, gems, and watches from wholesalers so they can resell the items to the public in retail stores. Buyers may take items with them or arrange to have them shipped to the retail establishment for which they work.

Requirements

A high school education usually is necessary for persons desiring to enter the jewelry trade. High school courses in chemistry, physics, mechanical drawing, and art are especially useful. Computer-aided design classes are helpful for those

planning to design jewelry. Sculpture and metalworking classes provide training in working with metals.

A large number and variety of educational and training programs are available for people interested in jewelry and jewelry repair. Trade schools and community colleges offer a variety of programs, including classes in basic jewelry-making skills, techniques, use and care of tools and machines, stone setting, casting, and polishing, and gem identification. Programs usually run from six to thirty-six months although individual classes are shorter and can be taken without enrolling in an entire program. Some colleges and universities offer programs in jewelry store management, metalwork, and jewelry design. Classes can also be taken at fashion institutes, art schools, and art museums. In addition, one can take correspondence courses and continuing education classes. For sales and managerial positions in a retail store, college experience is usually helpful. Recommended classes are sales techniques, gemology, advertising, accounting, business administration, and computers.

The work of the jeweler and jewelry repairer may also be learned through an apprenticeship or by informal on-the-job training. On-the-job training will often include instruction in design, quality of precious stones, and chemistry of metals. The apprentice becomes a jeweler upon the successful completion of a two-year apprenticeship. Also, the apprentice is usually required to pass written and oral tests covering the trade. The apprenticeship generally focuses on casting, stone setting, and engraving.

Most jobs in manufacturing require on-the-job training, although many employers prefer to hire individuals who have completed a technical education program.

Jewelers and jewelry repairers need to have extreme patience and skill to handle the expensive materials of the trade. Although the physically disabled may find employment in this field, superior eye-hand coordination is essential. Basic mechanical skills such as filing, sawing, and drilling are vital to the jewelry repairer. Jewelers who work from their own designs need to have creative and artistic ability, as well as good eyesight and finger dexterity. They also need to have a strong understanding of metals and their properties. Retail jewelers and those who operate or own trade shops and manufacturing establishments must possess the ability to deal with people and a knowledge of merchandising and business management and practices. Sales staff should be neat and friendly, and buyers must have good judgment, self-confidence, and leadership capabilities. Because of the expensive nature of jewelry, some of the people working in the retail industry need to be bondable, which generally means they pass the requirements for an insurance company to insure them.

Opportunities for Experience & Exploration

Students interested in becoming jewelers or jewelry repairers can engage in arts and crafts activities and take classes in crafts and jewelry making. Many community education programs are available through high schools, park districts, or local art stores and museums. Hobbies such as metalworking and sculpture also help one to become familiar with metals and many of the tools jewelers use. Students can also visit museums and fine jewelry stores to see collections of jewelry.

High school students interested in a career in the retail field may be able to find work in a retail jewelry store part time or during the summer. A job in sales, or even as a clerk can provide a firsthand introduction to the business. One will become familiar with a jewelry store's operations, its customers, and the jewelry sold. In addition, one will learn much of the terminology unique to the jewelry field. Working in a retail store with an in-house jeweler or jewelry repairer provides many opportunities to observe and speak with a professional engaged in this trade. If you live near a manufacturing factory you may be able to secure summer or part-time employment as a bench worker or assembly line worker. At a factory you may perform only a few of the operations involved in making custom jewelry, but you will be exposed to many of the skills used within a manufacturing plant.

You can also visit retail stores and shops where jewelry is made and repaired or visit a jewelry factory. Some boutiques and galleries are owned and operated by jewelers who enjoy the opportunity to talk to people about their trade as long as they are not busy with other tasks. It is also possible to go to art fairs and craft shows where jewelers exhibit and sell their products. In this more relaxed environment, jewelers are more likely to have the time to discuss their work.

Methods of Entering

While in high school, students could obtain a summer or part-time job in a jewelry store or the jewelry department of a department store to learn about the business. Another method of entering this line of work is to obtain employment in jewelry manufacturing establishments in major production centers. A trainee is thus able to acquire the many skills needed in the jewelry trade. The number of trainees accepted in this manner, however, is relatively small. Students who have completed a training program improve their chances of finding work as either an apprentice or trainee. They may find out about available jobs and apprenticeships through the placement offices of their training schools, local jewelers, or the personnel offices of manufacturing plants.

Persons desiring to establish their own retail business will find it helpful to first obtain employment with an established jeweler or a manufacturing plant. Considerable financial investment is required to open a retail jewelry store, and jewelers in such establishments find it to their advantage to be able to do repair work on watches as well as the usual jeweler's work. Less financial investment is needed to open a trade shop. These shops generally tend to be more successful in or near areas with large populations where they can take advantage of the large volume of jewelry business. Both of these establishments (retail stores and trade shops) are required to meet local and state business laws and regulations.

Advancement

There are many opportunities for advancement in the jewelry field. Jewelers and jewelry repairers can go into business for themselves once they have mastered the skills of their trade. They may create their own designer lines of jewelry that they market and sell, or they can open up a trade shop to make jewelry or a retail store. Many self-employed jewelers gain immense satisfaction from the opportunity to specialize in one aspect of jewelry or to experiment with new methods and materials and learn new aspects of jewelry making.

Workers in jewelry manufacturing have less opportunities for advancement than in other areas of jewelry because of the declining number of workers needed in this area. Plant workers in semiskilled and unskilled positions can advance based on the speed and quality of their work and by perseverance. Taking advantage of any on-the-job training can provide opportunities for higher-skilled positions. Workers in manufacturing who show proficiency in their skill can advance to supervisory and management positions, or they may leave manufacturing and go to work as a jeweler in a retail shop or trade shop.

The most usual avenue of advancement is from employee in a factory, shop, or store to owner or manager of a trade shop or retail store. Sales is an excellent starting place for people who want to own their own store someday. Sales staff receive firsthand training in customer relations as well as knowledge of the different aspects of jewelry store merchandising. Sales staff may become gem experts who are qualified to manage a store, and managers may expand their territory from one store to managing several stores in a district or region. Top management in retail offers many interesting and rewarding positions to people who are knowledgeable, responsible, and ambitious. Buyers may advance by dealing less with inexpensive items to exclusively buying fine gems that are more expensive, and some buyers become diamond merchants, buying diamonds on the international market.

Jewelry designers' success depends not only on the skill with which they make jewelry but also on the ability to come up with creative designs and to keep in touch with current trends in the consumer market. They need to closely watch how their lines of jewelry sell to see whether the public accepts their designs or they need to create new ones. Jewelry designers attend many craft shows, trade shows, and jewelry exhibitions to see what other people are making and to get ideas for new lines of jewelry.

Employment Outlook

There were 32,000 jewelers employed in the United States in 1996; one-third were self employed. The majority of the self-employed jewelers own their own stores or repair shops or specialize in designing and creating custom jewelry. Opportunities in this field are expected to deline through the year 2006. Non-traditional markets for jewelry such as catalogs and cable television shopping networks are attracting consumers. Traditional markets, such as jewelry stores, are selling less merchandise, thus limiting the need for repairmen. Job opportunities are positive for people who are skilled in personnel, management, sales and promotion, advertising, floor and window display, and buying. There are also many opportunities in appraisals, with some stores employing a person to do nothing but appraisals. In most cases, though, appraisals are done by store owners or jewelers who have been in the business a long time.

The future of the jewelry industry will depend to a large degree upon economic conditions. In recessionary times people have less money to spend on nonessential items such as jewelry. However, there are a large number of baby boomers entering their prime earning years, in addition to many households with two-income wage earners, and as long as economic conditions stay fairly good, they generally have the money and desire to purchase high-ticket items such as jewelry.

Jewelers and jewelry repairers will continue to be needed to replace those workers who leave the workforce or move to new positions within it. Although opportunities in manufacturing plants are declining, opportunities in retail and as self-employed jewelers should remain steady or slightly improve.

Earnings

According to the U.S. Department of Labor, in 1996, retail jewelers earned an average annual salary of around $31,000. Starting salaries for beginning retailers and those with only a few years of experience are much less. The average annual salary for retail jewelry repairers is around $25,000. Retail sales staff earn between $5.15 to $7.00 an hour, with some workers earning a commission on what they sell. Jewelers and other workers in manufacturing have average annual salaries of $14,500 to $32,000, with jewelers making significantly more than those in unskilled or semiskilled positions. Retail store owners and jewelry artists and designers can earn anywhere between $25,000 to $50,000 or more yearly, based on their volume of business.

Most employers offer benefit packages that include paid holidays and vacations, and health insurance. Retail stores may offer discounts on store purchases.

Conditions of Work

Jewelers can work in a variety of environments. Some self-employed jewelers design and create jewelry out of their homes, and others work in small studios or trade shops. Some use computer-aided designing software to create their sketches. Jewelers who create their own designer lines of jewelry may travel to retail stores and other sites to show and promote their merchandise. Many designers also attend trade shows and exhibitions to learn more about current trends. Some sell their jewelry at both indoor and outdoor art shows and craft fairs. These shows can be on weekends, evenings, or during the regular workweek and may require extensive travel. Many jewelry artists live and work near tourist areas or in artist communities.

Workers in jewelry manufacturing plants usually work in clean, air-conditioned, and relatively quiet environments. Workers in departments such as polishing, electroplating, and lacquer spraying may be exposed to the fumes from chemicals and solvents used. Workers may do bench work where they sit at a workstation or work on an assembly line where they may either be standing or sitting. Assembly line workers may operate machinery. Many times, workers in a manufacturing plant may only perform one or two types of operations so the work can become repetitious. Most employees in a manufacturing plant work thirty-five-hour workweeks, with an occasional need for overtime.

Retail store owners, managers, jewelers, and sales staff work a variety of hours and shifts that include weekends (especially during the Christmas season,which is the busiest time of year). Buyers may work more than forty hours a week because they make appointments to see wholesalers and must travel to see them.

Work settings vary from small shops and boutiques to large department stores. Most jewelry stores are clean, quiet, pleasant, and attractive. However, most jewelry store employees spend many hours on their feet dealing with customers, and buyers travel a great deal.

Sources of Additional Information

For career information and a listing of schools offering jewelry programs, please contact:

■ **Jewelers of America**
1185 6th Avenue, 30th Floor
New York, NY 10036
Tel: 800-223-0673

For career information, please contact:

■ **Jewelry Information Center**
19 West 44th Street
New York, NY 10036-5903
Tel: 212-398-2319

For career information, a listing of schools offering jewelry programs, and scholarship information, please contact:

■ **Manufacturing Jewelers and Silversmiths of America**
1 State Street, 6th Floor
Providence, RI 02908-5035
Tel: 800-444-MJSA

Laboratory Testing Technicians

Definition

Laboratory testing technicians usually assist materials science engineers in conducting tests on various substances and products. They perform a variety of laboratory duties such as measuring, testing, and preparing materials and are responsible for quality control. Laboratory testing technicians work in many industries, including medicine, metallurgy, manufacturing, geology, and meteorology, to name a few. Since laboratory testing technicians work in a variety of fields, students interested in this career should also refer to such job titles as *metallurgical technicians, pharmaceutical technicians,* and *medical technicians.*

Nature of the Work

There are many types of laboratory testing technicians, but in general, they all usually assist scientists in conducting tests on various substances and products. They are trained in the use of the specialized tools and instruments pertinent to their area. Some laboratory testing technicians, often called *quality control technicians,* conduct tests on products to determine whether they are safe and whether they correctly perform the tasks they are designed to do. Most of these technicians either work for testing laboratories that test products made by a wide variety of companies or work in the research and development branch of a specific production plant. These laboratory technicians might test toys for safety by looking for specific aspects such as small, removable parts, sharp edges, and overall durability. Or a technician might test electrical appliances such as toasters to make sure that they are wired correctly, do not smoke or make sparks, and meet all safety standards. In short, laboratory testing technicians in quality control are responsible for making sure a product or material will do exactly what it is supposed to do. Not only do these technicians test new products for safety and per-

School Subjects
Physics
Shop (Trade/Vo-tech education)

Personal Interests
Figuring out how things work
Science

Work Environment
Primarily indoors
Primarily one location

Minimum Education Level
Some postsecondary training

Salary Range
$17,500 to
$26,500 to
$37,900+

Certification or Licensing
Voluntary

Outlook
About as fast as the average

DOT
029

GOE
02.04.01

NOC
2211

formance, they also analyze failed products in order to determine the cause of the problem and remedy it.

Laboratory testing technicians who work with metals, ceramics, and chemicals assist engineers in testing these materials in order to process and convert them into usable forms. In recent years, these materials have increasingly overlapped and these technicians are now sometimes grouped under the name *materials technicians*. These laboratory testing technicians prepare specimens, set up equipment, run heating and cooling tests, and record test results. They may test to discover what happens to an alloy at certain temperatures or to find a new process for smelting iron. Not only do these technicians work with the test materials, they also work on and assess the equipment used to perform the tests. For example, a technician might run tests to determine the proper setting for a furnace that will heat the materials for a specific test. They might build and test a variety of these furnaces to determine which performs the test most effectively. Some of these technicians might supervise other workers as they perform tasks such as smelting to make sure that the equipment is being used in the right way and that it is functioning correctly. Technicians who specialize in testing ores and minerals (such as gold and iron) to determine value are known as *assayers*.

Laboratory testing technicians who work in the medical field are often called medical technicians or *clinical technicians*. These technicians work in hospitals, universities, doctors' offices, and research laboratories to set up equipment and perform tests on body fluids, tissues, and cells. Among other duties, they may perform blood counts, help identify parasites, and analyze bacteria. Medical technicians are also needed in the veterinary sciences and by pharmaceutical laboratories.

Some laboratory technicians in the field of geology test shale, sand, and other earth materials to determine petroleum and mineral content and other characteristics. These technicians often run tests on core samples during oil well drilling to determine the conditions of the earth in and surrounding the well.

Regardless of the specific nature of the tests conducted by testing technicians, they must keep detailed records of every step performed in working with the substance, as well as how the substance or product reacts to the test. Laboratory testing technicians often do a great deal of writing and must make charts, graphs, and other displays to illustrate their results. They may be called on to interpret test results, to draw overall conclusions, and to make recommendations to manufacturers. Occasionally, laboratory testing technicians are asked to appear as expert witnesses in court, often having to explain why a product failed and who might be at fault for the failure.

Requirements

A high school diploma is the minimum requirement for finding work as a laboratory testing technician. However, a two-year technical school degree in engineering technology, or in a more specific field such as medical technology or metallurgy, is highly recommended. While in high school, students should take at least two years of mathematics and develop their knowledge of the physical sciences, namely chemistry and physics. High school students interested in this field should take shop classes to become accustomed to working with tools and develop manual dexterity. Classes in English and writing will give prospective technicians good training for writing reports. Students who have specific interests such as geology or biology would do well to take subjects relevant to that branch.

Students who desire to become laboratory technicians should be detail oriented and enjoy figuring out how things work. They should like problem solving and trouble shooting. For example, students who enjoy such activities as disassembling and reassembling their own bicycles or installing and reinstalling their own car stereos would probably enjoy being laboratory testing technicians. Laboratory technicians must have the patience to repeat a test many times, perhaps even on the same material. They should be independent and motivated; often, once they receive their assignment, they will be left on their own until the tests are completed.

Opportunities for Experience & Exploration

Due to the precision and training required in the field, there is not much room for high school students to find actual jobs as laboratory testing technicians. However, it is possible to schedule tours of plants and laboratories that employ technicians to get a firsthand view of these workers on the job. Students can also contact local technical colleges to receive further information on the career. Some research companies and plants will hire students for internships and summer jobs in areas other than the laboratory (such as offices or mail rooms). While these jobs do not offer hands-on technical experience, they do allow students to experience the work environment of testing technicians.

Methods of Entering

Technical schools often help place graduating technicians with companies. Many laboratories contact these schools directly looking for student employees or interns. Students can also contact local manufacturing companies and laboratories to find out about job openings in their area. Often, jobs for laboratory technicians are listed in the classified section of the newspaper, and qualified technicians need only send a resume and cover letter and schedule an interview for the position.

Advancement

Skilled laboratory technicians may be promoted to manager or supervisor of a division in their company. For example, a quality-control technician who has become an expert in testing computer monitors may be put in charge of others who perform this task. This supervisor might assign project duties, organize how and when results will be recorded and analyzed, and help the other technicians solve problems they encounter when running the tests. Other technicians may open their own testing laboratories or return to school to become engineers, physicists, or geologists, depending upon their fields of interest.

Employment Outlook

Job opportunities for laboratory technicians are expected to grow as fast as the average through the year 2006. Environmental concerns and dwindling natural resources are causing many manufacturers to look for better ways to develop ores, minerals, and other substances from the earth. Laboratory technicians will be needed to test new production procedures as well as prototypes of new products. This growth will be especially high for metallurgical technicians.

Employment possibilities at testing laboratories will also grow, as many plants and companies rely on outside instead of in-house quality control. Also, as machinery grows increasingly complex, trained technicians will be needed not only to operate the equipment in tests, but to test and analyze the functioning of the equipment itself. The medical field, too, will need laboratory technicians who are well-versed in the latest medical and pharmaceutical technology and procedures.

Growth will be slower in industries focused on such materials as stone, clay, glass, fabricated metal products, and transportation equipment. However, laboratory testing technicians who remain flexible and up-to-date on new developments in the industry should have little trouble finding employment.

Earnings

According to the U.S. Department of Labor, beginning, full-time clinical laboratory testing technicians earned about $17,500 annually in 1996. Medium-range salaries for laboratory testing technicians range from about $21,000 to $26,500. The highest paid technicians earn about $37,900 or more per year. In a 1997 survey conducted by the Hay Group, hospital-employed technicians earned a yearly average of $26,500. Salaries increase as technicians gain experience and as they take on more responsibility, such as becoming a supervisor. Most companies that employ laboratory testing technicians offer medical benefits, sick leave, and vacation time, but these policies depend on the individual employer.

Conditions of Work

Laboratory testing technicians typically work a forty-hour week. During especially busy times, or if a test is not going well, they may be required to work overtime. Most technicians work in clean, well-lighted laboratories where attention is paid to neatness and organization. Some laboratory testing technicians have their own offices, while others work together in a large single laboratory, similar to a high school chemistry classroom in appearance. When tests are not going well, when new products are not working properly, or when equipment breaks down, stress levels in laboratories tend to rise. Laboratory testing technicians must remain level-headed and calm in these situations.

Depending on the field, some technicians will be required to leave the laboratory to collect samples or materials for testing. These locations can be hot, cold, wet, or muddy, and the work may be strenuous.

Sources of Additional Information

American Institute of Mining, Metallurgical, and Petroleum Engineers
345 East 47th Street, 14th Floor
New York, NY 10017
Tel: 212-705-7695

ASM International
Student Outreach Program
9639 Kinsman
Materials Park, OH 44073
Tel: 216-338-5151

Junior Engineering Technical Society (JETS)
1420 King Street, Suite 405
Alexandria, VA 22314-2794
Tel: 703-548-5387
Email: jets@nas.edu

Minerals, Metals, and Materials Society
420 Commonwealth Drive
Warrendale, PA 15086
Tel: 412-776-9000

Landscapers and Grounds Managers

Definition

Landscapers and grounds managers plan, design, and maintain gardens, parks, lawns, and other landscaped areas and supervise the care of the trees, plants, and shrubs that are part of these areas. Specific job responsibilities depend on the type of area involved. Landscapers and grounds managers direct projects at private homes, parks, schools, arboretums, office parks, shopping malls, government offices, and botanical gardens. They are responsible for purchasing material and supplies and for training, directing, and supervising employees. Grounds managers maintain the land after the landscapers' designs have been implemented. They may work alone or supervise a grounds staff. They may have their own business or be employed by a landscaping firm.

Nature of the Work

There are many different types of landscapers and grounds managers, and their specific job titles depend on the duties involved. One specialist in this field is the *landscape contractor,* who performs landscaping work on a contract basis for homeowners, highway departments, operators of industrial parks, and others. They confer with prospective clients and study the landscape design, drawings, and bills of material to determine the amount of landscape work required. They plan the installation of lighting or sprinkler systems, erection of fences, and the types of trees, shrubs, or ornamental plants required. They inspect the grounds and calculate labor, equipment, and materials costs. They also prepare and submit bids, draw up contracts, and direct and coordinate the activities of *landscape laborers* who mow lawns, plant shrubbery, dig holes, move topsoil, and perform other related tasks.

On golf courses, landscapers and grounds managers are employed as greenskeepers. There are two types of greenskeepers: *Greenskeepers I* supervise and coordinate the activities of

School Subjects
Biology
Chemistry

Personal Interests
The Environment
Plants/Gardening

Work Environment
Primarily outdoors
Primarily multiple locations

Minimum Education Level
High school diploma

Salary Range
$9,360 to
$15,600 to
$50,000+

Certification or Licensing
Required for certain positions

Outlook
About as fast as the average

DOT
408

GOE
03.01.03

NOC
2225

workers engaged in keeping the grounds and turf of a golf course in good playing condition. They consult with the greens superintendent to plan and review work projects; they determine work assignments, such as fertilizing, irrigating, seeding, mowing, raking, and spraying; and they mix and prepare spraying and dusting solutions. They may also repair and maintain mechanical equipment.

Greenskeepers II follow the instructions of greenskeepers I as they maintain the grounds of golf courses. They cut the turf on green and tee areas; dig and rake grounds to prepare and cultivate new greens; connect hose and sprinkler systems; plant trees and shrubs; and operate tractors as they apply fertilizer, insecticide, and other substances to the fairways or other designated areas.

Greens superintendents supervise and coordinate the activities of greenskeepers and other workers engaged in constructing and maintaining golf course areas. They review test results of soil and turf samples, and they direct the application of fertilizer, lime, insecticide, or fungicide. Their other duties include monitoring the course grounds to determine the need for irrigation or better care, keeping and reviewing maintenance records, and interviewing and hiring workers.

Industrial-commercial grounds managers maintain areas in and around industrial or commercial properties by cutting lawns, pruning trees, raking leaves, and shoveling snow. They also plant grass and flowers and are responsible for the upkeep of flower beds and public passageways. These types of groundskeepers may repair and maintain fences and gates and also operate sprinkler systems and other equipment.

Parks-and-grounds grounds managers maintain city, state, or national parks and playgrounds. They plant and prune trees; haul away garbage; repair driveways, walks, swings, and other equipment; and clean comfort stations.

Landscape supervisors supervise and direct the activities of landscape workers who are engaged in pruning trees and shrubs, caring for lawns, and performing related tasks. They coordinate work schedules, prepare job cost estimates, and deal with customer questions and concerns.

Landscapers maintain the grounds of private or business establishments. They care for hedges, gardens, and other landscaped areas. They mow and trim lawns, plant trees and shrubs, apply fertilizers and other chemicals, and repair walks and driveways.

Many arboriculture technicians work as landscapers or grounds managers. Below is a listing of some careers in this area.

Tree surgeons prune and treat ornamental and shade trees to improve their health and appearance. This may involve climbing with ropes, working in buckets high off the ground, spraying fertilizers and pesticides, or injecting chemicals into the tree trunk or root zone in the ground. *Tree-trimming supervisors* coordinate and direct the activities of workers engaged in cutting away tree limbs or removing trees that interfere with electric power lines. They inspect power lines and direct the placement of removal equipment. Tree-trimming supervisors answer consumer questions when trees are located on private property.

Pest management scouts survey landscapes and nurseries regularly to locate potential pest problems including insects, diseases, and weeds before they become hard to control in an effective, safe manner. Scouts may specialize in the treatment of a particular type of infestation, such as gypsy moths or boll weevils.

Lawn-service workers plant and maintain lawns. They remove leaves and dead grass and apply insecticides, fertilizers, and weed killers as necessary. Lawn-service workers also use aerators and other tools to pierce the soil to make holes for the fertilizer and dethatchers to remove built-up thatch.

Related jobs include the *horticulturist* who conducts experiments and investigations into the problems of breeding, production, storage, processing, and transit of fruits, nuts, berries, flowers, and trees. Horticulturists also develop new plant varieties and determine methods of planting, spraying, cultivating, and harvesting. A *city forester* advises communities on the selection, planting schedules, and proper care of trees. They also plant, feed, spray, and prune trees and may supervise other workers in these activities. Depending on the situation, landscapers and groundskeepers may perform these functions alone or with city foresters. *Turfgrass consultants* analyze turfgrass problems and recommend solutions. They also determine growing techniques, mowing schedules, and the best type of turfgrass to use for specified areas. Depending on the geographic area of the country, lawn-service companies regularly use such consultants.

Requirements

In general, a high school diploma is necessary for most positions, and at least some college training is needed for those with supervisory or specialized responsibilities. Aspiring landscapers and grounds managers should have "green thumbs," and an interest in preserving and maintaining natural areas. They should also be reasonably physically fit, have an aptitude for working with machines, and display good manual dexterity.

High school students interested in this career should take classes in English, mathematics, chemistry, biology, and as many courses as possible in horticulture and botany. Those interested in college training should enroll in a two or four-year program in horticulture, landscape management, or agronomy. Classes might include landscape maintenance and design, turf grass management, botany, and plant pathology. Course work should be selected with an area of specialization in mind. Those wishing to have managerial responsibilities should take courses in personnel management, communications, and business-related courses such as accounting and economics.

Many trade and vocational schools offer landscaping, horticulture, and related programs. Several extension programs are also available that allow students to take courses at home.

Licensing and certification differ by state and vary according to specific job responsibilities. For example, in most states landscapers and grounds managers need a certificate to spray insecticides or other chemicals. Contractors and other self-employed people may also need a license to operate their business.

All managerial personnel must carefully supervise their workers to ensure that they adhere to environmental regulations as specified by the EPA and other local and national governmental agencies.

Opportunities for Experience & Exploration

Part-time work at a golf course, lawn-service company, greenhouse, botanical garden, or other similar enterprise is an excellent way of learning about this field. Many companies gladly hire part-time help, especially during the busy summer months. In addition, there are numerous opportunities mowing lawns, growing flowers, and tending gardens. Interested students can also join garden clubs, visit local flower shops, and attend botanical shows.

The American Association of Botanical Gardens and Arboreta (AABGA) has a very strong internship program and offers a directory of internships in over one hundred public gardens throughout the United States. AABGA is a valuable resource to those individuals interested in gaining practical experience. Finally, a summer job mowing lawns and caring for a neighbor's garden is an easy, simple introduction to the field.

Methods of Entering

Summer or part-time jobs often lead to full-time employment with the same employer. Those who enroll in a college, university, or other training program can receive help in finding work from the school's job placement office. In addition, directly applying to botanical gardens, nurseries, or golf courses is common practice. Jobs may also be listed in newspaper help wanted ads.

Most landscaping and related companies provide on-the-job training for entry-level personnel.

Advancement

In general, landscapers and grounds managers can expect to advance as they gain experience and additional educational training. For example, a greenskeeper with a high school diploma usually must have at least some college training to become a greens superintendent. It is also possible to go into a related field, such as selling equipment used in maintaining lawns, parks, and other natural areas.

Those in managerial positions may wish to advance to a larger establishment or go into consulting work. In some instances, skilled landscapers and grounds managers may start their own consulting or contracting businesses.

Employment Outlook

Employment in this field is expected to grow about as fast as the average due to the greater use of landscaping in and around buildings, shopping malls, homes, highways, recreational facilities, and other structures. Jobs should be available with governmental agencies as well as in the private sector.

Earnings

Salaries depend on the experience and education level of the worker, the type of work being done, and geographic location. According to the *1998-99 Occupational Outlook Handbook*, landscapers and groundskeepers earned a median salary of $15,600 in 1996. Workers just starting out in the field earned as little as $9,360 per year, while those with the most experience earned as much as $29,120 a year. Landscape contractors and others who run their own businesses earn between $23,000 and $50,000 per year, with those with a greater ability to locate customers earning even more.

Conditions of Work

Landscapers and grounds managers spend much of their time outside. Those with administrative or managerial responsibilities spend at least a portion of their workday in an office. Most of the outdoor work is done during daylight but work takes place all year round in all types of weather conditions. Most people in the field work thirty-seven to forty hours a week, but overtime is especially likely during the summer months when landscapers and grounds managers take advantage of the longer days and warmer weather. Work weeks may be shorter during the winter. Weekend work is highly likely. Fringe benefits vary from employer to employer but generally include medical insurance and some paid vacation.

Much of the work can be physically demanding and most of it is performed outdoors in one extreme or another. Workers shovel dirt, trim bushes and trees, constantly bend down to plant flowers and shrubbery, and may have to climb ladders or the tree itself to prune branches or diagnose a problem. There is some risk of injury using planting and pruning machinery and some risk of illness from handling and breathing pesticides, but proper precautions should limit any job-related hazards. Managerial personnel should be willing to work overtime updating financial records and making sure the business accounts are in order.

Sources of Additional Information

American Association of Botanical Gardens and Arboreta
351 Longwood Road
Kennett Square, PA 19348
Tel: 610-925-2500
WWW: http://www.cissus.mobot.org/AABGA

For information on career opportunities and educational training, contact:

American Society for Horticultural Sciences
600 Cameron Street
Alexandria, VA 22314-2562
Tel: 703-836-4606
Email: ashs@ashs.org

Associated Landscape Contractors of America
12200 Sunrise Valley Drive, Suite 150
Reston, VA 22091
Tel: 703-620-6363

National Landscape Association
1250 I Street, NW, Suite 500
Washington, DC 20005
Tel: 202-789-2900

Professional Grounds Management Society
120 Cockeysville Road, Suite 104
Hunt Valley, MD 21031
Tel: 410-584-9754

Laser Technicians

Definition

Laser technicians produce, install, operate, service, and test laser systems and fiber optics equipment in industrial, medical, or research settings. They work under the direction of engineers or physicists who conduct laboratory activities in laser research and development or design. Depending upon the type of laser system—gas or solid state—a technician generally works either with information systems or with robotics, manufacturing, or medical equipment.

Nature of the Work

There are basically two types of laser systems with which laser technicians work. Those who work with semiconductor laser systems, which are the most compact and reliable, work mainly with computer and telephone systems. In addition to helping test, install, and maintain these systems, technicians work with engineers in their design and improvement.

Technicians who work with gas-type laser systems, which are larger and more expensive, usually assist scientists, engineers, or doctors. These systems are used primarily in the fields of robotics, manufacturing, and medical equipment.

Not all laser technicians are responsible for the same types of tasks. Much depends upon their positions and places of employment. For example, some repair lasers and instruct different companies on their use, while others work as technicians for very specific applications, such as optical surgery or welding parts in a manufacturing process. In general, most technicians are employed in one of five areas: materials processing, communications, military, medical, and research.

In any one of these areas, technicians may be involved in the process of building laser devices. To build a solid-state laser, they may construct, cut, and polish a crystal rod to be used in the laser. They put a flash tube around the crystal and place the

School Subjects
Mathematics
Physics

Personal Interests
Building things
Computers

Work Environment
Primarily indoors
Primarily one location

Minimum Education Level
Associate's degree

Salary Range
$21,000 to
$30,000 to
$38,000+

Certification or Licensing
None

Outlook
Faster than the average

DOT
019

GOE
05.01.01

NOC
2241

unit in a container with a mirror at each end. Using precision instruments, they position the mirrors so that all emitted or reflected light passes through the crystal. Finally, they put the laser body in a chassis, install tubing and wiring to the controls, and place a jacket round the assembly.

In addition, there are other duties that all technicians perform, no matter what application they work in. Taking measurements, cleaning, aligning, inspecting, and operating lasers, and collecting data are standard duties in almost all areas. Since the field of lasers is very technologically advanced, computers are used in many tasks and applications. Technicians may be responsible for programming the computers that control the lasers, inputting data, or outputting computer generated reports.

Lasers are used in the area of materials processing for machining, production, measurement, construction, excavation, and photo-optics. Technicians in this area often read and interpret diagrams, schematics, and shop drawings in order to assemble components themselves or oversee the assembly process. They may operate lasers for welding, precision drilling, cutting, and grinding of metal parts or for trimming and slicing electronic components and circuit elements. They may use lasers to measure parts to verify that they are the precise size needed. Finally, technicians may be involved in part marking—using a laser to mark an identifying number or letter on each component manufactured. If working in construction, they may use a laser as a surveying guideline or an aligning tool because of its ability to travel in a straight, or coherent, beam.

Laser technicians in communications use lasers to generate light impulses transmitted through optical fibers. They work to develop, manufacture, and test optical equipment, and they may design, set up, monitor, and maintain fiber fabrication facilities. This field also uses lasers for data storage and retrieval.

In military and space projects, lasers are frequently used for target-finding, tracking, ranging, identification, and communications. Technicians repair and adapt low-power lasers, which are widely used for these applications.

Technicians who work in the medical field serve as technical equipment experts and assist the physicians and surgeons who use the laser system. They advise the surgeons on which type of laser to use and which method of delivery to use, such as through a microscope, fiber optic tube, or contact tip that transfers the energy to tissue in the form of heat. They must be on hand during laser surgical procedures to offer recommendations, fine-tune attachments and machines, and troubleshoot should a technical problem occur. In addition, technicians help set up the reflection devices that are used to aim the laser beam into hard-to-reach spots.

There are many areas of research and development in laser technology. For example, lasers are being studied as a source to produce the multimillion degree temperatures needed to cause elements to develop controlled nuclear fusion. These studies are part of the continuing research to produce inexpensive electrical power for the nation's energy needs. Technicians on a research and development team use lasers and electronic devices to perform tests, take measurements, gather data, and make calculations. They may use the data to prepare reports for engineers, doctors, scientists, production managers, or lab workers.

Requirements

Most laser technicians enter the field by attending a two-year program in laser technology at a vocational, technical, or community college. The prospective technician can begin to prepare for the career while still in high school by taking certain classes. Important courses include four years of English and at least two years of mathematics, one of which should be algebra. At least one year of physical science, preferably physics, should be included, as should a class in basic computer programming. Machine shop, basic electronics, and blueprint reading classes are also useful.

The average course of study leading to an associate's degree in laser technology includes intensive technical and scientific study, with more hours spent in a laboratory or work situation than in the actual classroom. This hands-on experience is supplemented in the first year by courses in mathematics, physics, drafting, diagramming and sketching, basic electronics, electronic instrumentation and calibration, introduction to solid-state devices, electromechanical controls, computer programming, and English composition.

A second year's study might include courses in geometrical optics, digital circuits, microwaves, laser and electro-optic components, devices and measurements, vacuum techniques, technical report writing, microcomputers, and computer hardware. Special laser projects are often a part of the second year and can help students decide upon the specific field in which they want to work.

Even after completing their education, technicians typically require further training in the specific practices of their employers. This training is usually paid for by employers to help employees adapt their general knowledge to their specific positions.

There are several personal characteristics that are needed to ensure success as a laser technician. A reasonable degree of intelligence and a strong motivation to learn are important. An interest in instruments, laboratory apparatus, and how devices and systems work is also highly appropriate. Written and spoken communications are very important in the majority of positions for laser technicians, since they often have to work closely with many people of varied technological backgrounds.

Physical strength is not usually required for laser technicians, but good manual dexterity and hand-eye and body coordination are quite important. Because lasers can be extremely dangerous, it is necessary that technicians be careful and attentive and willing to follow safety precautions closely. The ability to work efficiently, patiently, and consistently is extremely important for laser technicians, as is a strong ability to solve problems and to do careful, detailed work.

Opportunities for Experience & Exploration

For high school students and others interested in a career as a laser technician, the high school vocational guidance counselor is a valuable resource person. If a community or technical college is nearby, its occupational information center and counseling staff can also be very helpful. In addition, there are several periodicals that are devoted to the field of lasers. Periodicals such as the *Journal of Laser Applications, Laser Bulletin,* and *Laser Focus World* may offer valuable insight into the field.

Lasers are used in so many places that it should be fairly easy to find a local laser technician, operator, or engineer in the community who can share knowledge about his or her job. It might be possible to find summer or part-time work in construction, manufacturing, or mining where lasers are used in measuring, cutting and welding, and surveying. This type of work can provide the interested student with exposure to jobs in laser technology.

Methods of Entering

Colleges that offer associate's degrees in laser technology usually work closely with industry, providing their graduating students with placement services and lists of potential employers. Most laser technicians graduating from a two-year program, in fact, are interviewed and recruited while still in school by representatives of companies who need laser technicians. If hired, they begin working soon after graduation.

Another way to enter the career is to join a branch of the U.S. armed forces under a technical training program for laser technicians. Military laser training is not always compatible to civilian training, however, and further study of theory and applications is needed to enter the field as a civilian.

Advancement

Opportunities for advancement in laser technology are excellent for technicians who keep abreast of advances in the field. In a relatively new technology such as that of the laser, new developments occur very rapidly; those workers who investigate and adapt to these changes become more valuable to their employers and advance to greater responsibilities.

Many employers designate various levels of employment for laser technicians, according to experience, education, and job performance. By being promoted through these levels, technicians can advance to supervisory or managerial positions. Supervisors manage a department, supervise other technicians, and conduct training of new or current employees.

Mature, experienced, and highly successful laser technicians may decide to become consultants or specialists for individual firms. A consulting position entails working closely with clients, conducting studies and surveys, and proposing improvements, changes, and solutions to problems.

Some technicians move into positions in sales or technical writing. Others become instructors in vocational programs, teaching intermediate or advanced laser and fiber optics technology courses.

Employment Outlook

Employment opportunities for laser technicians are expected to be very good through the year 2006. Rapid changes in technology and continued growth in the industry will almost certainly lead to an increase in the number of technicians employed.

One of the fastest growing areas for laser technicians is the area of fiber optic systems used in communications. Optical fiber is replacing wire cables in communication lines and in many electronic products. This trend is expected to continue, so the demand for technicians in the fiber optics field should be especially strong. Growth is also expected to be strong in production, defense, medicine, construction, and entertainment.

Technicians interested in the area of research and development, however, should keep in mind that growth in opportunities for jobs such as these often slows in the face of economic downturns.

Earnings

According to a survey done by the Laser Institute of America, the overall average starting salary for laser technicians is between $21,000 and $25,000 per year. Salaries for technicians with at least five years of experience average approximately $30,000 per year, depending on background, experience, and the industry where they are employed. Those in advanced supervisory positions, advanced sales and service, or in private consulting work earn between $35,000 and $38,000 a year or more.

In addition to salary, technicians usually receive benefits such as insurance, paid holidays and vacations, and retirement plans. Many employers have liberal policies of paying for professional improvement through continued study in school or at work.

Conditions of Work

Working conditions for laser technicians vary. They may spend their workday in a wide variety of environments, including laboratories, hospital operating rooms, offices, or manufacturing plants. In most cases, however, work areas are kept clean and temperature-controlled in order to protect the laser equipment.

Laser technicians may work at relatively stationary jobs, assembling or operating lasers in the same environment every day, or they may be required to move around frequently, in and out of laboratory areas, production sites, or offices. Some are office- or laboratory-based; others, especially those in sales and service positions, may travel the country.

Laser technicians typically work regular hours. Five eight-hour days per week is the standard, although certain projects may occasionally require overtime.

There are possible dangers present in most areas where lasers are used. Because the power sup-plies for many lasers involve high voltages, the technician frequently works around potentially deadly amounts of electricity. The laser beam itself is also a possible source of serious injury to users and bystanders, either through direct exposure to the beam or by reflected light from the laser. Close adherence to safety precautions, such as wearing protective glasses, reduces the danger of injury, however.

In addition to the pressure of working in potentially dangerous conditions, there is the stress of handling extremely valuable instruments. The parts used to make lasers are almost always costly. Mistakes that damage lasers or errors in applying lasers can be very costly, running into the thousands of dollars.

The laser technician often works as part of a production team or supervisory group, sometimes with scientists and engineers, sometimes as a member of a production team or supervisory group. Some technicians work alone but usually report directly to an engineer, scientist, or manager.

Among the greatest sources of satisfaction that laser technicians experience is the feeling of success whenever they meet a challenge and see their laser systems perform correctly. This is especially true in sales and service where new users are taught to use this complicated technology and where the technician can actually see customers discovering the effectiveness of lasers. The same satisfaction is felt in research when a new development is proved to be a success.

Sources of Additional Information

For information on becoming a laser technician, contact:

■ **Institute of Electrical and Electronics Engineers/LEOS**
445 Hoes Lane
Piscataway, NJ 08854
Tel: 908-562-3892

For information on colleges and universities that offer programs in laser technology and optics education, as well as general career information, contact:

■ **Laser Institute of America**
12424 Research Parkway, Suite 125
Orlando, FL 32826
Tel: 407-380-1553
Email: lia@laserinstitute.org
WWW: http://www.creol.ucf.edu/~lia/

Library Technicians

Definition

Library technicians, sometimes called library technical assistants, work in all areas of library services, supporting professional librarians or, in some situations, working on their own to help people access information. They order and catalog books; help library patrons locate books, periodicals, and reference materials; and make the library's various services and facilities available to its patrons.

Technicians verify bibliographic information on order requests before ordering books and perform routine cataloging of books received. They locate materials using the on-line computer catalog, the card catalog, the Library of Congress catalog, or the library's interlibrary loan system. They answer routine questions about library services and refer questions requiring professional help to librarians.

Library technicians also help with desk operations in the circulation department of the library and oversee the work of stack workers and catalog-card typists. They also often circulate audiovisual equipment and materials and inspect the materials when they are returned.

Nature of the Work

Work in libraries falls into three general categories: technical services, user services, and administrative services. Library technicians may be involved with the responsibilities of any of these areas.

In technical services, library technicians are involved with acquiring resources and then organizing them so the material can be accessed easily. They process order requests, verify bibliographic information, and prepare order forms for new materials, such as books, magazines, journals, videos, and CD-ROMs. They perform routine cataloging of new materials and record information about the new materials in computer files or on cards to be stored in catalog drawers. The *acquisitions technicians, classifiers*, and *catalogers* who perform these

School Subjects
Education
English
(writing/literature)

Personal Interests
Helping people: personal service
Reading/Books

Work Environment
Primarily indoors
Primarily one location

Minimum Education Level
Associate's degree

Salary Range
$15,000 to
$24,100 to
$45,000+

Certification or Licensing
Voluntary

Outlook
Faster than the average

DOT
100

GOE
11.02.04

NOC
5211

functions make information available for the library users. Technicians also arrange for one library to borrow materials from another library or for a library to temporarily display a special collection. They might make basic repairs to damaged books and collect late fines for overdue books. *Media technicians* operate audiovisual equipment for library media programs and keep the equipment in working order. They often prepare graphic artwork and television programs.

Working with librarians in user services, technicians work directly with library patrons and help them to access the information they need. They direct library patrons to the computer or card catalog in response to inquiries and assist with identifying the library's holdings. They describe the general arrangement of the library for new patrons and answer basic questions about the library's collections. They may also help patrons use microfiche and microfilm equipment. They may help them locate materials in an interlibrary system's computerized listing of holdings. *Reference library technicians* specialize in locating and researching information. *Children's library technicians* and *young-adult library technicians* specialize in getting children and young adults interested in books, reading, and learning by sponsoring summer reading programs, reading hours, and other fun activities.

Technicians who work in administrative services help with the management of the library. They might help prepare budgets, coordinate the efforts of different departments within the library, write policy and procedures, and work to develop the library's collection. If they have more responsibility they might supervise and coordinate staff members, recruit and supervise volunteers, organize fund-raising efforts, sit on community boards, and develop programs to promote and encourage reading and learning.

The particular responsibilities of a library technician vary according to the type of library: *academic library technicians* work in university or college libraries, assisting professors and students in their research needs. Their work would revolve around handling reference materials and specialized journals.

School library technicians work with *school library media specialists,* assisting teachers and students in utilizing the print and nonprint resources of a school library media center.

Library technicians also work in special libraries maintained by government agencies, corporations, law firms, advertising agencies, museums, professional associations, medical centers, religious organizations, and research laboratories. Library technicians in special libraries deal with information tailored to the specific needs and interests of the particular organization. They may also organize bibliographies, prepare abstracts and indexes of current periodicals, or research and analyze information on particular issues.

Library technicians develop and index computerized databases to organize information collected in the library. They also help library patrons use computers to access the information stored in their own databases or in remote databases. With the increasing use of automated information systems, many libraries hire *automated system technicians* to help plan and operate computer systems and *information technicians* to help design and develop information storage retrieval systems and procedures for collecting, organizing, interpreting, and classifying information.

In the past, library technicians functioned solely as the librarian's support staff, but this situation has evolved over the years. Library technicians continue to refer questions or problems requiring professional experience and judgment to librarians. However, with the increasing use of computer systems in libraries, library technicians now perform many of the technical and user service responsibilities once performed by librarians, thereby freeing librarians to focus more on acquisitions and administrative responsibilities. In some cases a library technician may handle the same responsibilities as a librarian, sometimes in place of a librarian.

Requirements

The technical nature of the work performed by library technicians, especially when working in technical services, is prompting more and more libraries to hire only high school graduates who have gone on to complete a two-year program in library technology. Certification for library technicians is voluntary at this point. The typical program leads to an associate of arts degree and includes courses in the basic purpose and functions of libraries; technical courses in processing materials, cataloging acquisitions, library services, and use of the Internet; and one year of liberal arts studies. Persons entering such programs should understand that the library-related courses they take will not apply toward a professional degree in library science.

Some smaller libraries, especially in rural communities, may hire persons with a high-school education for library technician positions. Some libraries may hire individuals who have prior work experience, and some may provide their own training for inexperienced individuals. On the other hand, some libraries may only hire library technicians who have earned bachelor's degrees.

High school students considering a career as a library technician should take courses in English, history, literature, foreign languages, computers, and mathematics. Strong verbal and writing skills are especially important. Any special knowledge of a particular subject matter can also be beneficial.

After employment, technicians may be encouraged to take more courses and to obtain training in special areas. It is also important for a technician to stay updated on new technical advances in library functions and computers.

Whatever their educational or training background, library technicians should demonstrate aptitude for careful, detailed, analytical work. They should enjoy problem solving and working with the public as well as with books. Good interpersonal skills are invaluable. A library technician should possess patience and flexibility and should not mind being interrupted frequently to answer questions from library patrons.

Opportunities for Experience & Exploration

Personal experience as a library patron would probably be the first and best way for a person to see if a library career would be of interest. Time spent browsing for books, searching in electronic encyclopedias for a school research project, or using a library's Internet connection to access all kinds of information would give a person a good idea of the general atmosphere of a library as well as of the types of services that a library provides for its patrons.

Persons interested in careers as library technicians should talk with their school and community librarians and library technicians. A visit to a large or specialized library would also be helpful in providing a view of the different kinds of libraries that exist.

There may also be opportunities to work as a library volunteer at a public library or school library media center. Some high schools have library clubs as a part of their extracurricular activities.

Methods of Entering

Since specific training requirements may vary from library to library, individuals interested in careers as library technicians should be familiar with the requirements of the libraries in which they hope to work. In some small libraries, for instance, a high school diploma may be sufficient, and a technician might not need a two-year associate's degree. However, since most libraries are requiring their library technicians to be graduates of two-year associate degree programs, most job applicants should have earned or be close to earning this degree.

In most cases, graduates of training programs for library technicians may seek employment through the placement offices of their community colleges. Job applicants may also approach libraries directly, usually by contacting the head librarian. Civil service examination notices, for those interested in government service, are usually posted in community colleges as well as in government buildings.

Many state library agencies maintain job hotlines listing openings for prospective library technicians. State departments of education also may keep lists of openings available for library technicians. Applicants interested in working in a school library media center should remember that most openings occur at the end of the school year and are filled for the following year.

Advancement

The trend toward requiring more formal training for library technicians suggests that advancement opportunities will be limited for those lacking such training. In smaller libraries and less-populated areas, the shortage of trained personnel may lessen this limitation. Nonetheless, those with adequate or above-average training will perform the more interesting tasks.

Generally, library technicians advance by taking on greater levels of responsibility. A new technician, for instance, may check materials in and out at the library's circulation desk and then move on to storing and verifying information. Experienced technicians in supervisory roles might be responsible for budgets and personnel or the operation of an entire department. Library technicians will find that experience, along with continuing education courses, will enhance their chances for advancement.

Library technicians might also advance by pursuing a master's degree in library and information science and becoming a librarian. With experience, additional courses, or an advanced degree, technicians can also advance to higher paying positions outside of the library setting.

Employment Outlook

In 1996, an estimated seventy-eight thousand library technicians worked in libraries of every kind in the United States. The profession of library technician is expected to grow faster than the average growth rate for all occupations through the year 2006.

At the present time, there is a greater demand for library technicians than for librarians. Since the government is decreasing funding for public and school libraries, budgets will have to be cut. Libraries might decide to hire two library technicians instead of one librarian, especially since library technicians now handle tasks once handled exclusively by librarians. The continued growth of special libraries in medical, business, and law organizations will lead to growing opportunities for technicians who develop specialized skills.

Earnings

Salaries for library technicians vary according to the type of library, geographic location, and specific job responsibilities. A survey by *Library Mosaics Magazine* reports that in 1996, library technicians employed by two-year colleges averaged $27,200; technicians employed by four year colleges or universities earned $30,200. The same survey reported median salaries of $24,100 for technicians in special libraries, while salaries for technicians in public libraries averaged $33,000. Salaries for library technicians in the federal government averaged approximately $26,500 a year in 1997.

Conditions of Work

Libraries usually have clean, well lit, pleasant work atmospheres. Hours are regular in company libraries and in school library media centers, but academic, public, and some specialized libraries are open longer hours and may require evening and weekend work, usually on a rotating basis.

Some tasks performed by library technicians, like calculating circulation statistics, can be repetitive. Technicians working in technical services may develop headaches and eyestrain from working long hours in front of a computer screen. Heavy public contact in user services may test a technician's tact and patience. However, a library's atmosphere is generally relaxed, and interesting. The size and type of library will often determine the duties of library technicians. A technician working in a small branch library might handle a wide range of responsibilities. Sometimes a technician working in a school, rural, or special library might be the senior staff member, with full responsibility for all technical, user, and administrative services and staff supervision. A technician working in a large uni-

versity or public library might focus on only one task all of the time.

Libraries are presently responding to decreased government funding by cutting budgets and cutting back on staff, often leaving an overwhelming workload for the remaining staff members. Since library technicians earn less money than librarians, libraries are replacing librarians with technicians. This situation can lead to resentment in the working relationship between these colleagues. In addition, there is also an ongoing struggle to define the different responsibilities of the librarian and technician. Despite the difference in the educational requirements for the two jobs—librarians require a master's degree and technician's a two-year associate's degree—some of the responsibilities do overlap. Library technicians may find it frustrating that, in some cases, they are performing the same tasks as librarians and yet do not command as high a salary.

Sources of Additional Information

■■American Library Association
Office for Library Personnel Resources
50 East Huron Street
Chicago, IL 60611
Tel: 800-545-2433
Email: ala@ala.org
WWW: http://www.ala.org/index.html

■■American Society for Information Science
8720 Georgia Avenue, Suite 501
Silver Spring, MD 20910
Tel: 301-495-0900
Email: asis@asis.org
WWW: http://www.asis.org/

For information on education programs, please contact:

■■Association for Library and Information Science Education
4101 Lake Boone Trail, Suite 201
Raleigh, NC 27607

To request information on education programs and scholarships, please contact:

■■Canadian Library Association
200 Elgin Street, Suite 602
Ottawa, ON K2P 1L5 Canada
Tel: 613-232-9625
WWW: http://www.cla.amlibs.ca/

Life Insurance Agents and Brokers

Definition

Life insurance agents sell policies that provide life insurance, retirement income, and various other types of insurance to new clients or to established policyholders. Some agents are referred to as *life underwriters,* since they may be required to estimate insurance risks on some policies.

Nature of the Work

Life insurance agents act as field sales representatives for the companies to which they are under contract. They may be under direct contract or work through a general agent who holds a contract. *Insurance brokers* represent the insurance buyer and do not sell for a particular company but place insurance policies for their clients with the company that offers the best rate and coverage. In addition, some brokers obtain several types of insurance (automobile, household, medical, and so on) to provide a more complete service package for their clients.

The agent's work may be divided into five functions: identifying and soliciting prospects, explaining services, developing insurance plans, closing the transaction, and following up.

The life insurance agent must use personal initiative to identify and solicit sales prospects. Few agents can survive in the life insurance field by relying solely on contacts made through regular business and social channels. They must make active client solicitation a part of their regular job. One company, for example, asks that each agent make between twenty and thirty personal contacts with prospective customers each week, through which eight to twelve interviews may be obtained, resulting in from zero to three sales. As in many sales occupations, many days or weeks may pass without any sales, then several sales in a row may suddenly develop.

Some agents obtain leads for sales prospects by following newspaper reports to learn of newcomers to the community, births, graduations, and business promotions. Other agents

School Subjects
Business
Economics

Personal Interests
Computers
Helping people: personal service

Work Environment
Primarily indoors
One location with some travel

Minimum Education Level
Some postsecondary training

Salary Range
$20,000 to
$49,000 to
$76,000+

Certification or Licensing
Required

Outlook
More slowly than the average

DOT
250

GOE
08.01.02

NOC
6231

specialize in occupational groups, selling to physicians, farmers, or small businesses. Many agents use general telephone or mail solicitations to help identify prospects. All agents hope that satisfied customers will suggest future sales to their friends and neighbors.

Successful contact with prospective clients may be a difficult process. Many potential customers already may have been solicited by a number of life insurance agents or may not be interested in buying life insurance at a particular time. Agents are often hard-pressed to obtain their initial goal—a personal interview to sit down and talk about insurance with the potential customer.

Once they have lined up a sales interview, agents usually travel to the customer's home or place of business. During this meeting, agents explain their services. Like any other successful sales pitch, this explanation must be adapted to the needs of the client. A new father, for example, may wish to ensure his child's college education, while an older person may be most interested in provisions dealing with retirement income. With experience, agents learn how best to answer questions or objections raised by potential customers. The agents must be able to describe the coverage offered by their company in clear, nontechnical language.

With the approval of the prospective client, the agent develops an insurance plan. In some cases, this will involve only a single standard life insurance policy. In other instances, the agent will review the client's complete financial status and develop a comprehensive plan for death benefits, payment of the balance due on a home mortgage if the insured dies, creation of a fund for college education for children, and retirement income. Such plans usually take into account several factors: the customer's personal savings and investments, mortgage and other obligations, Social Security benefits, and existing insurance coverage.

To best satisfy the customer's insurance needs, and in keeping with the customer's ability to pay, the agent may present a variety of insurance alternatives. The agent may, for example, recommend term insurance (the cheapest form of insurance since it may only be used as a death benefit) or ordinary life (which may be maintained by premium payments throughout the insured's life but may be converted to aid in retirement living). In some cases, the agent may suggest a limited payment plan, such as twenty-payment life, which allows the insured to pay the policy off completely in a given number of annual premiums. Agents can develop comprehensive life insurance plans to protect a business enterprise (such as protection from the loss resulting from the death of a key partner),

employee group insurance plans, or the creation and distribution of wealth through estates. The agent's skill and the variety of plans offered by the company are combined to develop the best possible insurance proposal for customers.

Closing the transaction is probably the most difficult part of the insurance process. At this point, the customer must decide whether to purchase the recommended insurance plan, ask for a modified version, or conclude that additional insurance is not needed or affordable.

After a customer decides to purchase a policy, the agent must arrange for him or her to take a physical examination; insurance company policies require that standard rates apply only to those people in good health. The agent also must obtain a completed insurance application and the first premium payment and send them with other supporting documents to the company for its approval and formal issuance of the policy.

The final phase of the insurance process is follow-up. The agent checks back frequently with policyholders both to provide service and to watch for opportunities for additional sales.

Successful life insurance agents and brokers work hard at their jobs. A majority of agents average over forty hours of work a week. Because arranging a meeting often means fitting into the client's personal schedule, many of the hours worked by insurance agents are in the evenings or on weekends. In addition to the time spent with customers, agents must spend time in their homes or offices preparing insurance programs for customer approval, developing new sources of business, and writing reports for the company.

Requirements

Formal requirements for the life insurance field are few. Because more mature individuals are usually better able to master the complexities of the business and inspire customer confidence, most companies prefer to hire people who are at least twenty-one years of age. Many starting agents are more than thirty years of age. Most companies insist on at least a high school education, although many strongly prefer college training. Courses in English, economics, finance, business law, sociology, psychology, and insurance are particularly helpful. A familiarity with computers and appropriate software, such as those that compile spreadsheets and databases, also is very helpful. There are more than sixty colleges and universities in the United States that offer a major in insurance.

The personal characteristics of the agents are of even greater importance. Although no insurance agent possesses all of them, the following traits are most helpful: a genuine liking and appreciation for people; a positive attitude toward others and sympathy for their problems; a personal belief in the value of life insurance coverage; a willingness to spend several years learning the business and becoming established; and persistence, hard work, and patience. Sales workers should also be resourceful and organized to make the most effective use of their time.

Requirements for success in life insurance are elusive, and it is this fact that contributes to the high turnover rate in this field. Despite the high rate of failure, life insurance sales offers a rewarding career for those who meet its requirements. It has been said that life insurance offers the easiest way to earn $1,000 to $2,000 a week, but the most difficult way to earn $300 or $400. People with strong qualifications may readily develop a successful insurance career, but poorly qualified people will find it a very difficult field.

Life insurance agents must obtain a license in each state in which they sell insurance. Agents are often sponsored for this license by the company they represent, which usually pays the license fee.

In most states, before a license is issued, the agent must pass a written test on insurance fundamentals and state insurance laws. Companies usually provide training programs to help prepare for these examinations. Often, the new agent may sell on a temporary certificate while preparing for the written examination. Information on state life insurance licensing requirements can be easily obtained from the state commissioner of insurance. Agents that sell securities, such as mutual funds, must obtain a separate securities license.

For full professional status, many companies recommend that their agents become chartered life underwriters (CLU) and/or chartered financial consultants (CHFC). To earn these designations, agents must successfully complete at least three years of work in the field and pass a series of examinations that test the agents' ability to apply their knowledge of life insurance fundamentals, economics, business law, taxation, trusts, and finance to common insurance problems. There are separate tests for the CLU and CHFC designations; both are conducted by the American Society of CLU and CHFC in Bryn Mawr, Pennsylvania. Only a small percentage of all life insurance agents are CLUs and/or CHFCs.

Opportunities for Experience & Exploration

Because of state licensing requirements, it is difficult for young people to obtain actual experience. The most notable exceptions are the student-agency programs developed by several companies to provide college students with practical sales experience and a trial exposure to the field.

Those wishing to learn about life insurance may be able to get a part-time or summer job as a clerical worker in an insurance agency. This work will provide background information on the requirements for the field and an understanding of its problems and prospects for the future. Formal college or evening school courses in insurance will also provide a clearer picture of this profession's techniques and opportunities.

Methods of Entering

Aspiring agents may apply directly to personnel directors of insurance companies or managers of branches or agencies. In most cases, the new agent will be affiliated with a local sales office almost immediately. To increase the agency's potential sales volume, the typical insurance office manager is prepared to hire all candidates who can be readily recruited and properly trained. Prospective life insurance agents should discuss their career interests with representatives of several companies to select the employer that offers them the best opportunities to fulfill their goals.

Prospective agents should carefully evaluate potential employers to select an organization that offers sound training, personal supervision, resources to assist sales, adequate financial compensating, and a recognizable name that will be well received by customers. Students graduating from college should be able to arrange campus interviews with recruiters from several insurance companies. People with work experience in other fields usually find life insurance managers eager to discuss sales opportunities.

In addition to discussing personal interests and requirements for success in the field, company representatives usually give prospective agents aptitude tests, which are developed either by their company or by LIMRA International (formerly the Life Insurance Marketing and Research Association).

Formal training usually involves three phases. In precontract orientation, candidates are provided with a clearer picture of the field through classroom work, training manuals, or other materials. On-the-job training is designed to present insurance fundamentals, techniques of developing sales prospects, principles of selling, and the importance of a work schedule. Finally, intermediate instruction usually provides company training of an advanced nature.

More than 30,000 agents a year take the insurance courses prepared by the Life Underwriter Training Council (LUTC), sponsored in most cities by local member associations of the National Association of Life Underwriters (NALU). After completing a certain number of courses, an agent may apply for the professional educational designation of life underwriter training council fellow.

Advancement

Continuing education has become essential for life insurance agents. Several professional organizations offer courses and tests for agents to obtain additional professional certification. Although voluntary, many professional insurance organizations require agents to commit to continuing education on a regular basis. Membership in professional organizations and the accompanying certification is important in establishing client trust. Many states also require continuing education to maintain licensing.

Unlike some occupations, many of the ablest people in the life insurance field are not interested in advancing into management. There can be many reasons for this. In some cases, a successful sales agent may be able to earn more than the president of the company. Experienced agents often would rather increase their volume of business and quality of service rather than their responsibility for the work of others. Others develop by specializing in various phases of insurance.

Still, many successful agents aspire to positions in sales management. At first, they may begin by helping train newcomers to the field. Later, they may become assistant managers of their office. Top agents are often asked by their companies (or even by rival insurance companies) to take over as managers of an existing branch or to develop a new one. In some cases, persons entering management must take a temporary salary cut, particularly at the beginning, and may earn less than successful agents.

There are several types of life insurance sales office arrangements. *Branch office managers* are salaried employees who work for their company in a geographic region. *General agency managers* are given franchises by a company and develop and finance their own sales office. General agents are not directly affiliated with their company, but they must operate in a responsible manner to maintain their right to represent the company. *General insurance brokers* are self-employed persons who place insurance coverage for their clients with more than one life insurance company.

The highest management positions in the life insurance field are in company headquarters. Persons with expertise in sales and field management experience may be offered a position with the home office.

Employment Outlook

About 409,000 life insurance agents and brokers were working in the United States in 1996. A number of factors should encourage moderate employment growth in this field. The percentage of citizens older than sixty-five is growing at a much faster rate than that of the general population. To meet the special needs of this group, agents are needed to convert some insurance policies from a death benefit to retirement income. The twenty-five-to-fifty-four age group is also growing, and this is the age group that has the greatest need for insurance. More women in the workplace will increase insurance sales. Employment opportunities for life insurance agents will also be aided by the general increase in the nation's population, the heavy turnover among new agents, and the openings created by agents retiring or leaving the field.

Despite these factors, employment growth will not keep pace with increased insurance sales. Some life insurance business has been taken over by multiline insurance agents who handle every type of insurance. Department stores and other businesses outside the traditional insurance industry have begun to offer insurance. Also, customer service representatives are increasingly assuming some sales functions, such as expanding accounts and occasionally generating new accounts. Many companies are diversifying their marketing efforts to include some direct mail and telephone sales. Increased use of computers will lessen the workload of agents by creating a database for tailor made policies. Rising productivity among existing agents also will hold down new job openings. In addition, the life insurance industry has come under increasing competition from financial institutions that offer retirement investment plans such as mutual funds.

Earnings

In 1996, the median annual salary of insurance agents was $49,000 according to the U.S. Department of Labor. The typical agent starting out earns about $20,200; those with five to ten years' experience earn about $55,200; while those with ten or more years' experience often exceed $76,000. Many offices also pay bonuses to agents that sell a predetermined amount of coverage. Beginning agents usually receive some form of financial assistance from the company. They may be placed on a moderate salary for a year or two; often the amount of salary declines each month on the assumption that commission income on sales will increase. Eventually, the straight salary is replaced by a drawing account—a fixed dollar amount that is advanced each month against anticipated commissions. This account helps agents balance out high- and low-earning periods.

Agents receive commissions on two bases: a first-year commission for making the sale (usually 55 percent of the total first-year premium) and a series of smaller commissions paid when the insured pays the annual premium (usually five percent of the yearly payments for nine years). Most companies will not pay renewal commissions to agents who resign.

Annual earnings of agents vary widely, from the beginning agent who may sell one policy a month up to the approximately 20,000 agents each year who qualify for the "Million Dollar Round Table" by selling policies with a face value of more than $1 million.

Conditions of Work

The job of the life insurance agent is marked by extensive contact with others. Most agents actively participate in groups such as churches, community groups, and service clubs, through which they can meet prospective clients. Life insurance agents also have to stay in touch with other individuals to keep their prospective sales list growing.

Because they are essentially self-employed, agents must be self-motivated and capable of operating on their own. In return, the life insurance field offers people the chance to go into business for themselves without the need for capital investment, long-term debt, and personal liability.

When asked to comment on what they liked least about the life insurance field, a group of experienced agents listed the amount of detail work required of an agent, the ignorance of the public concerning life insurance, the uncertainty of earnings while becoming established in the field, and the amount of night and weekend work. The last point is particularly important. Some agents work four nights a week and both days of the weekend when starting out. After becoming established, this may be reduced to three or two evenings and only one weekend day. Agents are often torn between the desire to spend more time with their families and the reality that curtailing evening and weekend work may hurt their income.

Sources of Additional Information

American Society of CLU and CHFC
270 South Bryn Mawr Avenue
Bryn Mawr, PA 19010
Tel: 610-526-2500

LIMRA International
PO Box 208
Hartford, CT 06141
Tel: 800-235-4672

National Association of Life Underwriters (NALU)
1922 F Street, NW
Washington, DC 20006
Tel: 202-331-6000

Line Installers and Cable Splicers

Definition

Line installers and cable splicers construct, maintain, and repair the vast network of wires and cables that transmit electric power, telephone, and cable television lines to commercial and residential customers. Line construction and cable splicing is a vital part of the communications system. Workers are involved in linking electricity between generation plants and homes and other buildings, merging phone communications between telephone central offices and customers, and bringing cable television stations to residences and other locations.

Nature of the Work

In the installation of new telephone and electric power lines, workers use power-driven machinery to first dig holes and erect the poles or towers that are used to support the cables. (In some areas, lines must be buried underground, and in these cases installers use power-driven equipment to dig and to place the cables in underground conduits.) These line installers, also called outside plant technicians and construction line workers, climb the poles using metal rungs (or they use truck-mounted work platforms) and install the necessary equipment and cables.

Installers who work with telephone lines usually leave the ends of the wires free for cable splicers to connect afterward; installers who work with electric power lines usually do the splicing of the wires themselves. For work on electric power lines, insulators must first be set into the poles before cables are attached. To join sections of power line and to conduct transformers and electrical accessories, line installers splice, solder, and insulate the conductors and related wiring. In some cases, line installers must attach other equipment—such as transformers, circuit breakers, and devices that deter lightning—to the line poles.

School Subjects
Mathematics
Shop (Trade/Vo-tech education)

Personal Interests
Building things
Fixing things

Work Environment
Primarily outdoors
Primarily multiple locations

Minimum Education Level
High school diploma
Apprenticeship

Salary Range
$17,000 to
$33,600 to
$45,500

Certification or Licensing
Voluntary

Outlook
About as fast as the average

DOT
821, 822, 829

In addition to working with lines for electric power and telephones, installers set up lines for cable television transmission. Such lines carry broadcast signals from microwave towers to customer bases. Cable television lines are hung on the same poles with power and phone lines, or they are buried underground. In some cases, installers must attach other wires to the customer's premises in order to connect the outside lines to indoor television sets.

After line installers have completed the installation of underground conduits or poles, wires, and cables, cable splicers complete the line connections; they also rearrange wires when lines are changed. To join the individual wires within the cable, splicers must cut the lead sheath and insulation from the cables. They then test or phase out each conductor to identify corresponding conductors in adjoining cable sections according to electrical diagrams and specifications. At each splice, they either wrap insulation around the wires and seal the joint with a lead sleeve or cover the splice with some other type of closure. Sometimes they fill the sheathing with pressurized air so that leaks can be located and repaired.

In the past, copper was the material of choice for cables, but fiber optics are now replacing the outdated material. Fiber optic cables are hair-thin strands of glass that transmit signals more efficiently than do copper wires. For work with fiber optic cable, splicing is performed in workshop vans located near the splice area. Splicers of copper cables do their work either on aerial platforms, down manholes, in basements, or in underground vaults where the cables are located.

In the mid-1990s, hybrid fiber/coax systems began to be used. These systems combine elements of fiber Preventive maintenance and repair work occupy major portions of the line installer's and cable splicer's time. When wires or cables break or poles are knocked down, workers are sent immediately to make emergency repairs. Such repair work is usually necessary after the occurrence of such disasters as storms and earthquakes. The line crew supervisor is notified when there is a break in a line and is directed to the trouble spot by workers who keep a check on the condition of all lines in given areas. During the course of routine periodic inspection, the line installer also makes minor repairs and line changes. Workers often use electric and gas pressure tests to detect possible trouble.

The use of hybrid fiber/coax systems requires far less maintenance than traditional copper-based networks. Line installers and cable splicers will spend significantly less time repairing broken wires and cables once hybrid fiber/coax systems become more prevalent.

Included in this occupation are many specialists, such as the following: section line maintainers, tower line repairers, line construction checkers, tower erectors, and cable testers. Other types of related workers include trouble shooters, test desk trouble locators, steel-post installers, radio interference investigators, and electric powerline examiners.

Requirements

Many companies prefer to hire applicants with a high school diploma or the equivalent. Although specific educational courses are not required, applicants must have certain qualifications because of the nature of the work involved in line and cable installation. Line installers and cable splicers need to be good with their hands and in good physical shape. Much of their work involves climbing poles and ladders, so they need to feel comfortable with heights. They also need to be strong in order to carry heavy equipment up poles and ladders. Also, because lines and cables are color coded, workers must have the ability to distinguish such colors. Installers may have extensive contact with the public and need to be polite and courteous. They also need to be able to interact well with people from diverse backgrounds, as their work will take them into a variety of neighborhoods.

It is helpful to have some knowledge of the basic principles of electricity and the procedures involved in line installation; such information can be obtained through attending technical programs or having been a member of the armed forces. Many employers, particularly for cable television installation, prefer to hire applicants who have received some technical training or completed a trade school or technical program that offers certification classes in technology such as fiber optics.

Training can also be obtained through special classes offered through trade associations. The Society for Cable Telecommunications Engineers offers seminars that provide hands-on, technical training. It also offers an Installer Certification Program. Certification is not a requirement in terms of being a license, but shows employers that a person has achieved a certain level of technical training and is qualified to perform certain functions. (The address for the Society for Cable Telecommunications Engineers is listed at the end of this article.)

Employers may also give pre-employment tests to applicants to determine verbal, mechanical, and mathematical aptitudes; some employers test applicants for such physical qualifications as stamina, balance, coordination, and strength.

Workers who drive a company vehicle need a driver's license and a good driving record.

Many workers are represented by unions, and union membership may be required. Two unions that represent many line installers and cable splicers are the International Brotherhood of Electrical Workers and the Communications Workers of America.

Opportunities for Experience & Exploration

In high school or vocational school, students may test their ability and interest in the occupations of line installer and cable splicer through courses in mathematics, electrical applications, and machine shop. Hobbies that involve knowledge of and experience with electricity also provide valuable practical experience. To observe line installers and cable splicers at work, it may be possible to have a school counselor arrange a field trip by calling the public relations office of the local telephone or cable television company.

Direct training and experience in telephone work may be gained in the armed forces. Frequently, those who have received such training are given preference for job openings and may be hired in positions above the entry level.

Methods of Entering

Those who meet the basic requirements and are interested in becoming either a line installer or a cable splicer may inquire about job openings by directly contacting the personnel offices of local telephone companies, utility companies, and cable television providers.

Persons enrolled in a trade school or technical institute may be able to find out about job openings through their schools' job placement services. Occasionally, employers will contact teachers and program administrators, so it is helpful to check with them also. Some positions are advertised through classified advertisements in the newspaper.

Advancement

Entry-level line installers are generally hired as helpers, trainees, or ground workers; cable splicers tend to work their way up from the position of line installer.

In many companies, entry-level employees must complete a formal apprenticeship program combining classroom instruction with supervised on-the-job training. These programs often last several years and are administered by both the employer and the union representing the employees. The programs may involve computer-assisted instruction as well as hands-on experience with simulated environments.

After successfully completing the training program, the employee will be assigned either as a line crew member under the guidance of a line supervisor or as a cable splicer's helper under the guidance of experienced splicers. Cable splicers' helpers advance to positions of qualified cable splicers after three to four years of working experience.

Both the line installer and the cable splicer must continue to receive training throughout their careers, not only to qualify for advancement but also to keep up with the technological changes that occur in the industry. Usually it takes line installers about six years to reach top pay for their job; top pay for cable splicers is earned after about five to seven years of work experience.

Opportunities for advancement can be limited due to the declining number of positions for line installers and cable splicers. A worker may qualify for a higher-level position, but have to wait a lengthy period before an opening may occur. In companies represented by unions, opportunities for advancement may be based on seniority. Workers who demonstrate technical expertise in addition to certain personal characteristics, such as good judgment, and planning skills and the ability to deal with people, may progress to foremen or line crew supervisors. With additional training, the line installer or the cable splicer may advance to telephone installer, telephone repairer, communications equipment technician, or another higher-rated position.

Employment Outlook

There are about 309,000 line installers and cable splicers in the United States in the late-1990s. More than half are telephone and cable television line installers and repairers, with the balance employed by electric companies and construction firms that specialize in installing power lines and cables.

There tends to be a low rate of employee turnover in this field. The U.S. Department of Labor anticipates that, in general, employment opportunities for installers and splicers will grow about as fast as the average for all occupations through the year 2006, though the trend will vary among industries. For example, opportunities will be good through the year 2006 for those working in the telephone and cable television industries; those working specifically for electric companies will face slower employment growth during this same time period.

Earnings

For line installers and cable splicers, earnings vary according to different regions of the country, and as with most occupations, work experience and length of service determine advances in scale. In general, however, line installers and repairers in 1996 earned an average weekly pay of $703; the highest of these wage earners were paid approximately $1,072 per week. When emergencies arise and overtime is necessary during unscheduled hours, workers are guaranteed a minimum rate of pay that is higher than their regular rate.

Beginning workers and those with only a few years of experience make significantly less than more experienced workers. As mentioned earlier, the turnover rate in these occupations is low; therefore, many workers are in the higher wage categories. Also, cable splicers who work with fiber optics tend to earn more than those who work with copper cables.

Telephone companies often provide workers with many benefits. Although benefits vary from company to company, in general, most workers receive paid holidays, vacations, and sick leaves. In addition, most companies offer medical, dental, and life insurance plans. Some companies offer pension plans.

Conditions of Work

Most line installers and cable splicers work standard forty-hour weeks, though evening and weekend work is not unusual. For example, line installers and cable splicers who work for construction companies may need to schedule their work around contractors' activities and then be required to rush to complete a job on schedule. Shift work, such as four ten-hour days or working Tuesday through Saturday, is common for many workers. Most workers earn extra pay for any work over forty hours a week.

Some workers are on call twenty-four hours a day and need to be available for emergencies. Both occupations require that workers perform their jobs outdoors, often in severe weather conditions when emergency repairs are needed. Construction line installers usually work in crews of two to five persons, with a supervisor directing the work of several of these crews. Work may involve extensive travel, including overnight trips during emergencies to distant locations.

There is a great deal of climbing involved in these occupations, and some underground work must be done in stooped and cramped conditions. Cable splicers sometimes perform their work on board a marine craft if they are employed with an underwater cable crew.

The work can be physically demanding and poses significant risk of injury from shocks or falls. The hazards of this work have been greatly reduced, though, by concerted efforts to establish safety standards. Such efforts have been put forward by the telephone companies, utility companies, and appropriate labor unions.

Sources of Additional Information

For information on the telephone industry, contact:

Communications Workers of America
Department of Apprenticeships
501 Third Street, NW
Washington, DC 20001
Tel: 202-434-1100
Email: cwa@capcon.net
WWW: http://www.cwa-union.org

International Brotherhood of Electrical Workers
Telecommunications Department
1125 15th Street, NW, Room 807
Washington, DC 20005
Tel: 202-833-7000
Email: IBEWnet@compuserve.com
WWW: http://www.ibew.com

For information on educational programs, contact:

Society for Cable Telecommunications Engineers
140 Philips Road
Exton, PA 19341-1318
Tel: 800-542-5040
Email: info@scte.org
WWW: http://www.scte.org

For a copy of Phonefacts, *please contact:*

United States Telephone Association
1401 H Street, NW, Suite 600
Washington, DC 20005-2164
Tel: 202-326-7372
WWW: http://www.usta.org

Locksmiths

Definition

Locksmiths, or *lock experts,* are responsible for all aspects of installing and servicing locking devices, such as door and window locks for buildings, door and ignition locks for automobiles, locks on such objects as combination safes and desks, and electronic access control devices. Locksmiths are often considered to be artisans—craftspeople who combine ingenuity with mechanical aptitude.

Nature of the Work

The precise aspects of locksmithing differ, depending on whether one works for one's own business, in a shop for a master locksmith, or as an in-house lock expert for a large establishment, such as an apartment complex or a high-rise office building. However, the essential nature of the work for all locksmiths can be described in general terms. Basically, they sell, service, and install locks, spending part of their working time in locksmith shops and part of it at the sites they are servicing. Locksmiths install locks in homes, offices, factories, and many other types of establishments. In addition to maintaining the working mechanics of lock devices, locksmiths usually perform functions that include metalworking, carpentry, and electronics.

The basic equipment used by the locksmith includes an appropriate workbench; tools and supplies, such as broken key extractors, code books, drills, files, key blanks, hammers, and screwdrivers; parts cabinets and storage boxes; and a key machine, which is used to cut blank pieces of metal keys into duplicates of other keys. Other utensils that a locksmith might use include tweezers, springs, C-clamps, circular hole cutters, flashlights, lock pick sets, and lubricants.

While at the shop, locksmiths work on such portable items as padlocks and luggage locks, as well as on an endless number of keys. When they need to do work at a customer's site, they usually drive to the site in a work van that carries an assort-

School Subjects
Mathematics
Shop (Trade/Vo-tech education)

Personal Interests
Figuring out how things work
Fixing things

Work Environment
Indoors and outdoors
Primarily multiple locations

Minimum Education Level
High school diploma

Salary Range
$11,440 to
$24,000 to
$48,000+

Certification or Licensing
Recommended

Outlook
About as fast as the average

DOT
709

GOE
05.05.09

NOC
7383

ment of the most common locksmithing equipment and supplies. On-site, they perform whatever function is needed for each specific job, be it opening locks whose keys have been lost, preparing master-key systems for such places as hotels and apartment complexes, removing old locks and installing modern devices, or rewiring electronic access control devices. Because locks are commonly found on doors and other building structures, lock experts often put their carpentry skills to use when doors have to be fitted for locks. And because locking devices are increasingly made with electronic parts, locksmiths must use their knowledge and skill to work with electronic door openers, electromagnetic locks, and electrical keyless locks.

Lock experts may spend part of their working day providing service to those who have locked themselves out of their houses, places of work, or vehicles. When keys are locked inside, locksmiths must pick the lock. If keys are lost, new ones often must be made. Locksmiths often repair locks by taking them apart to examine, clean, file, and adjust the cylinders and tumblers. Combination locks present a special task for locksmiths; they must be able to open a safe, for example, if its combination lock does not work smoothly. Manipulating combination locks requires expert, precise skill that is honed by much practice. The technique requires that the locksmith listen for vibrations and for the interior mechanism to indicate a change in direction, while the dial is carefully rotated; this is repeated until the mechanism has been accurately turned. If it isn't possible to open the lock through these methods, the device may be drilled.

Locksmiths work in any community large enough to need their services, but most jobs are available in large metropolitan areas. Some locksmiths work in shops for other professionals, and others work for large hardware or department stores. Also, many open their own businesses. Independent locksmiths must perform all the tasks needed to run any type of business, such as keeping books and tax records, preparing statements, ordering merchandise, and advertising. A locksmith's clients may include individual home or automobile owners as well as large organizations such as hospitals, housing developments, military bases, and federal agencies. Industrial complexes and huge factories may employ locksmiths to install and maintain complete security systems, and other establishments, such as school systems and hotels, employ locksmiths to regularly install or change locks.

Requirements

No special educational requirements are needed for a locksmithing occupation. Most employers prefer applicants who have graduated from high school. Helpful school classes include metal shop, mathematics, mechanical drawing, and electronics, if available.

There are locksmiths who have learned their skills from professionals in the business, but many workers learn the trade by either attending a community college or trade school that offers appropriate courses or completing an accredited correspondence course. A number of trade schools in the United States offer courses in locksmithing, following a curriculum based on all practical aspects of the trade. They teach the correct application of the current range of security devices, including the theory and practice of electronic access control, as well as the servicing and repairing of mortise, cylindrical, and bit-key locks. Students learn to recognize keys by their manufacturer and practice cutting keys by hand as well as by machine. Some courses allow students to set up a sample master-key system for clients such as a business or apartment complex. In addition to these fundamentals, pupils also learn to use carpentry tools and jigs to install common locking devices. Finally, they learn about automobile lock systems (how to enter locked automobiles in emergencies and how to remove, service, and repair ignition locks) and combination locks (how to service interchangeable core cylinders and manipulate combinations). The objective of such training is to teach the prospective locksmith all basic locksmithing responsibilities. After completing a training course, the graduate should be able to meet customer demand and standards of the trade with minimum supervision.

Many persons interested in a career in locksmithing learn the trade by taking correspondence courses, for which they receive instructions, assignments, tools, and model locks and keys. Lessons may be supplemented with supervised on-the-job training with a consenting master locksmith.

Locksmiths must be able to plan and schedule jobs and to use the right tools, techniques, and materials for each. Good vision and hearing are necessary for working with combination locks, and eye-hand coordination is essential when working with tiny locks and their intricate interiors. A good locksmith should have both a delicate touch and an understanding of the nature of mechanical devices.

Each lost key, broken lock, and security problem will present a unique challenge that the locksmith must be prepared to remedy on the spot. Locksmiths, therefore, must be able to think well on their feet. Locksmiths also have a responsibility to be reliable, accurate, and, most important, honest, since their work involves the security of persons and valuables. Customers must be able to count on their skill, dependability, and integrity. In addition, locksmiths must be aware of laws that apply to elements of their jobs, such as restrictions on duplicating master keys, making safe deposit box keys, and opening automobiles whose keys are not available. It is suggested that the locksmith-to-be consult with a lawyer to discuss the legal responsibilities he or she may have.

Opportunities for Experience & Exploration

Taking classes in machine shop while in high school provide the prospective locksmith a degree of experience in using a variety of hand tools, some of which may be used in the locksmithing trade. Those who are interested in learning specifically about types of locks and how to work with them can read *The Complete Handbook of Locks & Locksmithing* (C. A. Roper, Tab Books, 1991).

It is a good idea to contact organizations that are involved with the locksmithing trade. One might request information from the Associated Locksmiths of America, whose objective is to educate and provide current information to those involved in the physical security industry. Another method of finding out more about the career is to talk with someone already employed as a locksmith.

Methods of Entering

Since locksmithing is a vocation that requires skill and experience, it is unlikely that the untrained job seeker will be able to begin immediately in the capacity of locksmith. Beginners might consider contacting local shops to inquire about apprenticeships. In some cases, skilled locksmiths may be willing to teach their trade to a promising worker in exchange for low-cost labor. Another method is to check with state employment offices for business and industry listings of job openings for locksmiths.

Students enrolled in a trade school can obtain career counseling and job placement assistance. Trade school graduates should be qualified to begin work in established locksmith shops doing basic work both in the shop and on the road; others become in-house locksmiths for businesses and other establishments.

Advancement

Most locksmiths regard their work as a lifetime profession. They stay abreast of new developments in the field so that they can increase both their skills and earnings. As they gain experience, industrial locksmiths may advance from apprentices to journeyworkers to master locksmiths, to any of several kinds of supervisory or managerial positions.

After having worked in the field for a number of years, many lock experts decide to establish their own shops and businesses. In so doing, they tend to build working relationships with a list of clients and, in effect, can grow their business at their own flexible rate. Self-employed locksmiths are responsible for all the tasks that are required to run a business, such as planning, organizing, bookkeeping, and marketing.

Another advancement opportunity lies in becoming a specialist in any of a number of niches. Some locksmiths work exclusively with combination locks, for example, or become experts with automobile devices. One of the most promising recent specialty growth areas is that of electronic security. Such safety devices and systems are becoming standard equipment for large establishments such as banks, hotels, and many industries, as well as residences and autos, and their popularity is creating a need for skilled locksmiths to install and service them.

Employment Outlook

In the late 1990s, there are an estimated twenty-five thousand locksmiths and safe repairers employed in the United States, in small and large shops, as well as in-house for other businesses. This number is expected to grow slightly in the next several years, so opportunities for entry-level and skilled locksmiths should increase.

Population growth and an expanding public awareness of the need for preventive measures against home, business, and auto burglary continue to create needs for security devices and their maintenance. Also, many individuals and firms are replacing older lock and alarm systems with the latest developments in computerized equipment. Consequently, opportunities will be best for those workers who are able to install and service electronic security systems.

The locksmith trade itself has remained stable, with few economic fluctuations, and locksmiths with an extensive knowledge of their trade are rarely unemployed.

Earnings

Locksmithing can be a lucrative occupation, depending upon the geographic region of the country and the type of work done. Geographically, wages for locksmiths tend to follow the pattern of general earnings; that is, workers on the East coast tend to earn the most, and those in the South and Southwest the least.

Entry-level locksmiths with no experience generally start out with wages between $5.15 and $7.00 an hour, although in some areas wages may be higher. Experienced locksmiths earn an average of approximately $48,000 annually, and those who specialize in high-security electronic systems may earn much more than that. Self-employed locksmiths may be small business operators who earn less than some salaried employees, or they may head larger operations and earn more than the average through contracts with numerous clients.

Conditions of Work

Locksmiths who are self-employed often work up to sixty hours per week; apprentices and locksmiths working in industries and institutions, however, usually work standard forty-hour workweeks. Locksmiths stand during much of their working time, but they also often need to crouch, bend, stoop, and kneel. Sometimes they are required to lift heavy gates, doors, and other objects when dealing with safes, strong rooms, or lock fittings.

Locksmith workshops are usually well lit, well heated, and well ventilated. Some shops, particularly mobile ones, however, may be crowded and small, requiring that workers move carefully around fixtures and stock. Some locksmiths work outdoors, installing or repairing protective or warning devices, and some do much driving on assignments away from the shop. A proportion of locksmiths work alone much of the time, but many work at stores, banks, factories, or schools where there are usually other people. Physical injuries are not common, but minor ones can occur from soldering irons, welding equipment, electric shocks, flying bits from grinders, and sharp lock or key edges.

Sources of Additional Information

For information on careers as a locksmith and schooling options, contact:

Associated Locksmiths of America
3003 Live Oak Street
Dallas, TX 75204
Tel: 214-827-1701

For information on schools and colleges that offer locksmithing classes, contact:

Accrediting Commission of Career Schools and Colleges of Technology
2101 Wilson Boulevard, Suite 302
Arlington, VA 22201
Tel: 703-247-4212

For a list of accredited home study programs in locksmithing, contact:

Distance Education & Training Council
1601 18th Street, NW
Washington, DC 20009
Tel: 202-234-5100

Machine Tool Operators

Definition

Many of the countless manufactured products that we encounter in our everyday lives are composed of individual components—metal or plastic parts that have been shaped into specified dimensions by machine tools. Machine tools are pieces of equipment that cut, inject, extrude, or apply electricity, ultrasound, or chemicals to metal and plastic. These machines, including lathes, planers, drilling machines, blow-molding machines, injection-molding machines, and extruding machines, are run by *machine tool operators.* Some machine tool operators operate computerized numerical control machines.

Nature of the Work

An understanding of the type of work performed by machine tool operators begins with a description of machine tools themselves. Metalworking tools perform either the function of cutting metal or of shaping it. These are stationary, power-driven machines with holding devices for both the workpiece and the shaping tools. They may be either manually controlled or numerically controlled.

Machine tools used in plastics manufacturing include injection-molding machines, which heat plastic compounds and force them into a mold; extruding machines, which force plastic compounds through dies that then push out the parts in desired shapes; and blow-molding machines, which force hot air into molds of plastic compound and then inflate the plastic into desired shapes.

There are two categories of machine tool operators: those who set up the machines and those who tend to the machines' operations. *Setup operators,* also known as *job and die setter*s, plan the sequence of a machine's operations according to blueprints or other instructions. Although some workers are known by specific machines that they are responsible for (e.g., *lathe setup operator, plastics-molding machine setup operator*),

School Subjects
Mathematics
Shop (Trade/Vo-tech education

Personal Interests
Building things
Figuring out how things work

Work Environment
Primarily indoors
Primarily one location

Minimum Education Level
High school diploma
Apprenticeship

Salary Range
$24,700 to
$30,600 to
$36,400

Certification or Licensing
None

Outlook
Decline

DOT
601

GOE
05.05.07

NOC
9511

most are trained to work on a variety of machines. Skilled setup operators use micrometers and other gauges to ready their machines, which must be preset for speed and the amount of cutting, drilling, extruding, or injecting. This means that, in the case of a drill press, for example, the machine is set to drill only so deep and no further into the metal stock. No matter how much pressure is exerted on the tool's handle, the drill will go no deeper than the preset stop will allow. If this stop loosens, the machine tool operator must generally call the setup operator to remeasure the distance the drill should travel and lock it into place. During the course of the day, setup operators replace worn and broken belts, change cutting tools on their machines, and check measurements regularly to ensure continued accuracy.

Machine tool operators tend to machines that have already been set up. For example, the operator may be working with a drilling machine. He or she starts the drill, inserts a piece of metal stock into the guide that holds it during machining, pulls down the lever of the drill press until the piece is drilled the prescribed distance, and releases the lever. He or she then removes the stock from the machine and places it in a bin for completed parts.

During the machining process, the operator watches to make sure that the machine is working properly. He or she adds cutting and lubricating oils to the machinery and the workpiece as needed. Except during machinery breakdowns or while new stock is being brought up for machining, the machine tool operator generally continues to repeat the same process until the batch of pieces is completed.

The work of the machine tool operator has traditionally differed from that of the setup operator and the *machinist* in that machine tool operators often do not have the training necessary to set up and operate the diverse range of machines found in a machine shop. They generally perform simple, repetitive tasks connected within one particular specialty. In other words, whereas a machinist knows about numerous pieces of equipment—such as grinders, lathes, mills, shapers, honers, chippers, and planers—the machine tool operator is limited to one type or a few types of machines, usually does little or no hand fitting or assembly work, and depends on a setup operator to ready, adjust, and maintain the equipment. However, the proliferation of computerized numerical control machines has allowed tool operators to tend to larger numbers of machines at one time.

Numerical control machine tools use automatic operations to produce batch parts from metal-working and plastics-working devices. Preprogrammed coded information is fed into the machines so that the positioning and machining processes can run without total manual operation; in many machines, this coding is computerized. However, the machines still must be manually set up and monitored. In this regard, the duties of *numerical control machine tool operators* are similar to those of standard machine tool operators and setup operators. They include setting up the machine tools (in this case, loading programs into the controller), attaching the necessary accessories, securing workpieces, and maintaining coolants and lubricants.

Requirements

There are no special educational requirements for the job of machine operator, but a high school diploma is preferred by most employers. High school classes in algebra, geometry, and drafting or mechanical drawing are excellent preparation for workers in this job. Machine shop also is very helpful.

Most workers in this occupation learn their skills on the job. Trainees begin by observing and helping experienced workers, sometimes in formal training programs. As part of their training, they advance to more difficult and complex tasks, such as adjusting feed speeds or changing cutting tools. Eventually, they become responsible for their own machines.

Becoming a setup worker requires considerably more training. Although they perform many of the same functions as machine operators, they also need a complete knowledge of the machinery being used and the product being manufactured. Although most operators learn basic machine operations in a few weeks, it may take several years to become a setup operator.

Students interested in this work should have better than average mechanical aptitude, manual dexterity, and an interest in machines. The ability to pay close attention to the task, even when it becomes repetitive and dull, is essential. As machinery becomes more complex and shop floor organization changes, employers are increasingly looking for people with good communications skills. Finally, because machine tool operators spend most of their days standing at machines, a certain amount of physical stamina is required.

Opportunities for Experience & Exploration

Those who have hobbies such as building models and working with wood and other materials will gain practical experience in fundamental machining concepts. If students want to explore the occupation further, high school or vocational school shop classes teach technical theory and machining techniques.

There are several student organizations such as Vocational Industrial Clubs of America (VICA) and the Technology Student Association (TSA). Students who wish to see machine tool operators in action might ask school teachers or guidance counselors to set up a visit to a local plant.

Methods of Entering

Job seekers should apply directly to the personnel offices of machine shops and factories. Entry-level workers may start out by doing a wide variety of jobs at the plant, learning skills on the job by observing skilled operators at work. Afterward, they have the opportunity to work under supervision until they are completely familiar with the work. This type of training usually lasts about one to two years.

Job openings for machine tool operators may be listed in classified ads of newspapers as well as with state and private employment agencies.

Advancement

Becoming a professional, skilled operator with commensurate wages often takes a number of years. In addition, it is generally only after several years' experience as a basic operator that one can advance to the position of setup operator. The machine tool operator who knows how to read blueprints and use tools such as micrometers and gauges, and who is willing to try new methods, is more likely to be moved into supervisory jobs with more responsibility or to more varied and versatile positions, such as that of the programmer, who assists in planning the jobs. Operators may also transfer to training programs for other related occupations, such as that of general machinist or toolmaker.

Employment Outlook

Overall employment of machine tool operators is expected to decline in the coming years. The main reason for this decline is the increasing productivity resulting from computer-controlled equipment. Computer-controlled equipment allows operators to tend a greater number of machines simultaneously and thereby reduces the need for employees. Because of the proliferation of computer-controlled equipment, however, employment of operators who are skilled in the use of these machines is expected to increase, in spite of the decline in manual machine operators as a whole.

The demand for machine tool operators parallels the demand for the products they produce. In recent years, plastic has been substituted for metal in many manufacturing parts. If this trend continues, the demand for machine tool operators in plastics manufacturing will be greater than for those in metals.

Even with the decline in new positions, there should still be many job possibilities for machine operators. It is estimated that, within the next ten to fifteen years, 60 percent of the existing workforce in this field will be leaving the occupation and will have to be replaced.

Earnings

The average wage for machine tool operators is approximately $590 a week. Assuming a forty-hour workweek and full-time employment, this calculates to approximately $30,600 a year. Many workers often work more than forty hours a week and earn overtime pay and, hence, higher annual earnings.

Machine tool operators at the top end of the pay scale earn around $700 weekly, or $36,400 yearly; those at the low end may make $475 a week, or $24,700 a year.

Many machine tool firms have traditional benefit plans, including retirement programs to which both the employer and the employee contribute. Most operators are also eligible for paid vacations, sick leave, and group hospitalization insurance.

In many manufacturing operations, the plant closes during some parts of the year for changes in machinery necessary to make new models. The worker is seldom paid for this downtime. Machine tool operators must thus consider these layoffs when estimating their yearly salary.

Conditions of Work

This occupation requires at least forty hours of work per week, and often, when large orders have to be met quickly, workers are asked to work late and on Saturdays so that quotas are met. For each hour over the standard forty, workers receive time-and-one-half pay. Work is performed exclusively indoors.

Conditions can be somewhat dangerous, particularly because of the high speeds and pressures at which these machines operate. Therefore, protective equipment must be used, and safety rules must be observed. There are other minor hazards as well, including, for example, skin irritations from coolants used on cutting and drilling machines. Operators must wear goggles and avoid wearing loose clothing that could get caught in machinery. Most machine shops are clean, well lit, and well ventilated, although some older ones may be less so. The shops are often noisy as a result of the machinery being run.

The chief drawback to this profession is the repetitive and often boring nature of the work. Machine tool operators typically spend hours each day performing the very same task, over and over. However, the fairly high wage for work that is relatively easy to learn and perform may compensate for the tedium of the job.

Sources of Additional Information

■National Tooling and Machining Association
9300 Livingston Road
Fort Washington, MD 20744
Tel: 301-248-6200 or 800-248-6862
WWW: http://www.ntma.org

For literature on careers, apprenticeships, and earnings in the machine tools trades, contact:

■Tooling and Manufacturing Association
1177 South Dee Road
Park Ridge, IL 60068
Tel: 847-825-1120

For information on the career of machine tool operator, contact:

■International Union, United Automobile, Aerospace, and Agricultural Implement Workers of America
Skill Trades Department, Solidarity House
8000 East Jefferson Avenue
Detroit, MI 48214
Tel: 313-926-5000

■International Union of Electronic, Electrical, Salaried, Machine, and Furniture Workers
1126 16th Street, NW
Washington, DC 20036
Tel: 202-296-1200

Machinists

Definition

Many of the parts used in the production of such items as aircraft and automobiles are not manufactured in mass quantities, but in small batches. These pieces are produced by *machinists,* skilled tradesworkers with knowledge of machine shop practices, shop mathematics, and the machinability of various materials. These workers operate all kinds of machine tools and hand tools used for cutting, drilling, boring, turning, milling, planing, grinding, or otherwise forming pieces of material into desired shapes and sizes. Machinists finish and assemble parts by hand, and use scribers, gauges, and other measuring instruments to achieve an extremely high degree of accuracy.

Nature of the Work

With a working knowledge of the operation and uses of various machine tools, together with an understanding of the properties of various metals and other materials, the machinist is able to shape material into parts of precise dimensions. These workers are trained to operate most of the types of machine tools used to shape pieces of material—usually metal—to specifications. The work done by machine tools can be classified into one of the following categories: cutting, drilling, boring, turning (lathe), milling, planing (shaper, slotter, broach), and grinding.

The first task of the machinist, upon receiving a job assignment, is to review the blueprints or written specifications for the piece to be made. He or she then decides what machining operations should be used, plans their sequence, and calculates how fast to feed the metal into the machine. When this is complete, the machinist sets up the machine and the proper shaping tools and marks the metal stock (a process called layout work) to show where cuts should be made.

Once the layout work is done, machinists perform the necessary machining operations. They position the metal carefully

School Subjects
Mathematics
Shop (Trade/Vo-tech education)

Personal Interests
Building things
Computers

Work Environment
Primarily indoors
Primarily one location

Minimum Education Level
High school diploma
Apprenticeship

Salary Range
$16,100 to
$28,600 to
$45,200

Certification or Licensing
None

Outlook
Decline

DOT
600

GOE
05.05.07

NOC
7221

on the tool, set the controls, and make the cuts. During the shaping operation, they constantly monitor the feed of metal and the speed of the machine to ensure that the piece will turn out as planned. If necessary, they add coolants and lubricants to the workpiece.

At times, machinists produce a number of identical machined products by working at a single machine; at other times, they produce one item by working on a variety of machines. After completing the machining operations, they might finish the work by hand, using files and scrapers, for example, and then assemble the finished parts with such hand tools as wrenches and screwdrivers.

A high degree of accuracy is required in all work performed by machinists. Some specifications call for accuracy within one-ten-thousandth of an inch; to achieve this precision, machinists must use measuring instruments such as scribers, micrometers, calipers, verniers, scales, and gauges.

In the past, machinists have had direct control of their machines. However, the increasing use of numerically controlled machines and, in particular, computer numerically controlled machines, has changed the nature of the work. Machinists may now work alone or with tool programmers to program the machines that make the parts. They may also be responsible for checking computer programs to ensure that they run the machinery properly.

Some machinists, often called *production machinists,* may produce large quantities of one part. Others produce relatively small numbers of each item they make. Finally, some specialize in repairing machinery or making new parts for existing machinery. In repairing a broken part, the machinist might refer to existing blueprints and perform the same machining operations that were used to create the original part.

Requirements

For trainee or apprentice jobs, most companies prefer high school or vocational school graduates. Students' preparation should include courses in algebra, geometry, mechanical drawing, blueprint reading, machine shop, drafting, and computer applications. Courses in electronics and hydraulics are also helpful.

To qualify as a machinist, a person must complete either an apprenticeship or an on-the-job training program. Apprenticeships, which most employers prefer, generally consist of four to five years of carefully planned activity combining shop training with related classroom instruction. In shop training, apprentices learn filing, handtapping, and dowel fitting, as well as the operation of various machine tools. The operation and programming of computer-controlled tools are also covered. The classroom instruction, usually offered in the evenings, includes industrial math, blueprint reading, precision machining, computer numerical control concepts, machine tool technology, and manufacturing processes.

The other method of becoming a machinist, on-the-job training, involves working for four or more years under the supervision of experienced machinists, progressing from one machine to another. Trainees usually begin as machine operators; as they show necessary aptitude, they are given additional training in the machine they are operating. Further instruction in the more technical aspects of machine shop work is obtained through the studying of manuals and, occasionally, classroom instruction. The amount of progress depends on the skill of the worker.

A machinist must have an aptitude for using mechanical principles in practical applications. A knowledge of mathematics is important. In addition, the ability to understand and visualize spatial relationships is needed to read engineering drawings.

Machinists must have excellent manual dexterity, good vision and hand-eye coordination, and the concentration and diligence necessary to do highly accurate work. Because their work requires a great deal of standing and moving, good physical condition and stamina are important. Finally, it is necessary for machinists to be able to work independently in an organized, systematic way.

Opportunities for Experience & Exploration

Those interested in a career as a machinist have several avenues open for exploring the occupation. Courses in machine shop and mechanical drawing will test one's accuracy, patience, and ability in this type of work; courses in algebra and geometry will gauge one's skill in shop mathematics.

To observe machinists at work, field trips to machine shops can be arranged by the school counselor. An excellent opportunity for exploring this occupation would be a part-time job in a machine shop, perhaps during the summer months.

Methods of Entering

There are two ways an individual can enter the occupation of machinist: as an apprentice or as an on-the-job trainee. Those who wish to become apprentices may contact potential employers directly to ask about opportunities. Other sources of information are state employment offices, the Bureau of Apprenticeship and Training of the U.S. Department of Labor, and appropriate union headquarters (e.g., the International Association of Machinists and Aerospace Workers or the International Union, United Automobile, Aerospace, and Agricultural Implement Workers of America). School counselors or trade school information offices may also have information.

Entering the field through on-the-job training usually requires first taking a less-skilled job, such as machine shop helper or machine tool operator, and eventually working up to the position of machinist. In order to find an entry-level job, applicants can contact employers directly. Job listings may also be posted at state employment offices or in local newspaper ads.

Advancement

Successful completion of a training program is necessary before workers can become qualified machinists. After several years, when machinists have increased their skill level and have taken additional training, many advancement opportunities may become available. For instance, they may specialize in such niches as tool and die design or fabrication, sales, or instrument repairing. In large production shops, machinists have the opportunity to advance to such positions as setup operators and layout workers.

Those who have good judgment, excellent planning skills, and the ability to deal well with people may progress to supervisory positions, such as shop supervisor or even plant manager. With additional education, some machinists may become tool engineers. Finally, some exceptionally skilled and experienced workers eventually go into business for themselves.

Employment Outlook

Employment of machinists is expected to decline slightly through the year 2006. As the economy grows, so will the demand for goods that use machined metal parts. However, demand for workers will be limited by technological advances in metalworking. Increasing use of computer-numerically controlled (CNC) machine tools help machinists to work more productively and with better precision. However, such improvements have, as a result, decreased the demand for machinists. Increasing numbers of imports adversely affects domestic employment for all workers in industry. Finally, plastic and ceramic materials are replacing metals as the materials of choice for many products.

Even so, many openings will arise from the need to replace machinists who retire or transfer to other jobs. In recent years, employers have reported difficulty in attracting workers to machining occupations; if this trend continues, good employment possibilities should exist for candidates with the necessary skills.

Layoffs are often a factor affecting employment of machinists. When the demand for products declines, workers' hours may be either shortened or reduced completely for days, weeks, even months at a time. There is somewhat more job security for maintenance machinists because tending machines is required even when production is slow.

Earnings

Earnings for machinists compare favorably with those of other skilled factory workers. Since the industry is overtime-intensive, the typical workweek is between forty-five and fifty hours. With time-and-one-half pay after forty hours, the average apprentice could earn close to $28,600 a year, as reported by the U.S. Department of Labor's 1998-99 *Occupational Outlook Handbook*.

The average yearly pay for experienced and skilled machinists is $36,000, based on a fifty-hour workweek. At the top end of the pay scale, workers can earn in the low- to mid-$40,000s yearly. Benefits that generally are available to machinists include paid holidays and vacations; life, medical, and accident insurance; and pension plans.

Conditions of Work

The machining industry tends to require forty-five to fifty-five hour workweeks for machinists. For every hour worked over the standard forty, however, machinists receive time-and-one-half pay. Machinists work indoors in machine shops that usually are fairly clean with proper lighting and ventilation; however, noise levels are often quite high because of the nature of power-driven machinery.

Although machining work is not physically strenuous, machinists are usually on their feet for most of the day. Often, they must wear special shoes to reduce foot fatigue. Safety glasses are required as cutting tools, moving machine parts, and flying metal chips can cause injury to the eyes.

Because machinists can set up and operate almost every machine in the shop, their work may vary with the production needs of the company. They are often challenged by the needs of each job, and their accuracy and patience is tested by the precise demands of production. Machinists play an important role in the world of complex machinery and have the satisfaction of knowing that their contributions are valuable and seeing the results of their efforts.

Sources of Additional Information

For information on the career of machinist, contact:

International Union, United Automobile, Aerospace, and Agricultural Implement Workers of America
Skill Trades Department, Solidarity House
8000 East Jefferson Avenue
Detroit, MI 48214
Tel: 313-926-5000

National Tooling and Machining Association
9300 Livingston Road
Fort Washington, MD 20744
Tel: 301-248-6200 or 800-248-6862
WWW: http://www.ntma.org

For literature on careers, apprenticeships, and earnings in the machine tools trades, contact:

Tooling and Manufacturing Association
1177 South Dee Road
Park Ridge, IL 60068
Tel: 847-825-1120

Marine Services Technicians

Definition

Marine services technicians inspect, maintain, and repair marine vessels, from small boats to large yachts. They work on vessels' hulls, engines, transmissions, navigational equipment, and electrical, propulsion, and refrigeration systems.

Nature of the Work

Marine services technicians work on the more than sixteen million boats and other watercraft owned by people in the United States. They test and repair boat engines, transmissions, and propellers; rigging, masts, and sails; and navigational equipment and steering gear. They repair or replace defective parts and sometimes make new parts to meet special needs. They may also inspect and replace internal cabinets, refrigeration systems, electrical systems and equipment, sanitation facilities, hardware, and trim.

Workers with specialized skills often have more specific titles. For example, *motorboat mechanics* work on boat engines—those that are inboard, outboard, and inboard/outboard (I/O). Routine maintenance tasks include lubricating, cleaning, repairing, and adjusting parts.

Motorboat mechanics often use special testing equipment, such as engine analyzers, compression gauges, ammeters, and voltmeters, as well as other computerized diagnostic equipment. Technicians must know how to disassemble and reassemble components and refer to service manuals for directions and specifications. Motorboat workers often install and repair electronics, sanitation, and air-conditioning systems. They need a set of general and specialized tools, often provided by their employers; many mechanics gradually acquire their own tools, often spending up to thousands of dollars on this investment.

Marine electronics technicians work with vessels' electronic safety and navigational equipment, such as radar, depth

School Subjects
Mathematics
Shop (Trade/Vo-tech education)

Personal Interests
Boating
Fixing things

Work Environment
Indoors and outdoors
One location with some travel

Minimum Education Level
Some postsecondary training

Salary Range
$9.00 an hour to
$12.40 an hour to
$17.40 an hour

Certification or Licensing
Voluntary, except for radio technicians (required)

Outlook
About as fast as the average

DOT
806

GOE
05.05.02

NOC
7335

sounders, loran (long-range navigation), autopilots, and compass systems. They install, repair, and calibrate equipment for proper functioning. Routine maintenance tasks include checking, cleaning, repairing, and replacing parts. Electronics technicians check for common causes of problems, such as loose connections and defective parts. They often rely on schematics and manufacturers' specification manuals to troubleshoot problems. These workers also must have a set of tools, including hand tools such as pliers, screwdrivers, and soldering irons. Other equipment, often supplied by their employers, includes voltmeters, ohmmeters, signal generators, ammeters, and oscilloscopes.

Technicians who are *field repairers* go to the vessel to do their work, perhaps at the marina dock. *Bench repairers,* on the other hand, work on equipment brought into shops.

Some technicians work only on vessel hulls. These are usually made of either wood or fiberglass. *Fiberglass repairers* work on fiberglass hulls, of which most pleasure crafts today are built. They reinforce damaged areas of the hull, grind damaged pieces with a sander, or cut them away with a jigsaw and replace them using resin-impregnated fiberglass cloth. They finish the repaired sections by sanding, painting with a gel-coat substance, and then buffing.

Requirements

Although it is important to concentrate on high school classes such as shop and electronics, certain requirements may come naturally to many who become marine service technicians. Those who are familiar with boats and have had experience with them certainly are a step ahead. Some workers in this field have grown up with boats—perhaps they live near water or vacation each year near rivers or lakes.

Many marine services technicians learn their trade on the job; they find entry-level positions as general boatyard workers, doing such jobs as cleaning boat bottoms. Others attend vocational schools or technical colleges to get more formal training in skills such as engine repair and fiberglass work.

Most employers hire applicants with at least a high school diploma as long as they have good reading, writing, and math skills and a background in mechanics. High school students who are interested in work as marine services technicians, should take basic classes in English and math, as well as machine shop, woodshop, and electronics.

Further schooling is not required but can be helpful. Technical schools and community colleges offer basic mechanical and electronics courses. Many advanced electronics classes, including math, physics, electricity, schematic reading, and circuit theory, are offered at such schools, as well as at universities and the military services. Some schools—such as Northwest Technical College in Minnesota, Cape Fear Community College in North Carolina, and Washington County Technical College in Maine—have programs specifically for marine technicians. These schools often offer an associate's degree in areas such as applied science. Other types of institutions—such as the American Boatbuilders and Repairers Association, Mystic Seaport Museum, and the Wooden Boat School—offer skills training in less formal, short courses and seminars, often lasting days or a few weeks.

Marine services technicians do not usually need to have a special license, except for those who test and repair radio transmitting equipment. Those workers must have a general radiotelephone operator license from the Federal Communications Commission. Certification for electronics technicians is voluntary, administered by the National Marine Electronics Association.

Most technicians generally work outdoors some of the time, and they're often required to test-drive the vessels they work on. This often is considered an added benefit by many workers. Some workers in this field insist that one of the most important qualities for a technician is a pleasant personality. Boat owners are often very proud of and attached to their vessels, so workers need to have both respect and authority when communicating with customers.

Technicians also need to be able to adapt to the cyclical nature of this business. They are often under a lot of pressure in the summer months, when most boat owners are enjoying the water and calling on technicians for service. On the other hand, they often have gaps in their work during the winter; some workers earn unemployment compensation at this time.

Motorboat technicians' work can sometimes be physically demanding, requiring them to lift heavy outboard motors or other components. Electronics technicians, on the other hand, will probably not be required to do any heavy lifting but must be able to work with delicate parts, such as wires and circuit boards; they should have good eyesight, color vision, and good hearing (to listen for malfunctions revealed by sound).

Opportunities for Experience & Exploration

This field lends itself to a lot of fun ways to explore job opportunities. Of course, having a boat of one's own and working on it is one of the best ways of preparation. If friends, neighbors, or relatives have a boat, take trips with them and see how curious you are about what makes the vessel work. Offer to help do repairs to the boat, or at least watch while repairs are made and routine maintenance jobs are done. Clean up the deck, sand an old section of the hull, or polish the brass!

Some high schools have co-op training programs through which students can look for positions with boat-related businesses, such as boat dealerships or even marinas. Students also can read trade magazines such as *Boating Industry, Professional BoatBuilder,* and *Marine Mechanics.* These periodicals will have information monthly or bimonthly on the pleasure boat industry, as well as on boat design, construction, and repair.

Methods of Entering

A large percentage of technicians get their start by working as general boatyard laborers—cleaning boats, cutting grass, painting, and so on. After showing interest and ability, they can begin to work with experienced technicians and learn skills on the job. Some professional organizations, such as International Women in Boating, Marine Trades Association of New Jersey, and Michigan Boating Industries Association, offer scholarships for those interested in marine technician training.

Most motorboat mechanics find work in boat dealerships and marinas, which are usually located near water (the coasts, rivers, and lakes). The largest marinas are in coastal areas, such as Florida, New York, California, Texas, Massachusetts, and Louisiana; smaller ones are located near lakes and water recreation facilities such as campgrounds. Other technicians work for independent repair shops, boat rental firms, and resorts.

Some workers find jobs at boat engine manufacturers, where they make final adjustments and repairs to motors coming off the assembly line. Manufacturers of large fishing vessels also employ technicians for on-site mechanical support at fishing sites and competitive events. These workers often follow professionals on the fishing circuit, traveling from tournament to tournament maintaining the vessels.

Advancement

Many workers consider management and supervisory positions as job goals. After working for a number of years on actual repairs and maintenance, many technicians like to manage repair shops, supervise other workers, and deal with customers more directly. These positions require less physical labor but more communication and management skills. Many workers like to combine both aspects by becoming self-employed; they have their own shops, attract their own jobs, and still get to do the technical work they enjoy.

Advancement often depends on what individuals prefer to do at certain times in their careers. Some become marina managers, manufacturers' salespersons, or field representatives. Others take a different direction and work as boat brokers, selling boats. *Marine surveyors* verify the condition and value of boats; they are independent contractors hired by insurance companies and lending institutions such as banks.

Employment Outlook

The marine services technician's job can be considered secure for the near future. Although marine services technology is a small field, it is expected to grow. Employment opportunities are expected to increase at a rate that matches the national average for all occupations through the year 2006. As boat design and construction become more complicated, the outlook will be best for well-trained technicians. Many job opportunities will result from the need to replace retiring workers.

The availability of jobs will be related to the health of the pleasure boat industry. One interesting demographic trend that will influence job opportunities is the shift of the population to the South and West, where warm-weather seasons are longer and thus attract more boating activity.

An increase in foreign demand for U.S. pleasure vessels will mean more opportunities for workers in this field. U.S. manufacturers are expected to continue to develop foreign markets and establish more distribution channels. However, legislation in the United States may require boat operator licenses and stricter emission standards, which might lead to a decrease in the number of boats sold and maintained here.

Earnings

Most marine services technicians are paid by the hour, although some earn yearly salaries. Others earn a base salary and a commission, which is usually a percentage of the cost of labor and/or the parts used on the jobs. Wages vary by geographic location, skill levels, duties, and length of employment. The average pay for general technicians is about $12.40 per hour; for electronics technicians, $13.45 per hour; and for fiberglass technicians, about $12.00 per hour. Highly skilled technicians can command hourly fees of $17.00 or more.

Technicians tend to receive few fringe benefits in small shops, but larger employers tend to offer paid vacations, sick leave, and health insurance. Some employers pay for work-related training and provide uniforms and tools. Many technicians who enjoy the hands-on work with boats claim that the best benefit is being able to perform a craft they enjoy and to take repaired boats out for test-drives.

Conditions of Work

If you like boats, the best part about being a marine services technician is often the chance to take one of your jobs out on the water. At other times it could be that all your customers are pressuring you to finish their repairs in a few days, to make their boats fit for the water by the summer holidays. There is often a big cram for service just before Memorial Day and the Fourth of July. In the summer, workweeks can average sixty hours, whereas in winter the week can involve less than forty hours of work, with layoffs common at this time of year.

You might find yourself working in small, hot spaces on small boats, wishing for winter. Technicians often have to do a lot of squeezing and crawling around in tight, uncomfortable places to perform repairs. Sailboats have especially tight access to inboard engines.

Technicians working indoors often are in well-lit and ventilated shops. The work is cleaner than that on cars because there tends to be less grease and dirt on marine engines; instead, workers have to deal with water scum, heavy-duty paint, and fiberglass. In general, marine work is similar to other types of mechanical jobs, where you'll encounter such things as noise when engines are being run and potential danger with power tools and chemicals. Also similar to other mechanics' work, sometimes you'll do a job yourself and at other times you'll work on a boat with other technicians. Unless you are self-employed, your work will probably be overseen by a supervisor of some kind. For any repair job, you might have to deal directly with customers.

Sources of Additional Information

The following professional organization awards scholarships in the marine industry. Write for information on eligibility, application requirements, and deadlines:

■**International Women in Boating**
401 North Michigan Avenue
Chicago, IL 60611
Tel: 312-836-4747

To find out whether there is a marine association in your area, contact:

■**Marine Retail Association of America**
150 East Huron Street, Suite 802
Chicago, IL 60611
Tel: 312-944-5080

■**Marine Trades Association of New Jersey**
1999 Route 88
Brick, NJ 08724
Tel: 908-206-1400

■**Michigan Boating Industries Association**
41740 West Six-Mile Road, Suite 100
Northville, MI 48167
Tel: 810-344-1330

Massage Therapists

Definition

Massage therapy is a broad term referring to a number of health-related practices, including Swedish massage, sports massage, Rolfing, Shiatsu and acupressure, trigger point therapy, and reflexology. Although the techniques vary, most *massage therapists* or *massotherapists* rub or apply pressure to the body's soft tissues. Relaxed muscles, improved blood circulation and joint mobility, reduced stress and anxiety, and decreased recovery time for sprains and injured muscles are just a few of the potential benefits of massage therapy.

Massage therapists are sometimes called *bodyworkers*. The titles *masseur* and *masseuse,* once common, are now rare among those who use massage for therapy and rehabilitation.

Nature of the Work

Massage therapists work to produce physical, mental, and emotional benefits through the manipulation of the body's soft tissue. Auxiliary methods, such as the movement of joints and the application of dry and steam heat, are also used. Among the potential physical benefits are the release of muscle tension and stiffness, reduced blood pressure, better blood circulation, a shorter healing time for sprains and pulled muscles, increased flexibility and greater range of motion in the joints, and reduced swelling from edema (excess fluid buildup in body tissue). Massage may also improve posture, strengthen the immune system, and reduce the formation of scar tissue.

Mental and emotional benefits include a relaxed state of mind, reduced stress and anxiety, clearer thinking, and a general sense of well-being. Physical, mental, and emotional benefits are thought to be interconnected. A release of muscle tension, for example, may lead to reduced stress and anxiety.

There are many different approaches a massage therapist may take. Among the most popular are Swedish massage,

School Subjects
Anatomy and Physiology
Health

Personal Interests
Helping people: personal service
Helping people: physical health/medicine

Work Environment
Primarily indoors
Primarily one location

Minimum Education Level
Some postsecondary training

Salary Range
$10.00 per hour to
$40.00 per hour to
$70.00 per hour

Certification or Licensing
Required for certain positions

Outlook
Faster than the average

DOT
334

GOE
09.05.01

NOC
3235

sports massage, Rolfing, Shiatsu and acupressure, trigger point therapy, and reflexology.

In Swedish massage the traditional techniques are *effleurage, petrissage, friction,* and *tapotement.* Effleurage (French for stroking), the use of light and hard rhythmic stroking movements, is used to relax muscles and improve blood circulation. It is often performed at the beginning and end of a massage session. Petrissage (kneading) is the rhythmic squeezing, pressing, and lifting of a muscle. For friction, the fingers, thumb, or palm or heal of the hand are pressed into the skin with a small circular movement. The massage therapist's fingers are sometimes pressed deeply into a joint. Tapotement (tapping), in which the hands strike the skin in rapid succession, is used to improve blood circulation. During the session the client, covered with sheets, lies undressed on a padded table. Oil or lotion is used to smooth the skin. Swedish massage may employ a number of auxiliary techniques, including the use of rollers, belts, and vibrators; steam and dry heat; ultraviolet and infrared light; and saunas, whirlpools, steam baths, and packs of hot water or ice.

Sports massage is essentially Swedish massage used in the context of athletics. A light massage generally is given before an event or game to loosen and warm the muscles. This reduces the chance of injury and may improve performance. After the event the athlete is massaged more deeply to alleviate pain, reduce stiffness, and promote healing.

Rolfing, developed by American Ida Rolf, involves deep, sometimes painful massage. Intense pressure is applied to various parts of the body. Rolfing practitioners believe that emotional disturbances, physical pain, and other problems can occur when the body is out of alignment—for example, as a result of poor posture. This method takes ten sessions to complete.

Like the ancient Oriental science of acupuncture, Shiatsu and acupressure are based on the concept of meridians, or invisible channels of flowing energy in the body. The massage therapist presses down on particular points along the meridians to release blocked energy and knots of muscle tension. For this approach the patient wears loosely fitted clothes, lies on the floor or a futon and is not given oil or lotion for the skin.

Trigger point therapy, a neuromuscular technique, focuses in on a painful area, or trigger point, in a muscle. A trigger point might be associated with a problem in another part of the body. Using the fingers or an instrument, such as a rounded piece of wood, concentrated pressure is placed on the irritated area in order to "deactivate" the trigger point.

In reflexology, pressure is applied to specific points on the feet and hands thought to correspond to other areas of the body. The tips of the right foot, for example, correspond to the brain, while the palm of the left hand is associated with the stomach. The goal of reflexology is to not only promote a state of relaxation in the associated body part and increased blood circulation but also to return the body to a state of equilibrium.

Requirements

Massage therapists need to know more than just technical skills. In order to effectively use massage techniques, the therapist must be trained in physiology, anatomy, and psychology. A sensitivity toward the needs of the client is essential.

Those who wish to enter the field are advised to attend an accredited massage therapy school. In the United States, there are more than 60 schools accredited or approved by the American Massage Therapy Association (AMTA). Programs generally last one year. Accredited or approved schools provide at least 500 hours of classroom instruction, of which at least 300 hours are in massage theory and technique, 100 hours in the study of anatomy and physiology, and one hundred hours in program-specific coursework. First aid and cardiopulmonary resuscitation (CPR) must also be learned. Other organizations, such as some state medical boards, may require more than 500 hours of instruction. When choosing a school, an applicant should pay close attention to the philosophy and curriculum of the program, as a wide range of program options exist.

Interested high school and college students should consider taking basic science courses, such as chemistry and biology, as well as English, psychology, and other classes relating to communications and human development. A diverse course load is recommended.

In about one-fourth of the states, massage therapists must have a license to practice. Requirements may include a written test and a demonstration of massage therapy techniques. Since 1992 the National Certification Board for Therapeutic Massage and Bodywork has prepared a certification exam covering massage theory and practice, human anatomy, physiology, kinesiology, business practices, and associated techniques and methods.

Opportunities for Experience & Exploration

One way to become familiar with this field is to make appointments with various types of massage therapists. This provides firsthand experience in massage therapy and the opportunity to talk with therapists about the field.

A less costly approach is to find a book on massage instruction at a local public library or bookstore. Massage techniques can then be practiced at home. Books on self-massage are available. Many books discuss in detail the theoretical basis for the techniques.

Methods of Entering

After graduating from an accredited or approved school of massage therapy, there are a number of possibilities for employment. Doctors' offices, hospitals, clinics, health clubs, resorts, country clubs, community service organizations, and nursing homes, for example, all employ massage therapists. Massage therapy schools have job placement offices. Newspapers often list jobs. Some graduates are able to enter the field as self-employed massage therapists.

Advancement

For self-employed massage therapists, advancement is measured by reputation, the ability to draw clients, and the fee for services. Health clubs, country clubs, and other institutions have supervisory positions for massage therapists. In a community service organization, massage therapists may be promoted to the position of health service director.

Employment Outlook

The U.S. Bureau of Labor Statistics does not keep records on the number of massage therapists in the United States. In 1997, however, the industry estimated the number of practitioners to be about 200,000.

The employment outlook for massage therapists is good through the year 2006. For a ten-year period beginning in the early 1980s, the AMTA had a tenfold increase in the number of new members and a fourfold increase in the number of accredited or approved schools. The growing acceptance of massage therapy as an important health care discipline has led to the creation of additional jobs for massage therapists.

Earnings

The earnings of massage therapists vary greatly with the level of experience and location of practice. Some entry-level massage therapists earn as little as minimum wage, but with expe-

rience, a massage therapist can charge from $10.00 to $70.00 for a one-hour session. Additional earnings are made from tips. The average rate in the United States for a one-hour session is about $40.00. Massage therapists are not, however, paid for the time spent on recordkeeping, maintaining their offices, waiting for customers to arrive, and looking for new clients. Those who are self-employed—more than two-thirds of all massage therapists—must also pay a self-employment tax and provide their own benefits.

Conditions of Work

Massage therapists work in clean, comfortable settings. Because a relaxed environment is essential, the massage room may be dim, and soft music and scents are often used. Massage therapists employed by businesses may use a portable massage chair—that is, a padded chair that leaves the client in a forward-leaning position ideal for massage of the back and neck. Some massage therapists work out of their homes or travel to the homes of their clients.

The workweek of a massage therapist is typically thirty-five to forty hours. On average, fewer than twenty hours per week are spent with clients.

Sources of Additional Information

American Massage Therapy Association (AMTA)
820 Davis Street, Suite 100
Evanston, IL 60201-4444
Tel: 847-864-0123

Associated Bodywork and Massage Professionals
PO Box 1869
Evergreen, CO 80439
Tel: 800-458-2267
WWW: http://www.abmp.com/

National Certification Board for Therapeutic Massage and Bodywork
8201 Greensboro Drive, Suite 300
McLean, VA 22102
Tel: 800-296-0664
WWW: http://www.ncbtmb.com/

Meatcutters

Definition

Meatcutters cut animal carcasses into smaller portions and prepare meat, poultry, and fish for sale in food outlets or for cooking in hotels and restaurants.

Nature of the Work

Meatcutters receive animal carcasses in refrigerated trucks from food distributors. For easier handling, the carcasses have already been cut into sides or quarters at the meat packing plant or central distribution center before shipping. Meatcutters first divide the carcasses into rounds, loins, and ribs, and then into serving-size portions such as roasts, steaks, and chops. Less-expensive cuts and meat trimmings are cut into pieces for stewing or ground into hamburger. Meatcutters try to cut everything that can be sold or in some way used into appropriate sizes. About two-thirds of a cow can be processed as beef cuts; another one-fourth can be processed as ground beef, and about eight percent of a cow can be used for cold cut type products.

The large sides of beef are stored in refrigerated rooms until they are ready to be cut and packaged. In their work, meatcutters use special tools such as band saws, power cutters, butcher knives, cleavers, and electric grinders to divide animal carcasses into smaller portions. Meats intended for sale in food outlets and meat markets must then be weighed, priced, labeled, and graded according to government standards. Meatcutters also place the meat in trays, wrap the trays in plastic, and fill up the display case with them.

In retail stores, meatcutters are often called butchers. They are responsible for displaying the food properly, waiting on customers, and cutting orders to meet special needs. They may also filet fish, dress poultry, make sausage, and pickle meats. Other important aspects of the job include selecting meats from wholesale distributors, keeping accurate records, and

School Subjects
Business
Family and Consumer Science

Personal Interests
Cooking

Work Environment
Primarily indoors
Primarily one location

Minimum Education Level
High school diploma
Apprenticeship

Salary Range
$12,000 to
$19,240 to
$38,400

Certification or Licensing
Required

Outlook
Decline

DOT
316

GOE
05.10.08

NOC
6251

maintaining adequate inventory. Some meatcutters specialize as chicken and fish butchers.

In hotels and restaurants, meatcutters are usually referred to as *meat butchers*. Their duties involve preparing both large quantities and individual portions of meat. They may also estimate the amount of meat they need, order meat supplies, inspect and store meat upon delivery, and keep records. A head butcher has the responsibility of supervising the work of other butchers. To lessen the work of kitchen help, more and more hotel and restaurant kitchens now buy their meats already cut into portions.

Other related occupations include *schactos*, who slaughter meat according to Jewish dietary laws, *all-around butchers*, and *meat dressers*, who work in slaughterhouses killing animals and preparing carcasses. This type of work resembles an assembly line more than a butcher's kitchen.

Requirements

Most employers prefer applicants who have a high school diploma and the potential to develop into managers. The majority of meatcutters acquire their skills on the job, many through apprentice programs. A few attend schools specializing in the trade, but they still need additional training and experience after graduation before they can work as meatcutters. Prospective meatcutters applying for union jobs are required to complete an apprenticeship of two to three years before achieving full journeyworker status.

Trainees begin by doing odd jobs such as removing bones and fat from retail cuts. Gradually they are taught to use power tools and equipment, how to prepare various cuts of meat, poultry, and fish, and how to make sausage and cure meats. Later they may learn such things as inventory control, meat buying, and recordkeeping. Those in an apprentice program must pass a meatcutting test at the end of their apprenticeship.

Subjects that will help high school students in this career include business and business math, bookkeeping, home economics, and food preparation. Shop classes are also useful for helping students learn to handle and take care of tools and equipment.

Important skills for this occupation are manual dexterity, good depth perception, color discrimination, and good hand-eye coordination. Above-average strength is needed to lift large, heavy sides of meat. Meatcutters who wait on customers need a pleasant personality, a neat appearance, and the ability to communicate clearly.

Depending on local laws, a health certificate may be required. Many cutters are members of the United Food and Commercial Workers International Union.

Opportunities for Experience & Exploration

Summer or part-time employment in retail food stores, wholesale food outlets, or restaurant and institutional kitchens is one means of acquiring experience. Some vocational and trade schools offer courses in basic meatcutting techniques. Interviews with meatcutters and field trips to meat packing plants and slaughterhouses also are useful in exploring the conditions under which the prospective meatcutters work.

Methods of Entering

The usual path of entry to the meatcutting field is to apply for a job with a retail or wholesale food company that has an apprenticeship program. Interested people may also contact the local union office to find out about these programs. After two to three years of on-the-job training (sometimes coupled with classroom work), apprentices are given a meatcutting test in the presence of their employer and, in those establishments covered by a union, a union member. Those who fail the exam may take it again at a later time. In some areas, apprentices who can pass the test may not have to complete the training program. Employees at nonunion meat packing plants do not take part in an apprenticeship program but are given on-the-job training. Information about work opportunities can be obtained from local employers, union offices, or local offices of the state employment service.

Advancement

Experienced meatcutters may be promoted to supervisory positions, such as meat department manager in a supermarket or manager of the entire supermarket. A few become buyers for wholesalers and supermarket chains. Meatcutters working in restaurants and hotels may also become managers. Some become grocery store managers or open their own meat markets.

Employment Outlook

In 1996, meatcutters held around 217,000 jobs, mostly in retail stores and markets but also in wholesale stores, restaurants, hotels, hospitals, and other institutions. In recent years, the beef industry has been moving out of larger metropolitan areas such as Chicago; more and more meatcutting plants are located near the commercial feedlots of Kansas, Texas, Nebraska, and Oklahoma. The center of the pork industry continues to be in the Midwest, in the states of Illinois, Nebraska, Minnesota, Iowa, and Michigan. Poultry processing jobs are most likely to be found in the Southern and Southeastern states, such as Arkansas, Georgia, Alabama, North Carolina, Mississippi, Tennessee, and Virginia and occasionally in the Atlantic states and California.

During the past decade the number of meatcutters has slowly declined, and the decline in their numbers is expected to continue through the year 2006. One reason is the growing practice of central cutting, that is, the butchering and wrapping of meat in one location such as a meat packing plant for distribution to other outlets. Central cutting increases efficiency by permitting cutters to specialize in certain types of meats and cuts. Widespread use of automated cutting machines has decreased the demand for workers in this field. There will be fewer employment opportunities for meatcutters at the retail level, while many of the jobs at a central cutting plant can be performed by semiskilled workers, rather than journeyworker meatcutters.

The increasing health consciousness of the American public is another reason for the decline in demand for skilled meatcutters. The consumption of red meat has decreased as people eat greater quantities of fish and poultry. The increased consumption of poultry, which can be grown to a standard size and therefore are easier to process using automated equipment, has led to less demand for people skilled in manual meatcutting techniques.

Nevertheless, the consumer demand for meat will remain strong, and new workers will always be needed to replace older workers as they retire, change jobs, or leave the profession for other reasons.

Earnings

According to the 1998-99 Occupational Outlook Handbook, earnings for meatcutters vary according to location and whether or not they are members of a union. Union meatcutters generally earn between $19,240 and $38,400 per year. Meatcutters who work in urban areas are paid more than those in smaller cities. Beginning apprentices usually earn between 60 and 70 percent of an experienced cutter's wage, then receive increases every six months until they reach the rank of journeyworkers and earn full pay. Beginning meatcutters in nonunion jobs may start at about $12,000 per year. Among grocery store occupations, meatcutters usually earn the highest wages.

Conditions of Work

Health and safety standards require clean and sanitary work areas. The local board of health is usually in charge of inspecting food establishments and enforcing sanitation laws. Most meatcutters work in places that are comfortable, although handling and cutting carcasses is messy, and some workers must work their entire shift in refrigerated areas.

Meatcutters may face physical hazards from saws and other sharp instruments. Those working in slaughterhouses may develop carpal tunnel syndrome and other repetitive stress disorders if they have to repeat the same motions with their hands or arms all day long. In addition to much heavy lifting, meatcutters must stand most of the time they are on the job. Constant access to refrigerated areas exposes these workers to sudden temperature changes, which can increase fatigue.

Following proper safety habits and wearing protective garments eliminate much of the danger on the job. Taking care to use protective gloves and to rest when tired can help employees avoid serious injuries in the workplace.

Sources of Additional Information

American Association of Meat Processors
PO Box 269
Elizabethtown, PA 17022
Tel: 717-367-1168

American Meat Institute
PO Box 3556
Washington, DC 20007
Tel: 703-841-2400

United Food and Commercial Workers International Union
1775 K Street, NW
Washington, DC 20006

Mechanical Engineering Technicians

Definition

Mechanical engineering technicians work under the direction of mechanical engineers to design, build, maintain, and modify many kinds of machines, mechanical devices, and tools. They work in a wide range of industries and in a variety of specific jobs within every industry.

Mechanical engineering technicians review mechanical drawings and project instructions, analyze design plans to determine costs and practical value, sketch rough layouts of proposed machines or parts; assemble new or modified devices or components, test completed assemblies or components, analyze test results, and write reports. In addition, they may supervise the actual manufacturing process as it is carried out by skilled workers.

Nature of the Work

Mechanical engineering technicians are employed in an extremely broad range of industries. Virtually every type of application that involves mechanical principles and machinery employs mechanical engineers and their assistants, mechanical engineering technicians. Technicians may specialize in any of many areas including biomedical equipment, measurement and control, products manufacturing, solar energy, turbo machinery, energy resource technology, engineering materials and technology, heat transfer, and fluid mechanics.

Within each application, there are various aspects and phases of work with which the technician may be involved. One phase is research and development. In this area, the mechanical technician may assist an engineer or scientist in the design and development of anything from a ballpoint to a sophisticated measuring device. These technicians prepare rough sketches and layouts of the project being developed. In the design of an automobile engine, for example, they make drawings that detail the fans, pistons, connecting rods, and fly-

School Subjects
Mathematics
Physics

Personal Interests
Building things
Figuring out how things
work

Work Environment
Primarily indoors
Primarily one location

Minimum Education Level
Associate's degree

Salary Range
$15,500 to
$32,700 to
$54,800

Certification or Licensing
Voluntary

Outlook
About as fast as the
average

DOT
007

wheels to be used in the engine. They estimate cost and operational qualities of each part, taking into account friction, stress, strain, and vibration. By performing these tasks, they free the engineer to accomplish other research assignments.

A second common type of work for mechanical engineering technicians is testing. Technicians working in a testing laboratory use special devices to test the hardness, ductility, tensile strength, and other properties of materials. For products such as engines, motors, or other moving devices, technicians may set up prototypes of the equipment to be tested and run performance tests. Some tests require one procedure to be done over and over, while others require running equipment over long periods of time to observe any changes in operation. Technicians collect and compile all necessary data from the testing procedures and report to the engineer or scientist.

In the manufacture of a product, preparations must be made for its production. In this effort, mechanical engineering technicians assist in the product design by making design layouts and detailed drawings of parts to be manufactured and of any special manufacturing equipment needed.

These technicians, known as *drafting technicians,* usually work as *tracers, detailers,* or sometimes as *patent drafting technicians.* Tracers copy plans and drawings, usually by tracing with pencil on a transparent material in preparation for reproduction, often by using computer-aided equipment. They also may make some simple drawings under close supervision. Detailers make new drawings from layout drawings, to show the exact dimension, tolerances, finish, material, and other information necessary for production. Patent drafting technicians prepare mechanical drawings of many varieties of devices for use by patent attorneys in obtaining and recording patents.

Another specially trained mechanical technician who comes into play in the manufacturing process is the *tool designer.* Tool designers prepare sketches of designs for cutting tools, jigs, special fixtures, and other devices used in mass production. Frequently, they redesign existing tools to improve their efficiency.

Other mechanical engineering technicians, working as *engineering-specification technicians,* examine plans and drawings to determine what materials are needed and prepare lists of these materials, specifying quality, size, and strength. *Cost-estimating technicians* conduct studies to determine costs of required materials, labor, and plant space required for production. For efficient management, a product analysis must be completed before the product advances to the manufacturing stage. As a new product approaches this stage, mechanical engineering technicians called *plant-layout technicians* observe and direct the set-up of machinery and production lines as well as check the arrival and storage of raw materials.

After an item's production begins, the mechanical engineering technicians work toward perfecting the manufacturing process to make the product more profitable. This is accomplished by *time-and-motion study technicians* who observe and record the time required and motions involved when manufacturing parts. They then compare these time-and-motion values to accepted standards and may revise manufacturing methods to promote efficiency.

After the product is manufactured, some mechanical engineering technicians may help solve storage and shipping problems, while others assist in customer relations when product installation is required.

Depending on the employer's needs and technician's education or interests, many technicians are employed in very specialized positions. The following is a list of some of these specialized positions, all open to the appropriately trained entry-level technician:

Mechanical-design technicians develop mechanical drawings from engineering sketches and notes into complete, accurate working plans for a product. They also make necessary changes in drawings as requested by engineers. *Quality-control technicians* test and inspect components at various stages of manufacture, thus ensuring final quality of products as specified by engineering drawings and records. *Standards-laboratory technicians* test and calibrate measuring instruments used in manufacturing to assure precision and performance of these measuring tools. They also establish laboratory procedures to maintain the accuracy of measuring equipment. *Programmer technicians* prepare programs for numerically controlled and computer-operated machine tools using parts drawings. *Computer programmers* convert engineering problems to a language that a computer can process. They operate the computer, review results, and develop new routines for specific new computer uses. *Production-planning technicians* plan production schedules for the manufacture of industrial products, coordinating the supply of the product with its demand and forecasting needs for production.

Requirements

Preparation for this career should begin in high school. Although entrance requirements vary somewhat from school to school, mathematics and physical science form the backbone of a good preparatory curriculum. Coursework should include algebra, geometry, science, computer science, mechanical drawing, shop, and language skills.

Associate's degree or two-year mechanical technician programs are designed to prepare students for entry-level positions. Most programs offer one year of a basic program with a chance to specialize in the second year. The first year of the program generally consists of courses in mathematics, science, and communications skills. Other courses introduce students to the manufacturing processes, drafting, and language of the industry.

The second year's courses focus on mechanical technology. These include heating and cooling, internal combustion engines, tool and machine design, instruments and controls, production technology, electricity, and electronics. Many schools allow their students to choose a major in the second year of the program, which provides training for a specific area of work in the manufacturing industry.

Many mechanical engineering technicians choose to become certified by the National Institute for Certification in Engineering Technologies (NICET). To become certified, the technician must take and pass an examination. Such certification is not required for all mechanical technician positions; however, earning certification shows a high level of commitment and dedication that employers find highly desirable.

Mechanical engineering technicians are encouraged to become affiliated with professional groups that organize continuing education sessions for members. Some mechanical engineering technicians may be required to belong to unions.

Technicians need mathematical and mechanical aptitude. They must be able to understand abstract concepts and apply scientific principles to problems in the shop or laboratory, in either the design or the manufacturing process. They must be interested in people and machines and have the ability to carry out detailed work. They must be able to analyze sketches and drawings and possess patience, perseverance, and resourcefulness. Additionally, the ability to communicate in both spoken and written reports is an absolute necessity.

Opportunities for Experience & Exploration

There are several avenues that lie open to the person who wishes to gain experience or firsthand knowledge of the field of mechanical technology. High school courses in geometry, physics, mechanical drawing, and shop work will give a student a feel for the mental and physical activities involved in mechanical technology.

It may be possible to obtain part-time or summer work in a machine shop or factory. This type of work usually consists of sweeping floors and clearing out machine tools, but it offers an opportunity to view the field firsthand and also demonstrates interest to future employers.

Field trips to industrial laboratories, drafting studios, or manufacturing facilities can offer overall views of the type of work done in this field. Hobbies like automobile repair, model making, and electronic kit assembling can also be helpful. Finally, any high school student interested in the engineering field is encouraged to join the Junior Engineering Technical Society (JETS).

Methods of Entering

Both schools offering associate's degrees in mechanical engineering technology and two-year technician programs usually help graduates find employment. At most colleges, in fact, company recruiters interview prospective graduates during their final semester of school. As a result, many students receive job offers before graduation.

Other graduates may prefer to apply directly to employers, use newspaper classified ads, or apply through public or private employment services.

Advancement

As mechanical engineering technicians remain with a company, they become more valuable to the employer. Opportunities for advancement will be available to those who are willing to accept greater responsibilities, either by taking on more technically complex assignments or by assuming supervisory duties. Some technicians advance by moving into technical writing or technical sales. Mechanical technicians who further their education may become mechanical engineers.

The following paragraphs describe positions to which mechanical engineering technicians might reasonably expect to advance:

Tool designers design and modify the tools, such as milling machine cutters, broaches, fixtures, and jigs, that are used to produce the manufactured products.

Tool engineers (who are also called *machine designers*) design special machines and equipment that are used for manufacturing purposes as well as supervise drafters, detailers, and tracers.

Technical sales representatives show manufactured products to potential customers, provide the necessary advisory services, and sell the product.

Research designers develop new and better products through research and development procedures in laboratories.

Assistant production managers manage production through receiving, manufacturing, and shipping operations, including supervision of other employees.

Technical writers write reports, bulletins, and descriptive literature of all kinds, including specification sheets. They also write technical manuals that are required for manufactured products.

Production supervisors oversee specific production areas, assigning duties, interpreting engineering drawings, and checking for quality and quantity of production.

Production coordinators supervise a product's manufacture to expedite movement of supplies and finished parts; they are also responsible for completion of the product at a specified date.

Employment Outlook

Job opportunities for mechanical engineering technicians are expected to grow as fast as the average through the year 2006. There should be continuing efforts in the research and development field in search of new products, processes, and equipment. Manufacturing companies will be looking for more ways to apply the advances in mechanical technology to their operations. New manufacturing concepts, materials, designs, and consumer demands should require the need for more well-trained mechanical technicians.

However, the employment outlook for engineering technicians is influenced by the economy. Hiring will fluctuate with the ups and downs of the nation's overall financial situation. Many future job openings will be the result of retirement.

Earnings

Salaries for mechanical engineering technicians vary depending on the nature and location of the job, employer, amount of training the technician has received, and number of years of experience.

In general, mechanical engineering technicians earn salaries similar to other engineering technicians. According to the *1998-99 Occupational Outlook Handbook*, engineering technicians with little or no experience earned between $17,700 and $22,800 a year in 1995. Technicians with experience earned median salaries of $32,700, with those in supervisory or senior positions earning as much as $54,800 a year. Engineering technicians employed by the federal government, especially those at the beginning of their careers, average between $15,500 and $19,500, while some senior technicians with special skills and experience may earn as much as $42,000 or more. These salaries are based upon the standard workweek. Overtime or premium time pay may be earned for work beyond regular daytime hours or workweek.

Other benefits, depending on the company and union agreements, include paid vacation days, insurance, pension plans, profit sharing, and tuition-reimbursement plans.

Conditions of Work

Mechanical engineering technicians may find a variety of working conditions, depending on their field of specialization. Technicians who specialize in design may find that they spend most of their time at the drafting board or computer. Those who specialize in manufacturing may spend some time at a desk, but also spend considerable time in manufacturing areas or shops.

Conditions also vary according to industry. Some industries require technicians to work in foundries, die-casting rooms, machine shops, assembly areas, or punch-press areas. Most of these areas, however, are well lighted, heated, and ventilated. Moreover, most industries employing mechanical engineering technicians have fine safety programs.

Some technicians' jobs require working independently. However, most function as a part of a team and, as such, interact with other employees who may have either more or less training and authority.

Mechanical engineering technicians are often called upon to exercise decision-making skills, to be responsible for valuable equipment, and to act as effective leaders. They also sometimes carry out routine, uncomplicated tasks. Similarly, in some cases, they may be supervising the activities of others, while at other times, they are the ones supervised. They must be able to respond well to both types of demands. In return for this flexibility and versatility, mechanical engineering technicians are usually accorded considerable respect by their employers and coworkers.

Sources of Additional Information

For information on colleges and universities offering accredited programs in engineering technology, contact:

■**Accreditation Board for Engineering and Technology**
111 Market Place, Suite 1050
Baltimore, MD 21202
Tel: 410-347-7700

■**American Society of Certified Engineering Technicians (ASCET)**
PO Box 1348
Flowery Branch, GA 30542
Tel: 770-967-9173

■**American Society of Mechanical Engineers**
345 East 47th Street
New York, NY 10017
Tel: 212-705-7234
WWW: http://www.asme.org

For information on high school programs that provide opportunities to learn about engineering technology, contact:

■**Junior Engineering Technical Society (JETS)**
1420 King Street, Suite 405
Alexandria, VA 22314-2794
Tel: 703-548-5387
Email: jets@nas.edu

M dical Assistants

Definition

Medical assistants help physicians in offices, hospitals, and clinics. They keep medical records, help examine and treat patients, and perform routine office duties to allow physicians to spend their time working directly with patients. Medical assistants are vitally important to the smooth and efficient operation of medical offices.

Nature of the Work

Depending on the size of the office, medical assistants may perform clerical or clinical duties, or both. The larger the office, the greater the chance that the assistant will specialize in one type of work.

In their clinical duties, medical assistants help physicians by preparing patients for examination or treatment. They may check and record patients' blood pressure, pulse, temperature, height, and weight. Medical assistants often ask patients questions about their medical histories and record the answers in the patient's file. In the examining room the medical assistant may be responsible for arranging medical instruments and handing them to the physician as requested during the examination. Medical assistants may prepare patients for X-rays and laboratory examinations, as well as administer electrocardiograms. They may apply dressings, draw blood, and give injections. Medical assistants also may give patients instructions about taking medications, watching their diet, or restricting their activities before laboratory tests or surgery. In addition, medical assistants may collect specimens such as throat cultures for laboratory tests and may be responsible for sterilizing examining room instruments and equipment.

Medical assistants are responsible for preparing examining rooms for patients and keeping examining and waiting rooms clean and orderly. After each examination, they straighten the examinating room and dispose of used linens and medical supplies. Sometimes medical assistants keep track of office and

School Subjects
Biology
Mathematics

Personal Interests
Helping people: physical health/medicine
Science

Work Environment
Primarily indoors
Primarily one location

Minimum Education Level
Some postsecondary training

Salary Range
$14,500 to
$19,739 to
$24,793

Certification or Licensing
Voluntary

Outlook
Much faster than the average

DOT
079

GOE
10.03.02

NOC
6631

medical supply inventories and order necessary supplies. They may deal with pharmaceutical and medical supply company representatives when ordering supplies.

At other times medical assistants may perform a wide range of administrative tasks. Medical secretaries and medical receptionists also perform administrative activities in medical offices, but these workers are distinguished from medical assistants by the fact that they rarely perform clinical functions. The administrative and clerical tasks that medical assistants may complete include typing case histories and operation reports; keeping office files, X-rays, and other medical records up-to-date; keeping the office's financial records; preparing and sending bills and receiving payments; and transcribing dictation from the physician. Assistants may also answer the telephone, greet patients, fill out insurance forms, schedule appointments, take care of correspondence, and arrange for patients to be admitted to the hospital. Most medical assistants use word processors and computers for most recordkeeping tasks.

Some medical assistants work in ophthalmologists' offices, where their clinical duties involve helping with eye examinations and treatments. They use special equipment to test and measure patients' eyes and check for disease. They administer eye drops and dressings and teach patients how to insert and care for contact lenses. They may maintain surgical instruments and help physicians during eye surgery. Other medical assistants work as *optometric assistants,* who may be required to prepare patients for examination and assist them in eyewear selection. Others work as *chiropractor assistants,* whose duties may include treatment and examination of patients' muscular and skeletal problems.

Requirements

Medical assistants usually need a high school diploma, but in many cases they receive their specific training on the job. High school courses in the sciences, especially biology, are helpful to the prospective medical assistant, as are courses in algebra, English, bookkeeping, typing, computers, and office practices.

Formal training for medical assistants is available at many trade schools, community and junior colleges, and universities. College programs generally award an associate's degree and take two years to complete. Other programs can last as long as a year and award a diploma or certificate. Prior to enrolling in any school program, students should check its curriculum and verify its accreditation.

Schools for medical assistants may be accredited by either the Commission on Accreditation of Allied Health Education Programs, which has approved more than 200 medical and ophthalmic programs, or the Accrediting Bureau of Health Education Schools, which accredits over 150 medical assisting programs. Students in these programs do coursework in biology, anatomy, physiology, and medical terminology, as well as typing, transcribing, shorthand, recordkeeping, and computer skills. Perhaps most important, these programs provide supervised, hands-on clinical experience in which students learn laboratory techniques, first-aid procedures, proper use of medical equipment, and clinical procedures. They also learn about administrative duties and procedures in medical offices and receive training in interpersonal communications and medical ethics.

Medical assistants generally do not need be licensed. However, they may voluntarily take examinations for credentials awarded by certain professional organizations. The registered medical assistant (RMA) credential is awarded by American Medical Technologists and the American Registry of Medical Assistants, and the American Association of Medical Assistants (AAMA) awards a credential for certified medical assistant (CMA). Ophthalmic assistants can be certified at three levels by the Joint Commission on Allied Health Personnel in Ophthalmology: certified ophthalmic assistant, certified ophthalmic technician, and certified ophthalmic technologist.

Medical assistants must be able to interact with patients and other medical personnel, and they must be able to follow detailed directions. In addition, they must be dependable and compassionate and have the desire to help people. Medical assistants must also respect patients' privacy by keeping medical information confidential. Overall, medical assistants who help patients feel at ease in the doctor's office and have good communications skills and a desire to serve should do well in this job.

Opportunities for Experience & Exploration

Students in post–high school medical assistant programs will have the chance to explore the field through the supervised clinical experience required by the various programs. Others may wish to gain additional experience by volunteering at hospitals, nursing homes, or clinics to get a feel for the work involved in a medical environment. People interested in this field may want to talk with the medical assistants in their own or other local physicians' offices to find out more about the work they do.

Methods of Entering

Students enrolled in college or other post–high school medical assistant programs may learn of available positions through their school placement offices. High school guidance counselors may have information about positions for students about to graduate. Newspaper want ads and state employment offices are other good places to look for leads. Workers may also wish to call local physicians' offices to find out about unadvertised openings.

Advancement

To advance, many medical assistants must change occupations. Medical assistants may be able to move into managerial or administrative positions without further education, but moving into a more advanced clinical position such as nursing requires more education. As more clinics and group practices open, more office managers will be needed, and these are positions that well-qualified, experienced medical assistants may be able to fill. As with most occupations, today's job market gives medical assistants with computer skills more opportunities for advancement.

Employment Outlook

In 1996, about 225,000 medical assistants worked in physicians' offices, clinics, hospitals, health maintenance organizations, and other medical facilities. Over 70 percent work in private doctors' offices. Another 10 percent work in optometrists' and chiropractors' offices and other health care facilities. The ratio of medical assistant personnel to physicians is about seven to one.

The employment outlook for medical assistants is expected to be exceptionally good through the year 2006. Most openings will arise to replace workers who leave their jobs, but many will be the result of a predicted surge in the number of physicians' offices and outpatient care facilities. Technological advances and the growing number of elderly Americans who need medical treatment is also a factor in this increased demand for health services. In addition, new and more complex paperwork for medical insurance, malpractice insurance, government programs, and other purposes will create a growing need for assistants in medical offices.

Experienced and formally trained medical assistants are preferred by many physicians, so these workers have the best employment outlook. Word-processing skills, other computer skills, and formal certification are all definite assets.

Earnings

The earnings of medical assistants vary widely, depending on experience, skill level, and location. According to a *1997 Staff Salary Survey*, published by the Health Care Group, the average starting salary for graduates of the medical assistant programs they accredit is about $14,500. With experience, medical assistants may eventually earn an average of $24,793 a year. Earnings are higher in the Northeast and the West as compared to other regions of the United States.

Conditions of Work

Most medical assistants work in pleasant, modern surroundings, although older hospitals and clinics may be less-well ventilated. Sterilizing equipment and handling medical instruments require care and attentiveness. As most professionals in the health sciences will attest, working with people who are ill may be upsetting at times, but it can also have many personal rewards.

Most medical assistants work forty hours a week, frequently including some Saturday and evening hours. They are usually given six or seven paid holidays a year, as well as annual paid vacation days. They often receive health and life insurance, a retirement plan, sick leave, and uniform allowances.

Sources of Additional Information

American Registry of Medical Assistants
69 Southwick Road, Suite A
Westfield, MA 01085-4729
Tel: 413-562-7336

For information on accreditation and testing, please contact:

■**Accrediting Bureau of Health Education Schools**
Oak Manor Office, 29089 US 20 West
Elkhart, IN 46514
Tel: 219-293-0124

For an information packet on a career as a medical assistant, please contact:

■**American Association of Medical Assistants**
20 North Wacker Drive, Suite 1575
Chicago, IL 60606
Tel: 312-899-1500

■**American Medical Technologists**
710 Higgins Road
Park Ridge, IL 60068
Tel: 847-823-5169

Medical Record Technicians

Definition

In any hospital, clinic, or other health care facility, permanent records are created and maintained for all the patients treated by the staff. Each patient's medical record describes in detail his or her condition over time; entries include illness and injuries, operations, treatments, outpatient visits, and the progress of hospital stays. *Medical record technicians* compile, code, and maintain these records. They also tabulate and analyze data from groups of records in order to assemble reports. They review records for completeness and accuracy; assign codes to the diseases, operations, diagnoses, and treatments according to detailed standardized classification systems; and post the codes on the medical record, thus making the information on the record easier to retrieve and analyze. They transcribe medical reports; maintain indices of patients, diseases, operations, and other categories of information; compile patient census data; and file records or supervise others who do so. In addition, they may direct the day-to-day operations of the medical records department. They maintain the flow of records and reports to and from other departments, and sometimes assist medical staff in special studies or research that draws on information in the records.

Nature of the Work

A patient's medical record consists of all relevant information and observations of any health care workers who have dealt with the patient. It may contain, for example, several diagnoses, X-ray and laboratory reports, electrocardiogram tracings, test results, and drugs prescribed. This summary of the patient's medical history is very important to the physician in making speedy and correct decisions about care. Later, information from the record is often needed in authenticating legal forms and insurance claims. The medical record documents the adequacy and appropriateness of the

School Subjects
Business
English
(writing/literature)

Personal Interests
Computers
Helping people: physical health/medicine

Work Environment
Primarily indoors
Primarily one location

Minimum Education Level
Associate's degree

Salary Range
$20,000 to
$35,500 to
$47,000

Certification or Licensing
Recommended

Outlook
Much faster than the average

DOT
079

GOE
07.05.03

NOC
321

care received by the patient and is the basis of any investigation when the care is questioned in any way.

Patterns and trends can be traced when data from many records are considered together. These types of statistical reports are used by many different groups. Hospital administrators, scientists, public health agencies, accrediting and licensing bodies, people who evaluate the effectiveness of current programs or plan future ones, and medical reimbursement organizations are examples of some groups that rely on health care statistics. Medical records can provide the data to show whether a new treatment or medication really works, the relative effectiveness of alternative treatments or medications, or patterns that yield clues about the causes or methods of preventing certain kinds of disease.

Medical record technicians are involved in the routine preparation, handling, and safeguarding of individual records as well as the statistical information extracted from groups of records. Their specific tasks and the scope of their responsibilities depend a great deal on the size and type of the employing institution. In large organizations, there may be a number of technicians and other employees working with medical records. The technicians may serve as assistants to the medical record administrator as needed or may regularly specialize in some particular phase of the work done by the department.

In small facilities, however, technicians often carry out the whole range of activities and may function fairly independently, perhaps bearing the full responsibility for all day-to-day operations of the department. A technician in a small facility may even be a department director. Sometimes technicians handle medical records and also spend part of their time helping out in the business or admitting office.

Although most medical record technicians work in hospitals, many work in other health care settings, including health maintenance organizations (HMOs), industrial clinics, skilled nursing facilities, rehabilitation centers, large group medical practices, ambulatory care centers, and state and local government health agencies. Records are maintained in all these facilities, although recordkeeping procedures vary.

Whether they work in hospitals or other settings, medical record technicians must organize, transfer, analyze, preserve, and locate vast quantities of detailed information when needed. The sources of this information include physicians, nurses, laboratory workers, and other members of the health care team.

In a hospital, a patient's cumulative record goes to the medical record department at the end of the hos-

pital stay. A technician checks over the information in the file to be sure that all the essential reports and data are included and appear accurate. Certain specific items must be supplied in any record, such as signatures, dates, the patient's physical and social history, the results of physical examinations, provisional and final diagnoses, periodic progress notes on the patient's condition during the hospital stay, medications prescribed and administered, therapeutic treatments, surgical procedures, and an assessment of the outcome or the condition at the time of discharge. If any item is missing, the technician sends the record to the person who is responsible for supplying the information. After all necessary information has been received and the record has passed the review, it is considered the official document describing the patient's case.

The record is then passed to a *medical record coder.* Coders are responsible for assigning a numeric code to every diagnosis and procedure listed in a patient's file. Most hospitals in the United States use a nationally accepted system for coding. The lists of diseases, procedures, and conditions are published in classification manuals that medical records personnel refer to frequently. By reducing information in different forms to a single consistent coding system, the data contained in the record is rendered much easier to handle, tabulate, and analyze. It can be indexed under any suitable heading; for example, under patient, disease, type of surgery, physician attending the case, and so forth. Cross-indexing is likely to be an important part of the medical record technician's job. Because the same coding systems are used nearly everywhere in the United States, the data may be used not only by people working inside the hospital, but may also be submitted to one of the various programs that pool information obtained from many institutions.

After the information on the medical record has been coded, technicians may use a packaged computer program to assign the patient to one of several hundred "diagnosis-related groupings," or DRGs. The DRG for the patient's stay determines the amount of money the hospital will receive if the patient is covered by Medicare or one of the other insurance programs that base their reimbursement on DRGs.

Because information in medical records is used to determine how much hospitals are paid for caring for insured patients, the accuracy of the work done by medical records personnel is vital. A coding error could cause the hospital or patient to lose money.

Another vital part of the job concerns filing. Regardless of how accurately and completely information is gathered and stored, it is worthless unless it can be retrieved promptly. If paper records are kept, technicians are usually responsible for preparing records for storage, filing them, and getting them out of storage when needed. In some organizations, technicians supervise other personnel who carry out these tasks.

In many health care facilities, computers, rather than paper, are used for nearly all the medical record-keeping. In such cases, medical and nursing staff make notes on an electronic "chart." They enter patient care information into computer files, and medical record technicians access the information using their own terminals. Computers have greatly simplified many traditional routine tasks of the medical records department, such as generating daily hospital census figures, tabulating data for research purposes, and updating special registries of certain types of diseases, such as cancer and stroke.

In the past, some medical records that were originally on paper were later photographed and stored on microfilm, particularly after they were a year or two old. Medical record technicians may be responsible for retrieving and maintaining those films. It is not unusual for a health care institution to have a combination of paper and microfilm files as well as computerized record storage, reflecting the evolution of technology for storing information.

Confidentiality and privacy laws have a major bearing on the medical records field. The laws vary in different states for different types of data, but in all cases, maintaining the confidentiality of individual records is of major concern to medical records workers. All individual records must be in secure storage but also be available for retrieval and specified kinds of properly authorized use. Technicians may be responsible for retrieving and releasing this information. They may prepare records to be released in response to a patient's written authorization, a subpoena, or a court order. This requires special knowledge of legal statutes and often requires consultation with attorneys, judges, insurance agents, and other parties with legitimate rights access information about a person's health and medical treatment.

Medical record technicians may participate in the quality assurance, risk management, and utilization review activities of a health care facility. In these cases, he or she may serve as a data abstractor and analyst, reviewing records against established standards to ensure quality of care. He or she may also prepare statistical reports for the medical or administrative staff that reviews appropriateness of care.

With more specialized training, medical record technicians may participate in medical research activities by maintaining special records, called registries, related to such areas as cancer, heart disease, transplants, or adverse outcomes of pregnancies. In some cases, they are required to abstract and code information from records of patients with certain medical conditions. These technicians also may prepare statistical reports and trend analysis for the use of medical researchers.

Not all medical record technicians are employed in a single health care facility; some serve as consultants to several small facilities. Other technicians do not work in health care settings at all. They may be employed by health and property liability insurance companies to collect and review information on medical claims. Government agencies also hire some medical record technicians, as do manufacturers of medical records systems and equipment. A few are self-employed, providing medical transcription services.

Requirements

Most employers prefer to hire medical record technicians who have completed a two-year associate's degree program accredited by the American Medical Association's Commission on Accreditation of Allied Health Professions (CAAHP) and the American Health Information Management Association (AHIMA). There are approximately 150 of these accredited programs available throughout the United States, mostly offered in junior and community colleges. They usually include classroom instruction in such subjects as anatomy, physiology, medical terminology, medical record science, word processing, medical aspects of recordkeeping, statistics, computers in health care, personnel supervision, business management, English, and office skills.

In addition to classroom instruction, the student is given supervised clinical experience in the medical records departments of local health care facilities. This provides the student with practical experience in performing many of the functions learned in the classroom and with the opportunity to interact with health care professionals.

An alternative educational method is open to individuals with experience in certain related activities. It requires completion of an independent study program offered by the AHMA. Students in this program must successfully complete a lesson series and clinical experience internship in a health care institution. They must also earn thirty semester hours of credit in prescribed subjects at a college or university.

For either entry method, a high school diploma is required. Students contemplating a career in medical records should take as many high school English classes as possible, because technicians need both written and verbal communication skills to prepare reports and communicate with other health care personnel. Basic math or business math is very desirable because statistical skills are important in some job functions. Biology courses help by familiarizing the student with the terminology that medical record technicians use. Other science courses, computer training, typing, and office procedures are also helpful.

Medical record technicians who have completed an accredited training program are eligible to take a national qualifying examination to earn the credential of accredited record technician (ART). Most health care institutions prefer to hire individuals with an ART credential as it signifies that they have met the standards established by the AHIMA as the mark of a qualified health professional.

Technicians who have achieved the ART credential are required to obtain twenty hours of continuing education credits every two years in order to retain their ART status. These credits may be obtained by attending educational programs, participating in further academic study, or pursuing independent study activities approved by the AHIMA.

Medical records are extremely detailed and precise. Sloppy work could have serious consequences in terms of payment to the hospital or physician, validity of the patient records for later use, and validity of research based on data from medical records. Therefore, a prospective technician must have the capacity to do consistently reliable and accurate routine work. Records must be completed and maintained with care and attention to detail. The medical record technician may be the only person who checks the entire record, and he or she must understand the responsibility that accompanies this task.

The technician needs to be able to work rapidly as well as accurately. In many medical record departments, the work load is very heavy, and technicians must be well organized and efficient in order to stay on top of the job. They must be able to complete their work in spite of interruptions, such as phone calls and requests for assistance. These workers also need to be discrete as they deal with records that are private and sometimes sensitive.

Computer skills also are essential, and some experience in transcribing dictated reports may be useful.

Opportunities for Experience & Exploration

Interested high school students may be able to find summer, part-time, or volunteer work in a hospital or other health care facility. Sometimes such jobs are available in the medical records area of an organization. This experience could provide an ideal chance to measure aptitude and interests against those of people already employed in the medical records field.

Students may also be able to arrange to talk with someone working as a medical record technician or administrator. Faculty and counselors at schools that offer medical record technician training programs may also be good sources of information. Interested students also can learn more about this profession by reading journals and other literature available at a public library.

Methods of Entering

Most successful medical record technicians are graduates of two-year accredited programs. Graduates of these programs should check with their schools' placement offices for job leads. For those who have taken the accrediting exam and become ARTs, the AHIMA offers a resume referral service.

Individuals may also apply directly to the personnel departments of hospitals, nursing homes, outpatient clinics, and surgery centers. Many job openings are also listed in the classified advertising sections of local newspapers and with private and public employment agencies.

Advancement

Medical record technicians may be able to achieve some advancement and salary increase without additional training simply by taking on greater responsibility in their job function. With experience, they may move to supervisory or department head positions, depending on the type and structure of the employing organization.

Another means of advancing is through specialization in a certain area of the job. Some technicians specialize in coding, particularly Medicare coding or tumor registry. With a broad range of experience, some technicians may be able to establish themselves as independent consultants. Generally, technicians with an associate's degree and the ART designation are most likely to advance.

More assured job advancement and salary increase come with the completion of a bachelor's degree in medical record administration. The bachelor's degree, along with AHIMA accreditation, makes the technician eligible for a supervisory position, such as department director. Because of a general shortage of medical record administrators, hospitals often assist technicians who are working toward a bachelor's degree by providing flexible scheduling and financial aid or tuition reimbursement.

Employment Outlook

Most employment opportunities exist in hospitals; however, opportunities can be found in extended-care facilities, ambulatory-care facilities, HMOs, medical group practices, nursing homes, and home-health agencies. Technicians also work for computer firms, consulting firms, and government agencies.

Employment prospects for this field are excellent. The demand for well-trained medical record technicians will grow rapidly and will continue to exceed the supply. It is estimated that 47,000 new medical tech jobs will be created by the year 2006, according to the U.S. Department of Labor's Bureau of Labor Statistics. This forecast is related to the health care needs of a population that is both growing and aging and the trend toward more technologically sophisticated medicine and greater use of diagnostic procedures. It is also related to the increased requirements of regulatory bodies that scrutinize both costs and quality of care of health care providers. Because of the fear of medical malpractice lawsuits, doctors and other health care providers are documenting their diagnoses and treatments in greater detail. Also, because of the high cost of health care, insurance companies, government agencies, and courts are examining medical records with a more critical eye. These factors combine to ensure a healthy job outlook for medical record technicians.

Technicians with two-year associate's degrees and ART status will have the best prospects, and the importance of such qualifications is likely to increase.

Earnings

The salaries of medical record technicians are greatly influenced by the location, size, and type of employing institution, as well as the technician's training and experience. Beginning technicians who have earned their ART status can expect to earn between $20,000 and $25,000 a year. The average salary for all ARTs is between $35,000 and $36,000. With experience and, perhaps, specialization in a particular area, technicians may earn as much as $47,000 annually. Technicians who are not accredited typically earn somewhat less.

By earning a bachelor's or master's degree, the technician becomes more valuable to an employer and can expect higher wages. These technicians eventually can reach salary levels in the high $70,000s or the low $80,000s as medical record administrators.

In general, medical record technicians working in large urban hospitals make the most money, and those in rural areas make the least. Like most hospital employees, medical record technicians usually receive paid vacations and holidays, life and health insurance, and retirement benefits.

Conditions of Work

Medical records departments are usually pleasantly clean, well-lighted, and air-conditioned areas. Sometimes, however, paper or microfilm records are kept in cramped, out-of-the-way quarters. Although the work requires thorough and careful attention to detail, there may be a constant bustle of activity in the technician's work area, a constant bustle of activity, which can be disruptive. The job is likely to involve frequent routine contact with nurses, physicians, hospital administrators, other health care professionals, attorneys, and insurance agents. On occasion, individuals who the technicians may interact with are demanding or difficult. In such cases, technicians may find that the job carries a high level of frustration.

A forty-hour workweek is the norm, but because hospitals must operate on a twenty-four-hour basis, the job may regularly include night or weekend hours. Part-time work is sometimes available.

The work is extremely detailed and may be tedious. Some technicians spend the majority of their day sitting at a desk, working on a computer. Others may spend hours filing paper records or retrieving them from storage.

In many hospital settings, the medical record technician experiences pressure caused by a heavy workload. As the demands for health care cost containment and productivity increases, medical record technicians may be required to produce a significantly greater volume of high-quality work in shorter periods of time.

Nonetheless, the knowledge that their work is significant for patients and medical research can be personally very satisfying for medical record technicians.

Sources of Additional Information

For information on careers in health information management and ART accreditation, contact:

American Health Information Management Association (AHIMA)
919 North Michigan Avenue, Suite 1400
Chicago, IL 60611
Tel: 312-787-2672
WWW: http://www.ahima.org

For a list of schools offering accredited programs in health information management, contact:

Commission on Accreditation of Allied Health Education Professions
American Medical Association
515 North State Street, Suite 7530
Chicago, IL 60610
Tel: 312-464-5000

Medical Technologists

Definition

Medical technologists, also called *clinical laboratory technologists,* are health professionals whose jobs include many health care roles. They perform laboratory tests essential to the detection, diagnosis, and treatment of disease. They work under the direction of laboratory managers and pathologists.

Nature of the Work

Medical technologists perform laboratory tests to help physicians detect, diagnose, and treat diseases. The work of medical technologists is generally done under the supervision of a senior medical technologist, a clinical laboratory supervisor, or a physician who has specialized in diagnosing the causes and nature of disease.

Technologists in clinical practice ensure the quality of laboratory tests done for diagnosis. They may be responsible for interpreting the data and results and reporting their findings to the attending physicians. Many also assist attending physicians in correlating test results with clinical data and recommend tests and test sequences. Medical technologists may also have management and supervisory tasks, including serving as laboratory manager, supervisor of lab sections, and staff supervisor over other technologists and laboratory personnel.

The specific tasks performed by medical technologists are determined by the kind of setting in which they work. Technologists employed by small laboratories conduct many kinds of tests, such as blood counts, urinalyses, and skin tests. They use microscopes to examine body fluids and tissue samples to determine the presence of bacteria, fungi, or other organisms. They sometimes prepare slides from sample tissues and body cells to ascertain, for example, whether an individual has developed cancer. Depending on the laboratory facilities and needs, they may be responsible for operating highly sophisti-

School Subjects
Biology
Chemistry

Personal Interests
Computers
Helping people: physical health/medicine

Work Environment
Primarily indoors
Primarily one location

Minimum Education Level
Bachelor's degree

Salary Range
$15,500 to
$27,000 to
$40,680

Certification or Licensing
Required in some states

Outlook
About as fast as the average

DOT
078

GOE
02.04.02

NOC
3219

cated medical instruments and machines. They conduct research and maintain and make minor repairs to the instruments and equipment used in testing. Medical technologists employed in large laboratories generally specialize.

Medical technology specialists normally have advanced degrees in their area of expertise. They are capable of handling sophisticated equipment and testings because of their education and training. They may be responsible for ordering, purchasing, maintaining, and repairing specialized equipment and instruments required for the laboratory tests. They design new laboratory procedures and establish or continue training and education of other employees in laboratory procedures and skills.

Clinical laboratory directors oversee the laboratory or the laboratory department. They usually hold an M.D., D.O., or Ph.D. degree. They are responsible for the supervision of the technologists on the staff and for the quality of the work done. They may be in charge of sustaining the budget and determining the financial needs and responsibilities of the lab. They will assign duties, hire and fire staff, and establish work rules and standards.

Clinical laboratory supervisors, or *medical technology supervisors,* are the managers of the staff on a day-to-day basis. The supervisor assigns work schedules and assignments, reviews work and lab results, and may assist in training and continued education of the staff. The supervisor may also continue performing duties of the medical technologist. The *chief medical technologist* supervises the work of the entire laboratory operations, assigns duties, and reviews the reports and analysis.

A *chemistry technologist,* or *biochemistry technologist,* tests specimens of blood, urine, gastric juices, and spinal fluid to detect the presence of chemicals, drugs, and poisons, as well as levels of substances made by the body, such as sugar, albumin, and acetone. This information may be used in the diagnosis of metabolic disease such as diabetes. Precise measurements are made with equipment maintained by the technologist.

A *microbiology technologist,* or *bacteriology technologist,* examines specimens for microorganisms, including viruses, fungi, parasites, and bacteria. It may be necessary to isolate and grow a specific organism to make a better identification for diagnosis. Treatment of a condition may depend on the results of testing various ways of dealing with the organism itself, before the patient can be treated.

Cytotechnologists stain and mount slides with specimens and examine them under a microscope to detect and diagnose disease or damage to the cells.

They study cell growth patterns to determine if the specimens have normal patterns or abnormal patterns. They look for changes in cell color, shape, or size. They may also assist doctors in the direct collection of cell samples from a patient's respiratory tract, urinary system, or gastrointestinal tract. A primary duty of cytotechnologists is diagnosing Pap smears.

Hematology technologists analyze blood and other body fluid samples by counting the cells and microscopically identifying them. The tests are performed to help identify illnesses such as anemia, leukemia, and other blood disorders.

Histotechnologists, or *tissue technologists,* prepare specimens of tissue and bone for examination by pathologists. The specimens are preserved in a variety of ways, called fixing. One method is to place tissues in special fluids, dehydrate the samples, and replace the water with wax, which supports the tissue. This allows the technologist to cut the tissue and section it into slices as small as one cell thick. The slices are then examined under a microscope. Many times tumors are submitted for biopsy while a patient is on the operating table. These specimens are fixed by freezing and then cut for examination under a microscope. The results help the surgeon to make a more exact diagnosis. These technologists may also assist pathologists at autopsies and preserve organs for later examination and reference.

Immunohematologists type blood and cross-match donor and recipient for compatibility. They perform other blood tests and maintain the equipment and supplies of blood in several different forms to be used for transfusion.

Phlebotomists are probably the most familiar medical technologist because they draw blood during physical examinations. Responsible for obtaining blood samples for whatever testing is required, phlebotomists draw the quantity of blood specified for the testing procedure from a vein, artery, or capillary. They label the vials and transport them to the testing facility without damage or heating of the samples.

Medical laboratory technicians perform routine tests in medical laboratories. They prepare samples of body tissue; perform laboratory tests, such as urinalysis and blood counts; and make chemical and biological analysis of cells, tissue, blood, or other body specimens.

Other medical technologists are employed in research, education, health policy development (particularly in government organizations), veterinary science, public health and epidemiology study and application, diagnostic equipment research and development, and other related fields to the theoretical and the practical applications of medical technology.

Requirements

High school students interested in a career in medical technology should take courses in the biological and physical sciences. For medical technologists, a bachelor's degree is required, consisting of at least three years of college studies, including work in chemistry, the biological sciences, and mathematics, in addition to a twelve-month program in a school of medical technology. Most of these approved schools are associated with colleges and universities and have affiliations with hospitals. Education requirements may vary according to specialty. Medical laboratory technicians must earn an associate's degree or complete a two-year accredited training program.

Advanced work in medical technology leading to graduate degrees and subsequent employment in teaching and research positions is available at an increasing number of universities.

Certification of medical technologists verifies that people in the profession have met the educational standards recognized by the certifying body. After passing appropriate examinations, candidates may be certified as medical technologists, MT (ASCP), by the Board of Registry of the American Medical Technologists; as Registered Medical Technologists (RMT) by the International Society for Clinical Laboratory Technology; or as Clinical Laboratory Scientists (CLS) by the National Certification Agency for Medical Laboratory Personnel. For the CLS, a bachelor's degree in medical technology or a bachelor's degree in biology or physical science plus additional training or education in medical technology are the minimum requirements for someone applying to take the examination.

Medical technologists need to secure a license in some states, including California, Florida, Georgia, Hawaii, Nevada, Tennessee, Louisiana, North Dakota, Montana, Rhode Island, and Puerto Rico. Licenses will be required with more regularity in all the states, as insurance companies involve the evaluation of laboratory certification (which affects the diagnoses of patients) in the cost of insurance to doctors and clinics.

Because of the nature of the work, students interested in careers in medical technology should possess the following characteristics: accuracy, patience, and the ability to work under pressure. Other essential characteristics are manual dexterity and good eyesight (with or without glasses). Because the medical technologist must survive a rigorous training program, above-average scholastic aptitude is also necessary.

Opportunities for Experience & Exploration

High school students may do volunteer work in hospitals or medical facilities to learn more about the work of medical technologists. Interested students will have difficulty gaining any direct experience in medical technology until they are in the clinical and laboratory phases of their training program. However, they can write to the sources listed at the end of this article for more reading material on medical technology, or they can visit a medical technologist to watch and learn about the work. A visit to an American Medical Association-approved school of medical technology to discuss career plans with the admissions counselor would also be valuable.

Methods of Entering

Graduates of schools of medical technology may receive assistance from placement services at the schools in securing their first jobs. Hospitals, laboratories, and other companies employing medical technologists often get in touch with these placement offices and notify them of job openings. Positions may also be secured with the assistance of various registries of medical technologists. Newspaper advertisements and commercial placement agencies are other sources of initial employment.

Advancement

Advancement can be relatively rapid in the field of medical technology. With satisfactory experience and perhaps more training, a medical technologist can advance to supervisory positions or specialist fields in clinical laboratory work. Considerable experience is required for advancement to a position as chief medical technologist in a large hospital. Graduate training is necessary for advancement to positions in research and teaching. Assistants can become technicians with further education and experience.

Advancement prospects may be better in large hospitals or independent laboratories that have many departments.

Employment Outlook

Employment growth in this field is expected to grow as fast as the average rate for all occupations through the year 2006. Because of a general shortage in hospital staffs, there will be a number of openings for new medical technologists. The benefits can be good, and there are many promotion possibilities. The greatest demand for medical technologists is expected to occur in independent medical laboratories. There will also be employment opportunities in physicians' offices and clinics.

Earnings

A 1997 Hay Group survey of acute care hospitals lists average starting salaries of about $15,500 for medical technologists in hospitals, medical schools, and medical centers, while experienced technologists earned $35,000 and higher. Specialists' starting salaries vary between about $25,000 and $30,000.

According to the *1998-99 Occupational Outlook Handbook,* the average medical technologists working for the federal government in 1997 received annual salaries of about $40,680, depending on academic records, education, and experience.

Conditions of Work

Most medical laboratory workers are employed in hospitals. Some work in clinics, physicians' offices, pharmaceutical labs, public health agencies, and research institutions. Others work in Veterans Administration hospitals and laboratories as well as in the armed forces and the U.S. public health service.

Medical laboratory personnel usually work a thirty-five to forty-hour week, with night or weekend duty often required in hospitals. However, with the current staff shortage, overtime in some facilities has become common, with required amounts of overtime hours assigned to staff.

Medical technologists must exercise meticulous care in their work to avoid risk of exposure to diseases or contamination of a testing sample, requiring the retesting of the patient. Plastics have replaced glass, so risk of cuts from broken equipment is greatly reduced. Chemicals and their containers and usage have also improved with the advancement of technology so chemical burns are rare.

Medical assistants may find the work repetitive and eventually tedious, but have chances for advancement with further education. Lab workers must often work under pressure at painstaking tasks. Work loads can be heavy because of staff shortage in the workplace.

Sources of Additional Information

Accrediting Bureau of Health Education Schools
3132 US 20 West
Elkhart, IN 46514
Tel: 219-295-0214

American Association for Clinical Chemistry
2101 L Street, NW, Suite 202
Washington, DC 20037-1526
Tel: 202-857-0717
Email: info@aacc.org
WWW: http://www.aacc.org

American Medical Technologists
710 Higgins Road
Park Ridge, IL 60068
Tel: 708-823-5169

American Society for Clinical Laboratory Science
7910 Woodmont, Suite 530
Bethesda, MD 20814
Tel: 301-657-2768

American Society of Clinical Pathologists
Board of Registry
2100 West Harrison Street
Chicago, IL 60612
Tel: 312-738-1336
WWW: http://www.ascp.org

International Society for Clinical Laboratory Technology
818 Olive, Suite 918
St. Louis, MO 63101
Tel: 314-241-1445

National Accrediting Agency for Clinical Laboratory Sciences
8410 West Bryn Mawr, Suite 670
Chicago, IL 60631
Tel: 312-714-8880

National Certification Agency for Medical Laboratory Personnel
PO Box 15945-489
Lenexa, KS 66285
Tel: 913-438-5110

Merchandise Displayers

Definition

Merchandise displayers design and install displays of clothing, accessories, furniture, and other products in windows and showcases, and on the sales floors of retail stores to attract potential customers. Display workers who specialize in dressing mannequins are known as *model dressers*. These workers use their artistic flair and imagination to create excitement and customer interest in the store. They also work with other types of merchandising to develop exciting images, product campaigns, and shopping concepts.

Nature of the Work

Using their imagination and creative ability, as well as their knowledge of color harmony, composition, and other fundamentals of art and interior design, merchandise displayers in retail establishments create an idea for a setting designed to show off merchandise and attract customers' attention. Often the display is planned around a theme or concept. After the display manager approves the design or idea, the display workers create the display by constructing backdrops, using hammers, saws, spray guns, and other hand tools, installing background settings, such as carpeting, wallpaper, and lighting; gathering props and other accessories; arranging mannequins and merchandise; and placing price tags and descriptive signs where they are needed.

They may be assisted in some of these tasks by carpenters, painters, or store maintenance workers. They may use merchandise from various departments of the store or props from previous displays. Sometimes they borrow special items that their store doesn't carry—toys or sports equipment, for example—from other stores. The displays are dismantled and new ones installed every few weeks. In very large stores that employ many display workers, one might specialize in carpentry, painting, making signs, or setting up interior or window displays. A *display director* usually supervises and coordinates

School Subjects
Art
Shop (Trade/Vo-tech education)

Personal Interests
Building things
Sculpting

Work Environment
Primarily indoors
Primarily one location

Minimum Education Level
High school diploma

Salary Range
$12,000 to
$23,400 to
$30,000+

Certification or Licensing
None

Outlook
About as fast as the average

DOT
297

GOE
01.02.03

NOC
5243

the display workers' activities and confers with other managers to select merchandise to be featured.

Ambitious and talented display workers have many possible career avenues. The importance of visual merchandising is being recognized more and more as retail establishments complete for consumer dollars. Some display workers can advance to display director or even a position in store planning.

In addition to traditional stores, the skills of *visual marketing workers* are now in demand in many other types of establishments. Restaurants often try to present a distinct image to enhance the dining experience. Outlet stores, discount malls, and entertainment centers also use visual marketing to establish their identities with the public. Chain stores often need to make changes in or redesign all their stores and turn to display professionals for their expertise. Consumer product manufacturers also are heavily involved in visual marketing. They hire display and design workers to come up with exciting concepts, such as "in-store shops," which present a unified image for the manufacturer's products and are sold as complete units to retail stores.

There are also opportunities for employment with store fixture manufacturers. Many companies build and sell specialized props, banners, signs, displays, and mannequins and hire display workers as sales representatives to promote their products. The display workers' understanding of retail needs and their insight into the visual merchandising industry make them valuable as consultants.

Commercial decorators prepare and install displays and decorations for trade and industrial shows, exhibitions, festivals, and other special events. Working from blueprints, drawings, and floor plans, they use woodworking power tools to construct installations—usually referred to as booths, no matter what their size—at exhibition halls and convention centers. They install carpeting, drapes, and other decorations, such as flags, banners, and lights. They arrange furniture and accessories to attract the people attending the exhibition. Special event producers, coordinators, and party planners might also seek out the skills of display professionals.

This occupation appeals to imaginative, artistic persons who find it rewarding to use their creative abilities to visualize a design concept and then apply their mechanical aptitude to transform it into reality. Original, creative displays grow out of an awareness of current design trends and popular themes. Although display workers use inanimate objects, such as props and materials, an understanding of human motivations helps them create displays with strong customer appeal.

Requirements

Display workers must have at least a high school degree. Important high school subjects include art, woodworking, mechanical drawing, and merchandising. Some employers require college courses in art, interior decorating, fashion design, advertising, or related subjects.

High schools and community and junior colleges that offer distributive education and marketing programs often include display work in the curriculum. Fashion merchandising schools and fine arts institutes also offer courses useful to display workers.

Much of the training for display workers is received on the job. They generally start as helpers for routine tasks, such as carrying props and dismantling sets. Gradually they are permitted to build simple props and work up to constructing more difficult displays. As they become more experienced, display workers who show artistic talent might be assigned to plan simple designs. The total training time varies depending on the beginner's ability and the variety and complexity of the displays.

Among the personal qualifications needed by display workers are creative ability, manual dexterity, and mechanical aptitude. Display workers should possess the strength and physical ability needed to be able to carry equipment and climb ladders. They also need agility to work in close quarters without upsetting the props.

Opportunities for Experience & Exploration

Display work is included in many of the marketing programs taught in high in community and junior colleges. Fashion merchandising schools and fine arts institutes offer courses that would be useful for this occupation. These courses usually combine hands-on activities with the study of fashion and merchandising.

Part-time and summer jobs in department stores and other retail stores or at exhibition centers provide interested students an overview of the display operations in these establishments. Photographers and theater groups need helpers to work with props and sets, although some may require previous experience or knowledge related to their work. Students active in school drama and photo clubs may be able to help with design. Interested persons also can read periodicals, such as *Display and Design Ideas,* that publish articles on the field or related subjects.

Methods of Entering

School placement offices may have job listings for display workers or related positions. Persons wishing to become display workers can apply directly to retail stores, decorating firms, or exhibition centers. Openings also may be listed in the classified ads of newspapers.

A number of experienced merchandise displayers choose to work as freelance designers. Competition in this area, however, is intense, and it takes time to establish a reputation, build a list of clients, and earn an adequate income. Freelancing part time while holding down another job provides a more secure income for many display workers. Freelancing also provides beginners opportunities to develop a portfolio of photographs of their best designs, which they can then use to sell their services to other stores.

Advancement

Display workers with supervisory ability can become regional managers. Further advancement may lead to a display director position (of a large store) and then head of store planning.

Another way to advance is by starting a freelance design business. This can be done with very little financial investment, although freelance design workers must spend many long hours generating new business and establishing their names in the field.

Experienced display workers also may be able to transfer their skills to jobs in other art-related fields, such as interior design or photography. These, however, will require additional formal training.

Employment Outlook

About 30,000 display workers are employed in the United States. Most of them work in department and clothing stores, but many are employed in other types of retail stores, such as variety, drug, and shoe stores. Some have their own design businesses, and some are employed by design firms that handle interior and professional window dressing for small stores. Employment of display workers is distributed throughout the country, with most of the jobs concentrated in large towns and cities.

The employment of display workers is expected to keep pace with the average for all occupations. Growth in this profession is expected due to an expanding retail sector and the increasing popularity of visual merchandising. Most openings will occur as older, experienced workers retire or leave the occupation.

Fluctuations of the economy affect the volume of retail sales because people are less likely to spend money during recessionary times. For display workers this can result in layoffs or hiring freezes.

Earnings

In the 1990s large employers pay beginning display workers approximately $12,000 a year, while those who have completed some college courses earn more. Experienced workers annually earn about $23,400. Display managers receive around $30,000 a year, with some directors in large metropolitan stores earning more. Freelancers may earn as much as $30,000 a year, but their income depends entirely on their talent, reputation, number of clients, and amount of time they work.

Conditions of Work

Display workers usually work thirty-five to forty hours a week, except during busy seasons, such as Christmas. Selling promotions and increased sales drives during targeted seasons can require the display staff to work extra hours in the evening and on weekends.

The work of constructing and installing displays requires prolonged standing, bending, stooping, and working in awkward positions. There is some risk of falling off ladders or being injured from handling sharp materials or tools, but serious injuries are uncommon.

Sources of Additional Information

National Retail Federation
325 7th Street, NW, Suite 1000
Washington, DC 20004
Tel: 202-783-7971

Millwrights

Definition

Millwrights install, assemble, and maintain heavy industrial machinery and other equipment. If necessary, they may have to construct foundations for certain large assemblies. They may also be called upon to dismantle, operate, repair, or lubricate these machines.

Nature of the Work

Millwrights are highly skilled workers whose primary function is to install heavy machinery. Their responsibilities begin when machinery arrives at the job site. The new equipment must be unloaded, inspected, and moved into position. To lift and move light machinery, millwrights may use rigging and hoisting devices such as pulleys and cables. In other cases, they require the help of hydraulic lifttruck or crane operators to position the machinery. Because millwrights often decide what device to use for moving machinery, they must know the load-bearing properties of ropes, cables, hoists, and cranes.

New machinery sometimes requires a new foundation. Millwrights either personally prepare the foundation or supervise its construction, so they must know how to read blueprints and work with building materials such as concrete, wood, and steel. They must also be able to read schematic diagrams in order to make any electrical connections.

When installing machinery, millwrights fit bearings, align gears and wheels, attach motors, and connect belts according to the manufacturer's blueprints and drawings. They may use hand and power tools, cutting torches, welding machines, and soldering guns. Some millwrights use metalworking equipment such as lathes or grinders to modify parts to specifications.

Precision leveling and alignment are important in the assembly process; millwrights must have good mathematical

School Subjects
Mathematics
Shop (Trade/Vo-tech education)

Personal Interests
Building things
Figuring out how things work

Work Environment
Primarily indoors
One location with some travel

Minimum Education Level
High school diploma
Apprenticeship

Salary Range
$19,700 to
$34,800 to
$53,500

Certification or Licensing
None

Outlook
Little change or more slowly than the average

DOT
638

GOE
05.05.06

NOC
7311

skills so that they can measure angles, material thicknesses, and small distances with tools such as squares, calipers, and micrometers. When a high level of precision is required, such as on a production line, lasers may be used for alignment.

In accordance with the trend toward employee specialization, workers in larger plants are usually responsible for a particular phase of the machinery. Once it is installed, they may be called upon to do repairs or perform preventive maintenance. Millwrights also may be responsible for oiling and greasing the machinery. They sometimes work with pipefitters and industrial machinery repairers to keep production lines in operating condition.

Millwrights may change the placement of existing machines in a plant or mill to set up a new production line or improve efficiency. Their skills are very important in the planning of complicated production processes. They talk with supervisors, planners, and engineers to determine the proper placement of equipment, floor loads, work flow, safety measures, and other important concerns.

In old shops and plants, millwrights may update and improve the production process by disassembling, moving, and reinstalling machines. In small factories, millwrights rarely replace and relocate machines and do so only to increase production and improve efficiency. In larger plants, they move and reassemble machinery each time a new production run starts.

The increasing use of automation in many industries means that millwrights are responsible for installing and maintaining more sophisticated machines. Because the machinery usually requires special care and knowledge, millwrights often work closely with computer or electronic experts, electricians, and manufacturers' representatives to install it.

Requirements

Millwrights receive their training either from a formal apprenticeship program or informally on the job. Apprenticeship programs last for four years and combine on-the-job training and related classroom instruction. During the program, apprentices receive training in dismantling, moving, erecting, and repairing machinery. They may also work with concrete and receive instruction in related skills such as carpentry, welding, and sheetmetal work. Classroom instruction is given in mathematics, blueprint reading, hydraulics, electricity, and computers.

Those millwrights who learn the trade on the job usually work as helpers and learn from experienced millwrights. This process takes six to eight years.

Applicants for this occupation should be between the ages of eighteen and twenty-six, be above average in size and strength, and be in excellent physical condition. A high level of mechanical aptitude is necessary. Applicants also must have successfully completed high school. Any class with an emphasis on mechanical reasoning—shop mathematics, blueprint reading, hydraulics, and machine shop—is of particular value. Experience with electrical systems is also beneficial.

Good hand-eye coordination, manual dexterity, and mechanical aptitude are necessary qualities for success in this job. The ability to visualize a layout by looking at blueprints and a memory for detail are also important.

Most millwrights are represented by a labor union. The unions to which most millwrights belong include the International Union of Electronic, Electrical, Salaried, Machine, and Furniture Workers; the International Union, United Automobile, Aerospace, and Agricultural Implement Workers of America; and the United Brotherhood of Carpenters and Joiners of America.

Opportunities for Experience & Exploration

One of the best ways for students to find out more about this career is to talk with someone who is already employed as a millwright. Visiting an industrial setting that employs millwrights could also be of value, by allowing the interested person to watch these workers in action. Local unions that represent millwrights can also provide information to students interested in this job.

Methods of Entering

Most young people pursuing millwright work are first hired for unskilled or semiskilled work in a plant or factory. Most companies post notices when job openings become available, and those employees who are interested and qualified may bid for the jobs. Openings are filled from lists of these employees according to experience and seniority.

Advancement

Most advancement for millwrights comes in the form of higher wages. With the proper training, skill, and seniority, however, workers can move to supervisory positions. Skilled and experienced employees may also work as trainers for apprentices.

Employment Outlook

Millwrights work in every state in nearly every plant and shop that uses heavy machinery and equipment. Most are employed in industries that manufacture durable goods, such as automobiles, steel, and metal products. Others work in plants that manufacture paper, chemicals, knit goods, and other items. Jobs are also available with utilities companies and in construction. Manufacturers and sellers of industrial machinery often employ millwrights to install machines for their customers. Employment is concentrated in industrial regions.

The employment of millwrights is expected to decline slightly through the year 2006. Although automation is replacing many manufacturing workers, millwrights are still needed to dismantle old machinery and install and maintain the modern replacements. Many openings will also arise each year as experienced millwrights transfer to other jobs or retire.

Downturns in the economy may affect the jobs of some millwrights. The impact is usually less for those working in manufacturing plants because, even though employers are not installing new equipment, existing machinery still needs to be maintained and repaired.

Earnings

Millwrights are typically paid an hourly wage. Those who are just beginning their careers may make around $10.00 per hour. Entry-level millwrights earn average salaries of $19,700 a year. Experienced workers earn annual wages between $26,500 and $42,000. Millwrights at the top end of the pay scale can earn $53,500 or more a year. Apprentices generally start at 50 percent of the millwright's salary and increase to the full pay rate by the end of the training program. In general, millwrights employed by construction companies earn more than those employed in manufacturing.

Most workers in this field receive a benefits package that includes life and health insurance, paid vacation and sick leave, and a retirement pension.

Conditions of Work

Millwrights generally work indoors, out of the elements, but their work is not, by any means, comfortable and relaxed. It is often hard physical labor, in surroundings made unpleasant by heat, noise, grime, and cramped spaces. In addition, it can be hazardous, although protective devices and an emphasis on safety have reduced the number of accidents in recent years.

Millwrights may be called to work at unusual times or for long hours in emergency situations. A breakdown in machinery can affect an entire plant's operation and be very costly, so machines need to be kept in operating condition at all times. Model changes in the production line can also require long hours. Millwrights who work for companies that manufacture and install industrial equipment may be required to travel.

Sources of Additional Information

■ **Associated General Contractors of America**
1957 E Street, NW
Washington, DC 20006
Tel: 202-393-2040

■ **International Union of Electronic, Electrical, Salaried, Machine, and Furniture Workers**
1126 16th Street, NW
Washington, DC 20036
Tel: 202-296-1200

For information on the career of millwright, contact:

■ **International Union, United Automobile, Aerospace, and Agricultural Implement Workers of America**
Skill Trades Department, Solidarity House
8000 East Jefferson Avenue
Detroit, MI 48214
Tel: 313-926-5000

For information on local chapters and apprenticeship opportunities, contact:

■ **United Brotherhood of Carpenters and Joiners of America**
101 Constitution Avenue, NW
Washington, DC 20001
Tel: 202-546-6206

Musicians

Definition

Musicians perform, compose, conduct, arrange, and teach music. Performers of music would include *singers* as well as *instrumental musicians. Performing musicians* may work alone or as part of a group, or ensemble. They may play before live audiences in clubs or auditoriums, or they may perform on television or radio, in motion pictures, or in a recording studio. Musicians usually play either classical, popular (including country and western), jazz or folk music, but many musicians play in several musical styles.

Nature of the Work

Instrumental musicians play one or more musical instruments, usually in a group and in some cases as featured soloists. Musical instruments are usually classified in several distinct categories according to the method by which they produce sound: strings (violins, cellos, basses, etc.), which make sounds by vibrations from bowing or plucking; woodwinds (oboes, clarinets, saxophones), which make sounds by air vibrations; brass (trumpets, French horns, trombones, etc.), which also make sounds by air vibrations, but differ from the woodwinds in shape and operation; and percussion (drums, pianos, triangles), which produce sound by striking. Instruments can also be classified as electric or acoustic, especially in popular music. Synthesizers are another common form of music, and computer and other electronic technology is increasingly used for creating music.

Musicians may play in symphony orchestras, dance bands, jazz bands, rock bands, country and western bands, or other groups or alone. Some of them may play in recording studios either with their group or as a *session player* for a particular recording. Recordings are in the form of records, tapes, compact discs, and videotape cassettes. Classical musicians perform in concerts, opera performances, and chamber music concerts, and they may also play in theater orchestras,

School Subjects
Music
Theater

Personal Interests
Entertaining/Performing
Music

Work Environment
Indoors and outdoors
Primarily multiple
locations

Minimum Education Level
High school diploma

Salary Range
$7,000 to
$26,000 to
$1,000,000+

Certification or Licensing
Required for certain
positions

Outlook
Faster than the average

DOT
152

GOE
01.04.04

NOC
5133

although theater music is not normally classical. The most talented ones may work as soloists with orchestras or alone in recital. Some classical musicians accompany singers and choirs, and they may also perform in churches and temples.

Musicians who play popular music make heavy use of such rhythm instruments as piano, bass, drums, and guitar. Jazz musicians also feature woodwind and brass instruments, especially the saxophone and trumpet, and they extensively utilize the bass. Synthesizers are also commonly used instruments; some music is performed entirely on synthesizers, which can be programmed to imitate a variety of instruments and sounds. Musicians in jazz, blues, country western, and rock groups play clubs, festivals, and concert halls and may perform music for recordings, television, and motion picture sound tracks. Occasionally they appear in a movie themselves. Other musicians compose, record, and perform entirely with electronic instruments, such as synthesizers and other devices. In the late 1970s, rap artists began using turntables as musical instruments, and later, samplers, which record a snippet of other songs and sounds, as part of their music.

Instrumental musicians and singers use their skills to convey the form and meaning of written music. Instrumentalists and vocalists work to achieve precision, fluency, and clarity of tone; vocalists attempt to express emotion through phrasing and characterization. Musicians practice constantly to perfect their techniques.

Many musicians supplement their incomes through teaching, while others teach as their full-time occupation, perhaps playing jobs occasionally. Voice and instrumental music teachers work in colleges, high schools, elementary schools, conservatories, and in their own studios; often they give concerts and recitals featuring their students. Many professional musicians give private lessons. Students learn to read music, develop their voices, breathe correctly, and hold their instruments properly.

Choral directors lead groups of singers in schools and other organizations. Church choirs, community oratorio societies, and professional symphony choruses are among the groups that employ choral directors outside of school settings. Choral directors audition singers, select music, and direct singers in achieving the tone, variety, intensity, and phrasing that they feel is required. *Orchestra conductors* do the same with instrumental musicians. Many work in schools and smaller communities, but the best conduct large orchestras in major cities. Some are resident instructors, while others travel constantly, making guest appearances with major national and foreign

orchestras. They are responsible for the overall sound and quality of their orchestras.

Musicians may also spend part or all of their time as *composers, arrangers, orchestrators, copyists, librettists,* and *lyricists.* The people in these occupations write and prepare the music that musicians play and sing. *Composers* write the original music symphonies, songs, or operas using musical notation to express their ideas through melody, rhythm, and harmony. *Arrangers* and *orchestrators* take a composer's work and transcribe it for the various orchestra sections or individual instrumentalists and singers to perform; they prepare music for film scores, musical theater, television, or recordings. *Copyists* assist composers and arrangers by copying down the various parts of a composition, each of which is played by a different section of the orchestra. *Librettists* write words to opera and musical theater scores, and lyricists write words to songs and other short musical pieces. Most songwriters compose both music and lyrics, and many are musicians who perform their own songs.

Requirements

Many musicians begin learning their musical skills at an early age, sometimes before they even enter elementary school. From that point on, the development of musical skills requires long hours of practice and study. Even after high school few students are prepared to take their place as professional musicians; more practice and study are needed. Further institutional study is not required, though, particularly for those seeking a career in the popular music field. College or conservatory degrees would only be required for those who plan to teach in institutions. However, it is probably a good idea for anyone going into music to acquire a degree, just to have a more versatile background in case of a career switch. Some musicians learn to play by ear, but for most, learning musical notation is a requirement.

Scores of colleges and universities have excellent music schools, and there are numerous conservatories that offer degrees in music. Many schools have noted musicians on their staff, and music students often have the advantage of studying under a professor who has a distinguished career in music. Having the means and a high grade average does not always assure entry into the top music schools. More than likely an audition is required and only the most talented are accepted. College undergraduates in music school will generally take courses in music theory, harmony, counterpoint, rhythm, melody, ear training, applied music, and music history. Courses in composing, arranging, and conducting are available in most comprehensive music schools. Students will also have to take courses such as English and psychology along with a regular academic program.

Hard work and dedication are key factors in a musical career, but music is an art form, and like those who practice any of the fine arts, musicians will succeed according to the amount of musical talent they have. Those who have talent and are willing to make sacrifices to develop it are the ones most likely to succeed. How much talent and ability one has is always open to speculation and opinion, and it may take years of studying and practice before musicians can assess their own degree of limitation.

There are other requirements necessary to becoming a professional musician that are just as important as training, education, and study. Foremost among these is a love of music strong enough to endure the arduous training and working life of a musician. To become an accomplished musician and to be recognized in the field requires an uncommon degree of dedication, self-discipline, and drive. Musicians who would move ahead must practice constantly with a determination to improve their technique and quality of performance. Musicians also need to develop an emotional toughness that will help them deal with rejection, indifference to their work, and ridicule from critics which will be especially prevalent early in their careers. There is also praise and adulation along the way, which is easier to take, but also requires a certain psychological handling.

Musicians who want to teach in state elementary and high schools must be state certified. To obtain a state certificate, musicians must satisfactorily complete a degree-granting course in music education at an institution of higher learning. About six hundred institutions in the United States offer programs in music education that qualify students for state certificates. Music education programs include many of the same courses mentioned earlier for musicians in general. They also would include education courses and supervised practice teaching. To teach in colleges and universities or in conservatories generally requires a graduate degree in music. Widely recognized musicians, however, sometimes receive positions in higher education without having obtained a degree.

For musicians interested in careers in popular music, however, little to no formal training is necessary. Many popular musicians teach themselves to play their instruments, which often results in the creation of new and exciting playing styles. Quite often, popular musicians do not even know how to read music. Some would say that many rock musicians do not even know how to play their instruments—this was especially true in the early days of the punk era. Most musicians, however, have a natural talent for rhythm and melody.

Musicians playing popular music, such as rock, jazz, or blues, often go through years of "paying their dues"—that is, receiving little money, respect, or attention for their efforts. They must have a strong sense of commitment to their careers and to their creative ideas.

Opportunities for Experience & Exploration

Opportunities for aspiring musicians to explore the field and find early musical experiences are fairly plentiful. Elementary schools, high schools, and institutes of higher education all present students with a number of options for musical training and performance, including choirs, ensembles, bands, and orchestras. Musicians may also have chances to perform in school musicals and talent shows as well. Music students taking private lessons usually are able to display their talents in recitals arranged by their teachers. College, university, and conservatory students also gain valuable performance experience by appearing in recitals and playing in bands, orchestras, and school shows. The more enterprising students in high school and in college form their own bands and begin earning money by playing while still in school.

It is important for aspiring musicians to take advantage of every opportunity to audition as they present themselves. There are numerous community amateur and semi-professional theater groups throughout the United States that produce musical plays and operettas, in which beginning musicians can gain playing experience. Churches provide numerous opportunities for singers, instrumentalists, and directors to perform and learn. Musical summer camps give young music students a chance to perform with others, gain experience on stage, and begin to find out if they have what it takes to become a professional musician.

Methods of Entering

Young musicians need to enter as many playing situations as they can in their school and community musical groups. They should audition as often as possible, because experience at auditioning is very important. Whenever possible they should take part in seminars and internships offered by orchestras, colleges, and associations. The National

Orchestral Association offers training programs for musicians who want a career in the orchestral field.

Musicians who want to perform in established groups, such as choirs and symphony orchestras, enter the field by auditioning. Recommendations from teachers and other musicians often help would-be musicians obtain the opportunity to audition. Concert and opera soloists are also required to audition. Musicians must prepare themselves thoroughly for these auditions, which are demanding and stressful. A bad audition can be very discouraging for the young musician.

Popular musicians often begin playing at low-paying social functions and at small clubs or restaurants. If people like their performances, they usually move on to bookings at larger rooms in better clubs. Continued success leads to a national reputation and possible recording contracts. Jazz musicians tend to operate in the same way, taking every opportunity to audition with established jazz musicians.

Music teachers enter the field by applying directly to schools. College and university placement offices often have listings of positions. Professional associations, in their newsletters and journals, also frequently list teaching openings, as do newspapers. An excellent source to check for instrumental jobs is *The International Musician,* the newsletter of The American Federation of Musicians. Other music-oriented journals and associations, such as the American Symphony Orchestra League, can also be contacted for leads and information.

Advancement

Advancement is not easy to define. Popular musicians, once they have become established with a band, advance by moving up to more famous bands or by taking leadership of their own group. Bands may advance from playing small clubs to larger halls and even stadiums and festivals. They may receive a recording contract; if their songs or recordings prove successful, they can command higher fees for their contracts. Symphony orchestra musicians advance by moving to the head of their section of the orchestra. They can also move up to a position such as assistant or associate conductor. Once instrumental musicians acquire a reputation as accomplished artists, they receive engagements that are of higher status and remuneration, and they may come into demand as soloists. As their reputations develop, both classical and popular musicians may receive attractive offers to make recordings and personal appearances.

Popular and opera singers move up to better and more lucrative jobs through recognition of their talent by the public or by music producers and directors and agents. Their advancement is directly related to the demand for their talent and their own ability to promote themselves.

Music teachers in elementary and secondary schools may, with further training, aspire to careers as supervisors of music of a school system, a school district, or an entire state. With further graduate training, teachers can qualify for positions in colleges, universities, and music conservatories, where they can advance to become department heads. Well-known musicians can become artists-in-residence in the music departments of institutions of higher learning.

Employment Outlook

It is difficult to make a living solely as a musician, and this will continue because competition for jobs will be as intense as it has been in the past. Most musicians must hold down other jobs while pursuing their music career. Many thousands of musicians are all trying to "make it" in the music industry. Musicians are advised to be as versatile as possible, playing various kinds of music and more than one instrument. More importantly, they must be committed to pursuing their craft.

A variety of factors will affect musician employment through the year 2006, which the U.S. Bureau of Labor Statistics predicts will grow faster than the average for all other occupations. The demand for musicians will be greatest in bands, orchestras, and religious organizations. The outlook is less favorable in bars and restaurants. Bars—regular employers of musicians—are predicted to grow more slowly in the next decade; the number of musicians employed by restaurants that also feature live entertainment will decrease as the consumption of alcoholic beverages outside the home continues to decline. The increasing numbers of cable television networks, and increasing numbers of new television programs, will likely see an increase in employment for musicians. The number of record companies has grown dramatically over the last decade, particularly among small, independent houses. Digital recording technology has also made it easier and less expensive for musicians to produce and distribute their own recordings. However, few musicians will earn substantial incomes from these efforts. Popular musicians may receive many short-term engagements in nightclubs, restaurants, and theaters, but these engagements offer little job stability.

The opportunities for careers in teaching music are expected to grow at an average rate in elementary schools and in colleges and universities but at a slower rate in secondary schools. Although increasing numbers of colleges and universities have begun to offer music programs, enrollments in schools at all levels have been depressed and are not expected to increase until early in the next century. Some public schools, facing severe budget problems, have had to eliminate music programs altogether, making competition for jobs at that level even keener. In addition to these, private music teachers are facing greater competition from instrumental musicians who increasingly must turn to teaching because of the oversupply of musicians seeking playing jobs. The job supply is also diminishing because of the advent of electronic instruments such as synthesizers, which can replace a whole band, and the increasing trend to use recorded music.

Earnings

It is difficult to estimate the earnings of the average musician, because what they can earn is dependent upon the performer's skill, reputation, geographic location, type of music, and number of engagements per year.

Musicians in the major U.S. symphony orchestras earn minimum salaries of between $140 and $1,200 a week. The season for these major orchestras, generally located in the largest U.S. cities, ranges from twenty-nine to fifty-two weeks. In major orchestras during the 1996-97 performing season, musicians earned annual salaries that ranged from $22,000 to $90,000, according to the American Federation of Musicians. Featured musicians and soloists can earn much more, especially those with an international reputation.

Popular musicians are usually paid per concert or "gig." A band just starting out playing a small bar or club may be required to play three sets a night, and each musician may receive next to nothing for the entire evening. Often, bands receive a percentage of the cover charge at the door. Some musicians play for drinks alone. On average, however, pay per musician ranges from $30 to $300 or more per night. Bands that have gained national recognition and a following may earn far more, because a club owner can usually be assured that many people will come to see the band play. The most successful popular musicians, of course, can earn millions of dollars each year. In the late-1990s, some artists have signed recording contracts worth $20 million and more.

Musicians are well paid for studio recording work, when they can get it. For recording film and television background music, musicians are paid a minimum of about $185 for a three-hour session; for record company recordings they receive a minimum of about $234 for three hours. Instrumentalists performing live earn anywhere from $30 to $300 per engagement,

depending on their degree of popularity, talent, and the size of the room they play.

Church organists, choir directors, and soloists make an average of $40 to $100 each week, but this is often part-time work supplemented by pay from other jobs.

The salaries received by music teachers in public elementary and secondary schools are the same as for other teachers. In public elementary schools the salary received by teachers in the 1990s is about $25,000 per year. The figure for public secondary school teachers is about $27,000. Music teachers in colleges and universities have widely ranging salaries. Most teachers supplement their incomes through private instruction and by performing in their off hours.

Most musicians do not, as a rule, work steadily for one employer, and they often undergo long periods of unemployment between engagements. Because of these factors, few musicians can qualify for unemployment compensation. Unlike other workers, most musicians also do not enjoy such benefits as sick leave or paid vacations. Some musicians, on the other hand, who work under contractual agreements do receive benefits, which usually have been negotiated by artists unions, such as the American Federation of Musicians.

Conditions of Work

Work conditions for musicians vary greatly. Performing musicians generally work in the evenings and on weekends. They also spend much time practicing and rehearsing for performances. Their workplace can be almost anywhere, from a swanky club to a high school gymnasium to a dark, dingy bar. Many concerts are given outdoors and in a variety of weather conditions. Performers may be given a star's dressing room or share a mirror in a church basement or find themselves changing in a bar's storeroom. They may work under the hot camera lights of film or television sets or tour with a troupe in subzero temperatures. They may work amid the noise and confusion of a large rehearsal of a Broadway show or in the relative peace and quiet of a small recording studio. Seldom are two days in a performer's life just alike.

Many musicians and singers travel a great deal. More prominent musicians may travel with staffs who make their arrangements and take care of wardrobes and equipment. Their accommodations are usually quite comfortable, if not luxurious, and they are generally playing in major urban centers. Lesser known musicians may have to take care of all their own arrangements and put up with lesser accommodations in relatively remote places. Some musicians perform on the streets or in subway tunnels and other places likely to have a great deal of passersby. Symphony orchestra musicians probably travel less than most, but those of major orchestras travel largely under first-class conditions.

The chief characteristic of musical employment is its lack of continuity. Few musicians work full-time and most experience periods of unemployment between engagements. Most work day jobs to supplement their incomes. Those who are in great demand generally have agents and managers to help direct their careers.

Music teachers affiliated with institutions work the same hours as other classroom teachers. Many of these teachers, however, spend time after school and on weekends directing and instructing school vocal and instrumental groups. Teachers may also have varied working conditions. They may teach in a large urban school, conducting five different choruses each day, or they may work with rural elementary schools and spend much time driving from school to school.

College or university instructors may divide their time between group and individual instruction. They may teach several musical subjects and may be involved with planning and producing school musical events. They may also supervise student music teachers when they do their practice teaching.

Private music teachers work part- or full-time out of their own homes or in separate studios. The ambiance of their work place would be in accordance with the size and nature of their clientele.

Most musicians work in large urban areas and are particularly drawn to the major recording centers, such as Chicago, New York City, Los Angeles, Nashville, and Miami Beach. Most musicians find work in churches, templcs, clubs and restaurants, at weddings, in opera and ballet productions, and on television and radio. Religious organizations are the largest single source of work for musicians.

Professional musicians generally hold membership in the American Federation of Musicians (AFL-CIO), and concert soloists also hold membership in the American Guild of Musical Artists, Inc. (AFL-CIO). Singers can belong to a branch of Associated Actors and Artistes of America (AFL-CIO). Music teachers in schools often hold membership in the Music Educa-tors National Conference, a department of the National Education Association.

Sources of Additional Information

American Federation of Musicians of the United States and Canada
Paramount Building
1501 Broadway, Suite 600
New York, NY 10036
Tel: 212-869-1330
Email: info@afm.org

American Guild of Musical Artists
1727 Broadway
New York, NY 10019
Tel: 212-265-3687

International Guild of Symphony, Opera, and Ballet Musicians
5802 16th, NE
Seattle, WA 98105
Tel: 206-524-7050

Music Teachers National Association
Carew Tower
441 Vine Street, Suite 505
Cincinnati, OH 45202
Tel: 513-421-1420
Email: smcray@mtna.org
WWW: http://www.mtna.org

National Association of Schools of Music
11250 Roger Bacon Drive, Suite 21
Reston, VA 22091
Tel: 703-437-0700
Email: kpmnasm@aol.com
WWW: http://www.arts-accredit.org/nosm

Women In Music
31121 Mission Boulevard, Suite 300
Hayward, CA 94544
Tel: 510-232-3897
Email: womeninmusic@pacbell.net
WWW: http://www.womeninmusic.com

Nannies

Definition

Nannies, also known as *au pairs,* are child monitors who care for children in the same family in the family's home. The children usually range in age from infancy to eleven years old. The nanny's responsibilities may include supervising the nursery, organizing play activities, taking the children to appointments or classes, and keeping the children's quarters clean and intact. They may be responsible for supervision for part or all of the day.

Nature of the Work

Nannies perform their child care duties in the homes of the families that employ them. Unlike other kinds of household help, nannies are specifically concerned with the needs of the children in their charge. Nannies prepare the children's meals, making sure they are nutritious, appealing, and appetizing. They may do grocery shopping specifically for the children. Nannies may accompany the children during their mealtimes and oversee their training in table manners and proper etiquette. They also clean up after the children's meals. If there is an infant in the family, a nanny will wash and sterilize bottles and feed the infant. It is not part of a nanny's regular duties to cook for the adult members of the household or do domestic chores outside of those required for the children.

Nannies are responsible for keeping order in the children's quarters. They may clean up the bedrooms, nursery, and playroom, making sure beds are made with clean linens and sufficient blankets. Nannies may also wash and iron the children's clothing and do any necessary mending. They make sure that the clothing is put neatly away. With older children, the nanny may begin instruction in orderliness and neatness, teaching children how to organize their possessions.

Nannies bathe and dress the children and instill proper grooming skills. Children often seek the assistance of their

School Subjects
Family and Consumer Science
Psychology

Personal Interests
Babysitting/Child care
Helping people: personal service

Work Environment
Primarily indoors
One location with some travel

Minimum Education Level
High school diploma

Salary Range
$7,800 to
$10,500 to
$23,400

Certification or Licensing
Voluntary

Outlook
Much faster than the average

DOT
301

GOE
10.03.03

NOC
6474

nanny in getting ready for family parties or holidays. As the children get older, she or he helps them learn how to dress themselves and take care of their appearance.

Not only are nannies responsible for the care and training of their charges, but they also act as companions and guardians. They plan games and learning activities for the children and supervise their play, encouraging fairness and good sportsmanship. They may be responsible for planning activities to commemorate holidays, special events, or birthdays. These activities may center around field trips, arts and crafts, or parties. Nannies may travel with families on trips and vacations or they may take the children on short excursions without their families.

Nannies must be detail oriented when it comes to the children entrusted in their care. They keep records of illnesses, allergies, and injuries. They also note learning skills and related progress as well as personal achievements, such as abilities in games or arts and crafts. Later, they relate these events and achievements to the parents.

The nanny acts as the parents' assistant by focusing closely on the children and fostering the behavior expected of them. He or she is responsible for carrying out the parents' directions for care and activities. By setting good examples and helping the children follow guidelines established by their parents, the nanny encourages the development of happy and confident personalities.

Requirements

Although nannies usually come to love the children with whom they work, they must possess an even and generous temperament when working with them. They must be kind, affectionate, and genuinely interested in the child's well-being and development. Good physical condition, energy, and stamina are also necessary for success in this career. Nannies must be able to work well on their own initiative and have sound judgment to handle any small crises or emergencies that arise. They must know how to instill discipline and carry out the parents' expectations.

They should be loyal and committed to the children and respectful of the families for which they work. In some cases, this is difficult, since nannies are often privy to negative elements of family life, including the emotional problems of parents and their neglect of their children. Nannies need to recognize that they are not part of the family and should not allow themselves to become too familiar with its members. When they disagree with the family on matters of raising the children, they should do so with tact and the realiza-

tion that they are only employees. Finally, it is imperative that they be discreet about the confidential family matter. A nanny that gossips about family affairs is likely to be rapidly dismissed.

From an educational standpoint, nannies usually are required to have at least a high school diploma or equivalent (e.g., GED). Helpful high school classes include health, psychology, and home economics. English and communications classes also are useful as they provide skills that will help in everyday dealings with the children and their parents. Nannies must also have a valid driver's license since they may be asked to chauffeur the children to doctors' appointments or other outings.

There are several schools that offer specialized training on becoming a nanny, which usually last between twelve and sixteen weeks. These programs are typically accredited by individual state agencies. Employers generally prefer applicants who have completed an accredited program. Graduates of accredited programs also can command higher salaries. Two- and four-year programs are available at many colleges and includes courses on early childhood education, child growth and development, and child care.

College course work on nanny training also may focus on communications, family health, first aid, child psychology, and food and nutrition. Classes may also include play and recreational games, arts and crafts, children's literature, and safety and health. Because nannies may be responsible for children of various ages, the coursework focuses on each stage of childhood development and the needs of individual children. Special emphasis is given to the care of infants. Professional nanny schools may also give instruction on family management, personal appearance, and appropriate conduct. Although nannies are not required to be certified, it is important that they select accredited and professional training so they may enter the field as skillful and prepared nannies.

Opportunities for Experience & Exploration

Babysitting is an excellent way to gain experience in taking care of children. Often, a baby-sitter cares for children without any supervision, thereby learning child management and personal responsibility. Volunteer or part-time work at day care centers, nurseries, or elementary schools can also be beneficial.

Talk to a nanny to get further information. There are several placement agencies for prospective nannies, and one of them might be able to setup a meeting or phone interview with someone who works in the field.

Methods of Entering

Most schools that train nannies offer placement services. In addition it is possible to register with an employment agency that places child care workers Some agencies conduct recruitment drives or fairs to find applicants. Newspaper classified ads may also list job openings for nannies.

When the prospective nanny starts interviewing families as potential employers, they should be sure to screen them carefully. Applicants should ask for references of previous nannies, particularly if a family has had many prior nannies, and talk with one or more of them, if possible. There are many horror stories in nanny circles about past employers, and the prospective worker should not assume that every employer is exactly what they appear to be at first. Nannies also need to ensure that the specific duties and terms of the job are explicitly specified in a contract. Most agencies will supply sample contracts.

Advancement

Over half the nannies working in this country are under the age of thirty. Many nannies work in child care temporarily as a way to support themselves through school or may leave to start families of their own. Some nannies, as their charges grow older and start school, may be employed by a new family every few years. This may result in better paying positions.

Other advancement opportunities for nannies depend on the personal initiative of the nanny. Some nannies enroll in college to get the necessary training to become teachers or child psychologists. Other nannies may establish their own childcare agencies or schools for nannies.

Employment Outlook

The continuing trend of both parents working outside the home ensures that nannies will remain in demand. As more women enter the workforce, the demand for good, qualified nannies will increase.

Presently, the demand for nannies outweighs the supply, and graduating nannies may find themselves faced with several job offers. It may be years before the gap between the demand for nannies and availability of nannies closes.

Earnings

According to the U.S. Department of Labor, hourly wages for nannies can range from minimum wage to over $10.00 an hour. Nannies almost always work more than forty hours per week, so clearly those on the lower end of the pay scale are rather poorly compensated for their time. This salary range also depends on such factors as the number of children cared for, length of time with a family, and amount of previous experience. Some employers provide room and board. Presently, the highest demands for nannies are in large cities on the West and East coasts. High demand can result in higher wages.

Some nannies may be asked to travel with the family. If it is a business-oriented trip, a nanny may be compensated with wages as well as additional days off upon return. If the travel is for vacation, a nanny may get a paid bonus for working additional days off. Some employers choose not to take their nannies along when they travel, and these nannies may not earn any wages while the family is gone. Such situations can be financially disadvantageous for the nanny who has been promised full-time work and full-time pay. It is recommended that nannies anticipate possible scenarios or situations that may affect their working schedules and wages and discuss these issues with employers in advance.

Nannies often have work contracts with their families that designate wages, requirements, fringe benefits, and salary increases. Health insurance, worker's compensation, and Social Security tax are sometimes included in the benefits package. Annual pay raises vary, with increases of seven or eight percent being on the high end of the scale.

Conditions of Work

No other job involves as intimate a relationship with other people and their children as the nanny's job. Because nannies often live with their employers, it is important that they choose their employer with as much care as the employer chooses them. All necessary working conditions need to be negotiated at the time of hire. Whether a day's or a week's notice for weekend work is required should be established at the time of hire. A long list of demands may make a nanny less employable not more, so prospective nannies need to determine what factors are priorities and which ones are negotiable. Nannies should be fair, flexible and able to adapt to changes easily.

Because nannies work in their employers' homes, their working conditions vary greatly. Some nannies are "live-ins," sharing the home of their employer, because of convenience or because of the number or age of children in the family. Newborn babies require additional care that may require the nanny to live on the premises.

It is also common for a nanny to live with the family during the week and return to her or his own home on the weekends. When nannies live in the family's home, they usually have their own quarters or a small apartment that is separate from the rest of the family's bedrooms and offers some privacy. Sometimes the nanny's room is next to the children's room so it is possible for the nanny to hear right away if help is needed.

Nannies who do not live in may expect to stay at the home for long periods of time, much longer than a traditional nine-to-five job warrants. Since it often is the nanny's responsibility to put the children to bed in the evening, a nanny may not return home until late evening. Often nannies are asked to stay late or work weekends if the parents have other engagements.

The work of a nanny can often be stressful or unpleasant. Many employers expect their nannies to do things unrelated to their job, such as clean the house, run errands, walk dogs, or babysit for neighborhood children. Some employers may be condescending, rude, and critical. Some mothers, while they need and want the services of a nanny, grow resentful and jealous of the bonds the nanny forms with the children.

Nannies have very few legal rights with regard to their jobs and have few recourses to deal with unfair employers. Job security is very poor as parents have less need for nannies as their children get older and start school. In addition, nannies are often fired with no notice and sometimes no explanation, due to the whims of their employers. Leaving behind a job and the children they have taken care of and grown close to can be emotionally difficult for workers in this field.

The work is often strenuous, requiring a great deal of lifting, standing, and walking or running. The work is also mentally taxing as young children demand constant attention and energy. However, it can be very rewarding for nannies as they grow close to the children, helping with their upbringing and care. In the best cases, the nanny becomes an integral part of the family he or she works for and is treated with professionalism, respect, and appreciation.

Sources of Additional Information

For information on training and careers as a nanny, contact:

■**American Council of Nanny Schools (ACNS)**
Delta College
University Center, MI 48710
Tel: 517-686-9417

■**International Nanny Association (INA)**
125 South 4th Street
Norfolk, NE 68701
Tel: 402-691-9628

The following organization is a private training school for nannies that also offers placement services.

■**National Academy of Nannies, Inc.**
1681 South Dayton Street
Denver, CO 80231
Tel: 303-333-NANI or 800-222-NANI

The following organization is a national support group run by nannies for nannies. In addition to offering a national network, it publishes a newsletter and sponsors a yearly conference.

■**National Association of Nannies (NAN)**
7413 Six Forks Road, Suite 317
Raleigh, NC 27615
Tel: 800-344-6266

The following organization is an exchange program that places foreign students between the ages of eighteen and twenty-five in American homes as au pairs for one year. A reciprocal program arranges for Americans to spend a year abroad as au pairs.

■**Au Pair in America**
American Institute for Foreign Study Scholarship Foundation
102 Greenwich Avenue
Greenwich, CT 06830
Tel: 800-574-8889

The following company places full-time, live-in child care workers nationwide.

■**Childcrest**
6985 Union Park Center, Suite 340
Salt Lake City, UT 84047
Tel: 203-869-9090

Nuclear Medicine Technologists

Definition

Nuclear medicine technologists prepare and administer chemicals known as radiopharmaceuticals (radioactive drugs) used in the diagnosis and treatment of certain diseases. These drugs are administered to a patient and absorbed by specific locations in the patient's body, thus allowing technologists to use diagnostic equipment to image and analyze their concentration in the patient's body. Technicians also perform laboratory tests on patients' blood and urine to determine certain body chemical levels.

Nature of the Work

Nuclear medicine technologists work directly with patients, preparing and administering radioactive drugs. All work is supervised by a physician. Because of the nature of radioactive material, the drug preparation requires adherence to strict safety precautions. All safety procedures are overseen by the Nuclear Regulatory Commission (NRC).

After administering the drug to the patient, the technologist operates a gamma scintillation camera that take pictures of the radioactive drug as it passes through or accumulates in parts of the patient's body. These images are then displayed on a computer screen, where the technologist and physician can examine them. The images can be used to diagnose diseases or disorders in such organs as the heart, brain, lungs, liver, kidneys, and bones. Nuclear medicine is also used for therapeutic purposes, such as to destroy abnormal thyroid tissue or ease the pain of a terminally ill patient.

Nuclear medicine technologists also have administrative duties. They must keep thorough records of the procedures performed, check all diagnostic equipment and record its use and maintenance, and keep track of radioactive drugs administered. Laboratory testing of a patient's body specimens, such as blood or urine, may also be performed by technologists.

School Subjects
Anatomy and Physiology
Chemistry

Personal Interests
Helping people: physical
health/medicine
Science

Work Environment
Primarily indoors
Primarily one location

Salary Range
$25,000 to
$33,400 to
$39,400

Minimum Education Level
Associate's degree

Certification or Licensing
Required for certain
states

Outlook
About as fast as the
average

DOT
078

GOE
10.02.02

NOC
3215

They are also responsible for maintaining medical records for review by the attending physician.

Requirements

Those interested in the field of nuclear medicine must complete at minimum a two-year certificate program, a two-year associate's degree program, or a four-year bachelor's degree program. Professional training is available at some colleges as part of a bachelor's or associate's program, and it ranges from two to four years in length. Some hospitals and technical schools also offer certificate training programs. All programs should be accredited by the Joint Review Committee on Educational Programs in Nuclear Medicine Technology.

Interested high school students should take courses such as algebra, biology, chemistry, physics, anatomy, and computer science.

Some educational programs are designed for individuals who already have a background in a related health care field, such as radiologic technology, sonography, or nursing. These programs are usually one year in length. A good knowledge of anatomy and physiology is helpful. Coursework in nuclear medicine technologist programs includes radiation biology and protection, radioactivity and instrumentation, radiopharmaceuticals and their use on patients, and therapeutic nuclear medicine.

Nuclear medicine technologists must know the minimum federal standards for use and administration of nuclear drugs and equipment. Approximately half of all states require technologists to be certified or registered by the American Registry of Radiologic Technologists (ARRT) or the Nuclear Medicine Technology Certification Board (NMTCB). Many nuclear medicine technologist positions, especially those in hospitals, are open only to certified or registered technologists. Information on becoming registered or certified is available from the ARRT and NMTCB.

Those interested in a nuclear medicine technology career should have a strong sense of teamwork, compassion for people, and self-motivation.

Opportunities for Experience & Exploration

Individuals cannot get hands-on experience without the necessary qualifications. However, it is possible to become familiar with the job responsibilities by talking with practicing nuclear medicine technologists or teachers in the subject. In addition, volunteer experience at local hospitals or nursing homes provides a good introduction to what it is like to work in a health care setting.

Methods of Entering

Graduates of specialized training programs and two- and four-year programs usually receive placement assistance from their educational institutions, which have a vested interest in placing as many graduates as possible. Help wanted ads in local papers and professional journals are also good sources of job leads, as is participation in professional organizations, which gives members opportunities to network.

Advancement

Growth in the field of nuclear medicine should lead to advancement opportunities. Advancement usually takes the form of promotion to a supervisory position, with a corresponding increase in pay and responsibilities. Due to increased competition for positions in large metropolitan hospitals, technologists who work at these institutions may need to transfer to another hospital or city to secure a promotion. Hospitals in rural areas have much less competition for positions and therefore are more likely to give promotions.

Promotions, which are more easily attained by earning a bachelor's degree, are normally to positions of supervisor, chief technologist, or nuclear medicine department administrator. Some technologists may advance by leaving clinical practice to teach or work with equipment development and sales.

Employment Outlook

Employment for nuclear medicine technologists is expected to grow as fast as the average rate for all occupations through the year 2006. Advances in medical diagnostic procedures could lead to increased use of nuclear medicine technology in the diagnosis and treatment of more diseases, including cancer treatment and cardiology. A growing middle age and older population will need specialized diagnostic procedures, thus creating a need for qualified technicians.

In 1996, there were approximately 13,000 nuclear medicine technologists, with most employed by hospitals. Most new job opportunities are expected to be in areas with large hospitals. Jobs are also available in health clinics, research facilities, and private laboratories. The actual number of new positions will be low because of the occupation's small size.

Earnings

According to a 1997 Hay Group survey of acute care hospitals, the starting salaries for nuclear medicine technologists average about $25,000 per year for entry-level positions. Technologists with experience can expect to make from $33,400 to $39,400 annually. Those who work overtime and are on-call can earn even higher salaries. Typical benefits for hospital workers include health insurance, paid vacations and sick leave, and pension plans.

Conditions of Work

Nuclear medicine technologists usually set their own schedules and can expect to work thirty-five to forty hours a week, although larger hospitals often require overtime. Night and weekend work can also be expected. Because the job usually takes place inside a hospital or other health care facility, the environment is always clean and well lighted. The placing or positioning of patients on the diagnostic equipment is sometimes required, so a basic physical fitness level is necessary. There is a small chance of low-level contamination from the radioactive material or from the handling of body fluids. Strict safety precautions, including the use of shielded syringes and gloves and the wearing of badges that measure radiation, greatly reduce the risk of contamination.

Sources of Additional Information

For information about career opportunities as a nuclear medicine technologist, contact:

■**American Society of Radiologic Technologists**
15000 Central Avenue, SE
Albuquerque, NM 87123-3917
Tel: 505-298-4500

For information on certification, contact:

■**American Registry of Radiologic Technologists**
1255 Northland Drive
St. Paul, MN 55120-1155
Tel: 612-687-0048

■**Nuclear Medicine Technology Certification Board**
2970 Clairmont Road, Suite 610
Atlanta, GA 30329-1634
Tel: 404-315-1739

■**Society of Nuclear Medicine**
1850 Samuel Morse Drive
Reston, VA 22090-5316
Tel: 703-708-9000

Numerical Control Tool Programmers

Definition

Numerical control tool programmers, also called *computer numerical control tool programmers,* use their knowledge of machining operations and blueprint reading to write programs that enable machine tools to make metal parts automatically.

Nature of the Work

Tool programmers write the programs that direct machine tools to make parts automatically. Programmers must understand how the various machine tools operate and know the working properties of the metals and plastics that are used in the process. Tool programmers should have an aptitude for mathematics and blueprint reading.

Writing a program for a numerically controlled tool involves several steps. Before tool programmers can begin writing a program, they must first analyze the blueprints of the various items to be made. After the blueprints have been analyzed, the programmers determine the steps that must be taken and the cutting tools that will be needed to machine the workpiece into a desired shape. The programmers must determine not only the size and position of the cuts that must be made, but the speed and rate that will be needed as well.

After all necessary computations have been made, the programmers write a program in the language of the electronic controller and store the program on punched tape, magnetic tape, or disks.

Programmers usually use computers to write the programs. They write a series of simple commands in a computer language; the computer then computes the necessary mathematics, translates the program into the language of the controller, and stores it. It is more and more common today for programmers to use computer-aided design (CAD) systems. CAD systems can be used to write the program for the computer. Tool

School Subjects
Computer science
Mathematics

Personal Interests
Computers
Figuring out how things work

Work Environment
Primarily one location
Primarily indoors

Minimum Education Level
High school diploma
Apprenticeship

Salary Range
$24,960 to
$28,000 to
$36,400

Certification or Licensing
None

Outlook
Decline

DOT
007

GOE
05.01.06

NOC
2233

programmers use computers and CAD systems as aids in their work; they do not, however, write the computer software themselves.

To ensure that a program has been properly designed, tool programmers often perform a test or trial run. Trial runs help ensure that a machine is functioning properly and that the final product is correct. Some computers run a simulation program to check a specific program.

Requirements

Numerical control tool programmers need to have an understanding of machine tool operations, analytical skills, and strong mathematical and computer aptitudes. In high school, students should take courses in algebra, geometry, trigonometry, computer science, physics, blueprint reading, computer-aided design and drafting, and English. Shop classes in metalworking are also useful.

Many employers prefer to hire experienced machine workers and then provide them with training either through programming courses offered by a machine manufacturer or a technical school. An individual who has completed courses in tool programming, however, may be hired in spite of a lack of experience. It is valuable for those interested in tool programming to have a background knowledge of mathematics, blueprint reading, metalworking, data processing, physics, and drafting.

Technical schools and community colleges offer courses in computer numerical control (CNC) tool programming through various programs. One such program is offered through the manufacturing technology department of a community college and awards associate's degrees to students who complete the two-year coursework. Associate's degrees are available in different areas, such as manufacturing technology and automated manufacturing systems. Typical classes include machine shop, numerical control (NC) fundamentals, technical mechanics, advanced NC programming, introduction to robotic technology, and computer-assisted manufacturing. Certificates, which generally take one to two years to complete, are also available in such areas as drafting/design and manufacturing technology. These programs usually offer a few classes related to numerical control tool programming.

Some workers learn this trade through apprenticeship programs that combine on-the-job training with classroom instruction. Apprenticeship programs last four years and include training in writing programs for machine operations, computer-aided design and manufacturing, analyzing drawings and design data, and machine operations. Classes include courses in blueprint reading and drawing, machine tools, industrial mathematics, trigonometry, computers, and operation and maintenance of CNC machines.

Opportunities for Experience & Exploration

Students who are interested in a career as a tool programmer may test their interest and aptitude by taking shop and vocational classes.

Students can also visit firms that employ numerical control tool programmers. Talking directly with tool programmers is an excellent way to gain practical information on what this type of work is like.

Summer jobs at manufacturing firms and machine shops may provide insight into the work, as will part-time work. A person may start out in an entry-level job to gain machining experience before deciding to obtain formal training in machine tool programming.

Methods of Entering

Tool programming generally is not considered an entry-level job; most employers prefer to hire those with experience and technical training. However, firms may promote skilled machine workers to programming jobs and then pay for their technical training. On the other hand, employers may hire individuals who have no direct job experience if they have completed technical courses. Some workers enter this field through apprenticeship programs.

Students who are enrolled in a community college or technical school may learn of job openings through their schools' job placement services. Prospective programmers also may learn of openings through state and private employment offices and newspaper ads. Students also can apply directly to a manufacturing firm or machine shop that uses tool programmers.

Advancement

Advancement opportunities are somewhat limited for tool programmers. Employees may advance to higher-paying jobs by transferring to larger or more established manufacturing firms or shops. Experienced tool programmers who demonstrate good interpersonal skills and managerial ability may be promoted to supervisory positions. Tool programmers also have the option of transferring to related positions such as that of a tool designer.

Employment Outlook

Employment for numerical control tool programmers is expected to decline in the years leading up to 2006. Computer numerical control machines have replaced cam-actuated machines in many companies, but new advances in technology will limit the demand for many new programmers.

Some positions may become available as demand for industrial machinery, aircraft, motor vehicles, and other products that use machined parts increases during the late1990s as companies recover from a worldwide recession in the early 1990s. Two of the largest users of NC equipment are the aerospace and electronics industries. Both of these industries are rebounding from earlier slumps in production and may provide employment opportunities to tool programmers. The automotive industry is another large user of NC machinery. Although the automotive industry experienced some growth in the mid-1990s, it is subject to cyclical swings in production, and employment opportunities in this area may fluctuate during the next decade.

Earnings

Based on limited salary information, tool programmers earn approximately $12.00 to $17.50 an hour. Apprentices begin at about half the journeyworker rate and earn incremental raises as they progress through training. Tool programmers generally work a forty-hour week, although overtime is common during peak periods. Overtime may include evening and weekend work during production periods when the tool programs are operating.

Benefits vary but may include paid vacations and holidays, personal leaves; medical, dental, vision, and life insurance; pension plans; 401(k) plans; profit sharing; and tuition assistance programs.

Conditions of Work

Tool programmers usually work in comfortable surroundings. Their work is less physically demanding than those who operate machine tools. In addition, the areas in which they work are separated from the noisier areas where machine tools are in use. Most tool programmers work in cities, where the majority of factories and machine shops are located.

Numerical control tool programmers are highly skilled workers who must be able to work both individually and as part of a team.

Sources of Additional Information

For information on apprenticeships, please contact:

International Union, United Automobile, Aerospace and Agricultural Implement Workers of America (UAW)
Public Relations Department
8000 East Jefferson Avenue
Detroit, MI 48214
Tel: 313-926-5000

For information on careers and educational programs, please contact the following sources:

National Tooling and Machining Association
9300 Livingston Road
Fort Washington, MD 20744
Tel: 301-248-6200 or 800-248-6862
WWW: http://www.ntma.org

Precision Machined Products Association
6700 West Snowville Road
Brecksville, OH 44141-3292
Tel: 216-526-0300

Operating Engineers

Definition

Operating engineers operate various types of power-driven construction machines such as shovels, cranes, tractors, bulldozers, pile drivers, concrete mixers, and pumps.

Nature of the Work

Operating engineers work for contractors who build highways, dams, airports, skyscrapers, buildings, and other large-scale projects. They also work for utilities companies, manufacturers, factories, mines, steel mills, and other firms that do their own construction work. Many work for state and local public works and highway departments.

Whatever the company, operating engineers run power shovels, cranes, derricks, hoists, pile drivers, concrete mixers, paving machines, trench excavators, bulldozers, tractors, and pumps. They use these machines to move construction materials, earth, logs, coal, grain, and other material. Generally, operating engineers move the materials over short distances—around a construction site, factory, or warehouse, or on and off trucks and ships. They also do minor repairs on the equipment, as well as keep them fueled and lubricated. They often are identified by the machines they operate.

Bulldozer operators operate the familiar bulldozer, a tractor-like vehicle with a large blade across the front for moving rocks, trees, earth, and other obstacles from construction sites. They also operate trench excavators, road graders, and similar equipment.

Crane and tower operators lift and move materials, machinery, or other heavy objects with mechanical booms and tower and cable equipment. Although some cranes are used on construction sites, most are used in manufacturing and other industries.

School Subjects
Mathematics
Shop (Trade/Vo-tech education)

Personal Interests
Building things
Fixing things

Work Environment
Primarily outdoors
Primarily multiple locations

Minimum Education Level
High school diploma
Apprenticeship

Salary Range
$13,700 to
$23,700 to
$41,900

Certification or Licensing
None

Outlook
About as fast as the average

DOT
859

GOE
05.11.01

NOC
7421

Excavation and loading machine operators handle machinery equipped with scoops, shovels, or buckets to excavate earth at construction sites and to load and move loose materials, mainly in the construction and mining industries.

Hoist and winch operators lift and pull heavy loads using power-operated equipment. Most work in loading operations in construction, manufacturing, logging, transportation, public utilities, and mining.

Operating engineers use various pedals, levers, and switches to run their machinery. For example, crane operators may rotate a crane on its chassis, lift and lower its boom, or lift and lower the load. They also use various attachments to the boom such as buckets, pile drivers, or heavy wrecking balls. When a tall building is being constructed, the crane and its operator may be positioned several hundred feet off the ground.

Operating engineers must have very precise knowledge about the capabilities and limitations of the machines they operate. To avoid tipping over their cranes or damaging their loads, crane operators must be able to judge distance and height and estimate their load size. They must be able to raise and lower the loads with great accuracy. Sometimes operators cannot see the point where the load is to be picked up or delivered. At these times, they follow the directions of other workers using hand or flag signals or radio transmissions.

The range of skills of the operating engineer is broader than in most building trades as the machines themselves differ in the ways they operate and the jobs they do. Some operators know how to work several types of machines, while others specialize with one machine.

Requirements

A high school education or the equivalent technical training is valuable for the operating engineer and is a requirement for apprenticeship training. Operators must have excellent mechanical aptitude and skillful coordination of eye, hand, and foot movements. In addition, because reckless use of the machinery may be dangerous to other workers, it is necessary to have a good sense of responsibility and seriousness on the job.

There are two ways to become an operating engineer: through a union apprentice program or on-the-job training. The apprenticeship, which lasts three years, has at least two advantages: the instruction is more complete, which results in greater employment opportunities, and both labor and management know that the apprentice is training to be a machine operator.

Besides learning on the job, the apprentice also receives some classroom instruction in grade-plans reading, elements of electricity, physics, welding, and lubrication services. Despite the advantages of apprenticeships, most apprenticeship programs are difficult to enter because the number of apprentices is limited to the number of skilled workers already in the field.

Operating engineers should be healthy and strong. They need the temperament to withstand dirt and noise and endure all kinds of weather conditions. Applicants to an apprenticeship program generally must be between the ages of eighteen and thirty. Many operating engineers belong to the International Union of Operating Engineers.

Opportunities for Experience & Exploration

Young people may be able to gain practical experience by operating machines by observing them in action by working as a laborer or machine operator's helper in construction job during the summer. Such jobs may be available on local, state, and federal highway and building construction programs.

Methods of Entering

Once apprentices complete their training and become journeyworkers, their names are put on a list; as positions open up, they are filled in order from the list of available workers. People who do not complete an apprenticeship program may apply directly to manufacturers, utilities, or contractors who employ operating engineers for entry-level jobs as machine operator's helpers.

Advancement

Some operating engineers—generally those with above-average ability and interest, as well as good working habits—advance to job supervisor and occasionally construction supervisor. Some are able to qualify for higher pay by training themselves to operate more complicated machines.

Employment Outlook

Approximately 1,097,000 operating engineers were employed in 1996. Increased spending planned for the nation's infrastructure indicates a good employment outlook for this type of work. Employment of all operating engineers is projected to grow about as fast as the average. Employment of hoist and winch operators and industrial truck and tractor operators is expected to grow more slowly than average, however, because of increased efficiency brought about by automation (factories and plants are increasingly relying on computer-controlled material handling systems, many of which do not require a human operator).

About 75 percent of the operating engineers work in construction and local government—industries that are associated with the construction and repair of highways, bridges, dams, harbors, airports, subways, water and sewage systems, power plants, and transmission lines. Construction of schools, office and other commercial buildings, and residential property will also stimulate demand for these workers. However, the construction industry is very sensitive to changes in the overall economy, so the number of openings may fluctuate from year to year. Many job openings will result in the need to replace older workers.

Earnings

According to 1997 statistics from the U. S. Department of Labor, the median annual salary for all operating engineers is about $23,700. Rates vary according to the area of the country and the type of machine being operated. Crane and tower operators earn a median annual salary of $28,600; excavation and loading machine operators, $25,200; bulldozer operators, $25,400; and other material moving equipment operators, $23,400. Other factors affecting wages are the experience of the operator and purpose for which the machine is being used.

Conditions of Work

Operating engineers consider dirt and noise a part of their jobs. Some of the machines on which they work constantly shake and jolt them. This constant movement, along with the strenuous, outdoor nature of the work, makes this a physically tiring job. Since the work is done almost entirely outdoors in almost any kind of weather, operating engineers must be willing to work under conditions that are often unpleasant.

Sources of Additional Information

Associated General Contractors of America
1957 E Street, NW
Washington, DC 20006
Tel: 202-393-2040
Email: 73264.15@compuserv
WWW: http://www.laborers.agc.org

International Union of Operating Engineers
1125 17th Street, NW
Washington, DC 20036
Tel: 202-429-9100

Painters and Paperhangers

Definition

For both practical purposes and aesthetic appeal, building surfaces are often painted and decorated with various types of coverings. Although painting and paperhanging are two separate skills, many building trades craft workers do both types of work. *Painters* apply paints, varnishes, enamels, and other types of finishes to decorate and protect interior and exterior surfaces of buildings and other structures. *Paperhangers* cover interior walls and ceilings with decorative paper, fabric, vinyls, and other types of materials.

Nature of the Work

Workers in the painting and paperhanging trades often perform both functions; painters will often take on jobs that involve hanging wallpaper, and paperhangers will sometimes work in situations where they are responsible for painting walls and ceilings. However, although there is some overlap in the work done by painters and paperhangers, each trade has its own characteristic skills.

Painters must be able to apply paint thoroughly, uniformly, and rapidly to any type of surface. To do this, they must be skilled in handling brushes and other painting tools and have a working knowledge of the various characteristics of paints and finishes—their durability, suitability, and ease of handling and application.

Preparation of the area to be painted is an important duty of painters, especially when repainting old surfaces. They first smooth the surface, removing old, loose paint with a scraper, paint remover (usually a liquid solution), a wire brush, or paint removing gun (similar in appearance to a blowdryer for hair) or a combination of several of these items. If necessary, they must also remove grease and fill nail holes, cracks, and joints with putty, plaster, or other types of filler. Often, a prime coat or a sealer is applied to further smooth the surface and make the finished coat level and well blended in color. Once the surface

School Subjects
Mathematics
Shop (Trade/Vo-tech education)

Personal Interests
Building things
Drawing/Painting

Work Environment
Indoors and outdoors
Primarily multiple locations

Minimum Education Level
High school diploma
Apprenticeship

Salary Range
$11,180 to
$19,812 to
$35,776

Certification or Licensing
None

Outlook
About as fast as the average

DOT
840

GOE
05.10.07

is prepared, painters select premixed paints or prepare paint themselves by mixing required portions of pigment, oil, and thinning and drying substances. (For purposes of preparing paint, workers must have a thorough knowledge of the composition of the various materials they use and of which materials mix well together.) They then paint the surface using a brush, spray gun, or roller; choosing the most appropriate tool for applying paint is one of the most important decisions a painter must make because using incorrect tools often slows down the work and produces unacceptable results. Spray guns are used generally for large surfaces or objects that do not lend themselves to brush work, such as lattices, cinder and concrete block, and radiators.

Many painters specialize in working on exterior surfaces only, painting house sidings and outside walls of large buildings. When doing work on tall buildings, scaffolding (raised supportive platforms) must be erected to allow the painter to climb to his or her position at various heights above the ground; workers also might use swinglike and chairlike platforms hung from heavy cables.

The first task of the paperhanger is similar to that of the painter: to prepare the surface to be covered. Rough spots must be smoothed, holes and cracks must be filled, and old paint, varnish, and grease must be removed from the surface. In some cases, old wallpaper must be removed by brushing it with solvent, soaking it down with water, or steaming it with portable steamer equipment. In new work, the paperhangers apply sizing, which is a prepared glazing material used as filler to make the plaster less porous and to ensure that the paper sticks well to the surface.

After erecting any necessary scaffolding, the paperhangers measure the area to be covered and cut the paper to size. They then mix paste and apply it to the back of the paper, which is then placed on the wall or ceiling and smoothed into place with brushes or rollers. In placing the paper on the wall, paperhangers must make sure that they match any design patterns at the adjacent edges of paper strips, cut overlapping ends, and smooth the seams between each strip.

Requirements

Basic skills requirements are the same for both painters and paperhangers. Most employers prefer to hire applicants in good physical condition, with manual dexterity (or the equivalent) and a good sense of color. Although a high school education is not essential, it is preferred that workers have at least the equivalent of a high school diploma (i.e., a GED). For protection of their own health, applicants should not be allergic to paint fumes or other materials used in the trade.

To qualify as a skilled painter or paperhanger, a person must also complete either an apprenticeship or an on-the-job training program. The apprenticeship program, which often combines painting and paperhanging, consists of three years of carefully planned activity, including work experience and related classroom instruction (approximately 144 hours of courses each year). During this period the apprentice becomes familiar with all aspects of the craft: use of tools and equipment, preparation of surfaces as well as of paints and pastes, application methods, coordination of colors, reading of blueprints, characteristics of wood and other surfaces, cost-estimating methods, and safety techniques. Courses often involve the study of mathematics as well as practice sessions on the techniques of the trade.

On-the-job training programs involve learning the trade informally while working for two to three years under the guidance of experienced painters or paperhangers. The trainees usually begin as helpers until they acquire the necessary skills and knowledge for more difficult jobs. Workers without formal apprenticeship training are more easily accepted in these crafts than in most of the other building trades.

Opportunities for Experience & Exploration

In high school and vocational school there are several ways to explore the skills of the painter and paperhanger. Courses in art, industrial arts, and wood shop will test students' interest and ability in this type of work, while courses in chemistry and mathematics will gauge their aptitude in the characteristics of materials (such as paints, varnishes, and pastes) and in cost estimation.

Other opportunities can be explored by reading trade journals and watching instructional videos or television programs. Those who already have some experience in the trade should keep up with the news by reading such publications as the monthly *Painters and Allied Trades Journal,* available to members of the painters and allied trades union. Look for educational videos at your local library, and check your TV listings for such programs as *This Old House.*

Certainly, painting and paperhanging in one's own home or apartment provides valuable firsthand experience, often impossible to obtain in other fields. Also valuable is the experience gained with a part-time or summer job as a helper to skilled workers who are already in the trade. Those who have done satisfactory part-time work sometimes go to work full-time for the same employer after a certain period of time.

Methods of Entering

There are two ways that individuals can enter the painting and paperhanging trades: as apprentices or as on-the-job trainees. If they wish to become apprentices, the applicants usually contact employers (such as painting and paperhanging contractors), the state employment service bureau, the state apprenticeship agency, or the appropriate union headquarters (International Brotherhood of Painters and Allied Trades). They must, however, have the approval of the joint labor-management apprenticeship committee before they can enter the occupation by this method.

If the apprentice program is filled, applicants may wish to enter the trade as on-the-job trainees. In this case, they usually contact employers directly and begin work as helpers.

Advancement

Successful completion of one of the two types of training programs is necessary before individuals can become qualified, skilled painters or paperhangers. If workers have management ability and good planning skills, and if they work for a large contracting firm, they may advance to the following positions: supervisor, who supervises and coordinates activities of other workers; painting and decorating contract estimator, who computes material requirements and labor costs; and superintendent on a large contract painting job.

Some painters and paperhangers, once they have acquired enough capital and business experience, go into business for themselves as painting and decorating contractors. These self-employed workers must be able to take care of all standard business affairs, such as bookkeeping, insurance and legal matters, advertising, and billing.

Employment Outlook

In the late 1990s, there are about 449,000 painters and paperhangers employed in the United States; most of these workers are painters, and most are members of the trade union. Over 40 percent of these workers are self-employed. Jobs are found mainly with contractors who work on projects such as new construction, remodeling, and restoration; others are found as maintenance workers for such establishments as schools, apartment complexes, and high-rise buildings.

Employment of painters and paperhangers is expected to grow about as fast as the average for all occupations through the year 2006. Most job openings will occur as other workers retire, transfer, or otherwise leave the occupation. Turnover is very high in this trade. Openings for paperhangers will be fewer than those for painters, however, because this is a smaller specialized trade.

Increased construction will generate a need for more painters to work on new buildings and industrial structures. However, this will also lead to increased competition among self-employed painters and painting contractors for the better jobs. Newer types of paint have made it easier for inexperienced persons to do their own painting, but this does not affect the employment outlook much because most painters and paperhangers work on industrial and commercial projects and are not dependent on residential work.

Earnings

Painters and paperhangers tend to earn more per hour than other workers, but their total annual incomes may be less because of work time lost due to poor weather and periods of layoffs between contract assignments. The average annual beginning salary in 1996 for painters and paperhangers who were not self-employed was $11,180; for more experienced workers, $19,812; and for the top wage earners, $35,776. Paperhangers generally earn more than painters. Wages often vary depending on the geographic location of the job. Apprentices tend to earn starting wages that are about 40 to 50 percent less than those of more experienced workers.

Conditions of Work

Most painters and paperhangers have a standard forty-hour workweek, and they usually earn extra pay for working overtime. Their work requires them to stand for long periods of time, to climb, and to bend. Painters work both indoors and outdoors, because their job may entail painting interior surfaces as well as exterior siding and other areas; paperhangers work exclusively indoors.

Because these occupations involve working on ladders and often with electrical equipment such as power sanders and paint sprayers, workers must adhere to safety standards.

Sources of Additional Information

International Brotherhood of Painters and Allied Trades
United Unions Building
1750 New York Avenue, NW
Washington, DC 20006
Tel: 202-637-0700
Email: mail@ibpat.org
WWW: http://www.ibpat.org

National Association of Home Builders
1201 15th Street, NW
Washington, DC 20005
Tel: 800-368-5242
Email: info@nahb.com
WWW: http://www.nahb.com

National Joint Painting, Decorating, and Drywall Apprenticeship and Training Committee
1750 New York Avenue, NW
Washington, DC 20006
Tel: 202-637-0740

Painting and Decorating Contractors of America
3913 Old Lee Highway
Suite 33B
Fairfax, VA 22030
Tel: 703-359-0826
WWW: http://www.masterpainter.com/pdca

Painters and Sculptors

Definition

Painters use watercolors, oils, acrylics, and other substances to paint a variety of subjects, including landscapes, people, and objects. *Sculptors* design and construct three-dimensional artwork from various materials, such as stone, concrete, plaster, and wood.

Nature of the Work

Painters and sculptors use their creative abilities to produce original works of art. They are generally classified as fine artists rather than commercial artists because they are responsible for selecting the theme, subject matter, and medium of their artwork. As fine artists, painters and sculptors create works to be viewed and judged for aesthetic content. Visual art can take as many forms as the people who create them.

Painters use a variety of media to paint portraits, landscapes, still lifes, abstracts, and other subjects. They use brushes, palette knives, and other artist's tools to apply color to canvas or other surfaces. They work in a variety of media, including oil paint, acrylic paint, tempera, watercolors, pen and ink, pencil, charcoal, crayon, pastels, but may also use such nontraditional media as earth, clay, cement, paper, cloth, and any other material that allows them to express their artistic ideas. Painters develop line, space, color, and other visual elements to produce the desired effect. They may prefer a particular style of art, such as realism or abstract, and they may be identified with a certain technique or subject matter. Many artists develop a particular style and apply that style across a broad range of techniques, from painting to etching to sculpture.

Sculptors use a combination of media and methods to create three-dimensional works of art. They may carve objects from stone, plaster, concrete, or wood. They may use their fingers to model clay or wax into objects. Some sculptors create

School Subjects
Art
Computer science

Personal Interests
Painting
Sculpting

Work Environment
Indoors and outdoors
One location with some travel

Minimum Education Level
High school diploma

Salary Range
$30 or less for a piece by a little-known artist, to $300 for a piece by an artist with some experience and exposure, to $10,000 or more for a piece created by an established, well-known artist

Certification or Licensing
None

Outlook
Faster than the average

DOT
144

GOE
01.02.02

NOC
5136

forms from metal or stone, using various masonry tools and equipment. Others create works from found objects, whether parts of a car, branches of a tree or other objects. Like painters, sculptors may be identified with a particular technique or style. Their work can take monumental forms or they may work on a very small scale.

Many artists, of course, combine both elements of painting and sculpture in their art. They may also combine techniques of music, dance, photography, and even science, engineering, mechanics, and electronics in their work.

Sculptors creating large works, especially those that will be placed outdoors and in public areas, usually work under contract or commission. Most artists, however, create works that express their personal artistic vision and then hope to find someone to purchase them. Artists generally seek out a gallery to display their work and function as the sales agent for the work. The gallery owner and artist set the prices for pieces of art, and the gallery owner receives a commission on any work that sells. The relationship between the gallery owner and artist is often one of close cooperation, and the gallery owner may encourage the artist to explore new techniques, styles, and ideas, while helping to establish a reputation for the artist. As an artist becomes well-known, selling his or her work often becomes easier, and many well-known artists receive commissions for their art.

There is no single way to become or to be an artist. As with other areas of the arts, painting and sculpting usually are intensely personal endeavors. If it is possible to generalize, most painters and sculptors are people with a desire and need to explore visual representations of the world around them or the world within them, or both. Throughout their careers, they seek to develop their vision and the methods and techniques that allow them to best express themselves. Many artists work from or within a tradition or style of art. They may develop formal theories of art or advance new theories of visual presentation. Painters and sculptors are usually aware of the art that has come before them as well as the work of their contemporaries.

Every painter and sculptor has his or her own way of working. Many work in studios, often separate from their homes, where they can produce their work in privacy and quiet. Many artists, however, work outdoors. Most artists probably combine both indoor and outdoor work during their careers. An artist may choose complete solitude in order to work; others thrive on interaction with other artists and people. Artists engaged in monumental work, particularly sculptors, often have people who assist in the creation of a piece of art, working under the artist's direction.

They may contract with a foundry in order to cast the finished sculpture in bronze, iron, or another metal.

As film, video, and computer technology has developed, the work of painters and sculptors has expanded into new forms of expression. The recently developed three-dimensional computer animation techniques in particular often blur the boundaries between painting, sculpture, photography, and cinema.

The work of an artist usually continues throughout his or her lifetime. Creating fine art is rarely a career choice but rather a way of life, a following of a desire or need that may exhibit itself at an extremely early age. Visual artists use their work to communicate what they see, feel, think, believe, or simply are in a form other than language. For some artists, this may be the only way they feel they can ruly communicate.

Requirements

There are no educational requirements for becoming a painter or sculptor. However, most artists benefit from training, and many attend art schools or programs in colleges and universities. There are also many workshops and other ways for artists to gain instruction, practice, and exposure to art and the works and ideas of other artists. The artist should learn a variety of techniques, be exposed to as many media and styles as possible, and gain an understanding of the history of art and art theory. By learning as much as possible, the artist is better able to choose the appropriate means for his or her own artistic expression.

An important requirement for a career as a painter or sculptor is artistic ability. Of course, this is entirely subjective, and it is perhaps more important that artists believe in their own ability, or in their own potential. Apart from being creative and imaginative, painters and sculptors should exhibit such traits as patience, persistence, determination, independence, and sensitivity.

Because earning a living as a fine artist is very difficult, especially when one is just starting out, many painters and sculptors work at another job. With the proper training and educational background, many painters and sculptors are able to work in art-related positions, such as art teachers, art directors, or graphic designers, while pursuing their own art activities independently. For example, many art teachers hold classes in their own studios.

Both painters and sculptors should be good at business and sales if they intend to support themselves through their art. As small-business people, they must be able to market and sell their products to wholesalers, retailers, and the general public.

Artists who sell their works to the public may need special permits from the local or state tax office. In addition, artists should check with the Internal Revenue Service for laws on selling and tax information related to income received from the sale of artwork.

Many artists join professional organizations that provide informative advice and tips as well as opportunities to meet with other artists.

Opportunities for Experience & Exploration

Experience drawing, painting, and even sculpting can be had at a very early age, even before formal schooling begins. Most elementary, middle, and high schools offer classes in art. Aspiring painters and sculptors can undertake a variety of artistic projects at school or at home. Many art associations and schools also offer beginning classes in various types of art for the general public.

Students interested in pursuing art as a career are encouraged to visits museums and galleries to view the work of other artists. In addition, they can learn about the history of art and artistic techniques and methods through books, videotapes, and other sources.

The New York Foundation for the Arts sponsors a toll-free hotline, 800-232-2789, that offers quick information on programs and services and answers to specific questions on visual artists. The hotline is open Monday through Friday, between 2 and 5 PM, Eastern Standard Time.

Methods of Entering

Artists interested in exhibiting or selling their products should investigate potential markets. Reference books, such as *Artist's Market,* may be helpful, as well as library books that offer information on business laws, taxes, and related issues. Local fairs and art shows often provide opportunities for new artists to display their work. Art councils are a good source of information on upcoming fairs in the area.

Some artists sell their work on consignment. When a painter or sculptor sells work this way, a store or gallery displays an item; when the item is sold, the artist gets the price of that item minus a commission that goes to the store or gallery. Artists who sell on consignment should read contracts very carefully.

Many art schools and universities have placement services to help students find jobs. Although fine artists are generally self-employed, many need to work at another job, at least initially, to support themselves while they establish a reputation.

Advancement

Painters and sculptors are self-employed; thus, the channels for advancement are not as well defined as they are at a company or firm. An artist may become increasingly well-known, both nationally and internationally, and as an artist's reputation increases, he or she can command higher prices for his or her work. The success of the fine artist depends on a variety of factors, including talent, drive, and determination. However, luck often seems to play a role in many artists' success, and some artists do not achieve recognition until late in life, if at all. Artists with business skills may open their own galleries to display their own and others' work. Those with the appropriate educational backgrounds may become art teachers, agents, or critics.

Employment Outlook

The employment outlook for painters and sculptors is difficult to predict. Because they are usually self-employed, much of their success depends on the amount and type of work created, the drive and determination in selling the artwork, and the interest or readiness of the public to appreciate and purchase the work. According to the *1998-99 Occupational Outlook Handbook,* visual artists are expected to enjoy faster than average growth through the year 2006.

Success for an artist, however, is difficult to quantify. Individual artists may consider themselves successful as their talent matures and they are better able to present their vision in their work. This type of success goes beyond financial considerations. Few artists enter this field for the money. Financial success depends on a great deal of factors, many of which have nothing to do with the artist or his or her work. Artists with good marketing skills will likely be the most successful in selling their work. Although artists should not let their style be dictated by market trends, those interested in financial success can attempt to determine what types of artwork are wanted by the public.

It often takes several years for an artist's work and reputation to be established. Many artists have to support themselves through other employment. There are numerous employment opportunities for commercial artists in such fields as publishing, advertising, fashion and design, and teaching. Painters and sculptors should consider employment in these and other fields. They should be prepared, however, to face strong competition from others who are attracted to these fields.

Earnings

The amount of money earned by painters and sculptors varies greatly. Most are self-employed and set their own hours and prices. Artists often work long hours and earn little, especially when they are first starting out. The price they charge is up to them, but much depends on the value the public places on their work. A particular item may sell for a few dollars, a few hundred, or a few thousand or tens of thousands of dollars and more. Often, the value of an artwork may increase considerably after it has been sold. An artwork that may have earned an artist only a few hundred dollars may earn many thousands of dollars the next time it is sold.

Some artists obtain grants that allow them to pursue their art; others win prizes and awards in competitions. Most artists, however, have to work on their projects part time while holding down a regular, full-time job. Many artists teach in art schools, high schools, or out of their studios. Artists who sell their products must pay social security and other taxes on any money they receive.

However, 1997 statistics from the U.S. Department of Labor show average earnings for all visual artists to be about $27,000.

Conditions of Work

Most painters and sculptors work out of their homes or in studios. Some work in small areas in their apartments; others work in large, well-ventilated lofts. Occasionally, painters and sculptors work outside. In addition, artists often work at fairs, shops, museums, and other places where their work is being exhibited.

Artists often work long hours, and those who are self-employed do not receive paid vacations, insurance coverage, or any of the other benefits usually offered by a company or firm. However, artists are able to work at their own pace, set their own prices, and make their own decisions. The energy and creativity that go into an artist's work brings feelings of pride and satisfaction. Most artists genuinely love what they do.

Sources of Additional Information

American Society of Artists
PO Box 1326
Palatine, IL 60078

National Art Education Association
1916 Association Drive
Reston, VA 20191-1590
Tel: 703-860-8000
WWW: http://www.naea-reston.org

National Endowment for the Arts
Nancy Hanks Center
Arts and Education
Education and Access Division
1100 Pennsylvania Avenue, NW
Washington, DC 20506-0001
Tel: 202-682-5400
WWW: http://www.arts.endow.gov

Sculptors Guild
The Soho Building
110 Greene Street
New York, NY 10012
Tel: 212-431-5669
WWW: http://www.artincontext.com

Paralegals

Definition

Paralegals, also known as *legal assistants*, assist in trial preparations, investigate facts, prepare documents such as affidavits and pleadings, and, in general, do work customarily performed by lawyers.

Nature of the Work

Paralegals perform a variety of functions to assist lawyers. Although the lawyer assumes responsibility for the paralegal's work, the paralegal may take on all the duties of the lawyer except for setting fees, appearing in court, accepting cases, and giving legal advice.

Paralegals spend much of their time in law libraries, researching laws and previous cases and compiling facts to help lawyers prepare for trial. After analyzing the laws and facts that have been compiled for a particular client, the paralegal often writes a report that the lawyer may use to determine how to proceed with the case. If a case is brought to trial, the paralegal may help prepare legal arguments and draft pleadings to be filed in court. They also organize and store files and correspondence related to cases.

Not all paralegal work centers on trials. Paralegals also draft contracts, mortgages, affidavits, and other documents. They may help with corporate matters, such as shareholder agreements, contracts, and employee benefit plans. Paralegals may also review financial reports.

Some paralegals work for the government. They may prepare complaints or talk to employers to find out why health or safety standards are not being met. They often analyze legal documents, collect evidence for hearings, and prepare explanatory material on various laws for use by the public.

Other paralegals are involved in community or public-service work. They may help specific groups, such as poor or elderly members of the community. They may file forms, research laws, and prepare documents. They may represent

School Subjects
English
(writing/literature)
Government

Personal Interests
Law
Writing

Work Environment
Primarily indoors
Primarily multiple
locations

Minimum Education Level
Some postsecondary
training

Salary Range
$23,800 to
$32,900 to
$50,000

Certification or Licensing
Recommended

Outlook
Much faster than the
average

DOT
119

GOE
11.04.02

NOC
4211

clients at hearings, although they may not appear in court on behalf of a client.

Many paralegals work for large law firms, agencies, and corporations and specialize in a particular area of law. Some work for smaller firms and have a general knowledge of many areas of law. Paralegals have varied duties, and a large number use computers in their work.

Requirements

Requirements for paralegals vary by employer. Some paralegals start out as legal secretaries or clerical workers, and gradually are given more training and responsibility. The majority, however, choose formal training and education programs. These formal programs usually range from one to three years and are offered in a variety of educational settings: four-year colleges and universities, law schools, community and junior colleges, business schools, proprietary schools, and paralegal associations. Admission requirements vary, but good grades in high school and college are always an asset. There are over eight hundred paralegal programs, about two hundred of which have been approved by the American Bar Association.

Some paralegal programs require a bachelor's degree for admission; others do not require any college. In either case, those with a college degree usually have an edge over those without. High school students should take a broad range of subjects, including English, social studies, and languages, especially Spanish. Strong communications and research skills are crucial.

Presently, paralegals are not required to be licensed or certified. Instead, when lawyers employ paralegals, they often follow guidelines designed to protect the public from the practice of law by unqualified persons.

Paralegals may, however, opt to be certified. To do so, they may take and pass an extensive two-day test conducted by the National Association of Legal Assistants Certifying Board. Paralegals who pass the test may use the title Certified Legal Assistant (CLA) after their names. In 1996, the National Federation of Paralegal Associations established the Paralegal Advanced Competency Exam, a means for paralegals with bachelor's degrees and at least two years experience to acquire professional recognition. Paralegals who pass this exam may use the designation Registered Paralegal (RP).

Opportunities for Experience & Exploration

There are several ways interested students can explore the career of a paralegal. They may work part time as a secretary or in the mailroom of a law firm to get an idea of the nature of the work. Students may join an organization affiliated with the legal profession or talk directly with lawyers and paralegals. They can write to schools with paralegal programs or to the organizations listed at the end of this article for general information.

Methods of Entering

Although some law firms promote legal secretaries to paralegal status, most employers prefer to hire individuals who have completed paralegal programs. Those interested in becoming paralegals should consider attending paralegal school. In addition to providing a solid background in paralegal studies, most schools help graduates find jobs. Even though the job market for paralegals is expected to grow very rapidly over the next ten years, those with the best credentials will get the best jobs.

The American Association for Paralegal Education (AAPE) is a national organization that was established in 1981 to promote high standards for paralegal education and, in association with the American Bar Association, to develop an approval process for paralegal education programs. A complete list of member institutions is available from the AAPE headquarters(see address listed at the end of this article).

Advancement

There are no formal advancement paths for paralegals; paralegals usually do not become lawyers or judges. There are, however, some possibilities for advancement, as large firms are beginning to establish career programs for paralegals.

For example, a person may be promoted from paralegal to a head legal assistant who supervises others. In addition, a paralegal may specialize in one area of law, such as environmental, real estate, or medical malpractice. Many paralegals also advance by moving from small law firms to larger ones.

Expert paralegals who specialize in one area of law may go into business for themselves. Rather than work for one firm, these freelance paralegals often contract their services to many lawyers. Some paralegals with bachelor's degrees obtain additional education to become lawyers.

Employment Outlook

In 1997, there were about 113,000 paralegals in the United States; most employed by private law firms. The employment outlook for paralegals through the year 2006 is excellent, representing one of the fastest-growing professions in the country. One reason for the expected growth in the profession is the financial benefits of employing paralegals. The paralegal, whose duties fall between those of the legal secretary and those of the attorney, helps make the delivery of legal services more cost effective to clients. The growing need for legal services among the general population and the increased popularity of prepaid legal plans is creating a tremendous demand for paralegals in private law firms. In the private sector, paralegals can work in banks, insurance companies, real estate firms, and corporate legal departments. In the public sector, there is a growing need for paralegals in the courts and community legal service programs, government agencies, and consumer organizations.

The growth of this occupation, to some extent, is dependent on the economy. Businesses are less likely to pursue litigation cases when profit margins are down, thus curbing the need for new hires.

Earnings

Salaries vary. The size and location of the firm and the education and experience of the employee are some factors that determine the annual earnings of the paralegal.

According to 1997 statistics from the National Federation of Paralegal Associations, beginning paralegals average about $23,800 a year. Paralegals with seven to ten years' experience make about $32,900. Top paralegals in large offices can earn as much as $40,000 a year; and paralegal supervisors, $40,000 to $50,000. Many paralegals receive year end bonuses, some averaging $1,900 or more.

Paralegals employed by the federal government averaged $44,000 annually in 1997, as reported by the U.S. Department of Labor.

Conditions of Work

Paralegals often work in pleasant and comfortable offices. Much of the work is performed in a law library. Most paralegals work a forty-hour week, although long hours are sometimes needed to meet a court-imposed deadline.

Many of the paralegal's duties involve routine tasks. However, the paralegal may be given increasingly difficult assignments over time. The paralegal often compiles facts and writes reports for the lawyer.

Paralegals work in a variety of settings. In addition to law firms, paralegals also work for banks, accounting firms, insurance companies, and government agencies. Some work for groups interested in specific issues, such as ecology or consumer protection. Because much of the paralegals' work involves researching facts in a law library, they must be able to work independently and have good writing and communications skills. They also must have a great deal of patience as much of the work is routine.

Sources of Additional Information

For information regarding accredited educational facilities, contact:

American Association for Paralegal Education
PO Box 40244
Overland Park, KS 66204
Tel: 913-381-4458

American Bar Association
750 North Lake Shore Drive
Chicago, IL 60611
Tel: 312-988-5000
WWW: http://www.abanet.org

National Association of Legal Assistants
1516 South Boston Avenue, Suite 200
Tulsa, OK 74119
Tel: 918-587-6828
Email: naoa.org

National Federation of Paralegal Associations
PO Box 33108
Kansas City, MO 64114-0108
Tel: 816-941-4000
Email: info@paralegals.org
WWW: http://www.paralegals.org

Patternmakers

Definition

In the manufacturing industry, many items are produced from molds, hollow forms into which liquid substances such as molten metal are poured and hardened. Such items include things as small as jewelry and as large as airplane parts. *Patternmakers* build the patterns used to make the molds in which foundry castings are formed. They prepare the patterns from metal stock or, more commonly, from rough castings made from original wood patterns; they may also construct patterns from wax, ceramic, or plastic. To complete their jobs, patternmakers use their knowledge of blueprint reading and the operation of such machines as lathes, drill presses, and shapers.

Nature of the Work

Patternmakers are skilled workers. This means that they are fairly independent of close supervision on the job. At the same time, they must accept the responsibility of having a pattern ready in accordance with the plant production schedule. Precision and accuracy are the key skills of the patternmaker's job, whether the patternmaker is creating a small pattern on a workbench by hand or a large pattern made by machine to be used in floor molding. The guiding hands of patternmakers determine the proper dimensions of each pattern created; they have the responsibility of ensuring that each molding made from the pattern will be smooth and flawless.

The most general title for a worker in this occupation is *all-around patternmaker*. This person makes patterns from a variety of materials, including wood, metal, and plastic.

Patternmakers work from blueprints prepared by the engineering department of the foundry. They begin their work by studying a blueprint of the part to be cast, and from this they compute the dimensions and plan the sequence of operations. They measure, mark, and inscribe the pattern layout on a

School Subjects
Art
Shop (Trade/Vo-tech education)

Personal Interests
Building things
Sculpting

Work Environment
Primarily indoors
Primarily one location

Minimum Education Level
High school diploma
Apprenticeship

Salary Range
$17,000 to
$24,000 to
$35,000

Certification or Licensing
None

Outlook
Decline

DOT
693

GOE
05.05.07

NOC
7232

metal or wood sample, set up and operate appropriate machine tools to cut and shape the mold, pour the liquid substance into the mold, and shape the piece into the specified finished dimensional pattern.

Certain workers are more specialized than the all-around patternmaker. For example, the *wood patternmaker* selects an appropriate wood stock, lays out the pattern, marks the design for each section on the proper piece of wood, and saws each piece roughly to size. This worker then shapes the rough pieces into final form, using various woodworking machines, such as lathes, planers, handsaws, and sanders, as well as many small hand tools. Finally, the wood patternmaker assembles the pattern segments by hand.

The *metal patternmaker* follows the same basic sequence of operation that the wood patternmaker follows, using metal stock and the proper metalworking tools. Other patternmaking specialists include *spring patternmakers*, *sample patternmakers*, and *last-pattern graders*.

Much of the patternmaker's work consists of checking dimensions with extremely accurate tools so that the work will always be according to specifications. From the patternmaker, the pattern passes to the coremakers and molders for actual production of castings.

Requirements

Although a high school education is not always required, it is generally recommended. In high school, a person interested in becoming a patternmaker should take mechanical drawing, geometry, blueprint reading, English, and any other courses that provide practice in exact measurement and construction of items such as are found in machine and woodworking shops. Along with this experience comes the training involved in working with hand tools and power-driven equipment.

The usual way to learn to become a patternmaker is through an apprenticeship program or on-the-job training. Apprenticeships last for four or five years and include a combination of classroom study and working experience. Apprentices work under the supervision of a journeyworker patternmaker and learn all phases of the occupation. Initially, they perform relatively routine duties. As they acquire skills and experience, they perform more complex tasks and work with less supervision.

Some vocational schools offer courses in patternmaking; however, the skills needed for this occupation require more intensive training than that provided by vocational schools, and most employers require additional on-the-job training. Gaining practical experience, though, before applying for a job does assist

young people in appraising their aptitude for work of this kind.

Patternmakers require a high degree of mechanical aptitude and the ability to do precision work that entails periods of intense concentration. Patternmakers also need the ability to visualize three-dimensional objects and readily see spatial relationships. Most patternmakers work with little direct supervision and need to be highly self-disciplined and motivated.

Opportunities for Experience & Exploration

Foundries are factories in which both skilled and unskilled workers are employed. It may be possible to get a summer job as a laborer at a foundry, which provides a good introduction to the working environment and help interested persons decide if they want to further pursue the profession.

Persons who are inquisitive and not afraid to ask questions may be able to find a patternmaker who is willing to talk about what is involved in his or her work.

Other opportunities involve getting in touch with an accredited related organization, such as the American Foundrymen's Society. This group is a technical and trade association whose members are foundry workers, patternmakers, technologists, and educators. It sponsors training courses through the Cast Metals Institute on all subjects related to the castings industry. The society's Pattern Division furnishes information on issues related to the patternmaker's livelihood. Those who are already involved in the field can read such trade publications as *Modern Casting*, a monthly journal that includes articles on current technology and industry news, as well as a calendar of association events.

Methods of Entering

It is unlikely for someone to take a job in a foundry and immediately and informally learn the trade of the patternmaker. Even those machinists who have worked closely with patternmakers and who have been able to transfer to patternmaking need additional on-the-job training.

The prospective patternmaker generally applies for an apprenticeship program either through a foundry or the trade union representing workers at a foundry. People who have worked during the summer at a foundry or who have taken a class in patternmaking at a vocational school may have an advantage in being accepted into an apprenticeship program.

Advancement

Because of the time involved in the patternmaker apprenticeship program, and because of the satisfaction of the job resulting from the creative aspect of it, many patternmakers do not look for further advancement beyond perhaps supervisory positions. Those who spend many years in the accomplishment of a difficult skill often want to spend the remainder of their working life developing this skill. In the same vein, foundry management personnel often hesitate to move employees who are capable and satisfied in their positions.

In large foundries, however, patternmakers may become supervisors. Employers generally promote those whose ability to supervise others seems more valuable to the foundry than the patternmaker's skill in this one trade alone. Useful traits for supervisory positions include good communications, leadership, and interpersonal skills.

Employment Outlook

Employment of foundry patternmakers has been declining steadily and is expected to continue declining in the coming years. Patternmakers are being replaced by other skilled workers who use computer-aided design (CAD) and computer-aided manufacturing (CAM) programs to make parts. The use of computers and other automated equipment allows the design of a part to be created using computer programs and transferred directly from the design stage to the manufacturing stage, eliminating the need for patterns. Patternmakers are being replaced by CAD/CAM engineers and numerical control tool programmers.

It is estimated that only a few hundred new patternmakers will be needed annually to replace workers who transfer to other fields, retire, or otherwise leave the occupation. Most of the job openings will be in metal patternmaking. Competition for these positions may be keen as craftspersons with experience stand the best chance of obtaining available positions.

Because patternmakers learn either basic metalworking or woodworking skills, they can find jobs in related fields when patternmaking employment is not available. Wood patternmakers can qualify for skilled woodworking positions, such as that of a cabinetmaker, and metal patternmakers can transfer their skills to machining occupations, such as that of a machinist or machine tool operator.

Earnings

Patternmakers earn wages that are higher than the average for all other manufacturing occupations. In the mid-1990s, workers in iron and steel foundries average from $25,000 to $35,000 annually, and those in nonferrous foundries make an average of $24,000. Metal patternmakers generally receive higher average hourly wages than wood patternmakers. There often are opportunities for overtime, which is reimbursed at the rate of one and a half times the regular rate. Apprentices usually start at wages that are approximately 50 percent of more experienced workers. As they gain experience and demonstrate competency, they receive incremental raises. Companies may offer fringe benefits such as paid holidays, vacations, and health insurance.

Conditions of Work

The patternmaker's job is not physically demanding in that it does not require great strength for lifting, nor does it require extraordinary physical endurance. However, patternmakers spend much of their time standing. The work can be mentally demanding, requiring periods of great concentration and careful scrutiny. Some people find this stressful, but most patternmakers take pride in their skills and realize that the exacting nature of their work is a necessary part of their jobs.

Most foundry jobs are located in large, highly industrial areas. Working environments vary depending on type of company. Foundries are generally noisy, sometimes dusty, places. Also, the indoor air at many plants is warmer than usual because of the nature of the materials that are used in the job. There is some danger working around high-speed machine tools, but with proper safety practices these risks are minimized.

Some companies are represented by unions. Two unions representing many patternmakers are the Glass Molders, Pottery, Plastics and Allied Workers International Union and the International Association of Machinists and Aerospace Workers.

Sources of Additional Information

For information on careers and the Cast Metals Institute, please contact:

■ **American Foundrymen's Society**
505 State Street
Des Plaines, IL 60016-8399
Tel: 800-537-4237

For information on careers and apprenticeships, please contact:

■ **Glass Molders, Pottery, Plastics and Allied Workers International Union**
PO Box 607
608 East Baltimore Pike
Media, PA 19063-0607
Tel: 610-565-5051

Perfusionists

Definition

Although *perfusionists*, formerly known as *cardiovascular perfusionists*, are not well known to the general public, they play a crucial role in the field of cardiovascular surgery by operating what is known as the "heart-lung machine." The perfusionist is responsible for all aspects of the heart-lung machine whenever it becomes necessary to interrupt or replace the functioning of the heart by circulating blood outside of a patient's body.

Nature of the Work

Perfusionists perform one of the most delicate and crucial services for patients during open-heart surgery, coronary bypass, or any other procedure that involves the heart or the lungs. The perfusionist operates equipment that literally takes over the functioning of the patient's heart and lungs during surgery. Such equipment may also be used in emergency cases of respiratory failure.

When surgeons pierce the patient's breast bone and the envelope surrounding the heart, which is known as the pericardial sac, they must transfer the functions of the patient's heart and lungs to the heart-lung machine before any surgery can begin on the heart itself. This process is known as establishing extracorporeal bypass, or outside heart and lung functions. The heart-lung machine is activated by inserting two tubes into the heart, one circulates blood from the heart to the machine and the other circulates blood from the machine back into the heart. It is necessary during this procedure not only to maintain circulation and pumping action but also to maintain the appropriate oxygen, carbon dioxide, and other blood gas levels. In addition, perfusionists must effectively control the body temperature of patients who are undergoing extracorporeal bypass circulation because the flow of blood through the body greatly influences body temperature.

School Subjects
Biology
Mathematics

Personal Interests
Computers
Helping people: physical health/medicine

Work Environment
Primarily indoors
Primarily one location

Minimum Education Level
Bachelor's degree

Salary Range
$40,000 to
$65,000 to
$125,000

Certification or Licensing
Recommended

Outlook
Faster than the average

DOT
078

GOE
10.03.02

NOC
3214

To slow metabolism and reduce the stress on the heart and other bodily systems, perfusionists often reduce the body temperature of patients during open-heart surgery to 70 degrees Fahrenheit or below. Perfusionists use various probes within the body to monitor body temperature, blood gases, kidney functioning, electrolytes, and blood pressure.

Although the ultimate responsibility for open-heart surgery and for decisions concerning blood circulation, temperature, and other matters rests with the surgeon in charge of the operation, surgeons tend to rely heavily upon the judgment of perfusionists, who are regarded as specialists in their own right. Although the perfusionist may never have a discussion with the patient, perfusionists almost always have preoperative conferences with surgeons to discuss the patient's condition and other characteristics, the nature of the operation, and the equipment to be used.

Because of the nature of their work, perfusionists work in hospitals in cardiac operating rooms. They are members of a cardiac surgery team, and it is not uncommon for perfusionists to work through several successive operations in a row as well as to work on emergency cases. Because open-heart surgery cannot be performed without these specialists, perfusionists are usually on call a great deal of the time.

Requirements

To work as a cardiovascular perfusionist requires formal training from one of over thirty-three schools throughout the United States accredited by the Commission for the Accreditation of Allied Health Education Programs. As a prerequisite to admission, these schools generally require a bachelor of science degree, although in some cases they accept applicants who have trained at nursing schools and other technical schools and have experience as nurses or health technicians. Accredited perfusion technology programs range in length from one to two years. Several accredited schools offer a combined undergraduate degree and a degree in perfusion technology, but more often perfusionists are trained once they have completed a bachelor's degree or other training.

Those desiring entry to an accredited perfusion technology program can expect intense competition as only 10 to 20 percent of applicants are accepted into such programs. The accredited schools carefully examine academic record, character, and even personal temperament before accepting new students. The admissions officers at these schools realize that it takes a special individual to function under the kind of pressure and long hours perfusionists frequently encounter.

A strong background in biology, mathematics, and other sciences is recommended for applicants to perfusion technology programs, as these programs are designed to convey a great deal of technical information as well as clinical training over a one-and-one-half- to two-year period. The perfusion technology program involves courses in physiology, cardiology, respiratory therapy, pharmacology, and heart surgery. Classroom experience is combined with extensive clinical experience where students learn about extracorporeal circulation, respiratory therapy, general surgical procedures, anesthesia, and other operating room procedures. Nearly all of the accredited perfusion technology programs attempt to involve students as early and as much as possible in clinical experience, as the practice of extracorporeal circulation relies so much upon actual operating room experience.

High school students interested in perfusion technology should prepare themselves by taking all available science, mathematics, and health science courses. American Society of Extracorporeal Technology (AmSECT) offers some financial aid and scholarships, and a number of schools offer work-study programs as well as financial aid.

Upon the completion of instruction from an accredited school of perfusion technology, perfusionists may take a written test administered by the American Board of Cardiovascular Perfusion. Those who pass it are then qualified to take an oral examination. The written and oral examinations are given once a year, and candidates are permitted to take these tests three times; candidates who are not able to pass the tests become ineligible for further examinations. Certified perfusionists pay an annual $75 fee to maintain their certification.

Certification currently is not an absolute requirement for perfusionists, but it is rapidly becoming a practical requirement, as more than two thirds of perfusionists nationally are now certified. At the present, perfusionists do not need separate state licenses to practice their profession. Students who graduate from a school accredited by the Accreditation Committee for Perfusion Education have a definite advantage.

To maintain their certification, perfusionists are expected to engage in continuing education programs to remain abreast of the latest techniques. The cardiovascular surgery field is constantly changing, and open-heart surgery, bypass surgery, heart transplants, and other complicated operations are becoming increasingly common throughout the health care system. Therefore, perfusion technology will become increasingly more complex in the future.

Opportunities for Experience & Exploration

As with any technical medical field, one of the best ways to learn about the work of perfusionists is to talk with an existing practitioner. All hospitals performing open-heart surgery have perfusionists on staff who may be available for interviews with students. AmSECT offers a list of accredited perfusion technology programs, and those interested in such programs can talk to the professors, instructors, and admissions officers in those respective schools.

Methods of Entering

The most important prerequisite for entering the field of perfusion technology is acceptance at an accredited school that offers such a program. Once students have entered a program they should begin to investigate the field first through their professors and teachers and then through AmSECT. This professional society of perfusion technologists, has an active student membership division that hosts meetings and conferences and is a good source of advice and information concerning various job openings in the field.

Advancement

Because there are relatively few perfusionists nationwide and the field of extracorporeal technology (open-heart surgery) is growing rapidly, perfusionists have advancement opportunities of both in terms of high salaries and the opportunities to perform more complicated work. However, the field of perfusion technology is so specialized and so small that the concept of advancement is related more to improving one's technical skills through experience than to administering large departments or large numbers of people. Qualified perfusionists, however, can advance into management or to the technological side of the field.

The practicing perfusionist advances through gaining higher pay, better working conditions, and the ability to be involved in more complicated procedures as well as to train less experienced perfusionists. Perfusionists may also obtain teaching positions in one of the accredited schools or conduct research funded by educational institutions, foundations, or professional societies.

Employment Outlook

The perfusion field is highly specialized and employs approximately 3,500 individuals nationwide. These professionals work in approximately 750 hospitals with open-heart surgery departments. Employment in this area is expected to grow at a rate faster than the average for all occupations through the year 2006. As with many medical fields, advancing technology calls for additional professionals as these procedures are performed on a more regular basis. The field of open-heart surgery and the expanded scope of extracorporeal technology grew dramatically during the 1980s and 1990s and are expected to continue to expand, so that the job opportunities and job stability for perfusionists are expected to be excellent.

Earnings

According to the American Society of Extracorporeal Technology, salaries for starting perfusionists average about $40,000 per year Experienced perfusionists may earn as much as $65,000 per year. Some perfusionists annually earn as much as $125,000, but those earning higher salaries are generally employed directly by a physician or are self-employed.

Roughly half of all perfusionists are directly employed by hospitals, and the other half are independent contractors or practitioners who make themselves available by contract to one or more hospitals. Independent contractors are responsible for their own business affairs including medical health insurance, uniforms, liability insurance, and other items.

Conditions of Work

Perfusionists typically work in operating rooms of hospitals. They work alongside the operating table as part of the surgical team; it is the responsibility of the perfusionist to see that the equipment is properly assembled and maintained at all times.

Perfusionists frequently must spend long hours in operating rooms, often under stressful conditions. Although most perfusionists average 125 procedures a year, some of these procedures can be quite lengthy, and they may occur at odd hours as well as under emergency conditions.

Sources of Additional Information

For information about perfusionists, please contact:

American Society of Extracorporeal Technology (AmSECT)
National Office
11480 Sunset Hills Road, Suite 200E
Reston, VA 22090-9955
Tel: 703-435-8556
WWW: http://www.amsect.org

For information about certification, please contact:

American Board of Cardiovascular Perfusion
207 North 25th Avenue
Hattiesburg, MS 39401
Tel: 601-582-3309

American Medical Association
515 North State Street
Chicago, IL 60610
Tel: 312-464-5000
WWW: http://www.ama-assn.org

For accreditation information, please contact:

Accreditation Committee for Perfusion Education
7108-C South Alton Way
Englewood, CO 80112-2106
Tel: 303-741-3598

Pet Groomers

Definition

Pet groomers comb, cut, trim, and shape the fur of all types of dogs and cats. They comb out the animal's fur and trim the hair to the proper style for the size and breed. They also trim the animal's nails, bathe it, and dry its hair. In the process, they check for flea or tick infestation and any visible health problems. In order to perform these grooming tasks, the pet groomer must be able to calm the animal down and gain its confidence.

Nature of the Work

Although all dogs and cats benefit from regular grooming, it is shaggy, longhaired dogs that give pet groomers the bulk of their business. Some types of dogs need regular grooming for their standard appearance; among this group are poodles, schnauzers, cocker spaniels, and many types of terriers. Show dogs or dogs that are shown in competition, are groomed frequently. Before beginning grooming, the dog groomer talks with the dog's owner to find out the style of cut the dog is to have. The dog groomer also relies on experience to determine how a particular breed of dog is supposed to look.

The dog groomer places the animal on a grooming table. To keep the dog steady during the clipping, a nylon collar or noose, which hangs from an adjustable pole attached to the grooming table, is slipped around its neck. The dog groomer talks to the dog or uses other techniques to keep the animal calm and gain its trust. If the dog doesn't calm down but snaps and bites instead, the groomer may have to muzzle it. If a dog is completely unmanageable, the dog groomer may ask the owner to have the dog tranquilized by a veterinarian before grooming.

After calming the dog down, the groomer brushes it and tries to untangle its hair. If the dog's hair is very overgrown or is very shaggy such as an English sheepdog's, the groomer may have

School Subjects
Biology

Personal Interests
Animals
Babysitting/child care

Work Environment
Primarily indoors
Primarily one location

Minimum Education Level
High school diploma

Salary Range
$15,000 to
$20,000 to
$26,000+

Certification or Licensing
None

Outlook
Faster than the average

DOT
418

GOE
03.03.02

NOC
6483

to cut away part of its coat with scissors before beginning any real grooming. Brushing the coat is good for both longhair and shorthair dogs as brushing removes shedding hair and dead skin. It also neatens the coat so the groomer can tell from the shape and proportions of the dog how to cut its hair in the most attractive way. Hair that is severely matted is actually painful to the animal because the mats pull at the animal's skin. Having these mats removed is necessary to the animal's health.

Once the dog is brushed, the groomer cuts and shapes the dog's coat with electric clippers. Next, the dog's ears are cleaned and its nails are trimmed. The groomer must take care not to cut the nails too short because they may bleed and cause the dog pain. If the nails do bleed, a special powder is applied to stop the bleeding. The comfort of the animal is an important concern for the groomer.

The dog is then given a bath, sometimes by a worker known as a *dog bather.* The dog is lowered into a stainless steel tub, sprayed with warm water, scrubbed with a special shampoo, and rinsed. This may be repeated several times if the dog is very dirty. The dog groomer has special chemicals that can be used to deodorize a dog that has encountered a skunk or has gone for a swim in foul water. If a dog has fleas or ticks, the dog groomer treats them at this stage by soaking the wet coat with a solution to kill the insects. This toxic solution must be kept out of the dog's eyes, ears, and nose, which may be cleaned more carefully with a sponge or washcloth. A hot oil treatment may also be applied to condition the dog's coat.

The groomer dries the dog after bathing, either with a towel, hand-held electric blower, or in a drier cage with electric blow driers. Poodles and some other types of dogs have their coats fluff-dried, then scissored for the final pattern or style. Poodles, which at one time were the mainstay of the dog grooming business, generally take the longest to groom because of their intricate clipping pattern. Most dogs can be groomed in about ninety minutes, although grooming may take several hours for shaggier breeds whose coats are badly matted and overgrown.

More and more cats, especially longhaired breeds, are now being taken to pet groomers. The procedure for cats is the same as for dogs, although cats are not dipped when bathed. As the dog or cat is groomed, the groomer checks to be sure there are no signs of disease in the animal's eyes, ears, skin, or coat. If there are any abnormalities, such as bald patches or skin lesions, the groomer tells the owner and may recommend that the animal be checked by a veterinarian. The groomer may also give the owner tips on animal hygiene.

Pet owners and those in pet care generally have respect for pet groomers who do a good job and treat animals well. Many people, especially those who raise show dogs, grow to rely on particular pet groomers to do a perfect job each time. Pet groomers can earn satisfaction from taking a shaggy, unkempt animal and transforming it into a beautiful creature. On the other hand, some owners may unfairly blame the groomer if the animal becomes ill while in the groomer's care or for some malady or condition that is not the groomer's fault. Because they deal with both the pets and their owners, pet groomers can find their work both challenging and rewarding.

Requirements

A high school diploma generally is not required for people working as pet groomers. A diploma or GED certificate, however, can be a great asset to people who would like to advance within their present company or move to other careers in animal care that require more training, such as veterinary technicians. Useful courses include English, business math, general science, zoology, psychology, bookkeeping, office management, typing, art, and first aid.

Presently, state licensing or certification is not required of pet groomers. To start a grooming salon or other business, a license is needed from the city or town in which a person plans to start a business.

The primary qualification for a person who wants to work with pets is a love of animals. Animals can sense when someone does not like them or is afraid of them. A person needs certain skills in order to work with nervous, aggressive, or fidgety animals. They must be patient with the animals, able to gain their respect, and enjoy giving the animals a lot of love and attention. Persistence and endurance are also helpful as grooming one animal can take several hours of strenuous work. Groomers should enjoy working with their hands and have good eyesight and manual dexterity to accurately cut a clipping pattern.

A person interested in pet grooming can be trained for the field in one of three ways: enrolling in a pet grooming school; working in a pet shop or kennel and learning on the job; or reading one of the many books on pet grooming and practicing on his or her own pet.

To enroll in most pet grooming schools, a person must be at least seventeen years old and fond of animals. Previous experience in pet grooming can sometimes be applied for course credits. Students study a wide range of topics including the basics of bathing, brushing, and clipping, the care of ears and nails, coat and skin conditions, animal anatomy terminology and sanitation. They also study customer relations, which is very important for those who plan to operate their own shops. During training, students practice their techniques on actual animals, which people bring in for grooming at a discount rate.

Students can also learn pet grooming while working for a grooming shop, kennel, animal hospital, or veterinarian's office. They usually begin with tasks such as shampooing dogs and cats , and trimming their nails, then gradually work their way up to brushing and basic hair cuts. With experience, they may learn more difficult cuts and use these skills to earn more pay or start their own business.

The essentials of pet grooming can also be learned from any of several good books available on grooming. These books contain all the information a person needs to know to start his or her own pet grooming business, including the basic cuts, bathing and handling techniques, and type of equipment needed. Still, many of the finer points of grooming, such as the more complicated cuts and various safety precautions, are best learned while working under an experienced groomer. There still is no substitute for on-the-job training and experience.

Opportunities for Experience & Exploration

To find out if they are suited for a job in pet grooming, students should familiarize themselves with animals. This can be done in many ways, starting with the proper care of the family pet. Youth organizations such as the Boy Scouts, Girl Scouts, and 4-H Clubs sponsor projects that give members the chance to raise and care for animals. Students also may do part-time or volunteer work caring for animals at an animal hospital, kennel, pet shop, animal shelter, nature center, or zoo.

Methods of Entering

The best way for most people to gain a thorough knowledge of dog grooming is by an accredited pet grooming course or enrolling in a pet grooming school. The National Dog Groomers Association of America (NDGAA) provides a referral listing of approximately forty dog grooming schools throughout the United States to persons who send a stamped, self-addressed envelope. Three schools of dog grooming are recognized by the National Association of Trade and Technical Schools (NATTS): the Pedigree Professional School of Dog Grooming, the

New York School of Dog Grooming (three branches), and the Nash Academy of Animal Arts. Many other dog grooming schools advertise in dog and pet magazines. It is important for students to choose an accredited, licensed school in order to increase both their employment opportunities and professional knowledge.

Graduates from dog grooming schools can take advantage of the school's job placement services. Generally, there are more job openings than qualified groomers to fill them, so new graduates may have several job offers to consider. These schools learn of job openings in all parts of the United States and are usually happy to contact prospective employers and write letters of introduction for graduates.

The NDGAA also promotes professional identification through membership and certification testing throughout the United States and Canada. The NDGAA offers continuing education, accredited workshops, certification testing, seminars, insurance programs, a job placement program, membership directory, and other services and products. Other associations of interest to dog groomers are the Humane Society of the United States and the United Kennel Club. Because dog groomers are concerned with the health and safety of the animals they service, membership in groups that promote and protect animal welfare is very common.

Other sources of job information include the classified ads of daily newspapers and listings in dog and pet magazines. Job leads may be available from private or state employment agencies or from referrals of salon or kennel owners. People looking for work should phone or send letters to prospective employers, inform them of their qualifications, and, if invited, visit their establishments.

Advancement

Pet groomers who work for other people may advance to a more responsible position such as office manager or dog trainer. If a dog groomer starts his or her own shop, it may become successful enough to expand or to open branch offices or area franchises. Skilled groomers may want to work for a dog grooming school as an instructor, possibly advancing to a job as a school director, placement officer, or other type of administrator.

The pet industry is booming, so there are many avenues of advancement for groomers who like to work with dogs. With more education, a groomer may get a job as a veterinary technician or assistant at a shelter or animal hospital. Those who like to train dogs may open obedience schools, train guide dogs, work with field and hunting dogs, or even train stunt and movie dogs. People can also open their own kennels, breeding and pedigree services, gaming dog businesses, or pet supply distribution firms. Each of these requires specialized knowledge and experience, so additional study, education, and work is often needed.

Employment Outlook

The demand for skilled dog groomers has grown faster than average, and is expected to continue through the year 2006. The NDGAA estimates that more than 30,000 dog groomers are currently employed, and expects that more than 3,000 new groomers will be needed every year during the next decade.

Every year more people are keeping dogs and cats as pets. They are spending more money to pamper their animals, but often don't have enough free time or the inclination to groom their pets themselves. Grooming is not just a luxury for pets, however, because regular attention makes it more likely that any injury or illness will be noticed and treated.

Earnings

Groomers charge either by the job or the hour. They earn around $7.50 an hour. If they are on the staff of a salon or work for another groomer, they get to keep 50 to 60 percent of the charged fees. For this reason, many groomers branch off to start their own businesses. Those who own and operate their own grooming services can earn anywhere from $20,000 to $50,000 annually, depending on how hard they work and the clientele.

Groomers generally buy their own clipping equipment, including barber's shears, brushes, and clippers. A new set of equipment costs around $325; used sets cost less. Groomers employed at salons, grooming schools, pet shops, animal hospitals, and kennels often get a full range of benefits, including paid vacations and holidays, medical and dental insurance, and retirement pensions.

Conditions of Work

Salons, kennels, and pet shops, as well as gaming and breeding services, should be clean and well lighted, with modern equipment and clean surroundings. Establishments that do not meet these standards endanger the health of the animals who are taken there and the owners of these estab-

lishments should be reported. Groomers who are self-employed may work out of their homes. Some groomers buy vans and convert them into grooming shops. They drive them to the homes of the pets they work on, which many owners find very convenient. Those who operate these groommobiles may work on thirty or forty dogs a week, and factor their driving time and expenses into their fees.

Groomers usually work a forty-hour week and may have to work evenings or weekends. Those who own their own shops or work out of their homes, like other self-employed people, work very long hours and may have irregular schedules. Other groomers may work only part time. Groomers are on their feet much of the day, and their work can get very tiring when they have to lift and restrain large animals.

When working with any sort of animal, a person may encounter bites, scratches, strong odors, fleas, and other insects. They may have to deal with sick or bad-tempered animals. The groomer must regard every dog and cat as a unique individual and treat it with respect. Groomers need to be careful while on the job, especially when handling flea and tick killers, which are toxic to humans.

Sources of Additional Information

The National Dog Groomers Association of America (NDGAA) publishes a newsletter for dog groomers that includes information on shows, new grooming products and techniques, and workshop and certification test sites and dates. For information and/or list of dog grooming schools across the country, send a stamped, self-addressed #10 envelope to:

National Dog Groomers Association of America
PO Box 101
Clark, PA 16113
Tel: 412-962-2711

For information on pet grooming, contact:

New York School of Dog Grooming
248 East 34th Street
New York, NY 10016
Tel: 212-685-3776

Nash Academy of Animal Arts
857 Lane Allen Plaza
Lexington, KY 40504
Tel: 606-276-5301

Pharmacy Technicians

Definition

Pharmacy technicians, also called *pharmacy technologists, pharmacy medication technicians,* and *pharmacy assistants,* provide technical assistance for registered pharmacists and work under their direct supervision. They usually work in chain or independent drug stores, hospitals, community ambulatory care centers, home health care agencies, nursing homes, and the pharmaceutical industry. They perform a wide range of technical support functions and tasks related to the pharmacy profession. They maintain patient records; count, package, and label medication doses; prepare and distribute sterile products; and fill and dispense routine orders for stock supplies such as over-the-counter products.

Nature of the Work

The roles of the pharmacist and pharmacy technician have expanded greatly over the past decade. The pharmacist's primary responsibility is to ensure that medications are used safely and effectively through clinical patient counseling and monitoring. In order to provide the highest quality of pharmaceutical care, pharmacists now focus on providing clinical services. As a result, pharmacy technicians' duties have evolved into a more specialized role known as pharmacy technology. Pharmacy technicians perform more of the manipulative functions associated with dispensing prescriptions. Their duties primarily include drug-product preparation and distribution, although they are also concerned with the control of drug products. They assemble, prepare, and deliver requested medication. They are responsible for record-keeping and record drug-related information on specified records and forms. Depending on their experience, technicians order pharmaceuticals and take inventory of controlled substances, such as Valium and Ritalin.

School Subjects
Biology
Chemistry

Personal Interests
Computers
Helping people: physical health/medicine

Work Environment
Primarily indoors
Primarily one location

Minimum Education Level
Some postsecondary training

Salary Range
$14,500 to
$21,000 to
$23,000

Certification or Licensing
Recommended

Outlook
About as fast as the average

DOT
074

GOE
10.03.02

NOC
3414

Technicians who work in hospitals have the most varied responsibilities of all pharmacy technicians. They fill TPNs (total parenteral nutrition preparations) and standard and chemotherapy IVs (intravenous solutions) for patients under doctors' orders. They may be required to fill "stat," or immediate, orders and deliver them. They prepare special emergency carts stocked with medications and monitor defibrillators and resuscitation equipment. In an emergency, pharmacy techs may respond with doctors and nurses, rushing the cart and other equipment to the emergency site. They also keep legal records of the events that occur during an emergency. Hospital pharmacy technicians may also work in the hospital's outpatient pharmacy, which is similar to a commercial drugstore, and assist the pharmacist in dispensing medication.

As their roles increase, trained technicians have become more specialized. Some specialized types of pharmacy technicians include *narcotics control pharmacy technicians, operating room pharmacy technicians, emergency room pharmacy technicians, nuclear pharmacy technicians,* and *home health care pharmacy technicians.* Specially trained pharmacy technicians are also employed as *data entry technicians, lead technicians, supervisors,* and *technician managers.*

Requirements

High school students interested in a pharmacy tech career should take courses in mathematics, science (especially chemistry and biology), and English. In addition, courses in speech, typing, computer science, and health are useful. Any extracurricular activities, such as drama, science clubs, or other activities, help in developing communications and interpersonal skills.

In the past, pharmacy technicians received most of their training on the job in hospital and community pharmacy–training programs. Since technician functions and duties have changed greatly in recent years, most pharmacy technicians today receive their education through formal training programs offered through community colleges, vocational/technical schools, hospital community pharmacies, and government programs throughout the United States. Program length usually ranges from six months to two years, and leads to a certificate, diploma, or associate's degree in pharmacy technology. Pharmacy technicians must possess a specific core of knowledge and skills that can be applied in the pharmacy setting. Training programs provide this knowledge to phar-

macy technician students. A high school diploma usually is required for entry into a training program. The Pharmacy Technology Educators Council is working toward implementing a standardized curriculum in all pharmacy technician training programs throughout the country and provides a guide to pharmacy technician training programs throughout Canada and the United States (see address at end of this article).

Students attending pharmacy technician training programs receive classroom instruction and participate in supervised clinical apprenticeships in health institutions and community pharmacies. Courses include introduction to pharmacy and health care systems, pharmacy laws and ethics, medical terminology, pharmacy calculations, pharmacology, anatomy, physiology, therapeutic agents, chemistry and microbiology, pharmacy operations, drug preparation, sterile products preparation, and clinical/practical experiences.

Most pharmacy technicians continue their education even after their formal training ends by reading professional journals and attending training or informational seminars, lectures, review sessions, and audiovisual presentations.

At least three states license pharmacy technicians. and all fifty states have adopted a written, standardized test for voluntary certification of technicians. The Pharmacy Technician Certification board offers a national certification program and examination. Those who pass the examination may use the title Certified Pharmacy Technician (CPhT). Certification indicates that a person has demonstrated knowledge in the pharmacy technician field and shows prospective employers that the holder possesses the proper training and knowledge to be an effective part of a health care team. Many employers—especially hospital employers—require certification as a condition of employment. Most employers other than retail pharmacies offer financial incentives to those with certification. Currently, there are over 18,000 certified pharmacy technicians in the United States.

Pharmacy technicians must be precision-minded, honest, and mature as they are depended on for accuracy and high levels of quality control, especially in hospitals. They need good communications skills in order to successfully interact with pharmacists, supervisors, and other technicians. They must be able to precisely follow written or oral instructions as a wide variety of people, including physicians, nurses, pharmacists, and patients rely on their actions. Pharmacy technicians also need some computer aptitude in order to effectively record pharmaceutical data.

Opportunities for Experience & Exploration

Volunteering at a local hospital or nursing home may provide opportunities to meet and talk with pharmacy technicians. Jobs at a local retail pharmacy also can provide relevant experience. Students may be able to arrange a talk by a trained pharmacy technician or a tour of a hospital pharmacy with the help of their guidance or career counselors.

Methods of Entering

Pharmacy technicians often are hired by the hospital, or agency where they interned. If employment is not found this way, aspiring technicians can use employment agencies or newspaper ads to help locate job openings. Other employers of pharmacy technicians include retail drugstores, nursing care facilities, and health care centers. States with high numbers of retirees, such as Arizona, Florida, California, and New Mexico, offer more job opportunities because of the increased need for medical services.

Advancement

Advancement opportunities for pharmacy technicians—although improving—are not clear-cut. Depending on where they are employed, experienced technicians may direct or instruct newer pharmacy technicians, make schedules, or moving to purchasing or computer work. Some hospitals have a variety of tech designations, based on experience and responsibility, with an according increase in pay. Some pharmacy techs return to school to pursue a degree in pharmacy.

Employment Outlook

The number of pharmacy technicians is expected to increase as fast as the average through the year 2006. In 1996, 83,000 pharmacy technicians were employed in a variety of health care settings. As the role of the pharmacist shifts to consultation, more technicians will be needed to assemble and dispense medications. Furthermore, new employment avenues and responsibilities will mirror that of the expanding and evolving role of the pharmacist. A strong demand for technicians with specialized training has emerged. Those who have completed the required training will be in high demand. Mechanical advances in the pharmaceutical field, such as robot-picking devices and automatic counting equipment, may eradicate some of the duties pharmacy technicians previously performed, yet there will remain a need for skilled technicians to clean and maintain such devices.

Pharmacy technicians will continue to gain recognition for their skill and specialized work. New advancement and educational opportunities will emerge. Those interested in a career as a pharmacy technician should keep abreast of current health care trends, especially the government debate concerning health care reform. Pharmacy technicians who are certified will be best equipped to acquire the best positions and salaries.

Earnings

Most technicians earn between $14,500 to $21,000 per year. Large hospitals pay more than retail pharmacies, averaging between $16,000 and $23,000. The average starting pay rate for pharmacy technicians is between $6.50 and $15.00 per hour, depending on location, type of facility, and level of training. Graduates of accredited training programs, along with those who are certified, usually receive higher pay than technicians without such training. Salaries are higher for those who live on the East and West coasts, and in large urban areas.

Benefits generally include medical and dental insurance, retirement savings plans, and paid sick, personal, and vacation days.

Conditions of Work

Pharmacy technicians usually work in clean, well-lit, pleasant, and professional surroundings. Technicians often wear scrubs or other uniforms in hospitals, especially in the IV room. Other technicians may only be required to wear casual clothing. Most pharmacy settings are extremely busy, especially hospital and retail. The job of pharmacy technician, like any other occupation that demands skill, speed, and accuracy, can be stressful. Because most hospitals, nursing homes, health care centers, and retail pharmacies are open between sixteen and twenty-four hours a day, multiple shifts, weekend, and holiday hours usually are required.

Sources of Additional Information

Contact the following organization for information on certification and to obtain the National Pharmacy Technician Certification Examination Handbook:

▬Pharmacy Technician Certification Board
111 Eight Avenue, Suite 526
New York City, NY 10011

To obtain a copy of The Journal of Pharmacy Technology, *which lists opportunities for pharmacy technicians and developments in technology, and the* PTEC Directory, *which lists pharmacy tech training programs in the United States and Canada, contact:*

▬Pharmacy Technology Educators Council
Harvey Whitney Book Publishing
PO Box 42696
Cincinnati, Ohio 45242
Tel: 513-793-3555

Photographers

Definition

Photographers take and sometimes develop pictures of people, places, objects, and events, using a variety of cameras and photographic equipment. The work may be ordered by individuals who want photographic records or keepsakes or by companies that use commercial photographers for various business purposes.

Nature of the Work

Photography is both an artistic and technical occupation because many still photographers produce pictures that not only reveal their own proficiency but are so beautifully composed that they are works of fine art.

In all kinds of photographic work, the photographer must be able to use a variety of cameras, lenses, and filters to achieve a desired effect. They must know many kinds of film and know which to use for different types of pictures, lighting conditions, cameras, and filters. They also need to know and be able to use a variety of types of lighting equipment. In addition, photographers must be familiar with film processing techniques that develop, enlarge, and print photographs. In many large studios, photographic technicians are employed to process film and technical reproduction while in smaller shops photographers may have to do it themselves.

Many professional still photographers specialize in areas such as portrait work, commercial photography, and industrial photography.

Portrait photographers take photos of individuals, couples, or small groups. They try to attain not only a natural-looking and attractive effect but also one that expresses the personality of the individuals. Most portrait photographers work in their own studios, although they may go to people's homes and other locations to take photographs.

Commercial photographers usually take photos of consumer and industrial products, such as machinery, fashions, and

School Subjects
Art
Business

Personal Interests
Drawing
Photography

Work Environment
Indoors and outdoors
Primarily multiple
locations

Minimum Education Level
Some postsecondary
training

Salary Range
$10,400 to
$26,343 to
$94,707

Certification or Licensing
Recommended

Outlook
As fast as the average

DOT
143

GOE
01.02.02

NOC
5221

retail merchandise, and building exteriors and interiors, to be used in advertising and marketing. A great variety of cameras, lights, and props are used in commercial photography, and the photographer must have a full command of all kinds of photographic techniques.

The *industrial photographer* does work that is similar to that of the commercial photographer. The main emphasis, however, is on taking pictures for a single company or firm that may lead to the improvement of factory organization and products. To accomplish this end, the industrial photographer takes pictures of workers on the job and of equipment and machinery operating at high speed. The pictures are generally used in company publications or for advertising company products or services.

Other photographic specialists include the following:

Photojournalists take pictures of newsworthy events, people, places, and things for newspapers and magazines, combining an ability to find and record dramatic action with photographic talent. Some photojournalists specialize in educational photography and prepare slides, film strips, videos, and motion pictures for use in classrooms and training programs.

Aerial photographers take photographs from aircraft in flight for news, business, industrial, scientific, weather, or military purposes.

Scientific photographers and *biological photographers* provide photographic illustrations and documentation for scientific publications and research reports. They usually specialize in a field such as engineering, aerodynamics, medicine, biology, or chemistry.

Finish photographers photograph the results of horse races as the horses approach and cross the finish line.

Nightclub and restaurant photographers circulate among guests and take photographs of customers who request them.

Some photographers write for trade and technical journals, teach photography in schools and colleges, act as representatives of photographic equipment manufacturers, sell photographic equipment and supplies, produce documentary films, or do freelance work.

Requirements

Formal educational requirements depend upon the nature of the photographer's specialty. For instance, photographic work in scientific and engineering research generally requires an engineering background with a degree from a recognized college or institute.

A college education is not required to become a photographer, although many employers prefer candidates with a four year degree in journalism or photojournalism in fields such as industrial, news, or scientific photography. In the late 1990s, over 100 community and junior colleges offer associate degrees in photography, more than 160 colleges and universities offer bachelor's degrees, and over 40 offered master's degrees. Many of these schools offer courses in cinematography, although very few have programs leading to a degree in this specialty. It should be noted that many men and women, however, become photographers with no formal education beyond high school.

Prospective photographers should have a broad technical understanding of photography plus as much practical experience with cameras as possible. They should take many different kinds of photographs with a variety of cameras and subjects. They should learn how to develop photographs and, if possible, should have a darkroom. Experience in picture composition, cropping prints (cutting to desired size), enlarging, and retouching are all valuable.

Students who hope to become photographers should possess manual dexterity, good eyesight and color vision, and artistic ability. They should have an eye for form and line, an appreciation of light and shadow, and the ability to use imaginative and creative approaches to photographs or film, especially in commercial work. In addition, they should be patient and accurate and enjoy working with detail. Many photographers regularly attend seminars to keep their knowledge and techniques current.

Self-employed, or freelance, photographers need good business skills. They must be able to manage their own studios, including hiring and managing photographic assistants and other employees, keeping records, and maintaining photographic and business files. Marketing and sales skills are also important to a successful freelance photography business.

Opportunities for Experience & Exploration

Photography is a field that almost every person with a camera can explore. Students can join high school camera clubs, yearbook of newspaper staffs, photography contests, and community hobby groups to gain experience. Students also may seek a part-time or summer job in a camera shop or work as a developer in a laboratory or processing center.

Methods of Entering

There is no one way in which to become a photographer. Some people enter the field as apprentices, trainees, or assistants. A trainee may work in a darkroom, camera shop, or developing laboratory. Trainees may move lights and arrange backgrounds for a commercial or portrait photographer or motion picture photographer. They may spend many months learning this kind of work before they move into a job behind a camera.

In many large cities, there are schools of photography, which may be a good way to start in the field. A press photographer may work for one of the many newspapers and magazines published in the United States and abroad. Some employers require a probationary period of thirty to ninety days before a new employee attains full job security. On publications where there is a full Newspaper Guild shop, a photographer will be required to join the guild.

Some go into business for themselves as soon as they have finished their formal education. Setting up a studio may not require a large capital outlay, but beginners may find that success does not come easily.

Advancement

Because photography is such a diversified field, there is no usual way in which to get ahead. Those who begin by working for someone else may advance to owning their own businesses. Commercial photographers may gain prestige as more of their pictures are placed in well-known trade journals or popular magazines. Press photographers may advance in salary and the kinds of important news stories assigned to them. A few photographers may become celebrities in their own right by making contributions to medical science, engineering science, or natural or physical science.

Employment Outlook

Of the 154,000 photographers and camera operators employed in 1996, about sixty percent were salaried employees; the other forty percent were self-employed. Most jobs for photographers are provided by photographic or commercial art studios; other employers include newspapers and magazines, radio and TV broadcasting, government agencies, and manufacturing firms. Colleges, universities, and other educational institutions employ photographers to prepare promotional and educational materials.

There will be a favorable employment increase in photography throughout the year 2006 as the use of visual images continues to grow in areas such as communications, education, entertainment, marketing, and research and development. In business and industry, for example, greater use will be made of photographs in meetings, stockholders' reports, annual reports, sales campaigns, and public relations programs. As the population grows, so should the demand for portrait photographers. Excellent opportunities should exist for scientific and medical photographers. Photojournalism is also expected to show growth as advancements in telecommunications create new markets—such as electronic newspapers and magazines—for the work of motivated photojournalists.

Earnings

The earnings of photographers in private industry vary according to the level of responsibility and experience. According to 1996 U.S. Department of Labor statistics, the median starting salary for photographers was $14,500. Photographers with experience earned $46,500 annually.

Photographers working for newspapers earn salaries that range from a low of $10,400 to a median of $26,343 to a high of $94,707, according to The Inland Press Association's 1997 Newspaper Compensation Survey. Salaries vary greatly by newspaper size and slightly by geographic region. Smaller newspapers offer smaller salaries; larger newspapers are able to offer their photojournalists higher salaries and better benefits.

Photographers in government service earn an average salary of about $30,000 a year. Self-employed photographers often earn more than salaried photographers, but their earnings depend on general business conditions. In addition, self-employed photographers do not have the benefits that a company provides its employees.

Photographers who combine scientific training and photographic expertise, as do scientific photographers, usually start at higher salaries than other photographers. They also usually receive consistently larger advances in salary than do others, so that their income, both as beginners and as experienced photographers, places them well above the average in their field. Photographers in salaried jobs usually receive benefits such as paid holidays, vacations, and sick leave and medical insurance.

Conditions of Work

Work conditions vary based on the job and employer. Many photographers work a thirty-five to forty-hour workweek, but freelancers and news photographers often put in long, irregular hours. Commercial and portrait photographers work in comfortable surroundings. Photojournalists seldom are be assured physical comfort in their work and may in fact face danger when covering stories on natural disasters or military conflicts. Some photographers work in research laboratory settings; others work on aircraft; and still others work underwater. For some photographers, conditions change from day to day. One day, they may be photographing a hot and dusty rodeo; the next they may be taking pictures of a dog sled race in Alaska.

In general, photographers work under pressure to meet deadlines and satisfy customers. Freelance photographers have the added pressure of continually seeking new clients and uncertain incomes.

For specialists in fields such as fashion photography, breaking into the field may take years. Working as another photographer's assistant is physically demanding when carrying equipment is required.

For freelance photographers, the cost of equipment can be quite expensive, with no assurance that the money spent will be recouped through income from future assignments. Freelancers in travel-related photography, such as travel and tourism, and photojournalism have the added cost of transportation and accommodations. For all photographers, flexibility is a major asset.

Sources of Additional Information

American Society of Media Photographers
419 Park Avenue, South
New York, NY 10016
Tel: 609-799-8300

Newspaper Guild
Education Department
8611 Second Avenue
Silver Spring, MD 20910
Tel: 301-585-2990

Professional Photographers of America
57 Forsyth Street, NW, Suite 1600
Atlanta, GA 30303
Tel: 404-522-8600

Photographic Equipment Technicians

Definition

Photographic equipment technicians, sometimes called *camera technicians,* maintain, test, disassemble, and repair cameras and other equipment used to take still and motion pictures. They are responsible for keeping the equipment in working order.

Photographic equipment technicians use a variety of hand tools (such as screwdrivers, pliers, and wire cutters) for maintenance and repair of the complex cameras used by motion picture and still photographers.

As hobbyists' cameras and equipment become more convenient to use, they become more complicated to maintain and repair. Professionals' cameras as well—especially those of filmmakers—have become increasingly more complicated and expensive. In both cases, photographic equipment is too valuable to entrust to the care of anyone but a trained photographic equipment technician. Today, there are thousands of these technicians working in the United States, providing services that range from quick and simple adjustments to complicated repairs requiring specialized equipment.

Nature of the Work

Many photographic equipment technicians work in shops specializing in camera adjustment and repair or in the service departments of large camera stores. Quite a few technicians work for camera manufacturers, repairing cameras and photographic equipment that customers have returned to the factory. Some camera dealers have their own in-house repair departments and sometimes hire technicians to adjust cameras on site. Technicians specializing in motion picture cameras and equipment may work for motion picture or television studios or companies renting such equipment to studios.

Technicians diagnose a camera's problem by analyzing the camera's shutter speed and accuracy of focus through the use

School Subjects
Mathematics
Shop (Trade/Vo-tech education)

Personal Interests
Building things
Figuring out how things work

Work Environment
Primarily indoors
Primarily one location

Minimum Education Level
Some postsecondary training

Salary Range
$13,500 to
$25,000 to
$35,000+

Certification or Licensing
None

Outlook
Faster than the average

DOT
714

GOE
05.05.11

NOC
9498

of sophisticated electronic test equipment. Once the problem is diagnosed, the camera is opened and checked for worn, misaligned, or defective parts. At least half of all repairs are done without replacing parts. All tests and adjustments are done to manufacturer's specifications, using blueprints, specification lists, and repair manuals.

Most repairs and adjustments can be made using small hand tools. A jeweler's loupe (magnifying glass) is used to examine small parts for wear or damage. Electronic and optical measuring instruments are used to check and adjust focus, shutter speed, operating speed of motion picture cameras, and light readings of light meters.

Many modern cameras designed for amateur use include built-in light meters as well as automatic focus and aperture (lens opening) settings. These features are convenient for the user, but the mechanisms require careful adjustment by a skilled technician when they malfunction.

Cameras must be kept clean and well lubricated to operate properly. Photographic equipment technicians use vacuum and air pressure devices to remove tiny dust particles and ultrasonic cleaning equipment to dislodge and remove hardened dirt and lubricant. Lenses are cleaned with a chemical solvent and soft tissue paper. Very fine lubricants are applied, often with the aid of a syringe or fine cotton swab.

Occasionally technicians, especially those employed by manufacturers or shops servicing professional studios, fabricate replacement parts. They employ small instrument-makers' lathes, milling machines, grinders, and other tools.

Technicians must be able to discuss a camera's working problems with a customer in order to extract the necessary information to diagnose the problem.

Requirements

Because their work is highly technical, photographic equipment technicians need specialized training, which is available through either classroom instruction or a correspondence course. The training provides basic technical background information to work with cameras as well as a thorough understanding and working knowledge of electronics. Not all camera models can be covered in the training course. More specialized training on additional models is obtained on the job or through specialized seminars.

Camera manufacturers and importers provide training for their technicians. This training usually covers only the technical aspects of the manufacturer's own products.

In order to work with extremely small parts, photographic equipment technicians need excellent vision, manual dexterity, and mechanical aptitude. Those who work directly with the public must be able to communicate easily with people.

Opportunities for Experience & Exploration

Larger camera stores often have an on-site employee who does limited camera adjustment and repair. This person can be a good source of information about opportunities in this field. Information may also be obtained from technical schools and institutes offering photographic equipment courses. In addition, many schools and community centers have photography clubs, some with their own darkrooms, that offer an excellent chance to explore the general field of photography.

Methods of Entering

Individual shops looking for technicians usually notify schools in their area or advertise through national photographic service publications. Manufacturers hire technicians through their personnel departments. The placement counselor of a student's training institute can help locate openings for graduates.

Advancement

Advancement in a photographic equipment repair facility is usually from trainee to experienced worker to a supervisory position. Many manufacturer's technicians also open their own shops, perhaps starting part time on weekends and evenings. Although technicians who have worked for a manufacturer usually know only one line of cameras well, they can learn other manufacturers' models on their own.

Independent technicians advance as their reputation grows for doing quality work. They must become familiar with all the major brands and models of camera equipment. In recent years, major camera manufacturers have been offering more training courses and seminars to inform independent technicians about their newer models—particularly those repairs that can be done efficiently in their shops and the types of repairs that need to be handled at the factory. Because of this increased cooperation, technicians who decide to open independent businesses are now much better able to provide quality services for the cameras they service.

Some independent technicians expand their activities into selling small "add-ons" such as film, accessories, and used equipment. Some photographic equipment technicians also work as professional photographers during their off-hours.

Employment Outlook

Employment for photographic equipment technicians is expected to grow faster than the average for all other occupations through the year 2006. The number of technicians required to service photographic equipment is predicted to increase as photography continues to grow as a hobby.

While the low price of many of today's point-and-shoot cameras and the high cost of labor make it uneconomical to do extensive service on these cameras, technicians with more extensive training will be needed to work on cameras that incorporate more sophisticated electronics. Because independent shops often perform only minor adjustments on models they are not specifically equipped to service, only moderate numbers of new technicians may be needed to work in these settings. Technicians whose training has covered a wide variety of equipment brands and models will be in greatest demand.

Earnings

Photographic equipment technicians employed by camera and equipment manufacturers and repair shops can expect to earn starting salaries in the range of $13,500 to $15,500 a year. The average salary for an experienced technician working for a manufacturer is often between $19,500 and $26,500 a year. A skilled and experienced technician working on commission in a busy repair shop can make over $35,000 a year. Self-employed technicians have earnings that vary widely. In the right location, independent technicians can build up businesses that give them earnings higher than those of technicians who work for manufacturers or shops.

Conditions of Work

Photographic equipment technicians work in clean, well-lighted shop conditions. They are usually seated at a bench for much of the time, working with hand tools. Eyestrain and stiffness from long hours of sitting are common physical complaints. Tedium can be a problem for some technicians.

Photographic equipment technicians work alone most of the time, concentrating on their work. Patience and steadiness are required to work successfully with the small mechanisms of modern camera equipment.

Sources of Additional Information

National Association of Photo Equipment Technicians
3000 Picture Place
Jackson, MI 49201
Tel: 517-788-8100
WWW: http://www.pmai.org

Society of Photo-Technologists
367 Windsor Highway, Suite 404
New Windsor, NY 12553
Tel: 914-782-4248
Email: sptechny.frontiercomm.net

Photographic Laboratory Occupations

Definition

Photographic laboratory workers develop black-and-white and color film, using chemical baths or printing machines, mount slides, and sort and package finished photographic prints. Some of these laboratory workers are known as *darkroom technicians, film laboratory technicians* and *developers*.

Nature of the Work

Developers work mainly in portrait studios, photo studios of newspapers, magazines, and advertising agencies, and commercial laboratories that process the work of professional photographers. They are highly skilled workers who can control the light contrast, surface finish, and other qualities of the photographic print by their mastery of the steps in the developing process. They perform many of their tasks in well-equipped darkrooms.

To develop black-and-white negative film, which accounts for a large percentage of the film used in commercial and art photography, the developer first places the unwound roll of film in a pan of developer solution to bring out the image. The technician then transfers the film to a stop bath to prevent overdevelopment, and then to a fixing bath, or hypo solution, to make it insensitive to light. These three steps are performed in darkness. The developer may vary the immersion time in each solution, depending on the qualities desired in the finished print. After the film is washed with water to remove all traces of chemical solutions, it is placed in a drying cabinet.

The developer may be assisted by a *projection printer*, who uses a projection printer to transfer the image from a negative to photographic paper. Light passing through the negative and a magnifying lens projects an image on the photographic paper. Contrast may be varied or unwanted details blocked out during the printing process.

School Subjects
Chemistry
Mathematics

Personal Interests
Figuring out how things work
Photography

Work Environment
Primarily indoors
Primarily one location

Minimum Education Level
High school diploma

Salary Range
$11,556 to
$16,328 to
$31,772+

Certification or Licensing
None

Outlook
More slowly than the average

DOT
976

GOE
05.10.05

NOC
9474

Most semiskilled workers, such as those who simply operate photofinishing machinery, are employed in large commercial laboratories that process color snapshot and slide film for amateur photographers. Often, they work under the supervision of a developer.

Automatic print developers tend machines that automatically develop film and fix, wash, and dry prints. These workers attach one end of the film to a leader in the machine; they also attach sensitized paper for the prints. While the machine is running, workers check temperature controls and adjust them as needed. The developers check prints coming out of the machine and refer those of doubtful quality to quality control workers.

Color-printer operators control a machine that makes color prints from negatives. Under darkroom conditions, they load the machine with a roll of printing paper. Before loading the negative film, they examine it to determine what machine setting to use to produce the best color print from it. After the photographic paper has been printed, they remove it from the machine and place it in the developer. The processed negatives and finished prints are inserted into an envelope to be returned to the customer.

Automatic mounters operate machines that cut apart rolls of positive color transparencies and mount them as slides. After trimming the roll of film, the mounter places it on the cutting machine, takes each cut frame in turn, and places it in a press that joins it to the cardboard mount.

Photo checkers and assemblers inspect prints, mounted transparencies, and negatives for color shading, sharpness of image, and accuracy of identifying numbers, using a lighted viewing screen. They mark any defective prints, indicating the corrective action to be taken, and return them with the negatives for reprocessing. Satisfactory prints and negatives are assembled in the proper order, packaged, and labeled for delivery to the customer.

Laboratories that specialize in custom work may employ a *retoucher* to alter negatives or prints in order to improve their color, shading, or content. The retoucher uses artists' tools to smooth features on faces, for example, or to heighten or eliminate shadows. (Some retouchers work in art studios or advertising agencies; others work as freelancers for book or magazine publishers).

Other photographic process specialists include *print controllers, photograph finishers, take-down sorters, black-and-white printer operators, hand mounters, print washers, splicers, cutters, print inspectors, automatic developers,* and *film processing utility workers.*

Requirements

High school graduates are preferred for photographic laboratory jobs. Courses in chemistry and mathematics are recommended. Many two-year colleges and technical institutes offer programs in photographic technology. Graduates of these programs can obtain jobs as developers and supervisors in photo labs.

An interest in photography and an understanding of its basic processes are natural assets for those applying for jobs in this field. Manual dexterity, good vision with no defects in color perception, and mechanical aptitude are also important. Students who plan to pursue careers as darkroom technicians for professional photographers need to have experience with developing procedures. Film convenience stores and camera stores are good places to get this experience.

Opportunities for Experience & Exploration

Many high schools and colleges have photography clubs, which can provide valuable experience for those interested in careers in this field. Evening courses in photography are offered in many technical schools and adult education programs. The armed forces also train personnel as photographic technicians.

There are several magazines that may be both interesting and helpful for prospective photographic laboratory workers. These include *American Photo, Darkroom Photography,* and *Photographic Processing.* Local libraries often have large collections of photography books as well. *The Darkroom Book,* edited by Jack Schofield, was published in 1985 by Watson-Guptill, and *Elementary Darkroom Practices,* by Eugene Groppetti, was published by Kendall/Hunt in 1987.

Methods of Entering

After receiving a high school diploma or its equivalent, prospective photographic laboratory workers usually apply for jobs at photofinishing laboratories. New employees in photographic laboratories begin as helpers to experienced technicians, moving into specialized jobs, such as printing and developing, as they gain more experience. Semi-skilled workers usually receive a few months of on-the-job training, while developers may take three or four years to become thoroughly familiar with their jobs.

Advancement

Advancement in this field is usually from technical jobs, such as developer, to supervisory and managerial positions. Semiskilled workers who continue their education in film processing techniques may move up to developer, all-around darkroom technician, and supervisory jobs.

Aspiring young photographers often take jobs in photo labs to provide themselves with a source of income while they attempt to establish themselves as professionals. There they can learn the most basic techniques of color, black and white, and slide reproduction. Those who accumulate sufficient capital may open their own commercial studios.

Employment Outlook

In 1996, about 63,000 people were employed in photographic laboratory occupations. More than half were semiskilled workers. The rest were developers or darkroom technicians.

Employment is expected to be slower than the average in this field through the year 2006, both for skilled developers and semiskilled machine operators. The increasing popularity of photography should provide some new job openings in film processing laboratories. However, during recessions, job openings for photographic laboratory occupations tend to decrease as photofinishing is considered a luxury by most consumers.

The introduction of digital cameras, which use electronic memory instead of a film negative to record an image, has not yet affected the employment of photographic laboratory workers. Digital cameras are still considered too cost prohibitive for most amateur photographers. Once digital cameras become affordable and widely used, demand for photographic laboratory workers is expected to decline.

Earnings

In 1996, the U.S. Department of Labor reported the median annual salary for photo process workers to be about $16,300. Weekly wages ranged from $203 for the lowest ten percent to $611 for the top ten percent. The average entry-level salary for darkroom technicians is about $10,500 per year. Those employees who go on to managerial positions can expect to earn $31,000 or more a year. Most employees worked a forty-hour week, with premium pay for overtime. Most photographic workers are eligible for benefits such as medical insurance.

Conditions of Work

Photographic laboratories are usually clean, well lighted (except for darkroom areas), and air-conditioned. There is usually no heavy physical labor. Many of the jobs performed by semiskilled workers are limited and repetitive and may become monotonous. The jobs often entail sitting or standing for a considerable amount of time in one place. Employees in these jobs need patience and ability to concentrate on details. Some employees, such as printer operators, photo checkers, and assemblers who examine small images very closely, may be subject to eyestrain.

The work of developers and darkroom technicians calls for good judgment, ability to apply specialized technical knowledge, and an appreciation of the aesthetic qualities of photography. Their contributions to the clarity and beauty of the finished photographs can be a great source of satisfaction.

Sources of Additional Information

Association of Professional Color Laboratories
3000 Picture Place
Jackson, MI 49201
Tel: 517-788-8146

Photo Marketing Association International
3000 Picture Place
Jackson, MI 49201
Tel: 517-788-8100
WWW: http://www.pmai.org

Professional Photographers of America, Inc.
57 Forsyth Street, NW, Suite 1600
Atlanta, GA 30303
Tel: 404-522-8600

Physical Therapist Assistants

Definition

Physical therapist assistants are skilled health care workers who assist physical therapists in a variety of techniques (such as exercise, massage, heat, and water therapy) to help restore physical function in people with injury, birth defects, or disease.

Physical therapist assistants work directly under the supervision of physical therapists. They instruct and assist patients in learning and improving functional activities required in their daily lives, such as walking, climbing, and moving from one place to another. The assistants observe patients during treatments, record the patients' responses and progress, and report these to the physical therapist, either orally or in writing. They fit patients for and help them learn to use braces, artificial limbs, crutches, canes, walkers, wheelchairs, and other devices. They may make physical measurements to assess the effects of treatments or to use in patient evaluations, determining the patients' range of motion, length and girth of body parts, and vital signs. Physical therapist assistants act as members of a team and regularly confer with other members of the physical therapy staff. In addition, they sometimes perform various clerical tasks in the department and order supplies, take inventories, and answer telephones.

Nature of the Work

Physical therapy personnel work to prevent, diagnose, and rehabilitate, to restore physical function, prevent permanent disability as much as possible, and help people achieve their maximum attainable performance. For many patients, this objective involves daily living skills, such as eating, grooming, dressing, bathing, and other basic movements that unimpaired people do automatically without thinking.

Physical therapy may alleviate conditions such as muscular pain, spasm, and weakness, joint pain and stiffness, and neu-

School Subjects
Anatomy and Physiology
Health

Personal Interests
Helping people: physical health/medicine
Helping people: emotionally

Work Environment
Primarily indoors
Primarily one location

Minimum Education Level
Associate's degree

Salary Range
$20,000 to
$25,000 to
$30,000

Certification or Licensing
Required in most states

Outlook
Much faster than the average

DOT
076

GOE
10.02.02

NOC
6631

romuscular incoordination. These conditions may be caused by any number of disorders, including fractures, burns, amputations, arthritis, nerve or muscular injuries, trauma, birth defects, stroke, multiple sclerosis, and cerebral palsy. Patients of all ages receive physical therapy services; they may be severely disabled or they may need only minimal therapeutic intervention.

Many kinds of equipment may be used in physical therapy, including mechanical devices such as parallel bars, stationary bicycles, and weightlifting equipment. Heat may be applied to the body using a whirlpool bath, paraffin bath, infrared lamp, heating pad, or diathermy (a technique for generating heat inside body tissue using a carefully controlled small electrical current). Other equipment is needed to produce ultrasound (sound vibrations of extremely high frequency that heat body tissue). Swimming pools are often found in physical therapy facilities. Therapy may involve teaching patients how to use corrective and helpful equipment, such as wheelchairs, canes, crutches, orthotic devices (orthopedic braces and splints), and prosthetic devices (artificial limbs and other body parts).

Physical therapy personnel must often work on improving the emotional state of patients, preparing them psychologically for treatments. The overwhelming sense of hopelessness and lack of confidence that afflict many disabled patients can reduce the patients' success in achieving improved functioning. The health team must be attuned to both the physical and nonphysical aspects of patients to assure that treatments are most beneficial. Sometimes physical therapy personnel work with patients' families to educate them on how to provide simple physical treatments and psychological support at home.

Physical therapist assistants always work under the direction of a qualified physical therapist. Other members of the health team may be a physician or surgeon, nurse, occupational therapist, psychologist, or vocational counselor. Each of these practitioners helps establish and achieve realistic goals consistent with the patient's individual needs. Physical therapist assistants help perform tests to evaluate disabilities and determine the most suitable treatment for the patient; then, as the treatment progresses, they routinely report the patient's condition to the physical therapist. If they observe a patient having serious problems during treatment, the assistants notify the therapist as soon as possible. Physical therapist assistants generally perform complicated therapeutic procedures decided by the physical therapist; however, assistants may initiate routine procedures independently.

These procedures may include physical exercises, which are the most varied and widely used physical treatments. Exercises may be simple or complicated, easy or strenuous, active or passive. Active motions are performed by the patient alone and strengthen or train muscles. Passive exercises involve the assistant moving the body part through the motion, which improves mobility of the joint but does not strengthen muscle. For example, for a patient with a fractured arm, both active and passive exercise may be appropriate. The passive exercises may be designed to maintain or increase the range of motion in the shoulder, elbow, wrist, and finger joints, while active resistive exercises strengthen muscles weakened by disuse. An elderly patient who has suffered a stroke may need guided exercises aimed at keeping the joints mobile, regaining the function of a limb, walking, or climbing stairs. A child with cerebral palsy who would otherwise never walk may be helped to learn coordination exercises that enable crawling, sitting balance, standing balance, and, finally, walking.

Patients sometimes perform exercises in bed or immersed in warm water. Besides its usefulness in alleviating stiffness or paralysis, exercise also helps to improve circulation, relax tense muscles, correct posture, and aid the breathing of patients with lung problems.

Other treatments that physical therapist assistants may administer include massages, traction for patients with neck or back pain, ultrasound and various kinds of heat treatment for diseases such as arthritis that inflame joints or nerves, cold applications to reduce swelling, pain, or hemorrhaging, and ultraviolet light.

Physical therapist assistants train patients to manage devices and equipment that they either need temporarily or permanently. For example, they instruct patients how to walk with canes or crutches using proper gait and maneuver well in a wheelchair. They also instruct patients in how to apply, remove, care for, and cope with splints, braces, and artificial body parts.

In addition, physical therapist assistants may perform office duties: they schedule patients, keep records, handle inventory, and order supplies.

Requirements

A degree from an accredited physical therapist assistant program is required; programs are usually offered in community and junior colleges. These programs, typically two years long, combine academic instruction with a period of supervised clinical practice in a physical therapy department setting. In recent years, admission to accredited programs has been fairly competitive, with three to five applicants for each available opening.

Some physical therapist assistants begin their careers while in the armed forces, which operate training programs. While these programs are not sufficient for state licensure and do not award degrees, they can serve as an excellent introduction to the field for students who later enter more complete training programs.

Licensure for physical therapist assistants is currently mandatory in forty-four states. Licensure requirements vary from state to state, but all require graduation from an American Physical Therapy Association–accredited two-year associate degree program and passing a written examination administered by the state. Conditions for renewing the license also vary by state. For information about licensing requirements, candidates should consult their schools' career guidance offices or the state licensure boards.

While still in high school, prospective physical therapist assistants should take courses in health, biology, mathematics, psychology, social science, physical education, computer data entry, English, and other courses that develop communications skills. In the physical therapist assistant training program, students can expect to study general education plus anatomy, physiology, biology, history and philosophy of rehabilitation, human growth and development, psychology, and physical therapist assistant procedures such as massage, therapeutic exercise, and heat and cold therapy. Other courses in mathematics and applied physical sciences help students understand the physical therapy apparatus and the scientific principles on which therapeutic procedures are based.

Physical therapist assistants must have large amounts of stamina, patience, and determination, but at the same time they must be able to establish personal relationships quickly and successfully. They should genuinely like and understand people, both under normal conditions and under the stress of illness. An outgoing personality is highly desirable as is the ability to instill confidence and enthusiasm in patients. Much of the work of physical retraining and restoring is very repetitive, and assistants may not perceive any progress for long periods of time. At times patients may seem unable or unwilling to cooperate. In such cases, assistants need boundless patience, to appreciate small gains and build on them. When restoration to good health is not attainable, physical therapist assistants must help patients adjust to a different way of life and find ways to cope with their situation. Creativity is an asset to devising methods that help disabled people achieve greater self-sufficiency. Assistants should be flexible and open to suggestions offered by their coworkers and willing and able to follow directions closely.

Because the job can be physically quite demanding, physical therapist assistants must be reasonably strong and enjoy physical activity. Manual dexterity and good coordination are needed to adjust equipment and assist patients. Assistants should be able to lift, climb, stoop, and kneel.

Opportunities for Experience & Exploration

While still in high school, students can get experience through summer or part-time employment or by volunteering in the physical therapy department of a hospital or clinic. Also, many schools, both public and private, have volunteer assistance programs for work with their disabled student population. Students can also gain useful direct experience by working with disabled children in a summer camp.

These opportunities provide prospective physical therapy workers with direct job experience that helps them determine whether they have the personal qualities necessary for this career. Students who have not had such direct experience should make an effort to talk to a physical therapist or physical therapist assistant during career-day programs, if available. It may also be possible to arrange to visit a physical therapy department, watch the staff at work, and ask questions.

Methods of Entering

The student's school placement office is probably the best place to find a job. Alternatively, assistants can apply to the physical therapy departments of local hospitals, rehabilitation centers, extended-care facilities, and other potential employers. Openings are listed in the classified ads of newspapers, professional journals, and with private and public employment agencies. In locales where training programs have produced many physical therapist assistants, competition for jobs may be keen. In such cases, assistants may want to widen their search to areas where there is less competition, especially suburban and rural areas.

Advancement

With experience, physical therapist assistants are often given greater responsibility and better pay. In large health care facilities, supervisory possibilities may open up. In small institutions that employ only one physical therapist, the physical therapist assistant may eventually take care of all the technical tasks that go on in the department, within the limitations of his or her training and education.

Physical therapist assistants with degrees from accredited programs are generally in the best position to gain advancement in any setting. They sometimes decide to earn a bachelor's degree in physical therapy and become fully qualified physical therapists.

Employment Outlook

Employment prospects are very good for physical therapist assistants, with job growth projected around 80 percent through the year 2006. Demand for rehabilitation services is expected to continue to grow much more rapidly than the average for all occupations, and the rate of turnover among workers is relatively high. Many new positions for physical therapist assistants are expected to open up as hospital programs that aid the disabled expand and as long-term facilities seek to offer residents more adequate services.

A major contributing factor is the aging of the U.S. population. People over age sixty-five tend to suffer a disproportionate amount of the accidents and chronic illnesses that necessitate physical therapy services. Many from the baby boom generation are reaching the age common for heart attacks, thus creating a need for more cardiac and physical rehabilitation. Legislation that requires appropriate public education for all disabled children also may increase the demand for physical therapy services. As more adults engage in strenuous physical exercise, more musculoskeletal injuries will result, thus increasing demand for physical therapy services.

Earnings

Salaries for physical therapist assistants vary considerably depending on geographical location, employer, and level of experience. The yearly income for a recently graduated assistant is usually between $20,000 and $24,000 a year, while experienced physical therapist assistants usually earn between $25,000 and $30,000. Fringe benefits vary, although they usually include paid holidays and vacations, health insurance, and pension plans.

Conditions of Work

Physical therapy is generally administered in pleasant, clean, well-lighted, and well-ventilated surroundings, located in hospitals, rehabilitation centers, schools for the disabled, nursing homes, community and government health agencies, physicians' or physical therapists' offices, and facilities for the mentally disabled. The space devoted to physical therapy services is often large, in order to accommodate activities such as gait training and exercises and procedures requiring equipment. Some procedures are given at patients' bedsides.

In the physical therapy department, patients come and go all day, many in wheelchairs, on walkers, canes, crutches, or stretchers. The staff tries to maintain a purposeful, harmonious, congenial atmosphere as they and the patients work toward the common goal of restoring physical efficacy.

The work can be exhausting. Physical therapist assistants may be on their feet for hours at a time, and they may have to move heavy equipment, lift patients, and help them to stand and walk. Most assistants work daytime hours, five days a week, although some positions require evening or weekend work. Some assistants work on a part-time basis.

The combined physical and emotional demands of the job can exert a considerable strain. Prospective assistants would be wise to seek out some job experience related to physical therapy so that they have a practical understanding of their psychological and physical capacities. By checking our their suitability for the work, they can make a better commitment to the training program.

Job satisfaction can be great for physical therapist assistants as they can see how their efforts help to make people's lives much more rewarding.

Sources of Additional Information

American Physical Therapy Association
1111 North Fairfax Street
Alexandria, VA 22314
Tel: 800-999-2782
WWW: http://www.apta.org

Pipefitters and Steamfitters

Definition

Pipefitters and *steamfitters* design, install, and maintain the piping systems for steam, hot water, heating, cooling, lubricating, sprinkling, and industrial processing systems.

Nature of the Work

Pipe systems carry more than just water. In power plants, they carry live steam to the turbines to create electricity. At oil refineries, pipes carry raw crude oil to processing tanks, then transport the finished products, such as petroleum, kerosene, and natural gas, to storage areas. In some manufacturing plants, pneumatic (air) pipe systems are used to monitor and adjust the industrial processes in the plant. Naval ships, submarines, aircraft, food processing plants, refrigerated warehouses, nuclear power plants, and office buildings all depend heavily on pipe systems for their operation. Pipe systems are also needed in the home for natural gas, hot and cold water, and sewage.

Pipefitters are the tradespeople who design, install, and maintain all of these different pipe systems. Steamfitters construct pipe systems that must withstand high amounts of pressure. It is a skilled and demanding line of work, because careless or incomplete work could cost lives.

Pipefitters can work both in existing buildings and buildings under construction. When working in an old building on a task such as installing a sprinkler system, a pipefitter (more appropriately, a *sprinkler fitter*) sometimes receives nothing more than a verbal description of the job to complete. The pipefitter then examines the blueprints of the building, makes the necessary measurements, and draws a layout for how the system is to be installed. Installing a new pipe system in an old building is trickier than in a new one because the system must adapt to the existing construction. Modifications made to accommodate the pipe system must not weaken the building's structure

School Subjects
Mathematics
Shop (Trade/Vo-tech education)

Personal Interests
Building things
Fixing things

Work Environment
Indoors and outdoors
Primarily multiple locations

Minimum Education Level
High school diploma
Apprenticeship

Salary Range
$16,224 to
$30,732 to
$54,444

Certification or Licensing
Recommended

Outlook
More slowly than the average

DOT
862

GOE
05.05.03

NOC
7252

or interfere with its other operations. Pipefitters also frequently are called on to repair the pipes in old buildings.

When installing pipe systems in buildings under construction, the pipefitter usually works under the supervision of the general contractor for the project. The blueprints for the piping are usually drawn up by the architect and the contractor and show the type of piping needed, what kind of fixtures are required, and where valves and connectors should be placed.

Pipefitters and steamfitters work with pipes made of many different types of materials, including steel, cast iron, copper, lead, glass, and plastic. As they study the blueprints, the pipefitters decide what types of materials they need and how much of each material. The first step in preparing the pipes is cutting them to the proper length. If pipes need to be screwed together, the pipefitter cut threads into the ends of the pipe using a pipe threader, which is attached to the end of the pipe and rotated to cut a slowly spiralling groove into the pipe. To remove any metal burrs after the thread is cut, the pipefitter cleans out using a pipe reamer. Pipes may also need to be bent to the proper angle, which is done with a bending device that can be either manually or electrically powered.

Once the pipes are sized and cut, they are put into position, and the pipefitter determines what needs to be done to support or give access to the pipes. Occasionally, holes may need to be cut through ceilings, floors, or walls, or the pipes may need to be bracketed to ceiling joists or along walls. Then the pipes are fitted together. This may be done by screwing the pipes into couplers, elbow joints, connectors, or special valves. Very large pipes, such as sewer pipes, have flat flanges that are bolted together when joined. At this stage, the pipefitter installs special mechanisms such as pressure gauges or meters.

Finally, the connections between the pipes are sealed and made airtight. Depending on the pipe's material, this is done by soldering, caulking, brazing, fusing, or cementing the joints of the pipes together. The pipe system is then tested to make certain it is completely sealed. Water, air, or gas is pumped into the system at a high pressure and leaks are checked either personally by the pipefitter or an apprentice, or mechanically by means of gauges attached to the pipes. Proper and complete sealing is extremely important. Leaks will affect the performance of the entire system, and in certain cases, such as high-pressure steam pipes or pipes carrying noxious chemicals, leaks can be deadly.

Requirements

Pipefitters and steamfitters learn their occupations through apprenticeship programs. These programs take five years to complete, combining on-the-job training with a minimum of 216 hours of related classroom instruction each year. To apply for apprenticeship programs, people must be at least eighteen years of age, in good physical condition, and have earned a high school diploma or its equivalent. Apprentice applicants are expected to have taken high school courses in shop, drafting, mathematics, physics, chemistry, and blueprint reading. Coursework from vocational schools and correspondence schools may supplement an apprentice's training. To measure their mechanical readiness for this profession, apprentice applicants take mechanical aptitude tests.

Apprentices sign a written agreement with the local apprenticeship committee, which is made up of members from both union and management. This committee sets the standards for work and training that ensures apprentices gain a broad range of experience through employment with several different contractors. In their training period, they learn to cut, bend, fit, solder, and weld pipes. They also learn the proper use and care of tools and equipment, materials handling, workplace operations and safety (including the regulations of the Occupational Safety and Health Administration), and how to make cost estimates.

Pipefitters and steamfitters learn related construction techniques, such as installing gas furnaces, boilers, pumps, oil burners, and radiators. They study and work on various heating and cooling systems, hot water systems, and solar and radiant heat systems. They explore industrial applications such as pneumatic control systems and instrumentation. Classroom work for apprentices includes subjects such as drafting, blueprint reading, applied math and physics, and local building codes and regulations.

Union membership often is a requirement for most pipefitters and steamfitters. The main union representing this trade is the United Association of Journeymen and Apprentices of the Plumbing and Pipe Fitting Industry of the United States and Canada. In certain industries such as the aerospace or petroleum industries, pipefitters and steamfitters may belong to other unions.

In some cities, pipefitters, steamfitters, and sprinkler fitters must be licensed. This requires passing a written test that covers local building and plumbing codes and offering proof of training and skills in the trade.

Opportunities for Experience & Exploration

To get an idea of the type of work done by pipefitters and steamfitters, students can look for jobs as construction helpers to these trades. This does not involve the commitment of an apprenticeship, and it is a good vantage point from which to consider whether one is interested in the type of work pipefitters do and the amount of training that the profession requires. A job as a helper is also a very good stepping-stone to apprenticeship programs.

Methods of Entering

After completing high school, those interested in a career as a pipefitter should seek information on the various apprenticeship programs available. To do this, job seekers can visit the nearest plumbing and pipefitting union local or nearby construction contractors to learn the details of apprenticeship programs and how to apply.

Another source for this information is the state employment service office of the U.S. Department of Labor, Bureau of Apprenticeship and Training. Applicants may have to take an aptitude test for admittance to apprenticeship programs.

For those who do not want to commit to an apprenticeship program, local unions and contractors are the best sources for work. Both unions and contractors may hire helpers to pipefitters and steamfitters.

Advancement

After their training, apprentice pipefitters become journeyworkers, which means more money and more employment opportunities. They may continue to work for the same contractor or switch to a new employer. If they gain experience in all the skills of the trade, they may rise to the position of supervisor. Some pipefitters and steamfitters decide to go into business for themselves as independent contractors, lining up job contracts and hiring their own employees. According to the Department of Labor, one out of every seven pipefitters is self-employed.

Employment Outlook

Employment prospects for pipefitters and steamfitters are expected to be slower than average for all occupations through the year 2006. While this field is not expanding, the U.S. Department of Labor predicts that 61,000 job openings will occur in the next decade. These openings will occur as workers retire or leave the profession and the number of replacement workers entering apprenticeship programs declines. As a result, job prospects will be good for the motivated person who is willing to work in sometimes strenuous or uncomfortable work situations.

Those pipefitters who work in construction may experience layoffs when there are lulls in construction activity, while those who maintain existing pipe systems generally have steadier work. Pipefitters and steamfitters are less sensitive to swings in the economy than other construction trades.

Expansion of certain industries, such as chemical and food-processing factories and those that rely on automated production, will be an important source of work for pipefitters. In office and home construction, air-conditioning and refrigeration systems will keep pipefitters busy, as will legislation requiring sprinkler systems in older buildings. Keeping existing pipe systems in good repair will employ many workers in the trade.

Earnings

Earnings for pipefitters and steamfitters are among the highest in the construction trades. According to the *1998-99 Occupational Outlook Handbook (OOH)*, median weekly earnings for plumbers and pipefitters in 1996 who were not self employed range from a low of $312 to over $1,047 for the most experienced workers. Pipefitters earn an average of $21.46 an hour in metropolitan areas, according to *OOH*. Geography is a factor in earnings; wages tend to be higher in the Midwest and West.

Apprentices typically earn about 50 percent of a journeyworker's wage at the beginning of their training. If their work is satisfactory, their wages are raised at regular intervals, usually six months, as stipulated in their apprenticeship agreements. Applicants with some relevant training or experience may receive a higher wage when they begin their apprenticeship. Pipefitters and steamfitters also enjoy a variety of benefits, including health insurance, pension plans, paid vacations, and training opportunities. Many pipefitters belong to unions which negotiate national or regional pay scales for members.

Conditions of Work

Like other construction and maintenance work, pipefitting is hard, dirty, and physically active. Much of their work is done in cramped quarters and uncomfortable positions. Lifting, joining, and installing heavy pipe work and operating large machinery can cause fatigue and muscle strain. Other hazards include cuts from sharp tools, burns from hot pipes and welding material, and related construction injuries. However, the injury rate for pipefitters and steamfitters is the same as the average for most construction employees.

Most pipefitters and steamfitters are employed by building contractors and perform their work at different sites every day. They may work for a few hours at one work site and then travel to another. However, the construction of a large housing or industrial complex may keep pipefitters at the same site for several months. Pipefitters work a regular forty-hour week, although they may work overtime to meet deadlines or complete assignments. Pipefitters on the maintenance staff of large processing plants generally work from thirty-five to forty hours a week.

Pipefitting, steamfitting, and sprinkler fitting are demanding trades. Aside from the physical strain the work requires, pipefitters must perform very careful, conscientious, and exacting work. Flaws in their work could lead to damage to property and injury to others. They must be able not only to follow instructions but to apply judgment and experience in making decisions and directing other workers when necessary.

Pipefitters and steamfitters invest a lot of time into their training for the profession, so relatively few of them leave the field to move into other lines of work. Work is usually available in all parts of the country, and the pay is above average. Pipefitters and steamfitters enjoy the satisfaction of working in one of the skilled construction trades.

Sources of Additional Information

■ Mechanical Contractors Association of America
1385 Piccard Drive
Rockville, MD 20850
Tel: 301-869-5800

■ National Association of Plumbing-Heating-Cooling Contractors
PO Box 6808
180 South Washington Street
Falls Church, VA 22040
Tel: 703-237-8100

Plasterers

Definition

Plasterers apply coats of plaster to interior walls, ceilings, and partitions of buildings to produce fire-resistant and relatively soundproof surfaces. They also work on exterior building surfaces and do ornamental forming and casting work. Their work is similar to that of *drywall workers,* who use drywall rather than plaster to build interior walls and ceilings.

Nature of the Work

Plasterers work on building interiors and exteriors. They apply plaster directly to masonry, wire, wood, metal or lath. (Lath is a supportive reinforcement made of wood or metal that is attached to studs to form walls and ceilings.) These surfaces are designed to hold the plaster in position until it dries. After checking the specifications and plans made by the builder, architect, or foreman, plasterers put a border of plaster of the desired thickness on the top and bottom of the wall. After this border has hardened sufficiently, they fill in the remaining portion of the wall with two coats of plaster. The surface of the wall area is then leveled and smoothed with a straightedged tool and darby (long flat tool used for smoothing). They then apply the third or finishing coat of plaster, which is the last operation before painting or paperhanging. This coat may be finished to an almost velvet smoothness or into one of a variety of decorative textures that are used in place of papering.

When plastering cinder block and concrete, plasterers first apply what is known as a brown coat of gypsum plaster as a base. The second coat, called the white coat, is lime-based plaster. When plastering metal lath foundations, they first apply a scratch coat with a trowel, spread it over the lath, and scratch the surface with a rake-like tool to make ridges before it dries so that the next coat—the brown coat—will bond tightly. Next, the plasterer sprays or trowels the plaster for the brown

School Subjects
Art
Shop (Trade/Vo-tech education)

Personal Interests
Building things
Fixing things

Work Environment
Primarily indoors
Primarily multiple locations

Minimum Education Level
High school diploma
Apprenticeship

Salary Range
$13,000 to
$27,600 to
$49,900

Certification or Licensing
None

Outlook
About as fast as the average

DOT
840

GOE
05.05.04

NOC
7284

coat and smooths it. The finishing coat is either sprayed on or applied with a hawk and trowel. Plasterers also use brushes and water for the finishing coat. The final coat is a mix of lime, water, and plaster of Paris that sets quickly and is smooth and durable.

The plasterer sometimes works with plasterboard or sheetrock, which are types of wallboard that come ready for installation. When working with such wallboard, the plasterer cuts and fits the wallboard to the studding and joists of ceilings and interior walls. When installing ceilings, workers perform as a team.

Plasterers who specialize in exterior plastering are known as *stucco masons*. They apply a weather-resistant decorative covering of Portland cement plaster to lath in the same manner as interior plastering or with the use of a spray gun. In exterior work, however, the finish coat usually consists of a mixture of white cement and sand or a patented finish material that may be applied in a variety of colors and textures.

Decorative and ornamental plastering is the specialty of highly skilled *molding plasterers*. This work includes molding or forming and installing ornamental plaster panels and trim. Some molding plasterers also cast intricate cornices and recesses used for indirect lighting. Such work is rarely used today because of the great degree of skill involved and the high cost.

In recent years, most plasterers began using machines to spray plaster on walls, ceilings, and structural sections of buildings. Machines that mix plaster have been in general use for many years.

Requirements

Most employers prefer to hire applicants who are at least seventeen years old, in good physical condition, and who have a high degree of manual dexterity. Although a high school or trade school education is not mandatory, it is highly recommended. To qualify as a journeyworker plasterer, a person must complete either an apprenticeship or on-the-job training program.

The apprenticeship program consists of three to four years of carefully planned activity combined with approximately 6,000 to 8,000 hours of work experience and an annual 144 hours of related classroom instruction. An apprenticeship is usually the best start, since it includes on-the-job training as well as supervision.

On-the-job training consists of working for four or more years under the supervision of experienced plasterers. The trainee usually begins as a helper or laborer and learns the trade informally by observing or being taught by other plasterers.

Opportunities for Experience & Exploration

In high school or vocational school, students have several avenues open for exploring the occupation of plasterer. Mechanical drawing, drafting, woodwork, and other shop courses test their ability and aptitude for this type of work, while courses in mathematics gauge their skill in the applied mathematics of layout work.

To observe the plasterer at work, field trips to construction sites may be arranged by a school counselor or students can arrange an interview on their own.

An excellent firsthand experience in this trade would be to obtain a part-time or summer job as a plasterer's helper or laborer.

Methods of Entering

There are two ways individuals can enter this field: as apprentices or on-the-job trainees. Those who wish to become apprentices usually contact local plastering contractors, the state employment service bureau, or the appropriate union headquarters. In most places, the local branch of the Operative Plasterers' and Cement Masons' International Association of the United States and Canada is the best place to inquire about apprenticeships. The Bureau of Apprenticeship and Training, U.S. Department of Labor, and the state employment office are also good places to contact for information.

If the apprenticeship program is filled, applicants may wish to enter the field as on-the-job trainees. In this case, they usually contact a plastering contractor directly and begin work as helpers or laborers. They learn about the work by mixing the plaster, helping plasterers with scaffolding, and carrying equipment.

Advancement

Successful completion of a training program is necessary before individuals can become qualified plasterers. It takes four years to become proficient in most plastering techniques. After increasing their skill and efficiency for a few years, several promotional opportunities are open to them.

Most plasterers learn the full range of plastering skills. They develop expertise in finish plastering as well as rough coat plastering. They also learn the spray gun technique and become proficient spray gun plasterers. With additional training, they may specialize in exterior work as stucco masons or in ornamental plastering as molding plasterers.

If they have certain personal characteristics such as the ability to deal with people and good judgment and planning skills, plasterers may progress to become supervisors or job estimators. Many plasterers become self-employed, and some eventually become contractors.

Employment Outlook

There were approximately 32,000 plasterers employed in the United States in 1996. Employment opportunities for plasterers are expected to increase as fast as average through the year 2006 because of the trend toward wider use of drywall construction. Plasterers' employment prospects usually rise and fall with the economy, and especially with the health of the construction industry.

However, recent improvements in both plastering materials and methods of application are expected to increase the scope of the craft and create more job opportunities. To name a few such developments: more lightweight plasters are being used because of excellent soundproofing, acoustical, and fireproofing qualities; machine plastering, insulating, and fireproofing are becoming more widespread; and the use of plaster veneer or high-density plaster in creating a finished surface is being used increasingly in new buildings. Plaster veneer is a thin coat of plaster that can be finished in one coat. It is made of lime and plaster of Paris and can be mixed with water at the job site. It is often applied to a special gypsum base on interior surfaces. Exterior systems have also changed to include Styrofoam insulation board and two thin coats of polymer and acrylic modified materials, called Exterior Insulated Finish Systems, or EIFS.

Earnings

The median annual salary for plasterers in 1996, according to the U.S. Department of Labor, was about $27,600. However, the minimum wage rate varies considerably according to geographic regions. Hourly wages vary from a low of $14.45 for apprentice plasterers to $39.08 for experienced union plasterers in certain areas. Average monthly wages range from $1,481 to $3,265. Apprentice workers usually receive fifty percent of an experienced plasterer.

Workers in this field may receive traditional fringe benefits, such as health insurance and paid vacation days.

Conditions of Work

Most plasterers have a regular forty-hour workweek with occasional overtime when necessary to meet a contract deadline. Overtime work is compensated at the rate of one and a half times the regular hourly wage. The workday may start earlier than most (7:00 AM, but it also usually ends earlier (3:00 PM). Some plasterers face layoffs between jobs, while others may work with drywall or ceiling tile as required by their contractors when there is no plastering work to be done.

Most of the work is performed indoors, plastering walls and ceilings and forming and casting ornamental designs. Plasterers also work outdoors, doing stucco work and EIFS. They often work with other construction workers, including carpenters, plumbers, and pipe- fitters. Plasterers must do a considerable amount of standing, stooping, and lifting. They often get plaster on their work clothes and dust in their eyes and noses.

Most plasterers work for independent contractors and are members of unions, either the Operative Plasterers' and Cement Masons' International Association of the United States and Canada or the Bricklayers and Allied Craftsmen International Union.

Most plasterers take pride in seeing the results of their work—something they have helped to build that will last a long time. Their satisfaction with progress on the job, day by day, may be a great deal more than in jobs where the worker never sees the completed product or where the results are less obvious.

As highly skilled workers, plasterers have higher earnings, better chances for promotion, and more opportunity to go into business for themselves than other workers. They also can usually find jobs in almost any part of the United States.

Sources of Additional Information

■**Foundation of the Wall and Ceiling Industry**
307 East Annandale Road, Suite 200
Falls Church, VA 22042
Tel: 703-534-1703

International Institute for Lath and Plaster
820 Transfer Road
St. Paul, MN 55114
Tel: 612-645-0208

International Union of Bricklayers and Allied Craftsmen
815 15th Street, NW
Washington, DC 20005
Tel: 202-783-3788

Operative Plasterers' and Cement Masons' International Association of the United States and Canada
1125 17th Street, NW
Washington, DC 20036
Tel: 202-393-6569

Mason Contractors of America
1550 Spring Road, Suite 320
Oak Brook, IL 60521
Tel: 630-782-6767

Plumbers

Definition

Plumbers assemble, install, alter, and repair pipes and pipe systems that carry water, steam, air, or other liquids and gases for sanitation and industrial purposes as well as other uses. Plumbers also install plumbing fixtures, appliances, and heating and refrigerating units.

Nature of the Work

Because little difference exists between the work of the plumber and the pipefitter in most cases, the two are often considered to be one trade. However, many craftsworkers specialize in one field or the other, especially in large cities.

The work of pipefitters differs from that of plumbers mainly in its location and the variety and size of pipes used. Plumbers work primarily in residential and commercial buildings, whereas pipefitters are generally employed by a large industry such as an oil refinery, refrigeration plant, or defense establishment where more complex systems of piping are used. Plumbers assemble, install, and repair heating, water, and drainage systems, especially those that must be connected to public utilities systems. Some of their jobs include replacing burst pipes and installing and repairing sinks, bathtubs, water heaters, hot water tanks, garbage disposal units, dishwashers, and water softeners. Plumbers also may work on septic tanks, cesspools, and sewers. During the final construction stages of both commercial and residential buildings, plumbers install heating and air-conditioning units and connect radiators, water heaters, and plumbing fixtures.

Most plumbers follow set procedures in their work. After inspecting the installation site to determine pipe location, they cut and thread pipes, bend them to required angles by hand or machines, and then join them by means of welded, brazed,

School Subjects
Mathematics
Physics

Personal Interests
Building things
Finding out how things work

Work Environment
Primarily indoors
Primarily multiple locations

Minimum Education Level
High school diploma
Apprenticeship

Salary Range
$16,200 to $30,700 to $54,400

Certification or Licensing
Required in most states

Outlook
More slowly than the average

DOT
862

GOE
05.05.03

NOC
7251

caulked, soldered, or threaded joints. To test for leaks in the system, they fill the pipes with water or air.

Specialists include *diesel engine pipefitters, ship and boat building coppersmiths, industrial-gas fitters, gas-main fitters, prefab plumbers,* and *pipe cutters.*

Plumbers use a variety of tools, including hand tools such as wrenches, reamers, drills, braces and bits, hammers, chisels, and saws; power machines that cut, bend, and thread pipes; gasoline torches; and welding, soldering, and brazing equipment.

Requirements

Most employers prefer to hire applicants who are at least eighteen years old, in good physical condition, and have a high degree of mechanical aptitude. Although a high school education is not required, it is generally preferred. The student's preparation should include coursework in mathematics, chemistry, and physics, as well as some shop courses.

To become a plumber, a person must complete either a formal apprenticeship or an informal on-the-job training program. To be considered for the apprenticeship program, individuals must pass an examination administered by the state employment agency and have their qualifications approved by the local joint labor-management apprenticeship committee.

The apprenticeship program for plumbers consists of four years of carefully planned activity combining direct training with at least 144 hours of formal classroom instruction each year. The program is designed to give apprentices diversified training by having them work for several different plumbing or pipe-fitting contractors.

On-the-job training, on the other hand, usually consists of working for five or more years under the guidance of an experienced craftsworker. Trainees begin as helpers until they acquire the necessary skills and knowledge for more difficult jobs. Frequently, they supplement this practical training by taking trade- or correspondence-school courses.

A license is required for plumbers in many places. To obtain this license, plumbers must pass a special examination to demonstrate their knowledge of local building codes as well as their all-around knowledge of the trade. To become a plumbing contractor in most places, a master plumber's license must be obtained.

Opportunities for Experience & Exploration

Although opportunities for direct experience in this occupation are rare for those in high school, there are ways to explore the field. Courses in chemistry, physics, mechanical drawing, and mathematics are all helpful to the work of the plumber and pipefitter. By taking these courses in high school, students can test their ability and aptitude in the theoretical aspects of the trade.

Methods of Entering

Applicants who wish to become apprentices usually contact local plumbing, heating, and air-conditioning contractors who employ plumbers, the state employment service bureau, or the local branch of the United Association of Journeymen and Apprentices of the Plumbing and Pipe Fitting Industry of the United States and Canada. Individual contractors or contractor associations often sponsor local apprenticeship programs. Before becoming apprentices, however, prospective plumbers must have the approval of the joint labor-management apprenticeship committee. Both union and nonunion apprenticeships typically last four to five years. The Bureau of Apprenticeship and Training, the U.S. Department of Labor, and state employment offices are also good places to contact for information.

If applicants are rejected from apprenticeship programs or if the programs are filled, they may wish to enter the field as on-the-job trainees. Others pursue plumbing training through the armed forces.

Advancement

Successful completion of a training program is necessary before an individual can become a qualified journeyworker plumber, and licenses are required in most communities. It takes two to four years to master most of the skills the plumber needs to perform everyday tasks.

If plumbers have certain qualities, such as the ability to deal with people and good judgment and planning skills, they may progress to such positions as supervisor or job estimator for plumbing or pipefitting contractors. If they work for a large industrial company, they may advance to the position of job superintendent.

Many plumbers go into business for themselves. Eventually they may expand their activities and become contractors, employing other workers.

Employment Outlook

There were approximately 389,000 plumbers and pipefitters working in the United States in 1996. Employment opportunities for plumbers are expected to grow slower than the average for all jobs through the year 2006. There are several reasons for this outlook. The most important factor is the anticipated decrease in construction activity. Plumbing and heating work in new homes for sprinkler systems, bathrooms, washing machines, waste disposals, air-conditioning equipment, and solar heating devices will use plastic pipes and fittings. Such materials are easier to use and maintain, thus creating a lighter workload for plumbers. The need to replace those who leave the field for retirement or other reasons will provide tens of thousands of job openings each year.

Earnings

According to 1996 U.S. Department of Labor statistics, the annual median salary for non-self-employed plumbers is $30,000. Wages vary, however, according to location. Plumbers working in the Midwest and West tend to earn more than others working elsewhere in the United States. Monthly wages for plumbers range from $1,600 to $3,200. Hourly pay rates for apprentices usually start at 50 percent of the experienced worker's rate, and increase by five percent every six months until a rate of 95 percent is reached. Benefits for union workers usually include health insurance, sick time, and vacation pay, as well as pension plans.

Conditions of Work

Most plumbers have a regular forty-hour workweek with extra pay for overtime. Unlike most of the other building trades, this field is little affected by seasonal factors.

The work of the plumber is active and strenuous. Standing for prolonged periods and working in cramped or uncomfortable positions are often necessary. Possible risks include falls from ladders, cuts from sharp tools, and burns from hot pipes or steam. Working with clogged pipes and toilets can also be smelly.

Those who would be successful and contented plumbers should like to solve a variety of problems and should not object to being called on during evenings, weekends, or holidays to perform emergency repairs. As in most service occupations, plumbers should be able to get along well with all kinds of people. The plumber should be a person who works well alone, but who can also direct the work of helpers and enjoy the company of those in the other construction trades.

Sources of Additional Information

National Association of Plumbing-Heating-Cooling Contractors
PO Box 6808
180 South Washington Street
Falls Church, VA 22040
Tel: 703-237-8100

United Association of Journeymen and Apprentices of the Plumbing and Pipe Fitting Industry of the United States and Canada
PO Box 37800
Washington, DC 20013
Tel: 202-628-5823

Police Officers

Definition

Police officers perform many duties relating to public safety. Their responsibilities include not only preserving the peace, preventing criminal acts, enforcing the law, investigating crimes, and arresting those who violate the law but also directing traffic, community relations work, and controlling crowds at public events. Police officers are employed at the federal, state, county, and city level. *State police officers* patrol highways and enforce the laws and regulations that govern the use of those highways, in addition to performing general police work. Police officers are under oath to uphold the law twenty-four hours a day.

Nature of the Work

Police officers are responsible for preserving law and order at all times. If they patrol a beat or work in small communities, their duties may be many and varied. In large city departments, their work may be highly specialized. Police officers are employed by state, county, and municipal governments.

Depending on the orders they receive from their commanding officers, police may direct traffic during the rush-hour periods and at special local events when traffic is unusually heavy. They may patrol public places such as parks, streets, and public gatherings to maintain law and order. Police are sometimes called upon to prevent or break up riots and to act as escorts at funerals, parades, and other public events. They may administer first aid in emergency situations, assist in rescue operations of various kinds, investigate crimes, issue tickets to violators of traffic or parking laws or other regulations, or arrest drunk drivers. Officers in small towns may have to perform all these duties and administrative work as well.

As officers patrol their assigned beats, either on foot, horseback, or in cars, they must be alert for any situations that arise and be ready to take appropriate action. Many times they must

School Subjects
Physical education
Psychology

Personal Interests
Helping people:
protection
Law

Work Environment
Indoors and outdoors
Primarily multiple
locations

Minimum Education Level
High school diploma

Salary Range
$19,200 to
$34,700 to
$64,500+

Certification or Licensing
None

Outlook
About as fast as the
average

DOT
375

GOE
04.01.02

NOC
6261

be alert to identify stolen cars, identify and locate lost children, and identify and apprehend escaped criminals and others wanted by various law enforcement agencies. While on patrol, they keep in constant contact with headquarters and their fellow officers by calling in regularly on two-way radios. Although their job may at times be dangerous, police officers are trained not to endanger their own lives or the lives of ordinary citizens. If they need assistance, they radio for additional officers.

In large city police departments, officers usually have more specific duties and specialized assignments. The police departments usually are comprised of special work divisions such as communications, criminal investigation, firearms identification, fingerprint identification and forensic science, accident prevention, and administrative services. In very large cities, police departments may have special work units such as the harbor patrol, canine corps, mounted police, vice squad, fraud or bunco squad, traffic control, records control, and rescue units. A few of the job titles for these specialties are *identification and records commanders and officers, narcotics and vice detectives or investigators, homicide squad commanding officers, detective chiefs, traffic lieutenants, sergeants, parking enforcement officers, public safety officers, accident-prevention squad officers, safety instruction police officers,* and *community relations lieutenants.*

In very large city police departments, officers may fill positions as *police chiefs, precinct sergeants and captains, desk officers, booking officers, police inspectors, identification officers, complaint evaluation supervisors and officers, crime prevention police officers,* and *internal affairs investigators,* whose job is to police the police. Some officers work as plainclothes detectives in criminal investigation divisions. Other specialized police officers include *police reserves commanders; police officer commanding officers III,* who act as supervisors in missing persons and fugitive investigations; and *police officers III,* who investigate and pursue nonpayment and fraud fugitives. Many police departments employ *police clerks,* who perform administrative and community-oriented tasks.

A major responsibility for *state police officers* (sometimes known as *state troopers* or *highway patrol officers*) is to patrol the highways and enforce the laws and regulations of those traveling on them. Riding in patrol cars equipped with two way radios, they monitor traffic for troublesome or dangerous situations. They write traffic tickets and issue warnings to drivers who are violating traffic laws or otherwise not observing safe driving practices. They radio for assistance for drivers who are stopped because of breakdowns, flat tires, illnesses, or other reasons. They direct traffic around congested areas caused by fires, road repairs, accidents, and other emergencies. They may check the weight of commercial vehicles to verify that they are within allowable limits, conduct driver examinations, or give safety information to the public.

In case of a highway accident, officers take charge of the activities at the site by directing traffic, giving first aid to any injured parties, and calling for emergency equipment such as ambulances, fire trucks, or tow trucks. They write up a report to be used by investigating officers who attempt to determine the cause of the accident.

In addition to these responsibilities, state police officers in most states do some general police work. They are often the primary law-enforcement agency in communities or counties that have no police force or large sheriff's department. In those areas, they may investigate such crimes as burglary and assault. They also may assist municipal or county police to capture lawbreakers or control civil disturbances.

Most police officers are trained in the use of firearms and carry guns. Police in special divisions, such as chemical analysis, handwriting, and fingerprint identification, have special training to perform their work. Police officers often testify in court regarding their knowledge of cases with which they have been involved. Police personnel are required to complete accurate and thorough records of their cases.

Requirements

Police job appointments in most large cities and in many smaller cities and towns are governed by local civil service regulations. Applicants are required to pass written tests designed to measure the candidates' intelligence and general aptitude for police work. Physical examinations are required and, usually include tests of physical agility, dexterity, and strength. Candidates' personal histories, backgrounds, and character undergo careful scrutiny as honesty and law-abiding characteristics are essential traits for law-enforcement officers. An important requirement is that the prospective police officer has a clean arrest record.

Job applicants must be at least twenty-one years of age (or older for some departments), and some municipalities stipulate an age limit of not more than thirty-five years. Candidates must have, in most cases, 20/20 uncorrected vision, good hearing, and weight proportionate to their height. Male and female applicants must meet locally prescribed weight and height rules for their sex. Most job regulations require that appliants be U.S. citizens, and many police departments have residency requirements.

The majority of police departments today require that applicants have a high school education. Although a high school diploma is not always required, related work experience is generally required. The best chance for advancement, however, is for officers with some postsecondary education, and many police departments now require a two-year or four-year degree, especially for more specialized areas of police work. There are more than 800 junior colleges and universities offering two-year and four-year degree programs in law enforcement. The armed forces also offer training and opportunities in law enforcement that can be applied to civilian police work.

High school students who are interested in pursuing this career will find the subjects of psychology, sociology, English, law, mathematics, U.S. government and history, chemistry, and physics most helpful. Because physical stamina is very important in this work, sports and physical education are also valuable. Knowledge of a foreign language is especially helpful, and bilingual officers are often in great demand. High school students interested in specialized and advanced positions in law enforcement should pursue studies leading to college programs in criminology, criminal law, criminal psychology, or related areas. Prospective police officers should enjoy working with people and be able to cooperate with others. Because of the stressful nature of much police work, police officers must be able to think clearly and logically during emergency situations, have a strong degree of emotional control, and be capable of detaching themselves from incidents.

Newly recruited police officers must pass a special training program. After training, they are usually placed on a probationary period lasting from three to six months. In small towns and communities, training may be given on the job by working with an experienced officer. Inexperienced officers are never sent out on patrol alone but are always accompanied by veteran officers.

Large city police departments give classroom instruction in laws, accident investigation, city ordinances, and traffic control. These departments also give instruction in the handling of firearms, methods of apprehension and arrest, self-defense tactics, and first-aid techniques. Both state and municipal police officers are trained in safe driving procedures and maneuvering an automobile at high speeds. Physical fitness training is a mandatory, continuing activity in most police departments, as are routine physical examinations. Police officers can have no physical disabilities that would prevent them from carrying out their duties.

Opportunities for Experience & Exploration

A good way to explore police work is to meet with police officers in the various areas of law enforcement. Most police departments have community outreach programs and many have recruiting programs as well. Students may also wish to visit colleges offering programs in police work or write for information on their training programs.

In some cases, people who have finished high school can explore this occupation by seeking employment as *police cadets* in large city police departments. These cadets are paid employees who work part time in clerical and other duties. They attend training courses in police science on a part-time basis. When they reach the age of twenty-one, they are eligible to apply for regular police work. Some police departments also hire college students as interns.

Methods of Entering

Applicants interested in police work should apply directly to local civil service offices or examining boards to qualify as a candidate for police officer. In some locations, written examinations may be given to groups at specified times. In smaller communities that do not follow civil service methods, applicants should apply directly to the police department or city government offices in the communities where they reside. Those interested in becoming state police officers may apply directly to their state civil service commissions or state police headquarters, which are usually located in the state capital.

Advancement

Advancement in these occupations is determined by several factors. An officer's eligibility for promotion may depend on a specified length of service, job performance, formal education and training courses, and results of written examinations. Those who become eligible for promotion are listed on the promotional list along with other qualified candidates. Promotions generally become available from six months to three years after starting, depending on the department. As positions of different or higher rank become open, candidates are promoted to fill them according to their position on the list. Lines of promotion usually begin with officer third grade and progress to grade two and grade one. Other possible promotional opportunities include the ranks of detective, sergeant, lieutenant, or captain. Many promotions require additional training and testing. Advancement to the very top-ranking positions, such as division, bureau, or department director or chief, may be made by direct political appointment. Most of these top positions are held by officers who have come up through the ranks.

Large city police departments offer the greatest number of advancement opportunities. Most of the larger departments maintain separate divisions, which require administration workers, line officers, and more employees in general at each rank level. Officers may move into areas that they find challenging, such as criminal investigation or forensics.

Most city police departments offer various types of in-service study and training programs. These programs allow police departments to keep up-to-date on the latest police science techniques and are often required for those who want to be considered for promotion. Training courses are provided by police academies, colleges, and other educational institutions. Some of the subjects offered are civil defense, foreign languages, and forgery detection. Some municipal police departments share the cost with their officers or pay all educational expenses if the officers are willing to work toward a college degree in either police work or police administration. Independent study is also often required.

Intensive twelve-week administrative training courses are offered by the National Academy of the Federal Bureau of Investigation in Washington, DC. A limited number of officers are selected to participate in this training program.

Advancement opportunities on police forces in small communities are considerably more limited by the rank and number of police personnel needed. Other opportunities for advancement may be found in related police, protective, and security service work with private companies, state and county agencies, and other institutions.

Employment Outlook

Employment of police officers is expected to increase about as fast as the average for all occupations through the year 2006. Federal "tough-on-crime" legislation passed in the mid-1990s created a short-term increase of new jobs in police departments at the federal, state, and local levels.

The opportunities that become available, however, may be affected by technological, scientific, and other changes occurring today in police work. Automation in traffic control is limiting the number of officers needed in this area, while the increasing reliance on computers throughout society is creating demands for new kinds of police work. New approaches in social science and psychological research are also changing the methodology used in working with public offenders. These trends indicate a future demand for more educated, specialized personnel.

This occupation has a very low turnover rate. However, new positions will open as current officers retire, leave the force, or move into higher positions. Retirement ages are relatively low in police work compared to other occupations. Many officers retire while in their forties and then pursue a second career. In response to increasing crime rates, some police departments across the country are expanding the number of patrol officers; however, budget problems faced by many municipalities may limit growth. In the past decade, private security firms have begun to take over some police activities such as patrolling airports and other public places. Some private companies have even been contracted to provide police forces for some cities. Many companies and universities also operate their own police forces.

Earnings

According to the U.S. Department of Labor, police officers in 1996 earned an annual average salary of $34,700; the lowest 10 percent earned less than $19,200 a year, while the highest 10 percent earned over $58,500 annually. Police officers in supervisory positions earned median salaries of $41,200 a year in 1996, with a low of $22,500 and a high of over $64,500. Sheriffs and other law enforcement officers earned median annual salaries of $26,700 in 1996. Salaries for police officers range widely based on geographic location. Police departments in the West and North generally pay more than those in the South.

Most police officers receive periodic and annual salary increases up to a limit set for their rank and length of service. Police departments generally pay special compensation to cover the cost of uniforms. They usually provide any equipment required such as firearms and handcuffs. Overtime pay may be given for certain work shifts or emergency duty. In these instances, officers are usually paid straight or time-and-a-half pay, while extra time off is sometimes given as compensation.

Because most police officers are civil service employees, they receive generous benefits, including health insurance and paid vacation and sick leave, and enjoy increased job security. In addition, most police departments offer retirement plans and retirement after twenty or twenty-five years of service, usually at half pay.

Conditions of Work

Police officers work under many different types of circumstances. Much of their work may be performed outdoors, as they ride in patrol cars or walk the beats assigned to them. In emergency situations, no consideration can be made for weather conditions, time of day or night, or day of the week. Police officers may be on call twenty-four hours a day; even when they are not on duty, they are usually required by law to respond to emergencies or criminal activity. Although they are assigned regular work hours, individuals in police work must be willing to live by an unpredictable and often erratic work schedule. The work demands constant mental and physical alertness as well as great physical strength and stamina.

Police work generally consists of an eight-hour day and a five-day week, but police officers may work night and weekend shifts and on holidays. Emergencies may add many extra hours to an officer's day or week. The occupation is considered dangerous and hazardous. Some officers are killed or wounded while performing their duties. Their work can involve unpleasant duties and expose them to many sordid, depressing, or dangerous situations. They may be called on to deal with all types of people under many types of circumstances. While the routine of some assigned duties may become boring, the dangers of police work are often stressful for the officers and their families. Police work, in general, holds the potential for the unknown and unexpected, and most people who pursue this work have a strong passion and commitment for police work.

Sources of Additional Information

■ **International Union of Police Associations**
1421 Prince Street, Suite 330
Alexandria, VA 22314
Tel: 703-549-7473

The educational arm of the American Federation of Police and the National Association of Chiefs of Police, the American Police Academy compiles statistics, operates a placement service and a speaker's bureau, and offers home study programs. For more information, contact:

■ **American Police Academy**
1000 Connecticut Avenue, NW, Suite 9
Washington, DC 20036
Tel: 202-293-9088

The following association maintains a speaker's bureau, conducts educational programs, and offers both recognition and scholarship awards. For more information, contact:

■ **National Police Officers Association of America**
PO Box 22129
Louisville, KY 40252-0129
Tel: 800-467-6762

The following organization compiles statistics, operates a hotline, hall of fame, and speaker's bureau, offers children's services, and sponsors competitions and scholarships. For more information, use the toll free number, 800-533-4649, or write:

■ **National United Law Enforcement Association**
256 East McLemore Avenue
Memphis, TN 38106
Tel: 901-774-1118

Preschool Teachers and Child Care Workers

Definition

Preschool teachers promote the education of children under age five in all areas. They help students develop physically, socially, and emotionally, work with them on language and communications skills, and help cultivate their cognitive abilities. They also work with families to support parents in raising their young children and reinforcing skills at home. They plan and lead activities developed in accordance with the specific ages and needs of the children. Many schools and districts consider *kindergarten teachers,* who teach students five years of age, to be preschool teachers. For the purposes of this article, kindergarten teachers will be included in this category. Regardless of whether they teach kindergartners or younger students, it is the goal of all preschool teachers to help students develop the skills, interests, and individual creativity that they will use for the rest of their lives.

Preschool teachers are part of the larger category of *child care workers;* however, all child care workers are not preschool teachers. Child care workers include such people as *day care center employees* (even those who work with infants), *day camp counselors, teacher aides,* and before- and after-school child care programs staff, among others.

Nature of the Work

Preschool teachers design and implement activities that build on children's abilities and curiosity and aid them in developing skills and characteristics that help them grow. Attention to the individual needs of each child is vital, and teachers need to be aware of these needs and capabilities and, when possible, adapt activities to the specific needs of the individual child. Teachers should be aware of the growth and developmental stages of children and plan activities accordingly. For example, a teacher should plan activities based on the understanding that a three-year-old child has

School Subjects
Education
Family and Consumer Science

Personal Interests
Babysitting/Child care
Teaching

Work Environment
Indoors and outdoors
Primarily one location

Minimum Education Level
High school diploma
Apprenticeship

Salary Range
$7,200 to
$13,000 to
$20,200+

Certification or Licensing
Recommended

Outlook
Faster than the average

different motor skills and reasoning abilities than a child of five years of age. A teacher should also understand the psychology of a young child.

To accommodate the variety of abilities and temperaments of children enrolled in a preschool program, a teacher should develop a flexible schedule with varying amounts of time for music, art, playtime, academics, rest, and other activities. Preschool teachers should plan activities that encourage children to develop skills appropriate to their developmental needs. Preschool teachers might work with the youngest students to learn the days of the week and recognize colors, seasons, and animal names and characteristics; they might help older students with number and letter recognition and even simple writing skills. Preschool teachers need to be aware that all children develop at different rates and although one child may not be ready to recognize individual letters, another may be ready to read. A preschool teacher helps children with such simple, yet important tasks as tying shoelaces and washing hands before snack time.

Self-confidence and the development of communications skills are encouraged in preschools. For example, teachers may give children simple art projects, such as finger painting and have children show and explain their finished projects to the rest of the class. Show and tell, or "sharing time" as it is often called, allows students opportunities to speak and listen to others. Preschool teachers help students develop problem-solving and social skills.

For most children, preschool is their first time away from home and family for an extended period of time. A major portion of a preschool teacher's day is often spent helping children adjust to being away from home and encouraging them to play together. This is especially true at the beginning of the school year. Preschool teachers need to be able to gently reassure children who become frightened or homesick.

A preschool teacher often has an assistant, also called an aide, to help with the children. The assistant helps the teacher manage the classroom throughout the day. Assistants might supervise nap time for the youngest children while the teacher supervises older children involved in an activity. Preschool teachers also work with the parents of each child. It is not unusual for parents to come to preschool and observe a child or go on a field trip with the class, and preschool teachers often take these opportunities to discuss the progress of each child as well as any specific problems or concerns. Scheduled meetings are available for parents who cannot visit the school during the day. Solutions to fairly serious problems are worked out in tandem with the parents, often with the aid of the director of the preschool, or in the case of an elementary school kindergarten, with the principal or headmaster.

The preschool teacher adopts many parental responsibilities while the child is in school. The teacher greets each child in the morning and supervises the child throughout the day. Often these responsibilities can be quite demanding and complicated. In harsh weather, for example, preschool teachers contend with not only boots, hats, coats, and mittens, but with the inevitable sniffles, colds, and generally cranky behavior that can occur in young children.

In both full-day and half-day programs, the teacher supervises snack time, helping children learn how to eat properly and clean up after themselves. Proper hygiene, such as hand washing before meals, is also stressed. Other activities include storytelling, music, and simple arts and crafts projects. Full-day programs involve a lunch period and at least one nap time. Programs usually have exciting activities interspersed with calmer ones. Even though the children get nap time, a preschool teacher must be energetic throughout the day, ready to face with good cheer the many challenges and demands of young children.

Because young children look up to adults and learn through example, it is especially important that a preschool teacher be a good role model. With more families putting children into child care settings, the age range in preschools can vary from two or three years old up to age five, sometimes in the same classroom. Preschool teachers must be able to work with children of all these ages.

Kindergarten teachers usually have their own classrooms, made up exclusively of five-year-olds. Although these teachers don't have to plan activities for a wide range of ages, they need to consider individual developmental interests, abilities, and backgrounds represented by the students. Kindergarten teachers usually spend more time helping students with academic skills than do other preschool teachers. While a teacher of a two-, three-, and four-year-old classroom may focus more on socializing and building confidence in students through play and activities, kindergarten teachers often develop activities that help five-year-olds acquire the skills they will need in grade school, such as introductory activities on numbers, reading, and writing.

Requirements

Specific education requirements for preschool and kindergarten teachers vary from state to state and also depend on the specific guidelines of the school or district. Many schools and child care centers require preschool teachers to have a bachelor's degree in education or a related field, but others accept adults with a high school diploma and experience working with children. Preschool facilities that accept applicants with a minimum of high school diploma often offer on-the-job training to their teachers, hiring them as assistants or aides until they are sufficiently trained to work in a classroom alone.

Several groups offer on-the-job training programs for prospective preschool teachers. For example, the American Montessori Society offers a career program for aspiring preschool teachers. This program requires a three-month classroom training period followed by one year of supervised on-the-job training.

A high school student interested in pursuing a career as a preschool teacher should take courses in early childhood development, English, math, art, music, and physical education. It is beneficial for a preschool teacher to be able to draw from the widest possible knowledge base and pursuing a well-rounded high school education provides an excellent foundation. A college degree program should include coursework in a variety of liberal arts subjects, including English, history, and science, as well as nutrition, child development, psychology of the young child, and sociology.

In some states, licensure may be required. Many states accept the Child Development Associate (CDA) credential or an associate or bachelor's degree as sufficient requirements for work in a preschool facility. Individual state boards of education can provide specific licensure information. Kindergarten teachers working in public elementary schools almost always need teaching certification similar to that required by other elementary school teachers in the school. Other types of licensure or certification may be required, depending upon the school or district. These may include first-aid or CPR training.

Opportunities for Experience & Exploration

High school students can gain experience in this field by volunteering at a child care or other preschool facility. Some high schools provide internships with local preschools for students interested in working as a teacher's aide. Many guidance counselors can provide information on these opportunities. Summer day camps or Bible schools with preschool classes also hire high school students as counselors or counselors-in-training. Discussing the field with preschool teachers and observing in their classes are other good ways to discover specific job information and explore one's aptitude for this career.

Methods of Entering

Qualified individuals can contact child care centers, nursery schools, Head Start programs, and other preschool facilities to identify job opportunities. Often jobs for preschool teachers are listed in the classified section of newspapers. In addition, many school districts and state boards of education maintain job listings of available teaching positions. If no permanent positions are available at a preschool, potential teachers can often gain entry into the field by applying as a substitute teacher. Most preschools and kindergartens maintain a substitute list and refer to it frequently. Substitutes who do good work in that capacity are often hired when a permanent position becomes open, provided they meet necessary qualifications.

Advancement

Many teachers advance by becoming more skillful in what they do. Skilled preschool teachers, especially those with additional training, usually receive salary increases as they become more experienced. A few preschool teachers with administrative ability and an interest in administrative work advance to the position of director. Administrators need to have at least a master's degree in child development or a related field and have to meet any state or federal licensing regulations. Some become directors of Head Start programs or other government programs.

A relatively small number of experienced preschool teachers open their own facility. This entails not only the ability to be an effective administrator, but also the knowledge of how to operate a business. Kindergarten teachers sometimes have the opportunity to earn more money by teaching at a higher grade level in the elementary school. This salary increase is especially true when a teacher moves from a half-day kindergarten program to a full-day grade school classroom.

Employment Outlook

Employment opportunities for preschool teachers are expected to increase through the year 2006. More women than ever are part of the workforce; of those who have children, many take only an abbreviated maternity leave. More teachers are needed to meet the demand of quality child care needed by those without satisfactory home child care. Specific job opportunities vary from state to state and depend on demographic characteristics and level of government funding. Jobs should be available at private child care centers, nursery schools, Head Start facilities, public and private kindergartens, and laboratory schools connected with universities and colleges. In the past, the majority of preschool teachers were female, and although this continues to be the case, more males are becoming involved in early childhood education.

Because of low pay and often poor working conditions, there is a very high turnover of child care workers, such as preschool teachers. On the one hand, this may lead to dissatisfaction with the career, but it means there are usually positions available to those willing to accept the limitations of the job.

Earnings

Although there have been some attempts to correct the discrepancies in salaries between preschool teachers and other teachers, salaries in this profession tend to be lower than teaching positions in public elementary and high schools. Because some preschool programs are only in the morning or afternoon, many preschool teachers work only part time. As part-time workers, they often do not receive medical insurance or other benefits and may get paid minimum wage to start.

In 1996, the lowest salaries for full-time preschool teachers averaged $7,200. A mid-range salary in the field is $13,000, and the highest paid teachers earn $20,200 or more per year. Kindergarten teachers, on average, have the highest salaries in this field. In addition, earnings depend on the geographic region in which the preschool facility is located. Some preschool teachers supplement their incomes by staying after standard teaching hours or arriving early to work in school-sponsored extended-day child care programs. Others tutor or babysit in the evenings or work other part-time jobs.

Conditions of Work

Preschool teachers spend much of the day on their feet in a classroom or a playground. Facilities vary from a single room to large buildings. Class sizes also vary; some preschools serve only a handful of children, while others serve several hundred. Classrooms may be crowded.

Many children do not go to preschool all day, so work may be part-time. Part-time employees generally work between eighteen and thirty hours a week, while full-time employees work thirty-five to forty hours a week. Part-time work gives the employee flexibility, and for many, this is one of the advantages of the job. Some preschool teachers teach both morning and afternoon classes, going through the same schedule and lesson plans with two sets of students. Some preschool teachers work nine months of the year (with summers off), but many others work year-round.

A preschool teacher should be able to deal with a wide variety of children and parents. Parents may sometimes be more difficult to deal with than the children, as parents have special concerns about their children and may be frustrated that they cannot spend more time with them. While a preschool or kindergarten classroom is usually an exciting place full of discovery and learning, it can also be stressful and tiring for the teachers. Teachers need the ability to be patient and calm.

Sources of Additional Information

For information on training programs, contact:

American Montessori Society
Teacher Education Program,
150 Fifth Avenue, Suite 203
New York, NY 10011-4384
Tel: 212-924-3209
Email: amspaul@aol.com

For general information on preschool teaching careers, contact:

National Association for the Education of Young Children
1509 16th Street, NW
Washington, DC 20036
Tel: 800-424-2460

National Council for Accreditation of Teacher Education
2010 Massachusetts Avenue, NW, Suite 500
Washington, DC 20036-1023
Tel: 202-466-7496

Printing Press Operators and Assistants

Definition

Printing press operators and *printing press operator assistants* set up, operate, clean, and maintain printing presses. Their principal duties include installing and adjusting printing plates; feeding, loading, and unloading paper; controlling ink flow; and matching colors. They may also be involved in making the printing plates used on the press.

Nature of the Work

The work of press operators and their assistants varies according to the size of the printing plant where they work. Generally, they are involved in all aspects of making the presses ready for a job, installing and adjusting printing plates, and monitoring and operating the presses during production of the job.

In small shops, press operators handle all of the tasks associated with these jobs, including oiling and cleaning the presses and making minor repairs. In larger shops, press operators are aided by assistants who handle most maintenance and minor repair jobs. In shops that run large web presses, the presses are monitored and run by a large crew of operators under the supervision of a press operator-in-charge.

In order to prepare a printing press for a job, printing press operators and their assistants inspect and oil all moving parts, clean and adjust ink rollers, and clean the ink fountains. When the printing plate arrives from the platemaker, they begin the make-ready stage. In this stage, they lock the plate into place on the printing surface or cylinder. Then they make adjustments so that the paper will be in the exact position to take the impression of type. They mix and match ink if necessary, fill the ink fountains, and adjust the flow. They also load the paper, feeding it through the cylinders and adjusting feed and tension controls. When this is done, the printing press operator runs off a trial sheet and submits it for approval.

School Subjects
Computer science
Shop (Trade/Vo-tech education)

Personal Interests
Figuring out how things work
Fixing things

Work Environment
Indoors and outdoors
One location with some travel

Minimum Educational Level
High school diploma

Salary Range
$13,884 to
$25,168 to
$43,992

Certification or Licensing
Recommended

Outlook
More slowly than the average

DOT
651

GOE
05.05.13

NOC
7381

When the set-up and make-ready are complete, the trial sheet approved, and the final adjustments made, the press run begins. During the run, press operators constantly check the printed matter to see that it is clear, properly aligned, and that ink is not offsetting (blotting) onto other sheets. If they are printing with colors, they make certain that the colors line up properly.

On a web press, they adjust the feed and tension mechanisms that control the pulling of the paper through the press. If the paper tears or jams, they rethread the paper through the press. On other kinds of presses, they may feed paper into the press by hand.

Throughout the run, operators pull sheets to check for imperfections, and they make adjustments accordingly. They monitor the chemical properties of the ink and correct temperatures in the drying chamber, if the press has one.

Other duties of press operators or, more likely, their assistants include performing preventive maintenance on the presses, such as lubrication, replacing small parts, and cleaning and adjusting rollers and other small parts. Printing press operators are also often responsible for handling and disposal of hazardous chemicals. Press assistants are usually responsible for cleaning up, keeping the work area neat and orderly, and washing the press.

Some modern printing plants now have computer-controlled printing presses that make use of sophisticated instrumentation. In plants with this kind of equipment, press operators work at a control panel that monitors the printing processes. If any aspect of the print run requires adjustment, the operator can make the change by pushing the proper buttons on the control panel.

In some plants, printing press operators perform some of the prepress tasks that are usually done by a platemaker. Often this involves carrying out some of the photographic and chemical processes necessary to transfer an image of the type from the typesetter's proof to the printing plate.

Requirements

The minimum educational requirement for printing press assistants is a high school diploma or its equivalent. While in high school, people interested in this field should take courses that offer an introduction to printing, chemistry, electronics, color theory, and physics. People who are seeking employment as printing press operators should complete post–high school training in a vocational or technical-degree program designed to train workers for printing occupations.

Press operators and assistants need the ability to carefully follow written and oral instructions. They should have mechanical aptitudes and basic mathematical skills.

Some people learn the necessary occupational skills through an apprenticeship program. A high school education is usually required for admission to an apprenticeship. Applicants are more likely to be admitted to such programs if they have taken courses in printing, mathematics, chemistry, and physics.

The length of apprenticeships varies according to the kind of press the applicant wants to work on. Commercial shops, which typically run smaller presses, may offer two-year apprenticeships leading to a job as press assistant or four-year apprenticeships leading to a job as press operator. In newspapers and other shops using large web presses, the required time is five years; however, specialized technical education or prior experience in a print shop can be counted toward the five years.

An apprenticeship program includes on-the-job training in caring for equipment, performing the necessary make-ready tasks, and running, cleaning, and maintaining a press. It also includes training in the various types of inks and papers that are commonly used in printing. Apprentices participate in related classroom or correspondence courses concurrent with on-the-job training.

Approximately 10 to 13 percent of printing press operators and assistants belong to a union.

Opportunities for Experience & Exploration

Many high schools offer a number of opportunities for exploring the occupation of printing press operator. A print shop class provides the most direct experience of this work. Working on the high school newspaper or yearbook are other ways of gaining some familiarity with printing processes. A part-time or summer delivery job with a print shop or a visit to a local printing plant can provide an opportunity to see presses in action and get the feeling of the environment in which press operators work. Part-time, temporary, and summer jobs may be available as cleanup workers and press feeders in printing plants.

Methods of Entering

Most printing press operators, even those with formal training, begin their careers doing entry-level work, such as loading, unloading, and cleaning the presses. Some people enter this field through apprenticeship programs. High school vocational counselors can assist students in finding such programs. Information on apprenticeships may also be available through the local offices of the state employment service. Some printers choose their apprentices from among the printing press assistants and others employed in the plant. Some workers may be employed in printing plants for years before they become apprentices.

Advancement

In large print shops, the line of promotion is usually from press helper to press assistant, press operator, press operator-in-charge, press room supervisor, and superintendent. Press operators can also advance in pay and responsibility by learning to work more complex printing equipment; for example by moving from a one-color press to a four-color press.

Printing press operators with advancement ambitions should be prepared to continue their training and education throughout their careers. Because of technological changes in the industry, skill-updating has become increasingly important. If a printer decides to switch from one kind of press to another, for example, from a sheet-fed press to a web press, the entire crew may have to be retrained, because different types of equipment require different skills. It is likely that in the future printing press operators may need to be retrained for new equipment and processes several times during their careers.

Press operators who are interested and knowledgeable in other aspects of the printing business may find advancement by transferring to their employer's sales or purchasing department. Those with business ability may do well by going into business for themselves and establishing their own print shops.

Employment Outlook

Approximately 244,000 press operators and assistants were employed in the printing industry as of 1996. Through the year 2006, employment of press operators is expected to grow at a lower rate than is average for all other occupations. The added jobs will be related to a growth in demand for printed materials, although some of the growth will be offset by the use of larger and more efficient machines. Principal areas of growth are expected in books and magazines for use in schools and adult education; in books for foreign markets, especially scientific and technical books; and in commercial printing, such as newspaper inserts, catalogs, direct mail enclosures, and other kinds of advertising. Growth will be slower for newspapers and other kinds of books and magazines, and printers of these materials may be able to handle most tasks with their existing number of staff.

In all fields of printing, applicants may encounter stiff competition for jobs, including competition from other experienced workers or workers who have completed retraining programs to update their printing skills. Postsecondary courses in printing are important in order to stay competitive.

Earnings

Average earnings of printing press operators on average-sized single-color offset printing presses in 1996 were approximately $34,000, as reported by the U.S. Department of Labor. Operators who work night shifts and overtime can earn additional money.

The pay of apprentices begins at about 40 to 50 percent of an experienced press operator's wage rate. Apprentices receive regular raises, usually every six months; in the last year of their apprenticeship, they usually receive 80 to 95 percent of the press operator's rate.

Conditions of Work

Many print shops are small and employ approximately five employees, but the largest ones may have 250 to 1,000 employees. Pressrooms are busy, noisy places; there is a great deal of vibration when presses are running and often so much noise that ear protection must be worn. Working around large machines can be hazardous, so printing press operators and assistants must constantly observe good safety habits.

There are frequent deadlines to meet, and tension and pressure are part of the atmosphere. Errors by press operators may require that an entire job be rerun, doubling the cost and delaying the finish time.

Workers in printing press occupations have considerable contact with ink and cleaning fluids that can cause irritation. Pressrooms may be uncomfortably hot because presses generate a lot of heat. The work can be fairly strenuous, including lifting of ink rollers and type forms.

Sources of Additional Information

Graphic Arts Technical Foundation
4615 Forbes Avenue
Pittsburgh, PA 15213
Tel: 412-621-6941

Graphic Communications International Union
1900 L Street, NW
Washington, DC 20036
Tel: 202-462-1400

Printing Industries of America
100 Daingerfield Road
Alexandria, VA 22314-2888
Tel: 703-519-8100
WWW: http://www.printing.org

Canadian Printing Industries Association
#906, 75 Albert Street
Ottawa, ON K1P 5E7 Canada
Tel: 613-236-7208

Property and Casualty Insurance Agents and Brokers

Definition

Property and casualty insurance agents and brokers sell policies that help individuals and companies cover expenses and losses from such disasters as fires, burglaries, traffic accidents, and other emergencies. These salespeople also may be known as *fire, casualty, and marine insurance agents or brokers.*

Nature of the Work

Property and casualty insurance salespeople work under one of two types of relationships with insurers and clients. An agent serves as an authorized representative of the insurance company or companies with which the agent has a contract. A broker, on the other hand, serves as the representative for the client and has no contracts with insurance companies.

Agents can be independent agents, exclusive agents, or direct writers. Independent agents may represent one or more insurance companies, are paid by commission, are responsible for their own expenses, and own the rights to the policies they sell. Exclusive agents represent only one insurance company, are generally paid by commission, are generally responsible for all of their own expenses, and usually own the rights to the policies that they sell. Direct writers represent only one insurance company, are employees of that company (and therefore are often paid a salary and are not responsible for their own expenses), and do not own the rights to the policies are owned by the company.

Regardless of the system that is used, salespeople operate in a similar fashion. Each one orders or issues policies, collects premiums, renews and changes existing coverage, and assists clients with reports of losses and claims settlement. Backed by the resources of the companies that they represent, individual agents may issue policies insuring against loss or damage for

School Subjects
Business
Speech

Personal Interests
Helping people: personal service
Selling/Making a deal

Work Environment
Primarily indoors
Primarily one location

Minimum Education Level
High school diploma

Salary Range
$21,100 to
$31,500 to
$76,900+

Certification or Licensing
Required

Outlook
About as fast as the average

DOT
250

GOE
08.01.02

NOC
6231

everything from furs and automobiles to ocean liners and factories.

Agents are authorized to issue a "binder" to provide temporary protection for customers between the time they sign the policy application and the policy is issued by the insurance company. Naturally, the agent must be selective in the risks accepted under a binder. Sometimes a risk will be refused by a company, which might cause the agent to lose goodwill with the customer. Since brokers do not directly represent or have contracts with insurance companies, they can not issue binders.

Some agents or brokers specialize in one type of insurance such as automobile insurance. All agents or brokers, however, must have a knowledge of the kind of protection required by their clients and the exact coverage offered by each company that they represent.

One of the most significant aspects of the property and casualty agent's work is the variety encountered on the job. An agent's day may begin with an important conference with a group of executives seeking protection for a new industrial plant and its related business activities. Following this meeting, the agent may proceed to the office and spend several hours studying the needs of the customer and drafting an insurance plan. This proposal must be thorough and competitively priced because several other local agents will likely be competing for the account. While working at the office, the agent usually receives several calls and visits from prospective or current clients asking questions about protection, policy conditions, changes, or new developments.

At noon, the agent may attend a meeting of a service club or have lunch with a policyholder. After lunch, the agent may visit a garage with a customer to discuss the car repairs needed as the result of a client's automobile accident. Back at the office, the agent may talk on the telephone with an adjuster of the insurance company involved.

In the late afternoon, the agent may call on the superintendent of schools to discuss insurance protection for participants and spectators at athletic events and other public meetings. If the school has no protection, the agent may evaluate its insurance needs and draft a proposed policy.

Upon returning to the office, the agent may telephone several customers, dictate responses to the day's mail, and handle other matters that have developed during the day. In the evening, the agent may call on a family to discuss insurance protection for a new home.

Requirements

Minimum educational requirements include a high school degree. Although college training is not a prerequisite, an increasing number of agents and brokers hold a college degree. Many have taken insurance courses, which are offered in hundreds of colleges and universities in the United States as well as by many professional insurance associations. Others find a general background in business administration, accounting, economics, or business law helpful. For some specialized areas of property insurance, such as fire protection for commercial establishments, an engineering background may prove helpful.

All agents and brokers must obtain licenses from the states in which they sell insurance. Most states require that the agent pass a written examination dealing with state insurance laws and the fundamentals of property and casualty insurance. Often, candidates for licenses must show evidence of some formal study in the field of insurance.

Those agents who wish to seek the highest professional status may pursue the designation of Chartered Property Casualty Underwriter (CPCU). The CPCU requires the agent to have completed at least three years in the field successfully, demonstrate high ethical practices in all work, and pass a series of ten examinations offered by the American Institute for Chartered Property and Casualty Underwriters. Agents and brokers may prepare for these examinations through home study or by taking courses offered by colleges, insurance associations, or individual companies. As an intermediate step, many agents complete a study and examination program conducted by the Insurance Institute of America. One such program is the Accredited Adviser in Insurance (AAI). To earn the AAI designation an agent must pass three national exams. Although independent study for the AAI is possible, most agents complete a series of three courses given at a state independent agents' association prior taking the exams.

An agent or broker must thoroughly understand insurance fundamentals and recognize the differences between the many options provided by various policies. This knowledge is essential for the salesperson to gain the respect and confidence of clients. To provide greater service to customers and increase sales volume, beginning agents must study many areas of insurance protection. This requires an analytical mind, the ability to teach oneself how to use standard manuals and computer information systems, as well as the capacity for hard work.

Agents or brokers must be able to interact with strangers easily and talk readily with a wide range of people. They may need to talk with teenagers about their first cars, business executives faced with heavy responsibilities, or widows confronted for the first time with financial management of a home. Agents must be resourceful, self-confident, conscientious, and cheerful. As in other types of sales occupations, a strong belief in the service being sold helps agents to be more successful in their presentations.

Because they spend so much of their time with others, agents must have a genuine liking for people. Equally important is the desire to serve others by providing financial security. To be successful, agents must be able to present insurance information in a clear, nontechnical fashion. They must be able to develop a logical sales sequence and presentation style that is comfortable for prospects and clients.

Successful agents usually participate in a number of social activities, such as church groups, community organizations, and service organizations. They must stay visible within their communities to keep their volume of business up. It is essential that people respond positively to them. They often have an unusual facility for recalling people's names and past conversations they've had with them.

Because they work in small organizations, agents must possess both personal sales and management abilities. Many insurance offices consist of the agent and a single secretary. The freedom enjoyed by the agent necessitates discipline and careful self-planning.

Opportunities for Experience & Exploration

Because of state licensing requirements, it is sometimes difficult for young people to obtain part-time experience in this field. Summer employment of any sort in a property and casualty insurance office may provide helpful insights into the field. Since many offices are small and must have someone on premises during business hours, students may find summer positions with individual agencies or brokerage firms. Colleges with work-study programs may offer opportunities for practical experience in an insurance agency.

Methods of Entering

College graduates are frequently hired through campus interviews for salaried sales positions with major companies. Other graduates secure positions directly with local agencies or brokerages through placement services, employment offices, or classified advertisements in newspapers. Many high school and college graduates apply directly to insurance companies. Sometimes persons employed in other fields take evening or home-study courses in insurance to prepare for employment in this field.

Once hired, the new agent or salesperson uses training materials prepared by the company or by industry trade groups. In smaller agencies, newcomers may be expected to assume most of the responsibility for their own training by using the agency's written resources and working directly with experienced agents. In larger organizations, initial training may include formal classroom instruction and enrollment in education programs such as those offered by the Insurance Institute of America. Sometimes insurance societies sponsor courses designed to help the beginning agent. Almost all agents receive directed, on-the-job sales supervision.

Advancement

Sales agents may advance in one of several ways. They may decide to establish their own agency or brokerage firm, join or buy out an established agency, or advance into branch or home office management with an insurance company.

Self-employed agents or brokers often remain with the organization that they have developed for the length of their careers. They may grow professionally by expanding the scope of their insurance activities. Many agents expand their responsibilities and their office's sales volume by hiring additional salespeople. Occasionally an established agent may enter related areas of activity. Many property insurance agents, for example, branch out into real estate sales. Many agents and brokers devote an increasing amount of their time to worthwhile community projects, which helps to build goodwill and probable future clients.

Employment Outlook

Approximately 409,000 people work as insurance agents and brokers in the United States. About 12 percent of these work primarily in the property and casualty insurance field.

The overall demand for insurance should increase as the general population grows and the amount of personal and corporate possessions rises. Most homeowners and business executives budget insurance as a necessary expense. Their dependence on insurance coverage is reflected in the fact that insurance premium rates have gone up about 100 percent in the past ten years.

Laws that require businesses to provide workers' compensation insurance and car owners to obtain automobile liability protection help to maintain an insurance market.

Despite increasing sales, however, employment of insurance agents will probably grow only as fast as the average for all occupations through the year 2006. Computers enable agents to perform routine clerical tasks more efficiently, and more policies are being sold by mail and phone. Also, as insurance becomes more and more crucial to their financial health, many large businesses are hiring their own risk managers, who analyze their insurance needs and select the policies that are best for them.

There is a high turnover in this field. Many beginning agents and brokers find it hard to establish a large, profitable client-base, and eventually move on to other fields. Most openings in this field will occur as a result of this turnover and as workers retire or leave the field for other reasons.

Earnings

The employed sales agent is usually paid a moderate salary while learning the business. After becoming established, however, most agents are paid on the basis of a commission on sales. Agents who work directly for an insurance company often receive a base salary in addition to some commission on sales production. Salespeople employed by companies often receive fringe benefits (such as retirement income, sick leave, and paid vacations), whereas self-employed agents or brokers receive no such benefits.

According to the U.S. Department of Labor, the median annual salary for all types of insurance agents and brokers was $31,500 in 1996. Agents and brokers with little experience or small client-base earned as little as 21,100 per year, while the most experienced agents and brokers with a large clientele earned over $76,900 annually.

Unlike life insurance agents, who receive a high first-year commission, the property and casualty agent usually receives the same percentage each time the premium is paid.

Conditions of Work

Property and casualty insurance agents must be in constant contact with people—clients, prospective clients, and the workers in the home office of the insurance companies. This can be very time-consuming, and occasionally frustrating, but it is an essential element of the work.

Two of the biggest drawbacks to this type of work are the long hours and irregular schedule. Agents often are required to work their schedules around their clients' availability. Especially in their first years in the business, agents may find that they have to work three or four nights a week and one or two days on the weekend.

Sources of Additional Information

▬ **Independent Insurance Agents of America**
127 South Peyton
Alexandria, VA 22314
Tel: 703-683-4422

▬ **Insurance Information Institute**
110 William Street
New York, NY 10038
Tel: 212-669-9200
WWW: http://www.iii.org

Property and Real Estate Managers

Definition

Property and real estate managers plan and supervise the activities that affect land and buildings. Most of them manage rental properties, such as apartment buildings, office buildings, and shopping centers. Others manage the services and commonly owned areas of condominiums and community associations.

Nature of the Work

Most property and real estate managers are responsible for day-to-day management of residential and commercial real estate and usually manage several properties at one time. Acting as the owners' agents and advisers, they supervise the marketing of space, negotiate lease agreements, direct bookkeeping activities, and report to owners on the status of the property. They also negotiate contracts for trash removal and other services and hire the maintenance and on-site management personnel employed at the properties.

Some managers buy and develop real estate for companies that have widespread retail operations, such as franchise restaurants and hotel chains, or for companies that build such projects as shopping malls and industrial parks.

On-site managers are based at the properties they manage and may even live on the property. Most of them are responsible for apartment buildings and work under the direction of property managers. They train, supervise, and assign duties to maintenance staffs; inspect the properties to determine what maintenance and repairs are needed; schedule routine service of heating and air-conditioning systems; keep records of operating costs; and submit cost reports to the property managers or owners.

They deal with residents on a daily basis and are responsible for handling their requests for service and repairs, resolving

School Subjects
Business
Economics

Personal Interests
Business management
Helping people: personal service

Work Environment
Primarily indoors
Primarily multiple locations

Minimum Education Level
Bachelor's degree

Salary Range
$12,000 to
$28,500 to
$60,700

Certification or Licensing
Recommended

Outlook
As fast as the average

DOT
186

GOE
11.05.01

NOC
0121

complaints concerning other tenants, and enforcing rules and lease restrictions.

Apartment house managers work for property owners or property management firms and are usually on-site managers. They show apartments to prospective tenants, negotiate leases, collect rents, handle tenants' requests, and direct the activities of maintenance staffs and outside contractors.

Building superintendents are responsible for operating and maintaining the facilities and equipment of such properties as apartment houses and office buildings. At small properties they may be the only on-site manager and report directly to property managers; at larger properties they may report to on-site managers and supervise maintenance staffs.

Housing project managers direct the operation of housing projects provided for such groups as military families, low-income families, and welfare recipients. The housing is usually subsidized by the government and may consist of single-family homes, multiunit dwellings, or house trailers.

Condominium managers are responsible to unit-owner associations and manage the services and commonly owned areas of condominium properties. They submit reports to the association members, supervise collection of owner assessments, resolve owners' complaints, and direct the activities of maintenance staffs and outside contractors. In some communities, such as planned unit developments (PUDs), homeowners belong to associations that employ managers to oversee homeowners' own jointly used properties and facilities.

Real estate asset managers work for institutional owners such as banks and insurance companies. Their responsibilities are larger in scope. Rather than manage day-to-day property operations, asset managers usually have an advisory role regarding the acquisition, rehabilitation, refinancing, and disposition of properties in a particular portfolio, and they may act "as the owner" in making specific business decisions, such as selecting and supervising site managers, authorizing operating expenditures, reviewing and approving leases, and monitoring local market conditions.

Specialized property and real estate managers perform a variety of other types of functions. *Market managers* direct the activities of municipal, regional, or state markets where wholesale fruit, vegetables, or meat are sold. They rent space to buyers and sellers and direct the supervisors who are responsible for collecting fees, maintaining and cleaning the buildings and grounds, and enforcing sanitation and security rules. *Public events facilities rental managers* negotiate contracts with organizations that wish to lease arenas, auditoriums, stadiums, or other facilities that

are used for public events. They solicit new business and renewals of established contracts, maintain schedules to determine the availability of the facilities for bookings, and oversee operation and maintenance activities.

Real estate firm managers direct the activities of the sales agents who work for real estate firms. They screen and hire sales agents and conduct training sessions. They confer with agents and clients to resolve such problems as adjusting selling prices, determining who is responsible for repairs, and deciding who is responsible for closing costs. *Business opportunity-and-property-investment brokers* buy and sell business enterprises and investment properties on a commission or speculative basis. They investigate such factors as the financial ratings of businesses that are for sale, the desirability of a property's location for various types of businesses, and the condition of investment properties.

Businesses employ real estate managers to find, acquire, and develop the properties they need for their operations and to dispose of properties they no longer need. *Real estate agents* often work for companies that operate retail merchandising chains, such as fast-food restaurants, gasoline stations, and apparel shops. They locate sites that are desirable for their companies' operations and arrange to purchase or lease them. They also review their companies' holdings to identify properties that are no longer desirable and then negotiate to dispose of them. (Real estate sales agents also may be called real estate agents, but they are not involved in property management.) *Land development managers* are responsible for acquiring land for such projects as shopping centers and industrial parks. They negotiate with local governments, property owners, and public interest groups to eliminate obstacles to their companies' developments, and they arrange for architects to draw up plans and construction firms to build the projects.

Requirements

Most employers prefer college graduates for property and real estate management positions. They prefer degrees in real estate, business management, finance, and related fields, but they also consider liberal arts graduates. In some cases, inexperienced college graduates with bachelor's or master's degrees enter the field as assistant property managers. High school students interested in this field should enroll in college preparatory programs.

Many property and real estate managers attend training programs offered by various professional and trade associations. Employers often send their managers to these programs to improve their management skills and expand their knowledge of such subjects as operation and maintenance of building mechanical systems, insurance and risk management, business and real estate law, and accounting and financial concepts. Many managers attend these programs voluntarily to prepare for advancement to positions with more responsibility.

Certification or licensing is not required for most property managers. Managers who have appropriate experience, complete required training programs, and achieve satisfactory scores on written exams, however, can earn certification and such professional designations as certified property manager (CPM), accredited residential manager (ARM), real property administrator (RPA), and certified shopping center manager (CSM). (Note that CPM and ARM are registered trademarks of the Institute of Real Estate Management.) Such designations are usually looked upon favorably by employers as a sign of a person's competence and dedication.

The federal government requires certification for managers of public housing that is subsidized by federal funds. Business opportunity-and-property-investment brokers must hold state licenses, and some states require real estate managers to hold licenses.

Property and real estate managers must be skilled in both oral and written communications and adept at dealing with people. They need to be good administrators and negotiators, and those who specialize in land development must be especially resourceful and creative to arrange financing for their projects. Managers for small rental or condominium complexes may be required to have building repair and maintenance skills, as well as business management skills.

Opportunities for Experience & Exploration

High school students interested in property and real estate management positions should seek activities that help them develop management skills, such as serving as an officer in an organization or participating in Junior Achievement projects. They also should seek part-time or summer jobs in sales or volunteer for work that involves public contact.

Students may be able to tour apartment complexes, shopping centers, and other real estate developments and should take advantage of any opportunities to talk with property and real estate managers.

Methods of Entering

Students who are about to graduate from college, can obtain assistance from their school placement offices in finding their first job. Persons also can apply directly to property management firms and check ads in the help wanted sections of local newspapers. Property and real estate managers often begin as on-site managers for small apartment house complexes, condominiums, or community associations.

Advancement

With experience, entry-level property and site managers may transfer to larger properties or they may become assistant property managers, working closely with property managers and acquiring experience in a variety of management tasks. Assistant managers may advance to property manager positions, where they most likely will be responsible for several properties. As they advance in their careers, property managers may be responsible for larger or more complex operations, may specialize in managing specific types of property, or may eventually establish their own companies.

To be considered for advancement, property managers must demonstrate the ability to deal effectively with tenants, contractors, and maintenance staff. They must be capable administrators and possess business skills, initiative, good organization, and excellent communications skills. Companies may offer management service to property owners, or experienced managers may choose to invest in properties to lease or rent.

Employment Outlook

About 271,000 people in the United States were employed as property and real estate managers in 1996. Most work for real estate operators and property management firms. Others work for real estate developers, government agencies that manage public buildings, corporations with large property holdings used for their retail operations, real estate investors, and mining and oil companies. Many work as self-employed developers, apartment building owners, property management firm owners, or owners of full-service real estate businesses.

Employment of property and real estate managers is expected to increase as fast as the average for all occupations in the United States through the year

2006. Job openings are expected to occur as older, experienced managers transfer to other occupations or leave the labor force. The best opportunities will be for college graduates with degrees in real estate, business administration, and related fields.

In the next decade, many of the economy's new jobs are expected to be in wholesale and retail trade, finance, insurance, real estate, and other service industries. Growth in these industries will bring a need for more office and retail properties and for people to manage them.

In housing, there will be a greater demand for apartments because of the high cost of owning a home. New home developments also are increasingly organized with community or homeowner associations that require managers. In addition, more owners of commercial and multiunit residential properties are expected to use professional managers to help make their properties more profitable.

Earnings

Managers of residential and commercial rental real estate are usually compensated by a fee based on the gross rental income of the properties. Managers of condominiums and other homeowner-occupied properties also are usually paid on a fee basis. Site managers and others employed by a management company are typically salaried.

According to the *1998-99 Occupational Outlook Handbook,* annual earnings for all property managers in 1996 ranged from a low of $12,000 or less to a high of more than $60,700. The median annual average for property managers in 1996 was $28,500.

Property and real estate managers usually receive such benefits as medical and health insurance. On-site apartment building managers may have rent-free apartments, and many managers have the use of company automobiles. In addition, managers involved in land development may receive a small percentage of ownership in their projects.

Conditions of Work

Property and real estate managers usually work in offices, but may spend much of their time at the properties they manage. On-site apartment building managers often leave their offices to inspect other areas, check maintenance or repair work, or resolve problems reported by tenants.

Many apartment managers must live in the buildings they manage so they can be available in emergencies, and they may be required to show apartments to prospective tenants at night or on weekends. Property and real estate managers may attend evening meetings with property owners, association boards of directors, or civic groups interested in property planned for development. Real estate managers who work for large companies frequently travel to inspect their companies' property holdings or locate properties their companies might acquire.

Sources of Additional Information

■ **Apartment Owners and Managers Association of America**
65 Cherry Plaza
Watertown, CT 06795
Tel: 860-274-2589

■ **Building Owners and Managers Association**
720 Light Street
Baltimore, MD 21230
Tel: 410-752-3318
WWW: http://www.boma.org

■ **Community Associations Institute**
1630 Duke Street
Alexandria, VA 22314
Tel: 703-548-8600
WWW: http://www.caionline.com

■ **Institute of Real Estate Management**
430 North Michigan Avenue
Chicago, IL 60611
Tel: 312-329-6000
WWW: http://www.irem.org

■ **National Apartment Association**
201 North Union Street, Suite 200
Alexandria, VA 22314
Tel: 703-518-6141

■ **Canadian Real Estate Association**
320 Queen Street, Suite 2100,
Ottawa, ON K1R 5A3 Canada
Tel: 613-237-7111

Psychiatric Technicians

Definition

Psychiatric technicians work hands-on with mentally ill, emotionally disturbed, or developmentally disabled people. Psychiatric technicians work in hospitals, clinics, mental health centers, halfway houses, and other settings.

Their duties vary considerably depending on place of work but may include helping patients with hygiene and housekeeping and recording patients' pulse, temperature, and respiration rate. Psychiatric technicians participate in treatment programs by having "one-on-one" sessions with patients, under a nurse's or counselor's direction.

Another prime aspect of the psychiatric technician's work is reporting observations of patients' behavior to medical and psychiatric staff. Psychiatric technicians may also fill out admitting forms for new patients, contact patients' families to arrange conferences, issue medications from the dispensary, and maintain records.

Nature of the Work

Such technicians often are graduates of two-year post-high school programs. In most cases they not only take over for or assist professionals in traditional treatment activities but also provide new services in innovative ways. They must be skilled and specially trained.

Psychiatric technicians work in a variety of settings: the military, hospitals, mental hospitals, community mental health centers, psychiatric clinics, schools and day centers for the developmentally disabled, and social service agencies. They also work at residential and nonresidential centers such as geriatric nursing homes, child or adolescent development centers, and halfway houses. They may work with alcohol and drug abusers, psychotic or emotionally disturbed children and adults, developmentally disabled people, or the aged.

School Subjects
Health
Psychology

Personal Interests
Helping people: emotionally
Helping people: personal service

Work Environment
Primarily indoors
Primarily one location

Minimum Education Level
Associate's degree

Salary Range
$11,440 to
$20,000 to
$27,000+

Certification or Licensing
Voluntary

Outlook
More slowly than the average

DOT
354

GOE
10.03.02

NOC
3413

Psychiatric technicians are supervised by health professionals, such as registered nurses, counselors, therapists, or, more and more frequently nowadays, senior psychiatric technicians. Psychiatric technicians work as part of a team of mental health care workers and provide physical and mental rehabilitation for patients through recreational, occupational, and psychological readjustment programs.

In general, psychiatric technicians help plan and implement individual treatment programs. Their specific activities will vary according to their work setting, but they may include the following: interviewing and information gathering; working in a hospital unit where they are responsible for admitting, screening, evaluating, or discharging patients; record-keeping; making referrals to community agencies; working for patients' needs and rights; visiting patients at home after their release from a hospital; and participating in individual and group counseling and therapy programs. These programs may include behavior modification. Psychiatric technicians endeavor to work with patients in a broad, comprehensive manner, seeing each patient as a person whose peculiar or abnormal behavior stems from an illness or disability. They strive to help each patient achieve a maximum level of functioning. This means helping patients strengthen social and mental skills, accept greater responsibility, and develop confidence to enter into social, educational, or vocational activities.

In addition, psychiatric technicians working in hospitals handle a certain number of nursing responsibilities. They may take temperatures, count pulses and respiration rates, measure blood pressures, and help administer medications and physical treatments. In many cases, technicians working in hospitals will find themselves concerned with all aspects of their patients' lives-from eating, sleeping, and personal hygiene to developing social skills and improved self-image.

Technicians working in clinics, community mental health centers, halfway houses, day hospitals, or other noninstitutional settings also perform some activities special to their situation. They interview newly registered patients and their relatives and visit patients and their families at home. They also administer psychological tests, participate in group activities, and write reports about their observations to supervising psychiatrists or other mental health professionals. They try to ease the transition of patients leaving hospitals and returning to their communities. They may refer patients to and arrange for consultations with mental health specialists. They may also help patients resolve problems with employment, housing, and personal finance. Psychiatric technicians generally provide assistance to their patients, helping them through a maze of services, agencies, and professionals.

According to the American Association of Psychiatric Technicians (AAPT), there are more than one hundred different job titles used to describe the work of the psychiatric technician. The many titles reflect the subtle differences in job emphasis and training that occur from organization to organization. Most psychiatric technicians are trained as generalists in providing mental health services. But some opportunities exist for technicians to specialize in a particular aspect of mental health care. For example, some psychiatric technicians specialize in the problems of mentally disturbed children. Others work as counselors in drug and alcohol abuse programs or as members of psychiatric emergency or crisis-intervention teams.

Another area of emphasis is working in community mental health. Technicians employed in this area are sometimes known as human-services technicians. They use rehabilitation techniques that do not involve hospitalization for patients who have problems adjusting to their social environment. These technicians may be primarily concerned with drug and alcohol abuse, parental effectiveness, the elderly, or problems in interpersonal relationships. Human-services technicians work in social welfare departments, child care centers, preschools, vocational rehabilitation workshops, and schools for the learning disabled, emotionally disturbed, and mentally handicapped. This concentration is particularly popular with college curriculums, nowadays, according to the AAPT, although it has yet to find wide acceptance in the job market.

With slightly different training, psychiatric technicians may specialize in the treatment of developmentally disabled people. *Developmentally disabled psychiatric technicians* work with patients by doing such things as teaching recreational activities. They generally work in halfway houses, state hospitals, training centers, or state and local service agencies. Jobs as a "DD" tech are among the easiest psychiatric technician jobs to get, and many techs start out in this area. On average, however, the pay of the DD tech is considerably less than that of other psychiatric technicians.

Other potential places of employment for psychiatric technicians include correctional programs and juvenile courts, nursing homes, senior citizen centers, schools for the blind and deaf, community action programs, family service centers, and public housing programs.

Requirements

A high school diploma is the minimum education requirement to find work as a psychiatric technician, although in many cases psychiatric technicians are expected to have two years of training beyond high school. Furthermore, many hospitals are now preferring to hire applicants with bachelor's degrees. Students should find out as early as possible in the high school years about the requirements of colleges they might want to attend, to be assured of meeting them. In general, high school students should take courses in English, biology, psychology, and sociology.

The two-year post-high school training programs usually lead to an associate of arts or associate of science degree. In general, study programs include human development, personality structure, the nature of mental illness, and, to a limited extent, anatomy, physiology, basic nursing, and medical science. Other subjects usually encountered in two-year programs include some introduction to basic social sciences, so that technicians can better understand relevant family and community structures; an overview of structure and functions of institutions that treat patients; and, most importantly, practical instruction in doing the essential work that psychiatric technicians are called upon to do.

On average, programs include about one-fourth general study, such as English, psychology, and sociology; about one-fourth mental health-related courses, such as early childhood development, general and abnormal psychology, the family, and social welfare institutions; about one-fourth specific topics such as psychopathology, concepts and techniques of its prevention, forms of therapy, rehabilitation, general and psychiatric nursing, and community mental health; and about one-fourth practical and field learning. The practical and field learning gives students a personal and realistic orientation to problems they will face on the job.

Psychiatric technicians must be licensed in California, Colorado, Kansas, and Arkansas. Certification is voluntary in most other states. Prospective technicians and technicians-in-training should consult their guidance or placement counselors for more information about requirements in their state. Certification is available through the American Association of Psychiatric Technicians. Level 1 techs must have a high school diploma and pass a written test. Level 2 techs must have thirty semester credits and one year of experience and pass a written test. Level 3 techs must have an associate's degree and two years of experience and pass a written test. Level 4 techs must have a bachelor's degree and three years of experience and pass a written test.

Most mental health technology programs emphasize interviewing skills. Such training guides technicians to correctly describe a patient's tone of voice and body language, so that they are well equipped to observe and record behavior that will be interpreted by the treatment team, and sometimes even a court of law. Some programs also teach administration of selected psychological tests. Students may also gain knowledge and training in crisis intervention techniques, child guidance, group counseling, family therapy, behavior modification, and consultation skills.

Psychiatric technicians need to have stable personalities; the ability to relate well to patients, their families, and fellow staff members; and the motivation to help others function at their highest potential.

Because psychiatric technicians interact with people, they must be sensitive to others' needs and feelings. Some aspects of sensitivity can be learned, but this requires a willingness to listen, be extremely observant, and risk involvement in situations that at first may seem ambiguous and confusing. In addition, psychiatric technicians need to be willing to look at their attitudes and behavior and be flexible and open about effecting changes in themselves. The more they know of themselves, the more effective they will be in helping others.

Patience, understanding, and a "thick skin" are required in working with people who may be disagreeable and unpleasant because of their illness. Patients can be particularly adept at finding a person's weaknesses and exploiting them. This is not a job for the tender hearted. A sense of responsibility and the ability to remain calm in emergencies are also essential characteristics.

Opportunities for Experience & Exploration

Prospective psychiatric technicians can gather personal experience in this field in a number of ways. They can apply for a job as a nurse's aide at a local general hospital. In this way they gain direct experience providing patient care. If such a job requires too much of a time commitment, students might consider volunteering at a hospital part time or during the summer. Volunteering is an excellent way to become acquainted with the field, and many techs' full-time jobs evolve from volunteer positions. Most volunteers must be twenty-one years of age to work in the mental health unit. Younger students who are interested in volunteering can often find places in the medical records department or other areas to get their feet in the door.

Other relevant job experiences include playground and summer camp counseling. These positions will give prospective technicians with an idea about how well they do in getting along with people, supervising group activities, as well as taking responsibility for others' behavior.

People interested in this career might also consider volunteering at their local mental health association or a local social welfare agency. In some cases, the mental health association can arrange opportunities for volunteer work inside a mental hospital or mental health clinic. Finally, students on their own, or with their teachers, can arrange a visit to a mental health clinic. If permission has been received ahead of time, students may be able to talk with staff members and observe first-hand how psychiatric technicians do their jobs.

Methods of Entering

Graduates from mental health and human services technology programs can usually choose from a variety of job possibilities. College placement officers can be extremely helpful in locating employment. Students can follow want ads or apply directly to clinics, agencies, or hospitals of their choice. Job information can also be obtained from the department of mental health in each state.

Advancement

Working as a psychiatric technician is still a relatively new occupation, and sequences of promotions have not yet been clearly defined. Seeking national certification through the AAPT is one way to help to set up a career path in this field. Advancement normally takes the form of being given greater responsibilities with less supervision. It usually results from gaining experience, developing competence and leadership abilities, and continuing formal and practical education. In cases where promotions are governed by civil service regulations, advancement is based on experience and test scores on promotion examinations.

As more technicians are employed in a given setting, needs will inevitably arise for additional supervisory personnel. This growth will provide advancement opportunities, because many supervisors will probably be picked from the ranks of senior psychiatric technicians.

In large part, advancement is linked to gaining further education. Thus, after working a few years, tech-

nicians may decide to obtain a baccalaureate degree in psychology. Advanced education, coupled with previous training and work experience, greatly enhance advancement potential. For instance, with a baccalaureate degree, experienced technicians may be able to find rewarding positions as instructors in programs to train future mental health workers.

Employment Outlook

The number of psychiatric technicians and aides in the United States is estimated at about two hundred thousand. Employment for psychiatric technicians is predicted to grow more slowly than average through the year 2006. Many opportunities will be available because turnover is high as a result of low pay and lack of advancement opportunities. Psychiatric technicians will also be needed as the older population in the United States increases and requires mental health services. The well-established trend of returning hospitalized patients to their communities after shorter and shorter periods of hospitalization will also continue. The trend has encouraged development of comprehensive community mental health centers and has led to an increased need for psychiatric technicians to staff these facilities.

Earnings

Salaries for psychiatric technicians vary according to geographical area and work setting; technicians in California generally receive substantially higher wages than in other areas of the country, and technicians in community settings generally receive higher salaries than those in institutional settings. On average, psychiatric technicians receive starting salaries ranging anywhere from minimum wage to as much as $20,000 a year or more. Most technicians are hourly employees, receiving $7.00 to $12.00 an hour, some even as high as $15.00 an hour. With increased experience technicians can expect at least modest increases in their salaries each year. Some senior psychiatric technicians earn as much as $27,000 a year or more (those in California can earn as much as $35,000 to $40,000 a year or more with ten to fifteen years of experience).

Most psychiatric technicians receive fringe benefits, including hospitalization insurance, sick leave, and paid vacations. Technicians working for state institutions or agencies will probably also be eligible for financial assistance for further education.

Conditions of Work

Psychiatric technicians work in a variety of settings and their working conditions vary accordingly. Typically they work forty hours a week, five days a week, although one may be a weekend day. Some psychiatric technicians work evening or night shifts, and all technicians may sometimes be asked to work holidays.

For the most part, the physical surroundings are pleasant. Most institutions, clinics, mental health centers, and agency offices are kept clean and comfortably furnished. Technicians who work with the mentally ill must nonetheless adjust to an environment that is normally chaotic and sometimes upsetting. Some patients are acutely depressed and withdrawn or excessively agitated and excited. Some patients may become unexpectedly violent and verbally abusive. However, institutions treating these kinds of patients maintain enough staff to keep the patients safe and to protect workers from physical harm. Psychiatric technicians who make home visits also may sometimes confront unpleasant conditions.

Work with mentally ill people demands a high degree of emotional stability. Psychiatric technicians may work with patients who are acutely ill and who have lost contact with reality. Some patients may be suicidal. Technicians must be absolutely honest, yet compassionate. Most importantly, they must maintain their perspective and not permit a patient's problems to become their own. They should not take insults to heart. They also need to realize the hard fact that many of the patients they work with may never be restored to good health; many are released only to return days, or sometimes even hours, later.

To help patients most effectively, technicians must learn to understand themselves and the effect their own behavior and attitudes have on others. They must be willing to become involved with the people they treat, and they must be able to communicate an optimistic attitude. Successful psychiatric technicians realize that their own optimistic expectations for their patients are crucial and integral to the kind of recovery the patients can make.

Finally, psychiatric technicians work not only with individuals but often with the community. In that role technicians can be called upon to advocate for their patients, by motivating community agencies to provide services or obtaining exceptions to rules when needed for individuals or groups of patients. Successful psychiatric technicians become competent in working and dealing with various decision-making processes of community and neighborhood groups.

Sources of Additional Information

For a two-page flyer on psychiatric technician careers or for information on becoming a nationally certified Psychiatric Technician, please contact:

■American Association of Psychiatric Technicians, Inc.
2059 South Third Street
Niles, MI 49120
Tel: 616-684-3164
Email: info@aapt.com
WWW: http://www.psych-health.com/aapt.htm

Purchasing Agents

Definition

Purchasing agents work for businesses and other large organizations, such as hospitals, universities, and government agencies. They buy raw materials, machinery, supplies, and services required for the organization. They must consider cost, quality, quantity, and time of delivery.

Nature of the Work

Purchasing agents generally work for organizations that buy at least $100,000 worth of goods a year. Their primary goal is to purchase the best quality materials for the best price. To do this, the agent must consider the exact specifications for the required items, cost, quantity discounts, freight handling or other transportation costs, and delivery time. In the past much of this information was obtained by comparing listings in catalog and trade journals, interviewing suppliers' representatives, keeping up with current market trends, examining sample goods, and observing demonstrations of equipment. Increasingly information can be found through computer databases. Sometimes agents visit plants of company suppliers. The agent is responsible for following up on orders and ensuring that goods meet the order specifications.

Most purchasing agents work in firms having fewer than five employees in the purchasing department. In some small organizations there is only one person responsible for making purchases. Very large firms, however, may employ as many as a hundred purchasing agents, each responsible for specific types of goods. In such organizations there is usually a *purchasing director* or *purchasing manager*.

Some purchasing agents seek the advice of purchase-price analysts, who compile and analyze statistical data about the manufacture and cost of products. Based on this information, they can make recommendations to purchasing personnel

School Subjects
Business
Economics

Personal Interests
Helping people: personal service
Selling/Making a deal

Work Environment
Primarily indoors
Primarily one location

Minimum Education Level
High school diploma

Salary Range
$18,400 to
$33,200 to
$63,000

Certification or Licensing
Voluntary

Outlook
More slowly than the average

DOT
162

GOE
11.05.04

NOC
1225

regarding the feasibility of producing or buying certain products and suggest ways to reduce costs.

Purchasing agents often specialize in a particular product or field. For example, *procurement engineers* specialize in aircraft equipment. They establish specifications and requirements for construction, performance, and testing of equipment.

Field contractors negotiate with farmers to grow or purchase fruits, vegetables, or other crops. These agents might advise growers on methods, acreage, and supplies and arrange for financing, transportation, or labor recruitment.

Head tobacco buyers are engaged in the purchase of tobacco on the auction warehouse floor. They advise other buyers about grades and quantities of tobacco and suggest prices.

Grain buyers manage grain elevators. They are responsible for evaluating and buying grain for resale and milling. They are concerned with the quality, market value, shipping, and storing of grain.

Grain broker-and-market operators buy and sell grain for investors through the commodity exchange. Like other brokers, they work on a commission basis.

Requirements

Although it is possible to obtain entry-level purchasing job with only a high school degree, many employers prefer to hire college graduates, and some require college degrees. College work should include courses in general economics, purchasing, accounting, statistics, and business management. A familiarity with computers is also desirable.

Some colleges and universities offer majors in purchasing. Those with a master's degree—in business administration, for example—tend to have the best jobs and highest salaries. Companies that manufacture machinery or chemicals may require a degree in engineering or a related field. A civil service examination is required for employment in government purchasing positions.

Purchasing agents should have calm temperaments and the self-confidence to be firm in decision making. Because they work with other people, they need to be diplomatic, tactful, and cooperative. A thorough knowledge of business practices and understanding of the needs and activities of the employer are essential.

There are no specific licenses or certification requirements imposed by law for purchasing agents. There are, however, several professional organizations to which purchasing agents frequently belong, including the National Association of Purchasing Manage-

ment, the National Institute of Governmental Purchasing, and the American Purchasing Society. These organizations confer certification on applicants who meet their educational and other requirements and who pass the necessary examinations. The American Purchasing Society, for example, offers two types of certification, the certified purchasing professional (CPP) and certified purchasing executive (CPE).

Although such certification is not essential, it is a recognized mark of professional competence that enhances a purchasing agent's opportunities for promotion to top management positions.

Opportunities for Experience & Exploration

Students interested in becoming a purchasing agent can learn more about the field through a summer job in the purchasing department of a business. They also talk with experienced purchasing agents about the job and read periodicals, such as *Purchasing Magazine,* that publish articles on the field.

Methods of Entering

Students without a college degree may be able to enter the field as clerical workers and then receive on-the-job training in purchasing. A college degree, though, is required for most higher positions. College and university placement services offer assistance to graduating students in locating jobs.

Entry into purchasing departments of private businesses is made by direct application to a company. Some purchasing agents start in another department, such as accounting, shipping, receiving, and transfer to purchasing when an opportunity arises. Many large companies send newly hired agents through orientation programs, where they learn about goods and services, suppliers, and purchasing methods.

Another means of entering the field is through the military. Service in the Quartermaster Corps of the Army or the procurement divisions of the Navy and Air Force can provide excellent preparation for either a civilian job or a career position in the service.

Advancement

In general, purchasing agents begin by becoming familiar with departmental procedures, such as keeping inventory records, filling out forms to initiate new purchases, checking purchase orders, and dealing with vendors. With more experience they gain responsibility for selecting vendors and purchasing products. Agents may become junior buyers of standard catalog items, assistant buyers, or managers, perhaps with overall responsibility for purchasing, warehousing, traffic, and related functions. The top positions are *head of purchasing, purchasing director, materials manager,* and vice-president of purchasing. These positions include responsibilities concerning production, planning, and marketing.

Many agents advance by changing employers. Frequently an assistant purchasing agent for one firm will be hired as a purchasing agent or head of the purchasing department by another company.

Employment Outlook

The number of purchasing agents is likely to grow slower than the average for all occupations through the year 2006. Computerized purchasing methods and the increased reliance on a select number of suppliers boost the productivity of purchasing personnel and reduce the number of new job openings. But as more and more hospitals, schools, state and local governments, and other service-related organizations turn to professional purchasing agents to help reduce costs, they will become good sources of employment. Nevertheless, most job openings will be to replace workers who retire or otherwise leave their jobs.

Demand will be strongest for those with a master's degree in business administration or an undergraduate degree in purchasing. Among firms manufacturing complex machinery, chemicals, and other technical products, the demand will be for graduates with a master's degree in engineering, another field of science, or business administration. Graduates of two-year programs in purchasing or materials management should continue to find good opportunities, especially in smaller companies.

Earnings

The earnings of purchasing agents vary with the size of the employing firm, experience, and amount of responsibility. According to U.S. Department of Labor statistics, college graduates hired in 1996 as beginning purchasing agents received an average starting salary of $18,400. Purchasing agents with one to three years of experience averaged $33,200 a year. Purchasing directors earn about $63,000. The average salary for all purchasing agents in the federal government is about $28,700.

Purchasing personnel usually receive the same benefits as other company employees such as paid holidays and medical insurance. When purchasing agents are required to travel, they are reimbursed for lodging, transportation, and other expenses.

Conditions of Work

Working conditions for a purchasing agent are similar to those of other office employees. They usually work in rooms that are pleasant, well lighted, and clean. Work is year-round and generally steady because it is not particularly influenced by seasonal factors. Most have forty-hour workweeks, although overtime is not uncommon. Agents may have to spend time in addition to regular hours to attend meetings, read, prepare reports, visit suppliers' plants, or traveling. While most work is done indoors, some agents occasionally need to inspect goods outdoors or in warehouses.

It is important for purchasing agents to have good working relations with others. They must interact closely with suppliers as well as with personnel in other departments of the company. Because of the importance of their decisions, purchasing agents sometimes work under great pressure.

Sources of Additional Information

American Purchasing Society, Inc.
11910 Oak Trail Way
Port Richey, FL 34668
Tel: 813-862-7998

National Association of Purchasing Management
PO Box 22160
Tempe, AZ 85285
Tel: 602-752-6276
WWW: http://www.napm.org

National Institute of Governmental Purchasing, Inc.
11800 Sunrise Valley Drive, Suite 1050
Reston, VA 22091
Tel: 703-715-9400

Radio and Television Newscasters, Reporters, and Announcers

Definition

Radio and television announcers present news and commercial messages from a script. They identify the station, announce station breaks, and introduce and close shows. Interviewing guests, making public service announcements, and conducting panel discussions may also be part of the announcer's work. In small stations the local announcer may keep the program log, run the transmitter, and cue the changeover to network broadcasting as well as write scripts or rewrite news releases.

Nature of the Work

Some announcers merely announce; others do a multitude of other jobs, depending on the size of the station. But the nature of their announcing work remains the same.

An announcer is engaged in an exacting career. The necessity for finishing a sentence or a program at a precisely planned moment makes this a demanding and often tense career. It is absolutely essential that announcers project a sense of calm to their audiences, regardless of the activity and tension behind the scenes.

The announcer who plays recorded music interspersed with a variety of advertising material and informal commentary is called a *disc jockey*. This title arose when most music was recorded on conventional flat records or discs. Today much of the recorded music used in commercial radio stations is on magnetic tape or compact discs. Disc jockeys serve as a bridge between the music itself and the listener. They may perform such public services as announcing the time, the weather forecast, or important news. It can be a lonely job, since many disc jockeys are the only person in the studio. But because their job is to maintain the good spirits of their audience and to attract new listeners, disc jockeys must possess the ability be relaxed and cheerful.

Unlike the more conventional radio or television announcer, the disc jockey is not bound by a written script. Except for the commercial announcements, which must be read as written, the disc jockey's statements are usually spontaneous. Disc jockeys usually are not required to play a musical selection to the end; they may fade out a record when it interferes with a predetermined schedule for commercials, news, time checks, or weather reports.

Announcers who cover sports events for the benefit of the listening or viewing audience are known as *sportscasters.* This is a highly specialized form of announcing as sportscasters must have extensive knowledge of the sports that they are covering, plus the ability to describe events quickly and accurately.

Often the sportscaster will spend several days with team members, observing practice sessions, interviewing people, and researching the history of an event or of the teams to be covered. The more information that a sportscaster can acquire about individual team members, company they represent, tradition of the contest, ratings of the team, and community in which the event takes place, the more interesting the coverage is to the audience.

The announcer who specializes in reporting the news to the listening or viewing public is called a *newscaster.* This job may require simply reporting facts, or it may include editorial commentary. Newscasters may be given the authority by their employers to express their opinions on news items or the philosophies of others. They must make judgments about which news is important and which is not. In some instances, they write their own scripts, based on facts that are furnished by international news bureaus. In other instances, they read text exactly as it comes in over a teletype machine. They may make as few as one or two reports each day if they work on a major news program, or they may broadcast news for five minutes every hour or half hour. Their delivery is usually dignified, measured, and impersonal.

The *anchorperson* generally summarizes and comments on one aspect of the news at the end of the scheduled broadcast. This kind of announcing differs noticeably from that practiced by the sportscaster, whose manner may be breezy and interspersed with slang, or from the disc jockey, who may project a humorous, casual, or intimate image.

The newscaster may specialize in certain aspects of the news, such as economics, politics, or military activity. Newscasters also introduce films and interviews prepared by *news reporters* that provide in-depth coverage and information on the event being reported. *Radio and television broadcasting news analysts* are often called *commentators,* and they interpret specific events and discuss how these may affect individuals or the nation. They may have a specified daily slot for which material must be written, recorded or presented live. They gather information that is analyzed and interpreted through research and interviews and cover public functions such as political conventions, press conferences, and social events.

Smaller television stations may have an announcer who performs all the functions of reporting, presenting, and commenting on the news as well as introducing network and news service reports.

Many television and radio announcers have become well-known public personalities in broadcasting. They may participate in community activities as master of ceremonies at banquets and other public events.

Requirements

Although there are no formal educational requirements for entering the field of radio and television announcing, many large stations prefer college-educated applicants. The general reason given for this preference is that announcers with broad educational and cultural backgrounds are better prepared to successfully meet a variety of unexpected or emergency situations. The greater the knowledge of geography, history, literature, the arts, political science, music, science, and of the sound and structure of the English language, the greater the announcer's value. Good diction and English usage, thorough knowledge of correct pronunciation, and freedom from regional dialects are very important. A factual error, grammatical error, or mispronounced word can bring letters of criticism to station managers.

A pleasing voice and personality are of great importance to prospective announcers. They must be levelheaded and able to react calmly in the face of a major crisis. People's lives may depend on an announcer's ability to remain calm during a disaster. There are also many unexpected circumstances that demand the skill of quick thinking. For example, if guests who are to appear on a program do not arrive or become too nervous to go on the air, the announcer must compensate immediately and fill the air time. He or she must smooth over an awkward phrase, breakdown in equipment, or other technical difficulty.

Those who aspire to careers as television announcers must present a good appearance and have no nervous mannerisms. Neatness, cleanliness, and careful attention to the details of proper dress are important. The successful television announcer must have the combination of sincerity and showmanship that attracts and captures an audience.

Broadcast announcing is a highly competitive field. Although there may not be any specific training program required by prospective employers, station officials pay particular attention to taped auditions of an applicant's delivery or, in the case of television, to videotaped demos of sample presentations.

Some vocational schools advertise training for broadcasting. Persons interested in preparing in this way should contact local station managers to find out if such training will improve the chances of employment. They also should contact broadcasting trade organizations and the local Better Business Bureau to find out if the school has been successful in training and placing candidates.

A Federal Communications Commission license or permit is no longer required for broadcasting positions. Union membership may be required for employment with large stations in major cities and is a necessity with the networks. The largest talent union is the American Federation of Television and Radio Artists (AFTRA). Most small stations, however, are nonunion.

Opportunities for Experience & Exploration

Students who think they may be interested in becoming announcers can seek summer jobs at radio and television stations. Although they will probably not have the opportunity to broadcast, they may be able to judge whether or not the type of work appeals to them as a career.

Any chance to speak or perform before an audience should be welcomed by the prospective announcer. Appearing as a speaker or performer can show whether or not one has the stage presence necessary for a career in front of a microphone or camera.

Many colleges and universities have their own radio and television stations and offer courses in radio and television. Students can gain valuable experience working at college-owned stations. Some radio stations, cable systems, and TV stations offer financial assistance, internships and co-op work programs, as well as scholarships and fellowships.

Methods of Entering

One way to enter this field is to apply for an entry-level job rather than an announcer position. It is also advisable to start at a small station. Most announcers start in jobs such as production secretary, production assistant, researcher, or reporter in small stations. As opportunities arise, they move from one job to another. Work as a disc jockey, sportscaster, or news reporter may become available. Network jobs are few, and the competition for them is great. An announcer must have several years of experience as well as a college education to be considered for these positions.

An announcer is employed only after an audition. Applicants should carefully select audition material to show a prospective employer the full range of one's abilities. In addition to presenting prepared materials, applicants may be asked to read material that they have not seen previously, such as a commercial, news release, dramatic selection, or poem.

Advancement

Most successful announcers advance from small stations to large ones. Experienced announcers usually have held several jobs. The most successful announcers may be those who work for the networks. Usually, because of network locations, announcers must live in or near the country's largest cities.

Some careers lead from announcing to other aspects of radio or television work. More people are employed in sales, promotion, and planning than in performing; often they are paid more than announcers. Because the networks employ relatively few announcers in proportion to the rest of the broadcasting professionals, a candidate must have several years of experience and specific background in several news areas before being considered for an audition. These top announcers generally are college graduates.

Employment Outlook

In 1996, there were about 52,000 people employed as radio and television announcers and newscasters in the United States. Almost all are staff announcers at one of the more than 11,800 radio stations or 1,550 television stations around the country. Some, however, work on a freelance basis on individual assignments for networks, stations, advertising agencies, and other producers of commercials.

Competition for entry-level employment in announcing during the coming years is expected to be keen as the broadcasting industry always attracts more applicants than are needed to fill available openings. There is a better chance of working in radio than in television because there are more small radio stations. Local television stations usually carry a high percentage of network programs and need only a very small staff to carry out local operations.

Opportunities for experienced broadcasting personnel are expected to decline through the year 2006 as a result of mergers, consolidation, and downsizing, Also, the increased use of automatic programming equipment is likely to weaken the demand for radio announcers. A few job openings will result from the need to replace retiring workers, or those leaving the field for better paying occupations. The trend among major networks, and to some extent among many smaller radio and TV stations is toward specialization in such fields as sportscasting or weather forecasting. Newscasters who specialize in such areas as business, consumer, and health news should have an advantage over other job applicants.

Earnings

The range of salaries for announcers is a rather wide one. In 1996, salaries for radio news announcers averaged $31,251 a year, according to a survey by the National Association of Broadcasters and the Broadcast Cable Financial Management Association. Annual salaries in small markets were as low as $7,100; the largest urban markets paid the highest reported salaries of $102,676. The same survey reports that television announcers in 1996 earned salaries that ranged from $24,935 in the smallest markets to $199,741 in the largest markets. Television sportscasters and weathercasters averaged lower annual salaries of $48,704 and $52,562, respectively.

For both radio and television, salaries are higher in the larger markets. Nationally known announcers and newscasters who appear regularly on network television programs receive salaries that may be quite impressive. For those who have become top television personalities for metropolitan-area television stations, salaries also are quite rewarding.

Most radio or television stations broadcast twenty-four hours. Although much of the material may be prerecorded, announcing staff must often be available and as a result may work considerable overtime or split shifts, especially in smaller stations. Evening, night, weekend, and holiday duty may provide additional compensation.

Conditions of Work

Work in radio and television stations is usually very pleasant. Almost all stations are housed in modern facilities. The maintenance of technical electronic equipment require temperature and dust control and people who work around such equipment benefit from the precautions taken to preserve it.

Announcers' jobs may provide opportunities to meet well-known or celebrity persons. Being at the center of an important communications medium can make the broadcaster more keenly aware of current issues and divergent points of view than the average person.

Announcers and newscasters usually work a forty-hour week, but they may work irregular hours. They may report for work at a very early hour in the morning or work late into the night. Some radio stations operate on a twenty-four-hour basis. All-night announcers may be alone in the station during their working hours.

The announcer who stays with a station for a period of time becomes a well-known personality in the community. Such celebrities are sought after as participants in community activities; television announcers especially are easily recognized by the public.

Sources of Additional Information

For information on its summer internship program, please contact:

■**Association of Independent Television Stations**
1320 19th Street, NW, Suite 300
Washington, DC 20036
Tel: 202-887-1970

For a list of schools offering degrees in broadcasting, write to:

■ **Broadcast Education Association**
1771 N Street, NW
Washington, DC 20036-2891
Tel: 202-429-5355

For college programs and union information, write to:

■ **National Association of Broadcast Employees and Technicians**
501 3rd Street, NW, 8th Floor
Washington, DC 20001
Tel: 202-434-1254

For general information, write to:

■ **National Association of Farm Broadcasters**
26 East Exchange Street, Suite 307
St. Paul, MN 55101
Tel: 612-224-0508

For a booklet on careers in cable, write to:

■ **National Cable Television Association**
1724 Massachusetts Avenue, NW
Washington, DC 20036
Tel: 202-775-3550

For scholarship and internship information, contact:

■ **Radio-Television News Directors Association**
1000 Connecticut Avenue, NW, Suite 615
Washington, DC 20036
Tel: 202-659-6510
Email: rtnda.@.org
WWW: http://www.rtnda.org/rtnda/

Radiologic Technologists

Definition

Radiologic technologists, sometimes called *radiographers,* operate equipment that creates images of the body's tissues, organs, and bones for medical diagnoses and therapy. These images allow physicians to know the exact nature of a patient's injury or disease, such as where a bone is broken or the confirmation of an ulcer.

Before an X-ray examination, radiologic technologists may administer drugs or chemical mixtures to the patient to better highlight internal organs. They place the patient in the correct position between the X-ray source and film and protect body areas that are not to be exposed from radiation. After determining the proper duration and intensity of the exposure, they operate the controls to beam X-rays through the patient and expose the photographic film.

They may operate computer-aided imaging equipment that does not involve X-rays and may help to treat diseased or affected areas of the body by exposing the patient to specified concentrations of radiation for prescribed times.

Nature of the Work

All radiological work is done at the request of and under the supervision of a physician. Just as a prescription is required for certain of drugs to be dispensed or administered, so also must a physician's request be issued before a patient can receive any kind of imaging procedure.

There are four primary disciplines in which radiologic technologists may work: radiography, which is taking X-ray pictures or radiographs; nuclear medicine; radiation therapy; and sonography. In each of these, the technologist works under the direction of a physician who specializes in interpretation of the pictures produced by X-rays, other imaging techniques, or radiation therapy. Technologists can work in more than one of these areas. Some technologists specialize in a particular part of the body or a specific condition.

School Subjects
Biology
Health

Personal Interests
Helping people: physical health/medicine
Science

Work Environment
Primarily indoors
Primarily one location

Minimum Education Level
Some postsecondary training

Salary Range
$23,400 to
$28,800 to
$37,300+

Certification or Licensing
Required

Outlook
Faster than the average

DOT
078

X-ray pictures or radiographs are the most familiar use of radiologic technology. They are used to diagnose and determine treatment for a wide variety of afflictions, including ulcers, tumors, and bone fractures. Chest X-ray pictures can determine whether a person has a lung disease. Radiologic technologists who operate X-ray equipment first help the patient prepare for the radiologic examination. After explaining the procedure, they may administer a substance that makes the part of the body being imaged more clearly visible on the film. They make sure that the patient is not wearing any jewelry or other metal that would obstruct the X-rays. They position the person sitting, standing, or lying down so that the correct view of the body can be radiographed, and then they cover adjacent areas with lead shielding to prevent unnecessary exposure to radiation.

The technologist positions the X-ray equipment at the proper angle and distance from the part to be radiographed and determines exposure time based on the location of the particular organ or bone and thickness of the body in that area. The controls of the X-ray machine are set to produce pictures of the correct density, contrast, and detail. Placing the photographic film closest to the body part being X-rayed, the technologist takes the requested images, repositioning the patient as needed. Typically, there are standards regarding the minimal number of views to be taken of a given body part. The film is then developed for the radiologist or other physician to interpret.

In a fluoroscopic examination, a more complex imaging procedure that examines the gastrointestinal area, a beam of X-rays passes through the body and onto a fluorescent screen, enabling the physician to see the internal organs in motion. For these, the technologist first prepares a solution of barium sulfate to be administered to the patient, either rectally or orally, depending on the exam. The barium sulfate increases the contrast between the digestive tract and surrounding organs, making the image clearer. The technologist follows the physician's guidance in positioning the patient, monitors the machine's controls, and takes any follow-up radiographs as needed.

Radiologic technologists may learn other imaging procedures such as computed tomography (CT) scanning, which uses X-rays to get detailed cross-sectional images of the body's internal structures, and magnetic resonance imaging (MRI), which uses radio waves, powerful magnets, and computers to obtain body part images. These diagnostic procedures are becoming more common and usually require radiologic technologists to undergo additional on-the-job training.

Other specialties within the radiography discipline include mammography and cardiovascular interventional technology. In addition, some technologists may focus on radiography of joints and bones, or they may be involved in such areas as angiocardiography (visualization of the heart and large blood vessels) or neuroradiology (the use of radiation to diagnose diseases of the nervous system).

Radiologic technologists perform a wide range of duties, from greeting patients and putting them at ease by explaining the procedures, to developing the finished film. Their administrative tasks include maintaining patients' records recording equipment usage and maintenance, organizing work schedules, and managing a radiologist's private practice or hospital's radiology department. Some radiologic technologists teach in programs to educate other technologists.

Requirements

Students who wish to become radiologic technologists must complete an education program in radiography. Programs range in length from two to four years. Depending on length, the programs award a certificate, associate's degree, or bachelor's degree.

Educational programs are available in hospitals, medical centers, colleges and universities, and vocational and technical institutes. It is also possible to get radiologic technology training in the armed forces.

To enter an accredited program, applicants must be high school graduates; some programs require one or two years of higher education. High school courses in mathematics, physics, chemistry, biology, and photography are useful background preparation. Courses in radiologic technology education programs include anatomy, physiology, patient care, physics, radiation protection, medical ethics, principles of imaging, medical terminology, radiobiology, and pathology. For some supervisory or administrative jobs in this field, a bachelor's or master's degree may be required.

Radiologic technologists may register with the American Registry of Radiologic Technologists after graduating from an accredited program in radiography, radiation therapy, or nuclear medicine. Sonographers may register with the American Registry of Diagnostic Medical Sonographers. Although registration and certification are voluntary, many jobs are open only to technologists who have acquired these credentials. In addition to being registered in the various imaging disciplines, radiologic technologists can receive advanced qualifications in each of the four radiography specializations: mammography, computed tomography (CT), magnetic resonance imaging (MRI), and cardiovascular interventional technology. As the work of radiologic technologists grows increasingly complex, and employment opportunities become more competitive, the desirability of registration and certification will also grow. An increasing number of states have licensing requirements. In 1995, licenses were needed by radiographers in thirty states.

Radiologic technologists should be responsible individuals, with a mature and caring nature. They should be personable and enjoy interacting with all types of people, including those who are very ill. A compassionate attitude is essential.

Opportunities for Experience & Exploration

There is no way to gain direct experience in this profession without the appropriate qualifications. However, it is possible to learn about the duties of radiologic technologists by talking with them and observing the facilities and equipment they use. It is also possible to have interviews with teachers of radiologic technology. Guidance counselors and teachers can contact local hospitals or schools with radiography programs to locate technologists who are willing to talk to interested students.

As with any career in health care, volunteering at a local hospital, clinic, or nursing home provides an excellent opportunity to test one's real interest in the field. Most hospitals are eager for volunteers, and working in such a setting gives a chance to see health care professionals in action as well as to have some patient contact.

Methods of Entering

With more states regulating the practice of radiologic technology, certification by the appropriate accreditation body for a given specialty is quickly becoming a necessity for employment. Persons who acquire training in schools that have not been accredited, or who learn on the job, may have difficulty in qualifying for many positions, especially those with a wide range of assignments.

Students enrolled in hospital educational programs often work for the hospital upon completion of the program. Those students who attend degree programs can get help finding jobs through their schools' placement offices.

Advancement

About three-quarters of all radiologic technologists are employed in hospitals, where there are opportunities for advancement to administrative and supervisory positions such as chief technologist or technical administrator. Other technologists develop special clinical skills in advanced imaging procedures such as computed tomography scanning or magnetic resonance imaging. Some radiologic technologists qualify as instructors. There are more chances for advancement for persons who hold a bachelor's degree. For those who wish to become teachers or administrators, a master's degree and considerable experience are necessary.

Employment Outlook

This field is estimated to grow faster than average for all occupations through the year 2006. A growing older population is a factor for this growth. Although enrollments in accredited schools have equalized in recent years, the demand for qualified people in some areas of the country far exceeds the supply. This shortage is particularly acute in rural areas and small towns.

In the years to come, increasing numbers of radiologic technologists will be employed in nonhospital settings, such as physicians' offices, clinics, health maintenance organizations, laboratories, government agencies, and diagnostic imaging centers. This pattern will be part of the overall trend toward holding down health care costs by delivering more care outside of hospitals. Nevertheless, hospitals will remain the major employers of radiologic technologists for the near future. Because of the increasing importance of radiologic technology in the diagnosis and treatment of disease, it is unlikely that hospitals will do fewer radiologic procedures than in the past. Instead, they try to do more on an outpatient basis, and on weekends and evenings. This should increase the demand for part-time technologists and thus open more opportunities for flexible work schedules.

At present, most of the nation's radiologic technologists are radiographers, and this is the field that will continue to employ most technologists. Radiation, either alone or in combination with surgery and chemotherapy, will continue in the near future to be an important weapon against cancer and certain other diseases. More widespread use of ultrasound testing, especially in cardiology and obstetrics/gynecology, will have a positive effect on the hiring of diagnostic medical sonographers.

Earnings

Salaries for radiologic technologists compare favorably with those of similar health care professions. According to a 1997 Hay Group Survey of acute care hospitals, the starting salary in a hospital or medical center averages about $28,800 a year for radiologic technologists. With experience, technologists earn average salaries of about $31,000 or more a year.

Technologists with specialized skills may make larger salaries. Radiation therapists earn an average salary of about $37,300. In ultrasound technology, the average pay for those with experience is about $36,000. Most technologists are covered by the same vacation and sick leave provisions as other employees in the organizations that employ them, and some receive free medical care and pension benefits.

Conditions of Work

Full-time technologists generally work eight hours a day, forty hours a week and may be on call for some night emergency duty or weekend hours, which pays in equal time off or additional compensation.

In diagnostic radiologic work, technologists perform most of their tasks while on their feet. They move around a lot and often are called upon to lift patients who need help in moving.

Great care is exercised to protect technologists from radiation exposure. Each technologist wears a badge that measures radiation exposure, and records are kept of total exposure accumulated over time. Other routine pre-cautions include the use of safety devices such as lead aprons, lead gloves, and other shielding and the use of disposable gowns, gloves, and masks. Careful attention to safety procedures has greatly reduced or eliminated radiation hazards for the technologist.

Radiologic technology is dedicated to conserving life and health. Technologists derive satisfaction from their work, which helps promote health and alleviate human suffering. Those who specialize in radiation therapy need to be able to handle the close relationships they inevitably develop while working with very sick or dying people over a period of time.

Sources of Additional Information

■ **American Society of Radiologic Technologists**
15000 Central Avenue, SE
Albuquerque, NM 87123
Tel: 505-298-4500

■ **Canadian Association of Medical Radiation Technologists**
294 Albert Street, Room 601
Ottawa, ON K1P 6E6 Canada
Tel: 613-231-4361

■ **Society of Diagnostic Medical Sonographers**
12770 Coit Road, Suite 508
Dallas, TX 75251
Tel: 214-239-7367

For information on accreditation, please contact:

■ **American Registry of Radiologic Technologists**
1255 Northland Drive
St. Paul, MN 55120
Tel: 612-687-0048

■ **American Cancer Society**
1599 Clifton Road
Atlanta, GA 30329
Tel: 404-320-3333
WWW: http://www.cancer.org

Receptionists

Definition

Receptionists—so named because they receive visitors places of business—have the important job of giving a business's clients and visitors a positive first impression. These front-line workers are the first communication sources who greet clients and visitors, answer their questions, and direct them to the people they wish to see. Receptionists also answer telephones, take and distribute messages for other employees, and make sure no one enters the office unescorted or unauthorized. Many receptionists perform additional clerical duties. *Switchboard operators* perform similar tasks but primarily handle equipment that receives an organization's telephone calls.

Nature of the Work

The receptionist is a specialist in human contact: the most important part of a receptionist's job is dealing with people in a courteous and effective manner. Receptionists greet customers, clients, patients, and salespeople, take their names, and determine the nature or their business and the person they wish to see. The receptionist then pages the requested person, directs the visitor to that person's office or location, or makes an appointment for a later visit. Receptionists often keep records of all visits by writing down the visitor's name, purpose of visit, person visited, and date and time.

Almost all types of companies hire receptionists. They work in manufacturing, wholesale, retail, real estate, insurance, medicine, advertising, government, banking, church administration, and law. Their day-to-day duties depend almost entirely on the nature of the place at which they work.

Most receptionists answer the telephone at their place of employment; many operate switchboards or paging systems. These workers usually take and distribute messages for other employees and may receive and distribute mail. Recep-

School Subjects
Business
English
(writing/literature)

Personal Interests
Computers
Helping people: personal service

Work Environment
Primarily indoors
Primarily one location

Minimum Education Level
High school diploma

Salary Range
$11,900 to
$21,240 to
$24,250+

Certification or Licensing
None

Outlook
Faster than the average

DOT
237

GOE
07.04.04

NOC
1414

tionists may perform a variety of other clerical duties, including keying in and filing correspondence and other paperwork, proofreading, preparing travel vouchers, and preparing outgoing mail. In some businesses, receptionists are responsible for monitoring the attendance of other employees. In businesses where employees are frequently out of the office on assignments, receptionists may keep track of their whereabouts to ensure they receive important phone calls and messages. Many receptionists use computers and word processors in performing their clerical duties.

Receptionists are partially responsible for maintaining office security, especially in large firms. They may require all visitors to sign in and out and carry visitors' passes during their stay. Since visitors may not enter most offices unescorted, receptionists usually accept and sign for packages and other deliveries.

Receptionists are frequently responsible for answering inquiries from the public about a business's nature and operations. To answer these questions efficiently and in a manner that conveys a favorable impression, a receptionist must be as knowledgeable as possible about the business's products, services, policies, and practices and familiar with the names and responsibilities of all other employees. They must be careful, however, not to divulge classified information such as business procedures or employee activities that a competing company might be able to use. This part of a receptionist's job is so important that some businesses call their receptionists *information clerks.*

A large number of receptionists work in physicians' and dentists' offices, hospitals, clinics, and other health care establishments. Workers in medical offices receive patients, take their names, and escort them to examination rooms. They make future appointments for patients and may prepare statements and collect bill payments. In hospitals, receptionists obtain patient information, assign patients to rooms, and keep records on the dates they are admitted and discharged.

In other types of industries, the duties of these workers vary. Receptionists in hair salons arrange appointments for clients and may escort them to stylists' stations. Workers in bus or train companies answer inquiries about departures, arrivals, and routes. *In-file operators* collect and distribute credit information to clients for credit purposes. *Registrars, park aides,* and *tourist-information assistants* may be employed as receptionists at public or private facilities. Their duties may include keeping a record of the visitors entering and leaving the facility, as well as providing information on services that the facility provides. *Information clerks, automobile club information clerks,*

and *referral-and-information aides* provide answers to questions by telephone or in person from both clients and potential clients and keep a record of all inquiries.

Switchboard operators may perform specialized work, such as operating switchboards at police district offices to take calls for assistance from citizens. Or, they may handle airport communication systems, which includes public address paging systems and courtesy telephones, or serve as *answering-service operators,* who record and deliver messages for clients who cannot be reached by telephone.

Requirements

Most employees require receptionists to have a high school diploma. Some businesses prefer to hire workers who have completed post–high school courses at a junior college or business school. Applicants need a friendly, outgoing personality, excellent people skills, neat appearance, and good grasp of English and grammar. Many employers require typing, switchboard, computer, and other clerical skills, but may provide some on-the-job training as the work is typically entry level.

High school students may prepare for receptionist or switchboard operator positions by taking courses in business procedures, office machine operation, keyboarding, computers, business math, English, and public speaking. Students interested in post–high school education may find courses in basic bookkeeping and principles of accounting helpful in finding higher-paying receptionist jobs with better chances for advancement.

Good receptionists need to be well-groomed, have pleasant voices, and be able to clearly express themselves. Because receptionists sometimes deal with demanding people, a smooth, patient disposition and good judgment are important. All receptionists need to be courteous and tactful. A good memory for faces and names also proves very valuable. Most important are good listening and communications skills and an understanding of human nature.

Opportunities for Experience & Exploration

A good way to obtain experience in working as a receptionist is through a high school work-study program. Students participating in such programs spend part of their school day in classes and the rest working for local businesses. This arrangement helps students gain valuable practical experience before they look for their first job. High school guidance counselors can provide information about work-study opportunities.

Methods of Entering

High school students may be able to learn of openings with local businesses through their school guidance counselors or newspaper want ads. Local state employment offices frequently have information about receptionist work. Students should also contact area businesses for whom they would like to work; many available positions are not advertised in the paper because they are filled so quickly. Temporary-work agencies are a valuable resource for finding jobs, too, some of which may lead to permanent employment. Friends and relatives may also know of job openings.

Advancement

Advancement opportunities are limited for receptionists, especially in small offices. The more clerical skills and education workers have, the greater their chances for promotion to such better-paying jobs as secretary, administrative assistant, or bookkeeper. College or business school training can help receptionists advance to higher-level positions. Many companies provide training for their receptionists and other employees, helping workers gain skills for job advancement.

Employment Outlook

According to the U.S. Department of Labor, over one million people were employed as receptionists in 1996, accounting for about a third of all information clerks. Factories, wholesale and retail stores, and service providers employ a large percentage of these workers. Nearly one-third of the receptionists in the United States work in health care settings, including offices, hospitals, nursing homes, urgent care centers, and clinics. Almost one-third work part time.

This field is expected to grow faster than the average through the year 2006. Many openings will occur due to the occupation's high turnover rate. Opppor-

tunities will be best for those with wide clerical skills and work experience. Growth in jobs for receptionists are expected to be greater than for other clerical positions because automation will have little effect on the receptionist's largely interpersonal duties and because of an anticipated growth in the number of businesses providing services. In addition, more and more businesses are learning how valuable a receptionist can be in furthering their public relations efforts and helping them convey a positive image.

Earnings

Earnings for receptionists vary widely with the education and experience of the worker and type, size, and geographic location of the business. According to the U.S. Department of Labor, receptionists earned starting salaries of over $11,900 in 1996. Those with experience earned $24,250 or more.

In 1997, the federal government paid beginning receptionists salaries ranging from $18,900 to $19,200 a year; the average annual salary for experienced receptionists in the federal government was $21,240.

Receptionists are usually eligible for paid holidays and vacations, sick leave, medical and life insurance coverage, and a retirement plan of some kind.

Most receptionists work five days, thirty-five to forty hours a week. Some may work weekend and evening hours, especially those in medical offices. Switchboard operators may have to work any shift of the day if their employers require twenty-four-hour phone service, such as hotels and hospitals. These workers usually work holidays and weekend hours.

Conditions of Work

Because receptionists usually work near or at the main entrance to the business, their work area is one of the first places a caller sees. Therefore, these areas are usually pleasant and clean and are carefully furnished and decorated to create a favorable, businesslike impression. Work areas are almost always air-conditioned, well lit, and relatively quiet, although a receptionist's phone rings frequently. Receptionists work behind a desk or counter and spend most of their workday sitting, although some standing and walking is required when filing or escorting visitors to their destinations. The job may be stressful at times, especially when a worker must be polite to rude or uncooperative callers.

Sources of Additional Information

■Accrediting Council for Independent Colleges and Schools
750 First Street, NE, Suite 980
Washington, DC 20002
Tel: 202-336-6780

■Accrediting Council of Career Schools and College of Technology
2101 Wilson Boulevard, Suite 302
Arlington, VA 22201
Tel: 703-247-4212

■OfficeTeam
2884 Sand Hill Road
Menlo Park, CA 94025
Tel: 800-804-8367

■Professional Secretaries International
PO Box 20404
10502 NW Ambassador Drive
Kansas City, MO 64195-0404
Tel: 816-891-6600

Recreation Workers

Definition

Recreation workers help people, as groups and as individuals, enjoy and use their leisure time constructively. They organize and administer physical, social, and cultural programs. They also operate recreational facilities and study recreation needs.

Nature of the Work

Recreation workers plan, organize, and direct recreation activities for people of all ages, social and economic levels, and degrees of physical and emotional health. The exact nature of their work varies and depends on their individual level of responsibility.

Recreation workers employed by local governments and voluntary agencies include *recreation supervisors* who coordinate *recreation center directors,* who in turn supervise *recreation leaders and aides.* With the help of volunteer workers, they plan and carry out programs at community centers, neighborhood playgrounds, recreational and rehabilitation centers, prisons, hospitals, and homes for children and the elderly, often working in cooperation with social workers and sponsors of the various centers.

Recreation supervisors plan programs to meet the needs of the people they serve. Well-rounded programs may include arts and crafts, dramatics, music, dancing, swimming, games, camping, nature study, and other pastimes. Special events may include festivals, contests, pet and hobby shows, and various outings. Recreation supervisors also create programs for people with special needs, such as the elderly or people in hospitals. Supervisors have overall responsibility for coordinating the work of the recreation workers who carry out the programs and supervise several recreation centers or an entire region.

Recreation center directors run the programs at their respective recreation buildings, indoor centers, playgrounds, or day camps. In addition to directing the staff of the facility, they oversee the safety of the buildings and equipment, handle financial matters, and prepare reports.

Recreation leaders, with the help of recreation aides, work directly with assigned groups and are responsible for the daily operations of a recreation program. They organize and lead activities such as drama, dancing, sports and games, camping trips, and other recreations. They give instruction in crafts, games, and sports, and work with other staff on special projects and events. Leaders help train and direct volunteers and perform other tasks, as required by the director.

In industry, recreation leaders plan social and athletic programs for employees and their families. Bowling leagues, softball teams, picnics, and dances are examples of company-sponsored activities. In addition, an increasing number of companies are providing exercise and fitness programs for their employees.

Camp counselors lead and instruct children and adults in nature-oriented forms of recreation at camps or resorts. Activities usually include swimming, hiking, horseback riding, and other outdoor sports and games, as well as instruction in nature and folklore. Camp counselors teach skills such as wood crafting, leather working, and basket weaving. Some camps offer specialized instruction in subjects such as music, drama, gymnastics, and computers. In carrying out the programs, camp counselors are concerned with the safety, health, and comfort of the campers. Counselors are supervised by a *camp director.*

Another type of recreation worker is the *social director,* who plans and organizes recreational activities for guests in hotels and resorts or for passengers aboard a ship. Social directors usually greet new arrivals and introduce them to other guests, explain the recreational facilities, and encourage guests to participate in planned activities. These activities may include card parties, games, contests, dances, musicals, or field trips and may require setting up equipment, arranging for transportation, or planning decorations, refreshments, or entertainment. In general, social directors try to create a friendly atmosphere, paying particular attention to lonely guests and trying to ensure that everyone has a good time.

Requirements

For some recreation positions, a high school diploma or an associate degree in parks and recreation, social work, or other human service discipline is sufficient preparation. However, most full-time career positions require a bachelor's degree, and a graduate degree is often a necessity for high-level administrative posts. Acceptable majors include parks and recreation management, leisure studies, fitness management, and related disciplines. A degree in any liberal arts field may be sufficient if the person's education includes courses relevant to recreation work.

In industrial recreation, employers usually prefer applicants with a bachelor's degree in recreation and a strong background in business administration. Some jobs require specialized training in a particular field, such as art, music, drama, or athletics. Others need special certifications, such as a lifesaving certificate to teach swimming. In addition to specialized training, students interested in recreation work should get a broad liberal arts and cultural education and acquire at least a working knowledge of arts and crafts, music, dance, drama, athletics, and nature study.

Over 200 community and junior colleges offer associate degrees in parks and recreation programs, and about 300 colleges and universities have similar, but more extensive programs leading to a bachelor's, master's, or doctoral degree. In 1997, there were ninety-three parks and recreation curriculums at the bachelor's degree level accredited by the National Recreation and Park Association.

Many recreation professionals apply for certification as evidence of their professional competence. The National Recreation and Park Association, the American Camping Association, and the National Employee Services and Recreation Association award certificates to individuals who meet their standards. In the 1990s, more than forty states had adopted NRPA standards for park/recreation professionals.

The federal government employs many recreation leaders in national parks, the armed forces, the Department of Veterans Affairs, and correctional institutions. It may be necessary to pass a civil service examination to qualify for these jobs.

Personal qualifications for recreation work include a desire to work with people, outgoing personality, even temperament, and ability to lead and influence others. Recreation workers should have good health and stamina, and should be able to stay calm and think clearly and quickly in emergencies.

Opportunities for Experience & Exploration

Young people interested in the recreation field should obtain related work experience while in high school or college as part-time or summer workers or volunteers in recreation departments, neighborhood centers, camps, and other organizations.

Methods of Entering

College placement offices are useful in helping graduates find employment. Most college graduates begin as either recreation leaders or specialists and, after several years' experience, may become recreation directors. A few enter trainee programs leading directly to recreation administration within a year or so. Those with graduate training may start as recreation directors.

Advancement

Recreation leaders without graduate training will find advancement limited, but it is possible to obtain better-paying positions through a combination of education and experience. With experience it is possible to become a recreation director. With further experience, directors may become supervisors and eventually head of all recreation departments or divisions in a city. Some recreation professionals go to work for themselves and become consultants.

Employment Outlook

There were about 233,000 recreation workers, not counting summer workers or volunteers, in 1996. More than 50 percent worked for government agencies, mostly at the municipal or county level. Nearly 20 percent were employed by civic, social, fraternal, or religious membership organizations such as the Boy Scouts, YWCA, or Red Cross. The rest worked in social service organizations such as centers for seniors and adult day care, and residential-care facilities, such as halfway houses, institutions for delinquent youths, and group homes or commercial recreation establishments and private industry.

Employment opportunities for recreation workers are expected to increase faster than the average through the end of 2006. The expected expansion in the recreation field will result from increased leisure time and income for the population as a whole combined with a continuing interest in fitness and health and a growing elderly population in nursing homes, senior centers, and retirement communities. There also is a demand for recreation workers to conduct activity programs for special needs groups.

Two areas promising the most favorable opportunities for recreation workers are the commercial recreation and social service industries. Commercial recreation establishments include amusement parks, sports and entertainment centers, wilderness and survival enterprises, tourist attractions, vacation excursions, hotels and other resorts, camps, health spas, athletic clubs, and apartment complexes. New employment opportunities will arise in social service agencies such as senior centers, halfway houses, children's homes, and day-care programs for the mentally or developmentally disabled.

Recreation programs that depend on government funding are most likely to be affected in times of economic downturns when budgets are reduced. During such times, competition will increase significantly for jobs in the private sector.

In any case, competition is expected to be keen because the field is open to college graduates regardless of major; as a result, there are more applicants than there are job openings. Opportunities will be best for individuals who have formal training in recreation and for those with previous experience.

Earnings

Full-time recreation workers earned an average of $18,700 a year in 1996. Some earned up to $37,500 or more, depending on job responsibilities and experience. Some top level managers can make considerably more.

Salaries in industrial recreation are higher. Newly hired recreation workers in industry have starting salaries of about $18,000 to $24,000 a year. Camp directors average about $1,600 per month in municipally operated camps; in private camps, earnings are higher. Camp counselors employed seasonally are paid anywhere from $200 to $800 a month. Recreation workers in the federal government start at about $14,800 a year.

Most public and private recreation agencies provide benefits such as paid vacation, sick leave, and hospital insurance.

Conditions of Work

Physical conditions vary greatly from outdoor parks to nursing homes for the elderly. A recreation worker can choose the conditions under which he or she would like to work. Recreation workers with an interest in the outdoors may become camp counselors. Those who have an interest in travel may seek a job as a social director on a cruise ship. There are opportunities for people who want to help the elderly or mentally handicapped, as well as for people with an interest in drama or music.

Generally, recreation workers must work while others engage in leisure activities. Most recreation workers spend forty hours a week working. But they should expect, especially those just entering the field, some night and weekend work. A compensating factor is the pleasure of helping people enjoy themselves.

Many of the positions are part time or seasonal, and many full-time recreation workers spend more time performing management duties than in leading hands-on activities.

Sources of Additional Information

American Association for Leisure and Recreation
1900 Association Drive
Reston, VA 22091
Tel: 703-476-3472
Email: aalr@aalrperd.org
WWW: http://www.aalr.org

American Camping Association
5000 State Road, 67 North
Martinsville, IN 46151-7902
Tel: 317-342-8456

For information on placement and accreditation, write:

National Recreation and Park Association
2775 South Quincy Street, Suite 300
Arlington, VA 22206
Tel: 703-820-4940
Email: info@nrpa.org
WWW: http://www.nrpa.org

National Employee Services and Recreation Association
2211 York Road, Suite 207
Oak Brook, IL 60521-2371
Tel: 630-368-1280

Reporters and Correspondents

Definition

Reporters and *correspondents* are the foot soldiers for newspapers, magazines, and television and radio broadcast companies. They gather and analyze information about current events and write stories for publication in newspapers and magazines or for broadcast on radio and television. Correspondents are reporters who cover the news in outlying areas or foreign countries.

Nature of the Work

Reporters and correspondents collect information on newsworthy events and prepare stories for newspaper or magazine publication or for radio or television broadcast. The stories may simply provide information about local, state, or national events, or they may present opposing points of view on issues of current interest. In this latter capacity, the press plays an important role in monitoring the actions of public officials and others in positions of power.

Stories may originate as an assignment from an editor or as the result of a lead or news tip. Good reporters are always on the lookout for good story ideas. To cover a story, they gather and verify facts by interviewing people involved in or related to the event, examining documents and public records, observing events as they happen, and researching relevant background information. Reporters generally take notes or use a tape recorder as they collect information, and write their stories once they return to their offices. In order to meet a deadline, they may have to telephone the stories to *rewriters,* who write or transcribe the stories for them. After the facts have been gathered and verified, the reporters transcribe their notes, organize their material, and determine what emphasis, or slant, to give the news. The story is then written to meet prescribed standards of editorial style and format.

The basic functions of reporters are to observe events objectively and impartially, record them accurately, and explain

School Subjects
English
(writing/literature)
Journalism

Personal Interests
Computers
Writing

Work Environment
Indoors and outdoors
Primarily multiple
locations

Minimum Education Level
Bachelor's degree

Salary Range
$16,000 to
$25,000 to
$100,000+

Certification or Licensing
None

Outlook
Decline

DOT
131

GOE
11.08.02

NOC
5123

what the news means in a larger, societal context. Within this framework, there are several types of reporters.

The most basic is the *newspaper reporter.* This job involves covering a beat, such as the police station or courthouse. It may involve receiving general assignments, such as a story about a school board meeting or an obituary of a community leader. Large daily papers may assign teams of reporters to investigate social, economic, or political events and conditions.

Many newspaper, *wire service,* and *magazine reporters* specialize in one type of story, either because they have a particular interest in the subject or because they have acquired the expertise to analyze and interpret news in that particular subject area. *Feature reporters* cover stories for a specific department, such as medicine, politics, foreign affairs, sports, consumer affairs, finance, fashion, art, theater, travel, social events, science, business, education, labor, and religion. They often write features explaining the history that has led up to certain events in the field they cover. *Editorial writers* and *syndicated news columnists* present viewpoints that, although based on a thorough knowledge, are opinions on topics of popular interest. *News columnists* write under a byline and usually specialize in a particular subject, such as politics or governmental activities. *Critics* review restaurants, books, works of art, movies, plays, musical performances, and other cultural events.

Specializing allows reporters to present the news most effectively because it focuses their efforts, talent, and knowledge on one area of expertise. Also, specializing in one field allows reporters more opportunities to develop contacts and sources necessary to gain access to the news and use them repeatedly.

Correspondents report events in locations distant from their home offices. They may report news by mail, telephone, fax, or computer from rural areas, large cities throughout the United States, or countries. Many large newspapers, magazines and broadcast companies have one correspondent who is responsible for covering all the news for the foreign city or country where they are based.

Reporters on small or weekly newspapers not only cover all aspects of the news in their communities, but they also may take photographs, write editorials and headlines, lay out pages, edit wire-service copy, and help with general office work. *Television reporters* may have to be photogenic as well as talented and resourceful: they may at times present live reports, filmed by a mobile camera unit at the scene where the news originates, or they may tape interviews and narration for later broadcast.

Requirements

A bachelor's degree is essential for aspiring reporters. Graduate degrees give students a great advantage over those entering the field with lesser degrees. Most editors prefer applicants with degrees in journalism because their studies include liberal arts courses as well as professional training in journalism. Some editors consider it sufficient for a reporter to have a good general education from a liberal arts college. Others prefer applicants with an undergraduate degree in liberal arts and a master's degree in journalism. The great majority of journalism graduates hired today by newspapers, wire services, and magazines have majored specifically in news-editorial journalism. High school courses that provide a firm foundation for a career as reporter include English, journalism, social studies, speech, typing, and computer science.

More than 400 colleges offer programs in journalism leading to a bachelor's degree. In these schools, around three-fourths of a student's time is devoted to a liberal education and one-fourth to the professional study of journalism, with required courses such as introductory mass media, basic reporting and copy editing, history of journalism, and press law and ethics. Students are encouraged to select other journalism courses according to their specific interests.

Journalism courses and programs are also offered by more than 350 community and junior colleges. Graduates of these programs are prepared to go to work directly as general assignment reporters, but they may encounter difficulty when competing with graduates of four-year programs. Credit earned in community and junior colleges may be transferable to four-year programs in journalism at other colleges and universities. Journalism training may also be obtained in the armed forces. Names and addresses of newspapers and a list of journalism schools and departments are published in the *Editor and Publisher International Year Book,* which is available for reference in most public libraries and newspaper offices.

A master's degree in journalism may be earned at more than 100 schools, and a doctorate at about 20 schools. Graduate degrees may prepare students specifically for news careers, careers as journalism teachers, researchers, and theorists, or for jobs in advertising or public relations.

A reporter's liberal arts training should include courses in English (with an emphasis on writing), sociology, political science, economics, history, psychology, business, speech, and computer science. Knowledge of foreign languages is also useful. To be a reporter in a specialized field, such as science or finance, requires concentrated coursework in that area.

A crucial requirement for reporters is typing skill. Reporters type their own stories using word processing programs. Although not essential, a knowledge of shorthand or speedwriting can make note taking easier, and an acquaintance with news photography is an asset.

Opportunities for Experience & Exploration

There are a number of ways in which interested students can explore a career as a reporter or correspondent. They can talk to reporters and editors at local newspapers and radio and TV stations. They can interview the admissions counselor at the school of journalism closest to their homes.

In addition to taking courses in English, journalism, social studies, speech, computer science, and typing, high school students can acquire practical experience by working on school newspapers or on a church, synagogue, or mosque newsletter. Part-time and summer jobs on newspapers provide invaluable experience to the aspiring reporter.

College students can develop their reporting skills in the laboratory courses or workshops that are part of the journalism curriculum. College students might also accept jobs as campus correspondents for selected newspapers. People who work as part-time reporters covering news in a particular area of a community are known as *stringers* and are paid only for those stories that are printed.

More than 3,000 journalism scholarships, fellowships, and assistantships are offered by universities, newspapers, foundations, and professional organizations to college students. Many newspapers and magazines offer summer internships to journalism students for the purpose of providing them with practical experience in a variety of basic reporting and editing duties. Students who successfully complete internships are usually placed in jobs more quickly upon graduation than those without such experience.

Methods of Entering

Jobs in this field may be obtained through college placement offices or by applying directly to the personnel departments of individual employers. Applicants with some practical experience will have an advantage; they should be prepared to present a portfolio of material they wrote as volunteer or part-time reporters or other writing samples.

Most beginners start out as general assignment reporters or copy editors for small publications. A few outstanding journalism graduates may be hired by large city newspapers or national magazines, but they are the exception, as large employers usually require several years' experience. As a rule, novice reporters cover routine assignments, such as reporting on civic and club meetings, writing obituaries, summarizing speeches, interviewing important visitors to the community, and covering police court proceedings. As reporters become more skilled, they are assigned to more important events or to a regular beat or they specialize in a particular field.

Many graduates of journalism schools accept jobs at small publications as general assignment reporters or copy editors and are promoted to more important, special assignments as they gain some experience and job openings develop. The small number of outstanding journalism graduates who are hired immediately by large city newspapers and national magazines are trained on the job.

Advancement

Reporters may advance by moving to larger newspapers or press services, but competition for such positions is unusually keen. Many highly qualified reporters apply for these jobs every year.

A select number of reporters eventually become columnists, correspondents, editorial writers, editors, or top executives. These important and influential positions represent the top of the field, and there is strong competition for them.

Many reporters transfer the contacts and knowledge developed in newspaper reporting to related fields such as public relations, advertising, or preparing copy for radio and television news programs.

Employment Outlook

According to the U.S. Department of Labor, of the approximately 70,000 reporters and correspondents employed in 1996, about 70 percent worked for newspapers of all sizes. The rest were employed by wire services, magazines, and radio and television broadcasting companies.

The employment outlook for reporters and correspondents is expected to decline through the year 2006. Newspapers folding, or consolidating with others, as well as smaller circulation numbers have decreased the number of reporters needed. Many job openings will occur as the result of retirement. Openings will be limited on big city dailies. Because of an increase in the number of small community and suburban daily and weekly newspapers, opportunities will be best for journalism graduates who are willing to relocate and accept relatively low starting salaries. With experience, reporters on these small papers can move up to editorial positions or may choose to transfer to reporting jobs on larger newspapers or magazines. Part time workers, or stringers, will be in demand, as will writers for on-line publications.

Applicants will face strong competition for jobs on large metropolitan newspapers. Experience is a definite requirement, which rules out most new graduates unless they possess credentials in an area for which the publication has a pressing need. Occasionally, a beginner can use contacts and experience gained through internship programs and summer jobs to obtain a reporting job immediately after graduation.

A significant number of jobs will be provided by magazines and in radio and television broadcasting, but the major news magazines and larger broadcasting stations generally prefer experienced reporters. For beginning correspondents, small stations with local news broadcasts will continue to replace staff who move on to larger stations or leave the business. Network hiring has been cut drastically in the past few years and will probably continue to decline.

Overall, the prospects are best for graduates who have majored in news-editorial journalism and completed an internship while in school. The top graduates in an accredited program will have a great advantage, as will talented technical or scientific writers. Small newspapers prefer to hire beginning reporters who are acquainted with the community and are willing to help with photography and other aspects of production. Without at least a bachelor's degree in journalism, applicants will find it increasingly difficult to obtain even an entry-level position.

An indication of the growing competition in this field is the expected rise in enrollments in journalism education programs through the 1990s. Those with doctorates and practical reporting experience may find teaching positions at four-year colleges and universities, while highly qualified reporters with master's degrees may obtain employment in journalism departments of community and junior colleges.

This occupation is affected by the health of the economy. During a recession, new hiring is curbed, or suspended; some reporters may lose their positions.

Earnings

There are great variations in the earnings of reporters. Salaries are related to experience, kind of employer for which the reporter works, geographical location, and whether the reporter is covered by a contract negotiated by the Newspaper Guild.

In 1996, reporters on daily newspapers having Newspaper Guild contracts received salaries that ranged from about $342 to $742 or more a week. The majority earn approximately $448 a week. Some top reporters on big city dailies earn even more, on the basis of merit or level of experience.

According to a 1996 survey conducted by the National Association of Broadcasters, reporters who work for radio earn an average salary of $16,000 a year. Some who work for stations in large cities may earn up to $38,500. Reporters who work in television earn between $17,500 and $79,600, depending on the size of the station. High-profile reporters and newscasters working for prestigious papers or network television stations earn over $100,000 a year.

Conditions of Work

Reporters and correspondents work under a great deal of pressure in settings that differ from the typical business office. Their jobs generally require a five-day, thirty-five to forty-hour week, but overtime and irregular schedules are very common because deadlines have to be met and late-breaking developments often make it necessary to update an earlier report. Reporters employed by morning papers start work in the late afternoon and finish around midnight, while those on afternoon or evening papers start early in the morning and work until early or mid-afternoon. Foreign correspondents often work late at night to send the news to their papers in time to meet printing deadlines.

The day of the smoky, ink-stained newsroom has passed, but newspaper offices are still hectic places. Reporters have to work amid the clatter of typewriters and other machines, loud voices engaged in telephone conversations, and the bustle created by people hurrying about. An atmosphere of excitement and bustle prevails especially as press deadlines approach.

Travel is often required in this occupation, and some assignments may be dangerous, such as covering wars, political uprisings, fires, floods, and other events of a volatile nature.

Sources of
Additional Information

◼️**Association for Education in Journalism and Mass Communication**
University of South Carolina
1621 College Street
Columbia, SC 29208
Tel: 803-777-2005

To receive a copy of The Journalist's Road to Success, which lists schools offering degrees in news-editorial, and financial aid to those interested in print journalism, please contact:

◼️**Dow Jones Newspaper Fund**
PO Box 300
Princeton, NJ 08543-0300
Tel: 609-452-2820
Email: newsfund@plink.geis.com

To receive a free copy of Newspaper: What's in It for Me? *write:*

◼️**Newspaper Careers Project**
Fulfillment Department
NAA Foundation
11600 Sunrise Valley Drive
Reston, VA 22091

Restaurant and Food Service Managers

Definition

Restaurant and food service managers are responsible for the overall operation of businesses that serve food. Food service work includes the purchasing of a variety of food, selection of the menu, preparation of the food, and, most importantly, maintenance of health and sanitation levels. It is the responsibility of managers to oversee staffing for each task in addition to performing the business and accounting functions of restaurant operations.

Nature of the Work

Restaurant and food service managers work in restaurants ranging from elegant hotel dining rooms to fast-food restaurants. They also may work in food service facilities ranging from school cafeterias to hospital food services. Whatever the setting, these managers coordinate and direct the work of the employees who prepare and serve food and perform other related functions. They are responsible for buying the food and equipment necessary for the operation of the restaurant or facility. They may help with menu planning. Periodically they inspect the premises to ensure the maintenance of health and sanitation regulations. They perform many clerical and financial duties, such as keeping records, directing payroll operations, handling large sums of money, and taking inventories. Their work usually involves much contact with customers and vendors, such as taking suggestions, handling complaints, and creating a friendly atmosphere. Restaurant managers generally supervise any advertising or sales promotion for their operation.

In some very large restaurants and institutional food service facilities, the manager is assisted by one or more *assistant managers* and an *executive chef* or *food manager*. These specially trained assistants oversee service in the dining room and other areas of the operation and supervise the kitchen staff and preparation of all foods served.

School Subjects
Business
Family and Consumer Science

Personal Interests
Business management
Cooking

Work Environment
Primarily indoors
Primarily one location

Minimum Education Level
High school diploma

Salary Range
$21,000 to
$30,000 to
$50,000+

Certification or Licensing
None

Outlook
Faster than the average

DOT
319

GOE
09.05.02

NOC
0631

Restaurant and food service managers are responsible for the success of their establishment. They continually analyze every aspect of its operation and make whatever changes are needed to guarantee its profitability.

These duties are common, in varying degrees, to both owner-managers of relatively small restaurants and to nonowner-managers who may be salaried employees in large restaurants institutional food service facilities. The owner-manager of a restaurant is more likely to be involved in service functions, sometimes operating the cash register, waiting on tables, and performing a wide variety of tasks.

Requirements

Educational requirements for restaurant and food service managers vary greatly. In many cases, no specific requirements exist and managerial positions are filled by promoting experienced food and beverage preparation and service workers. However, as more colleges offer programs in restaurant and institutional food service management—programs that combine academic work with on-the-job experience—more restaurant and food service chains are seeking individuals with this training.

In the 1990s, more than 160 colleges and universities offer four-year programs leading to a bachelor's degree in restaurant and hotel management or institutional food service management. Some individuals qualify for management training by earning an associate degree or other formal award below the baccalaureate from one of the more than 800 community and junior colleges, technical institutes, or other institutions that offer programs in these fields. Students hired as management trainees by restaurant chains and food service management companies undergo vigorous training programs.

Experience in all areas of restaurant and food service work is an important requirement for successful managers. Managers must be familiar with the various operations of the establishment: food preparation, service operations, sanitary regulations, and financial functions.

One of the most important requirements for restaurant and food service managers is to have good business knowledge. They must possess a high degree of technical knowledge in handling business details, such as buying large items of machinery and equipment and large quantities of food. Desirable personality characteristics include poise, self-confidence, and an ability to get along with people. Managers may be on their feet for long periods, and the hours of work may be both long and irregular.

Opportunities for Experience & Exploration

Practical restaurant and food service experience is usually easy to get. In colleges with curriculum offerings in these areas, summer jobs in all phases of the work are available and, in some cases, required. Some restaurant and food service chains provide on-the-job training in management.

Methods of Entering

Many restaurants and food service facilities provide self-sponsored, on-the-job training for prospective managers. There are still cases in which people work hard and move up the ladder within the organization's workforce, finally arriving at the managerial position. More and more, people with higher educational backgrounds and specialized training move directly into manager-trainee positions and then on to a managerial position.

Advancement

In large restaurants and food service organizations, promotion opportunities are frequent for employees with a knowledge of the overall operation. Experience in all aspects of the work is an important consideration for the food service employee who desires advancement. The employee with a knowledge of kitchen operations may advance from pantry supervisor to food manager, assistant manager, and finally to restaurant or food service manager. Similar advancement is possible for dining room workers with a knowledge of kitchen operations.

Advancement to top executive positions is possible for managers employed by large restaurant and institutional food service chains. A good educational background and some specialized training are increasingly valuable assets to employees who hope to advance.

Employment Outlook

The industry is rapidly growing and employs about 493,000 professional managers. Opportunities for well-qualified restaurant and food service managers appear to be excellent through the year 2006, especially for those with bachelor's or associate degrees. New restaurants are always opening to meet increasing demand. It has been estimated that at least 25 percent of all of the food consumed in the United States is eaten in restaurants and hotels.

Many job openings will arise from the need to replace managers retiring from the workforce. Also, population growth will result in an increased demand for eating establishments, and in turn, a need for managers to oversee them. As the elderly population increases, managers will be needed to staff dining rooms located in hospitals and nursing homes.

Economic downswings have a great effect on eating and drinking establishments. During a recession, people have less money to spend on luxuries such as dining out, thus hurting the restaurant business. However, with more women working outside the home, eating out, or purchasing carry out food from a restaurant is quickly becoming a necessity.

Earnings

The earnings of salaried restaurant and food service managers vary a great deal, depending on the type and size of the establishment. According to a 1995 salary survey conducted by the National Restaurant Association, manager-trainees earned an average salary of $21,000 a year. Those working in larger restaurants and food service facilities received about $30,000. In addition, most trainees earn annual bonuses or incentive payments ranging from $1,000 to $3,000. Experienced managers receive an average of approximately $30,000 a year. Those in charge of the largest restaurants and institutional food service facilities often earn over $50,000. Managers of fast-food restaurants average about $21,000 a year. In addition to a base salary, most managers receive bonuses based on profits, which can range from $2,000 to $7,500 a year.

Conditions of Work

Work environments are usually pleasant. There is usually a great deal of activity involved in preparing and serving food to large numbers of people, and managers usually work forty to forty-eight hours a week. In some cafeterias, especially those located within an industry or business establishment, hours are regular, and little evening work is required. Many restaurants serve late dinners, however, necessitating the manager to remain on duty during a late evening work period.

Many restaurants furnish meals to employees during their work hours. Annual bonuses, group plan pensions, hospitalization, medical, and other benefits may be offered to restaurant managers.

Sources of Additional Information

Council on Hotel, Restaurant, and Institutional Education
1200 17th Street, NW
Washington, DC 20036-3097
Tel: 202-331-5990
Email: alliance@access.digex.net

Educational Foundation of the National Restaurant Association
250 South Wacker Drive, Suite 1400
Chicago, IL 60606

Canadian Restaurant and Food Services Association
316 Bloor Street, West
Toronto, ON M5S 1W5 Canada
Tel: 416-923-8416
Email: 102477.3104@compuserve.com

Retail Managers

Definition

Retail managers are responsible for the profitable operation of retail trade establishments. They oversee the selling of food, clothing, furniture, sporting goods, novelties, and many other items. Their duties include hiring, training, and supervising other employees, maintaining the physical facilities, managing inventory, monitoring expenditures and receipts, and maintaining good public relations.

Nature of the Work

Retail managers are responsible for every phase of a store's operation. They are often one of the first employees to arrive in the morning and the last to leave at night. Their duties include hiring, training, and supervising other employees, maintaining the physical facilities, managing inventory, monitoring expenditures and receipts, and maintaining good public relations.

Perhaps the most important responsibility is hiring and training qualified employees. Managers then assign duties to employees, monitor their progress, and promote and increase salaries when appropriate. When an employee is not performing satisfactorily, a manager must find a way to improve the performance or, if necessary, fire him or her.

Managers should be good at working with other people. Differences of opinion and personality clashes among employees are inevitable, and the manager must be able to restore good feelings among the staff. Managers often have to deal with customers' grievances and must attempt to restore goodwill toward the store when customers are dissatisfied.

Retail managers keep accurate and up-to-date records of store inventory. When new merchandise arrives, the manager ensures items are recorded, priced, and displayed or shelved. When stock is getting low so that new items can be ordered.

School Subjects
Business
Mathematics

Personal Interests
Business management
Helping people: personal service

Work Environment
Primarily indoors
Primarily one location

Minimum Education Level
High school diploma

Salary Range
$13,000 to
$34,000 to
$100,000+

Certification or Licensing
None

Outlook
More slowly than the average

DOT
185

GOE
11.11.05

NOC
6211

Some managers are responsible for advertising and merchandise promotions. The manager might confer with an ad agency representative to determine appropriate advertising for the store. The manager also may decide what products to put on sale for advertising purposes.

The duties of store managers vary according to the type of merchandise sold, size of store, and number of employees. In small, owner-operated stores, managers are often involved in accounting, data processing, marketing, research, sales, and shipping. In large retail corporations, however, managers may be involved in only one or two activities.

Requirements

A minimum high school education is generally required for this position. Most retail stores prefer applicants with a college degree, and many hire only college graduates. Liberal arts, social sciences, and business are the most common degrees held by retail managers. One survey of retail store managers without college degrees suggested that many believed coursework in business and economics would have been helpful to their careers.

To prepare for a career as a retail store manager, students should take courses in accounting, business, marketing, English, and advertising. Those unable to attend college as a full-time student should consider obtaining a job in a store to gain experience and attending college part time. All managers, regardless of their education, must have good marketing, analytical, communications, and people skills.

Many large retail stores and national chains have established formal training programs, including classroom instruction, for their new employees. The training period may last a week or as long as one year. Training for a department store manager, for example, may include working as a salesperson in several departments in order to learn about the store's operations.

Opportunities for Experience & Exploration

People interested in becoming retail managers may be able to find part-time, weekend, or summer jobs in a clothing store, supermarket, or other retail trade establishment. Students can gain valuable work experience through such jobs and will have the opportunity to observe the retail industry to determine whether they are interested in pursuing a career in it. It also is useful to read periodicals, such as *Mass Market Retailers* and *Stores,* that publish articles on the retail field.

Methods of Entering

Many new college graduates are able to find managerial positions through their schools' placement service. Some of the large retail chains engage in campus recruitment.

Not all store managers, however, are college graduates. Many store managers have been promoted to their positions from jobs of less responsibility within the organization. Some may have been in the retail industry for more than a dozen years before being promoted. Those with more education often receive promotions faster.

Regardless of educational background, people who are interested in the retail industry should consider working, at least part time or during the summer, in a retail store. Although there might not be an opening when the application is made, there is often a high turnover of employees, and vacancies occur from time to time.

Advancement

Advancement opportunities in retailing vary according to the size of the store, where city the store is located, and type of merchandise sold. Advancement also depends on the individual's work experience and educational background.

A store manager who works for a large retail chain, for example, may be given responsibility for a number of stores in a given area or region or transferred to a larger store in another city. The willingness to relocate to a new city may increase an employee's promotional opportunities.

Some managers decide to open their own stores after they have acquired enough experience in the retail industry. After working as a retail manager for a large chain of clothing stores, for example, a person may decide to open a small boutique.

Sometimes becoming a retail manager involves a series of promotions. A person who works in a supermarket, for example, may advance from clerk, checker, or bagger to a regular assignment in one of several departments in the store. After a certain amount of time, the person may become an assistant manager and eventually, a manager.

Employment Outlook

The number of retail managers is expected to decrease compared to the average of all occupations through the year 2006. Competition for jobs will continue to increase as companies implement computerized systems for inventory control, reducing the need for some managers. Also, many companies are cutting their sales staff, choosing instead to give added responsibilities to current sales people and managers. Applicants with the best educational backgrounds and work experience will have the best chances of finding jobs.

Earnings

Salaries for retail managers vary with the size of the store, its ownership, and number of customers. Large retail chains generally offer higher salaries than small, individually owned stores. A typical starting salary for a store manager is about $13,000 a year. Assistant store managers begin at even less money. Managers in charge of several retail stores make at least $34,000 a year, and some earn more than $60,000. Some high-level retail managers—for example, those in charge of an entire region—make more than $100,000 a year.

In addition to a salary, some stores offer their managers special bonuses, or commissions, which are typically connected to the store's performance. Many stores also offer employee discounts on store merchandise.

Conditions of Work

Most retail stores are pleasant places to work, and managers are often given comfortable offices. Many, however, work long hours. Managers often work six days a week and as many as sixty hours a week, especially during busy times of the year, such as the Christmas season. Because holiday seasons are peak shopping periods, it is extremely rare that managers can take holidays off or schedule vacations around a holiday, even if the store is not open on that day.

Although managers can usually get away from the store during slack times, they often must be present if the store is open at night. It is important that the manager be available to handle the store's daily receipts, which are often put in a safe or taken to a bank's night depository at the close of the business day.

Sources of Additional Information

■ **National Retail Federation**
325 7th Street, NW, Suite 1000
Washington, DC 20004
Tel: 202-783-7971

Robotics Engineers and Technicians

Definition

Robotics engineers design, develop, build, and program robots and robotic devices, including peripheral equipment and computer software used to control robots. *Robotics technicians* assist robotics engineers in a wide variety of tasks relating to the design, development, production, testing, operation, repair, and maintenance of robots and robotic devices.

Nature of the Work

The majority of robotics engineers and technicians work within the field of computer integrated manufacturing (CIM) or programmable automation. Using computer science technology, engineers design and develop robots and other automated equipment, including computer software used to program robots.

The title, robotics engineer, may be used to refer to any engineer who works primarily with robots. In many cases, these engineers may have been trained as mechanical, electronic, computer, or manufacturing engineers. A small, but growing, number of engineers trained specially in robotics are graduating from colleges and universities with robotics engineering or closely related degrees.

Robotics engineers have a thorough understanding of robotic systems and equipment and know the different technologies available to create robots for specific applications. They have a strong foundation in computer systems and how computers are linked to robots. They also have an understanding of manufacturing production requirements and how robots can best be used in automated systems to achieve cost efficiency, productivity, and quality. Robotics engineers may analyze and evaluate a manufacturer's operating system to determine whether robots can be used efficiently instead of humans and other automated equipment.

School Subjects
Computer science
Mathematics

Personal Interests
Building things
Computers

Work Environment
Primarily indoors
Primarily one location

Minimum Education Level
Bachelor's degree for engineers
High school diploma for technicians

Salary Range
$19,500 to
$30,000 to
$60,000

Certification or Licensing
None

Outlook
About as fast as the average

Many other types of engineers are also involved in the design, development, fabrication, programming, and operation of robots. Following are brief descriptions of these types of engineers and how they relate to robotics.

Electrical and electronics engineers research, design, and develop the electrical systems used in robots and the power supply, if it is electrical. These engineers may specialize in areas such as integrated circuit theory, lasers, electronic sensors, optical components, and energy power systems.

Mechanical engineers are involved in the design, fabrication, and operation of the mechanical systems of a robot. These engineers need a strong working knowledge of mechanical components such as gripper mechanisms, bearings, gears, chains, belts, and actuators. Some robots are controlled by pneumatic or mechanical power supplies and these engineers need to be specialists in designing thcsc systems. Mechanical engineers also select the material used to make robots. They test robots once they are constructed.

Computer engineers design the computer systems that are used to program robots. Sometimes these systems are built into a robot and othertimes they are a part of separate equipment that is used to control robots. Some computer engineers also write computer programs.

Industrial engineers are specialists in manufacturing operations. They determine the physical layout of a factory to best utilize production equipment. They may determine the placement of robotic equipment. They also are responsible for safety rules and practices and for ensuring that robotic equipment is used properly.

CAD/CAM (computer-aided design/computer-aided manufacturing) engineers are experts in automated production processes. They design and supervise manufacturing systems that utilize robots and other automated equipment.

Manufacturing engineers manage the entire production process. They may evaluate production operations to determine whether robots can be used in an assembly line and make recommendations on purchasing robotic equipment. Some manufacturing engineers design robots.

Scientists are also involved in the design and development of robots. Some scientists, called *robotics designers,* study anatomy of the human body and kinesiology (the study of movement of muscles) to design robots with flexible parts that can perform very specific functions. For example, these scientists may work on designing robots with flexible wrist motions that are capable of performing precise turning motions. Researchers and scientists in biomechanics also study the human body and design and develop devices that simulate the working of the human body. For example, they may work on creating mechanical hands made of synthetic materials that resemble the texture of skin.

Some engineers and scientists specialize in a specific area of robotics, such as artificial intelligence (AI), vision systems, and sensor systems. These specialists are developing robots with "brains" that are similar to human beings. Robots with AI would have the ability to learn from their mistakes and would have exceptional powers. Vision systems is another highly specialized field of robotics. This technology allows a robot to receive a visual image, process it, and understand what it means. For example, computers with optical character recognition would have optical scanning built into their vision systems. This would allow them to read signs and labels. Another growing technology is speech recognition. This would allow robots to understand and respond to voice signals. Advanced sensor technology is being developed to increase robots' abilities to use sensors that resemble human senses. For example, robots are being developed that can detect carbon monoxide emissions through smell sensors and that can analyze a chemical sample through taste sensors.

Another important contributor to robotics is the *computer programmer,* or *robotics programmer.* These specialists write sets of instructions, called software programs, that control robots. Programmers use standard computer languages such as FORTRAN and Pascal to write computer programs. They also need to be familiar with manufacturing applications protocol programs that relate directly to robots and other types of automated equipment. Some robotics engineers and robotics technicians also program robots.

Robotics technicians assist in all phases of robotics engineering. They install, repair, and maintain finished robots. Others help design and develop new kinds of robotics equipment.

Technicians who install, repair, and maintain robots and robotic equipment need a knowledge of electronics, electrical circuitry, mechanics, pneumatics, hydraulics, and computer programming. They use hand and power tools, testing instruments, manuals, schematic diagrams, and blueprints.

Before installing new equipment, they review the work order and instructional information; verify that the intended site in the factory is correctly supplied with the necessary electrical wires, switches, circuit breakers, and other parts; position and secure the robot in place, sometimes using a crane or other large tools and equipment; and attach various cables and hoses, such as those that connect a hydraulic power unit with the robot. After making sure that the equipment is operational, technicians program the robot for specified tasks, using their knowledge of the robot's programming language. They may write the detailed instructions that program robots or reprogram a robot when changes are needed.

Once robots are in place and functioning, they may develop problems. Technicians are then called upon to test components and locate faulty parts. When the problem is found, they may replace or recalibrate parts. Sometimes they suggest changes in circuitry or programming, or may install different end-of-arm tools on robots to allow machines to perform new functions. They may train robotics operators in how to operate robots and related equipment and help establish in-house basic maintenance and repair programs at new installations.

Companies that only have one or a few robots may not hire their own robotics technicians. In this case, they use *robot field technicians* who work for a robotic manufacturer. These technicians travel to manufacturing sites and other locations where robots are used and repair and service robots and robotic equipment.

Technicians involved with the design and development of new robotic devices are sometimes referred to as *robotics design technicians*. As part of a design team, they work closely with robotics engineers. The robotics-design job starts as the engineers analyze the tasks and settings to be assigned and decide what kind of robotics system will best serve the necessary functions. They then establish the initial design for the system. Technicians become involved in the process by first familiarizing themselves with the specifications and with any diagrams, blueprints, or sketches provided. They then carry out prescribed tests on the systems and materials that have been proposed for the new robotic device. During this testing phase, they keep records of all test procedures and results. They may be asked to present written reports, tables, or charts to document the results of their tests. If a particular system, subsystem, or material has not met testing requirements, the technician may suggest a way to rearrange the system's components or to substitute alternate materials.

After this initial testing is completed, robotics design technicians often build a prototype of the robot. Often this phase requires technicians to make sketches or drafts of components. *Machine-shop workers* use these sketches and drafts to make the parts. Once all of the parts and materials have been collected, the technicians assemble and test the prototype. If it proves successful, they help produce the formal documentation, including blueprints and manufacturing specifications sheets, needed by the technicians and other workers who will assemble the production robots that will actually be put in use.

Technicians involved with robot assembly, sometimes referred to as *robot assemblers*, commonly specialize in one aspect of robot assembly. *Materials handling technicians* receive requests for components or materials, then locate and deliver them to the technicians doing the actual assembly or those performing tests on these materials or components. *Mechanical assembly technicians* put together components and subsystems and install them in the robot. *Electrical assembly technicians* do the same work as mechanical assembly technicians but specialize in electrical components such as circuit boards and automatic switching devices. Finally, some technicians test the finished assemblies to make sure the robot conforms to the original specifications.

Other kinds of robotics technicians include *robot operators,* who operate robots in specialized settings, and *robotics trainers,* who train other employees in the installation, use, and maintenance of robots.

Robotics technicians may also be referred to as *electromechanical technicians, manufacturing technicians, robot mechanics, robotics repairmen, robot service technicians*, and *installation robotics technicians*.

Requirements

Because changes occur so rapidly within this field, it is often recommended that engineers and technicians get a broad-based education that encompasses robotics but does not focus solely on robotics. Programs that provide the widest career base are those in automated manufacturing, which includes robotics, electronics, and computer science.

People planning to become engineers need to have the ability to think in scientific and technical terms, have an understanding of the theories behind scientific principles, and have strong academic backgrounds. Students need to have above-average grades in high school and score high on standardized tests such as the SAT or ACT.

In high school, students should take as many science, math, and computer classes as possible. Recommended courses are biology, chemistry, physics, algebra, trigonometry, geometry, calculus, graphics, computer science, English, speech, composition, social studies, and drafting. Classes in electronics and electricity are also helpful. People who plan on pursuing a degree beyond a bachelor of science need to have studied a foreign language.

In order to become an engineer it is necessary to earn a bachelor of science degree. These programs generally take four or five years to complete. Over 400 colleges and universities offer courses in robotics or related technology. Many different types of programs are available. Some colleges and universities offer robotics engineering degrees. Others offer engineering degrees with concentrations or options in robotics and manufacturing engineering. As previously mentioned, engineering programs that provide a strong base in automated manufacturing may provide more career options than one solely in robotics. Programs may be found in engineering, engineering technology, industrial technology, automated manufacturing, and manufacturing engineering technology.

Robotics programs are found under a variety of names. They may be called Industrial and Systems Engineering, Machine Intelligence and Robotics, Manufacturing Engineering, Manufacturing Science and Robotics, or Industrial Manufacturing. Coursework focuses on subjects such as robotics, CAD/CAM, hydraulics, pneumatics, microprocessors, logics, integrated systems, and numerical control.

Some colleges offer cooperative work programs or internships that require a student to work in the field for one or more semesters. In addition to being an excellent way to gain practical experience, many employers view this work experience as an important consideration when hiring recent college graduates.

Broad-based engineering programs that include automated manufacturing but do not focus exclusively on robotics may be found in any of the following programs: Mechanical Engineering, Industrial Engineering, Aeronautical Engineering, Aerospace Engineering, and Materials Engineering. Some engineers who work with robots get degrees in biomedical engineering.

For some higher-level jobs, such as robotics designer, a master of science or doctoral degree is required. These degrees require additional years of study beyond a bachelor's degree.

People planning on becoming robotics technicians need manual dexterity, good eye-hand coordination, and mechanical and electrical aptitudes. They also should take as many science, math, and computer classes as possible, with an emphasis on application rather than theory. In addition, they should take shop and vocational classes that teach blueprint and electrical schematic reading, the use of hand tools, drafting, and the basics of electricity and electronics.

Although the minimum educational requirement for a robotics technician is a high school diploma, many employers prefer to hire technicians who have received formal training beyond high school. Two-year programs are available in community colleges and technical institutes that grant an associate's degree upon completion. Programs that focus exclusively on

robotics may be named Robotics, Robotics Technology, Process Control, Robotics/Automation Option, Flexible Automation, or Industrial Engineering Technology. Programs with robotics-related degrees may be offered through community colleges with programs in manufacturing engineering, industrial technology, and other fields. These programs may be titled Engineering Technology, Manufacturing Technology, Manufacturing Engineering, Industrial Electromechanics, Industrial Electricity, Manufacturing Processes Technology, Industrial Production Technology, Machine Tool Technology, Electronics Technology, or Machine Design Technology.

Courses studied vary based on the specific type of program, but generally include classes in robotics, numerical control, microprocessors, tool design, manufacturing processes, CAD/CAM, maintenance and repair, hydraulics, integrated manufacturing systems, and logics.

The armed forces also offers technical programs that result in associate's degrees in electronics, biomedical equipment, and computer science. The military uses robotics and other advanced equipment and offers excellent training opportunities to members of the armed forces. This training is highly regarded by many employers and can prove to be an advantage in obtaining a civilian job in robotics.

Although most robotics technicians do not need to obtain a license or join a union in order to get a job, in some industrial settings or situations it may be required. People interested in careers in robotics need to have scientific and mathematical aptitudes, a desire to understand how things work, and problem-solving abilities.

Because robotics is a relatively young field, it is subject to many changes. Technology is changing very rapidly, and by the time finishes his or her education, new technologies will most likely be developed or be developing. Therefore, one of the most important requirements for a person interested in a career in robotics is the willingness to pursue additional training on an ongoing basis during his or her career. After completing their formal education, engineers and technicians may need to take additional classes in a college or university or take advantage of training offered through their employers and professional associations. Reading trade magazines and technical books about trends in the industry will also be essential in order to stay up-to-date on current technologies and employment trends.

Opportunities for Experience & Exploration

People interested in robotics can explore this field in many different ways. Because it is such a new field, it is important to learn as much as possible about current trends and recent technologies. Reading recently published materials, such as books and articles in trade magazines, provides an excellent way to learn about what is happening in terms of robotics technologies and expected future trends. Trade magazines with informative articles include *Robotics Engineering, Robotics Quarterly, Personal Robotics Magazine,* and *Robotics Today.*

Students can become robot hobbyists and build their own robots or buy toy robots and experiment with them. Complete robot kits are available through a number of companies and range from simple, inexpensive robots to highly complex robots with advanced features and accessories. A number of books are available that give instructions and helpful hints on building robots and can be found at most public libraries. People also may order books directly from publishers. In addition, relatively inexpensive and simple toy robots are available from electronics shops, department stores, and mail order companies.

Students may be able to find out the names of professionals working in the robotics industry and invite them to their school to speak about the work they do.

Students can also participate in competitions. The Robotics International of the Society of Manufacturing Engineers sponsors a contest called the Student Robotics Automation Contest. Held every year, it is open to middle school through university-level students. Eight different categories challenge students in areas such as problem-solving skills, robot construction, and teamwork ability. Another annual competition, the International Aerial Robotics Competition, is sponsored by the Association for Unmanned Vehicle Systems. This competition, which requires teams of students to build complex robots, is open to college students. (Addresses for both associations are listed at the end of this article.)

Before college, it is important to explore opportunities at educational institutions in depth. Library directories list many universities and colleges that offer robotics or related programs. Information about educational programs also may be obtained from professional associations, such as the Society for Manufacturing Engineers. Students should request information from as many schools as possible. If possible, arrange to visit a school and talk with students enrolled in a robotics program if possible.

College students may want to join student chapters of professional associations. Actively participating in meetings and events gives students the opportunity to meet and talk with people in the industry and to learn firsthand what these professionals do. In addition, many associations offer newsletters, trade publications, and other services. Associations charge a fee for membership, but in most cases student membership fees are relatively inexpensive.

Another great way to learn about robotics is to attend trade shows. Many robotics and automated machinery manufacturers exhibit their products at shows and conventions. Numerous such trade shows are held every year in different parts of the country. Information about these trade shows is available through association trade magazines and periodicals such as *Managing Automation.*

Other activities that foster knowledge and skills relevant to a career in robotics include membership in high school science clubs, participation in science fairs, and pursuing hobbies that involve electronics, mechanical equipment, and model building.

Methods of Entering

Many people entered robotics technician positions in the 1980s and early 1990s who were formerly employed as automotive workers, machinists, millwrights, computer repair technicians, and computer operators. In the mid- and late 1990s, some companies are retraining current employees to troubleshoot and repair robots rather than hiring new workers. Because of these trends, entry-level applicants without any work experience may have difficulty finding their first jobs. Students who have participated in a cooperative work program or internship have the advantage of some work experience.

Graduates of two- and four-year programs may be able to learn about available openings through their schools' job placement services. It also may be possible to learn about job openings through want ads in newspapers and trade magazines.

In many cases, it will be necessary to research companies that manufacture or use robots and apply directly to them. A number of directories are available that list such companies. One such directory is *Robotics and Vision Supplier Directory*. It is available for purchase from the Robotic Industries Association. Other directories that may be available at public or college libraries include *The CAD/CAM Industry Directory* and *Robotics, CAD/CAM Marketplace*.

Job opportunities may be good at small start-up companies or a start-up robotics unit of a large company. Many times these employers are willing to hire inexperienced workers as apprentices or assistants. Then, when their sales and production grow, these workers have the best chances for advancement.

Robotics engineers also may have difficulty finding their first jobs as many companies have retrained existing engineers in robotics. Job hunters may learn about job openings through their colleges' job placement services, advertisements in professional magazines and newspapers, or job fairs. In addition, recruiters may come to colleges to interview graduating students for prospective positions. In many cases, though, applicants will need to research a company using robotics engineers and apply directly to it.

Some companies give competency exams to applicants for technician positions to test their knowledge in such areas as engineering graphics, design of machine elements, industrial manufacturing, and safety principles.

Advancement

Engineers may start as part of an engineering team and do relatively simple tasks under the supervision of a project manager or more experienced engineer. With experience and demonstrated competency, they can move into higher-engineering positions. Engineers who demonstrate good interpersonal skills, leadership abilities, and technical expertise may become team leaders, project managers, or chief engineers. Engineers can also move into supervisory or management positions. Some engineers pursue an MBA, or master of business administration, degree. Coupled with an engineering degree, these engineers are able to move into top management positions. Some engineers also develop specialties, such as artificial intelligence, and move into highly specialized engineering positions.

After several years on the job, robotics technicians who have demonstrated their ability to handle more responsibility may be assigned some supervisory work or, more likely, will train or instruct new technicians. Experienced technicians and engineers may teach courses at their workplace or find teaching opportunities at a local school or community college.

Other routes for advancement include becoming a sales representative for a robotics manufacturing or design firm or working as an independent contractor for companies that use or manufacture robots.

With additional training and education, such as a bachelor's degree, technicians can become eligible for positions as robotics technologists or robotics engineers.

Employment Outlook

Employment opportunities for robotics engineers and robotics technicians are closely tied to economic conditions in the United States, Canada, and the global marketplace. During the late 1980s and early 1990s, the robotics market suffered because of a lack of orders for robots and robotic equipment and intense foreign competition, especially from Japanese manufacturers.

In addition, many manufacturers reduced their number of employees significantly. Some companies cut their staffs by as much as 70,000 employees. Many companies that use large numbers of robotics personnel, such as those in the automobile industry, are represented by unions. These unions have agreements with companies that human beings will not lose their jobs because of automation. When companies do downsize, existing workers are given priority over other workers and are retrained to work in positions such as robotics technicians. This makes it more difficult for inexperienced workers to enter the field.

However, in 1995, U.S. robot manufacturers shipped record numbers of robots and robotic equipment. In addition, some Japanese robot builders shifted production to U.S. facilities. After a slump of several years, it is expected that the robotics industry will once again pick up.

The use of industrial robots is expected to grow as robots become more programmable and flexible and as manufacturing processes become more automated. Growth is also expected in nontraditional applications, such as delivery and service robots and the use of robots for agricultural purposes.

It is difficult to predict whether recent sales and the rising production of robots will increase employment opportunities, but trends for automated manufacturing equipment and a willingness by manufacturers to invest in capital expenditures indicate promising signs of growth. For prospective robotics engineers and technicians, this expansion suggests that more workers will be needed to design, build, install, maintain, repair, and operate robots.

Earnings

Earnings and benefits in manufacturing companies vary widely based on the size of the company, geographic location, nature of the production process, and complexity of the robots. In general, engineers with a bachelor of science degree earn annual salaries between $32,000 and $35,000 in their first job after graduation. Engineers with several years of experience earn salaries ranging from $35,000 to $60,000 a year.

Robotics technicians who are graduates of a two-year technical program earn between $22,000 and $26,000 a year. With increased training and experience, technicians can earn much more. Technicians with special skills, extensive experience, or added responsibilities can earn $36,000 or more. Technicians involved in design and training generally earn the highest salaries, with experienced workers earning $45,000 or more a year; those involved with maintenance and repair earn relatively less, with some beginning at salaries around $19,500 a year.

Employers offer a variety of benefits that can include any of the following: paid holidays, vacations, personal days, and sick leave; medical, dental, disability, and life insurance; 401(k) plans, pension and retirement plans; profit sharing; and educational assistance programs.

Conditions of Work

Robotics engineers and technicians may work either for a company that manufactures robots or a company that uses robots. Most companies that manufacture robots are relatively clean, quiet, and comfortable environments. Engineers and technicians may work in an office or on the production floor. A large number of robotics manufacturers are found in California, Michigan, Illinois, Indiana, Pennsylvania, Ohio, Connecticut, Texas, British Columbia, and Ontario, although companies exist in many other states and parts of Canada.

Engineers and technicians that work in a company that uses robots may work in noisy, hot, and dirty surroundings. Conditions vary based on the type of industry within which one works. Automobile manufacturers use a significant number of robots, as well as manufacturers of electronics components and consumer goods and the metalworking industry. Workers in a foundry work around heavy equipment and in hot and dirty environments. Workers in the electronic industry generally work in very clean and quiet environments. Some robotics personnel are required to work in clean room environments, which keep electronic components free of dirt and other contaminants. Workers in these environments wear face masks, hair coverings, and special protective clothing.

Some engineers and technicians may confront potentially hazardous conditions in the workplace. Robots, after all, are often designed and used precisely because the task they perform involves some risk to humans: handling laser beams, arc-welding equipment, radioactive substances, or hazardous chemicals. When they design, test, build, install, and repair robots, it is inevitable that some engineers and technicians will be exposed to these same risks. Plant safety procedures will protect the attentive and cautious worker, but carelessness in such settings can be especially dangerous.

In general, most technicians and engineers work forty-hour workweeks, although overtime may be required for special projects or to repair equipment that is shutting down a production line. Some technicians, particularly those involved in maintenance and repairs, may work shifts that include evening, late night, or weekend work.

Field service technicians travel to manufacturing sites to repair robots. Their work may involve extensive travel and overnight stays. They may work at several sites in one day or stay at one location for an extended period for more difficult repairs.

Sources of Additional Information

To purchase a copy of Robotics and Vision Supplier Directory *and for information on educational programs and student membership in the International Service Robot Association and Global Automation Information Network, please contact:*

Robotic Industries Association
PO Box 3724
900 Victors Way
Ann Arbor, MI 48106
Tel: 313-994-6088
WWW: http://www.robotics.org

For information on educational programs, competitions, and student membership in SME, Robotics International, or Machine Vision Association, please contact:

■**Society of Manufacturing Engineers (SME)**
Education Department
PO Box 930
One SME Drive
Dearborn, MI 48121-0930
Tel: 313-271-1500
WWW: http://www.sme.org

For information on careers and educational programs, please contact:

■**Robotics and Automation Council**
Institute of Electrical and Electronic Engineers (IEEE)
Education Information
345 East 47th Street
New York, NY 10017
Tel: 212-705-7900

For information on competitions and student membership, please contact:

■**Association for Unmanned Vehicle Systems**
1735 North Lynn Street, Suite 950
Arlington, VA 22209
Tel: 703-524-6646
Email: robert.michelson@gtri.gatech.edu

Roofers

Definition

Roofers install and repair roofs of buildings using a variety of materials and methods, including built-up roofing, single-ply roofing systems, asphalt shingles, tile, and slate. They may also waterproof and damp-proof walls, swimming pools, and other building surfaces.

Nature of the Work

Although roofers usually are trained to apply most kinds of roofing, they often specialize in either sheet membrane roofing or prepared roofings such as asphalt shingles, slate, or tile.

One kind of sheet membrane roofing is called "built-up roofing." Built-up roofing, used on flat roofs, consists of roofing felt (fabric saturated in bitumen, a tar-like material) laid into hot bitumen. To prepare for putting on a built-up roof, roofers may apply a layer of insulation to the bare roof deck. Then they spread molten bitumen over the roof surface, lay down overlapping layers of roofing felt, and spread more hot bitumen over the felt, sealing the seams and making the roof watertight. They repeat this process several times to build up as many layers as desired. They then give the top a smooth finish or embed gravel in the top for a rough surface.

Single-ply roofing is a relatively new method of roofing using a waterproof sheet membrane. Single-ply roofing, which increasingly is being used for roofing work, employs any of several different types of chemical products. Some roofing consists of ploymeria-modified bituminous compounds that are rolled out in sheets on the building's insulation. The compound may be remelted on the roof by torch or hot anvil to fuse it to or embed it in hot bitumen in a manner similar to built-up roofing. Other single-ply roofing is made of rubber or plastic materials that can be sealed with contact adhesive cements, solvent welding, hot-air welding, or other methods.

School Subjects
Mathematics
Shop (Trade/Vo-tech education)

Personal Interests
Building things
Fixing things

Work Environment
Primarily outdoors
Primarily multiple locations

Minimum Education Level
High school diploma
Apprenticeship

Salary Range
$11,000 to
$18,800 to
$37,000+

Certification or Licensing
Required for certain positions

Outlook
More slowly than the average

DOT
866

GOE
04.10.01

NOC
7291

Still another type of single-ply roofing consists of spray-in-place polyurethane foam with a polymeric coating. Roofers who apply these roofing systems must be trained in the application methods for each system. Many manufacturers of these systems require that roofers take special courses and receive certification before they are authorized to use the products.

To apply asphalt shingles, a very common roofing on houses, roofers begin by cutting strips of roofing felt and tacking them down over the entire roof. They nail on horizontal rows of shingles, beginning at the low edge of the roof and working up. Sometimes they must cut shingles to fit around corners, vent pipes, and chimneys. Where two sections of roof meet, they nail or cement flashing, which is strips of metal or shingle that make the joints watertight.

Tile and slate shingles, which are more expensive types of residential roofing, are installed slightly differently. First, roofing felt is applied over the wood base. Next, the roofers punch holes in the slate or tile pieces so that nails can be inserted, or they embed the tiles in mortar. Each row of shingles overlaps the preceding row.

Metal roofing is applied by specially trained roofers or by *sheet metal workers*. One type of metal roof uses metal sections shaped like flat pans, soldered together for weather-proofing and attached by metal clips to the wood below. Another kind of metal roofing, called "standing seam roofing," has raised seams where the sections of sheet metal interlock.

Some roofers waterproof and damp-proof walls, swimming pools, tanks, and structures other than roofs. To prepare surfaces for waterproofing, workers smooth rough surfaces and roughen glazed surfaces. They brush or spray waterproofing material on the surface. Damp-proofing is done by spraying a coating of tar or asphalt onto interior or exterior surfaces to prevent the penetration of moisture.

Roofers use various hand tools in their work, including hammers, roofing knives, mops, pincers, caulking guns, rollers, welders, chalk lines, and cutters.

Requirements

Most employers prefer to hire applicants at least eighteen years of age who are in good physical condition and have a good sense of balance. Although a high school education or its equivalent is not required, it is generally preferred.

Roofers learn the skills they need through on-the-job training or by completing an apprenticeship. Most roofers learn informally on the job while they work under the supervision of experienced roofers. Beginners start as helpers, doing simple tasks like carrying equipment and putting up scaffolding. They gradu-

ally gain the skills and knowledge they need for more difficult tasks. Roofers may need four or more years of on-the-job training to become familiar with all the materials and techniques they need to know.

Apprenticeship programs generally provide more thorough, balanced training. Apprenticeships are three years in length and combine a planned program of work experience with formal classroom instruction in related subjects. The work portion of the apprenticeship includes a minimum of 1,400 hours each year under the guidance of experienced roofers. The classroom instruction, at least 144 hours per year, covers such topics as safety practices, how to use and care for tools, and arithmetic.

Some roofers are members of the United Union of Roofers, Waterproofers and Allied Workers.

Opportunities for Experience & Exploration

High school or vocational school students may be able to get firsthand experience of this occupation through a part-time or summer job as a roofer's helper. Students can also take courses that familiarize them with some of the skills that are a regular part of roofing work. Beneficial courses include shop, basic mathematics, and mechanical drawing.

It may be possible to visit a construction site to observe roofers at work, but a close look is unlikely as roofers do most of their work at heights.

Methods of Entering

People who are planning to start out as helpers and learn on the job can directly contact roofing contractors to inquire about possible openings. Job leads may also be located through the local office of the state employment service or newspaper classified ads. Graduates of vocational schools may get useful information from their schools' placement offices.

People who want to become apprentices can learn about apprenticeships in their area by contacting local roofing contractors, the state employment service, or the local office of the United Union of Roofers, Waterproofers and Allied Workers.

Advancement

Experienced roofers who work for roofing contractors may be promoted to supervisory positions in which they are responsible for coordinating the activities of other roofers. Roofers also may become estimators, calculating the costs of roofing jobs before the work is done. Roofers who have the right combination of personal characteristics, including the ability to deal with people and good judgment and planning skills may be able to go into business for themselves as independent roofing contractors.

Employment Outlook

There were approximately 138,000 people employed as roofers in the United States as of 1996. This occupation is expected to grow slower than the average for all occupations through the year 2006.

There are several reasons for this outlook. The need for roofers, in part, relies on the amount of new construction. Though some existing roofs will need repairs, better quality materials and techniques will decrease this number.

Though this occupation as a whole is expected to have little or no growth, there will be many job openings due to roofers leaving the workforce due to retirement, or other reasons. Because most roofing work is done during the warmer part of the year, job opportunities will probably be best during spring and summer.

Earnings

The earnings of roofers vary widely depending on how much time they work, geographical location, skills and experience, and other factors. Roofers work an average of thirty-three hours a week. Sometimes bad weather prevents them from working, and some weeks they work fewer than twenty hours. They make up for lost time in other weeks, and if they work longer hours than the standard workweek (usually forty hours), they receive extra pay for the overtime. While roofers in northern states may not work in the winter, most roofers work year round.

According to the trade magazine, *Engineering News Record,* the average hourly wage for union roofers is $25.75. Some workers make less, and a few make nearly twice as much. Skilled and experienced roofers may earn $37,000 or more a year. Annual earnings may not reflect hourly figures because layoffs in bad weather limit the number of hours roofers work.

Hourly rates for apprentices usually start at about 40 percent of the skilled worker's rate and increase periodically until the pay reaches 90 percent of the full rate during the final six months.

Conditions of Work

Roofers work outdoors most of the time they are on the job. They work in the heat and cold, but not in wet weather. Roofs can get extremely hot during the summer. The work is physically strenuous, involving lifting heavy weights, prolonged standing, climbing, bending, and squatting. Roofers must work while standing on surfaces that may be steep and quite high; they must use caution to avoid injuries from falls while working on ladders, scaffolding, or roofs.

Sources of Additional Information

National Roofing Contractors Association
10255 West Higgins Road, Suite 600
Rosemont, IL 60018-5607
Tel: 847-299-9070

Roofing Industry Educational Institute
14 Inverness Drive East
Building H, Suite 110
Englewood, CO 80112-5608
Email: richroof@eworld.com

United Union of Roofers, Waterproofers and Allied Workers
1660 L Street
Washington, DC 20036

Sales Representatives

Definition

Sales representatives represent manufacturers and wholesalers by selling their products and services. They look for potential customers or clients (such as retail stores, other manufactures or wholesalers, government agencies, hospitals, and other institutions), explain or demonstrate their products to these clients, and attempt to make a sale. The job may include follow-up calls and visits to ensure the customer is satisfied.

Sales representatives work under a variety of titles. Those employed by manufacturers are typically called *manufacturers' sales workers* or *manufacturers' representatives*. Those who work for wholesalers are sometimes called *wholesale trade sales workers* or *wholesale sales representatives*. A *manufacturers' agent* is a self-employed salesperson who agrees to represent the products of various companies. A *door-to-door sales worker* usually represents just one company and sells products directly to consumers, typically at their homes.

Nature of the Work

Manufacturers' representatives and wholesale sales representatives sell goods to retail stores, other manufacturers and wholesalers, government agencies, and various institutions. They usually do so within a specific geographical area. Some representatives concentrate on just a few products. An electrical appliance salesperson, for example, might sell ten to thirty items ranging from food freezers and air-conditioners to waffle irons and portable heaters. Representatives of drug wholesalers, however, might sell as many as 50,000 items.

The duties of a sales representative usually include locating and contacting potential new clients, keeping a regular correspondence with existing customers, determining their clients' needs and informing them of pertinent products and prices, traveling to meet with clients and showing them samples or

---

School Subjects
Business
Economics

Personal Interests
Selling/Making a deal
Travel

Work Environment
Indoors and outdoors
Primarily multiple
locations

Minimum Education Level
High school diploma

Salary Range
$16,700 to
$36,100 to
$75,000+

Certification or Licensing
None

Outlook
About as fast as the
average

DOT
250

GOE
08.02.06

NOC
6421

catalogs, taking orders, arranging for delivery and, when appropriate, installation, handling customer complaints, keeping up-to-date on new products, and preparing reports. Many salespeople also attend trade conferences, where they learn about products and make sales contacts.

Finding new customers is one of the most important tasks. Sales representatives often follow leads suggested by other clients, from advertisements in trade journals, and from participants in trade shows and conferences. They may make "cold calls" to potential clients. Sales representatives frequently meet with and entertain prospective clients during evenings and weekends.

Representatives who sell highly technical machinery or complex office equipment are often referred to as *sales engineers* or *industrial sales workers.* Because their products tend to be more specialized and their clients' needs more complex, the sales process for these workers tends to be longer and more involved. Before recommending a product, they might, for example, carefully analyze a customer's production processes, distribution methods, or office procedures. They usually prepare extensive sales presentations that include information on how their products will improve the quality and efficiency of the customer's operations.

Some sales engineers, often with the help of their company's research and development department, adapt products to a customer's specialized needs. They may provide the customer with instructions on how to use the new equipment or work with installation experts who provide this service. Some companies maintain a sales assistance staff for training customers and providing specific information. This permits sales representatives to devote a greater percentage of their time to direct sales contact.

Other sales workers, called *detail people,* do not engage in direct selling activities but strive instead to create a better general market for their companies' products. A detail person for a drug company, for example, may call physicians and hospitals to inform them of new products and distribute samples.

The particular products sold by the sales representative directly affects the nature of the work. Salespeople who represent sporting goods manufacturers may spend most of their time driving from town to town calling on retail stores that carry sporting equipment. They may visit with coaches and athletic directors of high schools and colleges. A representative in this line may be a former athlete or coach who knows intimately the concerns of his or her customers.

Food manufacturers and wholesalers employ large numbers of sales representatives. Because these salespeople usually know the grocery stores and major chains that carry their products, their main focus is to ensure the maximum sales volume. Representatives negotiate with retail merchants to obtain the most advantageous store and shelf position for displaying their products. They encourage the store or chain to advertise their products, sometimes by offering to pay part of the advertising costs or by reducing the selling price to the merchant so that a special sale price can be offered to customers. Representatives may check to make sure that shelf items are neatly arranged and that the store has sufficient stock of their products.

Sales transactions can involve huge amounts of merchandise, sometimes worth millions of dollars. For example, in a single transaction, a washing-machine manufacturer, construction company, or automobile manufacturer may purchase all the steel products it needs for an extended period of time. Salespeople in this field may do much of their business by telephone because the product they sell is standardized and, to the usual customer, requires no particular description or demonstration.

Direct, or door-to-door, selling has been an effective way of marketing various products, such as appliances and housewares, cookware, china, tableware and linens, foods, drugs, cosmetics and toiletries, costume jewelry, clothing, and greeting cards. Like other sales representatives, door-to-door sales workers find prospective buyers, explain and demonstrate their products, and take orders. A door-to-door sales worker usually represents only one company and thus becomes an expert about the features of just one or a few products. Direct selling is also an important method of selling encyclopedias (which often require considerable explanation) and newspaper and magazine subscriptions.

Several different arrangements are common between companies and their door-to-door sales workers. Under the "direct company plan," for example, a sales representative is authorized to take orders for a product, and the company pays the representative a commission for each completed order. Such workers may be employees of the company (and may receive a salary in addition to a commission), or they might be independent contractors. They are usually very well trained. Sales workers who sell magazine subscriptions may be hired, trained, and supervised by a *subscription crew leader,* who assigns representatives to specific areas, reviews the orders they take, and compiles sales records.

Under the "exhibit plan" a salesperson sets up an exhibit booth at a place where large numbers of people are expected to pass, such as a state fair, trade show, or product exposition. Customers approach booth and schedule appointments of the salespersons', for later demonstrations at home.

The "dealer plan" allows a salesperson to function as the proprietor of a small business. The salesperson, or *dealer*, purchases the product wholesale from the company and then resells it to consumers at the retail price, mainly through door-to-door sales efforts.

Under various "group plans," a customer is contacted by a salesperson and given the opportunity to sponsor a sales event. In the "party plan," for example, the sales representative arranges to demonstrate products at the home of a customer, who then invites a group of friends for the "party." The customer who hosts the party receives free or discounted merchandise in return for the use of the home and for assembling other potential customers for the salesperson.

Finally, the "COD plan" allows representatives to sell products on a cash-on-delivery (COD) basis. In this method, the salesperson makes a sale (perhaps collecting an advance deposit) and sends the order to the company. The company, in turn, ships the merchandise directly to the customer (who in this case gives money to the delivery person) or to the salesperson (who then delivers the product to the customer and collects the balance owed).

Whatever the sales plan, door-to-door sales workers have some advantages over their counterparts in retail stores. Direct sellers, for example, do not have to wait for the customer to come to them; they go out and find the buyers for their products. The direct seller often carries only one product or a limited line of products and thus is much more familiar with the features and benefits of the merchandise. In general, direct sellers get the chance to demonstrate their products where they will most likely be used—in the home.

There are drawbacks to this type of selling. Many customers grow impatient or hostile when salespeople come to their house unannounced and uninvited. It may take several visits to persuade someone to buy the product. In a brief visit, the direct seller must win the confidence of the customer, develop the customer's interest in a product or service, and close the sale.

Requirements

A high school diploma is required for most sales positions, although an increasing number of salespeople are graduates of two- or four-year colleges. The more complex a product, the greater the likelihood that it will be sold by a college-trained person. About 30 percent of all door-to-door sales workers have a college degree.

Some areas of sales work require specialized college work. Those in engineering sales, for example, usu-

ally have a college degree in a relevant engineering field. Other fields that demand specific college degrees include chemical sales (chemistry or chemical engineering), office systems (accounting or business administration), and pharmaceuticals and drugs (biology, chemistry, or pharmacy). Those in less technical sales positions usually benefit from coursework in English, speech, psychology, marketing, public relations, economics, advertising, finance, accounting, and business law.

Sales representatives should enjoy working with people. Other important personal traits include self-confidence, enthusiasm, and self-discipline.

Opportunities for Experience & Exploration

Students interested in becoming a sales representative may benefit from part-time or summer work in a retail store. Working as a telemarketer also is useful. Some high schools and junior colleges offer programs that combine classroom study with work experience in sales.

Various opportunities exist that provide experience in direct selling. Students can become involved in the Junior Sales Clubs of America, for example, or take part in sales drives for school or community groups.

Occasionally manufacturers hire college students for summer assignments. These temporary positions provide an opportunity for the employer and employee to appraise each other. A high percentage of students hired for these specialized summer programs eventually become career employees after graduation. Some wholesale warehouses also offer temporary or summer positions.

Methods of Entering

Firms looking for sales representatives sometimes list openings with high school and college placement offices, as well as with public and private employment agencies. In many areas, professional sales associations refer people to suitable openings. Contacting companies directly is also recommended. A list of manufacturers and wholesalers can be found in telephone books and industry directories which are available at public libraries.

Although some high school graduates are hired for manufacturers' or wholesale sales jobs, many join a company in a nonselling position, such as office, stock, or shipping clerk. This experience allows an employee to learn about the company and its products. From there, he or she may eventually be promoted to a sales position.

Most new representatives complete a training period before receiving a sales assignment. In some cases new salespeople rotate through several departments of an organization to gain a broad exposure to the company's products. Large companies often use formal training programs lasting two years or more, while small organizations frequently rely on supervised sales experience.

Direct selling is usually an easier field to enter. Direct-sale companies advertise for available positions in newspapers, in sales workers' specialty magazines, and on television and radio. Many people enter direct selling through contacts they have had with other door-to-door sales workers. Most firms have district or area representatives who interview applicants and arrange the necessary training. Part-time positions in direct selling are common.

Advancement

New representatives usually spend their early years improving their sales ability, developing product knowledge, and finding new clients. As sales workers gain experience they may be shifted to increasingly large territories or more difficult types of customers. In some organizations, experienced sales workers narrow their focus. For example, an office-equipment sales representative may work solely on government contracts.

Advancement to management positions, such as regional or district manager, is also possible. Some representatives, however, choose to remain in basic sales. They often earn more money (because of commissions) than their managers do, and many enjoy being in the field and working directly with their customers.

A small number of representatives decide to become manufacturers' agents, or self-employed salespeople who handle products for various organizations. Agents perform many of the same functions as sales representatives but usually on a more modest scale.

Door-to-door sales workers also have advancement possibilities. Some are promoted to supervisory roles and recruit, train, and manage new members of the sales force. Others become area, branch, or district managers. Many managers of direct-selling firms began as door-to-door sales workers.

Employment Outlook

In the United States, more than one and a half million people worked as manufacturers' and wholesale sales representatives in 1996. Of these, three fourths were in wholesale, many as sellers of machinery. Food, drugs, electrical goods, hardware, and clothing are among the most common products sold by sales representatives.

The number of manufacturers' and wholesale sales representatives is expected to grow about as fast as the average for all occupations through the year 2006. This in part is because of technological advances. Electronic data interchange (EDI), a system that improves communication between computers, for example, allows customers to order goods more easily from suppliers.

Future opportunities will vary greatly depending upon the specific product and industry. Products that are in high demand, computers for example, will require increased hiring of sales representatives to service consumers. Representatives with strong knowledge of their product and a winning sales attitude will succeed in this career. Many job openings in this field will result from workers leaving the field due to retirement or other reasons.

Almost five million people work as door-to-door sales workers in North America. Of these, nearly 90 percent are women. The number of direct-selling companies has remained fairly constant over the past few years, and the growth in sales volume has been about average for the retail field.

Earnings

Many beginning sales representatives are paid a salary while receiving their training. After assuming direct responsibility for a sales territory, they may receive only a commission (a fixed percentage of each dollar sold). Also common is a modified commission plan (a lower rate of commission on sales plus a low base salary). Some companies provide bonuses to successful representatives.

Because manufacturers' and wholesale sales representatives typically work on commission, salaries vary widely. Some make $16,700 or less a year. More successful representatives earn more than $75,000. Most, however, earn between $24,900 and $51,900. The average salary is about $36,100, according to statistics given by the U.S. Department of Labor.

Earnings can be affected by changes in the economy or industry cycles, and great fluctuations in salary from year to year or month to month are common. Employees who travel usually are reimbursed for transportation, hotels, meals, and client entertainment expenses.

Door-to-door sales workers usually earn a straight commission on their sales, ranging from 10 to 40 percent of an item's suggested retail price. A typical or average income for this occupation is hard to estimate. It is not uncommon, however, for an experienced, full-time door-to-door salesperson to make between $12,000 and $20,000 a year.

Sales representatives typically receive vacation days, medical and life insurance, and retirement benefits. Some receive use of a company car and airline milage. Manufacturers' agents and some door-to-door sales workers, however, do not receive benefits.

Conditions of Work

Salespeople generally work long and irregular hours. Those with large territories may spend all day calling and meeting customers in one city and much of the night traveling to the place where they will make the next day's calls and visits. Sales workers with a small territory may do little overnight travel but, like most sales workers, may spend many evenings preparing reports, writing up orders, and entertaining customers. Several times a year, sales workers may travel to company meetings and participate in trade conventions and conferences. Irregular working hours, travel, and the competitive demands of the job can be disruptive to ordinary family life.

Sales work is physically demanding. Representatives often spend most of the day on their feet. Many carry heavy sample cases or catalogs. Occasionally, sales workers assist a customer in arranging a display of the company's products or moving stock items. Many door-to-door sellers work in their own community or nearby areas, although some cover more extensive and distant territories. They are often outdoors in all kinds of weather. Direct sellers must treat customers, even those who are rude or impatient, with tact and courtesy.

Sources of Additional Information

Direct Marketing Association
1120 Avenue of the Americas
New York, NY 10036
Tel: 212-768-7277

Sales and Marketing Executives International
Statler Office Tower, Suite 977
Cleveland, OH 44115
Tel: 800-999-1414

Secretaries

Definition

Secretaries perform a wide range of jobs that vary greatly from business to business. However, most secretaries key in documents, manage records and information, answer telephones, handle correspondence, schedule appointments, make travel arrangements, and sort mail. The amount of time secretaries spend on these duties depends on the size and type of the office as well as on their own job training.

Nature of the Work

Secretaries perform a variety of administrative and clerical duties. The goal of all their activities, however, is to assist their employers in the execution of their work and to help their companies conduct business in an efficient and professional manner.

Secretaries' work includes processing and transmitting information to the office staff and to other organizations. They operate office machines and arrange for their repair or servicing. These machines include computers, typewriters, dictating machines, photocopiers, switchboards, and fax machines. These secretaries also order office supplies and perform regular duties such as answering phones, sorting mail, managing files, taking dictation, and composing and keying in letters.

Some offices have word processing centers that handle all of the firm's typing. In such a situation, *administrative secretaries* take care of all secretarial duties except for typing and dictation. This arrangement leaves them free to respond to correspondence, prepare reports, do research and present the results to their employers, and otherwise assist the professional staff. Often these secretaries work in groups of three or four so that they can help each other if one secretary has a workload that is heavier than normal.

In many offices, secretaries make appointments for company executives and keep track of the office schedule. They

School Subjects
Business
English
(writing/literature)

Personal Interests
Computers
Reading/Books

Work Environment
Primarily indoors
Primarily one location

Minimum Education Level
High school diploma

Salary Range
$15,000 to
$30,000 to
$40,600

Certification or Licensing
Voluntary

Outlook
Varies by specialty

DOT
201

GOE
07.01.03

NOC
1241

make travel arrangements for the professional staff or for clients, and occasionally are asked to travel with staff members on business trips. Other secretaries might manage the office while their supervisors are away on vacation or business trips.

Secretaries take minutes at meetings, write up reports, and compose and type letters. They often will find their responsibilities growing as they learn the business. Some are responsible for finding speakers for conferences, planning receptions, and arranging public relations programs. Some write copy for brochures or articles before making the arrangements to have them printed or microfilmed. Or, they might use desktop publishing to create the documents themselves. They greet and guide clients to the proper offices, and often supervise and train other staff members and newer secretaries, especially in computer software programs.

Many secretaries do very specialized work. *Legal secretaries* prepare legal papers including wills, mortgages, contracts, deeds, motions, complaints, and summonses. They work under the direct supervision of an attorney or paralegal. They assist with legal research by reviewing legal journals and organizing briefs for their employers. They must learn an entire specialized vocabulary that is used in legal papers and documents.

Medical secretaries make appointments; prepare and send bills to patients, as well as track and collect them; maintain medical files; and pursue correspondence with patients, hospitals, and associations. They assist physicians or medical scientists with articles, reports, speeches, and conference proceedings. They, too, need to learn an entire specialized vocabulary of medical terms and be familiar with laboratory or hospital procedures.

Technical secretaries work for engineers and scientists preparing reports and papers that often include graphics and mathematical equations that are difficult to format on paper. The secretaries maintain a technical library and help with scientific papers by gathering and editing materials.

Social secretaries, often called *personal secretaries,* arrange all of the social activities of their employers. They handle private as well as business social affairs, and may plan parties, send out invitations, or write speeches for their employers. Social secretaries are often hired by celebrities or high-level executives who have busy social calendars to maintain.

Many associations, clubs, and non profit organizations have *membership secretaries* who compile and send out newsletters or promotional materials while maintaining membership lists, dues records, and directories. Depending on the type of club, the secre-

tary may be the one who gives out information to prospective members and who keeps current members and related organizations informed of upcoming events.

Education secretaries work in elementary or secondary schools or on college campuses. They take care of all clerical duties at the school. Their responsibilities may include preparing bulletins and reports for teachers, parents, or students, keeping track of budgets for school supplies or student activities, and maintaining the school's calendar of events. Depending on the position, they may work for school administrators, principals, or groups of teachers or professors. Other education secretaries work in administration offices, state education departments, or service departments.

In recent years, many secretaries have been performing tasks that were previously the responsibility of professional staff members and managers. Personal computers have enabled secretaries to use complex word processing, graphics, database, and spreadsheet programs to help their businesses. As secretaries' jobs are changing, they are becoming even more important in their positions as information managers in today's fast-paced working world.

Requirements

Secretaries must have a high school education. They need good office skills that include rapid and accurate keyboarding skills, good spelling and grammar, and they should enjoy handling details. Some positions require typing a minimum number of words per minute, as well as shorthand ability. Knowledge of word processing, spreadsheet, and database management is important, and employers require it. Some of these skills can be learned in business education courses taught in many local vocational and business schools. Courses that are helpful include business, communications, English, keyboarding, and computers.

Personal qualities are also important for secretaries. They often are the first employees of a company that clients meet, and therefore must be friendly, poised, and professionally dressed. Because they must work closely with others, they should be personable and tactful. Discretion, good judgment, organizational ability, and initiative are also important. These traits will not only get them hired, but will also help them advance in their careers.

Some employers encourage their secretaries to take certain advanced courses and to be trained to use any new piece of equipment in the office. Requirements vary widely from company to company.

Opportunities for Experience & Exploration

High school guidance counselors can give interest and aptitude tests to help students assess their suitability to a career as a secretary. Local business schools often welcome visitors, and sometimes offer courses that can be taken in conjunction with a high school business course. Work-study programs also provide students with an opportunity to work in a business setting to get a sense of the work performed by secretaries.

Part-time or summer jobs as receptionists, file clerks, and office clerks are often available in various offices. These jobs are the best indicator of future satisfaction in the secretarial field. Students who are computer-literate may find part-time jobs. Cooperative education programs arranged through schools and "temping" through an agency also are valuable ways to acquire experience. In general, any job that teaches basic office skills is helpful.

Methods of Entering

Most people looking for work as secretaries find jobs through the newspaper want ads or by applying directly to local businesses. Both private employment offices and local state employment services place secretaries, and business schools help their graduates find suitable jobs. Temporary-help agencies also are an excellent way to find jobs, many of which turn into permanent ones.

Advancement

Secretaries often begin by assisting executive secretaries and work their way up by learning the way their business operates. Initial promotions from a secretarial position are usually to jobs such as secretarial supervisor, office manager, or administrative assistant. Depending on other personal qualifications, college courses in business, accounting, or marketing can help the ambitious secretary enter middle and upper management. Training in computer skills can also lead to advancement. Secretaries who become proficient in word processing, for instance, can get jobs as instructors or as sales representatives for software manufacturers.

Qualifying for the designation Certified Professional Secretary (CPS) rating is increasingly recognized in business and industry as a consideration for promotion. The examinations required for this certification are given by Professional Secretaries International. Legal secretaries can become similarly certified by the National Association of Legal Secretaries.

Employment Outlook

Secretaries held about 3,400,000 positions across the country in the late-1990s, making this one of the largest occupations in the U.S. economy.

The employment outlook for secretaries varies by specialty. The growth of the health care field will create faster than average growth for medical secretaries. As fast as the average growth is predicted for legal secretaries as the legal services industry continues to expand. Employment of secretaries who do not specialize in legal or medical work is predicted to decline through the year 2006.

All businesses hire secretaries, and despite the increasing trend toward automation, skilled secretaries—regardless of their specialty—are expected to be able to find jobs without great difficulty in the next several years. Technological advances may mean that more professionals are doing some of their own correspondence on personal computers, but some administrative duties will still need to be handled by secretaries. The personal aspects of the job and responsibilities such as making travel arrangements, scheduling conferences, and transmitting staff instructions have not changed. Many employers currently complain of a shortage of first-rate secretaries. As a result, well-qualified and experienced secretaries still continue to be in great demand. Every year, several hundred thousand secretaries transfer to other occupations or leave the labor force. In this occupation, as in most, replacement needs are the main source of jobs. Increasingly, secretaries who keep their skills current and learn to use new computerized systems will get the best jobs.

Earnings

Salaries for secretaries vary widely by region; type of business; and the skill, experience, and level of responsibility of the secretary. Secretaries earned an average annual salary of $19,700 in 1995, according to the *1998-99 Occupational Outlook Handbook,* although salaries range from $15,000 to $40,600. Legal secretaries earned a median salary of over $30,000 in 1995. Beginning salaries in the federal government are on the low end of the scale, about

$17,400 a year in 1997, while beginning salaries in the sales/marketing, legal, and public utilities industries are higher. Secretaries who specialize—especially in legal or health care services—and those with computer skills and other experience are likely to command higher salaries.

Conditions of Work

Most secretaries work in pleasant offices with modern equipment. Office conditions vary widely, however. While some secretaries have their own offices and work for one or two executives, others share crowded workspace with other workers.

Most office workers work a thirty-five to forty hour week. Very few secretaries work on the weekends on a regular basis, although some may be asked to work overtime if a particular project demands it. Most secretaries receive paid holidays and two weeks' vacation time after a year of work, as well as sick leave. Many offices provide benefits including health and life insurance, pension plans, overtime pay, and tuition reimbursement.

The work is not physically strenuous or hazardous, although deadline pressure is a factor and sitting for long periods of time can be uncomfortable. Long periods of time spent in front of a computer can lead to eyestrain or repetitive-motion problems for secretaries. Most secretaries are not required to travel. Part-time and flexible schedules are easily adaptable to secretarial work.

Sources of Additional Information

■National Association of Legal Secretaries
314 East 3rd Street, Suite 210
Tulsa, OK 74120
Tel: 918-582-5188
WWW: http://www.nals.org

■National Association of Secretarial Services
22875 Sari Ranch Parkway, Suite H
Yorba Linder, CA 92887
Tel: 714-282-9398
Email: abssi4you@aol.com

■Office and Professional Employees International Union
265 West 14th Street, Suite 610
New York, NY 10011
Tel: 800-346-7348
WWW: http://www.opeiu.org

■OfficeTeam
2884 Sand Hill Road
Menlo Park, CA 94025
Tel: 800-804-8367
WWW: http://www.officeteam.com

■Professional Secretaries International
PO Box 20404
Kansas City, MO 64195-0404
Tel: 816-891-6600
WWW: http://www.psi.org

Security Consultants and Technicians

Definition

Security consultants and technicians are responsible for protecting public and private property against theft, fire, vandalism, illegal entry, and acts of violence. They may work for commercial or governmental organizations or private individuals.

Nature of the Work

A security consultant is engaged in protective service work. Anywhere there is valuable property or information, or public figures at risk, a security consultant may be called in to devise and implement security plans that offer protection. Security consultants may work for a variety of clients, including large stores, art museums, factories, laboratories, data processing centers, and political candidates. They are involved in preventing theft, vandalism, fraud, kidnapping, and other crimes. Specific job responsibilities depend on the type and size of the client's company and the scope of the security system required.

A security consultant always works closely with company officials or other appropriate individuals in the development of a comprehensive security program that will fit the needs of the individual client. After discussing goals and objectives with the relevant company executives, the consultant studies and analyzes the physical conditions and internal operations of a client's operation. Much is learned by simply observing day-to-day operations.

The size of the security budget also influences the type of equipment ordered and methods used. For example, a large factory that produces military hardware may fence off its property and place electric eyes around the perimeter of the fence. They may also install perimeter alarms and use passkeys to limit access to restricted areas. A smaller company may only use entry control mechanisms in specified areas. The consul-

School Subjects
Physical education
Psychology

Personal Interests
Helping people: personal service
Law

Work Environment
Indoors and outdoors
One location with some travel

Minimum Education Level
Bachelor's degree for consultants
High school diploma for technicians

Salary Range
$26,000 to $100,000 (consultants)
$15,500 to $35,600 (technicians)

Certification or Licensing
Recommended

Outlook
Faster than the average

DOT
199

GOE
11.05.02

NOC
6651

tant may recommend sophisticated technology, such as closed circuit surveillance or ultrasonic motion detectors, alone or in addition to security personnel. Usually, a combination of electronic and human resources is used.

Security consultants not only devise plans to protect equipment but also recommend procedures on safeguarding and possibly destroying classified material. Increasingly, consultants are being called on to develop strategies to safeguard data processing equipment. They may have to to develop measures to safeguard transmission lines against unwanted or unauthorized interceptions.

Once a security plan has been developed, the consultant oversees the installation of the equipment, ensures that it is working properly, and checks frequently with the client to ensure the client is satisfied. In the case of a crime against the facility, a consultant investigates the nature of the crime (often in conjunction with police or other investigators) and then modifies the security system to safeguard against similar crimes in the future.

Many consultants work for security firms that have several types of clients, such as manufacturing and telecommunications plants and facilities. Consultants may handle a variety of clients or work exclusively in a particular area. For example, one security consultant may be assigned to handle the protection of nuclear power plants and another will be assigned to handle data processing companies.

Security consultants may be called on to safeguard famous individuals or persons in certain positions from kidnapping or other type of harm. They provide security services to presidents of large companies, media personalities, and others who want their safety and privacy protected. These consultants, like *bodyguards*, plan and review client travel itineraries and usually accompany the client on trips, checking accommodations and appointment locations along the way. They often check the backgrounds of people who will interact with the client, especially those who see the client infrequently.

Security consultants are sometimes called in for special events, such as sporting events and political rallies, when there is no specific fear of danger, but just a need for overall coordination of a large security operation. The consultants oversee security preparation, such as the stationing of appropriate personnel at all points of entry and exit, and then direct specific responses to any security problems.

Security officers develop and implement security plans for companies that manufacture or process material for the federal government. They ensure that their clients' security policies comply with federal regulations in such categories as the storing and han-

dling of classified documents and restricting access to nonauthorized personnel only.

Security guards have various titles, depending on the type of work they do and the setting in which they work. They may be referred to as *patrollers, merchant patrollers, bouncers* (people who eject unruly people from places of entertainment), *golf-course rangers* (who patrol golf courses), or *gate tenders* (who work at security checkpoints). They may work as *airline security representatives* in airports or as *armored-car guards and drivers.*

Many security guards are employed during normal working hours in public and commercial buildings and other areas with a good deal of pedestrian traffic and public contact. Others patrol buildings and grounds outside of normal working hours, such as at night and on weekends. Guards usually wear uniforms and may carry a nightstick. Guards who work in situations where they may be called upon to apprehend criminal intruders are usually armed. They may carry a flashlight, whistle, two-way radio, and a watch clock, which is used to record the time at which they reach various checkpoints.

Guards in public buildings may be assigned to a certain post or they may patrol an area. In museums, art galleries, and other public buildings, guards answer visitors' questions and give them directions; they also enforce rules against smoking, touching art objects, and so forth. In commercial buildings, guards may sign people in and out after hours and inspect packages being carried out of the building. Bank guards observe customers carefully for any sign of suspicious behavior that may signal a possible robbery attempt. In department stores, security guards often work with undercover detectives to watch for theft by customers or store employees. Guards at large public gatherings such as sporting events and conventions keep traffic moving, direct people to their seats, and eject unruly spectators. Guards employed at airports limit access to boarding areas to passengers only. They make sure people entering passenger areas have valid tickets and observe passengers and their baggage as they pass through X-ray machines and metal detection equipment.

After-hours guards are usually employed at industrial plants, defense installations, construction sites, and transport facilities such as docks and railroad yards. They make regular rounds on foot or, if the premises are very large, in motorized vehicles. They check to be sure that no unauthorized persons are on the premises, that doors and windows are secure, and that no property is missing. They may be equipped with walkie-talkies to report in at intervals to a central guard station. Sometimes guards perform custodial duties, such as turning on lights and setting thermostatic controls.

In a large organization, a security officer is often in charge of the guard force; in a small organization, a single worker may be responsible for all security measures. As more businesses purchase advanced electronic security systems to protect their properties, more guards are being assigned to stations where they monitor perimeter security, environmental functions, communications, and other systems. In many cases, these guards maintain radio contact with other guards patrolling on foot or in motor vehicles. Some guards use computers to store information on matters relevant to security such as visitors or suspicious occurrences during their time on duty.

Security technicians work for government agencies or for private companies hired by government agencies. Their task is usually to guard secret or restricted installations in this country or in foreign countries. They spend much of their time patrolling areas, which they may do on foot, horseback, or in automobiles or aircraft. They may monitor activities in an area through the use of surveillance cameras and video screens. Their assignments usually include detecting and preventing unauthorized activities, searching for explosive devices, standing watch during secret and hazardous experiments, and other routine police duties within government installations.

Security technicians are usually armed and may be required to use their weapons or other kinds of physical force to prevent some kinds of activities. They are usually not, however, required to remove explosive devices from an installation. When they find such devices, they notify a bomb disposal unit, which is responsible for removing and then defusing or detonating the device.

Requirements

Most companies prefer to hire security consultants who have at least a college degree. An undergraduate or associates degree in criminal justice, business administration, or related field is best. Coursework should be broad and include business management, communications, computer courses, sociology, and statistics. As the security consulting field becomes more competitive, many consultants chose to get a master's in business administration (MBA) or other graduate degree.

Although there are no specific educational or professional requirements, many security consultants have had previous experience with police work or other forms of crime prevention. It is helpful if a person develops an expertise in a specific area. For example, if a person wants to work devising plans securing data processing equipment, it is helpful if the consultant has had previous experience working with computers. Many security consultants are certified by the Certified Protection Professionals. To be eligible for certification, a consultant must pass a written test and have ten years' work and educational experience in security work. Information on certification is available from the American Society for Industrial Security, a professional organization to which many security consultants belong.

There are no specific educational requirements for security guards, although most employers prefer to hire high school graduates. General good health (especially vision and hearing), alertness, emotional stability, and the ability to follow directions are important characteristics for this job. Military service and experience in local or state police departments are assets. Prospective guards should have clean police records.

Some employers require applicants to take a polygraph examination or a written test that indicates honesty, attitudes, and other personal qualities. Most employers require applicants and experienced workers to submit to drug screening tests as a condition of employment.

For some hazardous or physically demanding jobs, guards must be under a certain age and meet height and weight standards. For top-level security positions in facilities such as nuclear power plants or vulnerable information centers, guards may be required to complete a special training course. They may also need to fulfill certain relevant academic requirements.

Guards employed by the federal government must be U.S. armed forces veterans, have some previous experience as guards, and pass a written examination. Many positions require experience with firearms. In many situations, guards must be bonded.

Virtually every state has licensing or registration requirements for those guards who work for contract security agencies. Registration generally requires that a person newly hired as a guard be reported to the licensing authorities, usually the state police department or special state licensing commission. To be granted a license, individuals generally must be eighteen years of age, have no convictions for perjury or acts of violence, pass a background investigation, and complete classroom training on a variety of subjects, including property rights, emergency procedures, and seizure of suspected criminals.

Security technicians are required to be high school graduates. In addition, they should expect to receive from three to six months of specialized training in security procedures and technology. While in high school, they should take mathematics courses to ensure that they can perform basic arithmetic operations with different units of measure, compute ratios, rates, and percentages, and interpret charts and graphs. They should take English courses to develop their reading and writing skills and be able to read manuals, memos, textbooks, and other instructional materials and write reports with correct spelling, grammar, and punctuation. They should also be able to speak to small groups with poise and confidence.

Security technicians need good eyesight and should be in good physical shape, able to lift at least fifty pounds, climb ladders, stairs, poles, and ropes, and maintain their balance on narrow, slippery, or moving surfaces. They should be able to stoop, crawl, crouch, and kneel with ease.

Opportunities for Experience & Exploration

Part-time or summer employment as a clerk with a security firm is an excellent way to gain insight into the skills and temperament needed to become a security consultant. Discussions with professional security consultants are another way of exploring career opportunities in this field. Young people may find it helpful to join a safety patrol at school.

Those interested in a particular area of security consulting, such as data processing, for example, can join a club or association to learn more about the field. This is also a good way to make professional contacts.

Opportunities for part-time or summer work as security guards are not generally available to high school students. Students may, however, work in jobs such as lifeguards, safety patrols, and school hallway monitors, which can provide helpful experience.

Methods of Entering

People interested in a career in security services generally apply directly to security companies. Some jobs may be available through state or private employment services. People interested in security technician positions should apply directly to government agencies. Military experience is particularly appreciated by employers of security personnel.

Beginning security personnel receive varied amounts of training. Training requirements are generally increasing as modern, highly sophisticated secu-

rity systems become more commonplace. Many employers give newly hired security guards instruction before they start the job and also provide several weeks of on-the-job training. Guards receive training in protection, public relations, report writing, crisis deterrence, first aid, and drug control.

Those who are employed at establishments that place a heavy emphasis on security usually receive extensive formal training. For example, guards at nuclear power plants may undergo several months of training before being placed on duty under close supervision. Guards may be taught to use firearms, administer first aid, operate alarm systems and electronic security equipment, handle emergencies and evacuations, and spot and deal with security problems.

Many of the less strenuous guard positions are filled by older people who are retired police officers or armed forces veterans. Because of the odd hours required for many positions, this occupation appeals to many people seeking part-time work or second jobs.

Most entry-level positions for security consultants are filled by those with a bachelor's or associate's degree in criminal justice, business administration, or a related field. Those with a high school diploma and some experience in the field may find work with a security consulting firm, although they usually begin as a security guard and, only after training become a consultant.

Because many consulting firms have their own techniques and procedures, most require entry-level personnel to complete an on-the-job training program, where company policy is introduced.

Advancement

In most cases, security guards receive periodic salary increases, and guards employed by larger security companies or as part of a military-style guard force may increase their responsibilities or move up in rank. Guards with outstanding ability, especially those with some college education, may move up to the position of *chief guard*, gaining responsibility for the supervision and training of an entire guard force in an industrial plant or department store, or become *director of security services* for a business or commercial building. A few guards with management skills open their own contract security guard agencies; other guards become *licensed private detectives*. Experienced guards may become bodyguards for political figures, executives, and celebrities or choose to enter a police department or other law enforcement agency. Additional training may lead to a career as a corrections officer.

Increased training and experience with a variety of security and surveillance systems may lead security guards into higher-paying security consultant careers. Security consultants with experience may advance to management positions or they may start their own private consulting firms. Instruction and training of security personnel is another advancement opportunity for security guards, consultants, and technicians.

Employment Outlook

Security services is one of the largest employment fields in the United States. About 995,000 persons are employed as security guards in the United States. Industrial security firms and guard agencies, also called contract security firms, employ over 50 percent of all guards, while the remainder are in-house guards employed by various establishments.

The demand for guards and other security personnel is expected to increase faster than the average through the year 2006, as crime rates rise with the overall population growth. The highest estimates call for more than 1.25 million guards to be employed by the year 2006. Many job openings will be created as a result of the high turnover of workers in this field.

A factor adding to this demand is the trend for private security firms to perform duties previously handled by police officers, such as courtroom security and crowd control in airports. Private security companies employ security technicians to guard many government sites, such as nuclear testing facilities. Private companies also operate many training facility for government security technicians and guards, as well as provide police services for some communities.

Earnings

Earnings for security consultants vary greatly depending on the consultant's training and experience. Entry-level consultants with a bachelor's degree commonly start at $26,000 to $32,000 per year. Consultants with graduate degrees begin at $34,000 to $41,000 per year, and experienced consultants may earn $50,000 to $100,000 per year or more. Many consultants work on a per-project basis, with rates of up to $75 per hour.

Average starting salaries for security guards and technicians vary according to their level of training, experience, and the location of where they work. Starting salaries generally range between $5.50 and $11.73 per hour in 1996, according to the U.S. Department of Labor. Experienced security guards average as high as $35,600 per year, with those employed in manufacturing facilities receiving the highest wages. Entry-level guards working for a contract agency may receive little more than the minimum wage, however. In-house guards generally earn higher wages and have greater job security and better advancement potential.

Security guards and technicians employed by federal government agencies earned starting salaries of $15,500 or $17,500 per year, and average $22,900 per year with experience. Location of the work also affects earnings, with higher pay in locations with a higher cost of living. Government employees typically enjoy good job security and generous benefits. Benefits for positions with private companies vary significantly.

Conditions of Work

Consultants usually divide their time between their offices and a client's business. Much time is spent analyzing various security apparatus and developing security proposals. The consultant talks with a variety of employees at a client's company, including the top officials, and discusses alternatives with other people at the consulting firm. A consultant makes a security proposal presentation to the client and then works with the client on any modifications. A consultant must be sensitive to budget issues and develop a security system that the client can afford.

Consultants may specialize in one type of security work (nuclear power plants, for example) or work for a variety of large and small clients, such as museums, data processing companies, and banks.

Although there may be a lot of travel and some work may require outdoor activity, there should be no strenuous work. A consultant may oversee the implementation of a large security system but is not involved in the actual installation process. A consultant may have to confront suspicious people but they are not expected to do the work of a police officer.

Security guards and technicians may work indoors or outdoors. In high-crime areas and industries vulnerable to theft and vandalism, there may be considerable physical danger. Guards who work in museums, department stores, and other buildings and facilities remain on their feet for long periods of time, either standing still or walking while on patrol. Guards assigned to reception areas or security control rooms may remain at their desks for the entire shift. Much of their work is routine and may be tedious at times, yet guards must remain constantly alert during their shift.

Guards who work with the public, especially at sporting events and concerts, may have to confront unruly and sometimes hostile people. Bouncers often confront intoxicated people and are frequently called upon to intervene in physical altercations.

Many companies employ guards around the clock in three shifts, including weekends and holidays, and assign workers to these shifts on a rotating basis. The same is true for security technicians guarding government facilities and installations. Those with less seniority will likely have the most erratic schedules. Many guards work alone for an entire shift, usually lasting eight hours. Lunches and other meals are often taken on the job, so that constant vigilance is maintained.

Sources of Additional Information

International Security Officers' Police and Guard Union
321 86th Street
Brooklyn, NY 11209
Tel: 718-836-3508

International Association of Security Service
PO Box 8202
Northfield, IL 60093
Tel: 847-973-7712

International Union of Security Officers
2404 Merced Street
San Leandro, CA 94577
Tel: 510-895-9905

For information on certification procedures, please contact:

American Society for Industrial Security
1655 North Fort Myer Drive, Suite 1200
Arlington, VA 22209
Tel: 703-522-5800

Sheet Metal Workers

Definition

Sheet metal workers fabricate, assemble, install, repair, and maintain ducts used for ventilating, air-conditioning, and heating systems. They also work with other articles of sheet metal, including roofing, siding, gutters, downspouts, partitions, chutes, and stainless steel kitchen and beverage equipment for restaurants. Not included in this group are employees in factories where sheet metal items are mass produced on assembly lines.

Nature of the Work

Most sheet metal workers handle a variety of tasks in fabricating, installing, and maintaining sheet metal products. Some workers concentrate on just one of these areas. Skilled workers must know about the whole range of activities involved in working with sheet metal.

Many sheet metal workers are employed by building contracting firms that construct or renovate residential, commercial, and industrial buildings. Fabricating and installing air-conditioning, heating, and refrigeration equipment is often a big part of their job. Some workers specialize in adjusting and servicing equipment that has already been installed so that it can operate at peak efficiency. Roofing contractors, the federal government, and businesses that do their own alteration and construction work also employ sheet metal workers. Other sheet metal workers are employed in the shipbuilding, railroad, and aircraft industries or in shops that manufacture specialty products such as custom kitchen equipment or electrical generating and distributing machinery.

Fabricating is often done in a shop away from the site where the product is to be installed. In fabricating products, workers usually begin by studying blueprints or drawings. After determining the amounts and kinds of materials required for the job, they make measurements and lay out the pattern on the

School Subjects
Mathematics
Shop (Trade/Vo-tech education)

Personal Interests
Figuring out how things work
Fixing things

Work Environment
Primarily indoors
Primarily multiple locations

Minimum Education Level
High school diploma
Apprenticeship

Salary Range
$13,000 to
$22,800 to
$40,000

Certification or Licensing
None

Outlook
Decline

DOT
804

GOE
05.05.06

NOC
7261

appropriate pieces of metal. They may use measuring tapes and rulers and figure dimensions with the aid of calculators. Then, following the pattern they have marked on the metal, they cut out the sections with hand or power shears or other machine tools. They may shape the pieces with a hand or machine brake, which is a type of equipment used for bending and forming sheet metal, and punch or drill holes in the parts. As a last step before assembly, workers inspect the parts to verify that all of them are accurately shaped. Then they fasten the parts together by welding, soldering, bolting, riveting, or cementing or by using special devices such as metal clips. After assembly, it may be necessary to smooth rough areas on the fabricated item with a file or grinding wheel.

Computers play an increasingly important role in several of these tasks. Computers help workers plan the layout efficiently, so that all the necessary sections can be cut from the metal stock while leaving the smallest possible amount of waste sheet metal. Computers also help guide saws, shears, and lasers that cut metal, as well as other machines that form the pieces into the desired shapes.

If the item has been fabricated in a shop, it is taken to the installation site. There, the sheet metal workers join together different sections of the final product. For example, they may connect sections of duct end to end. Some items, such as sections of duct, can be bought factory-made in standard sizes, and workers modify them at the installation site to meet the requirements of the situation. Once finished, duct work may be suspended with metal hangers from ceilings or attached to walls. Sometimes sheet metal workers weld, bolt, screw, or nail items into place. To complete the installation, they may need to make additional sheet metal parts or alter the items they have fabricated.

Some tasks in working with sheet metal, such as making metal roofing, are routinely done at the job site. Workers measure and cut sections of roof paneling, which interlock with grooving at the edges. They nail or weld the paneling to the roof deck to hold it in place and put metal molding over joints and around the edges, windows, and doors to finish off the roof.

Requirements

The best way to learn the skills necessary for working in this field is to complete an apprenticeship. Apprenticeships generally consist of a planned series of on-the-job work experiences plus classroom instruction in related subjects. The on-the-job training portion of apprenticeships, which last at least four years, includes about 8,000 hours of work. The classroom instruction totals approximately 600 hours, spread over the years of the apprenticeship. The training covers all aspects of sheet metal fabrication and installation.

Apprentices get practical experience in layout work, cutting, shaping, and installing sheet metal. They also learn to work with materials that may be used instead of metal, such as fiberglass and plastics. Under the supervision of skilled workers, they begin with simple tasks and gradually work up to the most complex. In the classroom, they learn blueprint reading, drafting, mathematics, computer operations, job safety, welding, and the principles of heating, air-conditioning, and ventilating systems.

Apprenticeships may be run by joint committees representing locals of the Sheet Metal Workers' International Association, an important union in the field, and local chapters of the Sheet Metal and Air Conditioning Contractors' National Association. Other apprenticeships are run by local chapters of a contractor group, the Associated Builders and Contractors. Requirements vary slightly, but usually applicants for apprenticeships must be high school graduates. High school courses that provide a good background include shop classes, mechanical drawing, trigonometry, and geometry. Applicants need to be in good physical condition, with good manual dexterity, eye-hand coordination, and the ability to visualize and understand shapes and forms.

A few sheet metal workers learn informally on the job while they are employed as helpers to experienced workers. They gradually develop skills when opportunities arise for learning. Like apprentices, helpers start out with simple jobs and in time take on more complicated work. However, the training that helpers get may not be as balanced as that for apprentices, and it may take longer for them to learn all that they need to know. Helpers often take vocational school courses to supplement their work experience.

Even after they have become experienced and well qualified in their field, sheet metal workers may need to take further training to keep their skills up-to-date. Such training is often sponsored by union groups or paid for by their employers.

Opportunities for Experience & Exploration

High school students can gauge their aptitude for and interest in some of the common activities of sheet metal workers by taking courses such as metal shop, blueprint reading, and mechanical drawing. A summer or part-time job as a helper with a contracting firm that does sheet metal work could provide an excellent opportunity to observe workers on the job. If such a job cannot be arranged, it may be possible to visit a construction site and perhaps to talk with a sheet metal worker who can give an insider's view of this job.

Methods of Entering

People who would like to enter an apprentice program in this field can seek information about apprenticeships from local employers of sheet metal workers, such as sheet metal contractors or heating, air-conditioning, and refrigeration contractors; from the local office of the Sheet Metal Workers' International Association; or from the local Sheet Metal Apprentice Training office, the joint union-management apprenticeship committee. Information on apprenticeship programs also can be obtained from the local office of the state employment service or the state apprenticeship agency.

People who would rather enter this field as on-the-job trainees can contact contractors directly about possibilities for jobs as helpers. Leads for specific jobs may be located through the state employment service or newspaper classified ads. Graduates of vocational or technical training programs may get assistance from the placement office at their schools.

Advancement

Skilled and experienced sheet metal workers who work for contractors may be promoted to positions as supervisors and eventually job superintendents. Those who develop their skills through further training may move into related fields, such as welding. Some sheet metal workers become specialists in particular activities, such as design and layout work or estimating costs of installations. Some workers eventually go into business for themselves as independent sheet metal contractors.

Employment Outlook

Employment in this field is expected to decline through the year 2006 due to several factors. While modern technology, tools and machinery have allowed for greater productivity, these advancements have also resulted in a decreased demand for sheetmetal workers. In addition, the need to stay competitive has forced many businesses to relocate their factories to other countries where foreign labor is less costly, compared to that in America.

Job prospects will vary somewhat with economic conditions. In general, the economy is closely tied to the level of new building construction activity. During economic downturns, workers may face periods of unemployment, while at other times there may be more jobs than skilled workers available to take them. But overall, sheet metal workers are less affected by economic ups and downs than some other craftworkers in the construction field. This is because activities related to maintenance, repair, and replacement of old equipment comprise a significant part of their job, and even during an economic slump, building owners are often inclined to go ahead with such work.

Earnings

The median annual earnings for all sheet metal workers in the United States is roughly $34,000, according to 1996 U.S. Department of Labor salary statistics. Earnings vary in different parts of the country and tend to be highest in industrialized urban areas. Apprentices begin at about 40 percent of the rate paid to experienced workers and receive periodic pay increases throughout their training. Some workers who are union members are eligible for supplemental pay from their union during periods of unemployment or when they are working less than full time. Many sheet metal workers are members of the Sheet Metal Workers' International Association.

Conditions of Work

Most sheet metal workers have a regular forty-hour workweek and receive extra pay for overtime. Most of their work is performed indoors, so they are less likely to lose wages due to bad weather than many other craftworkers involved in construction projects. Some work is done outdoors, occasionally in uncomfortably hot or cold conditions.

Workers sometimes have to work high above the ground, as when they install gutters and roofs, and sometimes in awkward, cramped positions, as when they install ventilation systems in buildings. Workers may have to be on their feet for long periods, and they may have to lift heavy objects. Possible hazards of the trade include cuts and burns from machinery and equipment, as well as falls from ladders and scaffolding. Workers must use good safety practices to avoid injuries and sometimes wear protective gear such as safety glasses. Sheet metal fabrication shops are usually well ventilated and properly heated and lighted, but at times they are quite noisy.

Sources of Additional Information

National Training Fund for the Sheet Metal and Air Conditioning Industry
Edward F. Carlough Plaza
601 North Fairfax Street, Suite 240
Alexandria, VA 22314
Tel: 703-739-7200

Sheet Metal and Air Conditioning Contractors' National Association
PO Box 221230
Chantilly, VA 22022
Tel: 703-803-2980

Sheet Metal Workers' International Association
1750 New York Avenue, NW
Washington, DC 20006
Tel: 202-783-5880

Shoe Industry Workers

Definition

Shoe industry workers turn materials such as leather, rubber, fabrics, and plastic into finished shoes, boots, moccasins, sandals, slippers, and other footwear. Most of these workers operate machines. *Shoe and leather repairers* repair and restyle shoes and other products, such as saddles, harnesses, handbags, and luggage. More highly skilled *custom shoemakers* and *orthopedic-boot-and-shoe designers and makers* may design, construct, or repair orthopedic shoes in accordance with foot specialists' prescriptions.

Nature of the Work

Even with competition from imports, shoe factories in America still produce 376 million pairs of shoes in thousands of styles every year. Most of this work is done on machines, although some work is done by hand. A single pair of shoes may consist of as many as 280 different parts and require 150 different machine steps. Nearly all shoes are made in batches, not in individual pairs. These batches may consist of a dozen or more pairs of shoes, which are kept together through the entire manufacturing process to ensure that the shoes are consistent in color, texture, size, and pattern.

The steps in manufacturing conventional leather shoes can illustrate the process in which shoe industry workers take part. The leather on the top side of a pair of shoes starts out as tanned animal hides that the manufacturer purchases and keeps in storage. Keeping track of these hides is the job of *upper-leather sorters*, who sort, grade, and issue the hides that will be cut into shoe uppers. The leather is spread out under a cutting machine, which stamps down and cuts the leather into the various sections used for the shoe. This machine, tended by *cut-out-and-marking-machine operators,* also marks patterns for stitching, beveling, and punching holes and eyelets. The workers take care to avoid the imperfections that are in each

School Subjects
Family and Consumer Science
Shop (Trade/Vo-tech education)

Personal Interests
Clothing
Fixing things

Work Environment
Primarily indoors
Primarily one location

Minimum Education Level
High school diploma
Apprenticeship

Salary Range
$9,000 to
$15,600 to
$35,000

Certification or Licensing
None

Outlook
Decline

DOT
788

GOE
06.04.33

NOC
7343

hide and to cut the leather against the grain to minimize stretching when the shoes are worn.

Next, the lining, tongue, toe, and other parts of the shoe are sewn together on machines operated by *standard machine stitchers*. Shoe parts may be attached by machine using glue, nails, staples, and other fasteners. Other workers taper leather edges, trim linings, flatten seams, and attach buckles or eyelets. The throat of the shoe is then laced together by *lacers*.

At this point the shoe upper is still mostly flat and is missing its insole (the inside sole, on which the foot rests), outsole (the outside sole), and heel. Before these are added, the shoe needs to be shaped and made into the proper shoe size. This is done using individually sized molds called lasts, which may be made of wood or plastic and are shaped like feet. The shoe upper and lining are steamed to soften the leather, and then are secured to the lasts and stretched to conform to the last shape. This task is done by *lasters*, either by hand or with a lasting machine.

While this is being done, other workers prepare insoles, outsoles, and heels to be attached to the shoe uppers. They include *stock fitters*, who stamp rough forms for soles out of tanned hides, and *rounders*, who trim the rough soles to the proper size. Meanwhile, other workers may cut heel blanks out of wood, leather, or fiberboard and glue strips of leather trim to the heels.

The insole is the first piece that is attached to the shoe upper. It will be sewn or glued on by *thread lasters*. Next, *bottom fillers* may insert foam filling between the insole and outsole to provide a cushion for the ball of the foot and an even surface for attaching the outsole. The outsole is then stitched to the shoe by the welt, or lip of leather, that runs along the outside of the shoe. Now the shoe can be removed from the last and made ready for finishing. Heels are nailed on by *heel-nailing-machine operators*, and any excess leather or glue is removed by *machine trimmers*. *Inkers* apply ink, stain, color, glaze, or wax to the shoe parts and along the seams to color and protect the shoe, after which *brushers* hold and turn the shoe against revolving brushes to clean and polish it. After a final inspection, the shoes are ready to pack and ship to stores. If shoes have come out of the manufacturing process damaged or unfit for sale, they are sent to *cobblers*, who may use hand tools and machines to fix defects.

For shoes made of rubber, plastic, fabric, or other material, the manufacturing process is approximately the same. The die that cuts out the basic shoe pieces, however, is usually heated. Many layers of material can be cut at once because, unlike leather, the layers are uniform in color, texture, and thickness. Also, cementing and heating are used more often to join the pieces of nonleather shoes.

Custom shoe makers may assemble shoes by hand individually or they may modify manufactured shoes to meet the needs of individual customers.

Most shoe and leather repair work is still done by hand. However, the work of shoe repairers has been made easier by such technological innovations as power-operated equipment and the introduction of mass-produced replacement parts and decorative ornaments. The most frequently performed task of shoe repairers is replacing worn heels and soles. In small shops, a single worker may perform all the tasks necessary to repair an item, but in large shops, individual workers may be assigned specialized tasks. For example, sewing, trimming, buffing, and dying may be the duties of different workers called *pad hands*. However, most workers eventually move from one task to another to learn and master different skills.

When filling orders for customized products, workers first choose and check a piece of leather for texture, color, and strength. Then they place a pattern of the item being produced on the leather, trace the pattern onto the leather, cut the leather, and sew the pieces together.

Custom shoe workers also modify existing footwear for people with foot problems and special needs. They may prepare inserts, heel pads, and lifts based on plaster casts of customers' feet.

Shoe and leather workers use both hand tools and machines in their work. The most commonly used hand tools are knives, hammers, awls (used to punch holes in leather), and skivers (for splitting leather). Power-operated equipment includes sewing machines, heel nailing machines, hole punching machines, and sole stitchers.

Between 30 and 50 percent of shoe and leather repairers own their own shops. Shoe repairers who run their own establishments must be business-minded. In addition to actual repair work, they may have such managerial duties as estimating repair costs, preparing sales slips, keeping records, buying supplies, and receiving payments. They may also supervise their employees.

A few shoe repairers are employed in the shoe repair services of department stores, shoe stores, and cleaning plants. Other related types of workers include *leather stampers*, who imprint designs on leather goods, and custom-leather-products makers such as *harness makers*, *luggage makers*, and *saddle makers*.

Requirements

Shoe production workers are usually trained on the job. Beginners may go through in-house training programs operated by their employer, or they may start out in helper positions and learn the skills they need as they assist experienced workers. The training period varies. For some kinds of tasks, training can last up to two years; other operations can be learned in much less time.

A high school diploma may not be required of applicants for jobs in this field. But as more people apply for a shrinking number of positions, employers are increasingly likely to prefer those who have completed high school and have some experience in operating machines. High school courses in shop and sewing are desirable for people seeking work in this field.

A few vocational schools offer courses in shoe and boot making. These courses, which last from six months to a year, can prepare workers to start out in positions with higher wages than those open to people with no specialized training. Shoe and leather workers and repairers generally learn their craft on the job, either through in-house training programs or working as helpers to experienced craftspeople. Helpers generally begin by performing simple tasks and progress to more difficult projects such as cutting or sewing leather. Trainees generally become fully skilled in six months to two years, depending on their aptitude and dedication and the nature of the work.

A limited number of schools offer vocational training in shoe repair and leather work. These programs may last from six months to one year and teach basic skills, including leather cutting, stitching, and dying. Students in these programs learn shoe construction, practice shoe repair, and study the fundamentals of running a small business. Graduates are encouraged to gain additional training by working with an experienced leather worker or repairer. National and regional associations also offer specialized training seminars and workshops in custom shoe making, shoe repair, and other leather work.

Shoe repairers should have considerable manual dexterity, eye-hand coordination, and general physical stamina. They must also have self-discipline to in order to work alone with little supervision. Mechanical aptitude and manual dexterity are desirable for many jobs in the shoe industry. For workers who do custom work, artistic ability is important. Although there are no special educational requirements, a high school or vocational school education may help in getting a job with an established leather worker.

Approximately half of the workers in the shoe industry are represented by a union. These unions include the United Food and Commercial Workers International Union and the Amalgamated Clothing and Textile Workers Union.

Opportunities for Experience & Exploration

Students may be able to find summer or part-time jobs in the shoe industry and thus gain valuable firsthand experience as maintenance workers or assistants to experienced shoe repairers or craftworkers. However, very few jobs are available for inexperienced people who want to work on a part-time or temporary basis.

If a job cannot be found, it may be possible to get an insider's view of this work by talking with someone employed in a production job in the shoe industry. Training programs for shoe repairers are offered under the provisions of the Manpower Development and Training Act. Many vocational and trade schools also provide courses in the area of shoe making and repair.

Methods of Entering

Job seekers should apply directly, in person, to shoe factories that employ entry-level workers. The usual method of entering the shoe repair field is to be hired as a helper in a shoe repair shop that offers on-the-job training or some sort of apprenticeship program. Leads to specific jobs may be located through the local offices of the state employment service or newspaper classified ads. Graduates of vocational training programs often can get assistance in finding jobs through the placement office of the school they attended. State employment services also may list job openings.

Advancement

In the shoe industry, advancement often involves learning new skills on more complex machines. It can take from six weeks to six months to become skilled at operating some processing machines. Skill in cutting shoe uppers may take up to two years to learn. Higher wages usually accompany a change to more complicated tasks.

Some people who begin as production workers may move into positions as supervisors and managers in factories. Those with the right combination of skills may be able to open their own shoe repair shops.

Shoe repair helpers begin doing such simple tasks as staining, brushing, and shining shoes. As they gain experience, they progress to more complex jobs. After approximately two years of apprenticeship, helpers who demonstrate ability and initiative can become qualified shoe repairers. Skilled craftsworkers employed in large shops may advance to become supervisors or managers. For those who open their own shops, hard work and friendly service usually translate into increased clientele and greater income.

Employment Outlook

Employment in the shoe manufacturing industry is expected to continue to decline through the year 2006. Foreign competition has resulted in many American shoe factories closing as the labor costs for the shoes they produced were too high compared to foreign-made shoes. In fact, the United States now exports raw materials for shoes to foreign countries where workers make shoes that are returned here to be sold.

Increased automation also is causing a decline in the number of workers needed in the shoe industry. Innovations in the shoe manufacturing process such as laser cutting of materials and computer-aided design and manufacturing mean that far fewer workers are needed for many tasks, and few new jobs will open up in the future. Most job openings in this field will come about only as experienced workers retire, switch to other jobs, or otherwise leave.

Prospects are better for workers who make custom-built shoes or modify shoes for special needs. As the average age of Americans increases, more people will need special footwear, and the demand for molded and orthopedic shoes may increase.

In 1996, 21,000 shoe and leather workers and repairers were employed in the United States—a drop of 6,000 from the early 1990's. Self-employed individuals who own and operate small shoe repair shops or specialty leather manufacturing firms hold about 6,000 of these jobs. Over half of the remaining workers are employed in the manufacture of footwear products, and an additional one-fifth are employed in the production of leather goods, such as luggage, handbags, and apparel. Another fifth work in shoe repair and shoeshine shops.

Factors that limit industry growth are the increasing popularity of footwear that cannot be repaired, more durable, longer-wearing materials that require less frequent repair, and inexpensive imports that have made the cost of replacing shoes and leather goods cheaper or more convenient than repairing them. Nevertheless, retirements and job changes of experienced repairers are expected to create numerous job openings each year.

Earnings

Limited information on earnings suggests that most new workers in the shoe industry start out at low wages, perhaps as low as the federal minimum wage level, according to the U.S. Department of Labor. Average hourly wages for production workers in footwear in 1995 (the most recent figures available) were $7.79. Those working in men's footwear earned $8.27 an hour, while those working in women's footwear earned hourly wages of $7.16. The highest paid shoe industry workers are cutters, who average about $18,000 per year. Often workers receive increases within a few months, after they have gained some experience and developed job skills. Many production workers with experience are paid piecework rates, meaning that their pay is related to how much work they accomplish. Their actual earnings vary greatly, depending on such factors as the company that employs them and the nature of the job they do.

Shoe repairers on average earn about $300 a week. One in ten earns $420 or more. Assuming a forty-hour week, these workers earn an average of $15,600 a year. Employees in large shops receive from one to four weeks' paid vacation and at least six paid holidays a year. Shop owners who do brisk business earn considerably more—approximately $25,000 to $35,000 a year.

Many shoe industry workers who are union members have their pay rates and benefits set by agreements between the union and company management. Fringe benefits may include health and life insurance, employer contributions to pension plans, and paid vacation days.

Conditions of Work

In many shoe factories, production workers generally work thirty-five hours a week or less. In companies that produce custom goods, the standard workweek is about forty hours.

The work is not strenuous, but it can require stamina. Many workers are on their feet much of the time. Many jobs involve repetitive tasks. Workers who are paid according to how much they get done have an incentive to work accurately and at a brisk pace.

Conditions in plants vary. Many factories have modern, air-conditioned, well-lighted work areas, but some older plants are not as comfortable. For the most part, hazards are few if safety precautions are followed. Because so much machinery is used, plants can be very noisy. Some workers are exposed to unpleasant odors from dyes, stains, and other chemicals.

Although some repair shops are crowded, noisy, poorly lit, and characterized by unpleasant odors, working conditions in large repair shops, shoe repair departments, and in more modern shoe service stores generally tend to be good. Most shoe repairers work eight hours a day for a five- or six-day week. Self-employed workers work considerably longer—often ten hours a day.

Sources of Additional Information

Amalgamated Clothing and Textile Workers Union
15 Union Square, West
New York, NY 10003
Tel: 212-242-0700

Brotherhood of Shoe and Allied Craftsman
PO Box 390
East Bridgewater, MA 02333
Tel: 508-587-2606

Footwear Industries of America
1420 K Street, NW, Suite 600
Washington, DC 20005
Tel: 202-789-1420

Leather Industries of America
1000 Thomas Jefferson Street, NW, Suite 515
Washington, DC 20007
Tel: 202-342-8086

Pedorthic Footwear Association
9861 Broken Land Parkway, Suite 255
Columbia, MD 21046-1151
Tel: 410-381-7278

Shoe Service Institute of America
5024-R Campbell Boulevard
Baltimore, MD 21236
Tel: 410-931-8100

Software Engineers

Definition

Software engineers are responsible for customizing existing software programs to meet the needs and desires of a particular business or industry. First, they spend considerable time researching, defining, and analyzing the problem at hand. Then, they develop software programs to resolve the problem on the computer. Software engineering work is done in many fields, including medical, industrial, military, communications, aerospace, scientific, and other commercial businesses.

Nature of the Work

Every day, businesses, scientists, and government agencies encounter difficult problems that they cannot solve manually, either because the problem is just too complicated or because it would take too much time to calculate the appropriate solutions. For example, astronomers receive thousands of pieces of data every hour from probes and satellites in space as well as telescopes here on earth. If they had to process the information themselves, that is, compile careful comparisons with previous years' readings, look for patterns or cycles, and keep accurate records of the origin of the various data, it would be so cumbersome and lengthy a project as to make it next to impossible. They can, however, process the data, but only thanks to the extensive help of computers. Computer software engineers define and analyze specific problems in business or science and help develop computer software applications that effectively solve them. The software engineers that work in the field of astronomy are well versed in its concepts, but many other kinds of software engineers exist as well.

The basic structure of computer engineering is the same in any industry. First, software engineers research specific problems and investigate ways in which computers can be programmed to perform certain functions. Then, they develop

School Subjects
Computer science
Mathematics

Personal Interests
Building things
Computers

Work Environment
Primarily indoors
Primarily one location

Minimum Education Level
Bachelor's degree

Salary Range
$24,000 to
$46,000 to
$76,000+

Certification or Licensing
Recommended

Outlook
Much faster than the average

DOT
030

GOE
11.01.01

NOC
2147

software applications customized to the needs and desires of the business or organization. For example, many software engineers work with the federal government and insurance companies to develop new ways of reducing paperwork, such as income tax returns, claims forms, and applications. There are currently several independent but major form automation projects taking place throughout the United States. As software engineers find new ways to solve the problems associated with form automation, more and more forms are completed online and less on paper.

Software engineers specializing in a particular industry, such as a particular science, business, or medicine, are expected to demonstrate a certain level of proficiency in that industry. Consequently, the specific nature of their work varies from project to project and industry to industry. Software engineers also differ by the nature of their employer. Some work for consulting firms, who complete software projects for different clients on an individual basis. Others work for large companies that hire engineers full time to develop software customized to their needs. Software engineering professionals also differ by level of responsibility. *Software engineering technicians* assist engineers in completing projects. They are usually knowledgeable in analog, digital, and microprocessor electronics and programming techniques. Technicians know enough about program design and computer languages to fill in details left out by engineers or programmers, who conceive of the program from a large-scale perspective. Technicians might also test new software applications with special diagnostic equipment.

Software engineering is extremely detail-oriented work. Since computers do only what they are programmed to do, engineers have to account for every bit of information with a programming command. Software engineers are thus required to be very well organized and precise. In order to achieve this, they generally follow strict procedures in completing an assignment.

First, they interview clients and colleagues in order to determine exactly what they want the final program to be able to do. Defining the problem by outlining the goal can sometimes be difficult, especially when clients have little technical training. Then, they evaluate the software applications already in use by the client to understand how and why they are failing to fulfill the needs of the operation. After this period of fact-gathering, the engineers use methods of scientific analysis and mathematical models to develop possible solutions to the problems. These analytical methods allow them to predict and measure the outcomes of different proposed designs.

When they have developed a good notion of what type of program is required to fulfill the client's needs, they draw up a detailed proposal which includes estimates of time and cost allocations. Management must then decide if the project will meet their needs, is a good investment, and whether or not it will be undertaken.

Once a proposal is accepted, both software engineers and technicians begin work on the project. They verify with hardware engineers that the proposed software program is completed with existing hardware systems. Typically, the engineer writes program specifications and the technician uses his or her knowledge of computer languages to write preliminary programming. Engineers focus most of their effort on program strategies, testing procedures, and reviewing technicians' work.

Software engineers are usually responsible for a significant amount of technical writing, including projects proposals, progress reports, and user manuals. They are required to meet regularly with the clients in order to keep project goals clear and learn about any changes as quickly as possible.

When the program is completed, the software engineer organizes a demonstration of the final product to the client. Supervisors, management, and users are generally present. Some software engineers may offer to install the program, train users on it, and make arrangements for ongoing technical support.

Requirements

A high school diploma is the a minimum requirement for software engineering technicians. A bachelor's or advanced degree in computer science or engineering is required for most software engineers. High school students interested in pursuing this career should take as many computer, math, and science courses as possible, since they provide fundamental math and computer knowledge and teach analytical thinking skills. Classes that rely on schematic drawing and flowcharts are also very valuable. English and speech courses help students improve their communications skills, which is very important for software engineers who must make formal business presentations and interact with people having different levels of computer expertise. The qualities developed by these classes, plus an ability to work well under pressure, are key to success in software engineering.

There are several ways to enter the field of software engineering, although it is becoming increasingly necessary to pursue formal postsecondary education. Individuals without an associate's degree may first be hired in the quality assurance or technical support departments of a company. Many complete associate degrees while working and then are promoted into software engineering technician positions. As more and more well-educated professionals enter the industry, however, it is becoming more important for applicants to have at least an associate's degree in computer engineering or programming. Many technical and vocational schools offer a variety of programs that prepare students for jobs as software engineering technicians.

Interested students should consider carefully their long-range goals. Being promoted from a technician's job to that of software engineer often requires a bachelor's degree. In the past, the computer industry has tended to be fairly flexible about official credentials; demonstrated computer proficiency and work experience has often been enough to obtain a good position. This may hold true for some in the future. The majority of young computer professionals entering the field for the first time, however, will be college educated. Therefore, those with no formal education or work experience will have less chance of employment.

Obtaining a postsecondary degree in computer engineering is usually considered challenging and even difficult. In additional natural ability, students should be hard working and determined to succeed. Software engineers planning to work in specific technical fields, such as medicine, law, or business, should receive some formal training in that particular discipline.

Another option for individuals interested in software engineering is to pursue commercial certification. These programs are usually run by computer companies that wish to train professionals in working with their products. Classes are challenging and examinations can be rigorous. New programs are introduced every year; interested individuals should investigate current opportunities.

Opportunities for Experience & Exploration

Interested high school students should try to spend a day with a working software engineer or technician in order to experience firsthand what a typical day is like. School guidance counselors can help arrange such visits.

In general, students should be intent on learning as much as possible about computers. They should learn about new developments by reading trade magazines and talking to other computer users. They also can join computer clubs and surf the Internet for information about working in this field.

Methods of Entering

Most software engineers work for computer companies or consulting firms. Individuals with work experience and perhaps even an associate's degree are sometimes promoted to software engineering technician positions from entry-level jobs in quality assurance or technical support. Those already employed by computer companies or large corporations should read company job postings to learn about promotion opportunities. Employees who would like to train in software engineering, either on the job or through formal education, can investigate future career possibilities within the same company and advise management of their wish to change career tracks. Some companies offer tuition reimbursement for employees who train in areas applicable to business operations.

Technical and vocational and university students of software engineering should work closely with their schools' placement offices, as many professionals find their first position through on-campus recruiting. Placement office staff are well trained to provide tips on resume writing interviewing techniques, and locating job leads.

Individuals not working with a school placement office can check the classified ads for job openings. They also can consider working with a local employment agency that places computer professionals in appropriate jobs. Many openings in the computer industry are publicized by word of mouth, so interested individuals should stay in touch with working computer professionals to learn who is hiring. In addition, these people may be willing to refer interested job seekers directly to the person in charge of recruiting.

Advancement

With additional education and work experience, software engineering technicians may be promoted to software engineer. Software engineers who demonstrate leadership qualities and thorough technical know-how may become project team leaders who are responsible for full-scale software development projects. Project team leaders oversee the work of technicians and engineers. They determine the overall parameters of a project, calculate time schedules and financial budgets, divide the project into smaller tasks, and assign these tasks to engineers. Overall, they do both managerial and technical work.

Software engineers with experience as project team leaders may be promoted to a position as software manager, running a large research and development department. Managers oversee software projects with a more encompassing perspective; they help choose projects to be undertaken, select project team leaders and engineering teams, and assign individual projects. In some cases, they may be required to travel, solicit new business, and contribute to the general marketing strategy of the company.

Many computer professionals find that their interests change over time. As long as individuals are well qualified and keep up-to-date with the latest technology, they are usually able to find positions in other areas within the computer industry.

Employment Outlook

The field of software engineering is expected to be one of the fastest growing occupations through the year 2006. Demands made on computers increase every day and from all industries. The development of one kind of software sparks ideas for many others. In addition, users rely on software programs that are increasingly user-friendly.

Since technology changes so rapidly, software engineers are advised to keep up on the latest developments. While the need for software engineers will remain high, computer languages will probably change every few years and software engineers will need to attend seminars and workshops to learn new computer languages and software design. They also should read trade magazines, surf the Internet, and talk with colleagues about the field. These kinds of continuing education techniques help ensure that software engineers are best equipped to meet the needs of the workplace.

Earnings

Software engineering technicians usually earn beginning salaries of $24,000. Software engineers with college degrees can expect to start in the high twenties or low thirties. They generally earn more in geographical areas where there are clusters of computer companies, such as the Silicon Valley in northern California.

Mid-level salaries for technicians with some experience average about $34,000 per year. High-end salaries for technicians usually do not exceed $30,000 per year; such salaries are reserved for technicians with experience and an associate's degree. Software engineers can earn over $76,000 a year. When they are promoted into management, as project team leaders or software managers, they earn even more.

Most software engineers work for companies who offer extensive benefits, including health insurance, sick leave, and paid vacation. In some smaller computer companies, however, benefits may be limited.

Conditions of Work

Software engineers usually work in comfortable office environments. Overall, they usually work forty-hour weeks, but this depends on the nature of the employer and expertise of the engineer. In consulting firms, for example, it is typical for engineers to work very long hours and frequently travel to out-of-town assignments.

Software engineers generally receive an assignment and a timeframe within which to accomplish it; daily work details are often left up to the individuals. Some engineers work relatively lightly at the beginning of a project, but work a lot of overtime at the end in order to catch up. Most engineers are not compensated over overtime, unless the employer realizes that the projects were too complex for the preallocated time schedule. Software engineering can be stressful, especially when working to meet deadlines. Working with programming languages and intense details is often frustrating. Therefore, software engineers should be patient, enjoy problem-solving challenges, and work well under pressure.

Many software engineers give formal presentations to clients, colleagues, and managers and thus need good communications skills.

Sources of Additional Information

For more information about careers in software engineering, contact:

■ **American Software Association**
c/o ITAA
1616 North Fort Meyer Drive, Suite 1300
Arlington, VA 22209-9998
Tel: 703-522-5055

Software Management Association
PO Box 12004
Vallejo, CA 20910-3602
Tel: 707-643-4423

Special Interest Group on Software Engineering
c/o Association for Computing Machinery
1515 Broadway
New York, NY 10036-5701
Tel: 212-869-7440

American Society of Information Science
8720 Georgia Avenue, Suite 501
Silver Spring, MD 20910-3602
Tel: 301-495-0900

IEEE Computer Society
1730 Massachusetts Avenue, NW
Washington, DC 20036
Tel: 202-371-0101

Stationary Engineers

Definition

Stationary engineers operate and maintain boilers, engines, air compressors, generators, and other equipment used in providing utilities such as heat, ventilation, light, and power for large buildings, industrial plants, and other facilities. They are called stationary engineers because the equipment they work with is similar to equipment on ships or locomotives, except that it is stationary rather than located on a moving vehicle.

Nature of the Work

Stationary engineers are primarily concerned with the safe, efficient, economical operation of utilities equipment. To do their job, they must monitor meters, gauges, and other instruments attached to the equipment. They take regular readings of the instruments and keep a log of information about the operation of the equipment, such as the amount of power produced amount of fuel consumed the composition of gases given off in burning fuel temperature, pressure, and water levels inside equipment and temperature and humidity of air that has been processed through air-conditioning equipment. When the instrument readings show that the equipment is not operating in the proper ranges, they may control the operation of the equipment with levers, throttles, switches, and valves. They may override automatic controls on the equipment, switch to backup systems, or shut the equipment down.

Periodically, stationary engineers inspect the equipment and look for any parts that need adjustment, lubrication, or repair. They may tighten loose fittings, replace gaskets and filters, repack bearings, clean burners, oil moving parts, and perform similar maintenance tasks. They may test the water in boilers and add chemicals to the water to prevent scale from building up and clogging water lines. They keep records of all t routine service and repair activities.

School Subjects
Mathematics
Shop (Trade/Vo-tech education)

Personal Interests
Figuring out how things work
Fixing things

Work Environment
Primarily indoors
Primarily one location

Minimum Education Level
High school diploma
Apprenticeship

Salary Range
$17,000 to
$32,000 to
$54,000

Certification or Licensing
Required

Outlook
Decline

DOT
950

GOE
05.06.02

NOC
7351

Stationary engineers try to prevent breakdowns before they occur. But if unexpected trouble develops in the system, they must identify and correct the problem as soon as possible. They may need only to make minor repairs, or they may have to completely overhaul the equipment, using a variety of hand and power tools.

In large plants, stationary engineers may be responsible for keeping several complex systems in operation. They may be assisted by other workers, such as boiler tenders, air-conditioning and refrigeration operators and mechanics, turbine operators, and assistant stationary engineers. In small buildings, one stationary engineer at a time may be in charge of operating and maintaining the equipment.

Often the instruments and equipment that stationary engineers work with are computer controlled. This means that stationary engineers can keep track of operations throughout a system by reading computer outputs at one central location, rather than checking each piece of equipment. Sensors connected to the computers may monitor factors such as temperature and humidity in the building, and this information can be processed to help stationary engineers make decisions about operating the equipment.

Requirements

Stationary engineers may learn the skills they need by completing apprenticeships or they may learn through informal on-the-job training, often in combination with coursework at a vocational or technical school. A high school diploma or its equivalent is a requirement for either kind of training, and some college may be an advantage. Mechanical aptitude, manual dexterity, and good physical condition are also important. Because of the similarities between marine and stationary power plants, training in marine engineering during service in the U.S. Navy or Merchant Marine can be an excellent background for people who plan on going into this field. However, even with such experience, additional training and study are necessary to become a stationary engineer.

Apprenticeships combine a planned program of on-the-job training with classroom instruction in related fields. Apprenticeships are administered by local committees representing both the management of companies that employ stationary engineers and the union to which many stationary engineers belong, the International Union of Operating Engineers. Although local committees may establish slightly different requirements, they generally prefer applicants for apprenticeships who have taken courses in computers, mathematics, physics, chemistry, mechanical drawing, and machine shop.

Apprenticeships usually last four years. In the practical experience part of their training, apprentices learn how to operate, maintain, and repair stationary equipment such as blowers, generators, compressors, motors, and refrigeration machinery. They become familiar with precision measurement devices such as calipers and micrometers; hand and machine tools, including electric grinders, lathes, and drill presses; and hoists, blocks, and other equipment used in lifting heavy machines. In the classroom, apprentices study relevant technical subjects such as practical chemistry and physics, applied mathematics, computers, blueprint reading, electricity and electronics, and instrumentation.

People who learn their skills on the job work under the supervision of experienced stationary engineers. They may start as boiler tenders or helpers, doing simple tasks that require no special skills, and learn gradually through practical experience. If their job offers few opportunities to learn new skills, it may take many years for workers to acquire all the skills they need. The process may go more quickly if they take courses at a vocational or technical school in subjects such as computerized controls and instrumentation.

Even after they are well trained and experienced in their field, stationary engineers should take short courses to update their knowledge of relevant equipment. Employers often pay for this kind of additional training. When new equipment is installed in a building, representatives of the equipment manufacturer may present special training programs to introduce its functions.

Most states and cities require licensing for stationary engineers to operate equipment. There are several classes of license, depending on the kind of equipment and its steam pressure or horsepower. A first-class license qualifies workers to operate any equipment, regardless of size or capacity. Stationary engineers in charge of large equipment complexes and those who supervise other workers need this kind of license. Other classes of licenses limit the capacities or types of equipment that the license holders may operate without supervision.

The requirements for obtaining these licenses vary from place to place. In general, applicants must meet certain training and experience requirements for the class of license, pass a written examination, and be at least eighteen years old and a resident of the city or state for a specified period of time. When licensed stationary engineers move to another city or state, they may have to meet different licensure requirements and take a different examination.

Opportunities for Experience & Exploration

A good way of to learn about this work is to get a part-time or summer job in an industrial plant or another large facility where utility equipment is run by a stationary engineer. Even an unskilled position, such as custodian in a boiler room, can provide an opportunity to observe the work and conditions in this occupation. A talk with a stationary engineer or a union representative may also prove helpful.

Methods of Entering

Stationary engineers often start out working as craftworkers in other fields. Information about job openings, apprenticeships, and other training for this field may be obtained through the local offices of the state employment service or the International Union of Operating Engineers. State and city licensing agencies can give details on local licensure requirements and perhaps possible job leads.

Advancement

Experienced stationary engineers may advance to jobs in which they are responsible for operating and maintaining larger or more complex equipment installations. Such job changes may become possible as stationary engineers obtain higher classes of licenses. Obtaining these licenses, however, does not guarantee advancement. Many first-class stationary engineers must work as assistants to other first-class stationary engineers until a position becomes available. Stationary engineers may also move into positions as boiler inspectors, chief plant engineers, building superintendents, building managers, or technical instructors. Additional training or formal education may be needed for some of these positions.

Employment Outlook

The total number of people employed in this field is expected to decline through the year 2006. Although industrial and commercial development will continue, and thus more equipment will be installed and need to be operated by stationary engineers, much of the new equipment will be automated and computerized. The greater efficiency of such controls and instrumentation will tend to reduce the demand for stationary engineers. Nonetheless, most job openings will develop in this field when workers transfer or leave the workforce due to retirement. Stationary engineering, due to the high salary it offers, has very little turnover. Opportunities will be best for workers who have completed apprenticeships or technical school training.

Earnings

Earnings of stationary engineers vary widely, usually falling between $17,000 and $54,000 a year. The median annual salary is $32,000. In metropolitan areas, where most jobs are located, earnings tend to be higher than in nonmetropolitan areas. Stationary engineers in metropolitan areas of the West have the highest average earnings; those in the South have the lowest; and workers in the Midwest and Northeast are close to the national average for metropolitan areas.

Most stationary engineers receive fringe benefits in addition to their regular wages. Benefits may include life and health insurance, paid vacation and sick days, employer reimbursement for work-related courses, and pension plans.

Conditions of Work

Stationary engineers usually work shifts of about eight hours, five days a week. Because the plants where they work may operate twenty-four hours a day, some stationary engineers regularly work afternoon or night shifts, weekends, or holidays. Some work rotating shifts. Occasionally overtime hours are necessary, such as when equipment breaks down and must be returned to full operation as soon as possible.

Most boiler rooms, power plants, and engine rooms are clean and well lighted, but stationary engineers may still encounter some uncomfortable conditions in the course of their work. They may be exposed to high temperatures, dirt, grease, odors, and smoke. At times they may need to crouch, kneel, crawl inside equipment, or work in awkward positions. They may spend much of their time on their feet. There is some danger attached to working around boilers and electrical and mechanical equipment, but following good safety practices greatly reduces the possibility of injury. By staying constantly on the alert, stationary engineers can avoid burns, electrical shock, and injuries from moving parts.

Sources of Additional Information

■ **International Union of Operating Engineers**
1125 17th Street, NW
Washington, DC 20036
Tel: 202-429-9100

■ **National Association of Power Engineers, Inc.**
5-7 Springfield Street
Chicopee, MA 01013
Tel: 413-592-6273

Stock Clerks

Definition

Stock clerks receive, unpack, store, distribute, and record the inventory for materials or products used by a company, plant, or store.

Nature of the Work

Stock clerks work in just about every type of industry, and no matter what kind of storage or stock room they staff—food, clothing, merchandise, medicine, or raw materials—the work of stock clerks is essentially the same. They receive, sort, put away, distribute, and keep track of the items a business sells or uses. Their titles sometimes vary based on their responsibilities.

When goods are received in a stockroom, stock clerks unpack the shipment and check the contents against documents such as the invoice, purchase order, and bill of lading, which lists the contents of the shipment. The shipment is inspected, and any damaged goods are set aside. Stock clerks may reject or send back damaged items or call vendors to complain about the condition of the shipment. In large companies this work might be done by a *shipping and receiving clerk*.

Once the goods are received, stock clerks organize them and sometimes mark them with identifying codes or prices so they can be placed in stock according to the existing inventory system. In this way the materials or goods can be found quickly and easily when needed, and inventory control is much easier. In many firms stock clerks use hand-held scanners and computers to keep inventory records up-to-date.

In retail stores and supermarkets stock clerks may bring merchandise to the sales floor and stock shelves and racks. In stockrooms and warehouses they store materials in bins, on the floor, or on shelves. In other settings, such as restaurants, hotels, and factories, stock clerks deliver goods when they are needed. They may do this on a regular schedule or at the

School Subjects
English
(writing/literature)
Mathematics

Personal Interests
Business
Figuring out how things work

Work Environment
Primarily indoors
Primarily one location

Minimum Education Level
High school diploma

Salary Range
$12,500 to
$19,000 to
$22,000

Certification or Licensing
None

Outlook
Little change or more slowly than the average

DOT
222

GOE
05.09.01

NOC
1474

request of other employees or supervisors. Although many stock clerks use mechanical equipment, such as forklifts, to move heavy items, some perform strenuous and laborious work. In general, the work of a stock clerk involves much standing, bending, walking, stretching, lifting, and carrying.

When items are removed from the inventory, stock clerks adjust records to reflect the products' use. These records are kept as current as possible, and inventories are periodically checked against these records. Every item is counted, and the totals are compared with the records on hand or the records from the sales, shipping, production, or purchasing departments. This helps identify how fast items are being used, when items must be ordered from outside suppliers, or even whether items are disappearing from the stockroom. Many retail establishments use computerized cash registers that maintain an inventory count automatically as they record the sale of each item.

The duties of stock clerks often vary depending on their place of employment. Stock clerks working in small firms perform many different tasks, including shipping and receiving, inventory control, and purchasing. In large firms, responsibilities may be more narrow. More specific job categories include *inventory clerks, stock-control clerks, material clerks, order fillers, merchandise distributors,* and shipping and receiving clerks.

At a construction site or factory that uses a variety of raw and finished materials, there are many different types of specialized work for stock clerks. *Tool-crib attendants* issue, receive, and store the various hand tools, machine tools, dies, and other equipment used in an industrial establishment. They make sure the tools come back in reasonably good shape and keep track of those that need replacing. *Parts-order-and-stock clerks* purchase, store, and distribute the spare parts needed for motor vehicles and other industrial equipment. *Metal-control coordinators* oversee the movement of metal stock and supplies used in producing nonferrous metal sheets, bars, tubing, and alloys. In mining and other industries that regularly use explosives, *magazine keepers* store explosive materials and components safely and distribute them to authorized personnel. In the military, *space-and-storage clerks* keep track of the weights and amounts of ammunition and explosive components stored in the magazines of an arsenal and check their storage condition.

Many types of stock clerks can be found in other industries. At printing companies, *cut-file clerks* collect, store, and hand out the layout cuts, ads, mats, and electrotypes used in the printing process. *Parts clerks* handle and distribute spare and replacement parts in repair and maintenance shops. In eyeglass centers, *prescription clerks* select (according to the optometrist's specifications) the lens blanks and frames for making eyeglasses and keep inventory stocked at a specified level. In motion picture companies, *property custodians* receive, store, and distribute the props needed for shooting. In hotels and hospitals, *linen-room attendants* issue and keep track of inventories of bed linen, table cloths, and uniforms, while *kitchen clerks* verify the quantity and quality of food products being taken from the storeroom to the kitchen. Aboard ships, the clerk in charge of receiving and issuing supplies and keeping track of inventory is known as the *storekeeper.*

Requirements

Although there are no specific educational requirements for beginning stock clerks, employers prefer to hire high school graduates. Reading and writing skills and a basic knowledge of mathematics are necessary; typing and filing skills are also useful. In the future, as more companies install computerized inventory systems, a knowledge of computer operations will important. Good health and good eyesight is important.

Depending on where they work, some stock clerks may be required to join a union. This is especially true of stock clerks who are employed by industry and who work in large cities with a high percentage of union-affiliated companies.

When a stock clerk handles certain types of materials, extra training or certification may be required. Generally those who handle jewelry, liquor, or drugs must be bonded.

Opportunities for Experience & Exploration

The best way to learn about the responsibilities of a stock clerk is to get a part-time or summer job as a sales clerk, *stockroom helper, stockroom clerk,* or, in some factories, *stock chaser.* These jobs are relatively easy to get and can help students learn about stock work, as well as about the duties of workers in related positions. This sort of part-time work can also lead to a full-time job.

Methods of Entering

Job openings for stock clerks are often listed in newspaper classified ads. Job seekers should contact the personnel office of the firm looking for stock clerks and fill out an application for employment. School counselors, parents, relatives, and friends can also be good sources for job leads and may be able to give personal references if an employer requires them.

Stock clerks usually receive on-the-job training. New workers start with simple tasks, such as counting and marking stock. The basic responsibilities of the job are usually learned within the first few weeks. As they progress, stock clerks learn to keep records of incoming and outgoing materials, take inventories, and place orders. As wholesale and warehousing establishments convert to automated inventory systems, stock clerks need to be trained to use the new equipment. Stock clerks who bring merchandise to the sales floor and stock shelves and sales racks need little training.

Advancement

Stock clerks with ability and determination have a good chance of being promoted to jobs with greater responsibility. In small firms, stock clerks might advance to sales positions or become assistant buyers or purchasing agents. In large firms, stock clerks can advance to more responsible stock-handling jobs, such as invoice clerk, stock control clerk, and procurement clerk.

Furthering one's education can lead to more opportunities for advancement. By studying at a technical or business school or taking home-study courses, stock clerks can prove to their employer that they have the intelligence and ambition to take on more important tasks. More advanced positions, such as warehouse manager and purchasing agent, are usually given to experienced people who have post–high school education.

Employment Outlook

More than 1.8 million people worked as stock clerks in 1996. Of these, 80 percent worked wholesale or retail trades. Many sales-floor clerks work part time. Nearly all sales-floor stock clerks are employed in retail establishments, with about two-thirds working in supermarkets. Jobs can be found throughout the country, but are most plentiful in larger urban areas.

Although the volume of inventory transactions is expected to increase significantly, employment for stock clerks is expected to grow more slowly than the average for all occupations through the year 2006. This is a result of increased automation and other productivity improvements that enable clerks to handle more stock. Manufacturing and wholesale trade industries make the greatest use of automation. In addition to computerized inventory control systems, firms in these industries are expected to rely more on sophisticated conveyor belts, automatic high stackers to store and retrieve goods, and automatic guided vehicles that are battery-powered and driverless. Sales-floor stock clerks will probably be less affected by automation as most of their work is done on the sales floor, where it is difficult to locate or operate complicated machinery.

Because this occupation employs a large number of people, many job openings occur each year to replace stock clerks who transfer to other jobs and leave the labor force. Stock clerk jobs tend to be entry-level positions, so many vacancies will be created by normal career progression to other occupations.

Earnings

Beginning stock clerks usually earn the minimum wage or slightly more. Experienced stock clerks can earn anywhere from $5.50 to $10.00 per hour, with time-and-a-half pay for overtime. Average earnings vary depending on the type of industry and geographic location. The U.S. Department of Labor lists the 1996 median annual income for stock clerks to be about $19,000. Stock clerks working in the retail trade generally earn wages in the middle range. In transportation, utilities, and wholesale businesses, earnings are usually higher; in finance, insurance, real estate, and other types of office services, earnings are usually lower. Those working for large companies or national chains may receive excellent benefits. After one year of employment, some stock clerks are offered one to two weeks of paid vacation each year, as well as health and medical insurance and a retirement plan.

Conditions of Work

Stock clerks usually work in relatively clean, comfortable areas. Working conditions vary considerably, however, depending on the industry and type of merchandise being handled. For example, stock clerks who handle refrigerated goods must spend some time in cold storage rooms, while those who handle construction materials, such as bricks and lumber, occasionally work outside in harsh weather. Most stock clerk jobs involve much standing, bending, walking, stretching, lifting, and carrying. Some may be required to operate machinery to lift and move stock.

Because stock clerks are employed in so many different types of industries, the amount of hours worked every week depends on the type of employer. Usually stock clerks in retail stores work a five-day, forty-hour week, while those in industry work forty-four hours, or five and one half day, a week. Many others are able to find part-time work. Overtime is common, especially when large shipments arrive or during peak times such as holiday seasons.

Sources of Additional Information

■ **National Retail Federation**
325 7th Street, NW, Suite 1000
Washington, DC 20004
Tel: 202-783-7971

■ **Food Marketing Institute**
800 Connecticut Avenue, NW
Information Service
Washington, DC 20006-2701
Tel: 202-452-8444

Surgical Technologists

Definition

Surgical technologists, also called *surgical technicians* or *operating room technicians,* are members of the surgical team who work in the operating room with surgeons, nurses, anesthesiologists, and other personnel before, during, and after surgery. They perform functions that ensure a safe and sterile environment for surgical procedures before, during, and after surgery. To prepare a patient for surgery, they may wash, shave, and disinfect the area where the incision will be made. They arrange the equipment, instruments, and supplies in the operating room according to the preference of the surgeons and nurses. During the operation, they adjust lights and other equipment as needed. They assist by counting sponges, needles, and instruments used during the operation, by handing instruments and supplies to the surgeon, and by holding retractors and cutting sutures as directed. They maintain specified supplies of fluids such as saline, plasma, blood, and glucose and may assist in administering these fluids. Following the operation, they may clean and restock the operating room and wash and sterilize the used equipment using germicides, autoclaves, and sterilizers, although in most larger hospitals these tasks are done by other central service personnel.

Nature of the Work

Surgical technologists are allied health professionals who work in the surgical suite with surgeons, anesthesiologists, registered nurses, and other surgical personnel delivering surgical patient care.

In general, the work responsibilities of surgical technologists may be divided into three phases: preoperative (before surgery), intraoperative (during surgery), and postoperative (after surgery). Surgical technologists may work as the scrub person, circulator, or surgical first assistant.

School Subjects
Biology
Health

Personal Interests
Helping people: physical health/medicine
Helping people: emotionally

Work Environment
Primarily indoors
Primarily one location

Minimum Education Level
Some postsecondary training

Salary Range
$20,900 to
$25,000 to
$28,000+

Certification or Licensing
Recommended

Outlook
Much faster than the average

DOT
079

GOE
10.03.02

NOC
3219

In the preoperative phase, surgical technologists prepare the operating room by selecting and opening sterile supplies such as drapes, sutures, sponges, electrosurgical devices, suction tubing, and surgical instruments. They assemble, adjust, and check non-sterile equipment to ensure that it is in proper working order. Surgical technologists also operate sterilizers, lights, suction machines, electrosurgical units, and diagnostic equipment.

When patients arrive in the surgical suite, surgical technologists may assist in preparing them for surgery by providing physical and emotional support, checking charts, and observing vital signs. They properly position the patient on the operating table, assist in connecting and applying surgical equipment and monitoring devices, and prepare the incision site by cleansing the skin with an antiseptic solution.

During surgery, surgical technologists have primary responsibility for maintaining the sterile field. They constantly watch that all members of the team adhere to aseptic technique so the patient does not develop a postoperative infection. As the *scrub person,* they most often function as the sterile member of the surgical team who passes instruments, sutures, and sponges during surgery. After "scrubbing," which involves the thorough cleansing of the hands and forearms, they put on a sterile gown and gloves and prepare the sterile instruments and supplies that will be needed. After other members of the sterile team have scrubbed, they assist them with gowning and gloving and applying sterile drapes around the operative site.

Surgical technologists must anticipate the needs of surgeons during the procedure, passing instruments and providing sterile items in an efficient manner. Checking, mixing, and dispensing appropriate fluids and drugs in the sterile field are other common tasks. They share with the *circulator* the responsibility for accounting for sponges, needles, and instruments before, during, and after surgery. They may hold retractors or instruments, sponge or suction the operative site, or cut suture material as directed by the surgeon. They connect drains and tubing and receive and prepare specimens for subsequent pathologic analysis.

Surgical technologists most often function as the scrub person, but may function in the nonsterile role of circulator. The circulator does not wear a sterile gown and gloves, but is available to assist the surgical team. As a circulator, the surgical technologist obtains additional supplies or equipment, assists the individual providing anesthesia, keeps a written account of the surgical procedure, and assists the scrub person in counting sponges, needles, and instruments before, during, and after surgery.

Surgical first assistants, those technologists with additional education or training, provide aid in retract-ing tissue, controlling bleeding, and other technical functions that help surgeons during the procedure.

After surgery, surgical technologists are responsible for preparing and applying dressings, including plaster or synthetic casting materials, and for preparing the operating room for the next patient. They may provide staffing in postoperative recovery rooms where patients' responses are carefully monitored in the critical phases following general anesthesia.

Some of these responsibilities vary depending on the size of the hospital and department in which the surgical technologist works; they also vary based on geographic location and health care needs of the local community.

Requirements

Surgical technology education is available through postsecondary programs offered by community and junior colleges, vocational and technical schools, the military, universities, and structured hospital programs in surgical technology. A high school diploma is required for entry into any of these programs. During their high school years, prospective technologists should take courses that develop their basic skills in mathematics, science, and English. They also should take all available courses in health and biology.

More than 150 of these programs are accredited by the Commission on Accreditation of Allied Health Education Programs (CAAHEP). The accredited programs vary from nine to twelve months for a diploma or certificate, to two years for an associate's degree. Students can expect to take courses in medical terminology, communications, anatomy, physiology, microbiology, pharmacology, medical ethics, and legal responsibilities. Students gain a thorough knowledge of patient preparation and care, surgical procedures, surgical instruments and equipment, and principles of asepsis (how to prevent infection). In addition to classroom learning, students receive intensive supervised clinical experience in local hospitals, which is an important component of their education.

Surgical technologists may earn a professional credential by passing a nationally administered certifying examination. Those who become certified are granted the designation of certified surgical technologist (CST). Increasing numbers of hospitals are requiring certification as a condition of employment. To take the examination, an individual must be currently or previously certified or be a graduate of a formal educational program or its equivalent (starting in the year 2000, only graduates of CAAHEP-accredited programs will be eligible to take the test). The Liaison Council on Certification for the Surgical Technologist (LCC-

ST), an independent affiliate of the Association of Surgical Technologists, is the certifying agency for the profession. Those who become certified demonstrate a commitment to maximum performance and quality patient care. To renew the six-year certificate, the CST must earn continuing education credits or retake the certifying examination. The LCC-ST also offers an advanced credential for surgical first assistants; this exam awards the designation of CST certified first assistant (CST/CFA).

Surgical technologists must possess an educational background in the medical sciences, strong sense of responsibility, concern for order, and ability to integrate a number of tasks at the same time. They need good manual dexterity to handle awkward surgical instruments with speed and agility. In addition, they need physical stamina to stand through long surgical procedures.

Opportunities for Experience & Exploration

It is difficult for interested students to gain any direct experience on a part-time basis in surgical technology. The first opportunities for direct experience generally come in the clinical and laboratory phases of their educational programs. However, interested students can explore some aspects of this career in several ways. They or their teachers can arrange a visit to a hospital, clinic, or other surgical setting in order to learn about the work. They also can visit a school with a CAAHEP-accredited program. During such a visit, a student can discuss career plans with the admissions counselor. In addition, volunteering at a local hospital or nursing home can give students insight into the health care environment and help them to evaluate their interests aptitude to work in such a setting.

Methods of Entering

Graduates of programs are often offered jobs in the same hospital in which they received their clinical training. Programs usually cooperate closely with hospitals in the area, which are usually eager to employ technologists educated in local programs. Available positions are also advertised in newspaper want ads.

Advancement

As of 1996, surgical technologists in the United States numbered over 49,000. Most technologists are employed in hospital operating rooms. They also work in delivery rooms, cast rooms, emergency departments, ambulatory care areas, and central supply departments. With increased experience, they can serve in management roles in surgical services departments and may work as central service managers, surgery schedulers, and materials managers. The role of surgical first assistant on the surgical team requires additional training and experience and is considered an advanced role. Surgical technologists may also be employed directly by surgeons as private scrubs or as surgical first assistants or they may work in clinics and surgicenters.

Surgical technologists function well in a number of diverse areas. Their multicompetency is demonstrated by their employment in organ and tissue procurement/preservation, cardiac catheterization laboratories, medical sales and research, and medical-legal auditing for insurance companies. A number are instructors and directors of surgical technology programs.

Employment Outlook

Job opportunities for competent surgical technologists far exceed the supply. According to the U.S. Bureau of Labor Statistics, the field of surgical technology is projected to experience rapid job growth through the year 2006. Population growth, longevity, and improvement in medical and surgical procedures have all contributed to a growing demand for surgical services and hence for surgical technologists. As long as the rate at which people undergo surgery continues to increase, there will continue to be a need for this profession. Also, as surgical methods become increasingly complex, more surgical technologists will likely be needed.

Many surgeries are also performed on an outpatient basis in clinics and surgeons' offices. This current trend will increase the demand for surgical technologists employed in such settings.

Staffing patterns are also changing in response to the need to control costs. Hospitals are changing their staffing ratios of registered nurses to other health care workers and are employing more allied health professionals such as surgical technologists who can provide cost-effective care. On the other hand, hospitals are also increasing their use of multiskilled workers who can handle a wide variety of tasks in different areas of the hospital. A number of health care workers, including surgical technologists, are being asked by their employers to participate in training programs to become multiskilled.

Earnings

Salaries vary greatly in different institutions and localities. The average salary for surgical technologists is $25,000, but ranges from $20,900 to $28,000 a year (excluding overtime). Some technologists with experience earn much more. Most surgical technologists are required to be periodically on-call—available to work on short notice in cases of emergency—and can earn overtime from such work. Graduates of educational programs usually receive salaries higher than technologists without formal education. In general, technologists working on the East and West coasts earn more than surgical technologists in other parts of the country. Surgical first assistants and private scrubs employed directly by surgeons tend to earn more than surgical technologists employed by hospitals.

Conditions of Work

Surgical technologists naturally spend most of their time in the operating room. Operating rooms are cool, well lighted, orderly, and extremely clean. Technologists are often required to be on their feet for long intervals during which their attention must be closely focused on the operation.

Members of the surgical team, including surgical technologists, wear sterile gowns, gloves, caps, masks, and eye protection. This surgical attire is meant not only to protect the patient from infection but also to protect the surgical team from any infection or blood-borne diseases that the patient may have. Surgery is usually performed during the day; however, hospitals, clinics, and other facilities require twenty-four-hour-a-day coverage. Most surgical technologists work regular forty-hour weeks, although many are required to be periodically on call.

Surgical technologists must be able to work under great pressure in stressful situations. The need for surgery is often a matter of life and death, and one can never assume that procedures will go as planned. If operations do not go well, nerves may fray and tempers flare. Technologists must understand that this is the result of stressful conditions and should not take this anger personally.

In addition, surgical technologists should have a strong desire to help others. Surgery is performed on people, not machines. Patients literally entrust their lives to the surgical team, and they rely on them to treat them in a dignified and professional manner. Individuals with these characteristics find surgical technology a rewarding career in which they can make an important contribution to the health and well-being of their community.

Sources of Additional Information

Association of Surgical Technologists (AST)
7108-C South Alton Way, Suite 100
Englewood, CO 80112-2106
Tel: 303-694-9130

Surveyors

Definition

Surveyors mark exact measurements and locations of elevations, points, lines, and contours on or near the earth's surface. They measure the distances between points to determine property boundaries and to provide data for mapmaking, construction projects, and other engineering purposes.

Nature of the Work

The surveyor's party chief and party are usually the first workers to be involved in any job requiring the precise determination of points, locations, lines, or elevations. On proposed construction projects—superhighways, airstrips, housing developments and bridges—it is the surveyor's responsibility to make the necessary measurements by conducting an accurate and detailed survey of the area.

The surveyor usually works with a field party consisting of several people. Instrument assistants handle a variety of surveying instruments including the theodolite, transit, level, surveyor's chain, rod, and different types of electronic equipment used to measure distance or locate a position. In the course of the survey, it is important that all readings be accurately recorded and field notes maintained so that the survey can be checked for accuracy by the surveyor.

Surveyors may become expert in one or more particular types of surveying.

Land surveyors establish township, property, and other tract-of-land boundary lines. Using maps, notes, or actual land title deeds, they survey the land, checking the accuracy of existing records. This information is used to prepare legal documents such as deeds and leases. Land surveying managers coordinate the work of land surveyors and their survey parties with that of legal, engineering, architectural, and other staff involved with the project. In addition, these managers develop

School Subjects
Geography
Mathematics

Personal Interests
Computers
Drawing

Work Environment
Primarily outdoors
Primarily multiple locations

Minimum Education Level
Bachelor's degree

Salary Range
$14,240 to
$35,088 to
$47,850+

Certification or Licensing
Required

Outlook
Decline

DOT
018

GOE
05.01.06

NOC
2154

policy, prepare budgets, certify work upon completion, and handle numerous other administrative duties.

A *highway surveyor* establishes points, grades, lines, and other points of reference for highway construction projects. This survey information is essential to the work of the numerous engineers and the construction crews who actually plan and build the new highway.

A *geodetic surveyor* measures such large masses of land, sea, or space that the measurements must take into account the curvature of the earth and its geophysical characteristics. This person's work is helpful in establishing points of reference for smaller land surveys, for determining national boundaries, and in preparing maps. *Geodetic computers* calculate latitude, longitude, angles, areas, and other information needed for mapmaking. They work from field notes made by an engineering survey party using reference tables and a calculating machine or computer.

A *marine surveyor* makes surveys of harbors, rivers, and other bodies of water. This person determines the depth of the water, usually by taking soundings or sound measurements, in relation to land masses. These surveys are essential in planning navigation projects, in developing plans for and constructing breakwaters, dams, piers, marinas, and bridges, and or in constructing nautical charts and maps.

A *mine surveyor* makes surface and underground surveys, preparing maps of mines and mining operations. Such maps are helpful in examining underground passages on and between levels of a mine and in assessing the strata and volume of raw material available.

A *geophysical prospecting surveyor* locates and marks sites considered likely to contain petroleum deposits. *Oil-well directional surveyors* use sonic, electronic, or nuclear measuring instruments to gauge the characteristics of earth formations in boreholes from which they evaluate the productivity of oil- or gas-bearing reservoirs. A *pipeline surveyor* determines rights-of-way for oil pipeline construction projects. This surveyor establishes the right of way, property lines and assembles the information essential to the preparation for and laying of the lines.

A *photogrammetric engineer* determines the contour of an area to show elevations and depressions and indicates such features as mountains, lakes, rivers, forests, roads, farms, buildings, and other landmarks. Aerial, land, or water photographs used in this work are taken with special photographic equipment installed in the airplane or ground station that permits pictures of large areas to be made. From these pictures, accurate measurements of the terrain and surface features can be made. These surveys are helpful in highway and engineering planning and the preparation of topographical maps. Photogrammetry, as photo surveying is termed, is particularly helpful in charting areas that are inaccessible or difficult to travel.

Requirements

High school students interested in a career as a surveyor should take algebra, geometry, trigonometry, physics, mechanical drawing, and other related science or drafting courses.

After high school, students should take a four-year college program in surveying or engineering. Civil engineering, with a surveying emphasis, is a common major selected by students wishing to become surveyors because the two fields are so closely allied. Graduate study is necessary for advancement in the highly technical areas.

Because the surveyor spends a great deal of time in field surveys, an interest in working outdoors is necessary. Surveying involves working with other people and often requires directing or supervising the work of others. Therefore, a surveyor must have leadership qualities for supervisory positions.

The ability to work with numbers and perform mathematical computations accurately and quickly is very important. Other helpful abilities are the ability to visualize and understand objects in two or three dimensions (spatial relationships) and the ability to discriminate between and compare shapes, sizes, lines, shadings, and other forms (form perception). Surveyors walk a great deal and carry equipment over all types of terrain. Endurance, coordination, and the ability to compensate for physical impairment are important physical assets in the surveyor.

All fifty states require that surveyors making property and boundary surveys are licensed or registered. The requirements for licensure vary, but in general they include one of the following: be a college graduate with two to four years of experience, have at least six years' experience and be able to pass an examination in land surveying, or have at least ten years' experience. Information on specific requirements can be obtained by contacting the appropriate state agency in the capital of the state in which one plans to work. Those seeking employment in the federal government must take a civil service examination and meet the educational, experience, and other specified requirements for the position in which they are interested.

Opportunities for Experience & Exploration

One of the best opportunities for experience is to seek a summer job with a construction outfit or company that is planning survey work. This may be private or government work. Even if the job does not involve direct contact with survey crews, it will offer an opportunity to observe surveyors and talk with them about their work.

Some colleges have work-study programs that offer periodic on-the-job experiences. These opportunities, like summer or part-time jobs, can be helpful to someone considering this field as a career.

Methods of Entering

Some people get jobs as instrument assistants with a surveying firm. College graduates can learn about job openings through their schools' placement services. In many cities, employment agencies specialize in positions in surveying and related fields.

Advancement

Surveyors with the highest level of education and initiative in keeping up with technological developments in the field can become party chiefs.

There are many who believe that surveying has been too long isolated from engineering, and that land surveying is engineering. With the increasing requirement of an engineering degree for entrance to surveying in several states, it will be easier to transfer to a larger number of related positions. Although a surveying or civil engineering program is recommended for a prospective surveyor, one could major in electrical, mechanical, or chemical engineering. Drafting is another related field to which a surveyor might move.

Employment Outlook

Nearly three-fifths of the estimated 101,000 surveyors in the United States are employed in engineering, architectural, and surveying firms. Federal, state, and local government agencies employ about one-fourth, and most of the rest work for construction companies, oil and gas extraction companies, and public utilities. Approximately 8,000 surveyors are self-employed.

The employment outlook in surveying is expected to decline slightly as compared to the average of most occupations through the year 2006. In view of the pressure for preparation in engineering as a prerequisite for professional status and licensure, opportunities will be better for those who have college degrees.

Technology has had a great impact on this field. Satellite systems such as the Global Positioning System (GPS), and geographic information system (GIS), have made it easier for surveyors to measure and map out areas. Though it may lessen workloads, such advances have decreased demand for new hires. The majority of job openings will result from current workers retiring from the workforce. Depending on the health of the economy, the government may or may not spend funds to repair roads, highways, recreation areas, and housing developments. Therefore, a strong economy will spur the demand for surveyors.

Earnings

The median 1996 annual earnings for surveyors, according to the U.S. Department of Labor, was about $35,088. The federal government hires high school graduates as surveyor helpers at about $14,240 per year and as instrument assistants at about $17,450 per year. The federal government hires land surveyors at about $19,520 per year, depending on their qualifications. The average salary for all land surveyors in the federal government in 1997 was $47,850.

In private industry, beginning salaries are comparable to those offered by the federal government, according to the limited information available. Most positions with the federal, state, and local governments and with private firms provide the usual medical, pension, insurance, vacation, and holiday benefits.

Conditions of Work

The surveyor works the usual forty-hour week except when overtime is necessary to complete a survey so that a project can be started immediately. The peak work period for the surveyor comes during the summer months when weather conditions are most favorable. However, it is not uncommon for the surveyor to be exposed to all types of weather conditions.

Some survey projects involve a certain amount of hazard, depending upon the region and climate as well as the plant and animal life. Field survey crews encounter snakes, poison ivy, and other plant and animal life; they are subject to heat exhaustion, sunburn, and frostbite. Some survey projects, particularly those being conducted near construction projects or busy highways, impose the danger of injury from heavy traffic, flying objects, and other accidental hazards. Much of the surveying of vast lands and large mountain formations is beginning to be done with satellite technology. Thus, remote area studies may become less frequent. However, small areas of study will be more cost effective when surveyed by teams on the ground. Unless the surveyor is employed for office assignments, where the working conditions are similar to those of other office workers, the work location most likely will change from survey to survey. Some assignments may necessitate being away from home for periods of time.

Sources of Additional Information

American Congress on Surveying and Mapping
5410 Grosvenor Lane, Suite 100
Bethesda, MD 20814
Tel: 301-493-0200
WWW: http://www.landsurveyor.com

American Society for Photogrammetry and Remote Sensing
5410 Grosvenor Lane, Suite 210
Bethesda, MD 20814
Tel: 301-493-0290

Tailors and Dressmakers

Definition

Tailors and *dressmakers* cut, sew, mend, and alter custom-made clothing. Typically, tailors work only with menswear, such as suits, jackets, and coats, while dressmakers work with women's clothing, including dresses, blouses, suits, evening wear, wedding and bridesmaids' gowns, and sportswear.

Nature of the Work

Some tailors and dressmakers make garments from start to completion. In larger shops, however, each employee usually works on a specific task, such as measuring, patternmaking, cutting, fitting or stitching. One worker, for example, may only sew in sleeves or pad lapels. Smaller shops may only measure and fit the garment, then send piecework to outside contractors. Some tailors and dressmakers specialize in one type of garment, such as suits or wedding gowns. Many also do alterations on factory-made clothing.

Tailors and dressmakers may run their own businesses, work in small shops, or work in custom tailoring sections of large department stores. Some work out of their homes. Retail clothing stores, specialty stores, bridal shops, and dry cleaners also employ tailors and dressmakers to do alterations.

Tailors and dressmakers first help customers choose the garment style and fabric, using their knowledge of the various types of fabrics. They take the customer's measurements, such as height, shoulder width, arm length, and waist, and note any special figure problems. They may use ready-made, paper patterns or make one of their own. The patterns are then placed on the fabric and the fabric pieces are carefully cut. When the garment design is complex, or if there are special fitting problems, the tailor or dressmaker may cut the pattern from inexpensive muslin and fit it to the customer; any adjustments are then marked and transferred to the paper pattern before it is used to cut the actual garment fabric. The pieces are basted

School Subjects
Art
Family and consumer science

Personal Interests
Clothing
Helping people: personal service

Work Environment
Primarily indoors
Primarily one location

Minimum Education Level
High school diploma

Salary Range
$12,369 to
$20,800 to
$40,000+

Certification or Licensing
None

Outlook
Decline

DOT
785

GOE
05.05.15

NOC
7342

together first and then sewn by hand or machine. After one or two fittings, which confirm that the garment fits the customer properly, the tailor or dressmaker finishes the garment with hems, buttons, trim, and a final pressing.

Some tailors or dressmakers specialize in a certain aspect of the garment-making process. *Bushelers* work in factories to repair flaws and correct imperfect sewing in finished garments. *Shop tailors* have a detailed knowledge of special tailoring tasks. They use shears or a knife to trim and shape the edges of garments before sewing, attach shoulder pads, and sew linings in coats. *Skilled tailors* put fine stitching on lapels and pockets, make buttonholes, and sew on trim.

Requirements

Tailors and dressmakers must have at least a high school education, although employers prefer college graduates with advanced training in sewing, tailoring, draping, patternmaking, and design. A limited number of schools and colleges in the United States offer this type of training, including the Philadelphia College of Textiles and Science, the Fashion Institute of Technology in New York City, and the Parsons School of Design, also in New York. Students who are interested in furthering their career, and perhaps expanding from tailoring into design, may want to consider studying in to one of these specialized institutions. It is, however, possible to enter this field without a college degree. While in high school, the prospective garment worker should take any sewing, tailoring, and clothing classes offered by vocational or home economics departments. There are also a number of institutions that offer either on-site or home study courses in sewing and dressmaking. Art classes in sketching and design are also helpful.

Workers in this field must obviously have the ability to sew very well, both by hand and machine, follow directions, and measure accurately. In addition to these skills, they must have a good eye for color and style. Strong interpersonal skills will also help tailors and dressmakers get and keep clients.

Opportunities for Experience & Exploration

Students who are interested in a career as a tailor or dressmaker can get a feel for what the work is like by taking courses in home economics and by mending, altering, and making their own clothes. In addition, they can take basic sewing or specialty classes from fabric and craft stores that offer them.

Students also can visit department stores, clothing specialty stores, and tailor's shops to observe workers involved in this field. In some cases, part-time jobs may be available in these stores or in small custom shops. Aspiring tailors or dressmakers also can offer their sewing services to friends and family.

Methods of Entering

Custom tailor shops or garment manufacturing centers sometimes offer apprenticeships to students or recent graduates, which gives them a start in the business. Beginners also may find work in related jobs, such as a sewer or alterer in a custom tailoring or dressmaking shop, garment factory, or clothing or department store. Students should apply directly to such companies and shops and monitor local newspaper ads for openings, as well. Students who have attended a trade school or college, may be able to register with its placement office to find work in a large company or store.

In some cases, it is possible for tailors or dressmakers to start their own businesses by making clothes and taking orders from those who like their work. They can set up their businesses with little overhead since the equipment needed, such as a sewing machine, iron and ironing board, scissors, and notions, is widely available and relatively inexpensive. Beginning a business, however, is usually easier for those who have first worked in other related jobs.

Advancement

Workers in this field usually start by performing simple tasks. As they gain more experience and their skills improve, they may be assigned to more difficult and complicated tasks. However, advancement in the industry is typically somewhat limited. In factories, a production worker might be promoted to the position of line supervisor. Tailors and dressmakers can move to better shops, that offer higher pay or open their own businesses.

Some workers may find that they have an eye for color and style and an aptitude for design. With further training at an appropriate college, these workers may find a successful career in fashion design and merchandising.

Employment Outlook

There is not much competition for jobs among tailors and dressmakers since it is a relatively small industry. Additionally, there has been some growth in businesses that help customers choose fabric and style, take the customer's measurements, and then hire garment houses, or section shops, to manufacture the garment. However, the low cost and ready availability of factory-made clothing has caused a decline in the number of custom-tailoring, made-to-measure shops, where complete garments are made on the premises. Since automation may replace some jobs in the next decade, employment is expected to decline through the year 2006. Tailors and dressmakers who do reliable and skillful work, particularly in the areas of mending and alterations, however, should be able to find employment.

Earnings

Salaries for tailors vary widely, depending on experience, skill, and location. An hourly wage of $7.50 is not uncommon for inexperienced workers who are just beginning in this field. With some experience, tailors can expect to average $10.00 per hour, which translates into $20,800 annually. Those with several years experience and a loyal, regular clientele can earn $40,000 or more.

The Economic Research Institute reports that in 1997 dressmakers earned salaries that ranged from a low of $12,369 for those just breaking into the field to $40,000 for the most experienced dressmakers with advanced skills and a large clientele.

For those who work in manufacturing jobs for large apparel manufacturers, the average pay is $7 to $9 per hour. With experience, the manufacturing worker can earn as much as $15 per hour, or $31,200 yearly.

Workers employed by large companies and retail stores receive benefits such as paid holidays and vacations, health insurance, and pension plans. They are often affiliated with one of the two labor unions of the industry—the International Ladies Garment Workers Union, and the Amalgamated Clothing and Textile Workers of America—which may offer additional benefits. Self-employed tailors and dressmakers and small-shop workers usually provide their own benefits.

Conditions of Work

Tailors and dressmakers in large shops work forty to forty-eight hours a week, sometimes including Saturdays. Union members usually work thirty-five to forty hours a week. Those who have their own businesses often work longer hours. Spring and fall are usually the busiest times.

Since tailoring and dressmaking requires a minimal a investment, some tailors and dressmakers work out of their homes. Those who work in the larger apparel plants may find the conditions less pleasant. The noise of the machinery can be nerve-wracking, the dye from the fabric may be irritating to the eyes and the skin, and some factories are old and not well kept.

Much of the work is done sitting down, in one location, and may include fine detail work that can be time consuming. The work may be tiring and tedious and occasionally can cause eye strain. In some cases, tailors and dressmakers deal directly with customers, who may be either pleasant to work with, or difficult and demanding.

This type of work, however, can be very satisfying to people who enjoy using their hands and skills to create something. It can be gratifying to complete a project properly, and many workers in this field take great pride in their workmanship.

Sources of Additional Information

■**American Apparel Manufacturers Association**
2500 Wilson Boulevard, Suite 301
Arlington, VA 22201
Tel: 703-524-1864

For a listing of home study institutions offering sewing and dressmaking courses, contact:

■**Distance Education and Training Council**
1601 18th Street, NW
Washington, DC 20009
Tel: 202-234-5100

For information packets on college classes in garment design and sewing, contact:

■**Philadelphia College of Textiles and Science**
School House Lane and Henry Avenue
Philadelphia, PA 19144
Tel: 215-951-2800

■■Parsons School of Design
2 West 13th Street
New York, NY 10011

■■Fashion Institute of Technology
27th Street and 7th Avenue
New York, NY 10001
Tel: 212-760-7230

Teacher Aides

Definition

Teacher aides perform a wide variety of duties to help teachers run a classroom. The work they do helps free the teachers' time so they can concentrate on instructing their pupils. Teacher aides may prepare instructional materials, help students with classroom work, and supervise students in the library, on the playground, and at lunch. They may perform administrative duties such as photocopying, keeping attendance records, and grading papers.

Nature of the Work

Teacher aides work in public, private, and parochial preschools and elementary and secondary schools. Their duties vary depending on the classroom teacher, school, and school district. Teacher aides often help a classroom run more smoothly by copying, compiling, and handing out class materials, setting up and operating audiovisual equipment, arranging field trip, and typing or word processing materials. They may organize classroom files, including grade reports, and attendance and health records. They may also obtain library materials and order classroom supplies.

Many teacher aides are in charge of keeping order in classrooms, school cafeterias, libraries, hallways, and playgrounds. Often, they wait with preschool and elementary students coming to or leaving school and make sure all students are accounted for. When a class leaves its room for such subjects as art, music, physical education, or computer lab, the teacher aide may go with them to help the teachers of these other subjects.

Another responsibility of teacher aides is correcting and grading homework and tests, usually for "objective" work—assignments and tests that require specific correct answers. Teacher aides often use answer sheets to mark students' papers and examinations and keep records of students' scores. In

School Subjects
Education
Psychology

Personal Interests
Babysitting/Child care
Teaching

Work Environment
Primarily indoors
Primarily one location

Minimum Education Level
High school diploma

Salary Range
$11,000 to
$13,000 to
$18,800

Certification or Licensing
Recommended

Outlook
Much faster than the average

DOT
099

GOE
11.02.01

NOC
4216

some large schools, an aide may be called a *grading clerk* and be responsible only for scoring objective tests and computing and recording test scores. Often using an electronic grading machine or computer, the grading clerk totals errors found and computes the percentage of questions answered correctly. The worker then records this score and averages students' test scores to determine their grade for the course.

Under the teacher's supervision, some teacher aides work directly with students in the classroom. They may listen to a group of young students read aloud or involve the class in a special project such as a science fair, art project, or drama production. With older students, teacher aides may provide review or study sessions prior to exams or give extra help with research projects or homework. Some teacher aides work with individual students in a tutorial setting, helping in areas of special need or concern. Teacher aides may work with the teacher to prepare lesson plans, bibliographies, charts, and maps. They may help to decorate the classroom, design bulletin boards and displays, and arrange work stations. They may even participate in parent-teacher conferences to discuss students' progress.

Some teacher aides specialize in one subject and some work in a specific type of school setting. These settings include bilingual classrooms, gifted and talented programs, classes for learning disabled students and those with unique physical needs, and multi-age classrooms. They conduct the same type of classroom work as other teacher aides, but may provide more individual assistance to students.

Requirements

Education and certification requirements for teacher aides depend on the school or school district and the kinds of responsibilities the aides have. In districts where aides perform mostly clerical duties, applicants may need only to have high school diploma or the equivalent, Graduation Equivalency Degree (GED). Those who work in the classroom may be required to take some college courses and attend in-service training and special teacher conferences and seminars. Some schools and districts help teacher aides pay some of the costs involved in attending these programs. Often community and junior colleges offer courses that prepare teacher aides for classroom work.

High school courses in English, history, social studies, mathematics, art, drama, physical education and the sciences provide teacher aides with a broad base of knowledge in a wide variety of areas. This enables them to help students learn in these same subjects. Knowledge of a second language can be an asset to teacher aides, especially those who work in schools with bilingual student, parent, or staff populations. Courses in child care, home economics, and psychology are also valuable for this career. High school students interested in this field should try to gain some experience working with computers, as students at many elementary schools and even preschools now do a large amount of computer work, and computer skills may be important to teacher aides as they perform clerical duties.

Newly hired aides participate in orientation sessions and formal training at the school. In these sessions, aides learn about the school's organization, operation, and philosophy. They learn how to keep school records, operate audiovisual equipment, check books out of the library, and administer first aid.

Many schools prefer to hire teacher aides who have some experience working with children and some schools prefer to hire workers who live within the school district. Some schools may require teacher aide applicants to pass a physical examination. All teacher aides must be able to work effectively with both children and adults and should have good verbal and written communications skills.

Teacher aides must enjoy working with children and be able to handle their demands, problems, and questions with patience and fairness. A teacher aide must be willing and able to follow instructions, but should also be able to take initiative in projects. Flexibility, creativity, and a cheerful outlook are definite assets for anyone working with children.

Students interested in becoming teacher aides should find out the specific job requirements from the school, school district, and state department of education where they would like to work. Requirements vary from school to school and state to state. It is important to remember that an aide who is qualified to work in one state, or even one school, may not be qualified to work in another.

Opportunities for Experience & Exploration

High school students who wish to become teacher aides can get experience in working with children by volunteering to help with religious education classes at their church, synagogue, or other place of worship. They may volunteer to help with scouting troops or work as counselors at summer camps. Often high school students can volunteer to help coach a children's athletic team or work with children in after-school programs at community centers.

Babysitting is common way to gain experience in working with children and learn about different stages of child development. College students can obtain experience by working in schools where aspiring teacher aides help with real classes while earning course credit.

Methods of Entering

Once they have fulfilled certification requirements, most workers apply directly to school district or schools for teacher aide positions. College students may contact their school placement offices for information about openings. Many school districts and state departments of education maintain job listings, or bulletin boards and hot lines that list available job openings. Teacher aide jobs are often advertised in the classified section of the newspaper.

Advancement

Teacher aides usually advance only in terms of increases in salary or responsibility, which come with experience. Aides in some districts may receive time off to take college courses. Some teacher aides choose to pursue bachelor's degrees and fulfill the licensing requirements of the state or school to become teachers.

Some aides, who find that they enjoy the administrative side of the job, may move into school or district office staff positions. Others choose to get more training and then work as resource teachers, tutors, guidance counselors, or reading, mathematics, or speech specialists. Some teacher aides go into school library work or become media specialists. While it is true that most of these jobs require additional training, the job of teacher aide is a good place to begin.

Employment Outlook

According to the American Federation of Teachers, approximately 981,000 paraprofessionals worked in teacher aide or aide-related jobs in 1996, ninety percent of which worked in an elementary school setting. Growth in this field is expected to be much faster than the average through the year 2006 because of an expected increase in the number of school-age children. As the number of students in a school or district increases, new schools and classrooms will be added and more teachers and teacher aides will be hired. Opportunities for teacher aides may be better in the South or West than in the Northeast and North Central regions of the country.

The field of special education—working with students with specific learning, emotional, or physical concerns or disabilities—is expected to grow rapidly, and more aides will be needed in these areas. Teacher aides who want to work with young children in day care or extended day programs will have a relatively easy time finding work because more children are attending these programs while their parents are at work. Also, there has been a movement for more personal instruction between teacher and student; teacher aides help fill this gap.

This job has a high turnover rate. Many aides leave to return to school or pursue other careers. In fact, most openings in the field are to replace workers who leave. It is important to note, however, that schools are highly dependent on the economy and the budgets of states, municipalities, and federal government programs. When education expenditures are reduced, teacher aides may be among the first to be laid off.

Earnings

Teacher aides are usually paid on an hourly basis and usually only during the nine or ten months of the school calendar. Salaries vary depending upon the school or district, region of the country, and the duties the aides perform. Some teacher aides may earn as little as minimum wage while others earn up to $15.00 an hour. Hourly wages average about $9.04 an hour. Yearly averages for full-time teacher aides in 1996, according to the U.S. Department of Labor's Bureau of Labor Statistics, ranged from $11,000 to $18,800. Benefits such as health insurance and vacation or sick leave may also depend upon the school or district as well as the number of hours a teacher aide works. Many schools employ teacher aides only part time and do not offer such benefits. Other teacher aides may receive the same health and pension benefits as the teachers in their school and be covered under collective bargaining agreements.

Conditions of Work

Teacher aides may work in either well-kept school or those needing painting and repairs and having unpredictable heating or cooling systems. Teacher aides may work outdoors in good weather. Those in elementary schools may spend some time kneeling, while all aides do a great deal of standing and walking. Although this work is not physically strenuous, working closely with children can be stressful and tiring. Because schools close during summer months, most aides work about ten months out of the year. They may, however, use this time to continue their own education or find other jobs for extra income. Some private and religious schools and day care centers hire teacher aides to work in summer programs, day camps, and Bible schools.

Sources of Additional Information

■ **American Federation of Teachers, Paraprofessionals and School-Related Personnel**
555 New Jersey Avenue, NW
Washington, DC 20001
Tel: 202-879-4400

For a brochure on careers in childhood education, send a self-addressed, stamped envelope to:

■ **Association for Childhood Education International**
11501 Georgia Avenue, Suite 315
Wheaton, MD 20902-1924

■ **National Resource Center for Paraprofessionals in Special Education**
CASE-SUNY
25 West 43 Street, Room 620
New York, NY 10036
Tel: 212-642-2948

Telemarketers

Definition

Telemarketers, or *telephone solicitors,* make and receive phone calls for a company to sell its goods, market its services, gather information, receive orders and complaints, or handle other miscellaneous business. Telemarketers may work directly for one company, for several companies who use the same service, or for a single firm.

Nature of the Work

Telemarketers generally work for one of two types of businesses. Some telemarketers are part of the in-house staff of a company or corporation and make and receive calls on behalf of that company. Others work for a telemarketing service agency and make or receive calls for the clients of the agency. Telemarketing agencies are useful for companies that don't want to or can't keep a full-time telemarketing staff on the payroll or that need such services only occasionally. Both large corporations and small firms employ telemarketing agencies, which sometimes specialize in particular fields, such as fund-raising, product sales, and insurance.

Telemarketers are generally responsible for either handling incoming calls or placing calls to outside parties. Incoming calls may include requests for information or orders for an advertised product such as clothing or a magazine. Telemarketers also staff the phones that handle toll-free, "800" numbers, which customers call to ask questions about the use of a product or register complaints. Airline reservations, concert and sports tickets, and credit card problems are all transactions that can be handled by telemarketers. Newspapers often employ *classified ad clerks* to transcribe classified ads from callers. A person whose sole job is taking orders from callers over the phone might called an *order clerk.*

Telemarketers make outside calls for a great many purposes as well. One of their most important jobs is to sell products and services to consumers. The names of the people they call usu-

School Subjects
Business
Speech

Personal Interests
Business
Helping people: personal service

Work Environment
Primarily indoors
Primarily one location

Minimum Education Level
High school diploma

Salary Range
$10,712 to
$17,000 to
$40,000

Certification or Licensing
None

Outlook
Much faster than the average

DOT
299

GOE
08.02.07

NOC
6623

ally come from a prepared list of previous customers, the phone book, reply cards from magazines, or a list purchased from another source. Sometimes randomly dialed "cold calls" are made. Once made, these calls often serve as a source of potential leads for the company's regular sales staff. A wide range of products can be successfully sold in this way—everything from newspaper subscriptions to time-share resort condominiums. Once the sale is made, the telemarketer records it so that order fillers can prepare the product for shipment.

Cultural organizations, such as ballet and opera companies, public television stations, and theater troupes, use telemarketers to solicit subscriptions and donations. Charity fund-raising also relies heavily on telemarketing.

In addition to selling, telemarketers make calls for other reasons. They may conduct marketing surveys of consumers to discover the reasons behind their buying habits or what they like and dislike about a certain product. They may call to endorse a candidate in an upcoming election or tell citizens about an important vote in their city council. When making calls business-to-business, telemarketers may try to solicit attendance at important meetings, assist a company in recruiting and job placement, or collect demographic information for use in an advertising campaign.

When making outbound calls, telemarketers usually work from a prepared script that they must follow exactly. This is especially true of market-research surveys because people need to be asked the same questions in identical manners if the survey data is to be valid. Often when a customer tries to resist a sales pitch, the telemarketer will read a standard response that has been prepared in anticipation of potential objections. At other times, the telemarketer must rely on persuasive sales skills and quick thinking to win over the customer and make the sale. Telemarketers have to be a little more skillful when selling business-to-business because these customers usually have a clear idea of the needs of their businesses and will ask specific questions.

business-to-business calls, people trained in that field may be hired and then instructed in telephone and sales techniques.

Because they must be able to speak persuasively and listen to customers carefully, telemarketers will find classes in communications, speech, drama, and broadcasting particularly useful. Business and sales classes, as well as psychology and sociology, are also valuable.

Even though their work is done over the phone, telemarketers must be able to deal well with other people. This work requires the ability to sense how customers are reacting, how to keep them interested in the sales pitch, how to listen carefully to their responses and complaints, and how to react tactfully to impatient and sometimes hostile people. These workers need to balance a sensitivity to their company's concerns with the needs of the customer.

Telemarketers must also have a warm, pleasant phone voice that conveys sincerity and confidence. They should be able to work well with details. While on the phone, they have to take orders, get other important information, and fill out complete sales records, all of which requires an accurate and alert mind.

Many federal, state, and local laws have been enacted governing the sort of language and sales tactics that can be used in phone soliciting. Such legislation is intended to protect consumers from unscrupulous telemarketers operating phone scams. Telemarketers must be aware of these laws and conduct their phone sales in an honest and unambiguous manner. To bolster the industry's image in the eyes of the public, several professional organizations exist to further the cause of ethical and effective telemarketing.

Some states have guidelines or legislation to regulate further the activities of telemarketers. In California, for example, certain types of telemarketing agencies must register each year with the state, although most business-to-business telemarketing is exempt because sales are usually not the main goal of such calls.

Requirements

The type of skills and education people need to become a telemarketer depends in part on the firm for which they plan to work. A high school diploma is usually required for any type of position, while some employers hire only people who have earned college degrees. If the phone calls involve a complex product or service, as is the case with many

Opportunities for Experience & Exploration

There are many ways to gain practice and poise in telemarketing. Many organizations use volunteer phone workers during campaigns and fund drives. One of the most visible of these is public television stations, which conduct fund-raising drives several times a year and are always looking for volunteer help to staff the phone banks. Other groups that routinely need volunteer telemarketers include local political campaigns, theaters and other arts groups, churches, schools, and nonprofit social organizations, such as crisis centers and inner-city recreation programs.

Methods of Entering

Agencies that hire telemarketers usually advertise for new employees in the classified section of newspapers. Another possible source of job leads is temporary employment agencies, many of which specialize in placing telemarketers with firms. A person who wishes to become an in-house telemarketer for a specific firm should call or write to the personnel office of that firm to find out about job openings. It is important to note that employers of telemarketers sometimes interview job applicants over the phone, judging a person's telephone voice, personality, demeanor, and assertiveness. Being prepared for such an interview before making that first call can make the difference between getting the job and having to continue to look.

Employees undergo a great deal of on-the-job training after they have been hired. Trainers instruct the novice telemarketers on the use of equipment, characteristics of the product or service they will be selling, and proper sales techniques and listening skills. They rehearse the trainees on the script that has been prepared and guide them through some practice calls.

Advancement

Within telemarketing agencies, employees can advance to jobs as assistant managers, managers, and supervisors. Other responsibilities can include preparing reports or writing telephone scripts. Salaries can increase rapidly because managers and supervisors sometimes earn a commission on the net sales made by the agency.

Some telemarketers move into telephone-sales training, either with an agency or as an independent consultant. Experienced telemarketers can sometimes find new jobs with higher-paying firms, and still others start their own telemarketing agencies.

Employment Outlook

Because of the phenomenal growth of the telemarketing industry, the outlook for telemarketers is excellent. Aiding this job outlook are advances in telephone technology and, more importantly, the cost effectiveness of phone sales. For example, a regular sales representative makes an average of five in-person sales calls a day, typically at a cost of about $225 for each visit. By contrast, in the course of one hour, an experienced telemarketer can make ten to fifteen phone calls. Innovations in marketing also allow firms to pinpoint target markets more accurately, which increases the chances of successful sales calls.

Many firms that had previously employed telemarketing agencies are now establishing their own telemarketing divisions because of the advantages of having a well-informed sales staff. Many other firms cannot afford to keep telemarketers on staff or are only beginning to explore the ways they can use telemarketing. These firms still employ independent telemarketing agencies.

It is estimated that some 275,000 firms are now using telemarketing, providing employment for about four million part-time or full-time telemarketers. Because of rapid growth in the field and high turnover among telemarketers, many opportunities exist for entering the industry.

Earnings

Telemarketers' earnings vary with the type of work they do. For part-time phone solicitors making basic calls to consumers, the pay can range from the minimum wage to around $8.00 per hour. Pay may be higher for those who deliver more elaborate sales presentations or make business-to-business calls. As telemarketers gain experience and skills, their pay scales rise. Seasoned telemarketers can earn from $17,000 to $40,000 per year. Those telemarketers who start their own companies have the chance to earn even higher amounts.

Conditions of Work

The offices in which telemarketers work can range from the very basic, with standard phones and desks, to the highly advanced, with computer terminals, the latest in phone technology, and machines that automatically dial numbers from a database. There may be just four or five telemarketers in an office or more than a hundred. While the work is not strenuous, it can be very repetitive. The amount of supervision depends on the employer and region of the country. California and a few other states have laws that prohibit call monitoring by supervisors unless both the telemarketer and the person being called are aware of it.

Telemarketing requires many hours of sitting and talking on the phone. Customer rejections, which can range from polite to rude, can cause a great deal of stress. Because of this, many telemarketers work only four- and five-hour shifts. Telemarketing is an ideal job for people looking for part-time work because workweeks generally run from twenty-four to thirty hours. Because many agencies need staff at unusual hours, telemarketers are usually able to find positions where the work hours match their own lifestyles. Many agencies require staffing twenty-four hours a day to handle such calls as airline reservations and reports of stolen credit cards. Telemarketers who make business-to-business calls work during normal business hours, while those who call consumers make most of their calls in the evening and on weekends, when more people are at home.

Sources of Additional Information

Direct Marketing Association
11 West 42nd Street
New York, NY 10036-8096
Tel: 212-768-7277

Title Searchers and Examiners

Definition

Title searchers and *examiners* conduct searches of public records to determine the legal chain of ownership for a piece of real estate.

Nature of the Work

Clients hire title searchers and examiners to determine the legal ownership of all parts and privileges of a piece of property. The client may need to have these questions answered for many reasons: in addition to land sales and purchases, a lawyer may need a title search to fulfill the terms of someone's will; a bank may need it to repossess property used as collateral on a loan; a company may need it when acquiring or merging with another company; or an accountant may need it when preparing tax returns.

The work of the title searcher is the first step in the process. When a request for a title search is received, the title searcher determines the type of title evidence that will have to be gathered, purpose for which it will be used, people involved, and legal description of the property. The searcher then compares this description with the legal description contained in public records to verify such facts as the deed of ownership, tax codes, tax parcel number, and description of property boundaries.

This task can take title searchers to a variety of places, including the offices of the county tax assessor, the recorder or registrar of deeds, the clerk of the city or state court, and other city, county, and state officials. Title searchers consult legal records, surveyors' maps, and tax rolls. Companies who employ title searchers may also keep records called indexes. These indexes are kept up-to-date to allow fast, accurate searching of titles and contain important information on mortgages, deeds, contracts, and judgments. For example, a law firm specializing in real estate and contract law would probably keep extensive indexes, using information gathered both in its own work and from outside sources.

School Subjects
Computer science
English
(writing/literature)

Personal Interests
Computers
Figuring out how things work

Work Environment
Primarily indoors
Primarily one location

Minimum Education Level
High school diploma

Salary Range
$15,000 to
$25,000 to
$45,000

Certification or Licensing
Required for certain positions

Outlook
About as fast as the average

DOT
209

GOE
07.05.02

NOC
4211

As the title searcher reviews the legal documents, the important information is recorded on a standardized work sheet. This information can include judgments, deeds, mortgages (loans made using the property as collateral), liens (charges against the property for the satisfaction of a debt), taxes, special assessments for streets and sewers, and easements. The searcher must carefully record what records are used to supply this information, where the records are located, the date on which any action took place, and the names and addresses of the people involved.

Using the data gathered by the title searcher, the *title examiner* then determines the status of the property title. Title examiners study all the relevant documents on a property, including records of marriages, births, divorces, adoptions, and other important legal proceedings, to determine the chain of ownership. To verify certain facts, they may need to interview judges, clerks, lawyers, bankers, real estate brokers, and other professionals. They may summarize the legal documents they have found and used and use these abstracts as references in later work.

Using this information, title examiners prepare reports that describe the full extent of a person's title to a property, that person's right to sell, buy, use, or improve it, any restrictions that may exist, and actions that would be required to clear the title. If employed in the office of a title insurance company, the title examiner provides information for the issuance of a policy that insures the title, subject to applicable exclusions and exceptions. The insured party can then proceed to use the property as he or she sees fit, protected against any problems that might arise.

Requirements

A high school diploma is necessary to begin a career as a title searcher. Helpful classes include business, business law, English, social studies, real estate, real estate law, computers, and typing. In addition, skills in reading, writing, and research methods are essential.

Title searchers must be very methodical, analytical, and detail-oriented in their work. As they study the many hundreds of documents that may contain important data, they need to be very thorough. Overlooking important points can damage the accuracy of the final report and may result in financial loss to the client or employer. It is important for title searchers not to lose sight of the reason for the title search, in addition to remembering the intricacies of real estate law.

Because their work is more complex, title examiners are usually expected to have completed some college coursework. Pertinent courses for title searchers

and examiners include business administration, office management, real estate law, and other types of law. In some locales, title examinations typically are performed by attorneys.

In addition to very detailed work, title examiners deal with clients, lawyers, judges, real estate brokers, and other people. This task requires good communications skills, poise, patience, and courtesy.

A few states require title searchers and examiners to be licensed or certified. Title firms may belong to the American Land Title Association, as well as regional or state title associations. These groups maintain codes of ethics and standards of practice among their members and conduct educational programs. Title searchers and examiners who work for a state, county, or municipal government may belong to a union representing government workers.

Opportunities for Experience & Exploration

There may be opportunities for temporary employment during the summer and school holidays at title companies, financial institutions, or law firms. These positions may involve making copies or sorting and delivering mail, but they offer an excellent chance to see the work of a title searcher or examiner firsthand. Some law firms, real estate brokerages, and title companies provide internships for students who are interested in work as a title searcher or examiner. Information on the availability of such internships is usually available from the regional or local land title association or school guidance counselors.

Methods of Entering

Those workers interested in a career as a title searcher or examiner should send resumes and letters of application to firms in their area who employ these types of workers, including abstract companies, title insurance companies, and law firms. Other leads for employment opportunities are local real estate agents or brokers, government employment offices, and local or state land title associations. Graduates from two- and four-year colleges usually have the added advantage of being able to consult their college placement offices for additional information on job openings.

Advancement

Title searchers and examiners, learn most of their skills on the job. A basic understanding of the title search process can be gained in a few months, as employees first use public records and indexes maintained by their employers maintain. As time goes on, however, it becomes more important for these employees to gain a broader understanding of the intricacies of land title evidence and record-keeping systems. This knowledge and a number of years of experience are the keys to advancement.

With experience, title searchers can move up to become tax examiners, special assessment searchers, or abstracters. With enough experience, a searcher or examiner may be promoted to title supervisor or head clerk. Other paths for ambitious title searchers and examiners include other types of paralegal work or, with further study, a law degree.

Employment Outlook

The health of the title insurance business is directly tied to the strength of the real estate market. In prosperous times, more real estate activity is transacted and more title searches are needed. While the real estate business in America continues to operate during periods of recession, activity does slow a little. In general, the outlook for title searchers and examiners is good. Title searchers and examiners can find consistent work in any area of the country with an active real estate market.

Earnings

Depending on their employer and locale, title searchers can earn anywhere from $15,000 to $25,000 per year. Title examiners generally earn more, with salaries ranging from $18,000 to $45,000. Title searchers and examiners may receive such fringe benefits as vacations, hospital and life insurance, profit sharing, and pensions, depending on their employer.

Conditions of Work

Title searchers and examiners generally work a forty-hour week. Because most public records offices are only open during regular business hours, title searchers and examiners usually will not put in much overtime work, except when using private indexes and preparing abstracts.

Title searchers and examiners work in a variety of settings. Some work for law firms, title insurance companies, or companies that write title abstracts. Others work for various branches of government at the city, county, or state level. In larger offices, a *title supervisor* may direct and coordinate the activities of other searchers and examiners.

The offices in which title searchers and examiners work can be very different in terms of comfort, space, and equipment. Searchers and examiners spend much of their day poring over the fine print of legal documents and records, so they may be afflicted occasionally by eyestrain and back fatigue. Generally, however, offices are pleasant and the work is not physically strenuous.

Because the work is conducted in a business environment, title searchers and examiners are usually expected to dress in a business-like manner. Dress codes, however, have become more casual recently and vary from office to office.

Sources of Additional Information

For information on the title insurance industry, please contact:

■**American Land Title Association**
1828 L Street, NW, Suite 705
Washington, DC 20036
Tel: 202-296-3671
WWW: http://www.alta.org/

Tool, Tap, and Die Makers

Definition

Tool, tap, and die makers are skilled workers who produce the tools, dies, cutting devices, and guiding and holding devices used in mass production of a variety of products. *Tool and tap makers* produce precision tools for cutting, shaping, and forming metal and other materials. They also produce jigs and fixtures—the devices for holding the tools and metal while it is being worked— and various gauges and other measuring devices. *Die makers* make precision metal forms, or dies, used in stamping and forging metal. They also may design metal molds for die casting and molding plastics, ceramics, and composite materials.

Nature of the Work

Tool, tap, and die makers may produce many different kinds of devices or they may specialize in just one item. In either case, a single worker is typically responsible for all the work necessary to complete a single device, from start to finish. He or she first analyzes instructions, blueprints, sketches, or models of the finished product. Using such information, he or she decides how to go about making the device. He or she may compute dimensions, either by hand or with a calculator, plan the layout and assembly processes, and decide on a sequence of operations for machining the metal.

When the plan is clear, workers select and lay out metal stock, measuring and marking the metal and, if necessary, cutting it into pieces of the approximate size needed for the project. They set up the machine tools, such as lathes, milling machines, drill presses, and grinders, and carefully cut, bore, and drill the metal according to their plan for making the product. In the machining process, they closely monitor the dimensions of the workpiece since their work must have a high degree of accuracy—frequently within ten-thousandths of an inch. Measuring equipment, such as micrometers, gauge blocks, and dial indicators, are used to ensure precision.

School Subjects
Mathematics
Shop (Trade/Vo-tech education)

Personal Interests
Building things
Computers

Work Environment
Primarily indoors
Primarily one location

Minimum Education Level
High school diploma
Apprenticeship

Salary Range
$24,900 to
$37,400 to
$60,300

Certification or Licensing
None

Outlook
Decline

DOT
601

GOE
05.05.07

NOC
7232

When satisfied that the parts are accurately machined in accordance with the original specifications for the item, tool and die makers fit the pieces together to make the final product. They may need to do finishing work on the product, such as filing and smoothing surfaces.

The first part made is the master tap, which sets the markings or shape on the die. After the master tap is made, it is often used to thread a master die. The die is used as the reverse image from the final shapes will be created. Tool, tap, and die makers use the master taps and dies and other machine tools to make working taps and dies.

Modern technology is changing tool, tap, and die makers' jobs. Firms now commonly use computer-aided design (CAD) to develop products. Specifications from the computer program are used to develop designs electronically for the required tools and dies. Designs are then sent to computer numerically controlled (CNC) machines to produce the component parts of a tool.

In shops that use numerically controlled (NC) machine tools, tool, tap, and die makers' duties may be somewhat different. Although they still manually check and assemble each tool or die, the component parts are made by machines that are programmed to do the actual work of shaping the metal. Tool, tap, and die makers often take part in planning and writing the computer programs.

Requirements

Applicants for jobs in this field usually need to have at least a high school or vocational school education. Increasingly, an associate's degree is becoming preferred by many employers. Tool, tap, and die makers must have a much broader knowledge of machining operations, mathematics, and blueprint reading than most other machining workers. They also need a good knowledge of the properties of common metals and alloys, such as hardness and heat tolerance. They need to be familiar with a variety of machine tools and precision measuring instruments. To begin developing these types of knowledge, a good high school background would include courses in mathematics, blueprint reading, drafting, computers, metalworking, and machine shop.

Workers also need a combination of various personal characteristics, including mechanical aptitude, manual dexterity, and the ability to work with care and attention to detail. To ensure the absolute precision of their work, they need to be very methodical and careful. Good eyesight is a must. In some jobs, workers need the ability to lift moderately heavy objects.

Workers also need to be able to work as efficiently as possible, with a minimum waste of time or materials.

Because they often work without close supervision, tool, tap, and die makers need to be self-motivated and organized in their work habits. In addition, good communications skills are important because they may have to deal with and work in cooperation with other departments within the shop.

Tool, tap, and die makers can learn their trade through informal on-the-job training or formal apprenticeships. Most employers prefer to hire workers who learn their skills by completing an apprenticeship because apprentices receive more thorough training. Lasting four to five years, apprenticeships combine a planned and supervised on-the-job training program with classwork in related fields. On the job, apprentices learn how to set up and operate machine tools such as lathes, milling machines, grinders, and jig borers. They also learn to use other mechanical equipment, gauges, and various hand tools that are needed for fitting together and assembling items they fabricate. In addition, they receive classroom instruction covering subjects such as blueprint reading, mechanical drawing, tool programming, shop theory, shop mathematics, properties of various metals, and tool design.

Workers who become on-the-job trainees may have little background in tool, tap, and die making. Initially they are assigned simple tasks that usually involve operating machines; later they are given increasingly difficult work. They pick up skills gradually. One drawback of this method is that it may take many years to learn all the skills that a qualified craftworker must know.

Some tool, tap, and die makers start out as machinists. They supplement their metalworking experience with additional training in order to move into tool-making or die-making. Part of their additional training, which may include layout work, shop mathematics, blueprint reading, heat treating, and the use of precision tools, can be obtained through vocational schools or correspondence schools.

Opportunities for Experience & Exploration

There are several ways to find out about this occupation. High school courses such as geometry, trigonometry, mechanical drawing, and shop can help students decide whether they like some of the types of work involved in this occupational field.

Hobbies such as tinkering with cars, making models, and assembling electronic equipment may be helpful in testing patience, accuracy, and mechanical ability, all of which are important qualities for tool, tap, and die makers.

A field trip to a machine shop or tool and die shop can provide a glimpse of the work in this field and may offer the opportunity to talk to experienced workers. Even better would be a part-time or summer job in such a setting. Although the work would probably be basic labor, such as sweeping or mopping floors, the experience could provide a valuable opportunity to observe firsthand the day-to-day activities in a machine shop.

Methods of Entering

Prospective tool, tap, and die makers can contact various sources for information on job openings and apprenticeship programs. These sources include the local offices of the state employment service, local employers such as tool and die shops and manufacturing firms, and the local offices of unions to which some workers belong, such as the United Auto Workers or the International Association of Machinists and Aerospace Workers. Listings for some jobs may appear in newspaper classified ads. Additionally, high school, vocational school, and technical institute students may get help from their teachers or the placement office at their schools.

Advancement

After completing apprenticeship training, workers often need several more years' experience to learn the most difficult and specialized skills. Well-qualified, experienced workers may have several avenues of advancement open to them. Some may move into supervisory positions, in charge of directing the activities of other workers. Others may become tool designers or specialists in programming numerically controlled machine tools.

Another possibility for some tool, tap, and die makers is becoming a tool inspector in an industry that requires an extremely high degree of accuracy in producing components. A few workers go into business for themselves, opening their own independent job shops to make items for manufacturing firms that do not maintain their own tool-making and die-making department.

Employment Outlook

Most tool and die makers work in industries that manufacture machines and equipment for metalworking, automobiles, and other motor vehicles, aircraft, and plastics products. They also work in independent job shops where tools and dies are tailor-made for a variety of manufacturers.

Although the industries that use precision tools and dies are expected to expand and require a larger quantity of such items, the employment of tool and die makers is expected to decline through the year 2006. More numerically controlled machine tools and other automated equipment are being used to make these items and thus fewer operations are being done by hand, resulting in fewer workers being needed to accomplish a given amount of work. Furthermore, some products that are mass-produced using tools and dies are being imported from abroad, as are some tools and dies.

Despite the expected decline in employment, there should still be openings for new workers each year. Many of the workers presently employed in these occupations are approaching retirement, which will result in some openings. As fewer people are currently entering training programs to become tool, tap, and die workers, employers in some areas may have significant trouble filling positions. Highly skilled workers in these areas can expect to have very good job opportunities if the shortage grows more acute. Continuing demand for products that use machined metal parts, such as cars and aircraft, may create some new jobs and offset this occupation's decline.

As a group, tool, tap, and die makers have a more secure job situation than many other industrial workers. Since they serve industry, rather than consumers, they are not as subject to layoffs when the economy is slack. Also, tool, tap, and die makers have more mobility and a larger job market than less-skilled workers.

Earnings

Earnings for tool, tap, and die makers are generally good. In 1996, the overall national average wage, as reported by the U.S. Department of Labor, was $17.57 per hour. Assuming full-time employment and a forty-hour workweek, this translates into $37,400 on a yearly basis. The lowest paid workers in this field earn $24,900, while those in the highest paid positions can earn 60,300 or more.

Salary levels vary somewhat in different areas of the country, with workers in the West and Midwest earn ing approximately $2.00 more per hour than workers in the Northeast and South. The size of the employing institution is also a factor in salary level. Tool and die makers who work for larger establishments tend to have proportionately higher wages. For example, workers in establishments that employ between 50 and 499 people average $15.35 hourly, or $31,928 yearly, while those in establishments employing 2,500 or more people average $20.63 hourly, or $42,910 yearly.

In addition to regular earnings, most tool, tap, and die makers receive benefits such as health insurance, paid vacation days, and pension plans.

Conditions of Work

Tool, tap, and die makers typically work forty hours per week, although there is often the potential for overtime. Most plants that employ these workers operate only one shift per day. In plants that have two or three shifts, however, workers may work the second or third shift.

Tool, tap, and die makers usually work in shops that are adequately lighted, temperature-controlled, and well ventilated. Their work areas are not typically very noisy, as opposed to production departments, because at any one time only some of the machines are in operation. There are exceptions, however—tool and die departments that are near production areas or heat-treating or casting areas may be hot and noisy. Workers spend much of the day standing and moving about, and they may occasionally have to lift moderately heavy objects.

To avoid injury from machines and flying bits of metal, workers must follow good safety practices and use appropriate protective gear, including safety glasses and hearing protectors. In some settings, workers are exposed to smoky conditions and they may get oil, coolants, and other irritating substances on their skin.

Since most tool, tap, and die makers make a broad range of devices, their work is seldom routine.

Depending upon the complexity of the device they make however, they could spend anywhere from a week to several months on one job. In some cases, workers are engaged in completing several jobs at once.

Many who choose this field find the work to be very satisfying. They typically work with little supervision. They also have the pleasure of seeing a project through from start to finish and knowing that they have done a precise and skillful job. The work can be frustrating in some cases, however. Occasionally, a mistake is made during the fabrication process that cannot be corrected. When this happens, the worker may have to start over again from the beginning, even if he or she has spent many hours on the original project.

Sources of Additional Information

For information on careers in the machining industry, including tool, tap, and die making careers, contact:

Tooling and Manufacturing Association
1177 South Dee Road
Park Ridge, IL 60068
Tel: 847-825-1120

National Tooling and Machining Association
9300 Livingston Road
Fort Washington, MD 20744
Tel: 301-248-6200

International Union of Electronic, Electrical, Salaried, Machine, and Furniture Workers
1126 16th Street, NW
Washington, DC 20036
Tel: 202-296-1200

International Union, United Automobile, Aerospace, and Agricultural Implement Workers of America
Skill Trades Department, Solidarity House
800 East Jefferson Avenue
Detroit, MI 48214
Tel: 313-926-5000

Tour Guides

Definition

Tour guides plan and oversee travel arrangements and accommodations for groups of tourists. They assist travelers with questions or problems and may provide travelers with itineraries of their proposed travel route and plans. Tour guides research their destinations thoroughly so that they can handle any unforeseen situation that

Nature of the Work

Acting as knowledgeable companions and chaperons, tour guides escort groups of tourists to different cities and countries. Their job is to make sure that the passengers in a group tour enjoy an interesting and safe trip. To do this, they have to know a great deal about their travel destination and about the interests, knowledge, and expectations of the people on the tour.

One basic responsibility of tour guides is handling all the details of a trip prior to departure. They may schedule airline flights, bus trips, or train trips, as well as book cruises, house boats, or car rentals. They also research area hotels and other lodgings for the group and make reservations in advance. If anyone in the group has unique requirements, such as a specialized diet or a need for wheelchair accessibility, the tour guide will work to meet these.

Tour guides plan itineraries and daily activities, keeping in mind the interests of the group. For example, a group of music lovers visiting Vienna may wish to see the many sites of musical history there, as well as attend a performance by that city's orchestra. In addition to sight-seeing tours, guides may make arrangements in advance for special exhibits, dining experiences, and side trips. Alternate outings are sometimes planned in case of inclement weather conditions.

The second major responsibility of tour guides is, of course, the tour itself. Here, they must make sure all aspects of transportation, lodging, and recreation meet the itinerary as it was

School Subjects
History
Foreign language

Personal Interests
The Environment
Travel

Work Environment
Indoors and outdoors,
Primarily multiple
locations

Minimum Education Level
Some postsecondary
training

Salary Range
$9.75 per hour to
$20.00 per hour to
$75,000

Certification or Licensing
Recommended

Outlook
Faster than the average

DOT
353

GOE
07.05.01

NOC
6441

planned. They must see to it that travelers' baggage and personal effects are loaded and handled properly. If the tour includes meals and trips to local establishments, the guide must make sure that each passenger is on time for the various arrivals and departures.

Tour guides provide the people in their groups with interesting information on the locale and alert them to special sights. Tour guides become familiar with the history and significance of places through research and previous visits and endeavor to make the visit as entertaining and informative as possible. They may speak the native language or hire an interpreter so as to get along well with the local people. They are also familiar with local customs so their group will not offend anyone unknowingly. They see that the group stays together so that they do not miss their transportation arrangements or get lost. Guides may also arrange free time for travelers to pursue their individual interests, although time frames and common meeting points for regrouping are established in advance.

Even with thorough preparation, unexpected occurrences can arise on any trip and threaten to ruin everyone's good time. Tour guides must be resourceful to handle these surprises, such as when points of interest are closed or accommodations turn out to be unacceptable. They must be familiar with an area's resources so that they can help in emergencies such as an ill passenger or lost personal items. They often intercede on their travelers' behalf when any questions or problems arise regarding currency, restaurants, customs, or necessary identification.

Requirements

Although tour guides do not need a college education, they should at least have a high school diploma. Courses such as speech, communications, art, sociology, anthropology, political science, and literature often prove beneficial. Some tour guides study foreign languages and cultures, as well as geography, history, and architecture.

Some cities have professional schools that offer curricula in the travel industry. Such training may take nine to twelve months and offer job placement services. Some two- and four- year colleges offer tour guide training that are six to eight weeks long. Community colleges may offer programs in tour escort training. Programs such as these often may be taken on a part-time basis. Classes may include world geography, psychology, human relations, and communication courses. Sometimes students go on field trips themselves to gain experience. Some travel agencies and tour companies offer their own training so that

their tour guides may receive instruction that complements the tour packages the company offers.

Tour guides are outgoing, friendly, and confident people. They are aware of the typical travelers' needs and the kinds of questions and concerns they might have. Tour guides are comfortable being in charge of large groups of people and have good time-management skills. They need to be resourceful and able to adapt to different environments. They are also fun-loving and know how to make others feel at ease in unfamiliar surroundings. Tour guides should enjoy working with people as much as they enjoy traveling.

Opportunities for Experience & Exploration

One way to become more familiar with the responsibilities of this job is to accompany local tours. Many cities have their own historical societies and museums that offer tours, as well as opportunities to volunteer. To appreciate what is involved with speaking in front of groups and the kind of research that may be necessary for leading tours, students may prepare speeches or presentations for class or local community groups.

Methods of Entering

A person interested in a career as a tour guide may begin as a guide for a museum or state park. This would be a good introduction to handling groups of people, giving lectures on points of interest or exhibits, and developing confidence and leadership qualities. Zoos, theme parks, historical sites, or local walking tours often need volunteers or part-time employees to work in their information centers, offer visitors directions, and answer a variety of inquiries. When openings occur, it is common for part-time workers to move into full-time positions.

Travel agencies, tour bus companies, and park districts often need additional help during the summer months when the travel season is in full swing. Societies and organizations for architecture and natural history, as well as other cultural groups, often train and employ guides. Students interested in working as tour guides for these types of groups should submit applications directly to the directors of personnel or managing directors.

Advancement

Tour guides gain experience by handling more complicated trips. Some workers may advance through specialization, such as tours to specific countries or to multiple destinations. Some tour guides choose to open their own travel agencies or work for wholesale tour companies, selling trip packages to individuals or retail tour companies.

Some tour guides become travel writers and report on exotic destinations for magazines and newspapers. Other guides may decide to work in the corporate world and plan travel arrangements for company executives. With the further development of the global economy, many different jobs have become available for people who know foreign languages and cultures.

Employment Outlook

Because of the many different travel opportunities for business, recreation, and education, there will be a significant need for tour guides through the year 2006. This demand is due in part to the fact that when the economy is strong—which it is currently—people earn more and are able to spend more on travel.

Tours for special interests, such as to ecologically significant areas and wilderness destinations, continue to grow in popularity. Although certain seasons are more popular for travel than others, well-trained tour guides can keep busy all year long.

Another area of tourism that is on the upswing is inbound tourism. Many foreign travelers view the United States as a dream destination, with tourist spots such as Hollywood, Disney World, and Yellowstone National Park drawing millions of foreign visitors each year. Job opportunities in inbound tourism—guiding foreign visitors through famous American tourist sites—will likely be more plentiful than those guiding Americans in foreign locations. The best opportunities in inbound tourism are in large cities with international airports and in areas with a large amount of tourist traffic. Opportunities will also be better for those guides who speak foreign languages.

Aspiring tour guides should keep in mind that this field is highly competitive. Tour guide jobs, because of the obvious benefits, are highly sought after, and the beginning job seeker may find it difficult to break into the business. It is also important to remember that the travel and tourism industry is affected by the overall economy. When the economy is depressed, people have less money to spend and, therefore, travel less.

Earnings

Tour guides may find that they have peak and slack periods of the year that correspond to vacation and travel seasons. Many tour guides, however, work eight months of the year. Salaries range from $9.75 to $20.00 an hour. Experienced guides with managerial responsibilities can earn up to $65,000 a year, including gratuities. The 1997 U.S. News Career Guide Online lists the average salary for an entry-level inbound tour guide as $20,000. Average mid-level earnings are $35,000 and the top are $75,000, according to the Career Guide.

Guides receive their meals and accommodations free while conducting a tour, as well as a daily stipend to cover their personal expenses. Salaries and benefits vary depending upon the tour operators that employ guides and the location they are employed in. Generally, the Great Lakes, Mid-Atlantic, Southeast, and Southern regions of the country offer the highest compensation.

Tour guides very often receive paid vacations as part of their fringe benefits package; some may also receive sick pay and health insurance as well. Some companies may offer profit sharing and bonuses. They often receive discounts from hotels, airlines, and transportation companies in appreciation for repeat business.

Conditions of Work

The key word in the tour guide profession is variety. Most tour guides work in offices while they make travel arrangements and handle general business, but once on the road they experience a Tours to distant cities involve maneuvering through busy and confusing airports. Side trips may involve bus rides, train transfers, or private car rentals, all with varying degrees of comfort and reliability. Package trips that encompass seeing a number of foreign countries may require the guide to speak a different language in each city.

The constant feeling of being on the go, plus the responsibility of leading a large group of people, can sometimes be stressful. Unexpected events and uncooperative people have the capacity to ruin part of a trip for everyone involved, including the guide. However, the thrill of travel, discovery, and meeting new people can be so rewarding that all the negatives can be forgotten (or eliminated by preplanning on the next trip).

Sources of Additional Information

■■American Society of Travel Agents
1101 King Street, Suite 200
Alexandria, VA 22314
Tel: 703-739-2782
Email: kristil@astahq.com
WWW: http://www.astanet.com

For general information on the career of tour guide, as well as a listing of tour operators who are members of the association, contact:

■■National Tourism Foundation & National Tour Association
546 East Main Street
Lexington, KY 40508
Tel: 800-682-8886
WWW: http://www.ntaonline.com

For information regarding its certification program and other general information concerning a career as a tour guide, contact:

■■The Professional Guides Association of America
2416 South Eads Street
Arlington, VA 22202
Tel: 703-892-5757

■■Travel Educational Center
One Westbrook Center, Suite 200
Westchester, IL 60154
Tel: 800-945-2220
Email: tec@ultranet.com

Travel Agents

Definition

Travel agents assist individuals or groups who will be traveling, by planning their itineraries, making transportation, hotel, and tour reservations, obtaining or preparing tickets, and performing related services.

Nature of the Work

The travel agent may work as a salesperson, travel consultant, tour organizer, travel guide, bookkeeper, or small business executive. If the agent operates a one-person office, he or she usually performs all of these functions. Other travel agents work in offices with dozens of employees, which allows them to specialize in certain areas. In such offices, one staff member may become an authority on sea cruises, another may work on trips to the Far East, and a third may develop an extensive knowledge of either low-budget or luxury trips. In some cases, travel agents are employed by national or international firms and can draw upon very extensive resources.

As salespeople, travel agents must be able to motivate people to take advantage of their services. Travel agents study their customers' interests, learn where they have traveled, appraise their financial resources and available time, and present a selection of travel options. Customers are then able to choose how and where they want to travel with a minimum of effort.

Travel agents consult a variety of published and computer-based sources for information on air transportation departure and arrival times, airfares, and hotel ratings and accommodations. They often base their recommendations on their own travel experiences or those of colleagues or clients. Travel agents may visit hotels, resorts, and restaurants to rate their comfort, cleanliness, and quality of food and service.

As travel consultants, travel agents give their clients suggestions regarding travel plans and itineraries, information on

School Subjects
Business
Geography/Social studies

Personal Interests
Computers
Travel

Work Environment
Indoors and outdoors
One location with some travel

Minimum Education Level
High school diploma

Salary Range
$16,400 to
$24,500 to
$32,600+

Certification or Licensing
Recommended

Outlook
Faster than the average

DOT
252

GOE
08.02.06

NOC
6431

transportation alternatives, and advice on the available accommodations and rates of hotels and motels. They also explain and help with passport and visa regulations, foreign currency and exchange, climate and wardrobe, health requirements, customs regulations, baggage and accident insurance, traveler's checks or letters of credit, car rentals, tourist attractions, and welcome or escort services.

Many travel agents only sell tours that are developed by other organizations. The most skilled agents, however, often organize tours on a wholesale basis. This involves developing an itinerary, contracting a knowledgeable person to lead the tour, making tentative reservations for transportation, hotels, and side trips, publicizing the tour through descriptive brochures, advertisements, and other travel agents, scheduling reservations, and handling last-minute problems. Sometimes tours are arranged at the specific request of a group or to meet a client's particular needs.

In addition to other duties, travel agents may serve as *tour guides*, leading trips ranging from one week to six months to locations around the world. Agents often find tour leadership a useful way to gain personal travel experience. It also gives them the chance to become thoroughly acquainted with the people in the tour group, who may then use the agent to arrange future trips or recommend the agent to friends and relatives. Tour leaders are usually reimbursed for all their expenses or receive complimentary transportation and lodgings. Most travel agents, however, arrange for someone to cover for them at work during their absence, which may make tour leadership prohibitive for self-employed agents.

Agents serve as bookkeepers to handle the complex pattern of transportation and hotel reservations that each trip entails. They work directly with airline, steamship, railroad, bus, and car rental companies. They make direct contact with hotels and sight-seeing organizations or work indirectly through a receptive operator in the city involved. These arrangements require a great deal of accuracy, because mistakes could result in a client being left stranded in a foreign or remote area. After reservations are made, agents write up or obtain tickets, write out itineraries, and send out bills for the reservations involved. They also send out confirmations to airlines, hotels, and other companies.

Travel agents must promote their services. They present slides or movies to social and special interest groups, arrange advertising displays, and suggest company-sponsored trips to business managers.

Requirements

Travel courses are available from certain colleges, private vocational schools, and adult education programs in public high schools. Some colleges and universities grant bachelor's and master's degrees in travel and tourism. Although college training is not required for work as a travel agent, it can be very helpful and is expected to become increasingly important for these workers in the future. It is predicted that in the future most agents will be college graduates. Travel schools that provide basic reservation training and other training related to travel agents' functions are helpful but not required.

A liberal arts or business administration background is recommended for college students interested in this field. Useful liberal arts courses include foreign languages, geography, English, history, anthropology, political science, art and music appreciation, and literature. Pertinent business courses include transportation, business law, hotel management, marketing, office management, and accounting. As in many other fields, computer skills are increasingly important. High school students desiring to enter the field of travel should study English, social studies, business mathematics, typing, computers, and foreign languages.

To be able to sell passage on various types of transportation, a travel agent must be approved by the conferences of carriers involved. These are the Airlines Reporting Corporation (ARC) , the International Air Transport Association, Cruise Lines International Association, and the Rail Travel Promotion Agency. To sell tickets for these individual conferences, the agent must be clearly established in the travel business and have a good personal and business background. Not all travel agents are authorized to sell passage by all of the above conferences. Naturally, those who wish to sell the widest range of services should seek affiliation with all four.

Currently, travel agents are not required to be federally licensed, except in the state of Rhode Island. However, Ohio, California, and Hawaii do require their travel agents to be registered. In California, agents not approved by a corporation must be licensed. The American Society of Travel Agents certifies those agents who complete a travel and tourism course at Baruch College.

The prime requisite for success in the travel field is a sincere interest in travel. An agent's knowledge of and travel experiences with major tourist centers, various hotels, and local customs and points of interest make that person a more effective and convincing source of assistance. Yet the work of travel agents is not one long vacation. They operate in a highly competitive industry.

Travel agents must be able to make quick and accurate use of transportation schedules and tariffs. They must be able to handle addition and subtraction quickly. Almost all agents make use of computers to get the very latest information on rates and schedules and to make reservations.

Most travel agents work with a wide range of personalities, so their skills in psychology and diplomacy are always in use. They must also be able to generate enthusiasm among their customers and be resourceful in solving any problems that might arise. A knowledge of foreign languages is useful, because many customers come from other countries and agents are in frequent contact with foreign hotels and travel agencies.

Opportunities for Experience & Exploration

Any type of part-time experience with a travel agency would be helpful for those interested in this career. A small agency may welcome help during peak travel seasons or when an agent is away from the office. If their high school or junior college arranges career conferences, students may be able to invite a speaker from the travel industry. Visits to local travel agents also provide helpful information.

Examining the various travel magazines should provide a broader picture of the field and some of its current issues and newest developments. Students who are able to travel will, of course, learn some of the joys and problems of travel.

Methods of Entering

Young people seeking careers in the travel field usually begin by working for a company involved with transportation and tourism. Fortunately, a number of positions exist that are particularly appropriate for young people and those with limited work experience. Airlines, for example, hire *flight attendants, reservation agents,* and *ticket clerks.* Railroads and cruise line companies also have clerical positions; the rise in their popularity in recent years has resulted in more job opportunities. Those with travel experience may secure positions as tour guides. Organizations and companies with extensive travel operations may hire employees whose main responsibility is making travel arrangements.

Since travel agencies tend to have relatively small staffs, most openings are filled as a result of direct application and personal contact. In evaluating the merits of various travel agencies, job seekers may wish to note whether the agency's owner belongs to the American Society of Travel Agents (ASTA). This trade group may also help in several other ways. It sponsors adult night school courses in travel agency operation in some metropolitan areas. It also offers a fifteen-lesson travel agency correspondence course. Also available, for a modest charge, is a travel agency management kit containing information that is particularly helpful to people considering setting up their own agencies. ASTA's publication *Travel News* includes a classified advertising section listing available positions and agencies for sale.

Advancement

Advancement opportunities within the travel field are limited to growth in terms of business volume or extent of specialization. Successful agents, for example, may hire additional employees or set up branch offices. A travel agency worker who has held his or her position for a while may be promoted to become a *travel assistant.* Travel assistants are responsible for answering general questions about transportation, providing current cost of hotel accommodations, and providing other valid information.

Travel bureau employees may decide to go into business for themselves. Agents may show their professional status by belonging to ASTA, which requires its members to have three years of satisfactory travel agent experience and approval by at least two carrier conferences.

In addition to the regular travel business, a number of travel jobs are available with oil companies, automobile clubs, and transportation companies. Some jobs in travel are on the staffs of state and local governments seeking to encourage tourism.

Employment Outlook

About 142,000 people are currently employed as travel agents. About one in ten travel agents is self-employed. Although future prospects in the travel field will depend to some degree on the state of the economy, the travel industry is expected to expand rapidly as more Americans travel for pleasure and business. New travel agencies will open and existing ones will expand, causing employment of these workers to grow faster than the average for all occupations through the year 2006. The U.S. Department of Labor estimates that the number of travel agents will increase by at least 77,000 by the year 2006. Many of the expected job openings will result from workers leaving the field due to retirement or other reasons.

Certain factors may hinder growth for travel agents. On-line computer systems now enable people to make their own travel reservations. Electronic ticketing and a reduction on commissions paid to travel agencies by the airline industry may also hinder the growth of the travel industry. Since these innovations are recent, their full effect on travel agents has not yet been determined.

Earnings

Travel agencies earn their income from commissions from airlines, cruise lines, car rental companies, hotels, and other entities with whom agencies do business. The rate of commission varies, depending on the type of sale, from 8 to 10 percent of the cost to the customer. Air travel commissions vary on both domestic and international flights. Cruise lines pay a commission on a sliding scale depending upon the season. Bus tours, sight-seeing trips, and resort hotels often pay a commission of 10 percent or higher. From these commissions, travel agencies pay employee salaries and overhead costs.

The enterprising agency will be able to supplement transportation and hotel sales by offering automobile rentals, travel books, baggage forwarding, currency exchange, gift services, house rentals, insurance, letters of credit, prepaid meals, traveler's checks, and transfers. Many of the companies supplying such services also offer commissions.

Employed travel agents may be hired either on a regular salary, paid entirely on a commission basis, or receive a salary plus a modified commission or bonus. Salaries of travel agents ranged from $16,400 to $32,600, with an average of $24,500 in 1996, according to the Bureau of Labor Statistics. Those with five years of experience earn an average of $22,300. Managers with ten years of experience may earn from $26,300 to over $32,600 annually. In addition to experience, location also determines agent salaries, with those operating in large cities earning more.

In addition to income, travel agents receive a number of attractive opportunities for personal travel. Major airlines and cruise lines, knowing that agents who have used their services may recommend them more highly, offer some trips to agents at only 25 percent of the usual cost. Occasionally, the opening of a new hotel, airline route, or resort area leads to free trips for agents, as these companies encourage agents to recommend them to customers. If they organize tours, agents may be able to take advantage of the fact that transportation carriers and hotels usually offer one free trip for every fifteen to twenty paid members of a travel group.

Conditions of Work

While this is an interesting and appealing occupation, the job of the travel agent is not as simple or glamorous as might be expected. Travel is a highly competitive field. Since almost every travel agent can offer the client the same service, agents must depend upon repeat customers for much of their business. Their reliability, courtesy, and effectiveness in past transactions will determine whether they will get repeat business.

Travel agents also work in an atmosphere of keen competition for referrals. They must resist direct pressure or indirect pressure from travel-related companies that have provided favors in the past (free trips, for example) and book all trips based only on the best interests of clients.

Most agents work a forty-hour week, although this frequently includes working a half-day on Saturday or an occasional evening. During busy seasons (typically from January through June) overtime may be necessary. Agents may receive additional salary for this work or be given compensatory time off.

As they gain experience, agents become more effective. One study revealed that 98 percent of all agents had more than three years' experience in some form of the travel field. Almost half had twenty years or more in this area.

Small travel agencies provide a less-than-average amount of fringe benefits such as retirement, medical, and life insurance plans. Self-employed agents tend to earn more than those who work for others, although the business risk is greater. Those who own their own businesses may experience large fluctuations in income because the travel business is extremely sensitive to swings in the economy.

Sources of Additional Information

◼◼American Society of Travel Agents
1101 King Street, Suite 200
Alexandria, VA 22314
Tel: 703-739-2782

For information regarding certification, contact:

◼◼The Institute of Certified Travel Agents
PO Box 812059
48 Linden Street
Wellesley, MA 02181-0012
Tel: 617-237-0280

◼◼Society of Travel Agents in Government
6935 Wisconsin Avenue
Bethesda, MD 20815-6109

Truck Drivers

Definition

Truck drivers generally are distinguished by whether they drive a certain area or travel longer distances. *Local drivers,* also known as, *short-haul drivers* or *pickup and delivery drivers,* operate trucks that transport materials, merchandise, and equipment within a limited area, usually a single city or metropolitan area. Local drivers may be responsible for loading and unloading their trucks. Sometimes, they are expected to make minor mechanical repairs in order to keep their trucks in working order.

Over-the-road drivers, also known as *long-distance drivers* or *tractor-trailer drivers,* haul freight over long distances in large trucks and tractor-trailer rigs that are usually diesel-powered. Depending on the specific operation, over-the-road drivers also load and unload the shipments and make minor repairs to vehicles.

Nature of the Work

Truckers drive trucks of all sizes, from small straight trucks and vans to tanker trucks and tractors with multiple trailers. The average tractor-trailer rig is no more than 102 inches wide, excluding the mirrors, and is 13 feet and 6 inches tall and just under 70 feet in length. The engines in these vehicles range from 250 up to 600 horsepower.

Local truck drivers generally operate the smaller trucks and transport a variety of products. They may travel regular routes or routes that change as needed. Local drivers include delivery workers who supply fresh produce to grocery stores and drivers who deliver gasoline in tank trucks to gas stations. Other local truck drivers, such as those who keep stores stocked with baked goods, may sell their employer's products as well as deliver them to customers along a route. These drivers are known as *route driver*s or *route-sales drivers.*

Often local truck drivers receive their assignments and delivery forms from dispatchers at the company terminal each day.

School Subjects
Business
Shop (Trade/Vo-tech education)

Personal Interests
Travel

Work Environment
Primarily outdoors
Primarily multiple locations

Minimum Education Level
High school diploma
Apprenticeship

Salary Range
$15,000 to
$27,000 to
$50,000

Certification or Licensing
Required

Outlook
About as fast as the average

DOT
905

GOE
05.08.01

NOC
7411

Some drivers load goods or materials on their trucks, but in many situations dockworkers have already loaded the trucks in such a way that the unloading can be accomplished along the route with maximum convenience and efficiency.

Local drivers must be skilled at maneuvering their vehicles through the worst driving conditions, whether they are traffic-congested streets or rutted roads. The ability to pull into tight parking spaces, negotiate narrow passageways, and back up to loading docks is essential.

Some drivers have helpers who travel with them and assist in unloading at delivery sites, especially if the loads are heavy or bulky or when there are many deliveries scheduled. Drivers of some heavy trucks, such as dump trucks and oil tank trucks, operate mechanical levers, pedals, and other devices that assist with loading and unloading cargo. Drivers of moving vans generally have a crew of helpers to aid in loading and unloading customers' household goods and office equipment.

Once a local driver reaches his or her destination, he or she sometimes obtains a signature acknowledging that the delivery has been made and may collect a payment from the customer. Some drivers serve as intermediaries between the company and its customers by responding to customer complaints and requests.

Each day, local drivers have to make sure that their deliveries have been made correctly. At the end of the day, they turn in their records and the money they have collected. Local drivers may also be responsible for doing routine maintenance on their trucks to keep them in good working condition. Otherwise, any mechanical problems are reported to the maintenance department for repair.

Over-the-road drivers operate tractor-trailers and other large trucks that are often diesel-powered. These drivers generally haul goods and materials over long distances and frequently drive at night. Whereas many other truck drivers spend a considerable portion of their time loading and unloading materials, over-the-road drivers spend most of their working time in actual driving.

At the terminal or warehouse where they receive their load, drivers get ready for long-distance runs by checking over the vehicle to make sure all the equipment and systems are functioning and that the truck is loaded properly and has on board the necessary fuel, oil, and safety equipment.

Some over-the-road drivers travel the same route repeatedly and on a regular schedule. Other companies require drivers to do unscheduled runs and work when dispatchers call with an available job. Some long-distance runs are short enough that drivers can get to the destination, remove the load from the trailer, replace it with another load, and return home all in one day. Many runs, however, take up to a week or longer, with various stops. Some companies assign two drivers to long runs, so that one can sleep while the other drives. This method ensures that the trip will take the shortest amount of time possible.

In addition to driving their trucks long distances, over-the-road drivers have other duties. They must inspect their vehicle before and after trips, prepare reports on accidents, and keep a daily log. They may load and unload some shipments or hire workers to help with these tasks at the destination. Drivers of long-distance moving vans, for example, do more loading and unloading work than most other long-haul drivers. Drivers of vehicle-transport trailer trucks move new automobiles or trucks from manufacturers to dealers and also have additional duties. At plants where the vehicles are made, transport drivers drive new vehicles onto the ramps of transport trailers. They secure the vehicles in place with chains and clamps to prevent them from swaying and rolling. After driving to the destination, the drivers remove the vehicles from the trailers.

Over-the-road drivers must develop a number of skills that differ from the skills needed for operating smaller trucks. Because trailer trucks vary in length and number of wheels, skilled operators of one type of trailer may need to undergo a short training period if they switch to a new type of trailer. Over-the-road drivers must be able to maneuver and judge the position of their trucks and must be able to back their huge trailers into precise positions.

Over-the-road and local drivers may be employed by either private carriers or for-hire carriers. Food store chains and manufacturing plants that transport their own goods are examples of private carriers. There are two kinds of for-hire carriers: trucking companies serving the general public (common carriers) and trucking firms transporting goods under contract to certain companies (contract carriers).

Drivers who work independently are known as *owner-operators*. They own their own vehicles and often do their own maintenance and repair work. They must find customers who need goods transported, perhaps through personal references or by advertising their services. There is now an "Internet truckstop" on the world wide web where drivers can advertise their services and companies can post locations of loads they need transported. Some independent drivers establish long-term contracts with just one or two clients, such as trucking companies.

Requirements

Truck drivers must meet federal requirements and any requirements established by the state where they are based. All drivers must obtain a state commercial driver's license. Applicants for commercial driver's licenses must pass tests of their knowledge and driving ability, and they must not have had a previous license suspended or revoked.

Truck drivers involved in interstate commerce must meet requirements of the U.S. Department of Transportation. They must be at least twenty-one years old and pass a physical examination that requires good vision and hearing, normal blood pressure, and normal use of arms and legs (unless the applicant qualifies for a waiver).

In addition to meeting standards set by the state and federal governments, drivers must learn skills appropriate for the kind of driving they do. In some companies, new employees can learn these skills informally from experienced drivers. They may ride with and watch other employees of the company or they may take a few hours of their own time to learn from an experienced driver. For jobs driving some kinds of trucks, companies require new employees to attend classes that range from a few days to several weeks. During this time, potential drivers learn company policies and procedures, as well as how to load, unload, and operate the trucks.

One of the best ways to prepare for a job driving large trucks is to take a tractor-trailer driver training course. These courses are offered at many vocational and technical schools and include instruction in driving under various road and traffic conditions, complying with laws and regulations, and inspecting trucks and freight. However, programs vary in the amount of actual driving experience they provide. Programs that are certified by the Professional Truck Driver Institute of America meet established guidelines for training and generally provide good preparation for drivers. Another way to determine whether programs are adequate is to check with local companies that hire drivers and ask for their recommendations. Completing a certified training program helps potential truck drivers learn specific skills, but it does not guarantee a job.

Vehicles and the freight inside trucks can represent a large investment to companies that employ truck drivers. Therefore, they seek to hire the responsible and reliable drivers in order to protect their investment. For this reason many employers set various requirements of their own that exceed state and federal standards. For example, employers may require a high school diploma, several years of driving experience, a minimum age of twenty-five, the ability to lift heavy weights, annual physical examinations, and periodic screenings for drug use.

High school students interested in working as a truck driver should take courses in driver training and automobile mechanics. In addition, some bookkeeping, mathematics and business courses will help a truck driver learn methods that help in keeping accurate records of customer transactions.

Many drivers work with little supervision, so they need to have a mature, responsible attitude toward their job. In jobs where drivers deal directly with company customers, it is especially important for the drivers to be pleasant, courteous, and able to communicate well with people. Helping a customer with a complaint can mean the difference between losing and keeping a client.

Many truck drivers are members of the International Brotherhood of Teamsters, Chauffeurs, Warehousemen and Helpers of America and other unions that organize plant employees in various companies.

Opportunities for Experience & Exploration

High school students interested in becoming truck drivers may be able to gain experience by working as drivers' helpers during summer vacations or in part-time delivery jobs. Many people get useful experience in driving vehicles while they are serving in the armed forces. It may also be helpful to talk with employers of local or over-the-road truck drivers or with the drivers themselves.

The Internet provides a forum for prospective truck drivers to explore their career options. *Road King*, a magazine for truckers, has a World Wide Web site at WWW: http://www.roadking.com, with a chat group called "the driver's lounge." Feature articles about the lives of truck drivers are posted regularly. There is also a truck driver's news group, WWW: misc.transport.trucking, where potential truck drivers can pose questions.

Methods of Entering

Most truck drivers hold other jobs before they become truck drivers. Some local drivers start as drivers' helpers, loading and unloading trucks and gradually taking over some driving duties. When a better driving position opens up, helpers who have shown they are reliable and responsible may be promoted. Members of the armed forces who have gained appropriate experience may get driving jobs when they are discharged.

Job seekers may apply directly to firms that use drivers. Listings of specific job openings are often posted at local offices of the state employment service and in the classified ads in newspapers. Many jobs, however, are not posted. Looking in the yellow pages under trucking and moving and storage can provide names of specific companies to solicit. Also, large manufacturers and retailing companies sometimes have their own fleets. Many telephone calls and letters may be required, but can lead to a potential employer. Personal visits, when appropriate, sometimes get the best results.

Prospective over-the-road drivers can gain commercial driving experience as local truck drivers and then attend a tractor-trailer driver training program. Driving an intercity bus or dump truck is also suitable experience for aspiring over-the-road truck drivers. Many newly hired long-distance drivers start by filling in for regular drivers or helping out when extra trips are necessary. They are assigned regular work when a jobs opens up. Some companies provide in-house training.

Advancement

Local truck drivers can advance by learning to drive specialized kinds of trucks or by switching to better schedules or other job conditions. Some may move into positions as dispatchers and, with sufficient experience, eventually become supervisors or terminal managers. Other local drivers decide to become over-the-road drivers to receive higher wages. A few local truck drivers with business ability and sufficient capital establish their own independent local trucking companies.

Many over-the-road drivers look forward to going into business for themselves by acquiring their own tractor-trailer rigs. This step requires a significant initial investment and a continuing good income to cover expenses. Like many other small business owners, independent drivers sometimes have a hard time financially. Those who are their own mechanics and have formal business training are in the best position to do well.

Some over-the-road drivers who stay with their employers advance by becoming safety supervisors, driver supervisors, or dispatchers.

Employment Outlook

The employment of truck drivers is expected to increase as fast as the average for all other occupations through the year 2006. This increase will be related to overall growth in the nation's economy and in the volume of freight moved by trucks, both locally and over long distances. Currently, there is a shortage of both local and over-the-road drivers. There were 3,050,000 truck drivers employed in 1996.

The need for trucking services is directly linked to the growth of the nation's economy. During economic downturns, when the pace of business slows, some drivers may receive fewer assignments and thus have lower earnings or they may be laid off. Truck drivers who are self employed suffer the most during these times. Drivers employed in some vital industries, such as food distribution, are less affected by an economic recession. Even though our rail system is a popular choice in transporting goods across the country, perishable items, such as fruits and vegetables, are best delivered by refrigerated trucks.

A large number of driver jobs become available each year. Most openings develop when experienced drivers transfer to other fields or leave the workforce entirely. Beginners are able to get many of these jobs. Some positions offer much better pay, hours, and working conditions than others. Competition is expected to remain strong for the more desirable jobs, and people who have the best training and experience will have an advantage.

Earnings

Wages of truck drivers vary according to their employer, size of the truck they drive, product being hauled, geographical region, and other factors.

Although some local truck drivers are guaranteed minimum or weekly wages, most are paid an hourly wage and receive extra compensation for overtime work. In contrast, long-distance drivers are usually paid by the mile at rates that depend on their employer, number of miles driven in a pay period, seniority, and type of truck they drive.

On average, truck drivers can expect earnings at least in the range of $8.56 to $14.64 per hour. Drivers who are employed by for-hire carriers have higher earnings than those who work independently or for private carriers. In 1996, the U.S. Department of Labor's Bureau of Labor Statistics reported a median hourly rate of $13.39. Tractor-trailer drivers usually have the highest earnings; average hourly pay generally increases with the size of the truck. Drivers in the South have lower earnings than those in the Northeast and West. The annual earnings of long-distance drivers can range from about $20,000 to well over twice that amount. Owner-operators have average earnings between $20,000 and $25,000 per year, after subtracting expenses.

In addition to their wages, the majority of truck drivers receive benefits, many of which are determined by agreements between their unions and company management. The benefits may include health insurance coverage, pension plans, paid vacation days, and work uniforms.

Conditions of Work

Although there is work for truck drivers in even the smallest towns, most jobs are located in and around larger metropolitan areas. About a third of all drivers work for for-hire carriers, and another third work for private carriers. Less than 10 percent are self-employed.

Even with modern improvements in cab design, driving trucks is often a tiring job. Although some local drivers work forty-hour weeks, many work eight hours a day, six days a week, or more. Some drivers, such as those who bring food to grocery stores, often work at night or very early in the morning. Drivers who must load and unload their trucks may do a lot of lifting, stooping, and bending.

It is common for over-the-road truck drivers to work at least fifty hours a week. However, federal regulations require that drivers cannot be on duty for more than sixty hours in any seven-day period. Furthermore, after drivers have driven for ten hours, they must be off duty for at least eight hours before they can drive again. Drivers often work the maximum allowed time to complete long runs in as little time as possible. In fact, most drivers drive ten to twelve hours per day and make sure they have proper rest periods. A driver usually covers between 550 and 650 miles daily. The sustained driving, including at night, can be fatiguing, boring, and sometimes very stressful, as when traffic or weather conditions are bad.

Local drivers may operate on schedules that easily allow a social and family life, but long-distance drivers often find that difficult. They may spend a considerable amount of time away from their homes and families, including weekends and holidays. After they try it, many people find they do not want this way of life.

On the other hand, some people love the lifestyle of the over-the-road driver. Many families are able to find ways to work around the schedule of a truck driving spouse. In some cases, the two people assigned to a long-distance runs are a husband and wife team. Although the romantic notion of a truck driver being master of his or her own destiny is far from the reality of everyday life, the allure of the open road and the opportunity to see the country make this career attractive and satisfying to many.

Sources of Additional Information

For further information and literature about a career as a truck driver, contact the following organizations:

American Trucking Associations
Office of Public Affairs
2200 Mill Road
Alexandria, VA 22314
Tel: 703-838-1700
WWW: http://www.trucking org

International Brotherhood of Teamsters, Chauffeurs, Warehousemen, and Helpers of America
25 Louisiana Avenue, NW
Washington, DC 20001
Tel: 202-624-6800

Professional Truck Driver Institute of America, Inc.
8788 Elk Grove Boulevard
Elk Grove, CA 95624
Tel: 916-686-5146

Typists and Word Processors

Definition

Using typewriters, personal computers, and other office machines, *typists* and *word processors* convert handwritten or otherwise unfinished material into clean, readable, typewritten copies. Typists create reports, letters, forms, tables, charts, and other materials for all kinds of businesses and services. Word processors create the same types of materials using a computer that stores information electronically instead of printing it directly onto paper. Other typists use special machines that convert manuscripts into braille, coded copy, or typeset copy.

Nature of the Work

Typists and word processors are employed in almost every kind of workplace, including banks, law firms, factories, schools, hospitals, publishing firms, department stores, and government agencies. They may work with groups of employees in large offices or with only one or two other people in small offices.

Some typists perform few duties other than typing. These workers spend approximately 75 percent of their time at the keyboard. They may input statistical data, medical reports, legal briefs, addresses, letters, and other documents from handwritten copies. They may work in pools, dividing the work of a large office among many workers under the supervision of a *typing section chief*. These typists may also be responsible for making photocopies of typewritten materials for distribution.

Beginning typists may start by typing address labels, headings on form letters, and documents from legible handwritten copy. More experienced typists may work from copy that is more difficult to read or needs to be printed in tabular form.

Clerk-typists spend up to 50 percent of their time typing. They also perform a variety of clerical tasks such as filing,

School Subjects
Computer science
English
(writing/literature)

Personal Interests
Computers
Reading/Books

Work Environment
Primarily indoors
Primarily one location

Minimum Education Level
High school diploma

Salary Range
$15,500 to
$20,000 to
$30,750

Certification or Licensing
None

Outlook
Decline

DOT
203

GOE
07.06.02

NOC
1412

answering the phone, acting as receptionists, and operating copy machines.

Many typists type from recorded tapes instead of written or printed copy. *Transcribing-machine operators* sit at keyboards and wear headsets, through which they hear the spoken contents of letters, reports, and meetings. Typists can control the speed of the tape so they can comfortably type every word they hear. They proofread their finished documents and may erase dictated tapes for future use.

Many typists work at computer terminals. *Magnetic-tape-typewriter operators* enter information from written materials on computers to produce magnetic disks or tapes for storage and later retrieval. *In-file operators* use terminals to post or receive information about people's credit records for credit-reporting agencies. When an agency subscriber calls with a question about a person's credit, the typist calls up that record on the video screen and reads the information. Word processors also can send electronic files to people via email or modems to people in different locations.

Most common of the computer typists, however, are word processors. These employees put documents into the proper format by entering codes into the word processing software, telling it which lines to center, which words to underline, where the margins should be set, and how the document should be stored and printed. Word processors can edit, change, insert, and delete materials instantly just by pressing keys. Word processing is particularly efficient for form letters, in which only certain parts of a document change on each copy. When a word processor has finished formatting and keying in a document, it is electronically sent to a printer for a finished copy. The document is normally saved on a disk or the computer's hard drive so that any subsequent changes to it can be made easily and new copies produced immediately.

Certain typists use special machines to create copy. *Perforator typists* type on machines that punch holes in a paper tape, which is used to create typewritten copy automatically. *Telegraphic-typewriter operators* receive and transmit telegrams by typing messages using typewriter-like keyboards. In publishing and printing, *photocomposing-perforator-machine operators*, *photocomposing-keyboard operators*, *veritype operators*, and *typesetter-perforator operators* type on special machines that produce photographic negatives or paper prints of the copy. Some of these typists must also code copy to show what size and style of letters and characters should be used and how the layout of the page should look.

Braille typists and *braille operators* use special typewriter-like machines to transcribe written or spoken English into braille. By pressing one key or a combination of keys, they create the raised characters of the braille alphabet. They may print either on special paper or on metal plates, which are later used to print books or other publications.

Cryptographic-machine operators operate typewriter-like equipment that codes, transmits, and decodes secret messages for the armed forces, law enforcement agencies, and business organizations. These typists select a code card from a code book, insert the card into the machine, and type the message in English on the machine, which converts it to coded copy. A decoding card is used to follow the same process for decoding.

Requirements

Most employers require that typists and word processors are high school graduates and able to type accurately at a rate of at least forty or fifty words per minute. Typists need a good knowledge of spelling, grammar, and punctuation and may be required to be familiar with standard office equipment. Good listening skills are important for transcribing functions of the typist.

Keyboarding skills are taught in high schools, colleges, business schools, and home-study courses. Some people learn keyboarding through self-teaching materials such as books, records, and computer programs. Business schools and community colleges often offer certificates or associate's degrees for typists and word processors.

For those who do not pursue such formal education, temporary agencies will often train workers in these skills. Generally, it takes a minimum of three to six months of hands-on experience to become a skilled word processor.

Word processors must be able to type forty-five to eighty words per minute and should know the proper way to organize such documents as letters, reports, and financial statements. Increasingly, employers are requiring that employees know how to use various software programs for word processing, spreadsheet, and database management tasks.

All typists and word processors need manual dexterity and the ability to concentrate. They should be alert, efficient, and attentive to detail. Because these employees must often work directly with other people, they need good interpersonal skills, including a courteous and cheerful demeanor.

Opportunities for Experience & Exploration

As with many clerical occupations, a good way to gain experience as a typist is through high school work-study programs. Students in these programs work part-time for local businesses and attend classes part time. Temporary agencies also provide training and temporary jobs for exploring the field. Another way to gain typing experience is to do volunteer typing for friends, church groups, or other organizations and to create your own computerized reports.

Methods of Entering

Business school and college students may learn of typing or word processing positions through their schools' placement offices. Some large businesses recruit employees directly from these schools. High school guidance counselors also may know of local job openings.

People interested in typing or word processor positions can check the want ads in newspapers and business journals for companies with job openings. They can also apply directly to the personnel departments of large companies that hire many of these workers. They also can register with a temporary agency. To apply for positions with the federal government, job seekers should apply at the nearest regional Office of Personnel Management. State, county, and city governments may also have listings for such positions.

Advancement

Typists and word processors usually receive salary increases as they gain experience and are promoted from junior to senior positions. These are often given a classification or pay scale, such as typist or word processor I or II. They may also advance from clerk typist to technical typist, or from a job in a typing pool to a private-office typing position.

A degree in business management or executive secretarial skills increases a typist's chances for advancement. In addition, many large companies and government agencies provide training programs that allow workers to upgrade their skills and move into other jobs, such as secretary, statistical clerk, or stenographer.

Once they have acquired enough experience, some typists and word processors go into business for themselves and provide typing services to business clients on their premises working from their homes. They may find work typing reports, manuscripts, and papers for professors, authors, business people, and students.

The more word processing experience an employee has, the better the opportunities to move up. Some may be promoted to word processing supervisor or selected for in-house professional training programs in data processing. Word processors may also move into related fields and work as word processing equipment salespeople or servicers, or word-processing teachers or consultants.

Employment Outlook

In 1996 about 1.1 million people worked as typists and word processors in all industries. Business organizations employ one-third of these people, while education, medicine, and other services employ another third. About one-quarter work for various government agencies.

Employment in the typing field is expected to decline through the year 2006 due to the increasing automation of offices. However, the sheer size of the occupation means that many jobs will become available for typists and word processors, especially to replace those employees who change careers or leave the workforce.

Technological innovations such as optical character recognition readers, which scan documents and enter their copy into a computer, are being used in more and more workplaces. Voice recognition technologies that enable people to enter text and data by simply speaking to a computer are also being developed. Such machines will greatly reduce the demand for typists and word processors. Also, many businesses have been known to send their data entry work abroad where labor is less expensive. Thus, American workers with the best technical skills and knowledge of several word processing programs have the best chances of getting hired.

Earnings

Workers with word processing experience generally receive higher salaries than those without it. According to the U.S. Department of Labor, typists earned an average salary of about $20,000 in 1996. In the federal government, beginning clerk-typists earned about $15,500 per year in 1996, while the average salary for all clerk-typists in the federal government was about $21,500. The range for typists and word processors was from $15,500 to $30,750 in 1996.

Typists and word processors occasionally may work overtime to finish special projects and may receive overtime pay. In large cities workers usually receive paid holidays, two weeks' vacation after one year of employment, sick leave, health and life insurance, and a pension plan. Some large companies also provide dental insurance, profit sharing opportunities, and bonuses.

Conditions of Work

Typists and word processors usually work thirty-five to forty hours per week at workstations in clean, bright offices. They usually sit most of the day in a fairly small area. The work is detailed and often repetitious, and approaching deadlines may increase the pressure and demands placed on typists and word processors.

Recent years have seen a controversy develop concerning the effect that working at video display terminals can have on workers' health. Working with these screens in improper lighting can cause eyestrain, and sitting at a workstation all day can cause musculoskeletal stress and pain. The computer industry is paying closer attention to these problems and is working to improve health and safety standards in VDT-equipped offices.

Another common ailment for typists and word processors is carpal tunnel syndrome, a painful ailment of the tendons in the wrist that is triggered by repetitive movement. If left unchecked, it can require corrective surgery. However, proper placement of the typing keyboard can help prevent injury. Several companies have designed desks, chairs, and working spaces that accommodate the physical needs of typists and word processors in the best manner currently known.

The nature of this work lends itself to flexible work arrangements. Many typists and word processors work in temporary positions that provide flexible schedules. About 20 percent work part-time. Some offices allow word processors and typists to telecommute from home, whereby they receive and send work on home computers via modems. These jobs may be especially convenient for workers with disabilities or family responsibilities, but they often do not provide a full range of benefits and lack the advantages of social interaction on the job.

Sources of Additional Information

■ **National Association of Secretarial Services**
3637 Fourth Street North, Suite 330
St. Petersburg, FL 33704-1336
Tel: 813-823-3646

■ **OfficeTeam**
2884 Sand Hill Road
Menlo Park, CA 94025
Tel: 800-804-8367

■ **Professional Secretaries International**
PO Box 20404
10502 NW Ambassador Drive
Kansas City, MO 64195-0404
Tel: 816-891-6600

Veterinary Technicians

Definition

Veterinary technicians are professionals who provide support and assistance to veterinary doctors. They may work in a variety of environments, including zoos, animal hospitals, clinics, private practices, kennels, and laboratories. Work may involve large or small animals, or both. Although most veterinary technicians work with domestic animals, some professional settings may require treating exotic or endangered species.

Nature of the Work

Many pet owners depend upon veterinarians to maintain the health and well-being of their pets. Veterinary clinics and private practices are the primary settings for animal care. In assisting veterinarians, veterinary technicians play an integral role in the care of animals within this particular environment.

A veterinary technician is the person who performs much of the laboratory testing procedures commonly associated with veterinary care. In fact, approximately 50 percent of a veterinary technician's duties involves laboratory testing. Laboratory assignments usually include taking and developing X-rays, performing parasitology tests, and examining various samples taken from the animal's body, such as blood. A veterinary technician may also assist the veterinarian with necropsies in an effort to determine the cause of an animal's death.

In a clinic or private practice, a veterinary technician assists the veterinarian with surgical procedures. This generally entails preparing the animal for surgery by shaving the incision area and applying a topical antibacterial agent. Surgical anesthesia is administered and controlled by the veterinary technician. Throughout the surgical process, the technician tracks the surgical instruments and monitors the animal's vital signs. Sometimes, an animal patient is very ill and has no chance for survival or an overcrowded animal shelter may not be able to

School Subjects
Agriculture
Biology

Personal Interests
Animals
Science

Work Environment
Indoors and outdoors
Primarily one location

Minimum Education Level
Some postsecondary training

Salary Range
$15,000 to
$25,000 to
$40,000

Certification or Licensing
Required in some states

Outlook
Faster than the average

DOT
079

GOE
02.03.03

NOC
3213

find a home for a donated or stray animal. In these situations, the veterinary technician may be required to assist in euthanizing the animal.

During routine examinations and check ups, veterinary technicians will help restrain the animals. They may perform ear cleaning and nail clipping procedures as part of regular animal care. Outside the examination and surgery rooms, veterinary technicians perform additional responsibilities. In most settings, they record, replenish, and maintain pharmaceutical, equipment, and supply inventories.

Veterinary technicians may also work in a zoo. Here, job duties, such as laboratory testing, are quite similar, but practices are more specialized. Unlike in private practice, the *zoo veterinary technician* is not required to explain treatment to pet owners; however, he or she may have to discuss an animal's treatment or progress with zoo veterinarians, curators, and other zoo professionals. A zoo veterinary technician's work may also differ from private practice in that it may be necessary for the technician to observe the animal in its habitat, which could require working outdoors. Additionally, a zoo veterinary technician may work more with exotic or endangered species. This is a very competitive and highly desired area of practice in the veterinary technician field. Currently there are only fifty zoo veterinary technicians working in the United States. There are only a few zoos in each state; thus a limited number of job opportunities exist within these zoos. To break into this area of practice, veterinary technicians must be among the best in the field.

Another setting where a veterinary technicians work is research. Most research opportunities for veterinary technicians are presented in academic environments with veterinary medicine or medical science programs. Again, laboratory testing may comprise much of the job duties; however, the veterinary technicians participate in very important animal research projects from start to finish.

There is also a need for technicians in rural areas. Farmers require veterinary services for the care of farm animals such as pigs, cows, horses, dogs, cats, sheep, mules, and chickens. It is often essential for the veterinarian and technician to drive to the farmer's residence, as animals are usually treated on site.

An other area in which veterinary technicians work is that of animal training, for example, at an obedience school. Extraordinary positions in which a veterinary technician may practice, although quite rare, are those with a circus trainer and in information systems technology, where information on animals is compiled and provided by the veterinary technician via the Internet.

Veterinary technicians are the veterinarian's right arm. Despite the setting, a veterinary technician must be an effective communicator and proficient in basic computer applications. In clinical or private practice, it is usually the veterinary technician who conveys and explains treatment and subsequent animal care to the animal's owner. In research and laboratory work, the veterinary technician must record and discuss results among colleagues. In most practical veterinary settings, the veterinary technician must record various information on a computer.

Requirements

Employers look for many attributes when hiring a veterinary technician. A high school diploma is necessary in order to obtain additional required training. High school students who excel at math and science have a strong foundation on which to build. Those who have had pets or who simply love animals and would like to work with them also fit the profile of a veterinary technician.

The main requirement is the completion of a two- to four-year college-based accredited program. Upon graduation, the student receives an associate's or bachelor's degree.

Currently, there are sixty-five accredited programs in the United States. A few states do their own accrediting, using the American Veterinary Medical Association (AVMA) and associated programs as benchmarks. For a list of accredited schools, students can write to the AVMA (see address at end of this article).

Most accredited programs offer thorough coursework and preparatory learning opportunities to the aspiring veterinary technician. Typical courses includes mathematics, chemistry, humanities, biological science, communications, microbiology, liberal arts, ethics/jurisprudence, and basic computers.

Once the students complete this framework, they move on to more specialized courses. They take classes in animal nutrition, animal care and management, species/breed identification, veterinary anatomy/physiology, medical terminology, radiography and other clinical procedure courses, animal husbandry, parasitology, laboratory animal care, and large/small animal nursing.

Veterinary technicians must be prepared to assist in surgical procedures. In consideration of this, accredited programs offer surgical nursing courses. In these courses, a student learns to identify and use surgical instruments, administer anesthesia, and monitor the animal during and after surgery.

In addition to classroom study, accredited programs offer practical courses. Hands-on education and training are commonly achieved through a clinical practicum, or internship, where the student has the opportunity to work in a clinical veterinary setting. During this period, a student is continuously evaluated by the participating veterinarian and encouraged to apply the knowledge and skills learned.

Although the AVMA determines the majority of the national codes for veterinary technicians, state codes and laws vary from state to state. Most states offer registration or certification, and the majority of these states require graduation from an AVMA-accredited program as a prerequisite for taking the examination. Most colleges and universities assist graduates with registration and certification arrangements. To keep abreast of new technology and applications in the field, a practicing veterinary technician may be required to complete a determined amount of annual continuing education courses.

Opportunities for Experience & Exploration

High school students can acquire exposure to the veterinary field by working with animals in related settings. For example, a high school student may be able to work as a part-time animal attendant or receptionist in a private veterinary practice. Paid or volunteer part-time jobs may be available at kennels, animal shelters, and training schools. However, direct work with animals in a zoo is unlikely for high school students.

Some zoos do offer programs for adopting animals, though, which would probably not offer direct contact with the animal, it may provide an opportunity to learn more about zoos and certain animals.

Methods of Entering

Veterinary technicians who complete an accredited program and becomes certified or registered by the state in which they plan to practice, are often able to receive assistance in finding a job through their college placement offices. Students who have completes internships may receive job offers from the place where they interned

Veterinary technician graduates may also learn of clinic openings through classified ads in newspapers.

Opportunities in zoos and research are usually listed in specific industry periodicals such as *Veterinary Technician Magazine* and *AZVT News,* a newsletter published by the Association of Zoo Veterinary Technicians.

Graduates also can apply directly to potential employers by sending a letter of inquiry and resume.

Advancement

Where a career as a veterinary technician can lead is entirely up to the individual. Opportunities are unlimited. With continued education, veterinary technicians can move into allied fields. Among these are veterinary medicine, nursing, medical technology, radiology, and pharmacology. By completing two more years of college and receiving a bachelor's degree, a veterinary technician can become a veterinary technologist. Advanced degrees can open the doors to a variety of specialized fields. There are currently efforts to standardize requirements for veterinary technicians. A national standard would broaden the scope of educational programs and may create more opportunities in instruction for veterinary professionals with advanced degrees. Extremely rare areas into which veterinarian technicians can moved are those of circus training and focused information systems technology, through which information on animals is passed to industry professionals via the Internet.

Employment Outlook

The employment outlook for veterinary technicians is very good through the year 2006. Veterinary technicians are constantly in demand. Veterinary medicine is a field that is not adversely affected by the economy, so it does offer stability.

In 1996, there were 33,000 veterinary technicians employed in the United States. Currently, there is a shortage of veterinary technicians. In fact, there were 4,000 job openings for every 1,000 graduates in the mid-1990's. The public's love for their pets, coupled with higher disposable incomes will increase the demand for this occupation.

Earnings

Earnings are generally low for veterinary technicians in private practices and clinics, but pay scales are steadily climbing due to the increasingly strong demand for veterinary technicians. Better-paying jobs are in zoos and in academic or animal research areas. Those fields of practice are very competitive, especially zoos, and only a small percentage of highly qualified veterinary technicians are employed in them.

About 70 percent of veterinary technicians are employed in private or clinical practice and research. Earnings for zoo veterinary technicians range from $17,000 to $35,000. Salaries in clinical or private practice range from $15,000 for recent graduates to $40,000 for experienced graduates working in supervisory positions. Earnings vary depending on practice setting, geographic location, level of education, and years of experience. Benefits vary and depend on individual employer's policies.

Conditions of Work

Veterinary technicians generally work forty-hour workweeks, which may include a few long weekdays and alternated or rotated Saturdays. Hours may fluctuate as veterinary technicians may need to have their schedules adjusted to accommodate emergency work.

A veterinary technician must be prepared for emergencies. In field or farm work, it can be expected for them to overcome weather conditions in treating the animal. Injured animals can be very dangerous, and veterinary technicians have to exercise extreme caution when caring for them. A veterinary technician also handles animals that are diseased or infested with parasites. Some of these conditions, such as ringworm, are contagious, so the veterinary technician must understand how these conditions are transferred to humans and the measures needed to prevent the spread of diseases.

People who become veterinary technicians care about animals. For this reason, maintaining an animal's well-being or helping to cure an ill animal is very rewarding work. In private practice, technicians get to know the animals they care for. This provides the opportunity to actually see the animals' progress. In other areas, such as zoo work, veterinary technicians work with very interesting, sometimes endangered, species. This work is very challenging and rewarding in the sense that they are helping to save a species and contributing efforts to educate people about these animals. Veterinary technicians who work in research gain satisfaction from knowing their work contributes to promoting both animal and human health.

Sources of Additional Information

For more information on careers and resources, write to the American Veterinary Medical Association. In addition, check out the AVMA's web page for career and education information, especially the "NetVet" link that provides access to information on specialties, organizations, publications, plus fun sites such as the "Electronic Zoo."

American Veterinary Medical Association (AVMA)
1931 North Meacham Road, Suite 100
Schaumburg, IL 60173-4360
Tel: 847-925-8070
WWW: http://www.avma.org

North American Veterinary Technician Association
PO Box 224
Battleground, IN 47920
Tel: 317-742-2216

Canadian Veterinary Medical Association
339 Booth Street
Ottawa, ON K1R 7K1 Canada
Tel: 613-236-1162
Email: mmcvma@magi.com

For more information on zoo veterinary technology and positions, contact:

Association of Zoo Veterinary Technicians (AZVT)
c/o Louisville Zoo
AZVT Office
PO Box 37250
Louisville, KY 40233
Tel: 502-451-0440, ext. 345
Email: virginia.crossett@louky.iglou.com

Wastewater Treatment Plant Operators

Definition

Wastewater treatment plant operators control, monitor, and maintain the equipment and treatment processes in wastewater (sewage) treatment plants. They remove or make harmless the chemicals, solid materials, and organisms in wastewater so that the water is not polluted when it is returned to the environment.

Nature of the Work

Wastewater from homes, public buildings, and industrial plants is transported through sewer pipes to treatment plants. The wastes include both organic and inorganic substances, some of which may be highly toxic, such as lead and mercury. Wastewater treatment plant operators regulate the flow of incoming wastewater by adjusting pumps, valves, and other equipment, either manually or through remote controls. They keep track of the various meters and gauges that monitor the purification processes and indicate how the equipment is operating. Using the information from these instruments, they control the pumps, engines, and generators that move the untreated water through the processes of filtration, settling, aeration, and sludge digestion. They also operate chemical-feeding devices, collect water samples, and perform laboratory tests, so that the proper level of chemicals, such as chlorine, is maintained in the wastewater. Operators may record instrument readings and other information in logs of plant operations.

Computers are commonly used to monitor and regulate wastewater treatment equipment and processes. Specialized software allows operators to store and analyze data, which is particularly useful when something in the system malfunctions.

Other routine tasks that plant operators perform include maintenance and minor repairs on equipment such as valves and pumps. Operators may use common hand tools such as

---

School Subjects
Chemistry
Shop (Trade/Vo-tech education)

Personal Interests
Figuring out how things work
Fixing things

Work Environment
Indoors and outdoors
Primarily one location

Minimum Education Level
Some postsecondary training

Salary Range
$16,200 to
$28,600 to
$42,000+

Certification or Licensing
Required

Outlook
Faster than the average

DOT
955

GOE
06.02.11

NOC
9424

wrenches and pliers and special tools adapted specifically for the equipment. In large facilities, they also direct attendants and helpers who take care of some routine tasks and maintenance work. The accumulated residues of wastes from the water must be removed from the plant, and operators may dispose of these materials. Some of this final product, or sludge, can be reclaimed for uses such as soil conditioners or fuel for the production of electric power.

Plant operators sometimes have to work under emergency conditions, such as when heavy rains flood the sewer pipes, straining the treatment plant's capacity or when there is a chlorine gas leak or oxygen deficiency in the treatment tanks. When a serious problem arises, operators must work quickly and effectively to solve it as soon as possible.

The duties of wastewater treatment plant operators vary somewhat with the size and type of plant where they work. In small plants one person per shift may be able to do all the necessary routine tasks. But in larger plants, there may be a number of operators, each specializing in just a few activities and working as part of a team that includes engineers, chemists, technicians, mechanics, helpers, and other employees. Some facilities are equipped to handle both wastewater treatment and treatment of the clean water supplied to municipal water systems, and plant operators may be involved with both functions.

Requirements

A high school diploma or its equivalent is required for a job as a wastewater treatment plant operator, and additional specialized technical training is generally preferred. A desirable background for this work includes high school courses in chemistry, biology, mathematics and computers; welding or electrical training may be helpful as well. Other characteristics that employers look for are mechanical aptitude and the ability to perform mathematical computations easily.

Many operators acquire the skills they need during a period of on-the-job training. Newly hired workers often begin as attendants or operators-in-training. Working under the supervision of experienced operators, they pick up knowledge and skills by observing other workers and by doing routine tasks such as recording meter readings, collecting samples, and general cleaning and plant maintenance. In larger plants, trainees may study supplementary written material provided at the plant or they may attend classes where they learn plant operations.

As treatment plants become more technologically complex, workers who have previous training in the field are increasingly at an advantage. Specialized education in wastewater technology is available in two-year programs that lead to an associate's degree and one-year programs that lead to a certificate. Such programs, which are offered at some community and junior colleges and vocational-technical institutes, provide a good general knowledge of water pollution control and prepare students to become operators. Beginners must still learn the details of operations at the plant where they work, but their specialized training increases their chances for better positions and later promotions.

In most states, workers who control operations at wastewater treatment plants must be certified by the state. To obtain certification, operators must pass an examination given by the state. There is no nationwide standard, so different states administer different tests. Many states issue several classes of certification, depending on the size of the plant the worker is qualified to control. Certification may be beneficial even if it is not a requirement, and no matter how much experience a worker already has. In Illinois, for example, operators who have the minimum state certification level are automatically eligible for a higher pay schedule than those without any certification although certification is not a requirement of hire.

Wastewater treatment plant operators often have various opportunities to continue learning about their field. To improve the skills and broaden the knowledge of operators, most state water pollution control agencies offer training courses for people employed in the field. Subjects covered by these training courses include principles of treatment processes and process control, odors and their control, safety, chlorination, sedimentation, biological oxidation, sludge treatment and disposal, and flow measurements. Correspondence courses on related subject areas also are available for operators. Some employers help pay tuition for workers who take related college-level courses in science or engineering.

Operators must be familiar with the provisions of the Federal Clean Water Act and various state and local regulations that apply to their work. Whenever they become responsible for more complex processes and equipment, they must become acquainted with a wider scope of guidelines and regulations.

In larger cities and towns especially, job applicants may have to take a civil service exam or other tests that assess their aptitudes and abilities.

Opportunities for Experience & Exploration

Taking shop courses in high school is one way for students to gauge their mechanical aptitude and experience working with machinery and tools. Math courses help students learn to do computations similar to those that plant operators do on the job. Perhaps with the help of a guidance counselor or teacher, it may be possible to arrange to visit a wastewater treatment plant to observe its operations. It can also be helpful to investigate courses and requirements of any programs in wastewater technology or environmental resources programs offered by a local technical school or college.

While part-time or summer employment as a helper in a wastewater treatment plant could be very helpful experience, such a job may be hard to find. However, a job in any kind of machine shop can provide an opportunity to become familiar with handling machinery and common tools.

Methods of Entering

Graduates of most postsecondary technical programs and some high schools can get help in locating job openings from the placement office of the school they attended. Another source of information is the local office of the state employment service. Job seekers may also directly contact directly state and local water pollution control agencies and the personnel offices of wastewater treatment facilities in desired locations.

In some plants, a person must first work as a *wastewater treatment plant technician* before becoming an operator or working in a supervisory position. Wastewater treatment plant technicians have many of the same duties as a plant operator, but less responsibility. They inspect, study, and sample existing water treatment systems and evaluate new structures for efficacy and safety. Support work and instrumentation reading make up the bulk of the technician's day. Communications, statistics, and algebra are useful for this career path: such courses enable the technician to prepare graphs, tables, sketches, and diagrams to illustrate surveys for the operators and engineers they support.

Advancement

As operators gain skills and experience, they are assigned tasks that involve more responsibility for more complex activities. Some operators advance to become plant supervisors or plant superintendents. The qualifications that superintendents need are related to the size and complexity of the plant. In smaller plants, experienced operators with some postsecondary training may be promoted to superintendent positions. In larger plants, educational requirements are increasing along with the sophistication and complexity of the systems in them, and superintendents usually have bachelor's degrees in engineering or science.

For some operators, the route to advancement is transferring to a related job. A few operators become technicians for state water pollution control agencies, monitoring plants throughout the state and providing technical assistance. These jobs normally require vocational-technical school or community college training. Other experienced operators find employment with industrial wastewater treatment plants, companies that sell wastewater treatment equipment and chemicals, consulting firms, or vocational-technical schools.

Employment Outlook

Through the year 2006, employment in this field is expected to grow at a faster rate than average for all occupations. The growth in demand for wastewater treatment will be related to the overall growth of the nation's population and economy. New treatment plants will probably be built, and existing ones will be upgraded, requiring additional trained personnel to manage their operations. Other openings will arise when experienced workers retire or transfer to new occupations. Operators with formal training will have the best chances for new positions and promotions.

Workers in wastewater treatment plants are rarely laid off, even during a recession, because wastewater treatment is essential to public health and welfare. In the future, more plant operators will probably be employed by private companies that contract to manage treatment plants for local governments.

Earnings

Salaries of wastewater treatment plant operators vary depending on factors such as the size of the plant, workers' job responsibilities, and their level of certification. Entry-level plant operators can expect to make $16,200 per year. Average earnings of operators exceed $28,600 per year. Experienced certified workers can make over $42,000, depending on the size of the plant and staff they supervise. In addition to their pay, most operators receive benefits such as life and health insurance, a pension plan, and reimbursement for education and training related to their job.

Conditions of Work

Most of the approximately 98,000 wastewater treatment plant operators in the United States are employed by local governments; others work for the federal government, utilities companies, or private sanitary services that operate under contracts with local governments. Jobs are located throughout the country, with the greatest numbers found in areas with high populations. In small towns, plant operators may only work part time or may handle other duties as well as wastewater treatment.

Wastewater treatment plants operate twenty-four hours a day, every day of the year. Operators usually work one of three eight-hour shifts, often on a rotating basis so that employees share the evening and night work. During emergencies, operators often work extra hours.

The work takes operators both indoors and outdoors. They must contend with noisy machinery and may have to tolerate unpleasant odors, despite the use of chlorine and other chemicals to control odors. The job involves moving about, stooping, reaching, and climbing. Operators often get their clothes dirty. Slippery sidewalks, dangerous gases, and malfunctioning equipment are potential hazards on the job, but by following safety guidelines, workers can minimize their risk of injury.

Sources of Additional Information

For current information on the field of wastewater management, contact:

American Water Works Association
6666 West Quincy Avenue
Denver, CO 80235
Tel: 303-794-7711

For information on education and training, contact:

Coalition of Environmental Training Centers
c/o National Environmental Training Association
2930 East Camelback Road, Suite 185
Phoenix, AZ 85016
Tel: 602-956-6099

The following is a professional organization monitoring developments in the field of wastewater management:

Water Environment Federation
601 Wythe Street
Alexandria, VA 22314-1994
Tel: 703-684-2400

Welders

Definition

Welders operate a variety of special equipment to join metal parts together permanently, usually using heat and sometimes pressure. They work on constructing and repairing automobiles, aircraft, ships, buildings, bridges, highways, appliances, and many other metal structures and manufactured products.

Nature of the Work

Welders use various kinds of equipment and processes to create the heat and pressure needed to melt the edges of metal pieces in a controlled fashion so that the pieces may be joined permanently. The processes can be grouped into three categories. The arc welding process derives heat from an electric arc between two electrodes or between an electrode and the workpiece. The gas welding process produces heat by burning a mixture of oxygen and some other combustible gas, such as acetylene or hydrogen. The resistance welding process obtains heat from pressure and resistance by the workpiece to an electric current. Two of these processes, the arc and gas methods, can also be used to cut, gouge, or finish metal.

Depending on which of these processes and equipment they use, welders may be designated *arc welders, gas welders,* or *acetylene welders; combination welders* (meaning they use a combination of gas and arc welding); or *welding machine operators* (meaning they operate machines that use an arc welding process, electron beam welding process, laser welding process, or friction welding process). Other workers in the welding field include *resistance machine welders; oxygen cutters,* who use gas torches to cut or trim metals; and *arc cutters,* who use an electric arc to cut or trim metals.

Skilled welders usually begin by planning and laying out their work based on drawings, blueprints, or other specifica-

---

School Subjects
Physics
Shop (Trade/Vo-tech education)

Personal Interests
Building things
Fixing things

Work Environment
Indoors and outdoors
Primarily multiple locations

Minimum Education Level
High school diploma
Apprenticeship

Salary Range
$17,900 to
$31,400 to
$42,000+

Certification or Licensing
Required for certain positions

Outlook
More slowly than the average

DOT
810

GOE
05.05.06

NOC
7265

tions. Using their working knowledge of the properties of the metal, they determine the proper sequence of operations needed for the job. They may work with steel, stainless steel, cast iron, bronze, aluminum, nickel, and other metals and alloys. Metal pieces to be welded may be in a variety of positions, such as flat, vertical, horizontal, or overhead.

In the most commonly used the manual arc welding processes, welders grasp a holder containing a suitable electrode and adjust the electric current supplied to the electrode. Then they strike an arc (an electric discharge across a gap) by touching the electrode to the metal. Next, they guide the electrode along the metal seam to be welded, allowing sufficient time for the heat of the arc to melt the metal. The molten metal from the electrode is deposited in the joint and, together with the molten metal edges of the base metal, solidifies to form a solid connection. Welders determine the correct kind of electrode to use based on the job specifications and their knowledge of the materials.

In gas welding, welders melt the metal edges with an intensely hot flame from the combustion of fuel gases in welding torches. First, they obtain the proper types of torch tips and welding rods, which are rods of a filler metal that goes into the weld seam. They adjust the regulators on the tanks of fuel gases, such as oxygen and acetylene, and light the torch. To obtain the proper size and quality of flame, welders adjust the gas valves on the torch and hold the flame against the metal until it is hot enough. Then they apply the welding rod to the molten metal to supply the extra filler needed to complete the weld.

Maintenance welders, another category of welding workers, may use any of various welding techniques. They travel to construction sites, utility installations, and other locations to make on-site repairs to metalwork.

Some workers in the welding field do repetitive production tasks using automatic welding equipment. In general, automatic welding is not used where there are critical safety and strength requirements. The surfaces that these welders work on are usually in only one position. Resistance machine welders often work in the mass production of parts, doing the same welding operations repeatedly. To operate the welding machine, they first make adjustments to control the electric current and pressure and then feed in and align the workpieces. After completing the welding operation, welders remove the work from the machine. Welders must constantly monitor the process in order to make sure that the machine is producing the proper weld.

To cut metal, oxygen cutters may use hand-guided torches or machine-mounted torches. They direct the flame of burning oxygen and fuel gas onto the area to be cut until it melts. Then, an additional stream of gas is released from the torch, which cuts the metal along previously marked lines. Arc cutters follow a similar procedure in their work, except that they use an electric arc as the source of heat. As in oxygen cutting, an additional stream of gas may be released when cutting the metal.

Requirements

Many welders learn their skills in formal training programs in welding, such as those available in many community colleges, technical institutes, trade schools, and in the armed forces. Some programs are short term and narrow in focus, while others provide several years of thorough preparation for a variety of good jobs. A high school diploma or its equivalent is required for admission into these programs.

Beginners can also learn welding skills in on-the-job training programs. The length of such training programs ranges from several days or weeks for jobs requiring few skills to a period of one to three years for skilled jobs. Trainees often begin as helpers to experienced workers, doing very simple tasks. As they learn, they are given more challenging work. To learn some skilled jobs, trainees supplement their on-the-job training with formal classroom instruction in technical aspects of the trade.

Various programs sponsored by federal, state, and local governments provide training opportunities in some areas. These training programs, which usually stress the fundamentals of welding, may be in the classroom or on the job and last from a few weeks to a year. Apprenticeship programs also offer training. Apprenticeships that teach a range of metalworking skills, including the basics of welding, are run by trade unions such as the International Association of Machinists and Aerospace Workers.

Employers generally prefer to hire applicants who are in good enough physical condition that they can bend, stoop, and work in awkward positions. Applicants also need manual dexterity, good eye-hand coordination, and good eyesight, as well as patience and the ability to concentrate for extended periods as they work on a task. High school graduates are preferred for trainee positions for skilled jobs, although applicants with at least two years of high school or vocational school may be considered.

Useful high school courses that prospective welders include mathematics, blueprint reading, mechanical drawing, applied physics, and shop. If possible, the shop courses should cover the basics of welding and working with electricity.

Many people in welding and related occupations belong to unions, including the International Association of Machinists and Aerospace Workers; the International Brotherhood of Boilermakers, Iron Ship Builders, Blacksmiths, Forgers and Helpers; the International Union, United Automobile, Aerospace and Agricultural Implement Workers of America; the United Association of Journeymen and Apprentices of the Plumbing and Pipe Fitting Industry of the United States and Canada; and the United Electrical, Radio, and Machine Workers of America.

To do welding work where the strength of the weld is a critical factor (such as in aircraft, bridges, boilers, or high-pressure pipelines), welders may have to pass employer tests or standardized examinations for certification by government agencies or professional and technical associations.

Opportunities for Experience & Exploration

In many high schools, students can to learn the basics of welding, related metalworking skills, and the working with electricity in shop courses. Courses in drafting, blueprint reading, general science, mathematics, and applied physics and chemistry also introduce concepts that welders need to use in their work.

Perhaps with the help of a teacher or a guidance counselor, students may be able to arrange to visit a workplace where they can observe welders or welding machine operators on the job. Ideally, such a visit can provide a chance to see several welding processes and various kinds of welding work and working conditions, as well as an opportunity to talk with welders about their work.

Methods of Entering

Graduates of good training programs in welding often receive help in finding jobs through their schools' placement offices. The classified ads section of newspapers often carry listings of local job openings. Information about openings for trainee positions, apprenticeships, and government training programs, as well as jobs for skilled workers, may be available through the local offices of the state employment service and local offices of unions that organize welding workers. Job seekers can also apply directly to the personnel offices at companies that hire welders.

Advancement

Advancement usually depends on acquiring additional skills. Workers who gain experience and learn new processes and techniques are increasingly valuable to their employers, and they may be promoted to positions as supervisors, inspectors, or welding instructors. With further formal technical training, welders may qualify for welding technician jobs.

Some experienced welders go into business for themselves and open their own welding and repair shops.

Employment Outlook

Through the year 2006, overall employment in welding and related occupations is expected to change little. Most job openings will develop when experienced workers leave their jobs. However, the outlook varies somewhat by industry. In manufacturing industries, the trend toward increasing automation, including more use of welding robots, is expected to decrease the demand for manual welders and increase the demand for welding machine operators. In construction, wholesale trade, and repair services, more skilled welders will be needed as the economy grows, because the work tends to be less routine in these industries and automation is not likely to be a big factor.

During periods when the economy is in a slowdown, many workers in construction and manufacturing, including some welders, may be laid off.

Earnings

The earnings of welding trades workers vary widely depending on the skills needed for the job, industry, location, and other factors. On average, welders and welding machine operators can expect earnings in the range of $17,900 to $31,400 or more. Highly skilled welders may have earnings ranging from about $42,000, and sometimes much more. In addition to wages, employers often provide fringe benefits, such as health insurance plans, paid vacation time, paid sick time, and pension plans. About one-fourth of welders belong to a union.

Conditions of Work

Workers in welding occupations work in a variety of settings. About two-thirds of welders are employed in manufacturing plants that produce motor vehicles, ships, boilers, machinery, appliances, and other metal products. Most of the remaining welders work for repair shops or construction companies that build bridges, large buildings, pipelines, and similar metal structures. Welding machine operators all work in manufacturing industries. Thus workers may spend their workday inside in well-ventilated and well-lighted shops and factories, outside at a construction site, or in confined spaces, such as in an underground tunnel or inside a large storage tank that is being built.

Welders often encounter hazardous conditions and may need to wear goggles, helmets with protective face plates, protective clothing, safety shoes, and other gear to prevent burns and other injuries. Many metals give off toxic gases and fumes when heated, and workers must be careful to avoid exposure to such harmful substances. Other potential dangers include explosions from mishandling combustible gases and electric shock. Workers in this field must learn the safest ways of carrying out welding work and must always pay attention to safety issues. Various trade and safety organizations have developed rules for welding procedures, safety practices, and health precautions that can reduce the risks of the job to a minimum. Operators of automatic welding machines are exposed to fewer hazards than manual welders and cutters, and they usually need to use less protective gear.

Welding jobs can involve working in uncomfortable positions. Sometimes welders work for short periods in booths that are built to contain sparks and glare. In some jobs, workers must repeat the same process over and over.

Sources of Additional Information

American Welding Society
550 NW LeJeune Road
Miami, FL 33126
Tel: 305-443-9353

International Association of Machinists and Aerospace Workers
499 South Capitol Street
Washington, DC
Tel: 202-554-3034

Index